Yxsy Glyxsy

George Same

authorHOUSE®

AuthorHouse™ UK Ltd.
500 Avebury Boulevard
Central Milton Keynes, MK9 2BE
www.authorhouse.co.uk
Phone: 08001974150

First published by AuthorHouse   8/31/2009

ISBN: 978-1-4343-7902-3 (sc)

Printed in the United States of America
Bloomington, Indiana

This book is printed on acid-free paper.

Contents

The Man with Guts

The businessman was world famous. Those who knew him personally considered him a bit of a bastard. By the time he reached his 70's he was a world famous bastard. He had controlling stakes in virtually every major company in the world. No one was quite sure just how wealthy he was. Yet it was rumoured he possessed enough to build a new planet, if necessary.

For the moment he was content with satellite communications however. In his twenties he had shares in every major banking concern. In his 30's he bought into the manufacturing multinationals. In his forties he had bankrolled governments. In his 50's he created his own cosmopolitan city, with its own stock market. In his 60's he went into semi-retirement, buying into sports concerns and the media. While now, in his 70's, he was pursuing his hobby, buying up the worlds major religious, political and economic organisations, but only those with an international cachet. Bournemouth Hives, for that was his name, was the nearest thing to a world ruler. You could forget any of your past empire builders - your Genghiz Khans and your Adolf Hitlers, and all of the modern aspirants to world wealth. Not that Bournemouth was particularly superior to these people in any respect. But he was remorseless, and tireless, and would use any method to get a job done. He was a crude person. And crude people have a preference for crude methods. Bournemouth took pride in being unspeakably crude. A rising voice of protest had accompanied his surge to power. It was not heard by many. For Bournemouth could control publicity as he controlled money. Thus his crudity acquired a subtle edge. Indeed, the great mass of the population were unaware of his existence. Yet they worked in his offices, worked out in his gyms, watched his soap operas on T.V, bought houses from his banks, ate from his supermarkets, and even gained lifestyle tips from his fashion magazines. He was pervasive this Bournemouth Hives. Yet the feeble protests against his megalomania still bothered him. He disparaged his critics as lunatics, extremists and intellectuals. They were all interchangeable terms anyway, to him and the world's population.

However, it was noted, with faint perturbation, the numbers of these unstable critics had been growing. And their arguements appeared to achieve some faint credibility. Some critics infiltrated political parties, others business concerns, others became spokespeople moved by their own concerns. A propaganda war ensued. Bournemouth had all the strategic advantages, so he invariably won. Though the critics scored one or two successes. A general concern arose about too much power being concentrated in the hands of one man. There were also accusations over his motives. These penetrated the minds of that shrinking body of men and women known as intelligent. For large sections of the world's population had turned into dumb, passive crowds. Whole cities ground to a halt when a certain television programme was shown, or when certain vacuous celebrities were in town. This was not a problem for Bournemouth, as passive consumers were his sustenance. Yet the gatherings of dumb, massed ranks were always attended by the accidents overcrowding brings, fainting, hysteria, structures collapsing and emergency services not coping.

Now his critics would not let such matters rest. Yet they were accidents after all, tragedies even, fit copy for the evening bulletin. Think of all those future consumers lost. These things did happen however. And it was unfair to point out that Bournemouth valued human life too little in his quest for world domination. Ridiculous. He dominated the world already. Next stop was the Moon, Mars the Solar System and all the stars. Then the entire universe would fall under his dominion. Then perhaps he could seek other dimensions to purchase. He would not stop until the Multiverse was full of his accountants, where every sentient being watched a soap opera and brought a tabloid a day. But he must not get ahead of himself just yet. Some irritating activists and business rivals had still to meet with unfortunate accidents. A scientist accidentally ate some plutonium, some journalists accidentally got electrocuted at their VDU's. A politician accidentally bored herself to death, by inadvertently locking herself into her own room and listening to a tape loop of her own speeches. A musician was impaled to death, by his guitar, on stage. A fat general was constricted to death, by a pair of shrink-to -fit jeans. Finally, a whole team of stockbrokers were accidentally blown up playing paintball, they had picked up the wrong guns by mistake. Bournemouth's own son was found floating in a swimming pool full of flat champagne. He had choked to death, someone had stuck a massive tranquiliser in his mouth. The coroners verdict was open. And the cynics had a field day when they heard.

Some of Bournemouth's most dedicated employees looked over their shoulders for a moment, and then carried on working. Conspiracy theories had recently arisen. One religious leader called him the Anti Christ. This poor unfortunate was caught having sex with a tractor, dressed in a satin basque. His career was fortunately ruined, so he could continue his love life discretely. Those close to Bournemouth had always excused his manipulative tendencies and dictatorial commands, on the grounds that they received high salaries because of these character traits. However Bournemouth was also a huge glutton. Food was the only way he could unwind after a working day. He ate little while he conquered. His preference was to make up for lost time in the evening. Then he would have a banquet of several courses which usually lasted about three to four hours, at least. On one occaison, Bournemouth and a drug dealing dictator had made supper last two days. Two government ministers died of over indulgence at this feast. " It's just his way," was the platitude repeated by his closest employees. (He had no friends and was proud of that fact.) This was meant to be a way of excusing the man's gargantuan appetite. Otherwise, if they thought too much about it, they might reflect on the negative aspects of working for a rapacious monster. They only needed to pass over what happened to his family. Four wives - one drank herself to death, one drug overdose, one massive psychosis. The fourth only survived by retaining control of her own house and income. She had the doorways of her California hacienda narrowed by a mere three centimetres. It made little difference to the usual run of visitors. However her new ex-husband could not fit through the doorway, and Bournemouth had no jurisdiction over this desperate measure. So one person baulked the man of bulk. He retaliated by virtually putting her under house arrest, after calling a few favours from the appropriate authorities. Though his fourth wife was hurt she was still relieved. At least she would escape the fate of her two sons, who died from overwork.

" It's just his way," was repeated more often as Bournemouth climbed into silver haired age. It was begining to feel like an excuse, particularly among Bournemouth's older colleagues. Even the most brown-nosed of his followers felt events were culminating - too many suspicious deaths, too many acquisitions and too many food mountains disappearing. Could Bournemouth's health stand all of this ? He should be slowing down. He was supposed to be in semi-retirement, " God help us all if he ever goes back to working full time if that is the case." In view of his age they became concerned. This concern was not motivated by any regard for the worlds consumers. Nor had they any regard for the character of Bournemouth Hives. Their major worry was that Bournemouth would kick the bucket by driving himself too hard, and this would put them all out of a job.

Some very nervy meetings occurred, incognito, at discrete locations. This was because Bournemouth regularly bugged his staff, in the surveillance sense of the word, although he did get on their nerves as well. His senior accountants were the most worried as they had most to lose. While plenty of others had been badly treated by Hives, they usually consoled themselves in the benefits good salaries bring. So, once the whingers wheedled themselves out, there were five people who professed concern for Hives, in the person of their own persons. Through the cyncism, however, pulsed a faint beam of humanity. They feared for the future prospect of the human race if Hives was allowed to continue unchecked. Lines of tension appeared on their grey faces. After all, Hives had been with them from the begining. " He has grown on us over the years," said one, " Yes, like a disease," said another, " probably cancer," added a third.

Feeble attempts at humour did not enliven their furtive meetings. And so, they quickly got down to the serious business of choosing sacrifices, sorry, volunteers, to go and check the condition of Hives, to ask after his health. Then they were to assess his fitness to continue as the most powerful human being there was. What action to take then was totally unknown to them. Everyone secretly hoped Hives would be okay, so they would not have to consider drastic remedies, such as making decisions on their own. However, first things first, someone had to make an appointment. This premise was quite simple in theory, but almost impossible in practice. It became the five accountants Holy Grail. Various requests had to be made. Various procedures had to be adhered to. Preliminaries must be maintained. Forms were filled in, interviews conducted, while panels assessed and committees discussed. The five accountants had to fight their way through Bournemouth's administrative nightmare. Then came his press relations bureaucracy, his own civil service, his own security service. Then came various technicicans, scientists, hand-picked bodyguards, the remnants of his family, and his own medical team. And this was only to ask about the possibility of an appointment. It took five years, in total, before an audience with Hives was granted. However, only one person would be allowed to attend the master.

Now that their aim was achieved, the five accountants indulged in much hand wringing. It was all very well to discuss, make plans and fill out forms. Now something had to be done, and they all suffered from cold feet. The best way, it was agreed, was to discuss the matter again. Hopefully it would then emerge, just who was to be the sacrificial lamb, sorry, the honoured ambassador. Therefore they practised a combination of persuasion and intimidation on one another. The poor unfortunate to come out of this process the worst, and be granted the dubious honour, was a grey-haired dignitary named Reginald Splatt. Splatt and

Hives went way back. The others thought there was a certain symmetry about the arrangement, mainly because they had got out of going themselves. Splatt had been with Hives right from the begining, just as Bournemouth's epidemic of acquisition started. While Splatt readied himself for the worst a collective sigh of relief was heard around him.

And so, on the appointed day, Splatt's journey got under way. An interminable journey, full of pain and discomfort, was made. Splatt met up with various nondescript persons in uniforms. He was treated variously himself, as a combination of visiting dignitary, industrial spy and irritating pest. He was stuck in a hotel, in a middle of a desert, and left there for a couple of days. One morning he was picked up and whisked away, at Three A.M. Blindfolded, he was taken to a safe house and grilled by pointless questions for a few hours. Then he was sedated and helicoptered to another secret location. There he was examined, scanned, and interrogated again. He was informed he was now free to enter the Bournemouth enclave. This entailed a two mile hike up into some forbidding looking mountains. He reached a checkpoint where he was examined and scanned again, but only cross-questioned instead of being interrogated. Another four checkpoints had to be negotiated in this manner. Finally, Splatt was there, standing before a small but expensive ski-chalet. This was the supposed humble log cabin from which Hives had risen to achieve world domination. Splatt had visited Hives there in the remote past, before his boss became remote. No pleasant memories came flooding back. Splatt had found the place rather boring at the time. Still, there was a twinge of nostalgia, as a gun carrying guard, and a doctor with a hypoderm, permitted him to enter.

In fact, the chalet itself was largely unused, Splatt was informed. Mister Hives now resided exclusively within the large warehouse that had been carved out of the mountain. At the centre was a huge room to comfort a man of huge girth. This was reached through interlocking steel doors, that hissed and whirred as the small human figures passed along. The guard took his place before the central room, leaving Splatt and the doctor to be swallowed by Hive's massive hideaway. For the first time, in a period of weeks, Splatt was given some friendliness. Up till now he had been treated with sneering disdain and pedantic efficiency, the kind of skills only bureaucrats want to excel in. Indeed, he recognised the doctor as an acquaintance. It was Doctor Skuzz, one of Hive's personal physicians. It was the first time he talked to the man in over ten years. Skuzz was pleased to see Splatt. They reminisced, talking about old colleagues, most of whom had succumbed to stress related deaths, unfortunately. As they peered around this central control room, the conversation appeared to take on a strain. The pleasantries became forced. Splatt felt he was being prepared for something unpleasant. This suspicion comfirmed itself when Skuzz remarked, " Someone from the Corporation would have had to have come along sooner or later, and see for himself." But Splatt could see nothing. Some people milled about, walking around as if busy. This was obviously some kind of operations base. Skuzz asked for them to excuse the Doctor and Accountant for a short while. The staff hurried out efficiently, looking unnaturally pleased as they did so. The room was fringed by computer terminals and consoles. In the centre of which, a large bank of machinery supported a dirigible, floating almost plumb centre, within this great space.

" So where is Bournemouth ? " said Reginald Splatt.

" I don't see anyone else in the room, do you ? " replied Doctor Skuzz.

Splatt was wary of some kind of trick. However, he did not see the point of artifice at this stage.

" All I can see is that hot air balloon floating in the middle of the room."

" That is Bournemouth Hives."

" It can't be."

" Nevertheless it is."

Doctor Skuzz seemed to be enjoying the growing discomfiture on Splatt's face. Splatt peered closely at his employer. His attention divined the hot air balloon was pink. It was like one of those tacky, party balloons, with human features painted on.

" What has happened ? " he managed to gasp.

" Nothing really. We have just adapted Bournemouth's physiology to get the most out of his predominate characteristic..."

" You mean eating ? "

" Of course."

" But Hives was healthy, at one time anyway. Surely it didn't have to be this drastic ? "

" I thought that at first. But given the nature of the man's all consuming desire, and his immense power, I couldn't really say no."

" Can he talk ? "

" Not for another ten hours at least. His digestive system is absorbing the nutrients from his latest banquet. We use a process that combines liquid and gaseous action to break down the immense amounts of food this man eats. He is in the gaseous stage at the moment, which is why he looks like a hot air balloon, as you call it. It is a process not without its side effects. Bournemouth has been troubled with terrible flatulence lately. I suggest we remain here no more than ten minutes at least."

" In case he farts ? "

" Correct. But you will also experience what we call 'Repulsion Reaction' at some stage."

" I always did find Bournemouth a bit repulsive."

" In terms of character or appearance ? "

" In terms of everything."

" Quite, quite," Skuzz nodded in sympathy.

" But how ? "

" How we operated on him ? "

Splatt nodded eagerly.

" Well it was quite straightfoward in theory. Although it turned out to be very difficult in practice. Bournemouth wanted a stomach that could absorb anything he so desired, with no restraint. Basically, we substituted his stomach for a giant condom. A special kind of condom, admittedly, but the principle remains the same. Bournemouth's stomach is capable of expanding to over ten times his normal size. His skeleton had to be removed of course, and his internal organs flattened. We did this with the aid of several skin and tissue grafts. He is now, effectively, a rubber stomach, covered by strips of flesh, interspersed with strips of more rubber. Now he can eat until his stomach expands to maximum range, what we call ' Bloated Peak.' When this happens all his other bodily functions will shut down. The only process that will take place is digestion. This is why he cannot talk to you now, or do anything else for that matter. It is also why he is connected, via those tubes, to that bank of machines there. I'm not quite sure how they work myself, but they supply the gas and liquid for his digestion. And we need a lot of both believe me. "

" It's quite shocking this. I always knew he was a greedy, acquisitive glutton. But I never thought he'd go this far."

" I know what you mean. I must admit I was totally repelled by the whole concept at first. But it was what

Bournemouth wanted. Besides, he threatened to have me sacked and blacklisted if I refused..."

" Typical. And now we both end up being employed by a huge digestive system."

" In effect, yes. Although Bournemouth wants to take this process further. Did you know he is already connected to the internet."

Splatt found himself grasping at the implications of that statement,

" No I didn't."

" Well he's been online for some time. He is looking to make further modifications. He wants to be connected via all the phone cables, electricity wires, pipelines, satellite receivers and transmitters, etc, and every other man made object of transmission beside..."

" You mean now he's become a stomach, the internet will become his nervous sysytem and brain, power cables will become his muscles, phone lines his voice and hearing..."

" Television will become Bournemouth's imagination."

The thought of Burnemouth's imagination being transmitted around the globe was somewhat undermining to Splatt. What could the inside of an acquisitive monster's mind look like ? Would anyone want to know ? Would anyone survive knowing ? Splatt felt the ground underneath run away at the prospect.

" Splatt are you alright ? "

" I think so, I'm just feeling a little dizzy."

" Do you want to leave. It might be Repulsion Reaction starting up."

" No I'm fine, well fine enough.. What do you mean by Repulsion Reaction anyway."

" Basically it's our term for the combined disgust, nausea and fear that acummulates on everyone after being in the presence of a stomach for too long, a stomach that wants to eat everything in existence."

" It's too late isn't it ? the giant stomach rules the world already."

" In effect, yes. Although we have not been able to rid ourselves of the feeling of disgust this man causes at a visceral level."

" Though it seems to make no difference now."

" That is essentially true. It is already hard to make a distinction anymore, between Hives and the world. In effect he is the world, the technological world anyway. Although I do believe research is underway to enable Hives to absorb the natural world as easily as he would one of his banquets..."

Splatt shivered,

" What do you make of it Doctor ? "

" I'm both fascinated and appalled. But really, I have no choice in the matter. Either I work or Hives will ruin me, in one way or another."

" Does anyone have a choice ? "

" No, not really."

" And what if I were to blow the whistle on all this... that is assuming I don't meet with an occupational hazard that kills me..."

" Well, you know the Hives organisation is not that crude, not all the time. No one would believe you anyway. You would just become another ludricrous extremist, ridiculed then ignored. I wouldn't believe this myself if I wasn't involved in it. Besides, it's not as if you can plan anything, is it ? "

" I know, I know, all our conversations are monitored, our correspondance routinely read. It's all in our contracts. So the conversation we're having now is probably being recorded I bet."

" You bet correctly."

Splatt was begining to feel very tired and disheartened, even his shivering had subsided.

" I think I've seen enough now Doctor."

" Okay, what will you tell the others ? "

Splatt's eyebrows raised in mock surprise. Skuzz already knew of his colleagues deliberations. This in itself was routine. Privacy was a liability in the Hives organisation.

" Nothing really, What can I tell them ? Our Boss is a digestive system, a big stomach in the process of devouring the entire world... They always said Hives had guts, they wouldn't expect it to be literally true. I will tell them there is nothing much we can do, if they want to find out any more then they'll have to come here. It may be seen as unsatisfactory, it may cause some friction, but I can't see what else I can do, and at this moment I don't particularly care."

" I understand. Sometimes I feel I would love to tell people myself, just for the sake of telling really. But how would I get the opportunity ? how would anyone ? I'm sorry Mister Splatt."

" So am I. You know, I'm due for complete retirement soon, and I'm glad of that. I haven't got the stomach to work for Bournemouth Hives anymore. He's got more than enough for both of us. In fact he's got more guts than everyone else combined...What can you do against that ? "

" Nothing, you have to work with it."

" And how long before he starts swallowing us all, literally I mean ? "

" Shush, don't give him ideas," whispered Doctor Skuzz.

Splatt put his hand to his forhead and sighed.

" I think I know what should cheer you up," said Doctor Skuzz.

Splatt was guided rather than escorted from the room. The Doctor treated his colleague as if the accountant were one of his patients. And, in effect, he was. The trauma of finding out certain truths, and of seeing Hives in the flesh, had undone many lesser mortals. In fact Splatt held up quite well under the experience. Though of course the Doctor did consider that Splatt could have problems in the future, as he relived the memory, though this was hardly a major concern.

On this occaison the Doctor prescribed alcohol. Splatt was guided to a cosy, little room, a staff facility. And the first friendly space he had been in for weeks now. It was packed. The assorted group of technicians, guards and medical personel mingled in friendliness. The general hubub of relaxed conversation was itself a tonic to the good accountants frayed nerves. He felt his fellow imbibers had something of a kindred feeling. And this made him smile. Bottles of beer passed from hand to hand with a frequency Splatt would normally find uncomfortable. However, given the circumstances, Splatt felt his metabolism was in need of generous lubrication tonight.

The conversation was pleasant, inconsequential mostly, but all personnel let their words carry away into sentences that promoted solidarity. All that mattered was the fact they were here at this moment, in good company, having a good time.

But all good times come to an end. A pager device began beeping incessantly. It belonged to Doctor Skuzz. Splatt found himself carried along in the commotion that ran back to that dreaded room. It turned out to be a false alarm. There was nothing wrong with Hives. This statement amused Splatt. How could you tell whether anything was wrong about the big airbag called Hives ? what could you compare it to ? Like himself his companions were a bit tipsy, their usual trepidation had vanished. Instead they called Hives insulting names. One or two threw things at him. It made Splatt laugh, projectiles bouncing off the vacant face painted on that floating stomach. Splatt had a go himself. He threw whatever objects came to hand. However he realised he should have looked first. Something that felt like a compass left his hand. The next thing he knew there was a hissing sound. Hives had been punctured. Alarms went off. Concern arose on the faces of the tipsy staff. They sought to run around and rectify. But they began fainting. Splatt smelled something ghastly. Then he was grabbed by Skuzz and bundled through an automatic door. Without pausing to look back he pulled the confused Splatt with him. They scrambled through a service tunnel, pausing before another steel door. Skuzz fretted and moaned but eventually forced the little used exit ajar. Splatt tumbled out behind him. They knelt there on the mountainside, in the snow, swallowing great gulps of that wholesome mountain air. It rejuvenated Splatt. But Skuzz looked worried still.

" I have a car down at the bottom of the hill. I can give you a lift to the nearest town. But that is all. After that we never set eyes on each other again..."

" What ? "

" Don't you understand, you've killed Hives."

" Can't we do anything ? "

" Not a chance. Those digestive gases will have got into the ventilation system by now, they are extremely poisonous..."

" So why didn't you have safeguards ? "

" Because nobody would have dared to be as foolish, or as audacious, as to blow up his employer like a party balloon."

" But everyone else was throwing things at him..."

" Yes, paper darts mainly, not tools and implements like you were. I couldn't quite believe it I just stood and watched."

" So what do we do ? "

" We run away, naturally. We have to assume the Hives Organisation will find out what happened reasonably quickly, and then we will be called to account."

" So that's why we have to go our own separate ways ?
"

" Exactly, our chances of hiding, and survival, will be enhanced."

Splatt fell silent at these last words, both men walked tentatively on, brooding, to the waiting car.

The Hives Organisation continued to function for some months without the accident being detected. Indeed, it was a year before the mountain retreat was even visited. Unfortunately the accident investigators could not make much sense of the data they found. Some dark film of what appeared to be a party going on, and some barely audible, sarcastic remarks about a hot air balloon captured on audio. The unfortunate fact about the Hives retreat being the constant maintenance required for all his life support and spying systems. Once routine maintenance failed massive breakdown began to occur. Several records were corrupted, some fires had broken out, part of the complex had even caved in. Yet it was clear enough that Hives himself had exploded, gassing everyone within the mountain retreat it seemed. An unkind commentator likened the explosion to a gigantic fart, it was the kind of evil, malicious thing Hives would do. Unfortunately the source of this remark was never traced. In that respect it was similar to some of the staff present at the mountain, some of whose bodies were never recovered, among them Doctor Skuzz and Reginald Splatt, a visiting accountant.

Dog Chase

At the party Chris was enjoying himself, apart from a flirtation with paranoia. He was on his way to becoming well out of it. Elaine and Steve knew how to put on a good spread. Chris had smoked and drunk for about five hours solid. He was unable to talk to anyone much, which was a shame, since there were some gorgeous women running around. Chris tried it on several times, but only succeeded in scaring them away. He was left to flirt with his paranoia. It was the only way he could string a sentence together. Anyone within talking range was treated to his conspiracy theory. The Police were out to get him, backed by the CIA, with the sponsorship of the mafia and the dirty tricks of the Corporations. Everyone was in it together, leaving Chris as the lone paranoiac, left to convince unwary souls about the deviousness of everybody. Now he got on more peoples' nerves as well as scaring others away. Elaine and Steve talked about the best method of shutting Chris up. It was noted he was not far off unconsciousness. Therefore they spiked his drink. Chris was given a double helping of tequila and vodka. The slice of lemon contained acid. That was unnecessary, but Steve was feeling mischeivous, he fancied a laugh. Chris drank his drink in greedy gulps. His sense of taste had already died so he noticed nothing unusual. There were one or two expectant stares from people around. But he put this down to his resident paranoia. Then he put himself down, hoping for a relaxed conversation, with one of those females he kept pestering. But within minutes something began disturbing his stomach. Great waves of motion ran through it. It felt like a washing machine on the spin cycle. The motion spread through his whole body. Chris stood up in panic, but only succeeded in increasing his dizziness. He had to go outside. Every stimulus in the house began to push him round and round. Fresh air, space was required. Chris managed a staggering run outside, an achievement, as he was nearly bent double. Out on the street there was nowhere to go. A row of identikit, suburban houses stretched both in front and behind. His sense of direction became as detached as the buildings around him. The station was around somewhere. But he knew he would only get lost. Besides, he felt sick, and in need of a lie down. So he found the nearest hedge and fell asleep underneath it.

Some time passed. It was night and then it was day. Chris awoke to colourful dreams and a sour headache. It felt like morning. He guessed he had only been out a couple of hours. But better make sure. Better get up as well, he was begining to shiver. He noted the ground jumping up and down, but paid it no mind. However, as he stood up, he realised his swaying was not his usual swaying. There was something different about his hangover motion. He vaguely remembered drinking something that tasted vaguely weird. Then there was that expectant look as he played chug-a-lug for the final time that night. A horrible thought arose. But Chris discarded it in place of his need to urinate. He seemed to have urinated before, he noticed, for a wet stain made a cold compress on his thigh. He winced and staggered to the front door of the house. It looked so unfamiliar in the daylight. He usually picked out Elaine's house because it had the untidiest garden in the street. They must have done some clearing up. As Chris rang the bell he noticed the vomit stains on his shirt. He remembered he was pestering a lovely, big woman into making a smile. And she did laugh, because he was sick on himself in mid sentence, and after she had escaped from his presence. Chris cringed at the memory. And as he cringed the door opened. A huge, bald man answered and glowered at him,

" You've got five seconds to get out of here mate, before I set the dogs on you."

" Easy mate, I only want to talk to Steve."

" Who the fuck is Steve...Killer, Slasher, shut it will you."

Two monsters had come to Chris's attention. They were eager to get out from behind their master and chomp his legs.

" Er, what about Elaine ? "

" Elaine who ? "

Chris did not wait for an answer. The two black monsters became a bit frantic. So he ran away instead. The monsters got even more excited. They knocked their master sideways. Chris dived over the hedge onto the road. This move caught Baldy's admiration. Then he shook his head and mouthed " Stupid fucker". For the gate was already open. Baldy would usually be pleased about his dogs tearing up some smelly alkie. But he rembered his possession of these two fine breeds was not strictly legal. Two Japanese Tosas, acquired from a friend of a friend of a friend. It was a shame. Much as he would have enjoyed seeing that weirdo alkie get chewed up, he might himself get nicked if he were not careful. The chase was on. And it looked like being a short one.

Chris's running improved from a stumbling start. Yet the dogs gained on him in bounds. Their noise increased in its intensity. He also heard baldy bastard's voice, that soon tailed off. Chris weaved through quiet streets. He could not tell where he was going. In fact he felt he was running up and down the same street. In his fright his sense of perspective was going strange. For he could swear that one or two side streets lead directly into the clouds. So did the street he was on, sometimes. He could not work out if he was uphill or downhill.

Eventually Chris found himself at a main road. Now he could see the dogs panting, when they were not growling. So, the thought that perhaps he was at a dual carriageway, did not stop him running blindly across. He was lucky. A car swerved to avoid him, a few loud horns were heard. But he made it. As he continued running he heard a bump and a yelp behind him. But that still left one dog, so he ran on.

Chris ran into a sloping road. It was one he did not recognise, as usual. What area was this ? it was not familiar. It was lined with shops. Even as he ran, now down to jogging pace, he could not resist looking in the windows. Several tidy electrical goods were on display, he noticed, and this was his mistake. For the next thing he knew he had fallen on top of someone. Chris recoiled in horror, for this someone was a policeman. He felt he should better explain himself,

" I'm sorry Officer,I er didn't see you there, I was looking where I was going, except for a minute, but I didn't mean it, I didn't do it on purpose, it was an accident ,I wasn't trying to get away or anything, or get away with anything..."

" Will you shut up you brainless twat ."

" Er yes, er sorry."

" Now, what are you doing running down the road as if your arse was on fire ? "

" Erm, I was being chased by a big black dog."

" Really, one of those ghostly black dogs was it ? "

The policeman gave him a sarcastic look. Chris looked behind to find there was nothing remotely chasing him.

" It's true, it was chasing me."

The policeman looked him up and down with disgust.

" Look, I could easily think of an excuse to arrest you. But I just can't be bothered. You look such a state we'd probably have to fumigate the station afterwards. Go and sleep it off yeah, and no more running around like a nutter."

" Er yeah."

" Now piss off before I do arrest you."

Chris walked off timidly. He was still lost. But at least he might find a cafe or something, where he might sit down and regather his thoughts. Unfortunately, it was Sunday, and everywhere was closed. Or was it ? It did not feel like any day in particular. He could possibly get something at the train station. There were always train stations in these surburban parts. And all rails led to London. That was what he would do. Now came the embarassing part. He had to ask someone for directions. There were not many people around. And those that were around seemed to be walking their dogs. A few tentative words led to a mass of barking in each person he encountered. He was tempted to give up when another bald headed thug strolled up. This one had a bulldog.

Thuggy could barely contain his grin as Chris asked where the station was. But he was aimiable enough. He enquired after Chris's health, if " You look a state mate," could be called that. As the nice thug gave him some complex directions, his bulldog took a fancy to Chris. It kept sniffing his bollocks, as if they were on the menu for the day. Chris tried to shove it away. But he only encouraged it further. It embraced Chris's leg, trying to show its affection. The nice thug broke off from giving directions to have a good laugh. And after the tears welled up he tried to separate his dog from Chris's leg. It was a struggle to achieve. And as the bulldog was forced off, it became annoyed and went for its master. Chris decided the best thing to do was to run away. He was fairly sure he could remember the nice thug's directions.

But soon he became lost. Chris ran through more streets that confused him with their sameness. Although they were a bit more upmarket now. They had nice trees in them. Chris always took a nice tree as a sign of a posh street. As he rounded a leafy corner he came across a forbidding, white-haired woman, walking a combination of golden retrievers and collies. Before Chris could react he found himself walking by them. And all five dogs lept up at him, as if he were an old friend who wanted to play games with them. The woman barked orders at the dogs, in a voice that made Chris jump.

" Gervase, Charles, Tarquin, Tempest, Bimbo, behave yourself ."

She gave Chris a look of controlled disgust, at being forced to deal with a bad smell like himself. Then she broke into forced politeness,

" I'm terribly sorry. The dogs do get a bit excited sometimes."

" Er, that's okay."

The woman smiled a vinegar grin, and made to march off,

" Er, do you know where the nearest station is ? "

The vinegar grin became a frown. For a moment it looked as though she might hit him. Then she thrust an arm foward, a kung fu punch could not have been more dramatic.

" Left there, left, right, then right again," she barked.

She eyed him suspiciously,

" Clean yourself up you poor man, you stink."

" Er yeah, right."

" And stop mumbling, I can't hear you."

" Yeah right, I know, thanks."

" Do you live around here ? "

" No."

" Good, goodbye."

The woman marched on with her canine platoon. The mission was to go on manoevures at the nearest park, at 0900 hours.

" I heard that you cheeky young lout."

And, with an imperious motion, she snapped all five dogs from their leads,

" Get him boys and girls."

She burst out laughing,

" It's alright, they won't bite. They just think it's a game."

He did not stay around to verify this statement.

Chris was running away again. However he made the station in double quick time. The dogs could not be bothered chasing him too far. But he only noticed this when his panic subsided.

The station had a tiny snack bar, and it was open. This was the first bit of good news on this strange hangover day. But first he must make himself semi-presentable, and less smelly. He located some toilets and proceeded to eradicate his collection of stains. The urine patch on his leg seemed to have expanded, he could remember he was dying to go when he was at Baldy's house, but that was all. Still, a big emptying of various contents happened anyway. Chris tried to clean the sick and urine stains as he washed. But as he left the toilets it looked as if had taken a shower with his clothes on. And it still looked as if he had wet himself, more thoroughly this time. At least he got rid of the smell, a bit.

He would be soggy for a while yet. And, as he made his way back to the snack bar, in the station forecourt, it began to piss down with rain. So at least his wetness was evenly distributed. Chris walked into the snack bar shivering. The proprietor grinned at his discomfiture, his latest punter looked a bit of an idiot. A large mug of steaming, hot tea was in order, and this was what Chris got. As he moved into a squashed little booth, at the end of the counter, the mug nearly blistered his fingers. The proprietor stared at him with a bored expression. He was not alone. Some shuffling and growling were heard. And the next thing Chris knew, the triangular, hairy face of an alsatian was staring at him, with the same bored expression. Chris tried to be nonchalant. His fingers trembled in a nonchalant manner. Scalding tea spilled over the mug rim and warmed his hands a bit too much. A supercilious grin was begining to work its way round the proprietors face.

" Get off the counter Rufus," he barked.

The dog settled down out of sight. The proprietor resumed his staring.

Fortunately, another customer wandered in. He appeared to know the proprietor. Both their faces broke into friendliness. They began swapping gossip. Chris soon realised he prefered the silence, the conversation was so boring. A lot of crap about people seen in various places, stories about video shops, wine bars, and what was on cable T.V. Then they got round to the customers job, and that was even more boring. This punter was a painter and decorator. And he loved talking shop. Chris forced his hand into his pocket. He would pay now and get out, before his head went numb. The trouble was he could find no notes or coins as he rummaged around. A few bits of fluff and a frayed tissue were all he had. This was not what he had anticipated. He did not remember spending all his money, mind you, he did not remember having any money before he spent it. Although he was interested in cadging a lift home, he seemed to recall. The proprietor and his friend droned on. It was a conversation that could dry paint. Eventually, after an eternity, even the proprietor got bored. He forced things to an abrupt close with-

" Well, I've got to get on, see you."

The customer was in mid sentence. He forgot to finish it. Instead he shrugged his shoulders and said goodbye.

The proprietor moved back into the kitchen. Now was Chris's chance. He tried to be discrete sneaking out. But as he cleared the door he heard a shout of " oi " behind him. He ran into the station with an alsatian at his heels. Luckily there was a train waiting there. Unfortunately, he had the wrong platform. So Chris jumped down and scuttled across the rails. The dog would not follow him. Instead it ran back to station entrance, all the way around, until Chris heard barking coming nearer again. Chris jumped in a train, watching in panic as the alsatian gave several lumbering leaps to try and get in. The proprietors lumbering voice could also be heard getting nearer. But fortunately the train began pulling out.

Once he was moving, Chris felt it was safe to grab a seat. The carriage was empty. So he slumped into a long seat at the end of the carriage. Perhaps he might grab a bit of sleep, if he could stop shivering.

He must have dozed off. And someone must have woken him. For he opened his eyes to find an obnoxious teenager glaring at him. Another git with a dog. The teenager saw Chris's dishevelled state and obviously thought there was some profit to be had. His big doberman almost came up to his shoulders. In fact Chris was at eye level with the dog and the kid. The kid was dressed in bright clothes, all of which looked at least two sizes too big for him.

" Give me your money man, or I'll set the dog on you."

" I haven't got any money."

" Don't hold out on me man, this dog's nasty."

The kid tugged at the chain lead, and the dog growled menacingly on cue.

" I've told you, I've got no money, I'm skint, I'm bunking this train home."

" Wha ? "

This response did not meet the kid's limited intentions. And so he stood for a second, like an idiot, an idiot with a menacing dog, easy to see who wore the brains in that couple. What would have happened next was uncertain. For as the kid struggled to adapt to the new situation, a familiar cry of " Tickets please " was heard. A jobsworth of a rail guard stood there, trying to look authoritarian. It worked. The kid shuffled through his many pockets, looking for his ticket. Chris imitated the kid, for want of a better reaction. Luckily, the train began to slow. Platform signs whizzed pass the windows, they were pulling into a station. As it slowed to a stop the kid found his battered ticket. The jobsworth pored over it, expecting to find evidence the kid was a multimillion pound forger.

That moment was Chris's chance,

" Sorry, got to get off, late for an appointment."

In one swift move he swerved around the idiot kid and the jobsworth guard. The door was opened and slammed shut before they had a chance to move. The dog was quicker. It tried to take a chunk out of Chris's leg, for having the audacity to make a sudden move. But Chris was safe, he did not look back . The jobsworth shouted and the dog barked. Some kind of scuffle had started. Chris redoubled his steps, he tried to walk , nonchalantly, to disguise the rising panic. Two station staff ran hurriedly along the platform. This surprised Chris, for your never saw staff at places like this half the time, just when you do not want them, there they are. But he was well out of the station by the time the guards located the source of the noise. Someone might have pulled the emergency cord he realised, perhaps the jobsworth himself. Thank fuck he was out of that situation. It had stopped raining as well.

Another runout without paying. Trouble was he was only a couple of miles nearer home. He walked vaguely northward. It was less hilly now. Although he still saw brief glimpses of the inner city, in that sunken, central bowl, as he negotiated the inner suburbs. The inner city seemed to expand and contract, as if it were a huge heart. Individual noises of vehicles came to his ears. That was wrong, they would not carry that far usually, would they ? You might hear the general traffic hum. Chris could not figure it out. He strained his hearing to make sure he was not imagining things. But the noises were smothered by others closer at hand. New noises now emanated from the neat houses he passed. They were the individual sounds of labradors, alsatians, jack russells, plus a horde of assorted mongrels. It was a cacophony of barking. And every time he walked past a particular house he seemed to set more dogs off. As a precaution, Chris ran away again. He did not want to be pestered by another load of monsters. He ran in the general direction of home, trying to put a distance between himself and the noise. It was not easy. For every time Chris turned a corner, the barking kept pace, always at the same distance. He tried to be clever, weaving in and out of streets as he ran. But the barking could not be shaken off. He recognised a bit of mindless panic, as it grew at the base of his spine. The noise was attached to him by invisible threads, somehow.

He would never shake it off. Defeat welled up, Chris's sides began to pain. He could only stand there now, let the dogs catch him up. But then, as he turned automatically, into another semi-detached street, a new sight caught his eyes. A row of railings were stamped into a hill of green, obviously a park or common of some sort. He lept onto the railings, struggled to get over, caught his trousers twice, but he made it. As he landed he nearly sprained his foot, for he jumped onto a slope. The ground was hard, Chris limped on, better to be knackered and knocked about than molested by mangy hounds. He stumbled on, through rough grass, lots of bushes, and overhanging trees. The going was a little difficult, still at least the barking had faded away. Someone ought to give the plants a trim, he thought. Branches kept attaching themselves to him, stinging nettles nobbled his legs twice. And then he came across two more dogs. Thankfully they turned out to be the slobbering, friendly variety, not like the monsters who had chased him recently. However, they still insisted on sniffing him curiously, which was unnerving, until he heard voices calling them away, the commanding voices of possessive owners. Further weird sights awaited him, as he stumbled through the undergrowth. He saw a naked bum rise from a patch of long grass. Maybe he imagined that. But then another bum rose, hairier than the last, from a different patch. Telltale grunts soon made themselves known. Thankfully an open sky revealed itself toward Chris. He stumbled over a few remaining bushes onto a concrete path. At last he was out of the woods.

A bench loomed before him, a comforting thought after his most recent chase. Chris would catch his breath here. He sat down with his head in his hands. And as he sighed a pekingese came up and started yapping at him. This was not as scarey as the dogs Chris had met so far, but it was a bad tempered sod nevertheless. Chris measured up the distance for his foot to give the hairbag a swift kick, when the owner turned up. The owner was very camp, his pekingese obviously a fashion accessory.

" Sux, leave the man alone, shut up...sorry about that, he always investigates strangers."

He looked Chris up and down.

" Been cruising have we ? "

Chris was shocked,

" No, why would you think that ? "

The camp man pointed back into the bushes,

" That's where you go for a bit of rough, with a bit of rough, on a bit of rough."

" Eh ? "

" And you certainly look roughed up."

The penny eventually dropped.

" You mean it's a shagging spot."

" You could say that, if you were a bit of rough yourself."

" No no, I was was being chased by dogs, that's all."

" Not unusual, I've been chased by a few dogs around here, some pretty weird breeds as well. And you can stop looking at me like I'm going to pick you up. I'm not into fast food sex with something the cat looks like it's thrown up."

" Sorry I'm just paranoid, that's all."

" Yeah, you look it...are you tripping ? "

" Not that I know of. "

" well, if you are, you do now."

" Brrr, how can anyone go in for casual sex on a day like this ? "

" I don't know, I'm not into it myself. But at least I know I can take a walk without being molested by horrible, homophobic, hooligans. Instead I get pestered by horrible, horny, homos."

Chris laughed.

" Seriously, you do look bad, joking apart."

" Er. yeah, I had a bit of a rough night, er drink and drugwise, I don't mean sexwise."

" Really, you straights think the whole world is after your arse."

" It weren't meant, I'm still a bit all over the place. I could do with going home...How far away is Central London."

The camp man pointed,

" Three or four miles, you can see the dingy skyline from here."

" What's the quickest way there."

" Out the north entrance and down the hill, straight on."

" Okay then, I'll be off, thanks."

" You're off already."

" Eh ? "

" Only joking."

Chris got up to leave to find the pekingese curled up on his feet.

" Aaaah, Sux can always tell a nice character, even if it's hidden under a grubby exterior...get off Sux."

The pekingese was disentangled from his new friend. Chris loped away, awkwardly. He tried doing his best impression of a purposeful stride. It was a pity his limbs were made of rubber. He could feel the camp man's eyes burning into him. Maybe that was paranoia, but the suggestion he was tripping was all too agreeable, in his current state. It might explain a few things, because he felt vaguely weird. But then he felt vaguely weird most of the time, and most people thought he was vaguely weird. Based on his feelings, the evidence was inconclusive.

It must have been afternoon, or near enough. He was warming up, or was he ? as soon as this thought hit him he started shivering again. It helped Chris that he now felt on familiar ground. Walking down the hill was more reassuring than getting lost in all those suburban streets. Sure enough, he was only a couple of miles from the river. The dirt increased in layers as he neared the city centre. The whole area he walked through looked like it needed a soak in some washing up liquid. All the people around him seemed dirty as well. Chris was more secure now. A few bad smells would go unnoticed. But he could still not get away from dogs. Even here people were giving their monsters a Sunday airing. And the dogs were as dirty as their owners. No healthy, pure breeds here, instead a collection of mongrels with bad attitudes.

He was reminded his composure was still needed. For every dog he passed barked at him, or tried to leap at him. Dogs with strollers, dogs tied outside shops, and dogs tied to lampposts. Although they were all mixed breeds, they seemed to combine the worst traits of the more vicious types. They were big, mean and quick. The high street unravelled a fair distance. Chris barely noticed the traffic had picked up. Day trippers in cars turned up the noise. But it was what he expected. His concentration was taken up playing dodgems with the dogs. Fortunately his paranoia was simmering instead of boiling. After dodging a fair number of mutts they petered out, a few even ignored him. This cheered him up. The high street wandered into a nameless commuter road up ahead. But then he heard a familiar, scarey sound behind him.

A dog was padding behind him, keeping track with the pace of his walk. Chris took a turn to the left, through a housing estate, a favourite short cut. But the padding followed. Now the dog was giving off growls. Thoughts of running away appealed to Chris again. He ventured a glance behind. The dog was wearing some weird kind of ruff, it looked like a funnel. To convince himself he saw it, he glanced again. It was not a funnel but a muzzle. That was a relief, no worries about getting bitten. He tried to find his nonchalant mood again. Nevertheless, the dog charged him from behind. It hit the back of his knees, so he went tumbling. And, as he sprawled out in shock, the big, ugly monster stood on him. It gave Chris its best throaty growl. And that was all the husky-looking monster could give, its mouth being so restricted. Chris was reminded of a woman he had seen in a Dickens programme, a dog in a Victorian bonnet. He could not help laughing. His lying prone added a high pitched tone to his voice. The dog was somewhat perplexed at this reaction and ran off whimpering. Maybe it was self-conscious about its appearance. Luckily the estate was deserted, even if Chris fancied he heard sniggers from behind flat windows. So his embarassment was relatively minor, on a scale marked severe all over. Chris continued his walk, rather furtively. He tried to make as little sound as possible. Yet his boots still clop clopped, echoing from the walls of the various blocks.

Thankfully Chris managed to get through the rest of the estate without any more weird confrontations. The scenery shifted again. The roads were now very busy. Office blocks came to dominate over flats and houses. The smell of exhaust added a bouquet of monoxide, home sweet home, almost. A quick shuffle through an underpass, smelling of urine,across a bridge, where a mini dust storm was in progress. It always freezed his bollocks off as he crossed the bridge, and he always gazed fearfully at the brown water below. Over the river was home. Only one more short cut was left. This was one of his recent discoveries, a hole in a fence led across a patch of waste ground. However, someone had repaired the fence. There were signs indicating a property company was going to build another block there. Chris climbed over. He could not be bothered walking around. And, as he landed uncomfortably on the other side, he heard some familiar growls, yet another breed who wished to make his acquaintance. There were short bursts of exhaled sound, like the grunts a boxer would make as he threw a punch. But these dogs were not boxers, they were pitbulls. Chris instantly recognised the two solid slabs of meat, on their stumpy legs, as they bounced toward him. They almost looked cute, but pitbulls were the dogs he was scared of the most. This was quite an achievement, given his usual paranoia. So, for the umpteenth time that day, he ran away. This time he ran with much determination. Newly endowed with athletic ability, he sprinted the waste ground with ease, then flipped himself over a wire fence with gymnastic grace. The slabs of meat never got close. The monsters with cute faces looked sad as they continued their grunting noises. The promise of a free massacre, with lunch thrown in , had eluded them. Nevertheless, they still threw themselves at the fence in a show of aggression. Chris strolled away, this time attempting his controlled manner, undermined by his shooting wary glances behind. The two slabs of meat headbanged the fence until he was out of sight.

Now Chris was back in his own area. Claustrophobic buildings stood up all around him. And there was a traffic jam. But no one was walking the streets. It was the Sunday afternoon hour when everything was swamped in pleasant lethargy, even the cars crawled at a sleepy pace. Chris wandered left, right, left, through a main road. Then it was on to the deserted backstreets. Quiet was everywhere, along with rows of parked cars. It was so peaceful. Chris felt like letting his guard down as he walked, for the first time. Some shadowplay caught his attention. Something was flickering in the gaps between the parked cars, then its shadow slipped under a parked van. Chris tried to bring the object into focus, yet it always slipped out of his glance. The flickering shape was following him. With a sinking heart he prepared to run from another dog. However he wanted to make sure it really was a canine object first. Otherwise he would be running away from his own imagination. He half fancied he heard a growl,his spirits sank and his adrenalin rose. The black shape flitted expertly from vehicle to vehicle, in a deliberate attempt to keep out of Chris's vision. It was obviously trying to creep up on him and leap on him. So, at last, he ran away again. And all the while the black shape flitted from car to car. It would not come into the open. To do so would be to betray its presence. Yet Chris was aware of its intentions. The dog seemed to think that Chris was unaware of its actions. This thought struck Chris as a little ridiculous. Why should he try and imagine what a dog was thinking ? he was not sure the dog even existed, but then maybe that was part of its intention also ?

He stopped running, walking the remaining distance to the communal door at his block of flats. As he looked around, the sound of growling had disappeared, but a strange shape still flickered occaisonally, at the angle of his vision. Chris shrugged his shoulders then went in. As far as he was aware shadowplay had not attacked him previously. He put it down to over active imagination, if not hallucination. It seemed many aspects of the days journey could be put down that way. These were distinguished from the more scary aspects, which involved him running away.

Chris pondered as he walked up the stairwell, and onto the wrong balcony. He lived on the floor above. What reminded him of this was the fact he walked straight into the Morgan's dog. It was a big, stupid, lazy thing, much like its owner. But on this occaison it looked particularly vicious. It raised its head as Chris approached, sensing his trepidation. Its eyes woke up and Chris was serenaded by another menacing growl.

Chris ran away. The dog was tied to a rope, so it probably could not run far. This was his hope as he puffed up the stairs. But it must have been a long rope, for the dog easily kept pace with him. Chris fumbled along onto his balcony, with the dog in pursuit. Instead of turning right, in the direction of his flat, he turned left. He figured on running to the other stairwell, down the other stairs, back along the lower balcony. Then he would run up his own stairwell again, back to his own flat. The dog should have reached the limits of its rope by then. But it did not. The dog kept up the pace and the rope just kept coming. Chris passed previous lengths of this long lead as he approached his flat for the second time. Fortunately the dog was distracted as Chris struggled to get his key out. A neighbour passed his flight, and looked somewhat miffed as his hello was not returned. But then Chris always was a weirdo wanker, so his neighbour thought no more of it. Instead he stopped to stroke the friendly dog that lolloped up to him with its tongue hanging out. He recognised the Morgan's dog, and spent some time rubbing and patting the friendly mutt. Then he got bored and pissed off. Why would Chris run away from the Morgan's dog ? He must be a bigger wanker than previously thought.

For his part Chris had finally gained the sanctuary of home, after his panic stricken attempts to open his own front door that is. Fortunately that dozy neighbour had started playing with the dog, the neighbour who always stared through Chris's kitchen window. Chris stood in the landing, catching his breath. It was unusual for the Morgan's dog to chase him, usually it could not be bothered waking up. Maybe the dog could sense that he felt weirder than usual. Chris shrugged his shoulders, maybe he should put the whole day down to weird experience. Now he was ready to crash out. So the events of the day could fade away, like some strange film. But as he opened the door to his bedroom, a big, black mastiff stood there, growling heavily. Chris blinked in shock, and the dog disappeared. Now that one definitely was not real. With a sense of relief he made ready to fall on a smelly mattress. Yet as he pulled his curtains he was aware of the big, black dog again. This time it was on the back street outside. He rubbed his eyes, a second bout of relief came as the dog disappeared again. Perhaps now he could relax, perhaps not, for the doorbell rang. Chris nervously went to answer. Thankfully it was his sister, not a horrible monster, though she could be when she set her mind to it. She immediately launched into a flurry of speech,

" Where've you been, I thought you could've been back ages ago, Elaine was really worried about you, they played a mean trick on you, they spiked your drink, mind you, you were being a real pain apparently, they found it really funny, though you was really annoying at the time, they thought you might've freaked out, so they kept phoning me, they were really worried like I say, even if you was being a twat, I told them you always was a twat, but a harmless twat at that..."

She stopped and stared at Chris, who was somewhat taken back. For she appeared to have crammed those words into a mere ten seconds, or less.

" So, are you going to let me in or what ? "

" Er, yeah, I suppose so."

" Cor, thanks for the enthusiasm, you're such a melon sometimes Chris."

Chris frowned as she walked in. Something was dragged in with her. It was the big, black mastiff.

" This is Roy, aint he sweet ? "

The monster growled at Chris. All the past days events rebounded on him. He fainted. His sister sighed, for her wimpish brother was acting the twat again. Luckily she was often around to help out her brother when he started going all weird.

The Character of Mr Blight

" He always let himself go you know. The problem wasn't so much he overate, as he didn't know when to stop."

Resentment welled up in Mrs Bridget. How dare this secretary talk as if she knew Mr Blight. She only worked with him a couple of years, did Mrs Slaine. She was no confidante in the sense Mrs Bridget was. To be sure Mrs Slaine had worked with him for five years now, three more than Mrs Bridget. But it was quality rather then the length of friendship that mattered.

" Of course he did like his food, a bit too much at times," Mrs Bridget chimed in.

" If you mean he could be a pig at times, yes I agree."

" A pig? Why I would never suggest anything so insulting. He loved his food, just as he loved life, enormously."

" That's a description that fits his size well enough."

How dare this embittered employee talk in this way.

" There is a huge difference between enjoying what life has to offer and being a glutton," Mrs Bridget retorted.

" A gap he succeeded in bridging."

" That's completely wrong."

" You're right, I take it back, it was a gap he succeeded in smothering."

" You're just ungrateful. I know he treated his employees bad sometimes."

" Sometimes. Sometimes. He could be an old lecher. The amount of times I sat at my desk with his furnace breath on the back of my head, while his fingers, the size of bananas, nearly crushed my shoulder."

" He never made a pass at you did he ? "

" No but the intention was there."

" Really. You're not just a little paranoid are you ? Like the time you were convinced the ladies toilets were bugged."

" They were. But this isn't the same thing."

" You're right it isn't. Mr Blight would have no time for such a thing."

" True, he was too busy eating."

" Well he loved his food."

" Loved it to death."

" How do you mean ? "

" Well he was overweight, wasn't he ? "

" He was a little stout that's all."

" A little stout, like an elephant is a little heavy."

" How dare you."

" It's no more than he said himself anyway."

" I don't believe it."

" It's true. He used to say his bum and his belly flowed over his trousers like lava over the rim of a volcano."

" Ugh that's disgusting, what a horrible thought."

Mrs Bridget shuddered as the thought in question turned into a picture all too easily. She rushed to speak again before the picture in her mind prevented her.

" Well granted he could have shown a little more more restraint."

" Yes, like a gag or a muzzle perhaps."

" You're just being cynical. You know ,as well as I do, he was a generous man, a practical man, a decisive man..."

" A fat man."

" Really, you are intolerable."

" Perhaps, but I am the one who discovered him. And do you know how I discovered him ? "

" No. "

Mrs Bridget was starting to get uneasy.

" He was working late, apparently, on Friday night, with Ms Ronaldson. You know Ms Ronaldson don't you ? "

Mrs Bridget nodded, that awful show -off in the P.R. section, she had not seen her around lately.

" Well, needless to say, they didn't get much work accomplished, and, without going into too much detail, it would be a fair assumption to say they were involved in some kind of sexual activity."

" How ?...How can you infer this ? "

A look of shock appeared on Mrs Bridget's face. She could feel herself growing pale.

" Because both their bodies were discovered naked, wedged in that doorway there."

Mrs Slaine pointed to a small kitchenette at the back of the office.

" His bulk did it for both of them. She suffocated in the huge mound of his chest, while he died of hypothermia over the course of the weekend."

" Ugh," cried Mrs Bridget. Her stomach began moving of its own volition.

" Here dear I know exactly how you feel," said Mrs Slaine as she moved around to comfort the stricken Mrs Bridget.

YXSY
GLYXSY

II

Peter's Inheritance

They met in the same place on Friday night. It was the Bricklayers Arms. They had a swift pint, or two, then went home to their respective families. Any more drink and they would probably start enjoying themselves too much. And they were too responsible for that, nowadays. Peter, Ray and Pat went way, way back. They always kept in touch, even though they did not have much in common. But they loved swapping gossip and talking a lot of crap. It kept them down to earth, they said.

But one of their number had been absent recently, too often to escape comment indefinitely. Therefore, after the fourth Friday in a row, Pat thought he should raise the subject. Peter was a bit of a dozey sod. He probably went on holiday and forgot to tell anyone, Peter was like that. Ray shrugged his head, his shoulders following,

" Didn't you hear, Peter's dead."

" No."

" Where you been ? you plum."

" Working, just like you."

" So, everyone knows about it."

" Who's everyone ? "

" Everyone who knows us."

" But I didn't know about it."

" No, you're the exception that proves the rule."

" Well how am I supposed to find out unless I ask, eh ? "

" Why didn't you ask before ? "

" I thought he'd gone on holiday."

" What ? and leave his girlfriend an' kid behind ? "

" I didn't know that."

" You don't know nothing."

Pat was getting a bit wound up by this conversation.

" Look mate, I'm not a newsreader. How am I supposed to know everything that's going on ? "

Peter sensed his friend need placating.

" Easy man, easy...I thought you should've known, God, it's all over the place."

" What is ? "

" The fact that Peter's dead."

There was a thoughtful silence, which seemed to last too long.

" So how long ? "

" Four weeks."

" That long ? "

" Yeah."

" So how'd it happen ? "

" It's a long story."

" So tell me anyway."

" I told you, it's a long story."

" Can't be that long."

" Well it is."

" How long is long ? a couple of hours ? "

" I don't know, just long, and, er, a bit weird."

" Come on, you've got me interested now. Can't you just give me the extended highlights ? "

" The extended highlights, it's not a football match."

" You know what I mean, tell us the basic facts."

" The basic facts, well er..."

" Come on, it can't be that difficult."

" Well er."

" Come on mate, I known him for ages, just like you."

" Yeah, but you didn't miss him."

" Well I do now."

" Well, er, I suppose it started when Peter's Mum's boyfriend died."

" Peter's Mum's boyfriend ? "

" Yeah, you remember."

" Oh yeah, Claude."

" No, Clyde."

" Peter's Step Dad."

" Well, er, Peter was never keen on Clyde being called his step dad."

" You mean he didn't like him ? "

" No, he liked him alright, he just didn't like the term step dad."

" So ? "

" Well, Clyde had a heart attack, sitting in front of the telly one night."

" What was on ? "

" What do you mean what was on ? What's that got to do with it ? "

" Well, I know someone who collapsed and died watching Crystal Palace lose."

" Watching Crystal Palace is enough to make anyone top himself, and I should know, having supported them for twenty years."

" So you don't know."

" No I don't, and I don't think it's important either."

" Alright, sorry."

" Well, er, Clyde had all this stuff, you know, videos, magazines, a lot of dirty stuff."

" You mean it weren't clean ? "

" Yeah, I do, but not in the sense you mean. A lot of it was porn."

" Porn ? really ? "

" Yeah, only soft porn, but Peter's Mum was a bit embarassed by it. She just gave the lot to Peter."

" Wow."

" Yeah, he got a car and a stereo as well."

" A car stereo ? "

" No, you burglar, a car and a stereo."

" Oh right, sorry. So Peter did alright. "

" Well he would've but for Clyde's son, from his previous marriage, William."

" What about him ? "

" Well, er, William thought Peter's Mum had been a bit too hasty, just giving all his stuff away like that..."

" She probably was."

" Well, er, maybe she was, maybe she wasn't. Clyde had no will, so it was her choice."

" Still, William's got a point."

" I don't think so, man. Peter's Mum was entitled to dispose of the stuff how she liked."

" Still, I could understand William getting annoyed."

" He was annoyed, and he went...Hang on, I'm getting ahead of myself here...what happened next, oh yeah, Peter starts getting these dreams..."

" Dreams ? "

" Yeah, night after night, the same one..."

" The same what ? "

" Well, er, he dreamt he was lying in bed, when Clyde walks in and starts demanding all his stuff back. And he kept getting this dream every night..."

" Wow, brown trousers time."

" Yeah, it really freaked him out, you know, this kept going on for ages."

" So why didn't he tell anyone ? "

" It's just a dream innit. You don't want to sound like a soppy sod, do you ? "

" Unless you get scared."

" Well, er, he did get scared enough to tell a few people."

" And ? "

" I burst out laughing at first. I thought he was winding me up. But it turned out he was serious. I suggested he tell his Mum, and go and get some pills from his G.P. "

" And did he ? "

" Well yeah. Peter's Mum just laughed at him as well. And his G.P. didn't want to give him any pills, he wanted to send him to the Psycho Doctor."

" Wow, so Peter was going a bit loopy."

" Well, er, not quite. He just thought the Psycho Doctor could explain it, that's all..."

" Before he went gaga."

" I suppose so. Peter did say the dreams were driving him up the wall. He was becoming a nervous wreck."

" Wow, so he went flying off his trolley ? "

" Well no, coz he died before that happened."

" Yeah ? "

" Yeah, he had a heart attack one night, died of fright."

" Killed by a ghost in a dream ? "

" Eh ? well yeah, I suppose so, in a way, only it weren't that straightfoward."

" No ? "

" Well, er, no...You see William turns up at the Police Station a couple of days later, saying it's his fault..."

" Wow, did he put a curse on him or something ? "

" Don't be stupid...William went around Peter's house the night he died..."

" And he murdered him."

" Look, are you going to let me finish this story, or what ? "

" Alright, sorry."

" Well, er, anyway. William said he heard Peter was having the same dream all the time. So he goes over to Peter's place, after he's nicked Peter's Mum's spare key, and lets himself into Peter's flat...Thing is, he's all dressed up in Clyde's clothes, and you know, he looked a lot like his Dad. He was going to try a give Peter a fright."

" What ? just for a laugh ? "

" No man, he was annnoyed, he thought he might play on Peter's guilty feelings, and get some of his Dad's stuff back..."

" Sounds dodgy, anything could've happened."

" It was dodgy, man. But William was really upset, you know. He loved his Dad, and he thought he was a bit cheated..."

" So he tried to scare Peter into giving him the stuff back ? "

" Yeah."

" And it didn't work."

" It did work, too well. Peter was in bed when William walked in. As soon as Peter saw him, he died of fright."

" Wow, and William got done for it ? "

" Well, er, he's still awaiting trial. The police think there's some compassionate grounds for William, he'll probably only get a short spell in prison..."

" Wow."

Pat sat in silence, absorbing the story for a moment. He took a couple of swigs of beer. Something was not quite right.

" Listen, this don't make sense. If Peter's so scared of this dream ,right, so scared he goes to the doctor, why would he tell William about it ? someone he's not that friendly with."

Ray was taken aback.

" I don't know. Peter was a bit dozey sometimes."

" He wasn't that dozey, mate. When Peter was wound up, he was sharp."

Ray shrugged his shoulders.

" Don't know, maybe it was his Mum."

" Peter's Mum wouldn't tell William. She was sensible about things like that...Who else did he tell ?"

" Well, no one really, just Luke and me. Maybe Luke told him."

" Doubtful, Luke lives miles away now. He only comes down to visit Peter and his Mum."

" Well I did tell a few of the blokes in here one night, in confidence of course, they're not people who go blabbing things around..."

" Who was there ? "

" Well, just me, Carl, Danny, and...oh shit..."

" What ? William was there ? "

" He was, he weren't with us, but he was hovering around, glaring at us. He might have overheard, but I don't think so..."

" You don't think so. So where else would he have heard. Peter wouldn't tell, nor his Mum, nor Luke, not even Carl and Danny. I know these people as well as you...So it must have been you..."

Realisation dawned on Ray that it could have been his fault.

" Shit."

" You dipstick."

" No, it can't be..."

Pat got up to leave, but not before he landed a good right hand on Ray, whose head bounced back and foward in pain and surprise.

" Twat, you call me stupid, but you got our mate killed."

The Friday night meets at the Bricklayers Arms were suspended, for a short while, after that.

Making Babies

Location : an informal lecture in a small office, the office of Doctor Fabian Ratchets. Those present include Doctor Ratchets, Doctor Primley, Doctor Muggins, Doctor Mellow, and Doctor Norman.

The narrator first sets the scene -

Narrator : "Doctor Fabian Ratchets was presiding as the new doctors at the institute discussed their research. There were many willing volunteers for their revolutionary new fertility treatment. However, tests had to be stringent, given the fact their new research was highly controversial."

Doctor Ratchets : "You will appreciate we will be operating on largely untested hypotheses. The clinical evidence presented is inconclusive at best..."

The assembled Doctors nod in agreement,

Doctor Ratchets : "...However, our studies here indicate we may be on the verge of a possible breakthrough. We believe we have developed a technique which will make a baby as easy as making a cup of tea..."

One or two gasps are heard,

Doctor Ratchets : " Now I know this technique is new to most of you. But I can say it makes use of methods demonstrated by Doctor Belladona at Berkeley, research I presume you've heard of..."

There is a mixed reaction, two Doctors nod agreement, two others look blank.

Doctor Primley : " Wasn't that the woman who gave birth to a minotaur ? "

Doctor Ratchets : " Really Doctor Primley, I expect you not to believe that tabloid rubbish... No she did not give birth to a minotaur. The baby was stillborn."

Doctor Primley : " Yes, I remember, the Helen Killerwatt case. She Sued Doctor Belladona, and bankrupted both him and his financial backers."

Doctor Muggins : "But the medical report suggested abnormalities of the skull on the baby, abnormalities resulting from the use of a cow ovum, which made the baby look like a minotaur."

Doctor Ratchets : " Really Doctor Muggins. I have read that report as well. It was commissioned by an investigative journalist to discredit Doctor Belladona. I can categorically state that the woman did not give birth to a minotaur - or anything that looked like one.."

Doctor Mellow : " Doctor Ratchets ? "

Doctor Ratchets : " Yes Doctor Mellow.

Doctor Mellow : " What is a minotaur ? "

Doctor Ratchets shakes his head in disgust before speaking,

Doctor Ratchets : " Good God, I must say, for the record, that the standard of literacy, among the new intake of doctors is becoming appallingly low."

Doctor Mellow blushes with embarassment,

Doctor Ratchets : " Briefly, the minotaur is a figure from Greek Mythology, the offspring of a Queen of Crete and a bull. It is usually depicted as having a human body and a bull's head..."

Doctor Primley : " LIke Helen Killerwatt's baby..."

Doctor Ratchets : " Not at all like Helen Killerwatt's baby. The next person who mentions minotaurs in any context will be expelled from this group...now where was I ? "

Doctor Norman : " You were reminding us that Helen Killerwatt's baby did not look like a minotaur..."

Doctor Ratchets : " Get out of this room Doctor Norman."

Doctor Norman : " But Doctor Ratchets..."

Doctor Ratchets : " Get out now and don't come back."

Doctor Norman gets up shamefacedly and leaves the room with head bowed.

Doctor Ratchets : " Now... We have advanced Doctor Belladona's technique to the stage where we can combine human spermatozoa with portions of any mammalian or bird ova to produce a human embryo. This embryo can then be inserted into the woman who acts as host. This woman will have a normal pregnancy and then, hopefully, produce a happy faced cherubim..."

Doctor Primley : " I beg your pardon ? "

Doctor Ratchets : " A healthy baby to you, Doctor Primley. Of course, any woman who acts as host must be of a reasonable age, reasonable health, reasonable intelligence and reasonable sanity. Though, given the general standard of our volunteers, we may have to settle for three out these four, possibly two even."

Doctor Mellow : " Isn't that a little cynical Doctor Ratchets ? "

Doctor Ratchets : " Yes it is Doctor Mellow, but fortunately it does not cloud my judgement. Now, we have developed our course of action as follows, the proof of our claim rests on the supposition that any fresh mammal or bird egg will do. Therefore I propose we use an extreme example to begin with - a bird's egg. Then we will work our way up to compatible mammalian ova genetically, of the chimpanzee say. However, to begin our research, Doctor Primley will go to the supermarket and buy a half dozen eggs, free range naturally..."

Doctor Primley : " Why me ? "

Doctor Ratchets : " Because I asked you."

Doctor Primley : " But Sainsburys is closed now."

Doctor Ratchets : " I don't mean right now...God, as soon as is convenient would be fine. Just don't forget... Now, everyone here will be aware this research is ethically controversial to say the least..."

Doctor Muggins : " Or immoral."

Doctor Ratchets : " Yes, thank you Doctor Muggins. A lot of people would say that. But we are operating at the frontiers of research, where there is no clear morality. Therefore, whoever volunteers for our initial experiments, they will need to have a thorough grasp of the fact we are dealing with uncertainties, preferably. Now, I may have cast doubt on the fitness of our volunteers earlier. But there is one in particular who is head and shoulders above the others. She is intelligent, sophisticated, physically fit, mentally alert, and she is your wife Doctor Muggins."

Doctor Muggins : " My wife...but how ? "

Doctor Ratchets : " She has been in contact with us for some time, and she has passed all our tests with flying colours..."

Doctor Muggins : " She could have told me."

Doctor Ratchets : " She wanted it to be a surprise, as it is your birthday tomorrow."

Doctor Muggins : " Some surprise. I was expecting a new shaving kit, not this."

Doctor Ratchets : " Oh come now Doctor Muggins. Your wife is a pioneer, in the best traditions of medical research. You should be proud."

Doctor Muggins : " More like dumbfounded."

Doctor Ratchets : " Well you'll soon get over it. Now, once Doctor Primley gets our eggs tomorrow, we can start immediately..."

Doctor Mellow : " Just make sure you don't pick up a Cadbury's Creme Egg by mistake."

Doctor Ratchets : " Thank you Doctor Mellow. Please save your childish jokes for when you tour the Paedophile Ward..."

Doctor Primley : " I beg your pardon."

Doctor Ratchets : " Sorry Doctor Primley, I meant to say Paediatric Ward. I fear your irritating sense of humour is contagious Doctor Mellow..."

Doctor Mellow : " Like all the best diseases."

Doctor Ratchets : " Certainly the most irritable in their symptoms...Right, I believe we have all the required information for the present time. The techniques will be taught to you as we go along. Any questions ? "

Doctor Muggins : " Yes, I would like to protest at the way in which my wife has become involved."

Doctor Ratchets : " Very well Doctor Muggins. Your protest has been noted, and disregarded. Meeting adjourned gentlemen. "

Ten months later the good doctors are standing around a healthy baby boy sitting on an operating table. The baby is loving all their attentions. And it takes their minds away from Doctor Muggins wife. She is sitting in a hospital bed at the back of the room, glaring at them with impatience and barely concealed anger.

Doctor Ratchets : " I must say this turned a lot better than the original prognosis."

Doctor Muggins : " What was the original prognosis Doctor Ratchets ? "

Doctor Ratchets : " Erm...at best losing the baby, and at worst losing both mother and baby."

Doctor Muggins frowns,

Doctor Muggins : " Still, knowing Gladys, she would have volunteered whatever the risk."

Doctor Ratchets : " Who's Gladys ? "

Doctor Muggins : " My wife."

Doctor Ratchets shakes his head, unwilling to believe anyone in his hospital could be called Gladys.

Doctor Muggins : " You know she hasn't spoken to me since the baby was born, that's over two weeks now."

Doctor Ratchets tries to think of something sympathetic to say, but gives up.

Doctor Ratchets : " I believe that not everyone has seen the curious birthmark on Muggins Junior's back. This appears to be the only side effect of the technique."

The baby's back is exposed for all the waiting doctors to see.

Doctor Primley : " It can be, it's a tattoo surely."

Doctor Muggins : " It had better not be a prank."

Doctor Mellow : " More like an advertising logo."

Doctor Ratchets : " It's a birthmark I assure you gentlemen, even if it does take the form of a message."

Doctor Muggins : " Not every birthmark reads - Good Food Costs Less At Sainsburys."

Doctor Primley : " It really is extraordinary."

Doctor Mellow : " Yes, I thought they stopped using that slogan ages ago."

Doctor Ratchets : " We believe an inkstamp on the eggshell somehow seeped onto the portion of ovum we used. Although we are unsure just how this process occurred at the moment."

Doctor Mellow : " Still, there is great marketing potential to be had in this. Just think, we could sell advertising space on babies to fund hospitals and..."

Doctor Mellow stops talking when he realises the other doctors are not amused. If looks could kill he would have been stabbed a hundred times over.

Doctor Mellow : " Erm..or maybe not...just kidding... just an idea."

Doctor Ratchets gruffly takes Doctor Mellow aside,

Doctor Ratchets : " How dare you discuss such a matter in a hospital."

Doctor Mellow : " I'm so sorry Doctor Ratchets.'

Doctor Ratchets : " So you should be. Come to my office at 9.30 sharp tomorrow."

Doctor Mellow : " If you really think that's necessary."

Doctor Ratchets : " I certainly do, if we are to discuss the matter with our corporate sponsors and make pots of money. "

Doctor Mellow : " Don't you have any misgivings Doctor Ratchets ? "

Doctor Ratchets : " Yes, but I appear to have misplaced them somewhere."

Doctor Mellow : " Right you are. see you tomorrow then."

It Might Come True

" So what's the occaison ? " Dennis muttered, as he gulped the dregs of his fifth drink.

" Don't know," said Maurice, shrugging his shoulders. " Oh yes I do," He added. " Something about all our good work for the year, Hugo said."

" Great, so are we going to get a bonus ? "

" Er...no, we're not. I think it was either a bonus or a piss up this year. And a piss up's cheaper, so here we are."

" That shifty geezer Hugo. He said he was going to treat us all to a night of free drinks, like it was some kind of unexpected reward."

" Actually, it's not free anymore. The money he put behind the bar just ran out..."

Maurice interrupted himself by sticking his glass in his face and draining his fifth pint. The two sat in tipsy silence for awhile, punctuated by gassy burps. Hugo was walking up and down the floorspace between the bar and the tables, doing his public relations routine. This was rendered slightly less impressive by the fact he was wearing a pair of plastic antlers. Karen, the Assistant Director, would usually have tempered Hugo's twat tendencies. But this time she had a pair of springy antennae on her head. The pair of them looked like self-conscious retards.

Dennis was begining to get a headache, an irritable one. He gazed at Maurice, who in turn was gazing vacantly into space. Then he looked behind his seat to take in his fellow members of staff. They were grouped around three tables in a snug corner of the saloon bar. Everyone was talking about work as far he could make out. Though their individual voices tended to merge into a high pitched drone.

" Do you want a drink ? "

The voice startled Dennis. It was Maurice. Dennis barely nodded before his companion sloped off to the bar. Now he could be alone with his thoughts, except for the fact that someone irritating came over to talk to him. It was Shirley. She stood at the end of his seat and table, thus blocking his means of escape. Her huge body almost bent over double as she burbled out words, vodka breath was an uncomfortable thing.

" How are you finding it ? " she said.

" How am I finding what ? "

" The work, stupid."

" Oh I don't know, it's alright."

" You never say much do you, never give anything away."

" But I haven't got anything to give away."

" Oh yeah, everyone's got something to give away," and she winked at him.

Dennis was flummoxed by this, he struggled to get out a reply, and quickly.

" Er, I'm not a vending machine you know, giving out bars of chocolate."

This puzzled Shirley.

" What are you talking about ? "

" Oh nothing, it's alright."

Hugo was hovering nearer than usually welcome, Dennis might have been glad of his company, for once. But Shirley continued,

" They all say you're a bit of a shy one in the office. But I think you're just weird, but weird in a sweet way."

" Er... yeah, right. Hallo Hugo."

Shirley suddenly wheeled back, bumping into Hugo, and almost knocking him flying. He was slightly stunned but quickly regained his composure as Shirley disappeared. Dennis swapped a few pleasantries with him about work and the weather. Hugo offered him a cigarette. Dennis accepted with a forced gratitude. This evaporated when, after a couple of puffs, the cigarette exploded.

" Hee hee hee. I got hold of some french bangers recently. The fireworks I mean, not cars or women..."

" You're a twat Hugo," a female voice shouted.

" Worse than that," someone else said.

Dennis quite agreed with these remarks. However, all the pub's attention was still on the pair of them. To ease his self consciousness dilemma, he decided to have a real cigarette. So he fumbled around his jacket pocket.

" Who stuck a fucking saveloy sausage in my pocket."

More laughter. He slung the sausage into the crowd behind him, only to receive it back, in the face.

A good shot, Dennis thought. He turned back to see a grinning Maurice holding two pints. Luckily Hugo had sauntered off.

" At last, a welcome sight," he said, as Maurice sat down giggling," Don't you start as well. I get a bit fed up with these crappy pranks..."

" I agree they're crap, but they're funny as well."

" Really ? excuse me for not wetting myself."

" You're excused, young man. Though I expect to see you piss yourself at some stage."

" Why ? " Dennis giggled.

" Er, I don't know really, it's convention I suppose."

" Yeah right. Like all the practical jokes," Dennis' voice had turned more serious.

" That's right. You're one of the gang now. So you have to indulge in crappy jokes. It goes with the territory."

" Why can't they just supply me with free drinks all evening ? "

" That's a good idea. But it's too boring. You can't expect everyone to go along with it."

" Not a tight bastard like Hugo, anyway."

This time they both giggled.

" Oh no, Hugo's bringing out a fucking cake," Dennis observed.

" I never had fucking cake before."

" Ha bloody ha."

" I bet it's one of those cakes where you blow the candles and they re-light themselves."

" Yeah right. Only this cake hasn't got any candles, you twat."

" Oh well. It'll probably do something else."

" Like explode, you mean ?..."

" Or a woman in a bikini jumps out from inside..."

" Oh yeah, a cake that size, she'd only be a couple of centipedes high."

" What have centipedes got to do with anything ? "

" I give up, what ? "

" No. I'm asking you."

" Why ? "

" Because, you said the woman would only be a couple of sentimotors high."

" Sentimotors ?...Oh centimetres. But that's what I said."

" You said centipedes."

" No I didn't."

" Yes you did."

" Piss off."

" You piss off."

" Now now gentlemen, no conflict in the pub. Wait till we get outside, where we won't get barred for it, hee hee hee."

Hugo had wandered over to them while their exchange was in progress. He was still holding that cake.

" Oh, it was just a friendly arguement, er, sort of, " said Dennis.

" Er yeah," added Maurice.

" Only joking. I know you two are as thick as thieves, with the effasiss on thick. Even that's probly over-estinimating your intelligence."

" I'm sorry, could you repeat that ? " asked Maurice maliciously.

" Well yes...er no, because I've forgotten already. I'm sorry lads, all this drinks catching up with me a bit fast. How are you two at the moment ? "

Maurice lifted his right hand and shook it from side to side.

" I'm a little tiddly," said Dennis.

" Yeah, but only below the waist," added Maurice.

Maurice and Hugo collapsed with laughter. Which was a bit unfortunate. Since Hugo dropped his cake onto Dennis' lap. A little splodged onto Maurice beside him, but Dennis got the bulk of it. He heard an ominous crack when it landed. At first he thought it was his own bones. But no, the familiar whiff of rotten eggs told him something else had occurred. Hugo had laced the cake with stink bombs. Later Dennis learned there were six or seven in there. It was the intention that whoever cut the cake would crack these little capsules as he sliced with his knife. The intended victim was, of course, Dennis. Thanks to the laughing fit, they all went off prematurely, however. Amid cries of 'pooah,' and 'what's that stink,' the pub emptied quicker than a classroom at the end of lessons. Maurice and Dennis were left trying to mop up bits of cake from themselves, one with sniggers, the other with curses. Now they were the only two left in the saloon bar, the landlord strolled over, with a face ready to spit venom.

" All right you two, that's it. You, and the rest of your poxy office crowd are barred, get it. I never want to see your stupid faces in here again. Now get out. "

" But it wasn't us."

" No buts,out."

" But Peter..."

" Don't Peter me, out."

The two straightened up, casually. At least they wanted to be casual. The walk to the door seemed to take a couple of minutes. Maybe the fact they were holding onto each other, for balance, did not help. Once outside, the fresher air hit Dennis with stronger force than the hydrogen sulphide. He looked to the wall for support while he got his bearings. Maurice was talking some gibberish,

" Don't peter me out, right, no butts allowed out in my pub, hee hee..."

" Shut up will you, I feel sick."

" You look it, where'd the others go ?

" Fuck knows, and cares, but not me, I..."

Dennis was interrupted by a shower of chunder coming from his mouth.

" I think we better be off, are you okay ? "

Dennis held up his hand, a gesture that asked Maurice to wait a minute. Then he continued, with a couple more spasms, some coughing, and some gobbing.

" Whew, I needed that," he said.

" Are you finished now ? "

" Yeah, let's go."

Home was a comfortable option for both. However, they decided against it. They were feeling too rough and smelly, even if the outside air was working its recuperative powers. A coffee, or tea, was held to be needed. Anything that might lessen the effects of the inevitable hangover. Their staggers turned to walks as they homed in on the area they lived. They had a place to go to in mind, but had neglected to mention it to each other.

Dennis was dizzy. Waves of something kept rolling through him. He assumed Maurice was feeling similar, because Maurice kept bumping into him.

" God, I feel really weird, and it aint all pleasant. I aint been this fucked for ages...shit, I really shouldn't pile it down on an empty stomach. That's fair enough though, that's why I did the spew. But I can't work out why I'm the bumbling idiot all the time."

" Must be the joint we had in the toilets," said Maurice.

" Oh shit, I forgot that, no wonder, I hate blow."

" Sure, that's why you smoked half of it."

" But I didn't know what I was doing. You know I don't like that stuff, why'd you give it to me ? "

" Don't know, I don't like being the only one stoned at a place, I suppose. None of the other crowd will touch it."

" One thing about our workmates I agree with...God, I didn't even want to go on the piss with them. I knew this would happen. Eveyone chucks down the pints like their stomachs are on fire. And then you get all these twats with their pranks, which you've got to go along with, otherwise some nerdy type's going to get all offended. Sometimes, just sometimes, I wish we could go out and have a laugh without all this crap. I wish more people were like me in that way."

" Careful what you wish for mate, you might get it."

" Maybe, but at least I wouldn't have some wanker trying to put itching powder down my trousers, or something like that..."

" Dear oh dear. I think we better get you some refreshment, are we going to Maria's."

" Don't know, are we ? "

" Well, we're walking that way aren't we ? "

" Yeah, I suppose we are."

" Do you want to go then ? "

" I suppose so. "

" Well do you ? "

" I said yeah, didn't I. "

" You said 'I suppose so.'"

" Alright , yeah, I suppose, let's go."

Maria's was a cafe. They were regulars at this cafe, which was only around the corner from their respective flats. Yet Maria did not recognise them on this occaison. She would not let them in at first, thinking they were two dossers, just coming into the cafe for a bit of warmth. She eventually relented when she recognised them. But not without screwing up her face and waving her hand, a futile gesture intended to get rid of their smell. She informed Dennis she would tell his nan about the terrible way he was behaving. Dennis knew she was only half joking in her sternness, even if his nan would be told regardless, he would not hear the end of this. Maria plonked the two of them down, at the table by the old tea urn, the one Dennis hated. He was calmed by the sight of two huge mugs of tea moving toward him. Maria left them to their thoughts, not without giving a few of her own about their drunkeness. It was all their own fault, as per usual.

" It's always your fault if you get drunk, isn't it ? "said Dennis ,continuing the theme.

" Well no one else is using your body to get drunk, mate."

" No, I mean peer group pressure."

" Don't you mean beer group pressure."

" I'm serious, you know."

" Only coz you feel rough."

" No it isn't, sometimes I don't want to drink."

" Then don't."

" But everyone would take the piss."

" So what ? they take the piss anyway."

" It's a bad environment."

" Oh yeah. Listen mate, it's no one's fault you can't hold your drink."

" What ? as well as you, you mean ?

" Probably."

" I've seen you spew a good few times."

" Well maybe not then, who gives a shit ? "

" I don't know, I was just thinking. I just want to talk for a bit, It stops my head from spinning. If I stop I feel like I'm going to fall apart."

" That's quite natural."

" Oh yeah, it don't exactly feel natural. It feels like every part of my body wants to fly off in different directions."

" Better not, Think of the mess that'll have to be cleared up."

" Whew."

" Look, I know I've been taking the piss a bit, but I've had the deadly spins myself, a couple of times. You should put your head between your legs."

" What ? in here ? "

" No, drink your tea first."

Dennis looked at Maurice to see if he was serious. It was a huge effort. Maurice was a misty blur. He was a misty blur at the best of times. Dennis could never figure what his intentions were. Everything serious had a funny side, while everything funny was dead serious. Still, the conversations eased his spins to a tolerable degree. The hot, strong tea burned its way down their throats. It also served a little dose of sobriety. Both were flushed. Their staggers were less marked as they shuffled toward the door to leave. An angry shout soon brought their attention back to Maria at the counter. They had forgotten to pay. Some confused searching of pockets followed. Eventually Maria was paid, though not pacified. She waved a finger in front of them, accusing them of countless potential misdemeanours. After she had heard enough apologies, she let them go. At last Dennis could go home and crash out.

It was week or so before Dennis touched any alcohol again. No one had made any comments about the last episode with his workmates. But then he never expected anyone at work to, because no one ever did, at least not while he was around. Usually one of his charming neighbours would try to wind him up for no apparent reason, every time they heard a whisper of his escapades. It was a disadvantage living so close to work. Since his real mates thought his workmates were a bunch of wankers. Dennis could see their point. He never made such a distinction himself. For he could see his colleagues view of his close friends, who were little better than a bunch of hooligans and petty criminals. Both sets were exaggerating, at least he thought so, sometimes. It was boring to have to think about it too much, it gave him one of his headaches. At the same time, he did not wish to be seen by one group when he was with the other. Maurice was in the same predicament. Yet he managed the crossover with ease. Dennis had once asked him about this, and Maurice had burst out laughing,

" Just be yourself, you twat."

This was fine, if you knew which self to be,

" You think about it too much, you gonad."

There might be something in this, thought Dennis, but then he shrugged his shoulders and forgot about it.

He was due to meet Maurice that evening, and was already late. They were to go to one of their favourite haunts, the Kings Arms. Although it was not really a favourite, just an obvious place to meet. This place was a dark, grotty, little hole. Dennis thought it had character. Being located at the back of their estate, next to derelict builders yards, at least it was free from the office crowds. Although sometimes Dennis wondered. At least the pub he got banned from admitted daylight once in a while. In the Kings Arms no one was allowed in except locals, this was unwritten convention, though no one ever said anything about it. Any strangers would get the silent glares as they poked their heads around the door. That, and the grotty decor, usually dissuaded anyone from stopping. Both Dennis and Maurice were known here. And, as he walked in, he could see his friend bending the ear of a barmaid, who giggled intermittently. A fairly normal scene, Maurice was always trying it on with barmaids. Perhaps because they were the only women who would listen to him for any length of time. They could not run away, not too often anyway.

There was a feeling of something wrong. For a start, the pub was packed. This only happened on Fridays, and Christmas, never on Sundays. Secondly, the pub was packed with blokes, mainly. That last fact was not unusual. However, it magnified an uneasy feeling Dennis had. Whenever the Kings Arms was packed like this, a fight usually broke out. Mind you, the blokes in here did not look like troublemakers. In fact they looked like - a bunch of twats. Most of them had stupid mod type haircuts.

Dennis took a seat at the bar next to Maurice. Maurice's intended victim had made her excuses, and escaped. John the Landlord served Dennis as he bought the drinks. And he had time for a quick conversation, unfortunately.

" I'm going to have to change the barrel. I'd never have believed it..."

" What ? that Smile Ale is so popular," said Dennis.

" Well yeah, exactly, I mean, no disrespect, but Smile Ale is bottom of the range you know, cheap and nasty. Calling it piss is an insult to urine."

" But I drink Smile," said Dennis.

" Yeah, and there's no accounting for taste."

" It ought to be called Smeg Ale," said Maurice.

Dennis began to turn red.

" Look, we're only joking," said John.

" Er yeah, right," added Maurice with his hands up.

" There is no accounting for taste," droned on John. " It's a matter of opinion. But Smile's about the least popular of my beers. You're about the only one that drinks it," John nodded at Dennis. " Apart from tonight of course, never seen anything like it. Maybe it's flavour of the month, or some shit like that. That lot are welcome to it."

John finshed by giving a surly look to the crowd in his pub.

" Speaking of which," said Maurice. " Do you know any of them. They all look a bit familiar, like local casuals. Some of them look a bit like Dennis."

" Yeah sure," said Dennis. " So long as they haven't got your intelligence as well. What a poor combination."

" I'm not kidding, look."

Dennis felt this to be a waste of time. He did cast his glance over the clientele, automatically. He reluctantly admitted his two friends were right. Most of these blokes did look like him. There was not enough to suggest family resemblance, but enough to suggest similar types. And what types they were. Part of some weird club or clan, or what ? they were grouped randomly around tables and fruit machines, much as any pub crowd. He could hear the drone of their conversation, and was thankful he could not make out individual words. Dennis realised with a start he was admiring their clothes. They were not dressed uniformly. But they all appeared to be wearing something he liked, or, something associated with the many phases he went through in his impatient life. There was a biker jacket here, levi's there, a mop top here, pegs there, M and I jacket here, DM's there, baseball cap here, tracksuit bottoms there.

Even so, there was something exceedingly fucked up about the whole thing. These people were distorted reflections of his own life. He said nothing to Maurice or John about it. They were engaged in their own conversation anyway.

" Maybe, they're clones," said Maurice. " There's probably a factory down the road, churning out ready to wear twats."

" Why would anyone want to clone a twat ? " said John.

They both looked at Dennis. Having been satisfied he was not listening, they continued their comments. Dennis was engrossed in staring at his lookalikes, trying to figure it out himself, but with a steadily growing paranoia.

" Maybe it's cheap labour."

" What for ? "

" I don't know, shit jobs like bog cleaning, or a traffic warden."

" Maybe it's some kind of fashion, you know, like students or something," said John.

" Some of them look like trendy student wankers, yeah. But some some of them look like semi-decent blokes..."

" Like casuals ? "

" Don't know, does it matter ? it's more custom for you."

" Hmmm, up to a point, yeah. But if they are trendies, it might cause problems. These people only drink crappy drinks, like white wine... You seen what's happened with the Smeg Ale, I mean the Smile Ale. It might drive off all the regulars."

" Might be the price of progress, John."

" Progress my arse, it's the quality of the drinking experience that counts."

Maurice took a quick look at the decrepid surroundings before replying -

" Er...yeah, right."

Two lookalikes ambled to the bar.

" Anyway, I've got a job to do, rather than stand around talking crap to the likes of you."

John moved away to talk to his customers before disappearing to change the barrel.

Maurice prodded Dennis in the ribs.

" Oooww."

" God, take it easy mate."

" Sorry, I was miles away there."

" I know the feeling. You look a bit rattled by this."

" Slight fucking understatement, more like rampaging paranoia. The more I look at them and think about it, the more I remember what I said after we got chucked out the pub the other week..."

" What ? about Maria grassing you up to your nan..."

" Nooo...About wishing everyone was like me."

But Maurice had nicely reminded him of another worry. His nan did not like drunkeness. Not surprising, after being married to a drunk for forty years, another embarassment to deal with. She seemed to think the sniff of a vinegar bottle would turn you into a raging alkie. Maybe she was just being protective.

Maurice had begun to smile. But he noticed the look on Dennis' face.

" Take it easy, mate. It's all just coincidence. I do remember you making that wish. But so what ? Doesn't mean it's happened. You know lots of people come and go round here..."

" Apart from us lot."

" Apart from us lot, yeah. But the point still stands... Anyway, you always did fancy yourself as a trendy bastard. So it's not surprising that a bunch of trendy bastards looks a bit like you. What would really settle your fears is if you went over and talked to them."

Dennis thought this over for a few seconds, then shook his head.

" No way, I'm not mixing it with a bunch of twats."

Over the following days, however, the experience continued to bother him. Whenever something was bothering Dennis he might react in various ways. Though he never did. Usually he just got drunk or had some sex, if some was available. If lucky, he could get both. Although the combination had given him embarassing moments in the past, such as falling asleep on his girlfriend before he had even started. His girlfriend, she was someone he had been going out with for years, on and off, mostly off. Sue was very understanding. It did make Dennis guilty that he only saw her when he was either pissed or pissed off. And since he was good at being a miserable sod, she saw him more often than she would have liked. Sue had known him since childhood, this gave her loads of information, which she used to wind Dennis up to great advantage. She enjoyed telling him her sexual exploits at sixteen, while he was still waiting for his first bumfluff at fifteen. And as the years slowly progressed, you could always count on her to have a laugh while he complained. It was something that broke his bad mood and made him smile.

The walk along the main road, by the river, went quickly as Dennis daydreamed. His reverie shut out the monotonous moan of the heavy traffic. He walked up the stairs to Sue's second floor flat. A few minutes pause was needed before he walked along the balcony. His heart was pumping. This was not so much anticipation as the fact the stairs had made him knackered. Although anticipation took over when he rang the bell and heard those steps shuffling to the door. The door opened to reveal the petite features of Sue. Her black, curly hair seemed to cover half her body, draping aimlessly over her shoulders and halfway down her back. Her eyes seemed dreamy, but then she registered him and they nearly popped out.

" Wha...who are you ?

" Eh...it's me, Dennis."

" But I thought..."

" What ? "

" Oh nothing, er..."

" Is there something wrong ? "

" Yes, yes there is, as a matter of fact. Can you prove who you are ? "

" But you know who I am, and I know who I am."

" Look, just do it for me, okay."

Dennis pulled out his driving licence, holding it before her face.

" Satisfied. Do you want to take fingerprints as well ? Or maybe I should get a couple of references."

" Stop being a smartarse Dennis, it never did suit you."

Dennis frowned.

" Okay, fair enough, now are you going to let me in ? "

" It's a bit awkward at the moment."

" Why should it be awkward. We arranged it this morning. You said you were doing nothing all day."

Sue hesitated.

" Er, true, but I er..."

" There's something wrong isn't there ? "

Sue nodded.

" Look, I think you should come in. There's something you should see."

Having said this, Sue took Dennis' hand, marching him straight to the bedroom. This is great thought Dennis. Sue was never usually that foward. But on this occaison it seemed she was gagging for it.

That thought evaporated as they entered Sue's bedroom. Dennis saw one of his lookalikes lying naked in her bed, reading a marvel comic. The lookalike exchanged glances of surprise with him. It was Sue who broke the silence.

" Er..look, I think you better get out of my house, okay. You conned me into thinking you were him, and that gives me the fucking creeps..."

" Fucking right, you dirty bastard," said Dennis.

He stepped foward, ready to boot his adversary first, then punch him. But the lookalike's reaction stopped this. He held his arms in front of his face, as a gesture of self-protection, crossing them over at the wrists. It was a gesture Dennis had used several times in the past in threatening situations. Seizing his moment, the lookalike spoke -

" I'm sorry, I was only walking along the street. She came up to me and told me I was early, led me straight in here, undressed me, and forced me to have sex."

" I didn't force you," said Sue.

" No, but you didn't give me a chance to say anything."

Sue blushed as Dennis glared at her. It bothered him that, now, she had been foward on two occaisons, neither had the desired result. The marvel comic also bothered him, because he never read them.

" Is this true ? " he said.

" Look, er..yes, I thought it was you. He looked like you, walked like you, talked like you, dressed like..."

" But he aint me, is he. I'm me, for fuck's sake."

" Don't shout at me, it was a mistake okay."

While this exchange was going on, the lookalike had started dressing. After he had pulled his t-shirt and jeans on, he said,

" I'm really sorry, mate, I really am. I don't want to mess things up for you. If I'd have known, I never would have bothered to come here. But see it from my point of view. A woman comes out of nowhere, acts all friendly, and then invites me up here. I couldn't believe my luck. I thought Chrsitmas had come early..."

" Christmas didn't come early, but you did," snapped Sue.

The lookalike blushed as he did up his shoelaces. Dennis did understand. What happened has that Sue took the initiative, even if she took it more than usual. Sue always took the initiative. She just talked and led him along, "like a lemon," as she always put it. That was how he had first ended up in her flat himself. Personal history was repeating itself. He was not too keen on giving other people a stand in role, however. The lookalike continued to blush. He grabbed a jean jacket from a chair and hastily scuttled out the flat. After the front door slammed he looked at Sue wondering what to say.

" Um, look, this is all a bit weird. I think you should leave, Dennis."

" But I've only just got here."

" Look, can't you see I've had a disturbing experience."

" A disturbing experience, what ? shagging someone else..."

" I thought it was you."

" But I'm me. You supposed to be seeing me, not a bloody stunt double."

" It was a mistake, can't you see that...Now, I want to be on my own."

" What ? What about this afternoon ? "

" I don't feel like seeing anyone after something like this."

Dennis gave a heavy sigh.

" Alright, so I'll see you later on, yeah."

" I don't know...maybe."

" Maybe aint very definite."

" Look, I can't be very definite at the moment, okay."

" How do I know you haven't played some trick on me."

" Really ? not much of a trick is it. And why would I do something that backfired on me like that ? "

" I don't know, but I always seem to have to put with peoples' stupid pranks."

" No, don't be such a lemon..Oh I don't know. Look, I just want to be alone for the moment, okay, so get out."

" Alright, alright, I'm going...How about tomorrow ?

"Just go, you twat."

Dennis thought about prolonging the arguement, but ran out of things to say. After he left he pondered the past two weeks. Two disturbing experiences, and during this period work was even more a pain than usual. It was hard to keep his interest. And this fact was becoming known to his colleagues. It was commented that he looked more vacant than usual. Maurice gained wind of what had disturbed Dennis, by constantly asking what was wrong until Dennis gave up. Then he giggled relentlessly, much to Dennis' irritation. Maurice played down the events, as if they were talking about a telly programme. So, on the Friday, they went for their usual couple of pints, carefully avoiding their colleagues, as was custom. Maurice gained a rerun of the recent happenings. He was more sympathetic this time, although the giggles continued.

They were drinking in what looked like a converted office. It even had office chairs and tables as pub furniture. All that was needed was a broken photocopier and some dying rubber plants. The landlady heard this facetious remark, but thought it was a good idea, worth looking into. Dennis sighed heavily, a habit that had increased within the past week.

" An office pub ? it should be called the Admin Officer's Arms," Dennis sighed again.

" Or the Manager's Head...maybe we could get flexi-time drinking."

" How's that ? "

" Well, if you drank ten pints in a week usually, you could change and do it all in one session."

" What's the point in that ? "

" None really, but you could take a few days off to recover."

" I'd bet they'd make you clock in. And then you'd have to drink at least four pints every half hour..."

" With half an hour for lunch."

" And the manager would check your glasses afterwards to see you weren't skiving...shit...this is a crap conversation."

" I know, but it took your mind off Sue."

Dennis laughed.

" No it didn't, but thanks for trying anyway mate."

" Yeah she'll come round. It was a weird event."

" Yeah, but what if she don't come round."

" That's up to her, mate. I mean, you could go round there and kick the door in, and start throwing things around, like some people we know. But that isn't going to help. It's out of your hands at the moment."

" That's the problem. I feel like my whole life is out of my hands. I've been seeing more and more of these lookalikes, walking down the streets, in the pubs, in the market, even driving around in cars."

" Not much like you then. You can't drive."

" I can, and I've got a licence."

" Oh yeah."

" Yeah, and I've always liked it, what I've done of it."

" So ? "

" Don't you see. It's like they're all alike in some ways..."

" That's a lot of likes."

" Too much for my liking. Even the things I'd like to do."

" Yeah right. I've always wanted to be an astronaut. But every time I see one, I don't think, that geezer's copying me, because I wanted to be an astronaut as well."

" Oh yeah, how many astronauts do you see walking down the high street ? "

" It depends what day it is."

" I thought they sent out for something."

Maurice was unimpressed by this remark. But he gave Dennis a grin of admiration, to encourage him.

" That's the spirit, mate...Anyway, so what if a few geezers look like you, so what if they like some things you do, I mean, we've probably all got some things in common. And if you got a lot in common with a lot of other people, all it probably shows is what a boring, average, everyday bastard you are."

" Yeah, like I got a lot in common with someone like the Pope."

" Maybe, I mean, you're both unemployed down under at the moment."

" Fuck off."

" And you both like wearing old fashioned dresses."

" Right."

They both laughed. Dennis looked at his watch

" Look, I've got to go now. I promised my nan I'd go and see her."

" Why ? "

" Because she asked me."

" Why ? "

" How do I know ? probably some stupid errand."

" See you then."

" Aint you going to persuade me to stay and have another ? "

" Why would I want to do that ? "

" Because I'm good company."

" Yeah, like a medallion man at a feminist convention. "

This puzzled Dennis.

" What ? What does that mean ?

Maurice shook his head, the teacher despairing of his dumb student.

" It'll take too long to explain now, mate. I'll tell you later. If you got to go, you should go."

" Yeah right, see you."

" See you."

Dennis thought he half understood what Maurice had said. He wished he had pushed for an explanation though. Inevitably it played on his mind as he walked to his Nan's.

Still, at least it gave him a reprieve from the problem of the lookalikes. His Nan lived on the ground floor of the same block as Sue. Being reminded of this, the worries worked their way back into his deliberations. He met two people on the way, people he knew fairly well. They both remarked on the fact he got around a lot. He had not taken in their words at the time. But they had both said they had seen him in other places only minutes previously. With a sigh he knocked at his Nan's. The door was opened by one of his lookalikes.

" What the fuck are you doing here ? "

" Don't really know, mate. I just felt I should come round, that's all," said the lookalike.

" Well now you can feel like fucking off away from my Nan's."

" Don't get shirty, mate. It was an accident, that's all."

" You better go now, before you have another accident."

The lookalike fled quickly, thankfully, much as Dennis himself would, if confronted by the same situation. Dennis went inside and slammed the door. A voice hovered down the passageway, from the sitting room on the far right.

" Is that more of you turned up ? "

Dennis entered the sitting room to find it fully occupied. His Nan sat facing the telly. Adjacent to her were a settee and another armchair, of the same faded materials. Four lookalikes were seated altogether. They were all totally engrossed in watching some idiot chat show, laughing at all the required moments.

" What are you doing here ? "

" Shush," said his Nan.

" We're trying to watch this."

" I don't care. Look you lot, no disrespect, but get out, you don't belong here."

" But we feel perfectly at home here," said one of the lookalikes.

" I bet you do. But this aint your home, it's my Nan's."

" Don't be soft, son. They're not doing any harm."

" Sorry Nan, but I don't care. Everywhere I go I see these geezers, and it's begining to get on my tits."

" Dennis, I've always told you not to use crude and stupid language all the time."

Dennis blushed. He took out his discomfiture on the lookalikes.

" I'm sure you lot can go and pester someone else."

The lookalikes all stood and made to leave.

" Don't listen to this little berk, stay if you want to."

The lookalikes eyed Dennis and thought better of this suggestion. His flushed face and nervy twitch signalled anger.

" Thank you Mrs Thompson, but we better be off all the same.

Dennis walked his doubles to the door.

" What is it with you people ? aint you got Nan's of your own."

One of the lookalikes made as if to speak.

" Don't tell me, you just felt you should be here."

" Near enough, Mate. We can't explain it either. We don't particularly want to be near you. But we can't help it..."

" What's that supposed to mean ? "

" Well, no disrespect, mate, but we seem to be a lot alike in many ways...which is how we know you're a twat, a nice twat, true, but a bit slow on the uptake all the same. That's because we're twats as well."

" Well good for you. So why don't you go and act the twat somewhere else. Why do I have to see you everywhere ? you must have lives of your own."

" Course we do. But we drift through life, much as you do, just doing things on the spur of the moment."

" Oh really ? well you got some weird moments in your lives, the way you always end up hanging round me all the time."

" We might as well say the same."

" Oh yeah, I don't go and pester all the people you know."

" How can you be sure of that. Maybe you're just pestering our mates," said another lookalike.

" Yeah, you might be the one that's intruding," said a third.

" I might be but I'm not."

" Can you be sure of that ? "

" Listen, I've had about enough of this mind game shite. Please piss off now."

" That's exactly how we'd react."

" Well big gonads to you. Then you agree with my decsision."

" Not really, but we understand it."

" Good. Now understand my wish to have you fuck off."

With those words Dennis rudely slammed the door on his lookalikes. He turned around to see his Nan watching him from the sitting room doorway.

" That's no way to treat your gang, son."

" They're not my gang, Nan."

" Then what are they doing round here ? "

" How would I know ? "

" That's a shame."

" Why is it a shame ? "

" Well, the thought did occur to me, that maybe they came round to buy drugs."

" What, from you ? "

" Maybe, though I don't see what they'd want with prescription tranquilisers. Mrs Mason usually buys the lot from me anyway."

" You sell tranks, that's a bit dodgy."

" She needs them, she knows they're dangerous. Anyway, she doesn't take all of them, she sells a lot of them on..."

" I don't believe this, my Nan the junkie."

" Don't be stupid, son, junk is heroin, I can tell the difference. Tranquilisers are dangerous as well, but only if you take them like sweets. I wouldn't recommend them to everyone. Besides your gang was telling me you smoke a bit of dope occaisonally..."

" Nan, they're not my gang."

" But they still told me, and that nice Stanton lad."

" Nice ? you mean Maurice ? "

" That's the one. And that's the reason I asked you here. I'd like you to get some dope..."

" What ? I don't believe it."

" Don't be shocked, son."

" I'm not shocked, just, er, bewildered."

" Yes, you always were, pretty much. Listen son, this doesn't mean I'm on the road to ruin, like your poor old Grandad, god bless him, the poor sod took everything to excess. Besides, it's not as dangerous as drink. And it's the only thing that helps me with the pain, you know. I get terrible arthritis, as well as migraine. It doesn't kill the pain, but it helps me deal with it better. What do you say ? "

" I don't know."

" What do you mean, you don't know. You must be able to get it."

" Nan, I don't really smoke it. It makes me feel dizzy and sick."

" Just like your Grandad, can't handle anything stronger than a cup of tea. I heard abour your drunken behaviour at

Maria's place the other day. Give it up, son. Some people aint cut out for the life of Riley, and you're one of them."

" What ? other people'd be pleased I only drink."

" Yes, the dozey dipsticks who swallow everything the papers dish up. But I'm more realistic..."

" I still can't help you, I'm not into the stuff, and I don't want to get into it."

" Don't be gutless, son. Think of me, your poor, old Nan. I've not got many years left. It's a bit late to go down the sportscentre and do me Arabic classes..."

" You mean Aerobics ? "

" Same difference, now, will you help me ? "

" Oh alright, I'll talk to Maurice, but I don't promise you anything."

" You're a good lad, son, even if you're a bit of an idiot sometimes."

" Can I go now ? or do you want to me to do a bit of housebreaking for you."

" That's thoughtful of you, son, but I know you haven't got the bottle for it....I'm only joking, just talk to the Stanton lad for me."

" Right, right, bye then."

Another episode Dennis could make no sense of. Events were begining to pile up. Twice in the following week he arrived at work to find a group of lookalikes there. On the second occaison they had actually done most of his work, which he was not quite grateful for. It caused some disruption to his routine, and others. But, as usual, most of his colleagues found it amusing. There were serious jokes made about his 'Following.' After these came the complaints. He was accused of operating some kind of scam, getting his lookalikes to do his work for him. The complaints reached Hugo, and he was called into the Manager's office. Hugo was quite sympathetic, he managed to disentangle the fact that Dennis was powerless in this situation, indeed, as he was in most situations. However, it did not help that Hugo could not resist bursting out laughing couple of times. The whole series of happenings was just so, well, peculiar. Yet he was compassionate enough to grant Dennis two weeks leave, which would come out of his annual entitlement, naturally.

A couple of weeks twiddling his thumbs was the last thing Dennis needed. He wanted something to take his mind off events. He tried taking a train to the coast for a day. However, it was packed with lookalikes. So he had to stand most of the way. Everywhere he went they followed him like a huge parade. He could not even get served at a pub he went into because it was packed with his dopplegangers. He sneaked back to the train station hoping to leave them all behind. But they were already on the train. And once again he had to stand most of the way.

Back home, walking the streets became intolerable. Lookalikes wandered around everywhere. Some of the younger kids on his estate began copying them, in clothes, haircuts, even his unique slouching walk. His mates, meanwhile, continued to take the piss out of him, mercilessly. After giving out this eardrum bashing for two days, constantly, they admitted to Dennis that, yes, he might have a problem. This made Dennis even more worried. For when his friends got involved they usually messed things up. Although if they had noticed a problem, then things must be pretty severe indeed. Whatever, a meeting was arranged, Dennis was informed, for his benefit, at the Kings Arms. Dennis was rattled at the prospect. A further thought also occurred to him. Suppose it was full of his lookalikes. However, repeated going over of events of the past weeks had made some impression on him. He noticed he always ran into the lookalikes when he was in a dreamy passive state of mind, a quite common occurrence. When he was more alert, more active, nothing strange happened. Therefore, as he walked to the Kings Arms, he endeavoured to concentrate. He tried to plan what he would say and do over the coming evening. This concentration appeared to have the desired effect, as far as he could see. For when he peered into the Kings Arms there were no lookalikes present. However, all that concentration was giving him one of his headaches.

He could spy familiar faces, snug in one of the corners of the saloon. There was Maurice, Cheerful Charlie, his sister Rita, Danny Unfunny, and Lenny Guppy. John the Landlord was hovering around as well, pretending to be busy. Dennis timidly walked in. The pub was its usual self - dark, grotty and uninviting. The whole scene felt ridiculous to Dennis. There they were, all sitting around like they were some kind of war council. They would accomplish nothing apart from drinking excessively and talking bollocks. This meeting would end the same as their usual meets, everyone would get pissed and take the piss. Still, it was better than nothing. Dennis checked himself with this thought, no, it was not really. His paranoia was begining to ease into gear. And this lot would probably push it into overdrive. His wish was still to get away. And he said as much when he joined the gang.

" You don't want to bottle out now," said Cheerful Charlie, " You're always doing that."

" I didn't say run away, I said get away, take a break somewhere."

" But you tried that already," said Maurice, " And they all came with you."

" Ha ha, God, I'd love to have that. If I owned a B and B on the coast, I'd just phone Dennis when I was short of Business, and he could bring all his mates down."

This was Danny Unfunny. After this outburst everything went quiet for a few minutes, as it usually did when he tried to make a joke.

" It's a bit weird all this, isn't it ? " said Rita.

" But no weirder than Dennis himself," chipped in Maurice.

" Ha bloody ha."

" Yeah, don't take the piss...not yet anyway," said Lenny.

" So what brings it all on," Rita enquired.

" I've worked it out. When I'm in a certain state of mind, I get all these lookalikes ending up in the same place as me."

Dennis did not quite say that as he intended. He knew a pisstake was on the horizon.

" And what state of mind is that ? " demanded Cheerful.

Dennis looked at his friends in some trepidation before replying -

" When I'm feeling a bit dozey."

The whole table erupted in laughter. John the Lanldord came over to investigate, and the situation was explained. So everyone burst out laughing a second time. Dennis dropped quickly into a sulk.

The problem is worse than we thought," said Maurice.

" Fucking chronic," added Cheerful.

" You're as sick as a parrot," said Danny.

Conversation was killed for a brief minute, then -

" No wonder you've been so edgy lately," said Lenny.

" What are you saying ? that I've always been dozey."

" Yeah," Lenny replied.

" No, no, come on," said Maurice. " He's easy going, a lot of people would mistake this for dozey..."

" Yeah, practically everyone we know," interrupted Cheerful.

" Maybe, maybe, but you might just as well say laid back, yeah."

Everyone nodded except Cheerful.

" What ? you mean like a stoned hippy ? "

" Not quite, but close enough."

" All that's as maybe, but all these twats are still around, yeah. The only real way to get rid of them is to scare the shit out of them, or kick the shit out of them, or both."

Cheerful's solutions to problems always involved someone getting beaten up, with him giving the treatment. It accounted for his nickname, since he was a bad tempered bastard.

" You could always try talking to them," said Rita.

" What's the point in that ?" said Cheerful.

" Well, you could find out why they're here in first place."

Everyone nodded. This seemed sensible enough, except for Cheerful.

" No way. They're obviously taking the piss, these geezers, so something drastic has to be done..."

" I've tried talking to them, " Dennis interrupted, " But I don't get no sense out of them. They don't seem to be aware what's going on. They just wander about in the way they talk, the way they do things. It's a bit like..."

Dennis hesitated.

" Like talking to yourself," Maurice finished.

Everybody laughed.

" Yeah, like talking to yourself all at once," said Danny.

The laughter fizzled out quickly.

" They sound harmless enough, so what's the problem ? " said Rita.

" Yeah, I suppose they are harmless to me. But they keep turning up at places I'm supposed to be, and making life difficult for everyone else..."

" And embarassing for you," said Lenny.

" Well yeah."

" Then you do have to get rid of them somehow."

" Fucking do the bastards," shouted Cheerful.

" He may have a point," Maurice ventured.

" Fucking right I do."

" No, no, I mean about doing something drastic," Maurice paused to look warily at Cheerful, before going on. " It seems we don't where these people come from. But we know roughly when they're going to turn up, Don't we."

" Well maybe if you traced events back to when it all started, you might have some clue as to why Dennis attracts all these lookalikes, or whatever they are, when he's in a certain mood."

This was Rita. And her idea seemed to be the first sensible thing said all evening. So they all became briefly thoughtful.

" That's fucking brilliant, " Lenny finally said.

" Yeah, better a pork chop than a packed lunch."

Everyone gave Danny looks of confusion and distaste before the conversation resumed.

" So when did it all start ? " asked Rita.

" Easy peasy," Maurice said, " A few weeks ago, just after the weekend..."

" No, no, mate," Dennis said, " It was that same weekend."

" I remember, yeah, you kept complaining of feeling weird all the time, not that that means anything, you're always complaining."

" You complain more than an old bag."

Danny's unfunny remark fell on deaf ears. Conversation continued.

" It was the office do."

" I remember now."

" So what, a bunch of poncy tossers who can't handle their drink," growled Cheerful.

" Present company excepted of course," added Lenny diplomatically.

" Bloody office workers," Cheerful snorted.

" Did anything unusual happen in particular," Rita asked.

" Not really," said Maurice, " It was a typical office do, people wearing stupid hats, and someone let off a couple of stink bombs. Dennis got a bit annoyed because people kept doing things like sticking sausages in his pocket..."

" So long as they weren't attached to anything."

Danny had at last gained acknowledgement, though it was a fleeting grin on one or two faces rather than any laughs.

" But that's usual, Dennis always seem to cop it," Lenny was unsympathetic.

" Anyway," Maurice went on, " We got both real pissed and stoned, then we got the spins and Dennis was sick. Then we went to Maria's cafe and nearly got chucked out. Coz she thought we was a pair of methers..."

" Sounds pretty typical to me, " Lenny remarked.

Cheerful was shaking his head at Dennis.

" You never could handle anything, could you, always chucking up."

" That's not the point, though, is it ? " said Rita, " something happened, or you think something happened, that made all the difference."

" Well, er, I made a wish. I wished everyone could be like me."

All present burst out laughing yet again. It seemed ages before anyone got their guffaws under control. Cheerful was the first to speak.

" Fucking superstitious bollocks. You're telling us the good fairy granted your little wish."

" Or maybe it was someone come back from the future," said Lenny, " you know like in Star Trek."

" Hold on, hold on. It might sound ridiculous. So, maybe the only thing to do is to be ridiculous in return," Rita continued.

" What ? " this was said by all, nearly in unison.

" I mean just go through events the way the way you did last time."

" You don't half come out with some things sometimes," said Cheerful.

" I think I get what she means. It's like a hair of the dog cure, you know, when you drink to take the edge of the hangover you got the night before," Maurice said.

" Er, yeah, more or less," said Rita none too convincingly. She actually was not sure where the thought was leading her.

" Why ? why not just make a stupid wish again," said Cheerful.

" I'm wishing on a star-ar-ar," sung Danny self consciously.

" Shutup you, you got a shit voice," threatened Cheerful.

" I think conditions have got to be the same, is that it ? " ventured Lenny, " You do all the same things in the same way, like paying off a debt."

" Then wish it would all stop," said Rita.

Cheerful started laughing again.

" Fucking ridiculous, what are we ? a bunch of Aladdins ? This aint the forty thieves we're dealing with here..."

" Yeah, more like the forty twats," said Lenny.

Dennis went all quiet, so Maurice answered.

" True, true, it does sound like a load of old shite. But I don't see why we shouldn't try it. It can't do no harm, except to Dennis of course, only joking mate, plus, we get all the advantage of getting out of it along the way."

" But it's obviously not going to work," Lenny was having an attack of conscience, " getting out of it don't solve problems. It causes a lot, though."

" Maybe," said Maurice. " But I think we should try it before we try Cheerful's solution."

" You soppy sod, we can easily do them both at the same time, so why not ? " Cheerful growled at Maurice.

" Well, for a start, we'd have a hard time tracking down all these geezers."

" I'll go along with that," said Dennis, " We go with the piss up solution."

Dennis did not want to go with any solution. But he felt he must say something, otherwise they would all be dragged down Cheerful's path of casual mayhem.

Cheerful glared at Dennis but said nothing.

" Right that's it then. We get into the same mood and see what happens," Maurice was uncertain.

" Not much of a plan is it ? " said Rita.

" Too right, you got to go straight at the problem."

Like a bulldozer, thought Dennis, but he dare not say it. The mood of the group was drifting away from Cheerful's point of view anyway. Not that anyone preferred it in the first place. But Cheerful could be persuasive in his physically violent way. Now the conversation drifted out into murmurings between individuals rather than a group discussion.

Cheerful banged on at Maurice, and Maurice used all his diplomacy to avoid having to commit anyone to drastic action. While Danny continued to make unfunny remarks which nobody listened to, except for Lenny, who was unfortunate enough to sit next to him, and who constantly told him to shut up. Meanwhile, Rita turned to talk to Dennis. She had a lot of time for this 'little boy lost,' as she called him. He was so easy to talk to, and friendly. Yet he was always blundering into trouble. In the past she had actually quite fancied Dennis. But her protective brother had warned her off. Cheerful would be more than proud if she went out with someone who was a headcase. But a dozey twat like Dennis, forget it. The trouble was, most of the headcases were about as attractive as retarded gorillas, which is what most of them were already, according to Rita. And, in truth, Dennis was a bit of a dozey twat. However, she did not get very far before the random remarks of the others kept interrupting.

" So, are we going to do this, or what ? seems a bit pointless if you ask me."

" No one did."

" You're probably right. Still, I reckon this whole bit of weirdness started in a pointless way. So it's better to finish like that."

" Sounds like bollocks to me."

" You keep saying that."

" Well it is."

" I know, so stop telling me."

" I'm not telling anyone, I'm just saying."

No one could tell the provenance of these remarks, and, as drinking minutes were downed, nobody cared. Rita turned back to Dennis.

" You don't believe any of all this, do you Dennis ? "

" No."

" So why do you go along with it ? "

" Just in case, Rita."

She smiled.

" Well, just in case, would you include me in any future assignments ? "

" Signed what ?'

" Assignments you wally."

" Sorry."

" You really kill the moment sometimes, Dennis."

" Sorry."

" So, now you're in trouble with Sue, does this mean you're available ? "

" Er, how do you mean ? "

" Say, to come out for a drink sometime."

" Maybe, I'd love to come, I mean come along, not come come."

" What's the come come ? sounds like a dance."

" You know what I mean."

" Sorry, I'm too ladylike to discuss such matters."

Dennis narrowed his eyes to gain a good look at Rita. She was really intelligent, for the company she was in. It was a pity she came along with a growling brother like Cheerful. She was the good-natured, intelligent one of the family, while he was the bad-tempered, brawny bastard.

" There's a problem," Dennis nodded in the direction of Cheerful. " Your brother never trusts anyone. He acts like your bodyguard.

" Oh, I can handle him."

Well I can't, thought Dennis. But he said nothing and tried to smile at Cheerful, who gave him a glowering look in return.

" Oi twathead, you going to stick with this, then."

Dennis started, Cheerful's remark sounded like more of an order.

" Er, yeah."

" Well get them in then."

Cheerful waved his empty glass for emphasis. Dennis sloped off to the bar, feeling Cheerful's glare all the way. He looked unhappy, thought Maurice. But then, sloping off was one of Dennis' hobbies. Things were becoming blurry. Maurice continued in the general joviality. Dennis came staggering back with the drinks. John the Landlord was on his tail, because Dennis forgot to pay. This gave them all another good laugh. Danny Unfunny could not even make a funny remark about this. But nobody cared. They had a few more. Then they moved on. They had a few pubs to get through and a few joints to roll. Everything became dreamlike to Maurice. He remembered flashes of activity, usually Cheerful arguing with someone, between long spells of blackness, and that was it.

In fact Maurice missed the whole weekend. That evening really knocked the stuffing out of him. He could not even get out of bed till Tuesday. He was not that out of it, was he? Obviously he must have been. He had caught flu, or something similar. Although, at first, it was hard to distinguish from his usual hangover symptoms. The only clinching factor being the fact he was more spaced out than usual. He consistently forgot which day it was. People seemed to hear of his condition, so no one came round to see him. Only on Wednesday did Lenny Guppy feel safe enough from Maurice's germs to pay a visit. Even then he sat across the room from Maurice.

Something had gone wrong, apparently. Lenny could not remember much. But Rita disappeared early. They finally got rid of Danny Unfunny. Cheerful got into a fight, so everyone sneaked away from him. And the last he remembered seeing Maurice was when Maurice fell asleep on a seat. It was in some pub somewhere, but Lenny could not remember the name. Dennis had just vanished. One minute he was there and the next he was gone. Lenny was quite disturbed by this. Maurice could not really see why. Everything vanished when you got out of it, your money, your friends, your memory, then your consciousness. Why should one particular vanishing be any worse than the other. However, Dennis had not been seen since. Maurice was tempted to say 'so what.'

Whatever, Lenny had a copy of the local newspaper in his hand. He forced Maurice to read a short article on page four. Maurice protested, he could not even see his own way to the toilet at that moment. But Lenny was insistent. Words swam about before Maurice. He gradually focused his gaze, amidst a lot of dizziness, until he could read -

" DRUNKEN DEATHS MYSTERY ? "

" Police and hospital workers have been troubled by the rapid increase in deaths through misadventure recently, either as a result of alcohol poisoning, or accidents due to intoxication.

' The message regarding alcohol abuse does not seem to be getting through,' said a police spokesman. 'We have seen a marked rise in incidents related to the abuse of alcohol in recent weeks, and last weekend marked the worst yet.' He further appealed to people to be sensible in their enjoyment. ' You can have a good time without killing yourself.'

A significant factor in some of these recent casualties was held, by some, to be the fact a lot of them were of similar appearance. This has been dismissed as unimportant, however. 'Copycat behaviour always has happened, and probably always will. We can't stop this entirely, but we must stress the dangers of not thinking for yourself, becoming intoxicated just for the sake of it, just because somebody else does it. It is not " hard" or "cool", but a terrible by product of ignorance.'

The fact of so many people of similar appearance meeting a similar fate at roundabout the same time is seen by many as signicant however..."

" So what do you make of that ? " said Lenny.

" Er, am I supposed to make anything ? "

" Well yeah, it's a bit weird, isn't it ? "

Maurice gave out a hefty sigh.

" It's no weirder than usual, they're just trying to stir up something."

" I think it's creepy."

" I don't , I think it's bollocks, the press trying it on."

" But no one's seen Dennis."

" I don't blame him. I'd keep undercover, especially if he felt like me."

" Tell the truth, do you think there might be something in it ? "

Maurice tried to think. But if he did accept the nonsense article, that would have a lot of consequences. Ones he could not imagine but knew would come into being. It was the same of all mysteries. But his weary brain was not up to the prospect. Besides it really was bollocks, bollocks of a dog-sized degree and beyond. He shook his head. Lenny might have pursued the arguement, until he started thinking of germs again. Anyway, Maurice dozed off. So Lenny helped himself to one of his cigarettes, stuck it behind his ear, for later, then left.

Dennis was not seen again.

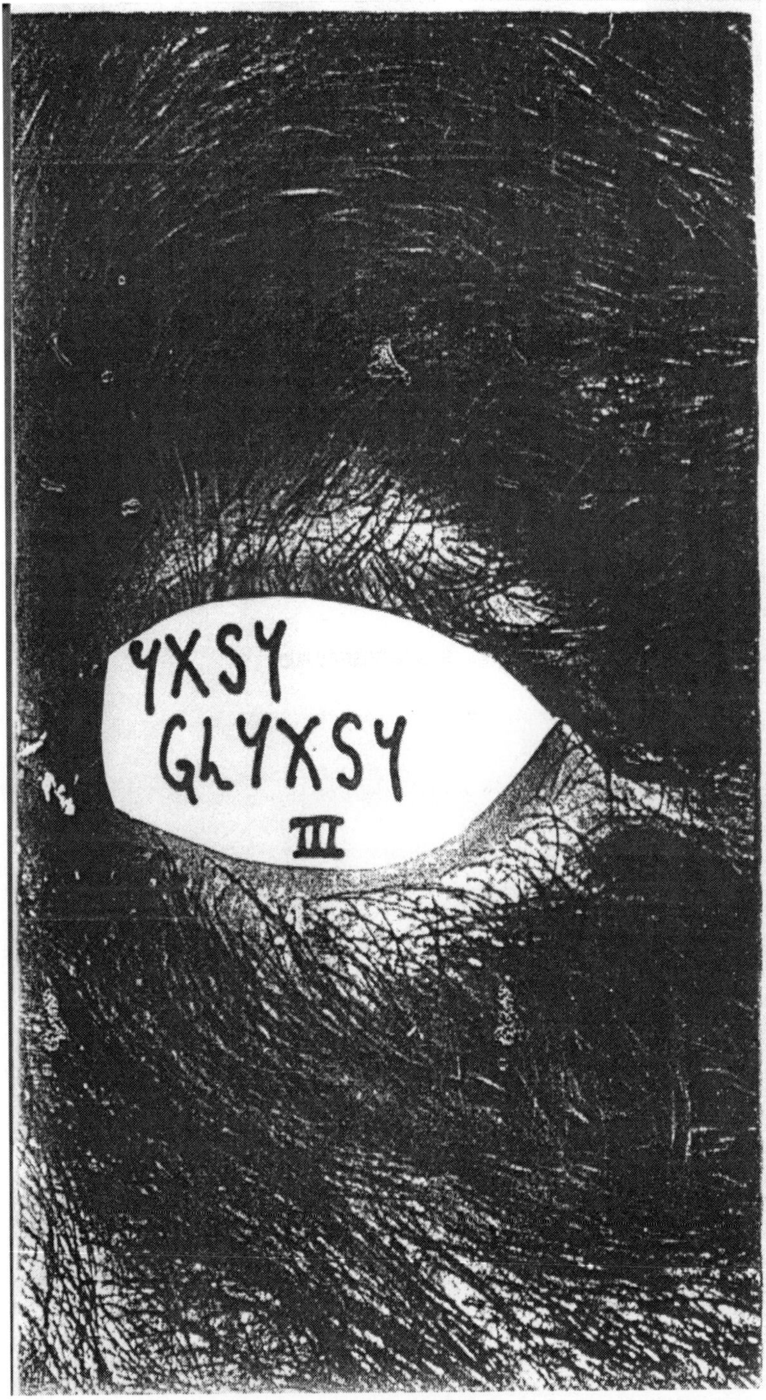
YXSY
GLYXSY
III

Handsome Glasses

" But Doctor Byfleet, it looks really painful."

" Please Rachel, call me Ronald...And I can assure you, once the glasses have been fitted, the wires insert quite easily into the eye socket. From then on, a pulse is sent to the temporal lobe area, and, well, we will wait and see what happens. There may be some discomfort, but no more than wearing an ordinary pair of glasses. "

" That's all very well Ronald, but these glasses do look a bit nerdy."

" I'm sorry but I cannot cater for your fashion sense Douglas. You know you may back out of this experiment at any time if you have reservations..."

" No, no, no, don't get me wrong. It was just a comment. After all the testing we've been through, I find the prospect quite exciting. I don't want to back out now."

" And how about you Paul ? "

" Oh I'm game Doctor Byfleet."

" Good, good...Now I cannot guarentee all the possible effects of this experiment. For you will not be under observation during the first phase. You will stay at the village, naturally, and go about your normal day to day activities, whatever that implies, ha ha. I would not recommend you wear the glasses for more than three hours at a time. And I also recommend, in fact I request, that you keep detailed notes as to your feelings, state of mind, and general physical well being. You will report back here after forty eight hours, when we can assess the initial results. I would also remind you, if any untoward effects occur, to contact us immediately, wherever you are, whatever the hour. You can use the pagers you have been supplied with. I must stress you are effectively under contract to myself and the company, " Free Market Pharmaceuticals, " during the whole course of the experiment. If you breach confidentiality, or if you abscond, you will find yourself liable for prosecution. Now, any questions ? "

" Yes, what method would you recommend for keeping notes. "

" Actually, a traditonal pen and note book might be best..."

The volunteers looked uneasy.

"... or you could have a dictaphone, possibly, if I could obtain a suitable model."

The trio nodded eagerly.

" What if we get into trouble and aren't able to use our pagers ? "

" Well you know this is practically the company's village. So I have instructed a handful of people to keep a discrete watch on you."

" Won't that put us off a bit ? "

" I said a discrete watch will be kept. They will not be shadowing you, or watching your every move...No more questions ? good. Well then, here's to a happy outcome.

Rachel, Douglas and Paul made tentative steps as they walked down the drive of the company's building. Self-consciousness had gripped all of them. It did not seem right to try the glasses on within the grounds. Once past the gate they moved off into the trees.

" This is stupid, I feel like a schoolboy."

" Why should you Paul, unless your motives are in question."

" Perhaps they are. I must admit, it's like getting paid for being out of it..."

" Not a very scientific attitude."

" But one that's there all the same."

" How about you Rachel ? Rachel ? "

While the two men talked Rachel was already wearing her glasses.

" You don't waste much time, do you ? "

" And neither should you boys."

" I've got to admit, I'm a bit wary of placing these things...I might take my eye out."

" It's easy Paul. The extensions are touch sensitive. They slide around the eyeball, and squeeze between the skin into the socket..."

" Yuck."

" Yuck indeed," said Douglas.

" Well here goes something, I hope."

" Is that the best you can do ? We're pioneers here, like Hoffman taking his first acid trip," said Rachel.

" Why remind me of that, it took him a whole weekend to come down, didn't it ? " said Paul.

" Didn't he nearly have a psychotic breakdown in the process," Douglas added, none too helpfully.

" I don't remember. All I know is he took a heroic dose, that's all."

Douglas had gingerly put on his glasses while Paul was talking.

" Well, what are you waiting for Paul ? "

" My stagefright to wear off."

" That is anticipation kicking in," said Rachel, " It won't go away until you join us."

" I was afraid you'd say that."

Paul reluctantly raised his glasses to his head, as if the touch of the eyeglasses might kill him. All three started to giggle.

" Does this have an immediate effect," Paul wondered out loud.

" I can't tell," Douglas chuckled.

" I don't know," Rachel tried to be as serious as her big grin could allow, " maybe it's just butterflies in the stomach.."

" Or nausea."

" Shut up Douglas. Paul, you'll be alright, it might take a bit of getting used to at first."

" I suppose, yeah. I do feel a bit, well stoned I suppose."

" I suggest we stick together while we get used to this," Rachel said."

" Okay, how about a slow walk into town ? " Paul asked.

" Sure, lead on Macduff."

" What ? "

" I don't know. I just came out with it."

" Come on will you," Rachel demanded.

It was Spring, or near enough. The ground rippled and writhed, its grass clothing being too tight. While the countryside noises were a deafening racket. The insects in particular were a nuisance. They kept divebombing the trio, as if aware they were more vulnerable than usual. Heartbeat, perspiration and perception had all increased, but this was to be expected. They were forewarned. And by the time the village brought itself into view, they had accomodated themselves to their new state.

" I don't feel we've been walking at all, but the village has got up and come to meet us."

" I know what you mean, I think. I feel a bit off balance, like being on a waltzer at a fairground."

" It's not much I haven't experienced before. Mind you, I was getting a bit paranoid with those flying insects. I thought they were deliberately attacking us."

" You know all of this can be attributed to our heightened expectation."

This banal remark deflated them all. And sure enough, as they reached the village, the effects seemed quite mundane, although they still felt fresh and adventurous. It was that Christmas Morning feeling, as Douglas put it. When the delight experienced is one of childish pleasure at the pleasant surprises that lay ahead. This feeling gave them the confidence to go their own separate ways. At least it gave Paul the confidence.

" I'm gasping for a drink."

Before the others could react he strode off.

" Well, shall we go with him," Douglas asked.

" No, not at all. I don't want to go in some shady old pub."

" Well how about a drive then."

" You know we can't leave."

" It doesn't have to be far. We could go up to that church on the hill, that's still within limits."

" I like that, that seems like a nice spot."

The Spotted Ferret, what a name. Immediately a vision of a vicious rodent creature seeped into Paul's imagination, with a spotted coat as well, like a miniature leopard. Paul shrugged off these misgivings. It was only another ye olde worlde pub. They were always cleaner and friendlier than the originals. And he found as much when he walked inside. Huge oak beams threatened to decapitate unwary customers, strange archaic ornaments hung from the ceiling, small, stuffed animals sat in glass cases, on dark brown shelves. Even the landlord was a beery, cheery, mein host. A round, red face, invaded by a fluffy moustache, that threatened to fly off if left unattended. Paul liked this place. A gaggle of locals sat sprawled around a corner. Paul got his foaming ale. It was honey, or was it syrup ? so golden and thirst quenching. But when he tasted it he nearly threw up. Ugh. It was warm and flat. He was tempted to make a remark about its resemblance to water from an attic storage tank. But the landlord stood there, his fists dug into his hips, eyes beaming, smile gleaming. He looked so friendly. Paul did not want to upset such a generous man.

Why was he so generous if he gave Paul a crap pint ? Puzzling. Paul disregarded this thought in favour of something more comfortable. He sat within talking distance of the locals. Normally he could not stand the pompous twats. They either seemed to be hunting and fishing commuters, or shifty-eyed peasants. Both types made him uneasy. But then that was a prejudice, he knew that. At least he knew that now, for the glasses had opened up his mind. Or was it that they had made him aware of something he would not admit to himself. And now it was brought to the surface of his recognition, it seemed of no more importance than a speck of dust. He could not help smiling to himself. He was in such a good mood. The commuters turned into respectable figures, as in people he would want to respect. Here were persons who embodied the best of both worlds, the cosmopolitan graft of the city, with the easy-going endurance of the country. The other locals were perfect rustics, survivors of country lifestyles going back to the dawn of time. They had traditions going back as far. Paul beamed at them and they beamed back. They seemed so full of life. They answered Paul's queries courteously, laughing at his jokes. One strapping lad of six foot six leaned over to give Paul a friendly tap on the shoulder. But something was wrong. He saw the man give the friendly tap, but he felt a numb pain on his cheekbone. The man's friends also came up to acknowledge his sense of humour, to joke with him with complimentary words and gestures. It was a pleasant sight. But it made Paul feel sick. He gained a queasy feeling in his stomach. The pain on his cheekbone spread to his eyes and nose. The locals left. The cheerful mein host escorted Paul to the door. What a wonderful experience. Simple friendliness and courtesy, it made such an impact. Paul felt he was getting clumsy however. Somehow he managed to fall flat on his face on the gravel drive outside. This added to his previous queasiness, so he threw up.

Rachel and Douglas meantime were sampling the joys of a drive in a convertible. Douglas had to admit he never enjoyed a drive as much before. His memory opened up with similar drives, rakish, young men in e-type jaguars with leather driving gloves. All his memories were from films. He could feel the appeal of those images now. There was excitement in the air. Maybe they were on the trail of a leather jacketed, Eastern European, who possessed the secrets of a new anti-gravity device. Or maybe they were on the trail of a gorgeous, Italian actress in big sunglasses, her silk scarf billowing behind her in the wind. Rachel was struck with the fitness of everything. Every feature of the landscape complimented another. Normally she would look at rounded hills and hedgerows and think " picture postcard." But there really was a charm about this scene they drove through. Even Douglas did not look too out of place. She must admit she had him down as one of those public school, prefect types, all snotty nose, with the character of a cardboard cutout. But now, with his athletic build and jutting jaw, he was the faithful, reliable companion. Even his convertible did not seem like a garish, penis compensator anymore. Instead it was a natural object, as finely formed as a crystal.

There were no spies or actresses to be found at the top of the hill, nothing but a small church. Its square tower and vaulted roof were patched with green. Various pieces of masonry had crumbled away. It looked organic, and it smelt it too. Rachel's nose turned up as they got out of the car and approached the building. It had rained yesterday. Maybe that explained the smell, but why the strong flavour of sewage ?

On closer view the church was not as crumbling as first appeared. Shiny new doors filled in the tower, while the graveyard appeared to be still in use. One or two headstones were brand new. On the north side there was no perimeter wall. How gorgeous, thought Rachel, to be buried with a permanent view of the river and pastures below.

Both Rachel and Douglas found their dialogue did not match their feelings or surroundings. They kept going " gosh," " wow," at everything. Everything seemed to be nice. And, as they sat on the spongey grass between headstones, their sensations became nicer still. Rachel continued to look at Douglas' slim, athletc build with admiration. While they sat still the surroundings appeared to open up on them even more. Birdsong was heightened, the breeze gossiped through the grass. If it were not for the occaisonal whiff of sewage, it would have been perfect. Yet after a time even this smell turned sickly sweet, and then into a rare perfume. Douglas himself found his proximity to Rachel triggered his growing arousal. She was slender, a wildflower, at one with all the flowers that grew around. Her curves touched the surface of her dress so gently. While her red curls coiled round that elvish face, with its distant gaze. Those eyes started to gorge with colour. It meant she appreciated what he was talking about, to him anyway. And it appeared he was right. For he found himself with his tongue in her mouth. It was a natural progression. He stroked her arm as he kissed her greedily. She was begining to get aroused now. Their movement grew from slow to frantic. And before Douglas knew what had happened, he was naked on top of her. They were on the point of climax, at least he was, like a saucepan coming to the boil. However, just as Douglas was about to ejaculate, a small funeral procession walked by. Everyone peered at the couple,then stopped, faces frozen wide open. One or two camera flash bulbs went off. For a second time seemed to be breathless. And then life started again. Douglas groaned in ecstasy in front of the audience, while Rachel frowned. The incident had put her off completely. She had managed to stop herself, why could Douglas not do the same. The funeral procession consisted of six coffin bearers, a priest, plus two elderly mourners. They began to giggle, and had to move off before their laughter further embarassed the young couple, but not before the camera flashbulbs went off again. When these people were safely out of embarassment range, Rachel wriggled her way up, with some grace. Then she ran off. Douglas was different, unlike Rachel he had to get dressed somehow. And so he scrambled around in panic, trying to remember where he had thrown his clothes in the heat of passion. He tried to catch up with her, running and dressing at the same time. By now large guffaws of laughter followed them in their flight. Actually he would have prefered it if they were outraged. Then he and Rachel could be suitably apologetic. But their reaction made him feel silly and shy. Rachel did not seem as bothered. She was staring at him and tutting, was he too inconsiderate or something ? Then he realised that was not the reason. At the bottom of the hill was a drainage ditch, filled with smelly, brackish water. Douglas found this obstacle was not to be forded. He fell in and sank up to thigh level. Luckily the mess he steeped in was thick enough to halt his momentum. Something pierced his foot, then his trousers fell down. This set Rachel off laughing. The whole episode was a scene from a bedroom farce, so corny on stage, so funny now. Swearing liberally, Douglas struggled to regain his composure, as they both scrambled up the hill again. The attentive audience were still watching, still holding their coffin.

" There's no way out there."

" It's not summer yet, you know."

Douglas thanked them for their kind comments. While that irritating old woman was still taking photographs. Then he realised his erect penis was was standing out from his undone flies. Laughter followed them as they both trotted off, two embarassed schoolkids. Once at the car they were able to rescue some shred of dignity. Rachel had a fit of beserk laughter. She sunk to the ground for a minute, doubled up in agonising pleasure. This annoyed Douglas somewhat, but the barking noises of Rachel soon set off the giggles in himself. This stopped her, as she felt Douglas was now laughing at her. With a mutual frown they pulled themselves together. Giggles could not help breaking out however, regardless of their attempts to straighten their clothes and clean themselves up. Finally they managed to get into the car. Yet they had got halfway down the hill road before Rachels laughter evaporated into a fixed grin, which was a bit irritating. Douglas could see the funny side himself now, but it did not cover his bruised pride completely. The sun was going down in all its crimson glory. This made further dialogue unnecessary. The drive became easier, meditation through motion. But then something peculiar happened. Both became afflicted by an outbreak of prickly heat. Or at least it was prickly, rather than being hot it was cold and wet, and shivery. Rachel started sneezing. Depression crept up on them, but why ? they could not tell.

The glorious surroundings rubbed these negative feelings in. Rachel was glad when they made the village again. At the first opportunity the car was parked. Bright shades reflected from the village buildings. And there was Paul, wandering around with a stupid, fixed grin on his face.

" I'm taking these stupid goggles off," said Rachel.

" Something's not quite right here," said Douglas.

" You're just scared that's all,' said Paul.

" Really ? then I suggest you both take off your glasses right now."

" Why ? " said Douglas.

" You'll find out."

Rachel sounded angry. In fact she was. She was disappointed to find that Douglas did indeed look as he first appeared, a pompous wimp. Paul, on the other hand, looked scarey, a down and out drug dealer.

The other two had taken their glasses off to discover it was pouring with rain. All three of them were soaked to the skin. Douglas looked with disappointment at Rachel. She looked so boney, and sounded so bossy. Paul thought she deserved a slap. Then he recoiled in horror. He was happy go lucky and anti-violence, mind you, she still deserved a slap. Rachel seemed to pick up on this bottled meance,

" You keep your distance, you look drunk. God knows what effect that has had combined with the glasses."

" He's probably had one pair of glasses too many."

" That's a joke is it Douglas ? it's pathetic."

" Oh piss off you moany bitch."

" Piss off yourself tiny tadger."

" Tiny tadger ha ha ha."

" And you can shut up pisshead."

" Shut up yourself you public school creep."

" Bloody druggie."

" Boys will be boys."

" Shut up slag."

" What did you say ? "

" You heard me."

" I heard your arse opening before your mouth."

" More sense comes out of my arse than your face."

" Your arse is more attractive than his face."

" Shut up Paul."

" I'm on your side, don't turn on me you bolshie bitch."

" Bolshie bitch ? at least I know who my parents are."

" You mean he had parents," said Douglas, " I thought he was found by the roadside somewhere."

" I knew I'd get this kind of shit from you two wankers. You just can't handle situations like this, coz you're two spoilt little kids."

" Yeah right, all this from the bloke that scampers into the pub as soon as something happens."

" Oh yeah ? I've got more life than you've ever dreamed of bland man."

" Will you two pricks shut up, God, you sound like two babies who've shit their nappies."

" And you've got a voice like a seagull with an arrow up its arse."

" It's always arses with you two prize prunes, isn't it ? "

" You started it, you dozey cow."

" No I didn't."

" You did Rachel."

" Fuck off Paul."

" Fuck off yourself ginger minge."

" You sexist streak of piss."

" Oh shut the fuck up the pair of you."

" You."

" No you."

They continued in this vein until they noticed the rain had stopped. It was dark now, and they were drying. A couple of streetlights had come on. They stood in silence, blushing with severe embarassment. Apologies broke out all round.

" Look we really should get back to the centre. I can't really make sense of what's happened here. So I'd feel a lot safer back there."

Paul and Douglas mumbled their agreement. They set off on a footpath to the centre, one that avoided going through the village. No one trusted themselves to drive, as their nerves were more than a little frazzled. A few wrong turnings later they found themselves in the middle of a cow pasture. Swearing heavily, they eventually found their way back to where they started. So a drive it was. Ultra-caution was in evidence. They were pulled over by a police car, their slow driving had aroused suspicion. The officer could not keep a straight face once he found out who they were. Their shenanigans in the pub and on the hill had already passed into gossip. The officer had to let them go, for fear of getting the uncontrollable giggles. To cap it all the gates of the centre were locked when they arrived. After ringing and knocking frantically, a sleepyhead arrived to let them in the darkened building. No one was around. And once he had satisfied himself they were not burglars, the sleepy security guard vanished at the first opportunity. The trio were left to crash out where they could.

It was a perturbed, but not unduly surprised Doctor Byfleet who arrived next morning, to find squatters in his office. He thought of pressing the security alarm, with its direct link to the police station. Fortunately, he realised in time that these unwashed individuals were in fact his volunteers. Doctor Byfleet gently woke them. He supervised breakfast, morning coffee, and a wash. Now they looked a bit presentable, if still a little ragged.

" While you've been cleaning up, I have been going through your notes, the ones that aren't entirely garbled. There are some interesting effects. But before we take this any further, I would like for you to relate all that happened while you wore the glasses..."

The trio related the previous day's events. Doctor Byfleet was perfectly neutral. He took notes constantly and had their summaries videoed.

" well, seems like a lot of interesting material here," he said, neutrally.

" Just what is the point of these glasses Doctor Byfleet ? "

" You know that already Rachel."

" No, I was just told it was for research."

Douglas and Paul nodded agreement.

" Their purpose... Well, my employers are looking at the commercial possibilities of marketing this product."

" Isn't that a little dangerous ? "

" Not at all Rachel, really, there's little difference between the glasses and some of the virtual reality hardware that's for sale..."

" I think there is Doctor," said Douglas, " I found it harder to distinguish things."

" You mean between different stimuli ? "

" Er.. partly. I mean really between different senses, and the imagination..I mean I would see something lovely, but hear something horrible. And that lovely something would overwhelm my imagination, but that horrible something would still effect me without my knowing it."

" I see..well, this explains the goings on at the church does it ? "

Both Rachel and Douglas blushed and nodded.

" It would also explain why we drove in an open top car, thinking it was a sunny day. I mean it was a sunny day, but later it poured with rain, and we didn't notice..."

" We didn't even see it getting cloudy,we didn't even feel the rain particularly," Rachel added.

" How did geting soaked mesh with your view of a sunny day ? "

" It didn't really, " Rachel continued, " I felt as if getting soaked was a minor irritation, a bit like a low noise in the background while you're trying to read...AH CHOO."

" Obviously the effects were not as minor as perceived... I take it this explains your episode in the pub Paul ? "

" Yeah , maybe, I'm still having trouble working it out..."

" Perhaps I can enlighten you. I've already talked to the landlord of the pub. He described you as acting the typical loudmouthed tourist, patronising and condescending. Despite attempts to warn you off, you continued talking down to everyone. In the end a fight broke out. The landlord was obliged to have you forcibly ejected from the pub..."

" You mean I was thrown out ? That explains how I ended up lying on the gravel patch. It wasn't my intention to be patronising, or condescending. I was really excited by the prospect of being in that place. It was like the first day of a holiday. I was just overcome by it all...'

" Hmmm, yes, the landlord did mention they became a bit afraid of you. One or two of them thought you might be having a psychotic episode...'

" Ha ha ha. Far from it. I just felt really good. The village looked superb. The pub did. I just wanted to share that feeling."

" You didn't appreciate that vision might effect us the most Doctor," said Rachel.

" The glasses just effected sight ? "

" No there were emotional effects and imaginative effects as well..."

" Could you be more specific ? "

" Well, it was like Paul says, everything had that wonderful air..erm, no disrespect Douglas, but you became my knight in shining armour, which is not my everyday opinion of you."

" The feeling was mutual, except that you were this gorgeous goddess. But once I took the glasses off, you were just another..."

" I think you should leave it there Douglas," interjected Doctor Byfleet.

" I suppose what I am trying to say Doctor," continued Rachel, " is that these were experiences where the world looked like a garden of roses, these were rose tinted glasses in effect. And every other thing we felt seemed to back up this view. Every thing I saw became beautiful, my feelings and imagination only served to increase this feeling..."

" You mean it was a kind of wish fulfillment ? "

" No, it was more like - everything is beautiful in its own way, every single object was one of an infinite series of types, each unique, yet every object fitted together perfectly with the others, I'm sorry, I don't think I'm describing it too well."

" On the contrary Rachel, that's very fascinating," said Doctor Byfleet.

" Really, I just felt like gosh, wow."

" Well you would Douglas, you would."

Douglas frowned before continuing,

" I mean, I know what you're getting at, though to me it only hints at what I was feeling. Because I cannot describe it."

" I was struck by the fact this was the weirdest trip I took," said Paul, " I was appreciating everything, apart from the irritating sensations from my other four senses."

" Interesting, did the rest of you feel your other senses were an intrusion ? "

Both Rachel and Douglas nodded.

" Exactly. The only experience I can think of at the moment that compares, is when we were watching telly, when we first arrived here. I was so intent on this programme..."

" Bloody soap operas," interrupted Paul.

"...I was so intent on this programme, that I didn't realise Paul was acting the stupid bastard..."

" What ? " Paul looked shocked.

" Really ? what was he doing ? "

" He was using his lighter to burn my bottom."

" Really Paul, such childish behaviour."

" I was only doing it to see if she'd flinch."

" And did you ? " asked Doctor Byfleet.

" No, I punched him in the face..."

Paul looked embarassed.

" Er, that's not really the point now," continued Rachel, " what I'm trying to say is that I ignored the effects of his lighter for some time. I didn't think it was important, like a bothersome itch that can wait. But once I saw what he was doing, I cried out and reacted, especially when I saw him laughing."

" Interesting. I thought maybe this effect would predominate. You see, in Western cultures the sense of sight is arguably considered the most important sense. That much has been verified. But I thought the main effect of the glasses would be to retrieve memories in pictoral form. These memories might then appear as outward projections on the glasses, rather like viewing your own personal film...

Though from what you are all saying, they intensified the way you saw the world, increasing the importance that is placed on sight, to the detriment of the other senses..."

" They made everything look handsome all right," said Paul.

" I had no time for memories at all," said Douglas.

" Although they did stimulate fantasy," said Rachel.

" Interesting...This may point to some therapeutic value in these glasses, in the treatment of depression for instance..."

" Mind you, the glasses did have their dangerous moments..."

" As you've already told me Paul."

" No, I mean potentially lethal... I remember I bought this pint that looked like amber nectar. The trouble was it tasted like sewage water. But I completely ignored the taste because I fell in love with the appearance.."

"Typical male," Rachel's sarcasm was obvious, everyone ignored the remark.

" You're familiar with the taste of sewage water then, are you Paul ? " asked Douglas.

" I am now."

" True, there could be psychotic implications. It seems the glasses can cause a division between sight and the rest of the senses. But this need not detract from its marketing potential..."

" So you are going to sell these things ? " asked Rachel.

" Only to select individuals."

" Like who ? "

"Anyone we can trust basically, anyone with a reasonable degree of sanity and maturity..."

How do you judge that ? " asked Douglas.

" Carefully."

" Sounds a bit vague to me," said Rachel.

Doctor Byfleet's Handsome Glasses did not make it onto the market however, not since the tragic accident. The doctor was giving an informal lecture to research students, in his laboratory. It was a hot day. In the midst of his enthusiastic proposals for the glasses, he paused to wipe his brow, and to wet his throat with a glass of his favourite cider. Unfortunately he picked up the wrong glass, so he drank some nitric acid instead. After his agonising death, mercifully short, the handsome glasses were shelved, at least for the time being. It was felt they may have possibilities in future. For the fact that people always mistook things for other things was not in itself a deterrent. Indeed, some of the greatest discoveries of science had happened because of such mistakes. The trouble was no one seemed willing to pick up on Doctor Byfleets research as yet. And so we await developments.

As for the volunteers, they pursued their own careers. Paul became a politician for a right wing political party, one that always churned out literature on the country's betrayal of its heritage, but which never got any votes. Douglas became a nightclub owner, who was arrested several times for sex with underage girls, and boys. He underwent a course of tranquilisers to tame his sexual appetite, after fear of a hefty prison sentence. Finally, Rachel joined a group of bad tempered journalists and scientists. These people saw themselves as guardians of public morality, out to expose the various cons and hoaxes perpetrated on gullible consumers. They eventually went bankrupt after several damaging lawsuits.

This Repulsive Matter

Some fresh air was needed. He had overdone it, yet again. His eyes were bigger than his belly, and his intention more powerful than his constitution. The room began to spin around, cloying pub fumes of stale beer and smoke made him choke. But the fresh breeze made him feel worse as he staggered outside. The cold bath of air brought his nausea to a nice pitch. He doubled up and retched as he staggered into the yard. This was the last time he would get this out of it again. This was a weekly promise he made after his heavy indulgence. And it would only last until he recovered.

But finally, the fresh air did give him its promise. His faculties began to grind into gear as the waves of nausea dissipated. Walking helped. Something to get that blood pumping again. He always walked to the same place. The nearby hill was always the place to contemplate, after his lurching metabolism had allowed his mind to reactivate. The mechanical climb, now a familiar routine, was the best cure he could think of. And so he slumped down, perched against a bush, in a half sitting, half lying posture. He peered at the pub below. That source of his Friday night pleasure that consistently became a solitary pain. He was in a philosophical mood. Propped up on his elbow, he surveyed the usual scene around. He could not feel the cold yet, and the lights of the village helped him focus. His bearings came back. Why did he do it all the time ? But what else was there to do, in a one horse village that could not even afford a horse. What else, except get tanked up until semi-comatose. These were his usual musings, and he quickly got bored with them. This night did feel a bit different, weird, at least weirder than usual. There was something else in the air, despite his routine nausea. It was not just his trouble in retaining balance. But then this could just be paranoia. For it was one of those perfectly mundane nights. Except for the fact of that light descending, very rapidly.

Obviously it was a shooting star, he tried to convince himself. It was too near, and made a noise, similar to food being fried at a rapid rate. This thought reactivated his nausea. But then the frying sound echoed again. The light flared up until it filled the sky, and then it disappeared behind his hill. It was no meteorite, probably an aircraft, a helicopter even. There was an army firing range nearby. That often produced weird sounds. Yet never so close as these. Well, so long as they stayed out of the way. He did not like those army types. They were either miserable or drunk and miserable. They had a habit of starting fights in the village. It was the looks that got him. They always tried to stare him out, so he believed. This gave them the pretext to start a fight. Not that anything had ever happened to him to confirm his fear. But he had seen it happen to other people. What if they decided to come over the hill ? They might be doing some exercises. Then they would see him and stare at him, and probably get all aggressive. He tried to remember if the army were still banned from the village, as they had been many times before, but gave up.

Then the light shone on him. Two men in close fitting uniforms had somehow crept above his position. They gave him stern looks, as far as he could see, for the light dazzled.

" Oh no, what's this ? " said the one with what appeared to be a torch, but looked more like a hair dryer.

They could have been twins, if twins could be born at least ten years apart, for one was apparently older. His black hair was lined with streaks of grey. But what kind of family did they come from ? What strange accented English. They were nearly seven feet tall, swarthy. The man with the hair dryer torch was the streaky one. As they moved closer they seemed to walk in a very un-army like way, almost effeminate. Maybe they came from a camp regiment. Instead of making him laugh however, this perception seemed to add to the sinister atmosphere around the two soldiers.

" It's half frightened and half savage, Lieutenant."

The Lieutenant was the one with the torch. That torch which managed always to keep him in its beam no matter how he turned his head. Wherever he looked the beam faced him head on and surrounded him. He tried to shift his eyes to escape the dazzle, but the beam followed his gaze everywhere. It was hypnotic.

" I'm not doing anything."

" We can see that, thank you...Orderly, what are we supposed to do with it ? "

The shorter one was known as Orderly. He found that discovery uninteresting. Orderly shrugged his shoulders and said nothing.

" Look, if I was trespassing, I didn't mean it. I didn't realise you had manoevures going on, or whatever it is you get up to."

" You cannot go until we decide how to deal with you."

" What ? I've done nothing wrong."

" It is not a question of you doing anything wrong. You look incapable of doing anything. But you might have interfered with our calculation."

" Calculations ? Look, I'm harmless. I was just sobering up in the fresh air. Can you get that torch out of my face please. Thank you. I'll say nothing about this..."

The beam was modified so it did not dazzle him anymore. Yet a halo of light still surrounded him.

" You are in no position to make requests or demands."

" It might be good idea to let it go."

" Orderly, you know we cannot do that. The creature might disrupt its environment as a consequence of our meeting."

" It looks disruptive enough to me already."

" Yes, but that is purely in terms of its own habitat."

" Oh no, don't tell me you're frigging aliens, " he interjected.

" We are not frigging anything, we are conducting a survey," said Orderly.

" I believe it is a dialect he is speaking, Orderly. His speech may not be the standard variety we have learnt. Nevertheless it contains interesting rhythms and cadences. It also appears to have more subtlety than the standard variety."

" The creature sounds like a choice subject for study, Lieutenant. You know we lack any subjects with vitality. Most of them die of fright."

" I am not sure. A coarser variety such as this might present its own problems. Look at it. It has ingested a variety of poisons, and yet it sits there with an expression an invertebrate would be ashamed of. And for what purpose ? a temporary lapse of consciousness ? "

" But Lieutenant, we both know that all beings of higher intelligence find existence painful at times. Therefore they take measures to deal with pain."

" By poisoning themselves ? "

" Well maybe it is perverse. But in its own primitive manner it shows potential. The experience of adjusting its own thoughts and feelings, through the process of intoxication, might actually make him more adaptable in dealing with a variety of situations in future, situations where different thoughts and feelings are required."

" I'm not convinced Orderly. I think you just want it for a pet..."

His eyes had progressively widened as this discussion was under way. He felt like the object of someone else's bargaining.

" Look, I don't want any trouble, okay."

He stood up with difficulty. He tried to muster his hardman pose. It was difficult. The two aliens still towered above him.

" You're not going to abduct me and take me to some weird planet and stick needles in me."

" Fascinating, Orderly. It shows a rudimentary understanding. It appears to have some knowledge of what are called Unidentified Flying Objects in this backwater, together with a basic awareness of abduction experiences..."

" I'm not convinced of that, Lieutenant. I think it is merely trying to impress us... Listen, inferior being, you are in no danger from us. But we do have a job to do. We are from the government. Our work here is highly important."

" Don't give me that. No one in government wears rubber jumpsuits, except maybe at home on the weekends, ah..."

A burbling and plopping sound exploded. It was as if a giant with flatulence also had a bad cough. The he realised it was laughter. So aliens could have a sense of humour.

" Okay, Incapacitated person," said the Lieutenant, " Let us suppose for an instant you are correct. Suppose we are two aliens. You can appreciate out meeting you here was quite an unforeseen circumstance..."

He tried to back away. But the beam held him.

" Stop behaving like a frightened animal. We mean you no harm. We are being truthful. We are genuinely conducting a survey. "

" Listen to the Lieutenant, although you might be of slight interest, we are not prepared to take too much trouble over you."

He could not make out if that last remark was a threat. Still, it was delivered in a soothing monotone. But then all their speech had a montonous tone. Whatever, he was placated. And those last words piqued his curiosity.

" What kind of survey is it ? "

" It is beyond your faculties."

" No no, Orderly. You said yourself it might have some intelligence, to a small degree... How can I put it creature ? so it will not overwhelm your basic powers of comprehension ? I know, you are familar with the concept of attraction and repulsion are you not ?"

" What ? like when someone fancies you ?

" Fancies ? "

" I think he is speaking of attraction and repulsion on the gross, physical level, Lieutenant."

" I understand, Orderly. You mean sexual desire. I forget how much we have to talk down before we can reach the level of these creatures... Yes creature, although I was postulating a more empirical, physically, quantifiable process, such as magnetism. "

" What have magnets got to do with shagging ? "

" Perhaps something, for both may be said to involve an object which either draws another object toward it, or pushes it away. Do you understand this simple concept ? "

" Er, yeah, sort of."

" Right, how can I put it... All the objects, of any size, around this mudball planet, are currently being pushed away. We are measuring the rate at which this phenomena is occuring."

" You mean, everything's running away from the earth because it don't like it."

" Primitive, but it will serve.... Yes, the planets, stars and galaxies are running away from this mudball because they do not find it attractive. "

" And the rate is increasing rapidly, " Orderly added unhelpfully.

" What you're saying is the stars are repulsed by the earth."

"As is most other matter in the universe, apart from a few stray pieces of debris."

" No one fancies the earth then."

Both the aliens nodded.

" It is not wholly proven of course, and that is why we are here, to verify...I believe even your fellow primitives may have perceived something similar, in their own fumbling way. They talk of the universe expanding..." The Lieutenant was begining to sound like a schoolteacher.

" Yeah I've heard of that, it's called Big Boom Theory..."

" You mean Big Bang Theory," said Orderly, rather patronisingly.

" Yeah, sort of... you mean the universe don't like us then..."

" And you do not care," added the Lieutenant unhelpfully.

" That's why you have never had any substantial contact with so-called aliens, as you call them, because you're both primitive and repulsive," said Orderly.

" So what are we having now ? "

" This ? This is a statistical anomaly. It is not common, though it happens. These anomalies account for all your weird literature, written by weirder people, who claim they have met aliens. These instances are miniscule however, compared to the number of times our surveying teams have actually visited here. Not that we would want to invade this mudball. It is not worth the effort. But it has a certain scientific interest, both to our teams of anthropologists, who study your primitive ways, and to us, who have to make sure you are not upsetting the universe any more than you do already."

" You're saying we're too unstable, aren't you ? Too unreliable to trust."

" It's quick, I'll give it that, " said Orderly.

" Quick is a relative term, Orderly. Single celled creatures in ponds, on our planet, can leave this creature looking as intelligent as a rock formation."

" Though it still has to be dealt with, Lieutenant."

" Quite so. Now , creature, what would you do in our position ? "

" I'd get a change of clothes for a start. Then I'd go down the gym. You two are a bit skinny."

" As per usual, intelligent conversation with these creatures soon breaks down. I am afraid will have to play with your perceptions a little, creature."

" Play with my what ? ugh. Look, you're not going to mess around with me."

" Why not ? You do it yourself," said Orderly.

" But that's my choice."

" Come along creature, or we might abduct you if you prove too troublesome."

" Look, you're not taking me to some godforsaken planet. Besides, I've got a dentists appointment on Tuesday."

" Lieutenant, you know I'd like a chance to take this primitive home. It would be hard work, but I'd get it housetrained. It's a bit feisty, which I like."

" No, I'll think we'll use the probe, it is much less effort."

The lieutenant produced what appeared to be a diamond-studded wand. He wondered if the Lieutenant was some kind of camp magician.

" But it can be dangerous, all sorts of of side effects have occurred in past cases. Why, it could melt the poor savage's brain in it's skull case."

He was now very afraid.

" Look, you're not meddling with my head, operating on me, or any other kind of weirdo things you might do..."

" You think so ? You are already in the probe's beam. It will only be a matter of a subtle adjustment in the beam's field for us to mould your metabolism accordingly."

" Eh ? What you going on about ? "

" You should stop teasing the creature, Lieutenant."

" You are quite right, let us get this over with."

The Lieutenant attached his magician's wand onto his hair dryer, he looked like a hairdresser preparing for a shampoo and set. But this was more likely to wash a brain and put a new set of memories in place.

The probe's beam expanded until it completely dazzled him. It effectively suspended all his movement. He could not even feel the ground anymore. But of course, this sensation was not entirely unknown to him, after a few too many, so he decided to enjoy it if he could. He floated there with an idiotic grin on his face.

" You may have lobotomised it, Lieutenant."

" No. I believe it is wearing one of it's usual expressions. Still, this is a calculated risk, because this creature is already severely intoxicated. It should make for some interesting side effects. Thankfully, I believe the creature will be so messed up after this, he will nor know which is memory or imagination."

" That could drive the poor creature insane."

" It could well do, Orderly. But I am trusting the creature to be a little more resilient than that."

As the Lieutenant had spoken the light continued to play on him. He was unaware of where he was now. But this was nothing to be concerned about. Those who knew him well had offered this opinion to him several times in the past. The light entered him, various colours manifested outside his vision, and strange sounds moved through his head. And then it happened. The Lieutenant located his memory of their specific encounter. This was removed with surgical precision. The beam shut off suddenly and he dropped to the ground, already snoring.

" A shame really, I would've liked to put this one on show back home."

" Yes, Orderly. We would have had difficulties obtaining a licence for it though, since it contains so many poisonous substances."

" I'm sorry to keep going on about this, Lieutenant."

" I understand. It is an interesting specimen... I have not even mentioned quarantine regulations yet. Think of all the trouble we would get from the Department of Inferior Life Forms..."

" And the League of Random Experimenters... I know Lieutenant. And the chances are I might have got fed up on the way home and jettisoned it out to space anyway."

" Problems all round, Orderly."

" Yes, how could it be otherwise, Lieutenant, when their planet is so repulsive..."

" Quite so, Orderly. Repulsive matter only causes a complex of chaos."

The two aliens walked casually off over the hill, gossiping as they did. Their conversation tailed off into the night. Moments later a ball of white light ascended into the sky. In the space of a thought it was gone.

He awoke the next morning, with a bad head and a shivering body. He clutched his brow as he staggered downhill. He was worried he might pick up a cold, or something. People had warned him against falling asleep outside before. Though he was not really sure he was awake now. Some strange memories lingered on. It was daylight now. And even at this early hour he knew there would be a couple of customers in his favourite pub, his only pub.

And so it was. He could not help talking about the strange dreams he had. Though instead of the sympathy he was expecting, the few people there went all quiet and edged away from him. His drink was spiked, with a tranquilliser. After that he was taken away. He was sedated further. Though after a couple of days he was free. Then he made a beeline for his favourite pub again, his only pub.

Our Intrepid Leader

Carlton Dempster felt some pride, standing in the Vatican halls, where so many pontiffs had blessed their congregations. Awe should have struck also, but he was too tense to bother himself with this feeling. Otherwise, the history of this fine venue might overwhelm him. No, history was about to be made, again, tomorrow, when the leader of the U.N. Alliance, one Ramires Okonkwo Jones, known affectionately as Roj, would address a new congregation. This congregation would be multi-cultural, multi-religious and multi-racial. Though all of them would be brought to St, Peter's Square by the overpowering humanity of the man, and the charisma of his words, not by any appeals to country, creed or community.

It had taken so much effort to get this far. Interminable conflict had dogged the world for a century. Although no official world war had been fought since 1945, a series of petty, localised conflicts had continued to engage the worlds attention. These conflicts proliferated at an alarming rate. The century itself was designated by the phrase " The Conflict." Carlton reflected on the many and confusing reasons for   the unrest - border wars, terrorist 'activities, propaganda wars, political wars, religious wars, nationalist wars, cultural wars, historical grievance wars. These were only the categories Carlton could remember, there were others, even more obscure. Every country in the world had engaged in some violent, protracted dispute, in which damage to life, limb and property became a feature of everyday life. There was one year in which no conflict occurred, by oversight rather than plan, and that was fifty years ago. It was jokingly referred to as the "Gap Year." Despite ongoing fighting, semblance of "normal" life continued, people rebuilt their lives as conflicts moved in and out like weather fronts. Of course, in this situation the Corporations reigned supreme. But then they had for some while now. Organised chaos suited their modus operandi and gave them their raison d'etre.

Those innumerable countries touched by conflict made a depressing parade in Carlton's memory. It was no exaggeration to say every high street in the world had known the impact of bombs or bullets.

Now, after complex negotiations Roj had emerged as the individual most likely to embody the peaceful wishes of all. Some kind of a treaty had been drafted, at least in outline. In essence it was amenable to all countries, corporations and communities. The major stumbling block in negotiations had been the international, corporate operatives. They were loth for any treaty to be presented in any binding form. But the serious good humour and humanity of Roj had persuaded them to the contrary. Any lingering doubts were removed by the endorsement of the treaty by the largest organisation to represent the international business community. This was the organisation formally known as The Coordinated Activities of Business and Leisure, otherwise known as the CABAL.

The way was thus cleared for a new begining. The standing of world leaders had been degraded throughout

" The Conflict." Cynicism was the everyday attribute of everyone. Roj was one of a small handful of public figures who had risen above this negativity. People genuinely had faith in him. They would accept no treaty without his endorsement. And so the agenda was set, the final reconciliation could at last be made concrete. Even the Pope gladly gave his permission for Roj to make his address. Rome would be just the start. Roj had a message for everyone to benefit, his further itinerary would include every major capital in the globe.

Carlton could feel the tension as something tactile. It was not so bad when when he was busy. Right now, however, it was just a matter of waiting, which he did not like. Left alone with his thoughts, the responsibility of his position became gargantuan. He was one of Roj's closest aides. Another was his colleague Maria D'alembert Istvaros. She was currently briefing Roj on his interview arrangements for the next week. She also arranged personal matters such as health and diet. The fact that Carlton was left alone to fidget was not unusual therefore. It had taken its toll on his nerves throughout the years. Carlton had been fighting a guerilla war against his nicotine addiction. And he was not winning. He had reached the point where he was prepared to do something radical to break the habit. Recently, in moments such as these, he had taken to playing his hypnotherapy discs, in order to aid his struggle. He also found their pleasant burble soothing. So far it was an option that did not have any marked results. He often found himself puffing away while listening to the discs. Those soothing tones urged him to give up. Unfortunately his mind was often elsewhere, contemplating his problems from a distance, before his nerves inevitably reminded him of something urgent needing to be taken care of.

So It was with a sense of relief he noticed Maria's imperious figure striding down the corridor toward him. He knew that determined walk of hers, it symbolised something was up. She was more curt in this mood, though always decisive.

" Dare I ask how it's going ? " Carlton said.

" You may dare ask, but I am afraid you will not like the answer."

Carlton's nerves went into overdrive,

" Oh no, he's not had another fainting attack has he ?
"

" Yes."

" Oh my God... so can he make the speech ? "

" I'm still working on that."

" And what is that supposed to mean ? "

" Well.. I think you had better sit down first Carlton."

Maria gestured toward a chair. Carlton felt the urgency of a new situation, one that was not going to be pleasing. He ignored his impulse to run out of the room.

" Roj is dead I'm afraid. He passed away in his sleep last night."

Carlton looked blankly at Maria with his mouth open.

" I know this must come as a shock Carlton. But given what we both knew already about his age and condition, it was not entirely unexpected. "

Carlton could not resist a sardonic smile.

" Yes, I know. We knew he was pushing himself too much, that he carried the burden of responsibility without regard to his health. But this is a bit too sudden."

" You think I don't know it's sudden. I've been going over events for hours, thinking what are we going to do ?... I'm sorry Carlton. I didn't mean to shout. You're right, it is a shock. And it's one that places us in a dilemma."

" You mean it's not as great a problem for us personally as it is for everyone else."

" Those are are my lines of thought exactly. I am glad to say you are acting rationally and thinking about the consequences..."

" Ha, right now I'm holding onto rationality the way a drowning man hangs onto a life preserver...I want to tell everyone about this. People must be informed, broadcast from the rooftops if necessary."

" That will not be necessary. You will appreciate I have had a little longer to consider the consequences. Right now only we two know, plus our immediate staff...We have to consider the wider impact as well."

" That's obvious," Carlton replied. " The people will not accept the treaty without Roj's endorsement. He was perhaps the only one who could have done this...This is one reason he's had the CABAL's support. Now it looks as though " The Conflict " will continue, as before, and indefinitely."

Maria nodded.

" This is all true. Yet there is an option which provides a solution to this problem. However, it would be easier to.... What is this insipid nonsense you're playing ?"

Carlton had neglected to stop his disc playing on Maria's arrival, she had only just noticed its soothing, mellow tones.

" Sorry, it's my hypnotherapy disc."

" Really, still trying to drop that habit. Well, we have other things to consider."

" Agreed. I wasn't actually aware it was still playing when you came in."

Carlton switched off those mellow, soothing tones and prepared for moments of nervous action.

" Sorry, you were saying ? "

" Yes, yes, there is a way out of this. But it is easier to show you rather than explain.'

At this Maria beckoned for Carlton to follow her. A long walk down mysterious corridors and hidden staircases followed. Roj's rooms were situated in a secluded corner, far from the maddening adulation of millions. Carlton would never have found them unaided. He felt a tinge of resentment, because she had always been closer to Roj. He also knew that one of her schemes was in operation. Schemes in which he was always ordered to take part. He tried to brace himself for unexpected events.

They walked into a grand room, which served as study and bedchamber and reception room. Roj was standing there, arms outstretched, a typical gesture. A few aides wandered around trying to look busy.

" Why Carlton, good morning, how are you ? "

" Fine thank you..." He turned to Maria.

" Is this some kind of loyalty test ? because it's in poor taste..."

" Why Carlton, good morning, how are you ? "

" I'm fine thank you sir, as I've just said...Maria, I expect better of you than such a cheap prank..."

" Why Carlton, good morning, how are you ? "

" I'm sorry sir, apparently you didn't hear me..." Carlton looked directly at Roj, "...Actually you don't look too well at all, you look a little pale, is there anything at all I can get you ? "

" Why Carlton, good morning, how are you ? "

" You are dead aren't you. I thought you were a bit rigid in your body language...What is the meaning of this outrage Maria ? "

Maria gestured toward Roj.

" Better switch him off Stephen."

One of the aides moved behind Roj and made a deft movement that suggested the flicking of a switch.

" This is the option I was talking about."

" And how can you justify such an obscenity ? "

" Don't get moral with me Dempster. You and I both know we serve a man who is far above the common run of humanity. Without him the prospect of world peace cannot even begin. Roj is truly a living legend. He is our El Cid, you remember the story of El Cid don't you ? "

" Vaguely, he cleared the Moors from Spain didn't he ? and died on the eve of what was to be his greatest battle. "

" Correct. But such was the inspiration of the man, his corpse was dressed in armour and led the Spanish troops on a charge toward the enemy, who fled before his very prescence. This Moorish army would have vanquished the Spanish without this act of inspiration that put fear into their hearts."

" I thought a lot of the Cid story was romantic legend."

" Does it matter if it is literally true ? What really counts is that it provided inspiration. From the Cid's death onwards the Moors were a declining force in Spain, until they were finally ejected... Come here, look out of the window."

Maria gestured outside while putting her other hand on Carlton's shoulder.

" Even from here you can see the gathering crowds, for an audience which will not begin for hours yet. What are we going to tell them ? "

" Well, the truth wouldn't be a bad idea, instead of all this trickery."

" The truth would cause a riot. You and I both know that. The crowd, cynical as they are, would believe the CABAL had him assassinated, despite the fact they are his sponsors."

" Well they did make two previous attempts on his life didn't they. "

" Precisely. And since Roj was in our care, they will not look too kindly on us, even if the man did die from natural causes. We will be victims of guilt by association. Of course, in later years people will view this as a horrible misunderstanding, but only after emotions have subsided and lots of people been murdered. "

" This trick you're trying will not prevent these events I'm afraid. Roj and I had rehearsed this complex speech over the past week. We are not going to get away with a statue that says good morning every minute. I am taking it that this is Roj of course, not some ridiculous robot figure..."

" Of course it's him. I've already had him embalmed. He will need further immersion in preservation drugs of course...However, from a distance he looks alive. Which leaves the problem of his speech..."

" I see where you're going with this. You're going to play a recording of Roj's voice, in such a way as to make it look as though the man is still alive, and in full control of his powers. I find the prospect of this working tenuous at best. We have a number of functions to attend, plus, approximately 150 addresses to be given across the world. People are going to want to speak to Roj, to shake his hand. They're going to be a bit suspicious when he just stands there arms open all the time."

" Really Carlton, you're not thinking straight. What we do is restrict his appearances in the first instance. No functions, no private parties, only events where he is seen at a distance will be allowed. We shall cite health reasons, that Roj needs to conserve his energy in view of his health. This is not so far from the truth. Secondly, I know you have recorded all of Roj's speeches, and a few of his private conversations, including, I'm hoping, a rehearsal of today's speech..."

" This is true, I do have tapes of him. But I haven't organised them in a systematic way. Roj only used these recordings for practice and amusement, so I've only got a few. Although I do happen to have the complete contents of today's speech, luckily. I usually wipe them once I've finished."

" That's all we need. We can splice together a few words of greeting. But we will need a recording with the entire contents of today's speech to be transmitted unaltered. Can this be done."

" Yes, yes. Oh God, it will involving some searching, but I can find the required recordings. I will need to go back to Roj's Rome office, and my hotel room, first."

" Good. So let's start now, because time is always going to be against us."

And so Carlton was required to rush through Rome. It did not do his nerves any good. But he moved with dexterity, a dexterity bred by urgency, given purpose by a possible solution to a problem. The only other alternaitve was to keep running until he left Rome, in fact until he found some obscure hiding place. He prefered the former option even though he considered the latter. Either option appeared horrible, but death would not come so quick on the first, he hoped. The crowds that thronged the streets gave his running a stop-start motion, which irritated him .People baulked him at every direction. He met some colleagues, but pleaded urgent business. Finally he located his apartment.

Carlton went through his belongings like a nervy burglar, afraid of getting caught. Eventually he found the required recordings. These were held in both hands and kissed. They made the negotiation of the streets less irritating on the way back. Back at St. Peters pandemonium reigned. Maria and the aides were running around with a pretence of efficiency. The thought of chattering budgies occurred to Carlton, then headless chickens. He reflected how their tensed actions mirrored his own uneasy state. Roj was installed on the balcony where so many popes had given their blessings. A black box was attached to his back, the only visible clue to his forthcoming speech. It made a discrete bump just below his shoulders. Wires ran intravenously, under the skin and into the mouth. They terminated in a round, black lump on the world leaders tongue. Carlton thought these devices made Roj look like a hunchback sucking a boiled sweet. It embarassed him to see the great man like this. Once Carlton's own appartment had been broken into, just after he had joined the diplomatic corps. The feeling was exactly the same - an intrusion of privacy by people with no respect for others, people whose life revolved around their own short term desires. This meant he too was one of the criminals now, he was part of their action. Maria, the aides and himself could justify their actions with reasonable arguements. But the feeling still remained.

Roj was up and running in time for the speech. Carlton excused himself to go off and brood somewhere. He found a quiet study with no windows, a place to enjoy a smoke or two, or three, or four. Even in this place he heard Roj's majestic tones. Though he could not make out the words. The tension was still unbearable. One of the junior aides interupted his thoughts, another escapee from the charged atmosphere of the balcony.

" Oh I'm sorry, I didn't realise you were here. If you like I'll... '

" It's alright Hanlon, I came down here for the same reason..."

Carlton raised his smoking cigarette for the junior to see.

" Thank you sir."

Hanlon lit up his own cigarette.

" So how is it going ? "

" It appears to be working sir. The speech has been well received, or at least the brief portion I heard. It was uplifting, even if it did start becoming a bit boring ? "

" Really ? "

" Er yes sir. Roj went into all these pleasantries and cliches, you know, the ones the nondescript politicians use. I mean no disrespect sir. It's just I've got used to such a high standard of eloquence from the man..."

Carlton had raised his eyebrows and creased his brow while Hanlon was talking.

" It's okay Hanlon, really. I was afraid the quality might slip myself. We did push Roj too hard. We can't have expected the man to be at his best always."

" That's true, although we had little control over events sir, then and now. The warring factions always wanted their say, and Roj was always the mediator."

" How true. Although I can't help thinking a precious resource has been abused nevertheless."

" I think we all feel a little guilty sir, given the fact we were all dedicated to the man, or were, rather..."

" Yes, and not a little nervous either. I think part of the guilt stems from our fear of the consequences of recent actions. We have had to act hastily, so we will not appreciate the full impact of events yet. With due consideration, we might have acted with a little more probity perhaps. And then.."

Carlton's potential monologue was rudely interupted by the door slamming open. Maria stood there, her voice always imperious, but more strident then usual.

" I cannot believe the stupidity of the whole episode. Why did you not tell me about the nature of these recordings ? "

" I did. I told you they were only for practice, that they were not systematically organised..."

As these words were exchanged Hanlon discretely slipped out of the room.

" Not systematcally, how true..."

" Maria, I didn't listen to the speech, I was too tensed up. Besides, I knew the content of it well enough...has something gone wrong ? "

Maria stood there glaring for a while, hands on hips. Her left eyebrow arched, as if it wished to travel backwards over her head. This was always a danger sign to Carlton. It presaged some dirty, emotional business ahead.

" Something has gone wrong. Roj's speech all went as planned. But there was an addendum, something we could not account for in our haste. For on the remnant of the recording we used was one of your ridiculous hypnotherapy sessions - " Part Three, The Steps to Self Hypnosis Preceeding the Implantation of a Suggestion," I believe it's called. Somehow, the fact of it's coming straight after the speech, means it has hypnotised the entire crowd. That ridiculous psychobabble of gibbering, new age nonsense has been given a potency it neither deserves nor has any claim to..."

" I don't believe it. It was, as you say, psychobabble. It couldn't have hypnotised a chicken, I should know. "

" Context is everything Carlton. They were in a situation of mass expectancy, where every word would be taken as literally gospel. They have been building up to this moment. They placed implicit trust in Roj in a way only the great and good of past ages have been able to equal..."

" Perhaps. Even so, I fail to see why I should take the blame. I was in such a panic I admit, but you could have checked yourself..."

" Panic is the word Carlton. We barely got Roj installed before his address was due to commence. If I am angry it is with the course events have taken, and the way they make us look like a pack of incompetent idiots..."

Further conversation might have followed, except for the fact that numerous men in black uniforms began streaming into the room. Their lack of insignia was disturbing. This meant they were part of The Honour Guard of the CABAL. They were both an official and a secret police. They were charged explicitly to defend the CABAL's select committee. It was a cause they dedicated their lives to under oath. There were also many rumours of their involvement in clandestine activities. They surrounded the aides with deft efficiency.

Carlton recognised their commander, Major Belinda Tyrone Dawson. He tried for some friendly eye contact, but gained a cold glare of acknowledgement in return.

" Good afternoon Ms D'alembert, Mr Dempster. You are cordially invited to attend the Emergency Session of the Select Committee of the CABAL..."

" I don't suppose this is R.S.V.P ? "

" Shut up Carlton...Major, you cannot just burst in and dictate to us, you must go through the proper channels."

" I beg your pardon, esteemed colleagues. But current events have bypassed the need for routine procedure. My invitation is at the behest of Committee members. I am afraid there are no alternative options..."

A brief, tense silence followed before the Major continued.

" Please do not render circumstances more difficult. We have our instructions. They will be implemented. We would be loth to use violence on Diplomatic Corps Members.

However necessity demands we fulfil our task. Therefore I would prefer to have your co-operation."

" Not that we have any choice in the matter," Maria said.

" None whatsover, the CABAL have invoked their rights as sponsors of the Peace Treaty. They are requesting your input on events of the past two days. So please, if you'll follow me."

Escorted on all sides by black clad officers, the two aides were led away. It was some walk before they reached The Discussion room, unofficial residence of the CABAL committee. This room was packed. The eighteen strong committee was already engrossed in discussion, around a large ebony table. Carlton and Maria were led to the front of the room and a silence descended. The guards filed around the room, lining the walls behind the seats of the Committee members. Carlton prepared for the interrogation. Both he and Maria gave their accounts of the past two days. He was surprised to find murmurs of sympathy from some. However there were scathing remarks made about their competency also. Yet it was quickly established that apportioning blame was not the issue here - it was recognised that planning for future events was more important. Both the aides were pledged under oath to serve the CABAL. The CABAL would handle Roj now, such as he was. Carlton's fellow aides and Maria's immediate staff had already been detained, as had everyone who had any knowledge of the situation. Loyalty contracts were already being drawn up. This would leave everyone under oath. An oath to the CABAL was total and final. It required no less than complete devotion and left a person's life under their jurisdiction. Carlton's head was spinning. It would mean some adjustments on his part. The committee members then went on to debate what course to take.

"...while I deplore the fact of not being informed. I can realise the motivation behind the corps members actions. I feel their oath to be sufficient recompense as it were... '' so said the North African member.

" You mean we have sold ourselves into slavery," said Maria despondently.

" A little crude perhaps, but true in essentials. You cannot have any complaints, given there are far worse penalties we could impose."

" Such as execution," the South Asian member remarked.

Maria bowed her head in silence.

" Obviously this charade will have to continue for a short while, then we can give Roj a public death." said the South American member.

" How about a plane crash ? " Carlton said. Maria glared at him.

" That is certainly an option..." said the Australasian member, " And one that is plausible. We should not continue the charade for too long however. I would suggest that Roj's second death be no more than a month's time. This gives an opportunity for the peace process to establish itself. and it minimises the possiblity of the ruse being discovered."

Nods and murmurs of agreement followed from all the committee members.

The North african delegate spoke again,

" There has been some concern raised over the the condition of the crowd outside. Not all of you will be up to date on this, but I can inform you all now that the situation is under control."

" But they haven't yet dispersed," said the Eastern European delegate.

" This could generate further problems," added the North Asian delegate.

" I don't think so."

" And why should we believe this ? " the hint of sarcasm was audible in the Western European member's tone, " Crowds cannot be trusted, we have all learnt this to our cost."

The North African showed a brief measure of impatience.

" My esteemed European colleague will be aware that I appreciate the dangers of crowds, particularly given past events. Yet this crowd remains docile. They are hypnotised in effect, completely under our guidance."

" And how long is this condition going to last ? " asked the North American member.

" We cannot be sure of this. Their trance condition may go of its own accord. But as yet they have not responded to commands to wake. At the other extreme one prognosis has suggested they could remain in a trance forever.."

" Which gives rise to the possibilty they may be suggestible for the rest of their lives ? " asked the South Asian member.

" That remains a strong possiblity."

A thoughtful silence followed before the acting chairman, the West African member, spoke up,

" I think I had better voice the growing feeling I am becoming aware of. I can see some of you are thinking along these lines also. Appalled as we are at events, it is because we are only human. Yet we are also business people. We have created, or rather we have had created, a population that is very susceptible to our commands. As such they are the perfect consumers. We can continue our plan for Roj to die within a month. But we can also prepare to avail ourselves of the business oportunities the remaining addresses of our intrepid leader can provide. If all goes as it did today, we will have created a large market, a market which will need whatever we instruct it to need. This will be a substantial proportion of the world's population. And the influence of these consumers will provide incentive for those unhypnotised to do likewise. For who can resist the fashion and fancy of the crowd ? You will all be aware the CABAL has found itself increasingly harassed during the course of the century, particularly from those who insist on putting mere human aspirations before the objectivity of the market. These misguided people have never realised it is the market that fuels human aspiration, at the request of business. We have an opportunity to re-establish the hold we once had on the world. For people have forgotten our role is that of financial caretakers who allow human life, in all its infinite variety, to flourish. Perhaps the course I am formulating here may strike some as immoral. What of it ? We have fought war after war on this planet to prove our claims of morality. I know we are practical. The CABAL is practical, objective in its aims, democratic in its means, a meritocracy that has always driven the world foward.

And once we have re-established our role in the world, we need not be distracted by the constant controversy that has so hampered out progress in the immediate past. We know our methods to be the best, for all. Therefore, I say to you all, that we use our skills to exploit this situation as we would any business opportunity. For I can forsee a possiblity whereby we can ensure the CABAL is entrenched in its position and completely unassailable to criticism..."

" I am in sympathy with the chairman's proposal," said the South Asian member with some readiness..

" It is exciting, and full of potential, for us all. I propose we vote to commend his words," said the North American member, whose own excitement was barely supressed.

" And to act them out in the building of a new era," said the Western European member.

The vote was carried with alacrity. Agreement was unanimous. Carlton and Maria both stood pale and open-mouthed. The North American spoke again,

" Here's to a new consumer era."

The room rang to resounding cheers.

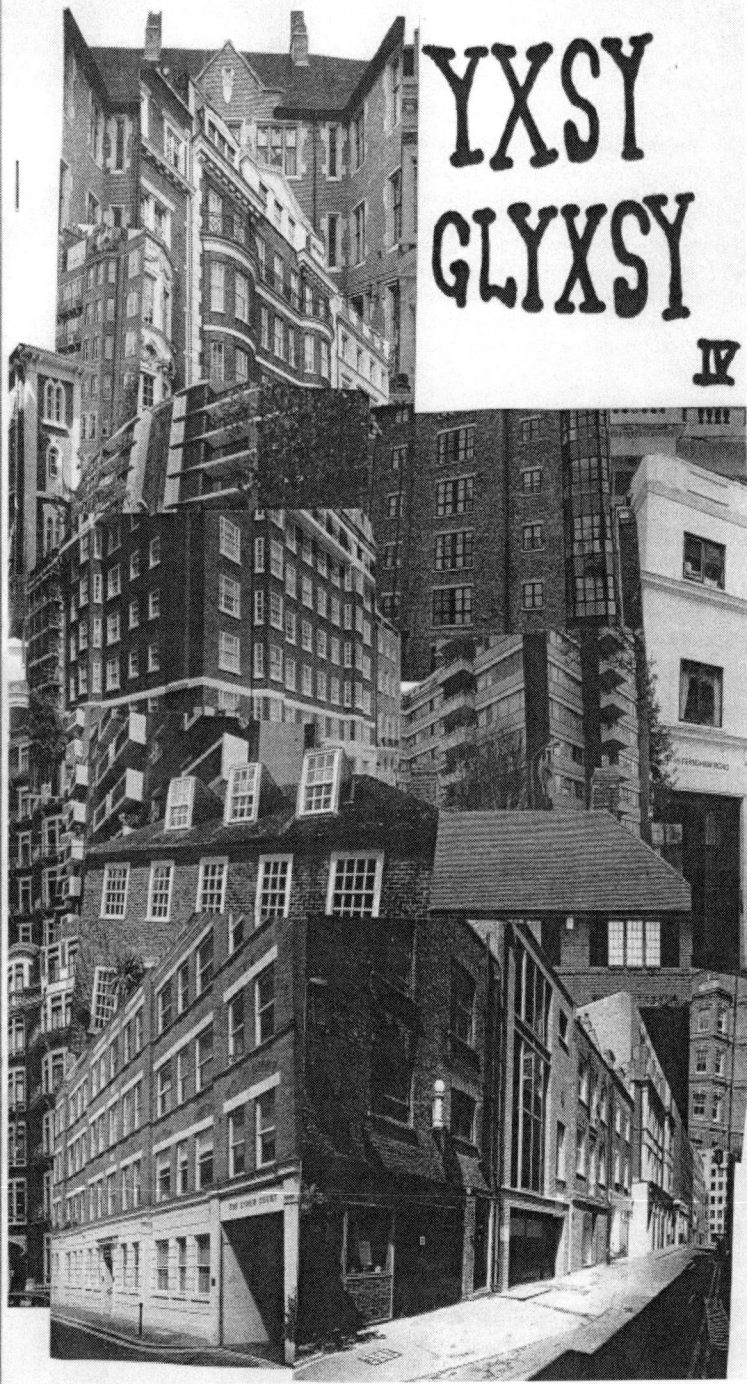

YXSY
GLYXSY
IV

The Palace of Thick Bastards

Four Eyes did not like this huge house. But then he had been wandering so long. Anywhere where he could get some rest and food would do. Anything but this constant wandering. Once, in the past, he had decided to wander the countryside. He wanted to be a walkabout wiseman, living close to nature. Actually that was only romantic justification. Debt had forced him from his wife and his home. He had been made redundant, three times in five years. Not good for someone who just fell into work in the first place. He never had any plan. So to have to look for jobs he was never interested in became extremely boring. Even the concern of his wife could not help. Her emotions just grated, her worry, anxiety, then her impatience and anger. The more extreme her emotions became the less he cared. He woke one morning to find her gone, having taken their three year old daughter. She had left a note that simply said " Bye."

She had done a runner. This placed the burden of debt upon him. There was the car, the fridge freezer, the dodgy finance company, and of course the crippling mortgage, to contend with. Four Eyes considered these payments carefully, and then said " Sod it, I'm off." He left a trail of court orders and bailiffs in his wake. It meant he could not settle anywhere long. Paranoid visions of huge fines, and huge men demanding huge fines, were always there. He could not relax, and it never occurred to him to face facts. He had given up the prospect of negotiating any kind of settlement with anyone.

The only solution was a clean break from everything. Although whenever he got time to stop and think it seemed everything caught up with him. Bad conscience and fear acted as a prod. They would never let him stop moving. He could never settle. But even he got fed up with his thoughts and feelings. He felt he would have to stop wandering or he would soon keel over. He was dirty, hungry, thirsty and light headed. And he saw this old house, perched on the hill overlooking the cliffs with their sheer drop. The sea boomed and nearly burst his eardrums. This was it. This last home in a shanty village of decaying timber and stone. All the habitations were uniform, their cracking sides painted dull white. They were holiday homes it was said. It looked like their owners had gone on permanent holiday. And it was peopled by the kind you would normally avoid. They looked like alkies, junkies, absconders and wanderers. Four Eyes considered himself one of the last, he was no different from the rest. Yet they scared him anyway. He kept fragments of his old, conventional views intact, somewhere.

Four Eyes, even that name was not his. The other tenants of the big house had given it to him, the way someone would give you a cold. But so what. He would have been too embarassed to tell them his real name, which was Drew Burke. What a name, it was more like a sound effect. But then his companions were not too inspiring in that department. There was Barry the Biker, Slobbo, Barbie and Stevey, what a bunch. Four Eyes could not even remember when he moved into the place. It was a gradual process. He used to go drinking, smoking, and consuming whatever else he could find. And these people pursued these activities with as much interest as him. One day he simply found he was living there. Although he could not get any benefit cheques delivered there, he had to go the nearest town, his address was considered unsafe. One of the others would probably have nicked his cheque anyway, if they could. The place was unsafe in other respects, it was damp, windy and falling apart. Luckily their drugged states seemed to nullify the environment. Also, their benefits were paid out on consecfutive weeks. It meant that careful financial management could leave them all with something to live on, even if it did not make them comfortable. This was the theory at least. In practice they were bored and starving for two weeks of the month.

Still, the occaisonal trip in to town became a highlight. Off they would plod. Already the town had a repuation as a D.S.S. backwater. It had declined from its daytripper status rather dramatically. Now there were armies of psychotic goons, just like themselves,all over the place. They had one occaisonal night out there, once in a while. But it always ended in trouble. Something got smashed up and someone got beaten up. Soon they were on first name terms with the police. And it became obvious, the officers would let no opportunity pass to hassle Four Eyes and his mates. It was an expression of their disgust.

Things could get bewildering and frightening. Four Eyes knew that none of his friends or associates were particularly evil. Yet bad things always followed them around. They had a bad smell about them, and not just in a literal sense. He tried to convince himself that his mates possessed some notions of friendship. For they often gave him moments that were too hairy, moments when he could feel his bowels loosening. And so, when he reached home, he would head straight for his room, pile the planks of wood, and boxes, against the door, and crash out. Unfortunately his companions could argue through closed doors. On one occaison Slobbo booted the whole pile, and the door, in an explosion of rubble. He was going to strangle Four Eyes for suggesting he had homosexual inclinations. Luckily Slobbo's rage effected his balance. He tripped over a chair leg and impaled himself. Slobbo liked to boast afterwards that he was not scared. He was fascinated by the orange colour of the wound. But Four Eyes saw the eyes widen and the blood drain from his face. After that he had one over on Slobbo, until Slobbo's memory gave out at least, which was no guarentee. But it meant The big slob was reasonably kind to him for a little while at least.

It was not as if Slobbo was particularly malicious. He was one of those big, clumsy dogs that just got angry as a matter of course. Usually he could be calmed down by someone acting as a nurse, soothing his wounded pride, then making continual suggestions. " No Slobbo, you didn't fuck up big time. You're not some clumsy twat. Actually you are king of the house, the village in fact." All of which would bring a gormless grin to his face, one that lasted for hours. Not that he had any real illusions about himself. He knew he was a slob and a clown, hence the nickname. Some wag suggested he was a famous clown, Slobbogigio. Slobbo laughed , then he kicked shit out of the wag. The name stuck regardless. He would freely admit he was a thick bastard, but no one else could, because he was as strong as a bull. More than once he came in handy when events became a little dodgy. He could pick up a bloke in each hand and throw them across a room, making the opposite wall shudder in the process. Whatever Slobbo did, whatever he consumed, his strength remained unimpaired. He had a body like a concrete slab, it was uniform and of industrial strength. And as he recognised his own stupidity, he kind of respected Four Eyes, because Four Eyes could string a sentence together. Once or twice he might call Four Eyes " the Boffin. " The others suggested it was only because Four Eyes had glasses that he gained this accolade.

Four Eyes was rather chuffed about this. It gave him a lever to unbalance the others, Stevey in particular. Stevey was the career alcoholic. While the others nursed their comedowns through the first half of the day, he started his with " some hair of the dog." It seemed to work, because he looked terrible when he woke. He was just a blotchy, red dishrag that had been wrung out while it slept. The morning gulp always seemed to bring him back to a semi-human state. The rest of the day was downhill from there. Stevey was unpredictable in his moods, they varied from bad to obnoxious. And you never knew when his obnoxiousness would surface. Tetchy he was just about bearable. He also had a dreamy, friendly state he might blunder into occaisonally. This was the worst of the lot. He became all pathetic pleading about how much he needed his mates. Once or twice an eloquent sentence escaped, like an unexpected fart. And like a fart it would soon disperse after causing an initial shock. You could only trust Stevey when he was sulking. Thankfully he often sulked. It was better than the stupid arguements he always tried to start. Obscure football teams and their cup runs, crap bands and their records, even crapper T.V. personalities and the boring shows they used to smile on. Yes Stevey was the one to watch okay, out of the corner of your eye, and constantly.

Barry the biker was the tetchy mechanic. Most of his time was spent tinkering outside on his putt putt Yamaha. One day he would transform his mickey mouse bike into a growling, demon machine. But that one day was forever far away. He could not even get the thing to start most of the time. And so he continued working, no one ever saw him drive anywhere. This was just as well, since Barry's appearance would probably scare everybody. To say he looked like an inbred hillbilly was putting it politely. His outsize head teetered on the brink of falling off his maladapted body. For all the time he spent outdoors he forever looked pale and sickly. His white flesh was given a grey tinge from constant exposure to grease and oil. These had entered his body and coloured it accordingly. Most of his conversation revolved on describing bike parts. It was enough to bore even the most hardened obsessive to death. And yet the dream kept him going. He was the easy rider, wild and free on the open road, involved in death defying stunts, romantic adventures, tense competition, and given the utmost respect from his fellow bikers. It was a pity no one else shared Barry's interest in the way he did. People usually found him boring and smelly.

Barbie was Barry's mirror opposite, in that he spent a corresponding amount of time indoors. This time was spent comatose, under the effects of tranquilisers. His career of tranquiliser abuse dated back years, he could quote forgotten names of long discarded pills and potions. He was an authority on the sedative, his particular favourites being the barbiturates, drugs which no one else seemed to have heard of. This gave him his nickname, which he was quite proud of, except when Stevey called him Barbie Doll. This almost wound up Barbie, but then Slobbo usually growled at Stevey. Therefore the others could never see if Barbie could get wound up.It was rumoured he had a character once, quite lively in fact. Certain comments which ventured to the surface of his brain, and crept out his mouth, seemed to confirm this. Although these were the few pearls to be found in a bed of oysters. Most of the time he spoke incoherent shit. Barbie did indeed look interesting. Women always came over to talk to him for some reason, perhaps they thought he was being cool instead of inert.

What happy memories Four eyes recalled. What happy memories were there ? none really. It was just one big blur. This blur had some moments more memorable than the unmemorable ones. That was about all he could express by way of any emotion on the matter. Perhaps he might have chuckled over memories of pool games in town. But these always degenerated into arguements about cheating. Strangers always bore the brunt of these accusations. A lot of the time a fight started, usually the others hid behind Slobbo, unless their adversaries were smaller than them. They invariably got banned from most pubs with a pool table. The bikers' pub was okay for a while. This was until the bikers lost patience with Stevey abusing everyone. Poor Stevey had the crap beaten out of him and spent six weeks in plaster. Slobbo would not help out on that occaison as the bikers were good mates and, more importantly, several of them were bigger then him. A tenuous goodwill was preserved with the bikers, mainly because they thought the foursome to be scumbags, and as such beneath their attention. However this did not stop fellow scumbags from attacking them. They had good reason besides the usual empty accusations scumbags make, unfortunately. Scumbags should never borrow money from scumbags. The foursome broke this golden rule regularly. They could never remember what was owed to whoever. Some canny scumbags tried to trade in on this memory loss, to claim money that never existed in the first place. This added further to the confusion. The matter was only settled by both parties keeping a respectful distance from each other, since they both became worried that someone else might found out something they had forgotten.

Even among the hazy brains of the four, they figured that somehow they had been cheating fate from witnessing a good kicking (apart from Stevey anyway). There was the added bonus that they alienated several people they could not be bothered with in the first place. As a method of conducting relations with people it was not entirely satisfactory. But it was about as far as they got. By degrees,however, their alcohol and drug intake had given them enough paranoia to manufacture their own grudges. No outside help was needed after that. Four Eyes never could figure out the mechanics of it all. It required someone technically minded, with a liking for masses of boring detail. But Barry the Biker could never be persuaded to go into town. He would only go when his bike was fixed. And so he never went. The other three soon adopted this habit. Going into town became a mythical date in the far future, when they would settle all accounts, grudges and loans, and live happily ever after.

Some problems followed because they could not find a safe address to have their giros delivered. The people known as the Miserable Old Gits performed this function for them, only after some embarassing begging and pleading on the part of Four Eyes. The Miserable Old Gits had gone to the village of white boxes to escape the crime and degradation of the city. Instead they found the crime and degradation of the village. They looked down on the foursome, but then everyone did. They were too cynical to be upset by having their dream of country retirement shattered. They were both extreme pissheads anyway. But they saw they had to keep the druggie scumbags at arms length. But only so much. Mister Pisshead could outscream Stevey in the verbal abuse stakes, while Mrs Pisshead proved to be a dab hand with the kitchen knives. Eventually some agreement was reached. The conditions were that Four Eyes and Co. should keep away from the Old Gits house all the time except to pick up their giro. The peace was nearly shattered when Barbie fell asleep in their flower bed one day. Mister Git was about to impale him with a pitchfork, when Slobbo grabbed him and proceeded to twist his arm behind his back. Mrs Git then ran out of the house, woodaxe in hand, ready to chop Slobbo into bite sized portions. Four Eyes feared the worst. He interceeded in the delicate negotiations that followed. Mrs Git's hysterics were calmed, Slobbo put the man's arm back in his socket, and the pitchfork was removed from Barbie's neck. To defuse the Old Gits ire, Four Eyes waved a couple of cans of extra strength lager in front of them. It was like waving a fish in front of a cat. The Miserable Old Gits were obviously impressed. Any remarks they made to the four were always addressed to Four Eyes after that, much to the amusement of the others, except Barbie, who was usually unconscious and had to be dragged home. And once home the other three, including Barry when it got dark, would fill him in on what a brown nosed crawler he was.

That was about as friendly as they could get with their fellow inhabitants. There was a psychotic, called Robbie, as their immediate neighbour. He lived with his doting sister. Robbie was dosed on medication most of the time. It stopped him running naked through the fields, which was his favourite hobby. Still, he visited the gangs' house a couple of times. He seemed to fit in pretty well. For some unknown reason he got on with Barbie best. Then there were the arty farty pagans, or so they claimed, a big, bruising hulk of a baldie, and his spiteful biker girlfriend. They were on friendly greeting terms with the foursome, at the start anyway. Slobbo and Barry got on best with them. But the Pagans tended to be erratic, the most erratic out of all the residents there. To tell the truth everyone was a bit afraid of them. This was mainly due to exaggerated fears about casting spells. In fact they were the most sober and relaible people there, which was not saying much. Since practically everyone else was violent, psychotic, drunken, or drugged up. The irony was not lost on Four Eyes, how a collection of weirdos could be afraid of people just because they had weird looks and beliefs ? This was amusing to him. He told Slobbo this, but Slobbo told him to shut up otherwise he would whack him one. And the others just shouted him down. Four Eyes was a fucking idiot, they said. The others believed the Pagans had cursed their home for some reason. Though why should the Pagans waste their time cursing something that was already a wreck ? It occurred to Four Eyes that the opportunity for a curse had long since gone. Stevey maintained that the Pagans curse would mean the village was populated by demons and that people would fall into evil ways. That day had long since gone, and everyone was too out of it to notice. Four Eyes wisely kept his observations on this matter to himself, the others became remarkably touchy about the subject. They threatened to give him a battering if he continued. It was too handy, the Pagans made a decent scapegoat, one that was too weird to do anything about. That was always the trouble with scumbags, they needed other scumbags to help them out too much when it came to attributing blame. But they could never admit to being scumbags themselves. This was something that was universally known but never acknowledged. Since, as Four Eyes was aware himself, the only way to live among scumbags is to become one yourself.

Four Eyes had to strain his wits to get through to his mates. These wits were walking wounded at the best of the times. Constant intoxication made him fumble his words and turned his actions into those of a bumbling idiot. Fortunately he was in good company. However, whenever he fell over, or spilt drink over himself, or set his fingers alight, you could be sure it would get the loudest laughs of the night. Four Eyes sought to divert their attention from these mishaps. One memorable, moonlit night, they were lying stoned on the dirty,dead grass outside their home. They had just had another escapade in town. The old shithole looked quite appealing in their relief at being back. Stevey took the old attitude that the home was the castle. Slobbo said it looked more like a palace. Barbie moaned something incomprehensible. This brought a volley of abuse from the others. They had just escaped a clutch of angry bikers. Barbie had vomited over one of their machines. The irate owner came up to them. Even then everything might have been alright. They made the placatory noises, explaining that Barbie was off his face. However, as they were doing so, Barbie vomited over the owner. Neither the owner nor his mates would let such a gross insult to go unpunished. Therefore the foursome legged it as fast as they could. They ran through the fields to try and throw the angry mob of bikers off the scent. They almost got away. But then they met the naked Robbie taking his midnight constitutional. Robbie was a strip of white light, and guided the bikers in their direction as sure as any beacon. The chase continued until everyone got hopelessly lost. It was nearly dawn by the time the gang all got back to their lovely white house.

Barry had a fit when he found out what happened. How could they be so disrespectful as to vomit over a motorbike ? But Slobbo punched him, and Barry fell over his own machine. Anyway, there they were, outside in the fading moonlight. Four Eyes stood up, all swaying arms and drunken eloquence. Stevey said he looked like an alcoholic computer nerd. Four Eyes expounded on the theme that a home is a home is a home is a house, sort of. The others nodded in agreement, they were not too sure what he meant, but it was Four Eyes talking, so it must be something intelligent. He granted Slobbo's claim that it was a palace, and they must do something in recognition of that fact. Actually it was old horses stables. Barely had the old owner gone bankrupt before a new one tried to convert them into holiday homes. Their resultant legal scrum meant the place fell into rapid neglect. To Four Eyes this explained the faint whiff of horse manure that was ever present, that is when the smell of themselves did not block it out. But that was bye the bye. They were all thick bastards, and this was as close as they would ever get to a palace. And so he tried to burn the title of their home on the peeling white paint outside, with a disposable lighter. Unfortunately the wind changed direction several times, fanning the flame onto his sensitive fingers, much to the others amusement. But Four Eyes did not mind. He settled for Palace of Thicko's instead. His companions cheered and shouted, and someone said shut up and someone else said fuck off. Four Eyes did not mind. It was his fondest memory of these times. Though he seldom revived it now. He was afraid it made him look too much like a sad bastard.

Four Eyes wallowed in that moment when it happened. He wallowed in a few other things as well. The Palace of Thick Bastards was famous for its smells, and its stains. Four Eyes always picked up stains he could never identify. Usually they came from his own body. In the midst of the haze he had some moments of clear consciousness, and they were horrifying. The part of his mind he used to call a conscience would emerge, gasping for breath. It would survey his surroundings and nag him with " You really have let things slip haven't you." The messed up over sensitivity of his emotions could not be hidden. Neither could the dire state of his companions. He glimpsed a blind panic in these moments. But a few seconds later he would forget everything. Something lingered however, and it was not the ill effects from his bad habits. He began to realise the sooner he left this place the longer he would live.

And he might have left sooner. But then the girls came to stay. Where did they come from ? he could not remember. Four Eyes saw Stevey with them first. Stevey boasted about how he picked them up, but no one paid any attention. Apparently they were promised endless drugs and music. Naturally the Foursomes thoughts turned to... well they could not be bothered really. Stevey fancied himself with the patter. And he could be quite charming. But you appreciated his charm most when he left the room. The girls were vague about where they stayed and where they came from. Four Eyes knew they were fellow loafers and wasters at once. You could tell because they wore stonewashed denim. The DSS must have cornered the market on this material, all their beneficiaries wore it. Four Eyes liked Joanne, the one with the black hair and big eyes. Unfortunately she was also the weird one. She was delighted Four Eyes had the same birth sign as herself. She endlessly quoted the accolades that went with this star sign. Four Eyes felt it made him sound like a completely boring bastard. There were the two Sues as well, big, bolshie, banshee women they were. They were great company. These bleach blonds went for muscle, consequently they were all over Slobbo, much to his enjoyment. This left Lisa, the hard headed, practical one, the one with half a brain. She took a shine to Barbie. All this was much to Stevey's annoyance. He had brought them home with evil designs on his mind. But they found him too abrasive. And when they discovered he was more bark than bite, they took the piss out of him, whenever they could.

Even so, all this change encouraged the gang to become a little more civilised. Some feeble efforts were made to tidy up. But the prospect of ever finishing was too far in the future. This made it too depressing. Besides, the girls were committed junkies. This suited three of the gang for a while. But Stevey was permanently narked. And so he did his best to disrupt proceedings for everyone else. A couple of beatings from Slobbo ensued. This could not disguise the fact they were getting on each others nerves, more so than usual. So it was suggested they get some money. A few thefts occurred in the village. There were one or two arguements, especially with the Miserable Old Gits. The girls stole their picket fence and sold it for firewood. Then they got Four Eyes and Barbie beaten up by an angry group of holidaymakers when they tried to steal a car. The girls ran away when they heard shouts. Four Eyes and Barbie were just standing there, watching, out of it. But it was assumed they were behind the whole affair. Others in the village had a laugh at this event. And they gossiped over others. There was talk of rounding up the Thick Bastards and giving them a good going over once and for all. Various peoples possessions kept going missing. No one ever quite knew the full facts. It was just the Thick Bastards up to their mischief again. Once or twice they got chased by a load of drunken farm labourers. In these events they relied on Slobbo's huge prescence. This was not a guarentee however, since some of these labourers were more insane than Slobbo. And poor old Barry the Biker got the worst of it. He became aware the bad name of his friends before he became aware there were girls living at the flat. This was because he was beaten up a couple of times. The others were chased into the house by drunken idiots while he continued working on his bike outside. While his friends locked themselves in, the drunken idiots vented their spleen on the poor twat outside. Friday night became a regular ordeal for Barry, in that one particular summer, for this was when the pubs turned out their biggest crowds of drunken idiots.

Things became excessively hairy for all the gang. There were threats their palace would be burned down. Even Slobbo got worried about going out. But then things were resolved, after a fashion. One day the police came and took the two Sues and Joanne. They had done a runner from some kind of institution, where Joanne was under constant medication. In fact all three girls were undergoing psychiatric treatment, as an alternative to prison, at least up until then.

Four Eyes was relieved. A lot of complications left their lives. But there was still Lisa. She moved from Four Eyes to Barbie, to Slobbo, to Four Eyes again, then Barry the Biker. Everyone was surprised at this, including Barry himself. If a woman had an internal combustion engine he could pull to bits, then he might have been interested. So he dealt with the advances of Lisa by looking bewildered and acting passive. In fact her moves were calculated to annoy Stevey, and they worked only too well. However, Stevey mistook the noises coming from outside and attacked Barbie, who was merely lying comatose. Slobbo then whacked Stevey, which usually ended things. But this time Stevey would not shut up. So everyone else pounced on Stevey. They tied him to a an old radiator, with a skipping rope and a bit of rusty chain, until he calmed down, which was a day later. After this Lisa had to go of course, though no one had the nerve to tell her. She had good ammunition. She could go for the withering blast of abuse that froze you in your tracks. And then she could turn on the charm offensive, making you feel wretched and pathetic for not sticking by her. If that failed she could go all weird. She seemed to have an uncanny knowledge of their moods, to them anyway, to others it might have been just as obvious. Yet it scared them the way she always seemed to know what they were feeling. The foursome could have used violence on her I suppose. But this was one residue of character they all shared, violence would never be an option. Apart from Stevey of course, who would consider anything he might get away with. But he was superstitious, he thought Lisa might throw a curse on him. Therefore he would have to involve the others. And so this meant they would have to use a dirty trick or two.

The gang waited for an opportune moment. They knew they would have to act fast. They conceieved of no brilliant plan, but it was the only one they could think of. And they had to do it before she could talk them out of anything. So one hazy evening, in the middle of a huge drugs session, they started an arguement about her sexual charms. She overheard of course, and stood there in their doorway, outlining all their peformance, and other deficiencies, in clinical detail. Their nerve nearly failed. But, on a desperate shout from Four Eyes himself, they shoved her out the door and locked it. She continued outlining their deficiencies from outside, alternating with pleas to be let in again. Barry was on the point of giving up, but that was really because he missed his bike, it was the longest he had spent indoors for ages. And when Lisa attacked his bike he nearly had a heart attack. But at least it would give him something to do in future.

Lisa's screaming attracted others as they came round to see what was going on. And she thought nothing of starting arguements with them. This was a mistake. For the Old Gits and the Pagans did not have the misgivings of the Foursome. Mrs Old Git gave Lisa a hefty right to the chin, while Mrs Pagan chased her away with a ceremonial dagger.

Some kind of order was restored to the village. But the gangs relationship with their neighbours cooled further. They were wary of the trouble in their midst. This was communicated to Four Eyes. On his advice it was decided to keep a low profile. And so they started going into town again. Despite an apologetic attitude to certain individuals they had offended in the past, word got around, the twats were back. And so the foursome got run out of the town centre. Four pubs refused to serve them. Then they were given a kindly warning by a large gang to behave in future. To round off the evening they were stopped by the police, who advised them to go home.

In the confusion Stevey had disappeared somewhere. With so many pubs in evidence he could have been anywhere. The four briefly thought about finding him. But as Stevey usually got up to dodgy antics it was decided to give him a miss. Besdies they got a free lift out of town in a police car. The police were not exactly concerned at the foursomes' plight, it was just, if the gang got massacred, then they might have to do some work. Still a free lift was a free lift, and nothing free was ever turned down. They promptly forgot Stevey's absence until next morning. Even the next week it barely got a mention. And the next month they finally assumed they had got rid of him.

A couple of months later a body was found in a ditch. It made all the local news. For its former occupant could not be identified. From post mortem analysis it was gathered he was a drifter and an alcoholic. He also appeared to have suffered stab wounds, although this was not conclusive. Nevertheless the inquest was treated as a murder inquiry for a short while. This inquiry never really got going to be honest. The body's description fitted a couple of hundred males in the area. However, the police narrowed the list down to twenty possibles. They went to the Palace of Thick Bastards to ask after Stevey, for he was one of the possibles. The gang could tell them nothing other than what actually happened. Although the gang's relationship with the police was one of mutual disgust, the police were actually reasonably sympathetic. Their questions covered all the ground it was possible to cover. And with that both parties were left shaking their heads. However the police delivered their customary threats. Some people around the area had taken an intense dislike to the Palace of Thick Bastards. They had seen situations like this before. People who were disliked often disappeared, it was more common than most would let on. This attempt at putting the frighteners on failed, because, as usual, the gang were well out of it.

Even when sobered up, Slobbo and Barry were not much bothered. Barbie was never bothered about anything. But Four Eyes' mind ran into overdrive for the first time in years. Not since the time he did a runner from his mortgage did he feel so panicky. If Stevey was stabbed were any of them safe ? probably not. Lucid, paranoid moments gained in strength in Four Eyes brain, in the midst of the drug haze. The thing with paranoia, Four Eyes believed, was that you were either completely right or completely wrong. Of course sometimes you were only half right. And then again your paranoia might only contain a hint of the truth. And going on from there you could easily manufacture a fear out of nothing. Four Eyes tried to talk to the others about this. But all he got were the usual blank looks. This redoubled his fears. What if Slobbo, Barbie, and Barry were in on some kind of conspiracy. But the thought of them being involved in something they could not even spell made him laugh, this soothed the paranoia.. But he still needed someone to talk to, someone reasonably well balanced and reasonably sane. He knew that was practically impossible in the village. All he got were the Pagans and the Old Gits. This showed how desperate Four Eyes was. For these people were sympathic but not that interested it seemed. Still, it was a start. Four Eyes was the only one of the Thick Bastards who was considered human. However, he was still a Thick Bastard, and needed to prove he was safe to talk to.

No one had any real answers for Four Eyes. Yet it was pleasing to note he could actually say hallo to others in the village without a confrontation starting. This caused no friction at all with his housemates, for they were too out of it to notice. In the Palace of Thick Bastards events pursued their own inexorable pace.

When walking home one evening, Slobbo was hit by a car. He limped home in a terrible mood. He was totally drunk and therefore unable to explain what happened. The others wanted him to go to hospital, but he would have none of it. He was terrified of hospitals. He did not even like doctors, he hated any suggestion there might be something wrong with him. The others could not persuade him. And he persuaded them to shut up or risk being hit themsleves. Uneasy peace was engendered. But in the morning Slobbo could not get up because he was in so much pain. An ambulance had to be called. Slobbo was picked up, while Four Eyes went with him. The other two were too scared to go along. It was depressing. Four Eyes waited ages and ages. He gleaned snippets of information - internal bleeding, possible organ damage, shock. Then there were the questions. What drugs had he taken ? what did he eat ? what did he drink ? how did he get hit ? Four Eyes answered as best he could. But most of the words he spoke were erms and aars.

As it was Slobbo was operated on. Four Eyes hung around for ages. But nothing else seemed to be going on, so he went home, disappointed. Slobbo was in there a couple of days. But things continued as usual - Barry worked on his bike while Barbie was crashed out somewhere. Four Eyes tried to get them to be concerned, but they were all too apathetic. It was a shame, since Slobbo had a certain deranged, simian charm. It was different with Stevey, everyone was relieved he was not around. All three of them assumed Slobbo would not be back though no one said anything. It was already a done thing. And of course he did not come back. Four Eyes only phoned the hospital a few times after his initial visit, thanks to the kindness of the Old Gits, who let him use their phone. Slobbo had left after a week. He checked himself out, against advice, and just disappeared.

It was then Four Eyes began to realise how boring their lives actually were. They just consumed poison and lay around. People had pointed it out before, but Four Eyes never believed it. All they did was get out of it and talk crap. Occaisonally they went out and took crap from someone else. Something had changed. Maybe it was the fact of Slobbo's and Stevey's disappearence. With one irritating and one intimidating twat off his back he now had room to think. The moments of lucidity were growing and he did not want to smother them. They made him aware he was bored, that his situation was inadequate, that the substances he took were not really doing much. An uncomfortable feeling grew on him. It took a while to put a name to it because Four Eyes had not known that feeling for years. He was begining to feel restless. He felt like doing things, but what ?

One day Barry actually got his bike working. He was as happy as a kid with a bag of sweets. Of course no one believed him. So he had to ride around the village, for hours on end, so enough people could see. Things were sufficiently patched up with the villagers, by this time, for them to enjoy a few drinks together. Everyone went to bed with sore heads. And that was the last anyone saw of Barry the Biker. Robbie disappeared as well. But then he always disappeared. However, after a few weeks people began to get worried. Had Robbie eloped with Barry in some kind of queer way. Everyone guessed but no one knew. A rusting bike and a decomposed body were found at the foot of the cliffs. The body turned out to be Robbie's. Barry was never found. It seemed a fair assumption he was dead also. For they were last seen driving drunkenly along the clifftop path. The fact that Robbie was naked whille riding pilion was a little weird, but Robbie was weird. Poor old Barry, it was always said he would rather tinker with his bike than ride it, because he did not know how to. Events would appear to have borne that out.

This left just Four Eyes and Barbie. By now Four Eyes was making arrangements to leave. The reasons were piling up. The main one was his health, it now seemed he had to leave if he wanted to live. If his own bad habits did not do it his paranoia would. It was not certain that Stevey and Slobbo were dead but everyone assumed so. And it was a bit suspicious the way Barry's body disappeared, the only virtue present among those deaths. Barbie was a problem however. Four Eyes knew if he left Barbie would not bother even waking up. Four Eyes concern reminded his mate he had to make some effort to stay alive. It was not that Barbie was unwilling to remain alive. He was just intensely forgetful all the time. Barbie was the household pet, he always needed feeding and cleaning up. Consciousness continued to work long forgotten ways on Four Eyes. He had completely misplaced the ablity to feel impatient or agitated. This proved an uncomfortable experience. By now the other villagers were his friends. They offered symapathy, even help. They had friends who had friends, and Barbie could stay with them. But no, Four Eyes could not treat Barbie like an old settee he did not want anymore, despite the fact he had not seen a settee for over four years now, and could just about remember what one looked like.

And so things continued after a fashion. The drugged up sessions rolled on, although it was less days a week now. Most of them were at the Pagans' house. It was becoming quite a routine. The Miserable Old Gits attended regularly. There were still miserable, but they actually talked to Four Eyes as if he were a human being, which was a step up. Robbie's sister became a frequent visitor. Even one or two old biker acquaintances turned up. These new arrangements did not bother Barbie too much. He usually lost consciouness at an early stage of the proceedings, then was dragged home as quickly as possible. He was left there while everyone else went back round the Pagans to enjoy themselves. Four Eyes feared the worst. He thought that Barbie might burn the place down by accident or die in his sleep, despite the reassurances of the others. Barbie was partial to paint thinner and other industrial products.

But one day Four Eyes went home, rather pie eyed, to find Barbie reading a book. This Four Eyes put down to hallucination on his own part. However, Barbie continued to do strange things, for him. He cleaned up the house, he began talking again. Four Eyes was disappointed to learn that he was just as boring in a state of sobriety. Barbie's drug abuse continued to decrease until he became a semi-rational human being. Then he told Four Eyes he was leaving, he had nothing against him, but nothing in common. Four Eyes shrugged, he was surprised to find he did not really care. So Barbie went back to the city to look for a job, to look for a different kind of anonymity to the type he had known for so long. Four Eyes waved, he felt too indifferent to say goodbye. That was that, well almost. One night when Four Eyes was round the Pagans, the Palace of Thick Bastards burned down. No one could do anything, except watch it burn. Still, it provided a good show for a couple of hours. Arson was suspected. But by now Four Eyes was thoroughly fed up of being paranoid. He was also fed up of getting out of it. One day he heard a friend of the Old gits was looking to employ someone. It was only part time but

Four Eyes went for it and , much to his surprise, got it. He moved out of the village, into town, started going out more, and getting out of it less. He still went round the Pagans' for for a huge session occaisonally. But this was now an anticipated pleasure rather than a routine habit.

This Was Your Life

A desperate,sweating man pushes through doors and bundles people out of the way. With his minders to protect him, he continues this process along winding corridors. The man is Mucus Aspic, all round telly bland man. Tonight he is presenting " This was Your Life," A most spectacular programme that intrudes into peoples' lives and shows them up in public. He is in a frantic haste because he wants to get to his latest victim before it is too late, before they figure out he is after them and run away. Besides, it is always better, from a viewing figures point of view, to surprise his victim in a situation that causes maximum embarassment. Once the victim is strangled by extreme self-consciousness Mucus can then manipulate proceedings accordingly.

As Mucus pushes his way through a final pair of double doors, he finds himself in an operating theatre. Some disgruntled surgeons make an effort to have him removed, but are quickly worked over by Mucus' minders. Now he has his quarry. He walks through a single door into a patient's room. There are two doctors here. They also attempt to have him removed. But some discrete intimidation again works wonders. The burly prescence of his minders secures Mucus his intended victim for that evening. She is a woman, looking worn out and in pain. She is on the final push of giving birth. This she does in some pain. And as the bloodied baby is held upside down for one of the doctors to slap life into it, Mucus thrusts a microphone in its face -

Mucus : Baby boy...it is isn't it ? yes, yes he's got a willy. I thought it was afterbirth for a minute. Baby boy, This Was Your Life...

Baby boy : WAAAAAAAAAAAAAAH.

Mucus : Yes I know this must come as something of a surprise.

1st. Doctor : You bet it is. He's only just been born. How can he be on ' This Was Your Life.'

Mucus : Baby boy is already a star, the main character in dozens of documentaries on human development.

2nd. Doctor : Is this true ?

Mother : I don't need this right now.

Mucus : But it's in your contract, Mother, any follow ups we want to do, we will.

Mother : Not in the delivery room.

Mucus : I'm afraid so. The contract was completely exclusive and intrusive.

Mother : Look, can you fuck off please.

Mucus : You're a bit emotional, I understand, but the show must go on.

1st. Doctor : Does the show have to go on at this moment ?

Mucus : Yes, or my minders will smash the place up.

2nd. Doctor : Oh very well then.

Mother : But he can't just barge in here with a T.V. camera. What about my right to privacy ? What about my baby's dignity ? what about my my dignity. This is a sensitive, delicate moment, when a new life comes into the world, where so many things can go wrong. How about showing a little decency, Mister Aspic ?

Mucus : How about you fulfilling your contract, Mother.

Mother : You could at least show a bit of common decency.

Mucus : I'll show a nice, juicy cheque that'll be yours when we finish this programme.

Mother : You can't bribe me.

Mucus : I'll throw in some gift vouchers.

Mother : Oh alright then.

1st. Doctor : Well, this will be the shortest programme on record.

Mucus : Not at all. Baby boy has appeared on camera several times over the past nine months. It all began on that evening of the drunken office party, nearly a year ago. Do you remember ?

Mother : No I don't.

Mucus : Probably because you were completely pie eyed at the time.

Mother : Nothing happened.

Mucus : Oh but it did.

Mother : No it didn't.

Mucus : Well then, do you remember this voice.

(A recorded voice booms out)

Voice : Oh no, the bag's burst.

Mucus : Yes, all the way from that office party a year ago, it's Roger, the office messenger. Roger who you rogered on the night in question.

Mother : But I didn't.

Mucus : Oh but you did.

(An embarassed man is bundled foward, squirming all the while. He struggles against the minders to no avail, who propel him foward until he is standing by the bedside.)

Mucus : So Roger, any anecdotes from the night in question ?

181

Roger : I'm sorry, Sue.

Mother : My name is Rita, you twat.

Roger : Oh, er sorry. You look different when you're not shit faced.

Mother : Can you get this idiot away from me ? I still cringe at the memory.

(Roger is unceremoniously shoved out of sight.)

Mucus : Now, Mother, do you remember this voice ?

Voice : Now, after the one sperm has penetrated the egg wall, the others cease trying. Imagine, if you can, a swimming pool full of tadpoles after a juicy tidbit, or better still, a classroom full of smelly boys competing to kiss a pretty girl, or better yet a school of sperm whales after a nice, juicy squid, or perhaps a horde of screaming teenagers about to molest a pop star, or even...

Mother : Oh no, it's that idiot from the documentary about me, Professor What's-His-Face.

Mucus : Yes, Professor Twatkins, from the University of Irrigation Ditch, who commissioned the documentary on your pregnancy.

Mother : Yeah, without my knowing about it.

Mucus : Stop moaning, you've been suitably reimbursed. Moving on quickly...

Mother : Do we have to ?

Mucus : Oh yes.

1st. Doctor : Wait a minute. Professor Twatkins is a fraud. He was exposed in the Mouth Baby Scandal.

Mucus : The Mouth Baby Scandal ?

2nd. Doctor : Yes, he claimed to be able to make a pregnant mother cough up her baby through her mouth, and so avoid all the pain of coming out through the womb.

Mucus : Wow, and did he succeed ?

2nd. Doctor : Of course he didn't, you moron. He was struck off the register, banned from teaching, and beaten up by disgruntled surgeons. Then he was exiled to a place where only charlatans and fantasists live.

Mucus : Wow, where was that ?

2nd. Doctor : Why Oxford of course.

Mucus : I went to Oxford.

1st. Doctor : That might explain a few things.

Mucus : I don't understand. I had a great time there, you two are just jealous.

2nd Doctor : I'm only jealous because that fraud Professor Twatkins got away with it for so long. I can't even get people people to send a letter to me.

Mucus : Oh cheer up. I'm sure you'll find a publisher at some point.

1st. Doctor : Nevertheless, the fact remains that Professor Twatkins is an embarassment now, even to an unintelligent, bad taste programme such as this.

Mucus : Really ? What do you have to say to all this, Professor Twatkins ?

Twatkins : When do I get my fee ?

Mucus : I see, erm, minders, could you beat up Professor Twatkins rather severely please and throw him out.

(A bout of unseemly thrashing, struggling and shouting follows as Professor Twatkins is massacred and thrown out.)

Twatkins : AAAAAAAARGH.

Mucus : Now, Baby boy, you were first filmed on a scan, naturally, erm, where it was determined, apparently, that you were possibly going to be a boy.

Baby boy : WAAAAAAAH.

Mucus : Yes quite.

1st. Doctor : This is all a bit tenuous isn't it ? Mister Aspic. You've hardly got enough material for a programme.

Mucus : That's not true. We have here a big bag of mail Baby boy received from the documentary series ' Womb Telly.'

(A big bag is shoved foward to Mucus, who grapples with it.)

2nd. Doctor : Wasn't ' Womb Telly,' withdrawn because you had faked some scenes.

Mucus : No, that was just a vicious slander...whew, here look at these.

(The 1st. Doctor reluctantly looks at a few letters.)

1st. Doctor : But they're all in the same handwriting.

Mucus : Obviously. All these people share the same obssession with the programme.

Mother : Look, can you hurry up and get this over with, so I can get back to real life.

Mucus : This is real life, Mother, from a mass media perspective.

Mother : It's about as real as a ballet dancing demon.

Mucus : Actually there's a programme about them on tonight, you shouldn't miss it.

Mother : Oh get on with it, Useless.

Mucus : It's Mucus.

Mother : Same difference as far as you're concerned.

Mucus : No it isn't. Show some patience. I know given your retarded upbringing this might be difficult...

1st. Doctor : Get on with it, Useless.

Mucus : I'm Mucus, not Useless...Please people, your cheques depend on my good mood...

Baby boy : WAAAAAAAAAH.

Mucus : Now, Baby boy, we have managed to round up your potential brothers and sisters...

Mother : But he's an only child.

Mucus : I said potential brothers and sisters.

(A trolley is wheeled in. It has a test tube rack on it, full of a cloudy susbstance, which is undoubtedly sperm.)

Mucus : Yes, we bribed the cleaner from the office party that night. He managed to scrape some sperm off the photocopier, Roger's sperm I might add, potential brothers and sisters.

2nd. Doctor : Reallly and what does all this sperm have to say for itself.

Mucus : Sperm can't talk, Doctor, I thought you'd know that.

2nd. Doctor : I was being sarcastic.

1st. Doctor : How pathetic this all is. What are you going to do next ? interview the poor woman's menstrual blood.

Mucus : Of course not. There was none available for comment.

2nd. Doctor : You really are a disgusting creep aren't you ?

Mucus : Yes, but only as an occupation. I don't sell my privacy the way you do.

2nd. Doctor : Why you...

Mucus : Ah ah ah, remember, I have a team of highly trained minders with me.

Baby boy : WAAAAAAH.

Mucus : Aren't you pleased to see all your tadpole relatives, Baby boy.

Baby boy : WAAAAAAH.

Mucus : No ? well shut up and let me get on with the show. This is your fiteen minutes of fame. So try to enjoy it, because it's going to be the only fame you're going to get in your life.

Mother : Stop shouting at my child, you obnoxious turd.

1st. Doctor : Have you finished interviewing the sperm now ?

Mucus : I wasn't interviewing it, it just made a guest appearance.

2nd. Doctor : Either way, let's get rid of it shall we.

(The trolley is wheeled out.)

Mother : This should be the best moment of my life and you've turned it into cheap and nasty crap.

Mucus : Patience, Mother. Remember, big, big, juicy chequey, with lots of zeros. That's a lot of rusks paid for....

2nd. Doctor : Can we please get this farcical situation over as soon as possible.

Mucus : A farcical situation that will produce high viewing figures, so don't be prejudiced.

2nd. Doctor : People will only watch this because it's cheap titilation.

Mucus : Well at least we have some understanding.

2nd. Doctor : Crass, cheap thrills to misinform morons about a world they barely understand in the first place.

Mucus : Have you been reading a copy of our policy manual ?

Mother : Get on with it, you idiot.

Mucus : Well Mother, you may not be so keen to get on with it. For our next guest is a chain-smoking, drunken coward, who we found hiding under the tables in the cafeteria.

Mother : Oh no, tell me it's not true.

Mucus : Unfortunately it is. Do you recognise this voice.

Voice : Wha ? What's going on ?

Mother : I wish I didn't.

Mucus : But you do, it's your husband Jerry.

(A drunken man lurches in smoking a cigarette, walking into walls and knocking things over.)

Jerry : It's hard to find your way round these hospitals.

1st. Doctor : Careful, you idiot.

2nd. Doctor : No smoking in the hospital.

(The cigarette is ripped out of Jerry's mouth.)

Jerry : Aaaah, you could have said please.

Baby boy : WAAAAAH.

Jerry : And don't you start, either.

Mother : You're drunk again, you twat.

Jerry : Yeah, but only accidentally.

Mother : Go and lie down somewhere, away from me.

Jerry : I love you, darling.

Mother : I know, go away.

Jerry : Even though it's not my baby, you bitch.

Mother : We'll talk about this later, Jerry.

Mucus : No, argue about it now. It'll make great telly.

Mother : Slither off and die, Mucus.

Mucus : Remember, chequey, chequey.

Jerry : Why didn't you tell me, Rita ?

Mother : Because most of the time you're too drunk to listen.

Jerry : So talk to me when I'm not drunk.

Mother : I can't talk to you when you're asleep, stupid.

Jerry : You can try.

Mother : There's no point.

Jerry : What ?

Mother : See what I mean.

Jerry : What're you talking about ?

Mother : You, you daft git.

Jerry : So let me in on the secret.

Mother : It's no secret.

Jerry : What isn't ?

Mother : The fact that you're a thick bastard who drinks too much, who's a total wimp, who's got stuck with me somehow...

Jerry : ...A big, spoilt baby who moans.

Mother : Well yeah, but I didn't want to show you up too much.

Jerry : I'm talking about you. It's always 'you're this and you're that' to me. Meanwhile you always 'just wanna do this' or, 'just wanna do that.' You go off and shag anything with trousers.

Mother : No I don't, I'm quite particular.

Jerry : Yeah, whoever happens to be available at a particular time.

Mucus : You mean she sleeps around quite a lot.

Mother : Shut up Mucus.

Jerry : Well, not that much, only during the week, er, and on weekends as well, um, and holidays as well.

Mother : Only because you've been too weak to raise your interest for the past five years.

Jerry : That's a total lie. It's four years.

Mother : You make it feel like forty.

Jerry : Which is about the number of blokes you've shagged.

Mother : You gormless idiot.

(Rita picks up a bedpan and whacks her husband with it. Jerry is knocked unconscious.)

Mother : I told you to go and lie down.

(Jerry is dragged away.)

Mucus : Well, I must say, you have a lively domestic life.

Mother : At least I have a life.

Mucus : Yes, and very sordid it is too.

1st. Doctor : No more sordid than prying into people's personal situations and passing judgement on them.

Mucus : But I'm a professional.

2nd. Doctor : Definitely a pro.

Mother : Are we finished yet ?

Mucus : No, I've got to bring on your probation officer, your social worker, and your psychiatrist, yet.

1st. Doctor : Good God man, how long are you going to drag this programme out for ?

Mucus : Oh I think we can fill up two programmes and take it from there.

2nd. Doctor : Maybe we're getting fed up with this.

Mucus : Remember chequey, chequey, nice, juicy chequey.

1st. Doctor : Nice, juicy chequey doesn't seem so appetising anymore.

2nd. Doctor : Perhaps we might be finding this programme too repulsive for money.

Mucus : What's the matter ? Aren't I paying enough ?

Mother : Why don't we pay you, to get lost.

Mucus : Watch it, I still have a small army of minders with me.

(The minders glare and growl on cue.)

Mucus : You will fulfill your contract, or we will print scurrilous stories in the tabloid press.

1st. Doctor : You wouldn't dare.

Mucus : That's in the contract as well.

2nd Doctor : Damn, outwitted by a slimy creep.

Mucus : Thank you.

Mother : Hmmm, I might be able to do something here. Doctors, could you help me out of bed please.

(The doctors support Rita while she stands upright.)

Mother : Now , hand me my baby.

(The doctors do so.)

Mother : Look, isn't he a lovely baby boy. Have you ever seen anything so sweet, so fragile, so dependant on us. But he's so lovely isn't he ? Would you like to take a look, go on, you can hold him if you like, don't be shy. I bet some of you have children of your own...

(While Rita is saying these words, the minders begin fidgeting uncontrollably. This reaches a crescendo of twitching. One or two whines escape from them as they can take no more and charge out of the room as though their lives depended on it.)

Mucus : How did you do that ?

Mother : I gambled on them being soft at heart, which of course minders can't afford to show, especially when they're at work.

1st. Doctor : Excellent. Now we can settle matters here.

2nd. Doctor : In a satisfactory manner.

Mucus : Er, what are you going to do ?

Mother : Oh, it looks like we can give this programme the right ending.

(Rita settles back down into bed. The two doctors turn on Mucus in a menacing manner.)

Mucus : I have lots of money you know, and power, and influence.

1st. Doctor : No you don't, you're a hack journalist with drink and sexual problems, and you sleep with all your colleagues.

Mucus : You have to get ahead somehow.

Mother : Every night by the sound of it.

Mucus : Look who's talking, Mrs Bow Leg herself.

Mother : No, it's Mister Slime Deposit.

1st . Doctor : Haven't we had enough of this ?

2nd. Doctor : We certainly have.

(The two doctors both jump Mucus and wrestle him to the ground. Rita looks on gleefully.)

(The scene changes. A News theme is heard. The nice, reassuring features of a newsreader appear, sitting behind a desk.)

Newsreader : Good evening. There is some confusion tonight concerning the whereabouts of T.V. presenter, slimy creep on the make, and git about town, Mucus Aspic. He was last heard of filming a sleazy programme in a hospital. Apparently, on the spur of the moment, he felt like a sex change operation. However, due to an administrative error, he was given several organs he did not need, including a pigs arse grafted onto his face, and horses' hooves sprouting out from his stomach. Mister Aspic, or Mrs Aspic as she is now known, checked out of the hospital in the company of two men in white coats carrying meat cleavers. He is said to be at home now, either resting, contemplating, fermenting or fulminating, er it says here. Matters are very confused at the moment, said a spokesperson for Mrs Aspic, but we should get a series or two out of it, plus some spin off merchandise as well. As soon as we have further details, we won't use them, because things move on pretty fast. Goodnight.

My Friends at Forest Glade

What was I doing at the time ? I do not know. I was bored, clinically bored. I was on one of my periodic bouts of unemployment. In between employment, I had been living like this for some years now. And I never got used to it. I worked for about eight months of the year, on contract work naturally. The rest of the year I spent running up huge debts. I was a casualty of the yuppie lifestyle I led, so I was told, gleefully, by too many people. Just because I was an accountant, and a good one at that.

Anyway, I am someone who prefers to be busy. When I am idle I just deteriorate. I become listless, lazy and apathetic. How could I be otherwise when I just hung around the house all day. I say the house, actually it was a block, a block of expensive apartments. They were prestige apartments, no mere flats. But they were the reason I always ran up huge debts. The payments were hard to keep up. It was not as if they they were really worth it. The average council flat was better maintained. In fact, I would have preferred a council flat. At least the leaseholders would stop going bankrupt, as mine always did.

There were cracks up and down the walls in my block, and a backlog of service repairs. Even if I wanted to sell

I doubt if I could have. I thought I was buying into the yuppie dream. Instead I bought into an upwardly mobile man's nightmare. And with these thoughts on my mind, I took to constantly moping around. Indoors got to be too claustrophic in this state of mind. So I thought I might explore the grounds.

The grounds, what a concept. As if it were the landscaped gardens of a manor house, instead of being the overgrown tip it had become. Still, that fact made it a bit interesting. There was a drive down the back of the block. I say was, because this drive was now lost in the undergrowth. Bushy plants sprung up everywhere, choking all remnants of a road, or even a path. Yet it looked, I imagined, as it did before it was first built upon, like a forest glade. That was the name of my block, Forest Glade. And this derelict remnant was all that remained of the woodlands that must have covered all of the hill on which my block perched precariously. (We had subsidence problems at Forest Glade.)

Halfway down this real glade, were three old garages. Their doors were long gone, but enough items of stray rubbish remained. Enough for me to take a seat and wonder what it must have once been like, and why was I in this place anyway.

That was it. That was all I did all day. So I cannot remember the date it actually happened. Although I remember what happened. I was always alone at this place. The other residents were a bit scared of the foxes. They never bothered me. In fact they always ran away from me. Good thing too. They were massive, some of them, like collie dogs at least. All that suburban rubbish must have been good for them. The foxes disuaded anyone else from coming to the glade, and that suited me down to the ground. I could be alone with my thoughts, what there was of them, since I usually enjoyed prolonged sulking. I often fancied I saw movement in the bushes, or in the trees that surrounded these bushes. I put this down to wishful thinking. Since, the state I was in, I wanted something to happen. But then I could always put that down to the wind, or the foxes.

Every now and then I would slip into a daydream, which I really liked. Because it was the only time I felt at peace with myself, instead of being bored or depressed. It was so still. It always was still in the suburb where I lived. But this was a different stillness, one of relaxation instead of boredom. On that, my last prolonged period of unemployment, it was summer, a gorgeous summer. That rubbed it in. For I had no real money to enjoy it. Yet as I sat in the middle garage, on an upturned crate, I could look at my own piece of summer magic. I could see the carpet of foliage before me, and on the edge of the path a wall of foliage protected me from the harsh glare of the sun. There were gaps of course, where the rays of light streamed through, and where I could catch a glimpse of the rolling suburban hills. In this light I could imagine I was in some kind of amazing hillscape, which I suppose I was. But I could make believe the endless rows of suburban houses did not exist. Sounds of a stray car, or of children playing, might find their way to my vantage point. But otherwise it was all quiet. It was the quiet of deserted houses, their occupants having gone to work in the city.

I hoped I would not need to mope long here. For I could feel myself getting very apathetic. I had stopped looking for work now. I was just waiting for others to contact me, to get me out of this situation, I could not really be bothered to do anything else. At the back of my mind was the thought I should be doing something. But I did not know what to do anymore.

Looking back now, I believe the stage was set. I was in a mood of expectation, though passive. The conditions were right, hot and listless, when what happened happened. I became aware of it by degrees. It was now a regular daily event, my sitting in that garage, fantasising I was in a real forest glade. First of all were the foxes. They became accustomed to my prescence, sniffing around me like curious dogs. I was alert enough to think of bringing them tidbits from my kitchen. Although maybe it was really because they scared me. Once they lost their initial shyness, they would pester me, in the manner of friendly dogs. But I have never really liked dogs. And it was a bit too insistent the way they pestered me. I was worried about fleas, and rabies. They smelled, these foxes, although they were striking to look at, well fed, mischievous, like household pets.

That thought was to recur to me. For after they became accustomed to me, about a week I should say, I began seeing something else. There were about four foxes in all, although I always heard shuffling beyond the trees in front of me that suggested more. Well one day these reluctant visitors decided to show themselves. And when they did I nearly fell off my crate. For they were mounted, or at least people were mounted on them. Short people, like midgets really, midgets in double breasted mohair suits. I was gobsmacked I have to say, I nearly fell off my crate. I had heard of hallucinations before, but I never thought they could look so ridiculous. The shock subsided, my mouth began to move, I was laughing uncontrollaby, hysterically. And that seemed the worst thing I could have done. For they became aware of my presence. No, that is not quite it, they became aware I could see them. For they could hardly have missed me, perched on my crate in the empty garage. They gave me a look so vile that it froze the mirth on my face. In unison they stared at me. It was a stare I had seen before, outside a few nightclubs, when some gang of drunken arseholes wanted to start a fight with me. But this look I was given by these fox riders, was a thousand times more malevolent.

I was frozen again. One of the riders dismounted and made to walk over to me, as if to inspect the nature of the threat I posed. Well that broke the spell they had me in. I leaped up and ran out of there. It struck me as curious I was formerly so apathetic. And now I was so panicky. I missed my former state. I had had anxiety before and I did not like it.

But I need not have worried, at least on this occaison. For, after a couple of hours, and a couple too many cigarettes, my regular torpor began to set in. The panic attack had worn me out, it seemed. Then the glade began to work its attraction on me again. I was back the next day, in my usual position. I waited for them to reappear. And they did. They came over warily and just stared at me. It was unnerving. I could feel the giggles rising, the urge to burst out laughing had control. Yet not for long. I supressed it. For there was that look of malevolence about them. It is funny. I never remember them actuallly talking. But I was always aware of what their moods and intentions were. I might call it telepathy. Except that was not it at all. Rather I became aware of their mood and intentions because they projected both toward me. And they seemed to know enough about me to know I was not an immediate threat. I would compare it to an extremely vivid dream. In such a dream, of which I have had a few, the emotional content was always very strong, making the need for speech redundant. In fact, that is how I cope with the experience now, to regard it as a dream. Yet it still disturbs me. For the contents of a dream were transfered out of my head into the prosaic surroundings of a suburban appartment block.

They were powerful, these supposed dream images. Yet in some ways they were frightened of me. I was glad of this at least. I became aware that some would do me physical harm, if they could. It seemed a matter of survival not to lose this advantage, whatever it was, for it was not that apparent. Indeed, they always appeared to have the upper hand in our meetings. They circled me rigorously. I could study their dress and manners. They were a bit ludicrous. They were dressed like office workers. Those double breasted mohair suits suggested well paid office workers, yuppies even. They looked like colleagues of mine. This undermined their malevolence. Although plenty of yuppies could be malevolent themselves, yuppie fairies were a different matter. There were one or two females now I noticed, dressed like PR people in smart, skirt suits. I had a notion I was partly responsible for these weird sights, even if they were out of my control. I could not put my finger on it though. The urge to just let myself go, into the vision that surrounded me, was powerful. It always seemed wrong to do that, even now I cannot understand why.

Well, these female fairies certainly were attractive. And they knew it. Their attraction was just that, it was magnetic. They grinned knowingly, daring me to come on and prove my desire. But I still held back. Mocking looks were cast at me. They knew, and so did I, I would try to find a way to consummate my desire with them, that is, if they existed in the sense women usually did. And this was when the doubt began to grow further. I would have to make some commitment, as is normal when making any kind of relationship, but what that committment involved was just too strange, if not unkown. On this second day of their company, I managed to tear myself away. I walked casually, as if I were inspecting them, as they did me, but took the opportunity to walk right on back to my flat, out of their grasp.

I had a shock. When I stepped out of the glade, and back into Forest Glade, it was night time. In the glade it was the usual hot summer afternoon. But as I walked around to the front of Forest Glade, it was midnight, and cold. I shivered as I walked bewildered up to my flat. I was in need of some reassurance. I did what I did after a hard day's work. I slumped out in front of the telly. This always banished anxiety from my head. There is nothing so soothing. Weird yuppie fairies mooching around in overgrown back gardens were a million miles away.

I must have fallen asleep in front of the telly. I assume I did. For the next thing I knew I was up and about, some miles away in fact. I was in a stationery shop. I had a large canvas suitcase with me, and I was helping myself to enveloppes, pens, folders, pads, paper, anything I could lay my hands on. I was extremely worried about how I was going to pay for this, since money was very tight at the time. But I solved that problem by simply running out of the shop with my full suitcase. I expected someone to stop me at any minute. But no one appeared to notice. As I got down the end of the street I did hear a voice shouting, and I turned around to see a large man pursuing me, but I was too far away now, I easily eluded him. Still, that moment of panic gave me extra incentive. I had to find somewhere to go, pretty quickly. So I walked and I walked, briskly, the suitcase growing heavier by the minute. I was sweating buckets. And there I found myself, back in the glade on a summer afternoon, surrounded by miniature malevolence. They rifled through the suitcase, chuckling as they did. I had done well, apparently. I was slightly annoyed. I have always been against shoplifting, I have worked in a few shops myself. Yet here were these greedy fairies who had somehow persuaded me into indulging their fetish for office stationery. They caught my mood, and they circled around, more menacing than usual. I grabbed the one nearest, an ugly little brute in a double-breasted, pin stripe suit. Yet as I grabbed him he vanished. I was baffled, until I received a hefty kick up the arse. This sent me flat on my face.

Malicious giggles erupted from the pint sized anomalies. I made to grab another, a blonde, arrogant, manicured type, but pain went coursing through me as I touched him. My hold was stuck fast on his sleeve. It numbed me, it was like an extreme case of pins and needles. I could feel the numbness moving into my shoulder. I got worried. And then I fainted.

When I came round I was further down in the glade, I suppose, I could not tell for sure. Those male fairies were behind me now. I could hear their whispered giggles. I was being tended, looked after. All those female, PR-looking fairies were fussing over me, rubbing some ointment into my arm, massaging me. I was enjoying this part of the adventure, no doubt. I wanted it to continue forever. Some people always have a way with massage. You just want to sit there and absorb their delicious touch, which is both relaxing and erotic. Although erotic was gaining the upper hand here. They knew this, in fact they were drawing out my desire. They stoked it up, like a fragile flame at first, and then they fanned the flame until a healthy blaze was developing. Then suddenly they stood up and backed away. They smiled that smile that women sometimes have, that dares you to pursue them and show what you are made of. Well, I was game. I made to get up to join the pursuit. But as I struggled to rise I leant on my injured arm, which, although better, had not yet recovered its circulation. So I fell over, face first , through the undergrowth. I gathered some momentum in my fall. A lot of malicious cackling echoed behind me. I must have rolled about ten feet at least, not a long way, except it feels long when it is vertical. The hill at the back of Forest Glade was quite steep in places. I rolled down ledges, across roots, until I went through a hole in a fence at the bottom of the hill. I ended up on a manicured lawn, set back from a suburban street. The mayflower trees were in full pink bloom above, and rows of desirable,if expensive, and identical, detached houses ran on either side of me. Except that this was no fantasy street. It was Maiden Avenue, which ran at the foot of the hill on which Forest Glade sat. I quickly got up and dusted myself down. I had no wish to be seen lying around here. Some irate soul would probably send a letter to the local newspaper, complaining about the arrival of down and outs. I shook myself to regain my composure, then walked out into this street casually. As I did a woman walked past with a gaggle of schoolgirls in attendance. They wore identikit uniforms, tilting their heads to look at me as they swarmed past. The giggly expressions reminded me of those whose company I had recently left. But the schoolgirls expressions were far less threatening. That thought shook me. School already, I thought it was the end of July. If school had started it must be September. Or was it?. I also remembered the telly programmes I had viewed recently. Many of them made reference to events I had no knowledge of. Me, who was usually so up to date with current affairs. Recently was becoming a relative term.

I thought it best not to go back up Forest Glade the way I had come down. Maiden Lane circumvented the bottom of the hill, then looped up to the right. I decided to use this path to go, where?

I had thought to go home, but events were moving at to fast a pace. It seemed I had no control over when I went to the little glade anymore. I had to find out what was happening, why was time so all over the place ? what was the month anyway ? and what was the date ? what exactly were these apparitions I kept encountering ? if they were apparitions, or fairies, or goblins, or mischievous, misshapen children, what ?

Questions buzzed through my head as I walked around the hill. I needed some answers. I remembered there was a library within walking distance of Forest Glade, well, half an hours walk. That did not matter. I did not want myself suddenly in a weird situation again, with no knowldege of how I arrived there. Once might have been interesting, even fun, but it was getting to be too much of a habit. I did not want these little monsters to have power over me, which I believed was now their intention. I had to find some way of stoppping them, somehow.

I found the library okay, and I went to their section that contained weird books. By weird I mean anything new age or related. Usually I found such stuff too stupid to be real. But what was happening to me was stupid and real, and scary. I could not find much on fairies. One book of folklore, and one on what appeared to be occultism generally. The folklore one contained all the kinds of stories I remembered from childhood. About people who went off dancing with the little folk, or who tried to steal from them, or who wanted to marry some gorgeous fairy female. At another time I might have been reasonably intrigued. But the stories did not seem too relevant. Although these tales did stress the fact that all human-fairy relations were never to the advantage of humans. Never take their gifts, never eat their food, never fall in love with them. In fact, keep a great distance away. That book depressed me. So I turned to the occult one. That took a different attitude. It related tales of men and women who supposedly had business with these 'spirits', as they were called. Transactions were possible with them, but certain precautions must be taken. Good, at last, I thought, something I could use to break the apparent spell I was under. The trouble was the precautions were so archaic. I did not have any silver armour with me, nor any iron weapons, and I certainly had no time to wait for the right phases of the moon to gather the right herbs.

I closed the book, not entirely disheartened. I could use nothing either book offered me. They both said fairies were afraid of modern technology. But these were yuppie fairies after all, modern, up to date spirits, if you will. None of these ancient charms would work, I knew intuitively. Yet I also intuited I might have a way of spoiling these malevolent pests' intentions. And maybe I had enough time to gather the necessary equipment before I was again whisked to do whatever they desired.

And so it happened I had some motivation again, for what seemed like, how long ? I never did find out the date. Never mind, I thought at the time. I had rushed around, in a blur, and I had the necessary equipment, I hoped, to get rid of the little pests. I manged to get home to change, also to stuff some items I needed into a carrier bag. I was feeling pleased with myself, until I found myself somewhere else again. It was midnight again, back in the city. I was loading up a van, with swivel chairs and a desk. Even now, I cannot remember how I got the van, or where it disappeared afterwards. Actually, the place I was taking the furniture from looked remarkably like the last place I worked. I was worried I might get arrested for stealing. But, as on the previous occaison, an air of unreality hung over the scene. No one else was around, and I proceeded to finish loading the van at my leisure. As I slammed the back door and slipped into the driver's seat, I thought I saw the same large man in the distance, the same one as before. But again I was too far away for him to do anything. As his shouts came nearer I started the van and slipped away easily. From then things got more hazy. The van just vanished somewhere along the way. I have never seen it since. And I was back at the little glade, at the back of Forest Glade. The desk and the office chairs were standing before me, just outside the garage, surrounded by a carpet of undergrowth. The yuppie fairies were trying out the furniture for size, spinning themselves around on the swivel chairs, and pretending to interview each other across the desk. They were pleased with me. I was something of an asset to them. I gained the impression they wanted to keep me there. I was too valuable to be let loose. I was a prisoner in actual fact. I felt as much. And they responded to my desperate feeling. A ring of foxes surrounded me, growling ominously. The fairies set a meal out. It smelt gorgeous. I would have done anything to have sat down, at the desk I had so recently stolen, and gorged myself. It looked like the mother of all curries. Plus, the drink they were passing around, in its colour alone, made me want to guzzle it uncontrollably.

The PR fairies also teased me into indulging myself. Their body language made clear that food and drink would be followed by another indulgence afterward. Yet as they stood around me and teased, they could not push their advantage, as they might have had before. Even the foxes kept a respectful distance.

They were a little taken back by my changed appearance. I suppose I lived the yuppie lifestyle even when off work, to keep up appearances. But instead of my usual designer, casual clothes I now wore a baseball cap, a cheap sweatshirt with a cheap and nasty logo, dirty, shapeless, tracksuit bottoms, and huge, white, lumpy trainers. I nearly made myself sick as I dressed in this stuff, it was so at odds with me, I could not even look in the mirror. But still, every embarassment in a person's wardrobe can have some uses. I guessed the yuppie fairies would feel likewise. And they did. There they were, with their weird designs of making a fairy office, but I had thrown a spanner in the works, like a slob who turns up at a party with a dress code. I hated slobs. And these yuppie fairies were enough like me to be disgusted by what disgusted me. They sensed this. They made to regroup, to overpower me, and strip me of my slob's outfit. That was when I revealed my secret weapon from its bag. It was a small cassette recorder, I turned the volume up full blast. It had an auto reverse function so it would play continously. And it played the dullest techno tracks imaginable. Repetative drums with a humming baseline that was far too loud. It was the sort of thing I always heard blaring from peoples' car stereos as they drove by on the street, and I hated it. My guess was right in the fact the fairies hated it too. They covered their ears and visibly shrank away. Though they still kept a watchful distance, waiting for their turn to strike. I decided to push my advantage while I had it. Out came the cold kebab and french fries, along with a burger that had the consistency of cardboard. This was too much for the PR fairies. They simply vanished. One second they were there, the next they were gone. I turned to face the remaining yuppie fairies. For the first time they were visibly scared. But they still came toward me. They might have overpowered me, despite all my advantages. Yet I produced my last weapon, the cheap tabloid newspaper. They screwed their faces up in horror as I produced it. And, as I crushed the paper between my hands, then threw it, they threw their own arms across their faces, to avoid being tainted by tabloid print. And, as the screwed up lump reached them, they too disappeared. Like their female companions they were simply not there anymore. Only the foxes remained, growling as ever. But they were easy to deal with. I just threw the junk food away, down the hill, and they went charging off after it. I never knew my snobbery could help me this effectively.

That was it. I never saw them after that. I never found myself in places I did not want to be anymore, at times I would not have chosen. If I went anywhere now I got there under my own volition. That fact alone was such a relief. It made me quite optimistic. This optimsim meant I was not suprised when a job offer came out of the blue, I took it in my stride. One of my colleagues came round to offer it me personally. She claimed she had been trying to contact me for weeks. I said I had took a prolonged holiday, nowhere special, just in the country, to recharge my batteries, as I was feeling low. This was no real lie. She could have sworn she saw me in the city a couple of times. In fact, she had gone so far as to call out my name and run up to me, but both times I eluded her. I let that last comment drop. I do not think she would be pleased to hear I mistook her for an overweight security guard.

Once I started work again, I could finish with that small patch of weirdness at the back of Forest Glade for good. I knew someone who did casual gardening work. I set him to work clearing away the back of all its undergrowth. He did a great job. It was something I was not supposed to do. But given the fact we were still looking for a new leaseholder, most people applauded. I never saw the foxes again. I have heard a few at night, occaisonally, but that is about it. As for the experience itself. I still cannot make head or tail of it. I think something in the setting acted on something in my psyche, or vice versa. That is as far as I get. And that is as far as I want to go. I thought writing this account down might help me. It has made me feel a bit better. But I still do not understand any clearer. Just as well, perhaps, since I am too busy now to give it much thought.

YXSY GLYXSY V

Eight Floors and Counting

It was hardly a dream home. But it was a start. A fourth floor flat in an eight storey block. High but not high, halfway high. Paula frowned at her new husband's humour, it could feel like a long marriage. It was no palace by any means. But it was something, and she was determined to stomach the place. The last ten years had not been kind to the block. No one would even live there at first, it was so desolate. And it was ugly, a concrete pimple on environmentally bad skin. The block was surrounded by waste sites. The estate was only half complete. The council had run out of money, five years ago. Still, you did not have to go far to dump your rubbish, there were some handy tips around, with full aroma provided. Corrulgated iron fences marked off areas that were supposedly undeveloped. Sometimes it was hard to tell the difference. But there were the beginings of something that might have been impressive, if the construction had been carried out with any kind of consideration, or even finished. There was an incomplete jigsaw puzzle of walls, windows, walkways and doorways. The first impression, on seeing the place, was of some kind of haphazard factory. Naturally the architect who designed the place won an award for this chaotic piece of geometry. But he did not have to live in the place, did he ?

Peter's thought ran along acid lines. But Paula repeated the mantra - a start is a start is a start. At least it was cheap. (Well it had to be.). It was right near Peter's work. The shops were just down the road. But unfortunately so was the pub. This was an area of friction between them. Paula hated alcohol, Peter loved it.

" What do you think, Paula ? "

" It'll do, but I don't like the look of it."

" What ? "

" Well I wouldn't fancy walking down here late at night. It don't look safe. But I suppose we have to start somewhere."

" Don't be too cheerful, will you. We're not exactly moving into a prison, you know."

" Aren't we ? Look at it. The place is an eyesore."

" You should have waited then."

" Till what ? "

" Till we saved up enough money, so we could put down a deposit on a home of our own."

" Look, don't start that again. Didn't we agree on this move. It's a stepping stone to a place of our own. That's what you said."

" Yeah I know. I was fed up of living round your mum's."

" It just looks grotty, that's all. "

It feels it too. But Peter kept that statment to himself. He merely sighed and shrugged. Her feelings were all too agreeable to him. The walls drifted past as they walked. The graffiti was childish, obscene. Various shades of smell wafted along, urine, dog shit and car exhaust. Smoke came out of a laundry window. It was better than Paula's mothers. Most things would be better than that, even prison would have its compensations, the interfering old bag. She used to lay it on, double thick - the criticism. And that was only the prelude to the moaning. Which itself led up to the second act of complaining, followed by the grand finale of the screaming arguement. Even when she was in a good mood she treated them like children.

Paula shuddered at the broken windows, that pockmarked the concrete avenue before them. They could not get above a trudge it seemed. This place appeared to sap the energy. A light drizzle of rain started, as the grey in the sky intensified. A miserable day to see them into a miserable flat. They would only be staying a year or two, she kept telling herself. It was no consolation. She threw a glance at the dingy sky, but the rain got into her eyes. It looked like she was crying. Peter pretended not to notice. At last the silhouette of their tower block arose before them. It looked very boring against the oncoming evening. Everything was so grey.

" Here we are, Mulberry Tower. Come on, let's get the lift, I don't fancy walking up...Good job we got your cousin to shift our gear round here yesterday. The way I feel at the moment, I couldn't handle lugging furniture up and down."

Silence.

" It's taking it's time innit."

Paula said nothing. Doubt was still working her over. The fact the place smelled like a public convenience did not help. At last the lift arrived.

" Here it is."

After they walked in a man literally jumped in behind them, just making it before the doors closed. A friendly enough looking bloke, but slightly seedy. He drinks too much, thought Paula, and he was begining to let things slip. This was part of her fear for Peter.

" Aren't you the people who were moving in yesterday ? "

" Yeah , that's right."

" Yeah, not long been here myself. I'm on the eighth, the top, good view, but traipsing up and down gets on my nerves a bit."

" Yeah ? " Peter was noncommittal. This was standard moaning.

" Yeah, these flats are okay, not exactly penthouse material, but they're a start."

Paula brightened just a little, " That's our opinion of it. Mind you, they're so cheap we couldn't resist."

" True."

Peter felt his head growing numb.

" See you," the man said, as they stepped out onto the fourth floor.

The lift door slammed closed, leaving them in a gloomy corridor.

" Where are we, number sixteen."

The key fitted into the lock with an empty metallic scrape. The door squealed open to reveal a jumble of bin bags and furniture. The full impact of what they had to do hit Peter's head. He looked at Paula's face, trying to read it, hoping she was not too against this place. After all, she had been moaning all the way up here. Still, at least she was not angry. The last thing he fancied was putting all their stuff in order. The sofa was free and the telly was plugged in. It could wait until tomorrow.

" I'll make some tea," said Paula.

The searing sound of an electronic alarm cut through Peter's dream. Half-dazed, with sleepy eyes, he went through the motions of getting ready for work. This took him longer than usual, as he could not find anything. There was some discussion the previous night about trying to get things in order. He tried to ignore this line of conversation, but Paula would insist. She insisted so much she switched off the telly. This caused an arguement. And it only stopped when Peter started moving a few objects around. Although the movement itself stopped when he broke a lamp, because this started another arguement. Paula said he did that on purpose and did not talk to him for the rest of the evening. He was finding it hard to concentrate. All these things that still needed to be done, to keep his new irate wife's temper at a minimum. He was glad when he got out of the house. Yet as he strolled out onto the walkway, he could not resist a mini glow of pride, their own place. He tilted his head to look at it. The sun had struggled through some clouds, it made his block look a bit more presentable. Unconsciously, he counted the floors, but he could not find his floor, he kept mistaking the number. He could not even remember where his flat was situated, which might have helped.

That bothered Peter, on his way back from work he made a point of counting them again, even moving his finger in front and talking out loud. There were seven. A worn and tired Paula greeted him at the door. She had been moving furniture all day, tidying up, cleaning, unpacking. Peter's puzzlement went straight out the window. He smiled. She always made an effort, did Paula, in everything she did. They spent the evening cleaning up the rest of the mess.

" It does look a bit more like home now."

Paula smiled, " Yes, it does look a bit more cosy."

A comfortable living space was actually developing. And they spent a cosy night together, reminiscent of when they first started going out. Peter had his contented grin on all of this time. It was not until they were in bed together that he remembered the floors.

" Paula, are you asleep ? "

" Not any more, no."

" Do you remember that man in the lift the other day ? "

" What man in the lift ? "

" Remember, the one who said he lived on the eighth floor."

" Not unless he lives on the roof. There's only seven floors on this block. "

" But you do remember the bloke who talked to us ? "

" Plenty of blokes talk to us, big deal."

" But he said he lived on on the eighth floor."

" Well he's as bad at arithmetic as you. Now shut up. I want to go to sleep.."

It was Saturday, Peter's favourite day. He woke up to find a tray of tea and toast in front of him. Spring sunlight poked its way through the net curtains. He surveyed their little kingdom, their home, theirs. Seen in the bright light of morning, his bewilderment over the floors looked ridiculous. He dismissed that confusion from his mind. Paula was aimiable this morning, singing to herself. She was warming to this place as well. Peter automatically crossed his fingers. A memory of the dull, depressing dinginess outside struck him. The view from outside would never be that good. But it was the inside that counted. And inside was comfortable. As if in response to his thought Paula grabbed his face in her hands and gave him a breathless kiss. Before he could say anything she said she was going to go out and do some shopping.

Peter felt satisfied. How could he continue the good mood ? He thought about phoning his mate Terry for a drink. It would be good to go outside anyway. The visit was easily arranged, Terry enjoyed getting out of his brains as much as Peter. Although both had partners that were trying to reform them.

Terry could hardly believe his luck.

" This is the third drink you've bought me, you sure you're feeling alright ? "

" Never better, now I got a place of me own."

" So that's it is it ? to celebrate your escape from mummy's apron strings."

" Ha ha ha... yeah, Paula's mum's apron strings at that. I can't tell you what it feels like, to come and go as I like..."

" Even if it's a bit grotty ? "

" Well yeah, but I still feel like someone who's just got out."

" Out of it, more like."

" In more ways than one."

" So how's Paula ? "

" Alright, alright. She was dead against it at first. But I think I swayed her."

" Good for you. Here's to you and your new found freedom then."

" Thanks mates, cheers."

Peter staggered out of the pub after Terry said his goodbyes. He did not have a clue what the time was. His head felt like a lead weight was pressing down on it, and he was enjoying the sensation. Walking proved difficult, but not insurmountable, and soon he found himself on the way home. As he approached on the walkway he could not resist a befuddled gaze upwards. Mechanically he counted the floors. He had to make allowances for his condition, so he counted them several times. But he never got beyond six. This was wrong. He tried to shake his head into some kind of sobriety. But both his condition and the number of floors resisted his attempts at reform. He was irritated by this. The irritation was compounded when he realised the lift was out of order. Still, it was only six floors, four floors, to his flat. He staggered manfully up the stairs, only falling over twice. And sticking the key in the door proved to be something of a mathematical puzzle. There was a little puddle of fear inside him now, but where it came form he could not place. Thought of puddles made him charge toward the toilet as soon as possible. But not quite soon enough. Some spray had got him, and so did Paula, who watched the whole farce as he blundered into the flat. Peter ignored her sour demeanour and began explaining about the missing floors. This served to convince her that her new husband really did have an idiot streak in him. But Peter insisted. And to placate the idiot drunk she walked with out to the lift, where he explained that someone had tampered with the lift display, which now only showed six floors."

" Look, don't you think it's suspicious there's only six floors now."

" There usually is in a six storey block."

" But there used to be eight."

" So what happened to the other two ? someone take them for a walk ? "

" I don't know, do I."

" Look, I told you before, I don't like your drinking, it always turns you into a dozy, stinking shitbag."

Peter tried telling her he had a real problem here, besides the drunkenness of course. He was still smarting at being called a dozy, stinking shitbag. And this did effect the arguement. Shouting was never a good way to talk to Paula. For she could shout back, she was a natural megaphone. Nothing was resolved, apart from the fact Peter had to sleep on the sofa, by himself.

Waking the next day, the military band beat a tattoo on his hungover skull. Peter tried in vain to compose himself. He did not remember the details of the arguement of the night before, merely that it concerned his inability to count the number of floors on the block, and that it felt bad. His body was like a wrung out flannel. Every noise was magnified. Paula was not talking to him. But he could even hear the menace of her malicious silence. Her eyes seemed to bore holes directly into his brain, already reeling from the past night's abuse. A breath of fresh air was the best help. And it would give Paula the chance to cool down.

And so he walked. His mood was intense, and so he walked some more. He had never walked much before, but he found it helped, and so he did it even more. It cleared his thoughts, but also brought his fear of his partner into sharp focus. He could not face Paula at the moment. But it was getting dark. So Peter opted for the shelter of his local.

The warm, cosy glow of the pub, with its delicious beery smell, was just what the doctor ordered. It was a shame the doctor was not a psychiatrist as well. It might have helped with those troublesome thoughts lurking under the surface. His dilemma, such as it was, did seem stupid. He tried telling the landlord about his irate wife and the disappearing floors. The landlord laughed, which was not what Peter intended. And when Peter tried to explain further, the landlord refused to serve him anymore. This was just as well, as Peter found, much to his surprise, he was completely ratarsed. This would not put him in Paula's good books. But he must go home now. He would try to hide his condition, as best he could, while he staggered home. As he found his way down the walkway, he did not want to look up and count the floors. He was afraid he would find another one missing. He resolutely kept his head staring straight ahead. Besides, he had half a mind to apologise profusely when he saw Paula. He had been a bit of a tit recently. He could not feel the cold. But he shuddered anyway when he saw the lift display. There were now only five buttons inside. To his credit, or his drunkeness, he never registered surprise. After the past few days it seemed inevitable. This made him angry. Someone was playing him for a fool. And why would no one believe him about something so blatant ? Obviously they were all in on the joke, trying to make him look like an idiot. And Paula must be in on it as well. How could she not be ?

So he charged into the flat demanding she explain.

" Explain what ? "

" This bloody practical joke you're playing on me."

" What practical joke ? "

" Look, don't give me that. What's happening to this building, eh. Why don't anyone say anything ? Why do all the floors keep vanishing."

" Look, don't start coming out to me with that drunken shit again. I hate it when you start going on like this."

" What about the vanishing floors ?"

" It's you, it's all in your mind, and in the drink. How else could you get stuck on stupid crap like vanishing floors, I ask you."

" But it's true."

" You've fallen out your pram, that's true."

" Look, how many floors did you say this place had yesterday ? "

" Five."

" No you didn't, you said six."

" I know what I said."

" You're winding me up."

" You're the one wound up."

" But you did say six yesterday."

" Alright I said six."

" No, you're just saying it now," Peter was near to tears. " Be truthful with me, Paula. "

" What do you want ? How could I lie about something so stupid ? You're a candidate for the funny farm, you know that. And you're getting me scared. So you can stay away from me."

Those were Paula's last words. For she stormed away and slammed the bedroom door, locking it behind her. Peter stood there in shock. It had gone disasterously, his attempt to find the truth. His drunkeness had muddled the attempt. He would have to start again tomorrow.

But Peter would not be given the opportunity by Paula. If she was part of some practical joke she played her part well. For she had left a note beside him, telling him she had left. She had gone round her mothers. And it asked him not to bother her for a few days. The note made little impression on him, numbness cancelled everything out.

He did not feel like going to work. He was two hours late anyhow. He fretted impatiently about the flat, wondering what to do. He just could not make any sense of the past few days. And he was unable to go about begining how to make sense. He had to get out. He tried not to look at any flat or floor numbers. He felt if he did not notice them, they might stay as they are, a stupid superstsition that made him feel a little better. He wandered around the concrete conurbation, taking care to avoid the more shady parts. And he saw building works, building works with notices pinned haphazard to fences. It was a council notice, explaining how if anyone had problems with their works, they could go to the office. Of course. Why did he not think of that sooner ? The council always made strange and arbitrary decisions, to him anyway. Random building works would always be springing up and finishing, while people in strange uniforms wandered around. This reminded him why he did not think of going to the council. He did not like these people in offices, they always confused him, with their jargon and their application forms. He had a terrible time even getting his flat. Only the extensive help of Paula and her family managed to enable him to complete the move. But he was desperate. He could see the end of his tether. And he would not like to go there. So it was off to see the people who wore ties, even in summer.

The council office was small, cramped and busy. Peter got an appointment with somebody. He settled down to wait, a long time. He tried to work out who was in front of him. But apparently people saw different people for different reasons. He was a 'housing problem,' so he would see the appropriate officer. Eventually he got to see a young, meek-looking lady. His usual housing officer was on holiday. Peter remembered Paula's calling him a madman. So he decided not the broach the subject of vanishing floors immediately. Instead he would talk about paying his rent monthly instead of weekly. Unfortunately, subtlety was a word he had never heard of. He blurted out a mish mash of confusion. His fears quickly rose to the surface and he felt to hell with it and laid out his concern about the vanishing floors. He braced himself for the laughter, and the taunts about his sanity. But these never came. Instead she was quite sympathetic. Even better, she appeared to know what was going on, at least at first. For he quickly lost the meaning of what she was saying. It sounded like she was talking from a text book, on a subject he never studied. It was full of phrases like - ' The law provides for this,' or ' The council requires you to do that.' But these were the only bits he understood. He asked her to explain but the gibberish only multiplied. He began to get a headache. Peter realised it was no use asking for sense, he had reached a dead end here. He had to leave. That meek-looking lady, still sympathetic, appeared to understand. He was escorted from the building. Maybe he should make an appointment in advance next time.

HIs head spun as left the office. He walked straight into a shower. He quickened his pace as the downpour increased, and made it to the space in front of the lift back at Mulberry Tower, wet, confused, frightened. He shuffled in, head down, avoiding a glance at the buttons, trying to hit the right button by touch alone. But an an old woman followed him, an old woman dressed in regulation old woman coat and woolly hat. But she did not make him jump. She seemed a friendly old dear.

" Would you press my floor please, young man, it's the third."

She smiled, a smile of warmth and friendliness. This made Peter forget his state momentarily. But it started up again when he registered -

" Only four floors now."

He stood there paralysed, until the lady's helpful clearing of her throat made him press the button automatically.

" Are you alright ? "

" There was five floors yesterday ? " he said, almost not knowing he was talking.

" So what, everything shrinks with age, some things more than others. I wouldn't be too frightened. But I wouldn't stick around long if something frightening was happening, hee hee hee."

The lift arrived at her floor and the woman walked out leisurely. Peter struggled to understand what she said. It was weird. But she knew something, she definetely knew something, not like that council woman who tried make out she knew something, this old woman really did. But by the time this realisation came to him, the lift doors had closed. He had to wait until he reached his own, floor, the fourth. Then he raced back down the stairs to the old woman's floor. There he found six doors, like his own floor. But five of them were boarded up, they looked pretty decrepid. Only one flat appeared to be occupied.

Peter rang the bell of this flat. A middle aged, balding man, with a pot belly, in a vest, answered.

" Excuse me, does an old lady live here ? "

" No."
" Do you know if one's lived on this floor ?"
" No."
" Or in the block ? "
" No."
" Even in the past ? "
Peter tried describing her.
" No."
" Are you sure you..."

The door was slammed in his face. Peter was left standing bewildered. The man looked like someone who could not be bothered to make the effort to lie, and too stupid to do it if he wanted to. Peter felt a momentary urge to smash something, he kicked the wall, then bit his fingers. The pain made him think. No, that was no answer, he stopped. This gave the despair room to come up and smother him. The feeling of powerlessness was even worse than the pain. He struggled to find some kind of balance. He had to find a way out of his condition. And something suggested itself to him. It was the council office. He should go back there, to the den of bureaucracy, much as it filled him with confusion. This horrible prospect made him wish for something to offset it first. He still had a reasonable amount of money, so he went and got drunk. At least it gave him a good nights sleep.

But he overslept. So he rushed down to the council office as soon as possible. He looked unshaven and felt smelly , or was it the other way round. This time he was lucky. He only waited twenty minutes, and he saw the correct person this time, the one who managed his block. But the interview was just as unsatisfactory. The man talked worse legalese than his predecessor, and a man in a uniform was present throughout. Peter tried to put his point across. But the man was oblivious, he did not seem to hear. So he tried shouting. That was a mistake. It did not make any difference whatsoever. The man simply disregarded his statement, issued his obscure warnings, couched in legal jargon, and had the uniformed man escort him from the premises. Apparently Peter was banned from the office. He was also warned not to come back. That much he did understand.

Having achieved nothing there, he thought he was still in need of help. But there was no one to turn to, no one to talk to, at that moment. There was a possibility however. And since it was his only possibility, he seized on it. He would go round Paula's Mum's. Even if he were told where to go, in the worst sense, at least that would shake him up a bit. But, as he walked toward her house, it occurred to him he could not remember the number. He found the street okay. And he remembered it was the house at the end of the street, next to the corrulgated iron fence of a rubbish dump. He lived there long enough. But a woman the wrong age, and with the wrong looks, answered the door, neither Paula nor her mother. She blinked at him and talked to him as though he were an idiot. Of course no one matching their description had ever lived in the street, she had been there since the War. That was a further blow to Peter. One of increasing numbness as he trudged his way back to the estate. A building, different from the others, met his gaze, then sidled up, with all the familiarity of an old friend. It was the pub. And he might as well go in as do anything else now. He drank well, until he felt unwell. Then he staggered home. He was too dizzy to look up at his block, nor to pay much attention to any display of floors, as he went in the lift back to his flat. And this suited him. Maybe he had beaten it now, this curse, this weird event, or whatever it was. Maybe he had broken the spell. This made him collapse into his bed with a hint of contentment.

There was no contentment when he awoke. For he found himself lying on a large, flattened cardboard box. He felt terrible. And what really rubbed this feeling in was the fact he was on the roof. But he forced himself up. He had to find a way out of course. Peter found his way back to the fire escape door he had barged through last night. Down some dingy staircase he went, until he found himself on a landing in front of the lift. The same lift of course, it was Mulberry Tower, and he was on the top floor. Only now the display said three floors. There was no earthly reason for this. His flat had disappeared. It was not as if someone had demolished his floor during the night. How could they ? How could they do something like that and get away with it ? without anyone noticing, that is, even if it was something like that, and who were they anyway ?

He recounted, a few times, and, sure enough there were only three floors. By now his simple arithmetic could work this out at a glance. Only three floors. He walked down, lightheaded, pausing outside before his now not-so-tall block, the block that had deleted his home from existence. Was the tower itself alive ? was it shedding its floors the way a snake shed its skin ? in some weird kind of renewal. In that case, would it grow the missing floors back at a later date ? This line of thinking was too off the wall for Peter. He started feeling dizzy. There was activity around him. A crocodile of schoolkids went by, and a few random office workers. They all gave Peter a wide berth. And As he caught a glimpse of himself in a shop window, he realised. He looked like he felt, dirty, smelly and confused. A policeman asked him to move on or else he would be arrested. This came as a shock to Peter, but only a minor one. He saw he had a bottle of some cheap and nasty spirit in his hand. He took big swigs from this as made his way to the high street. It was running low, and he needed a replacement if he was to drink himself unconscious tonight. He could not bear the thought of being sober while the floors vanished. Somehow it felt better when he was completely out of it. He could pretend it was not happening. But of course it was happening. And he begged for coins from passers by with some tenacity. Another bottle was purchased and he began to drain it liberally. He had to make his way back there. He had to see the whole sorry game through until the end.

Mulberry Tower looked less like a tower than a block now. Some kids saw him as he approached , and chased him away. They did not want his kind there. Peter hid from them among the rubbish bins, as the kids went back to their second floor flats. He saw the light come out of one of their doorways, heard womens' voices, and he was jealous. He was parked outside in a stinking heap, a stinking heap among stinking heaps. While they casually went about all the things he had once had, and more, and took it for granted. It was too late now, Peter knew that. Instead he settled down. If he could not get in the block he would at least stay awake outside, to see if yet another floor vanished.

And of course it did. When Peter woke up there was now only one floor. Naturally he missed it. He had an idea it would have not have happened, had he been awake. But he could not prove this. And he could not console himself by the fact the irritating kids had disappeared. He did not like this state of affairs. But he had now lost the will to do anything about it. Who could he go to anyway ? no one would stand and talk to him now. The council offices were off limits. He could not remember where his friends and relatives lived, or indeed many of their names. He thought the saw an old mate of his, though, briefly, on the High Street. Terry his name was. But this bloke crossed the road and walked round a corner when Peter began shouting at him.

There only remained the grand finale to be experienced. He would have to wake and see that the whole block had finally disappeared. Why this was so important he did not know. He had nothing else to do, so he might as well anyway. There was no fear or excitement, just a willingness to see it through. The day's routine hung in a bottle from his arm. It was slow, quick, slow. But eventually it started getting dark. Peter wandered over to Mulberry Tower, more like Mulberry floor now. He went up the stairs, noting the lift display as he did so. One floor to go. The block was looking pretty shabby now, almost condemned status. About two flats showed signs of habitation, the others were boarded up, except one. Its door had been forced. Whoever did it had not quite succeeded in opening it full. But there was enough of a gap to squeeze through. And once he squeezed through he wanted to squeeze back. The flat was grotty enough, dark, with rubbish strewn everywhere. But it was the two figures that stood before a small, bar, gas fire, with their hands out, that worried Peter. Two of the meanest looking tramps he had ever seen. They said nothing, they did not need to. Their glare told Peter he was not welcome. They were whitehaired and ragged, tramps of some years standing. One had longer hair and looked like he was intelligent once. So did the other one, but he was obviously more violent. He stormed over to Peter and immediately got him in a headlock.

" Trespassers will be prosecuted, m'boy."

" I was only looking, " Peter gasped.

" Leave him be now, Baz, he's only lookin for a doss. Is that not right now, fellar ?

" Y,yes,." said Peter hoarsely as Baz loosened his grip.

" He can't stop here, Napper."

" Indeed he can't. You can't be stopping here now boy. This territory's marked out for us for tonight."

" But you can't."

" And why can't we be doing that ? Are you about to try and stop us ? " Baz advanced on Peter, threateningly. Peter cringed.

" Now Baz, stop tormenting the boy now. He obviously has something on his noddle. Am I right fellar ? "

" So be telling us m'boy," Baz waved a length of pipe around for emphasis.

Peter cleared his throat. He then related recent events. He held nothing back. It felt good to get it all out. He was afraid they would laugh, or worse. But they listened, they were attentive.

Baz stood there rubbing his chin quizically.

" That's the best fucking yarn I heard in a while," said Napper.

" You just got out ,m'boy ? "

" Out from where ? "

Napper laughed, " He means an institution, the kind of establishment we've all made use of. But sure, if you don't want to tell us, that's fair enough. We'll not be going though, vanishing or no vanishing floors. What are such things to us, we are gents of the road, we seen more strange things than those that sleep in a comfortable bed. Besides, we have to be taking our chances, otherwise the life can get too boring. Is that not right, Baz."

' It is sure enough, now you'll be slinging your hook."

" Wait Baz, wait, where's your manners. The gent has entertained us, now we must repay with our hospitality."

" Sure, sure, here goes now. You get a swig of this down your neck, m'boy."

Baz repeated his headlock, not so tight this time, to allow him to pour some vile concoction down Peter's throat, from a metal can, that looked like a petrol can. It was irredeemably nasty. Disgust rampaged throughout his system.

" Don't puke now, we'll take that as a insult."

" No worries, Baz, he's one of us sure enough. It's my own secret recipe, storyman, top secret. I will say there's a hint of white spirit, with perhaps some lighter fuel, highly inflammable, in more ways than one..."

Peter lurched from the building. His insides managed to hold together till he got outside. Then the torrent came, from both ends, and he collapsed.

He expected not to wake, Peter managed it, but he was in bad shape. He was in waste ground now. Waste ground that surrounded the remnants of Mulberry Tower. There was still a building. He had forgotten about the ground floor flats, his maths would never be workable. They were derelict, fenced off. He did not wish to hang around while they disappeared, But now he found he could not even get up. He drifted in and out of consciousness. It was annoying, but sooner or later this process would stop and he would be able to stand up, or he would fall asleep one last time. As it was he got a helping hand, or foot. For he finally awoke after a boot continually prodded him. It was not a malicious action. But the man wearing the uniform did not want to touch Peter any more than necessary.

" Can you get up ? "

It was a request, but it would become an order if Peter did not make the move. He nodded.

" I'm sorry, but this area's off limits now, it's been earmarked for development in a couple of weeks."

Peter rose to his feet as one who rose from the dead. He was shaky, but felt remarkably well, considering. He looked over to where Mulberry Tower once was. There was now nothing left. Even the ground floor had gone. The security guard had said development. Had he simply been misinterpreting a straightfoward demolition. Perhaps. It did not seem likely however, because no explanation did, at least to him. The security guard and himself were standing in a desolate waste ground, full of rubbish, another man in a uniform prowled around in the background.

" Was there a block on this area before ? " he found himself blurting out.

The security guard was briefly taken aback before replying.

" No, it's been derelict at least twenty years I reckon, it's a new development, " as if that explained everything. None the wiser, and not particularly caring, Peter left. The guard was wrong of course. The last of the block had only disapppeared the previous evening. At least by his reckoning. Maybe his poor arithematic extended to his sense of time as well. Maybe his friends, his job, his flat and his wife never really existed anyway. But this line of thought repelled him, it was far too stupid to contemplate.

Of course he came back, it was only a few months. They never did develop the site. They would at some point, Peter knew that. But it always took them longer then they said, Peter knew that too. In the meantime, Peter would make his home here, among the rubble and detritus, with the occaisonal bottle or can of alcohol it could be quite homey. He knew this place, it felt like his territory. It felt like he knew it in different ways.

He was daydreaming again. Peter was snapped out of it, rudely. Stones hit him and he ran away into cover. Two boys had scrambled up holes in the corrulgated iron fence. They balanced precariously as they threw the stones and giggled at the retreating tramp.

" Does he live here, then ? "

" He's the local mether. Peter Pisshead they call him... He's been here ages, no one knows how long."

" He looks a bit scary."

" Ah, he's harmless. Everyone knows him. "

The two kids ran out of words. The tramp had disappeared. They stared at nothing for a while. Then they got bored and dropped down and went away.

Frisky Disko

The Frisky Disko ran at the Time Warp Club every Thursday. Seventies revival nights were very popular that year, as they had been every year since the 1970's. Some said the Frisky Disko was keeping a vital tradition alive. Others said it peddled nostalgia for those who liked retrograde crap.

One person who obviously disagreed with the nostalgia tag was the club's proprietor, Billy Shyte-Bucket. He said he was only catering for the needs of his punters. Taste was never a matter of consideration. It all depended on what got bodies through doors, for the cheapest possible expense. Rumours of Billy's financial malpractice were completely unfounded. As no one could be found who was not scared shitless of him. Any accusations that did fly around were met with Billy's usual honest violence.

His club was situated in a grubby back street, off a grubby high street, in a grubby part of London that will remain nameless (if anyone has any sense). Frisky Disko was moderately popular, it was frequented by moderate people with no where else to go. No scumbags or drug taking, or drug taking scumbags, were tolerated, said Billy. Though others said this was just a front, to keep him on good terms with the licensing authorities. I heard there were some weird goings on, in as much as a place as boring as Billy's could be said to be weird.

The first hint of trouble was when punters without platform shoes would not be admitted to the Frisky Disko. This decision was out of the blue and completely unnecessary. This only marked it down as one of Billy's normal arbitrary decisions. But the rumour spread around. The toilets had blocked up again. There was a big pool of piss everywhere. Only punters in platform shoes could wade through this pool in order to get to the toilet. Heavily built bouncers, in silk, bell-bottomed cat suits, turned away undesirables in sensible footwear.

Inside, the venue was only half full. A huge, homemade, glitter ball hung from the ceiling. Everyone could tell it was only a beach ball, with little squares of oven foil attached. People in huge shoes tottered around on the dancefloor, falling over in rhythm to the tinny disco hits, the ones played continuously in the lifts and supermarkets of yesteryear.

No respite could be had at the bar. The chill out room only sold melted lollys. At the bar you could have got warm, frothy shandy; flat, cheapo cider, and jelly and ice cream covered with hairs and mucus, the leftovers from an under fives' birthday party. This bar policy of Billy's was designed to tap into the hopeless nostalgia of his clientele, where everything that happened in the 1970's was magic, and they were too immature to have powers of discrimination.

However, it seemed the bar staff misunderstood the nature of the 70's night when they staged a wild cat strike, just because they were bored. They started ranting in good, old shop steward manner and went off to picket the toilets. Perhaps something could have been sorted out. But one of them found the power switch, and so all the lights went out. There was some confusion. Various screams and groans of people in pain were heard, and there was an explosion. The lights went back on to reveal the settling dust and the dazed punters. But the bar staff had disappeared. Billy explained it as a stunt. He had rigged up a bomb, just like all those 70's terrorist groups, to break the ice a bit. In the aftermath, several unwary punters found themselves promoted, at the point of a knife, to bar staff.

The disturbances continued. After 'Abba's greatest hits' was played for the tenth time that evening, some punters, dressed as 70's football hooligans, stormed the DJ's booth, to try and get him to play some Punk. However, these were stopped in their tracks when the DJ cleverly played Cliff Richard and Peters and Lee simultaneously. The resulting avalanche of soppy niceness sent the hooligans into fits of agony. It was a horrible way for anyone to go, smothered in dreary banality.

To take the punters' minds from these grisly events, Billy organised, or rather ordered, a dance competition. Everyone was ordered to take their massive shoes off, as nobody could dance in them. This did not help, as no one could dance without them. Eventually a person was discovered who knew all the 70's dances well. However, it turned out she was having epileptic episodes, and so she was rushed to hospital.

Billy tried to reorganise the competition, but again there were more casualties. One gang of punters distinguished themselves by wearing tight shirts with long, pointy collars. These collars stretched over their shoulders. And they had to be heavily starched as they had a habit of drooping like wilted plants. But in the close proximity of the dance floor these collars became dangerous. For they flailed around, slashing unwary passers-by, drawing blood continuously. These collars were as sharp as stanley knives.

An emrgency conference of the bouncers was held. It was decided it was time for the usual bouncers' massacre of lary punters. But they did not have it their own way. Several were slashed by the pointy collars before they could get a decent punch in themselves. Then someone had the bright idea of offering prizes to the pointy-collared punters. A free medallion and caveman chest wig were thown among them. In the ensuing scramble, the bouncers were enabled to drag all the pointy-collared punters away and throw them out into the street.

At this point Billy showed off what he considered to be the highlight of the evening. A back door was opened to reveal a pair of platform shoes several stories high. They were too big to fit inside the club itself. These shoes were known as babel platforms. Because, like the Tower of Babel, they seemed to reach the sky. The winner of the dance competition would be the lucky mug punter who walked away wearing these shoes. The shoes were a masterpiece of cack design. Massive cork effect soles and heels tapered upwards. The shoes narrowed the higher they went. A ladder ran up their sides. The lucky mug punter who won could climb all the way up to the top. Here the shoes narrowed sufficiently to fit normal human feet. A switch betrayed the fact they powered by massive batteries contained within the heels. For, as with normal platforms, no one could walk too far with them without having an auxillary source of power.

Since the epileptic punter had been disqualifed, the dance competition was resumed. However, now they had seen the prize, most punters felt daunted by the prospect of winning. Therefore they danced as badly as they could. Pulling gormless faces, falling over repeatedly, moving completely out of the time with the music, or just standing there with a gormless grin on the face, were some of the obvious tricks used. The judges commented that standard of 70's dancing had never been so high. It was so difficult to pick a winner. Eventually some unlucky dipstick was dragged out of the crowd. And the relieved punters filed out into the backyard, in the hope of seeing him plunge to his death as he attempted to scale the towering platforms.

People watched in awe as the dipstick did not flinch from his task. In fact the poor idiot looked eager to get on with it. He raced up the side of the platforms and strapped himself in. He shouted down that he imagined he was just putting on a pair of cheap 70's plimsolls, to reassure himself. However, as he said this, a dizzy spell set in. The dipstick started swaying. It was quite a windy night as well. It was some time before he managed to regain his balance. But then he managed to bend down and switch his new shoes on. A couple of unfortunate, fellow punters were crushed by his first two steps. But within five steps he was gone. Within ten steps he was out of the city. His stride was so large now that every step took in a few miles.

The watching crowd wondered how he had done it, when several of them expected the dipstick to fall to his death. In fact they were annoyed, because they had bet substantial amounts of money on that outcome. As they filed back into the club someone recalled they had seen the dipstick in the toilets, sniffing long lines of coke. This explained the fact that a dipstick now thought he could do anything. He was probably even more overconfident now, as he was high in two senses of the word.

But, unknown to the punters at the time, the dipstick did eventually fall over. He was stomping through the Essex countryside, at a rapid rate, when he tripped over some electricity pylons. His barbecued body was found by puzzled police the next day. They were criticised for being slow to respond to the plight of a fashion victim.

By this point of the night, the punters were getting a bit peeved. This whole 70's night was getting a bit too hairy. Recent casualties had reduced the number of punters considerably. But there were still more of them than the staff. Billy joined up with his bouncers to try and intimdate them. But as he was an obese bastard this did not work. Things would have turned very ugly if the staff had not run away. Unfortunately they ran out into the backyard again. This meant they were cornered. They literally had their backs to the wall as the disgruntled punters filed out, looks of glee on their faces. Then one of those miracles happened, one of those events that make you sit up and say, ' You jammy bastards.' The punters advanced slowly, relishing the anticipation of massacre to come. It was still windy. But then the wind whipped up further, it was gale strength at least. As several punters were wearing extremely baggy flares, their trousers filled with air. As the winds intensified, these flares acted like ships' sails. A number of unlucky punters were blown away. Screaming bodies were carried through the night air. It was chaotic. Some were carried a few miles, although one or two were blown out to sea. One lucky sod was blown to Amsterdam, where I am told she still lives.

Anyway, a shaken but unharmed staff were left to face what was left of the crowd, three young girls. Billy, and his crowd of bouncers, were always wary of harming girls, in public anyway. But he did want someone to suffer for all the fear they had felt. And who better than some outnumbered individuals. The girls ran to the main entrance. But the bouncers managed to block the only exit. Two of the girls had afro wigs on. They used these to tickle the bouncers until they collapsed in giggling heaps. However, the third girl was still trapped inside, and she had no afro wig to tickle her way to freedom. In a desperate bid to preserve her own safety she agreed to go out with Billy. But on one condition, all the staff had to wear a tight T-shirt. The girl was carrying a bundle of these in order to sell them at the 70's night. The staff grumbled but agreed, including Billy. They were horrible, wet look T-shirts. But what the girl had failed to mention was the fact these shirts actually were soaking wet. They were also made of rawhide leather. So, while the girl excused herself to go to toilet, the T-shirts constricted in the warm nightclub atmosphere. All the staff were asphyxiated, enabling the girl to step over their gasping bodies as she walked out.

The next week the 70's night at the Frisky Disko ran the same as usual.

Siddons the Healthworker

In this, the latest trouble spot, the healthworker cautiously drove his Red Cross van. Once around the corner Gerry Siddons could see the village. It had been cut off for three weeks now, medical supplies were needed urgently. Once the Provisional Government collapsed, the regular army had retreated to the hills in the north. Here they could hold out indefinitely against the guerillas who shelled them indiscriminately from the south. The village lay like an ampitheatre between the two sides. It was of little value strategically, but worth a little more in terms of prestige. Neither side would yield their claim to it. Subsequently, the village suffered the attentions and misdirections of both factions. Gerry Siddons, the healthworker, had gained what he thought could be a major concession from the guerillas. During the latest lull in fighting, events were still too haphazard to speak of a ceasefire, he gained permission to drive down to the village, to see just how serious the situation was. His was the only vehicle to be allowed. Hopefully the healthworker could gain further concessions, including perhaps an escort. For it was particularly eerie on that lonely and bumpy road. It felt as if hundreds of eyes kept track of him. There was expectancy around. The village grew larger as he began to descend to the outskirts.

It was then the trouble started. Explosions sounded behind him. They had their echoes in the Northern Hills. The opening salvos were quite distant. But they proceeded nearer, incendiary footsteps coming to meet him. It seemed he was being targeted, or was this just paranoia. One explosion shook the van, a mite too close to be comfortable. Another made his vehicles side panels shudder. His ears blocked, sound appeared to happen at a distance. Panic attacked him, his arms fought to keep his steering grip steady. He was only too aware the unpredictable road itself could finish him as much as any stray shell. Though he must get off this road quickly, he was too much out in the open here. The road seemed to even out, he put his foot down firmly on the accelerator. Then an explosion ripped apart beneath him, mines, it must be mines. A brief sensation of lurching or leaping followed, through a painful vaccuum, he had completely lost control, and that was it.

The next things he knew were sensations of pain, delirium and disorientation. Gradually these coalesced into the realisation he was in a hospital bed. His conversation progressed from groans to questions. He gathered the fact he had been lucky to survive. That he had driven over a mine, and been hit by a shell. The hospital was in some confusion. The shelling from the north was a cover for a surprise attack by the government troops. They had broken the guerilla lines and retaken the village. The fighting had been bloody, some revenge measures were in operation. Work in the makeshift hospital continued uneasily. It was only a bombed out hotel anyway. The rumble and roar of explosion formed the backing track to Gerry's delirium.

Safety was not assured. Events were out of control. He had gathered that much. There were one or two things more he wanted to ask. But he could never formulate the questions, pain and intermittent unconsciousness distracted him. The nature of his injuries was unclear. Although one of the doctors, whose English was poor, pointed repeatedly to his hands. The few doctors who had words of English kept referring to him as Mister Sidam. He put this down to simple mispronunciation. It was a trivial point, but it kept irritating him.

Staff at the hospital managed to convey to him he was being moved to a United Nations facility. Yet as the message dawned on him the pain rose again. The doctors became surreal beings, dressed like motor mechanics, working in a bombsite. Unreal feelings had hold of him. He could feel a dark and heavy dose of unconsciousness moving toward him. As his reason faded one ludicrous thought nagged him - " What are my thumbs doing upside down ? "

The next he knew he was back in England. A different hospital bed, but one located in more peaceful surroundings. Various minor aches acted themselves out, but otherwise he was fine, just a little groggy. Some time passed without much notice, then it moved into his awareness and began to hang heavy on him. How long was he out ? there was no way of telling, hours ? minutes ? days ? He seemed to be all in one piece, though his hands were heavily bandaged. Feelings poked through these bandages, so he was sure they were intact, it must be burns. Eventually, a serious looking doctor came into his room. He looked at Gerry with some thought before talking.

" So how are you feeling Mister Sidam ? "

" Ooh, fine, under the circumstances...it's Mister Siddons by the way, Gerry Siddons."

" I'm sorry, it's just you were referred to us as Mister Sidam."

" It doesn't matter, I feel okay, but is there anything else ? "

Gerry had begun to worry, since feeling okay did not necessitate feeling well. There was an uneasy tension in the air, a thing he felt in all conversations with doctors. The doctor began to look indecisive.

" My head's reasonably clear and my body feels alright. So if there is anything else doctor, I would appreciate you being straight with me."

A twitch of a frown appeared on the doctor's face as Gerry raised his hand to emphasise his last point.

" Well..if you really are quite alert ? "

Gerry nodded.

"...Then I must tell you some strange circumstances preceeded your deliverance to a U. N. base, and your final flight here. We know you were on a humanitarian mission to the village. And we also know you got caught in the middle of a massive government offensive. There have since been several counter attacks - from both sides. Any fragile ceasefire that operated in that region has been shattered, most civilians have been evacuated, those that could make it. Even the U.N. troops have pulled out. To say it is chaos there is an understatement. We have not been able to trace the guerillas who gave you permission to enter the village. Neither have we been able to trace the field hospital that stitched you up. Both government troops and guerillas are claiming you precipitated this present battle by the way..."

" That's ridiculous, I had permission from the guerillas. And my contacts on the government side knew I was negotiating for passage. Besides, the sides of my van were covered by the red cross. It was not an official vehicle, true, but one that was easily visible through a pair of field binoculars..."

" Nevertheless, there are numbers of people now, on both sides of the conflict, who hold you responsible for the fact the latest cease fire has collapsed..."

" It was never very much in evidence in the first place."

" That may well be true...But the fact these people hold you to blame may explain what happened to you in the field hospital..."

" What do you mean ? "

" I think it's easier to show you."

The doctor sat himself down beside Gerry and began unwrapping the bandage on his right hand. It felt fine, his fingers moved comfortably enough, even if they were a little stiff. Unfortunately it was not his real right hand. His left hand had been sown onto his right arm. He examined this fact with a blank stare. That delirious thought about his thumbs being upside down was true after all.

" I'm sorry..." the doctor began.

" No need doctor, I had an inkling this had happened. I was in a bit of a state at the field hospital, drifting in and out of consciousness. So it's not a total surprise even if it is a bit shocking, and pretty unpleasant to have it confirmed... Even so, if you wouldn't mind..."

Gerry held his left hand up for the doctor. The doctor unwrapped the bandage as he spoke.

" You're taking it very well. I can understand shock and disgust at this situation. To say it's a strange turn of events is an understatement. I'm not even sure if we can do anything to rectify this. The possibilty is there all right, to reattach your hands to their correct positions. But right now this would be too dangerous I fear. Odd as it sounds we need to make sure your hands are fit and working again after this first transplant before attempting a second."

Gerry's mind dwelt on these words for some time before he replied.

" You mean I'm going to have to walk around like this for a while."

" That's it exactly. I'm going to refer you to a specialist unit in London. I want your condition assessed and the likely course of action outlined, then we can suggest further measures..."

" You don't sound too certain."

" To be honest I'm not. Operations of this nature are tricky at the best of times. But two operations of this nature...well, I cannot give any prognosis. We'll just have to monitor events and see what we can do."

" Thank you for being straight with me doctor...Now, if you don't mind, I'd like a few hours alone to get my thoughts in order..."

" Certainly. If you need anything, don't hesitate to call."

Once left alone, Gerry's emotions went through the uncomfortable motions of shock, dismay, anger and depression. His thoughts perplexed him even more. How could this situation have come about ? He could not put the result down to front line surgery alone. The doctor had hinted there was perhaps some revenge carried out on him. But for what purpose ? There was plenty of strong feeling in such a conflict. Sometimes he had borne the brunt of some nasty intent. Yet usually he found he could work things out. He was a health worker after all, there to help. Surely he had given no one cause for such drastic measures. As far he knew he made no significant enemies in the conflict who would have cause to bear him a grudge. Yet the suggestion was there in the doctor's account, that he had almost become some kind of scapegoat. He had indeed been stitched up.

As time progressed he became accustomed to his new condition. However, his first examination was inconclusive, as he had expected. He was encouraged to get on with his life, as best he could, in the meantime. Everyone was very supportive, almost embarassingly so.

He had to go back to the office of course - The Worldwide Humanitarian Agency. They were a unique combination of charity and business, variously referred to as a charitable business, or a business charity, or a charity provider. Its exact status was never quite clear to its employees, or its auditors for that matter. This was something Gerry felt quite cynical about. The WHA portrayed itself as selfless organisation, and yet its funds were never quite located at their source. But these concerns were at the back of Gerry's mind at present. He would rather get back to work, even if it did present some physical difficulties, how would he hold a pen for example ? His meeting with the Chief Executive of WHA was - well not quite as expected. Gerry expected the same sympathy that was doled out to to colleagues who had gone through unhappy events, that same mixture of awkward politeness and concern, he had seen it many times before. True, events did not have his degree of strangeness most of the time, but his colleagues, once their weirdness was overcome, showed the traditional signs of understanding. Yet they kept their physical distance from Gerry, as if somehow they would fall victim to contagion. Even a feeble joke or two could not disguise this. There were undercurrents in the looks given Gerry he found distrurbing, or was this just the usual self-consciousness. His two immediate female colleagues were the most concerned. Both Martha and Sarah promised to visit him. This made him smile, mainly at the possibilities such a visit entailed.

This was in contrast to the Chief Executive himself. The man was cold with Gerry, even if the questions were polite. Of course returning to work was out of the question. But his position would be kept open The important thing was to get healed. Going back into the war zone was never a possibilty however. This response to Gerry's winsome query was dismissed out of hand. It was not explained why. But Gerry felt innuendo in the air. The suggestion was made that he acted as a catalyst in the events of the most recent conflict. Gerry denied this suggestion a little too vehemently. He mentioned the idea of scapegoating, but the Chief Executive merely laughed at this notion. There were always plenty of scapegoats in war, he reminded Gerry, and a lone healthworker was way down the list. He took Gerry's declarations of innocence with a snort, and his protestations of fitness to work with a sigh. Gerry felt somewhat guilty, even if no clear accusations had been made against him. Just what was he supposed to do now ? He did not know. Perhaps he could take time out as suggested, then he could become accustomed to the fact that strange rumour was borne out of many a conflict.

Yet the disturbance remained. Gerry felt unhealthy twinges of suspicion. The Chief executive's rather smug version of events was not to his liking. He had caught wind of one or two other rumours as well. These suggested lurid conspiracies that called him an agent for arms dealers. This kind of thing inspired enough hints, for those who were inclined, to make the leap of faith into giving an absurd explanation for a strange event. It was patently ludicrous. Though Gerry found himself wondering more at the probable causes and effects of his own behaviour. Along with the unsavoury rumours about himself, sat the more cynical ones about his employers links to arms dealers. These rumours were longstanding, much longer than those about Gerry. But not particularly reassuring. All the while Gerry felt there was something going on, but he could never really understand what it was. Of course he read the history of the convoluted conflict he was involved in. It was a parade of atrocity and revenge that made for depressing education. It was easier for him to unravel those twisted threads of past hatred then it was to read his current predicament. Gerry felt too vague to be certain of any particular anxiety. And so he went home. At least it might give him time to sort his feelings into some kind of order.

Martha phoned him a few days later. He was relieved to have someone contact him. She insisted on taking him out for a meal. That was pleasant enough. It was just what he needed, a large dose of the bland. Martha's life seemed pretty straightfoward as she told it. It was a confident rise from girls boarding school, to civil servant, to her present position at W.H.A. Even the vices of her past were pretty reasonable. A few parties, a few drugs, minor conflict with her mildly authoritarian father. The only real thing he took notice of was her interest in boats. She had been rowing since the age of fifteen for some club or other. Then he noticed the undeniable strength of those tree limbs she called arms. She had biceps, but this made her more attractive, she looked Scandinavian, he was not sure whether she said this or it it was just his fantasy. He liked the fact he was taller than her, and that her shortness did not run to fat. Indeed she was all muscle, it was his that was running to fat.

Perhaps Martha sensed his lack of confidence. It was her who proposed they go back to her flat. He nodded in ready agreement. He found her direct, but not too obvious. He could do with some confidence from someone else at that moment. It meant she wasted no time however. Shortly he found himself gasping for breath on the settee. Then shortly after that the bedroom gymnastics were in full flow. It was a bit like taking a pleasant row down the river, then suddenly finding yourself drawn onto the rapids. Gerry felt it best

247

to let the current take him, and hoped he could still keep his breath. She straddled him as if he were an exercise bike. And they indulged in all manner of positions. Gerry had not moved around so much since he laid the fitted carpet. Now he was the one being tacked to the floor.

How long this marathon went he could not remember. Needless to say, he finished as he started, lying flat out, unable to move. He must have drifted off, for when he awoke it was daylight. The dull grey light seeping in the window carried an early morning feel. Something smelled bad, really bad. Given the drain on their bodily fluids, this was not a surprise. Though once he recognised the smell he thought something embarassing or disgusting had happened. He began to notice a peculiar tingling in his hands, like pins and needles. Opening and closing them for a brief spell put paid to that feeling. Gerry tried to shake Martha awake, and got the shock of his life when his hand went straight through her body. Her body was completely mushy, it provided no resistance to touch. It was like dipping his hand into a mud puddle. The smell intensified at this action, so much so he felt he could taste it. And of course there was no denying it any longer. It smelt of shit. Gerry slowly backed up and away from what he thought had been his sleeping companion. He needed light to be sure in the early morning gloom, so he duly flicked the switch. And there it lay in all its glory, a representation of Martha's athletic figure, except for a gooey chunk missing where her left shoulder should have been. Gerry was reminded of photgraphs he had once seen of mud castles. He could not allow any doubt anymore, his model Martha was sculpted from excrement. Gerry stood coughing and spluttering before he thought it would be good idea to open the windows. Very slowly the painful suggestion took form, he would have to clear up the mess, gagging as he was. A bucket, deteregent, cloths and toilet rolls were collected from the kitchen and bathroom. As Gerry stared at the shit sculpture, psyching himself up for the task, he thought the colour reminded him of caramel. This was too much. Luckily the bucket was handy and he threw up. This cleared his mind and dissipated his squeamishness. So he set about his task of clearing up Martha - the big shit. He tackled this waste disposal task with a readiness to disappear quickly once it was completed. And disappear quickly he did.

Nothing more was heard from work. Gerry expected this with regard to himself. But no one even contacted him regarding Martha's whereabouts. Friends and family outside work seemed non-existent in all his colleagues. Gerry was not surprised on this count. His life was similar. He had lost contact with all influences outside of the workplace, apart from the privacy of his own flat. He had no time for another life. That is why he felt to be given leave of abscence like this was the cruelest act. Maybe they planned it way. Maybe they wanted him out of the way. His thoughts ran to conspiracy connecting the war and his workplace, the kind of imaginative speculation boredom provides. After a few days of this he felt he was going insane. It was impossible for him to tell anyone what had happened. Maybe a practical joke had been played on him. But why go to such an extent to make someone die of embarassment ? Whatever, he needed to be with someone, but did not want to talk to anyone. Eventually he decided to go for a walk, to try and drain the thoughts from his head.

Gerry never realised how grey and prosaic his surroundings looked. He lived in a company flat, in the middle of the financial district. The area looked dead, even in the middle of the working day. People and traffic abounded, but it all moved at a soporific pace. The hum of extractor fans whirled out through doorways and other apertures, the constant tune provided by underground car parks and ventilation systems, It formed the backdrop to the rhythm of workaday traffic. Gerry was worried he was losing it. He told himself it was because he was alone, with too much time on his hands. This gave him some reassurance. He turned away from the familiar walks associated with work. He found he had to make conscious effort to do this. Walking north, the office blocks decreased in height, though they still dominated the sky. Neighbouring areas too were dwarfed, dependant on their massive companions. Then Gerry realised he was walking through these neighbouring areas. He was surprised by the fact they were even more quiet. The bulidings gradually changed, they became smaller, older, more residential. They looked like poor relations compared with the office blocks. People were scarcer. But they stared at him, was he so different ? perhaps they considered him an intruder. He did know this area vaguely, although he thought it unimportant.

Some streets now began looking shabby, poor road repairs and broken lamposts began to appear. The buildings looked dirtier. Funnily enough the cars still looked the same, gleaming and expensive. Although traffic was scarce every parking space was filled, all the vehicles were relatively new. One or two gangs roamed about. Gerry was feeling like a stranger. He was still looking for somewhere to put his mind at rest. He could not go home yet. All his paranoia would flare up again. Instead he found a pub. Caution dictated it would have to be one on a main road, he did not trust some of the drinking establishments he passed.

Bright lights and a clean facade beckoned to him. A pub was found, it looked pretty clean, and it was moderately full. But it was so quiet, and so much darker inside than out. It looked a place that had just been given a spring clean, though a powerful detergent or two might still be needed to get rid of the general air of seediness about the place. What was it called ? the Intrepid Fox, you had to be intrepid to go for a night out here. One or two gorgeous women sat at separate tables, too gorgeous. Gerry wondered if this was was some kind of pick up place. The barman seemed affable enough, in his shirt and tie. Though his skinhead haircut made him look like an ex-boxer. Gerry sat at the bar. He was too nervous to go to one of the shady booths that lined the wall. Muffled whispers reached his ears from these places. He did not want to know the content of these conversations. His suspicion was they all ran to vice and drugs. A polite, bureaucratic place to ply these items, as there were some office workers around too. It still gave him the creeps. He would not have stayed. But the barman, once Gerry's thumbs were noticed, took a genuine interest in his latest customer. Gerry himself had gotten quite used to them in the past few days - well he had not seen anyone. The barman cracked a few jokes about Roman Emperors giving the thumbs down, and the perils of hitchhiking in such a condition. He was actually funny. It was ages since Gerry felt like he had had a decent laugh. The ice broken, Gerry gave his account of what had happened, and the barman was suitably impressed. He was an ex-marine himself, he regaled Gerry with tales of broken bones, bloody battles, and worsening wounds, which made the healthworker quite queasy. Gerry had seen a few disgusting things himself. But the barman seemed to have experienced a few thousand more. They sounded authentic enough, someone else's experience always effected Gerry more. That was partly why he became a healthworker in the first place. Yet it also had its depressing side. So much stamina, strength, skill and courage was used to inflict pain and suffering on others. It was a waste really, even when you hardened yourself to the emotional impact of events, the shake of the head to ask why remained.

Gerry said his goodbyes. He had stayed longer than necessary. Was it two or three hours ? he could not be sure. All he knew was it was late. It was pitch black outside. It was colder as well. Gerry hunched his shoulders and tried to walk determinedly. Retracing his steps was a mistake. He wandered aimlessly in the first place. So how could he remember to return aimlessy in the roundabout manner he had set out ? But somehow he found himself walking in the direction of home.

Something or someone walked alongside him, but what ? They were people, apparently. They looked young but walked like they were old. Why ? There were three of them. One was dressed in a huge coat/jacket that looked like a rubber life raft. The other had baggy trousers on, as if someone had sown two denim dresses together. The third was the big mouth, the leader. This was all Gerry could distinguish about them, apart from the fact they were male. They were caricatures, caricatures in baseball caps.

" Want to buy some hash geezer ? " said Big Mouth.

Gerry burst out laughing.

" Geezer thinks he's funny.."

Gerry turned round and punched Big Mouth, his fist was nearly swallowed in the process. Then he ran. Unfortunately he only got a few yards before he tripped on a loose paving stone. He thought of the possibilty of suing the council as he fell on the pavement. Luckily he got his hands in front of him to absorb the fall. Unluckily they hurt like hell. And the caricature gang caught up with him. He felt a combination of pain and tingling as kicks and punches rained on his crouched body. Then they stopped suddenly, or did he black out ?

He must have lost consciousness, for a few minutes at least. What had happened exactly ? he felt himself for bruises, and there were none to speak of. He brushed himself down and the smell began to hit him. He had no need to guess anymore. Three huge turds lay around him. They had splattered somewhat on impact. The caricature gang had all turned to shit in the action of hitting him. Once transformed they fell backwards and made a mess on the pavement. Poor Rubber Life Raft, Baggy Trousers and Big Mouth. Gerry felt it was his own fault. He could probably have bluffed his way out of the confrontation if he had kept his nerve. As it was it was lucky he did not receive a good kicking. There was poetic justice in operation nevertheless, for the gang who sought to kick crap out of him turned into crap themselves. There was a moral in there somewhere, but that was probably shit as well. Gerry shivered. He did not like such thoughts after a near escape. Panic was begining to simmer, his head was aching. He walked on feeling he had cheated someone perhaps. The blood in his temples beagn to throb. He was feeling dizzy now. Waves of giddiness began to ride through him. He steadied himself against a car, only to find his hands had sank right into it. The car had turned to shit. He noticed it was a Vauxhall Astra,

" I always thought they were shit cars anyway."

Was he in a bad way ? dizzy, disorientated, and the puns about shit kept forcing their way into his consciousness. A poor old woman, who had the temerity to ask the time, was also trasformed into a giant stool. A poor, kindly looking lady who looked as scared as he was. She was turned into shit for her pains. What a little shit he was, aaah. He ran, at a stagger at first. Then he got into his rhythm and built up speed. By the time running felt comfortable he realised he was back among the office blocks. His home was still a good twenty minutes away. At least he was in familiar surroundings.

Some kind of clean up was in order. Just the routine of it would do him good. There was sports centre he could use. What was the time ? eleven, not much chance then. Then again he did know Roland, who worked on the door. If this person was on duty, Gerry could get a quick shower, or swim even.

Roland was there, dozing in his little booth. Gerry's tapping at the window made him start. Roland's eyes remained wide as he took in the condition of his friend, well friend of a friend actually. He thought Gerry to be typical of that kind of creep that works in public services. Gerry told the truth about his condition, about the attempted mugging anyway. He did not tell Roland about his magical transformation of his antagonists. If he heard of that kind of thing from anyone else, Gerry would have figured them to be extremely loopy. Though he could not resist ending his account with " God, I really got dropped in the shit." Gerry cringed at himself. To Roland this looked like a grimace. Poor bloke - he thought. Gerry became less of a cipher in a suit and more like the rest of us, struggling gamely like the rest of us. Roland's sympathy went into overdrive, the poor suit was obviously shook up. Roland gave Gerry free use of the facilities. Officially the club was closed at ten, even to members. But the nod of the doorman and the back hand of the caretaker could work some concessions. Gerry headed for the swimming pool. One of the showers in that area would do him fine. The pool was only dimly lit by two strip lights. Someone else was there, a man on the diving board. Gerry waved to him and received acknowledgement. He wanted to act unconcerned, much as he would in any unreal situation. He heard the man dive off the board as he installed himself within a shower cubicle. After some playing around with the tap Gerry managed to find a balance between scalding hot and freezing cold. In fact the freezing cold made him jump before the temperature adjusted itself. The shock made his hands tingle. By now he realised strong emotion bought on this sensation, this consequently led to his manure inducing tendencies. As this thought plodded by him he noticed the water was turning to diarrhea as it struck his body. In effect he soon became covered in liquid squit. The panic made his acquaintance again, and things looked to go much the way of previous events that evening. But this time Gerry knew he was scared. Maybe if he tried to relax, since he was getting fed up of constant fear led palpitations. Gerry forced himself to breath deeply and slowly. His body remained in the same position, unwilling to move. Gradually some degree of relaxation reasserted itself. The shit became more runny, until it was running water again. Gerry looked down at his feet to see the last brown stains trickle into the gully by his feet, sailing off forever down the drain. This was quite a beautiful sight. He felt he had gained some measure of control over his condition at last. He enjoyed the water cascading down his body after this. Drying and getting dressed followed leisurely. The sounds of the man at the pool came along to him, alternate dives and lengths.

Gerry felt alive as he left his cubicle. Curiosity rather than fear began to dominate his perspective on events for the first time. He wondered if that thing was gone for good. Unmindful of the pool user, he resolved to test the water. As soon as he put his hand in he knew it was a mistake. The clear water turned into a pool of slurry. A short, though loud, plop followed. The water had transformed into shit as the man was in mid dive. Gerry moved out of the pool area as fast as he could. He tried to get out of the building by not touching anything. Unfortunately Roland saw he was still agitated and tried to stop him, out of concern. Gerry knew what happened. He did not turn around. The overpowering smell, and the soft flop of a huge turd hitting the floor, said more than enough to his senses.

He must not let anything excite or unnerve him. He knew this now. Some degree of resistance must be made to his condition. Otherwise he would be isolated and starved. He gained an unfortunate habit after the sports centre incident. Whenever he was performing an essential action, such as eating, his mind would run to the runs, and other associated excremental matters. For instance. as he gazed at a juicy forkful of curry, poised steaming before his lips, he would think about its resemblance to anal discharge, and he would think how terrible it would be if...Inevitably the food morsel then turned to shit as his mouth enclosed it. Gerry had gagged over three meals in this way. It also happened as he was reading a book. The book fell onto his chest as a little pile of droppings. Seeking something to draw off this anxiety he switched on his telly. He was not concerned, however, when the set turned into a huge chocolate log. He thought that incident was quite sweet, literally. It reminded him of the chocolate covered swiss rolls he used to enjoy as a kid. It looked far more appetising than most of the crap served up on television anyway. Gerry was glad his transformed telly reeked. Otherwise he might have been tempted to scoop a spoonful or two. As it was he ended up shovelling shit in his flat yet again. He had used so much detergent lately that his room was sterile enough for surgical operations, though only after shit sessions of course. Sometimes it was a pleasure to utilise his new found gift. He exercised it on a couple of garish, porcelin figures, a present from a girlfriend who ditched him. He also transformed two bottles of cheap and nasty wine into two earthy vintages, with a pungent bouquet of sewerage, and a hint of septic tank.

" I must be the only person who's ever turned piss into shit," he thought.

Such moments of pleasure were few however. Most of the time he prefered to mope around. He was intrigued by the fact that. although he could turn objects to shit, his range could not extend very far. Thankfully his brown stain capability was only directed outward. He could not turn himself to shit, by his own tingling hands. This meant he could masturbate quite free from anxiety. The clothes he wore and bed he slept in were likewise safe. Though once he got out of them they could also be potential shits. These kind of thoughts had driven him mad at first. He imagined the floor he was walking on turning into wall to wall cowpat, or the air he was breathing turning into farts. Even with these fears eased there was no guarentee he could control his condition. Events at the sport centre had proved that. And his anxiety always had a life of its own anyway. But it seemed the way out of his condition was to become as emotionless as possible, a nondescript automaton, a bit like most of his colleagues at the office. The doctors had given up on him for the moment, and he was wary of initiating contact with them. They always gave him the impression his condition was his fault. Gerry's paranoia insisted these doctors had their own agenda. By what reasoning he came to this conclusion he did not know. But he would wait until the hospital contacted him again. And then he would sit around wringing his hands a lot.

He thought maybe he should confide in a friend. Unfortunately he had no friends. There were no real close colleagues at work either. He did think of Sarah. He had often talked to her, mainly with the intention of getting inside her knickers. And she had kept her distance lately. Gerry was working out how he could approach her when another magical transformation happened. It was an awkward moment, for he was sitting on the toilet at the time. He was depositing waste when the toilet turned into a waste product itself. This was too much, he could not even have a shit without turning the surroundings into shit . The smell was horrendous. Gerry collapsed into a pile of cack. Somehow he struggled out of this mud bath and manged to turn the water off. After disposing of enough waste product to keep a sewage firm in business for a week, he called a plumber, with the lame excuse his toilet had been stolen.

Did Sarah look pleased to him ? or was she just laughing at him. He never could tell. Since she always laughed at him anyway. Not that she was being spiteful, she told him that herself. It was just she found him amusing, unintentionally so sometimes. This was unnerving to Gerry, since she often burst out laughing when he was being serious. And he felt he had to go along with the joke when this happened. It struck Gerry that she was the least suitable person to tell his problem to. But what else could he do ? He was not exactly spoilt for shoulders to cry on. So he must make the most of what he could find. They met in one of those places that call themselves brasseries, all glass and chrome, along with expensive prices for teeny amounts of food and drink. Gerry liked those places, and so did Sarah. They could toy with their Spanish beers and their cocktail sticks without spending too much. They were good for talking. It seemed Gerry's wariness was initially confirmed. Sarah was very sympathetic, but only after laughing herself breathless for a full minute.

" I'm sorry Gerry,whoooh, ha ha, I really am. But you must admit it's pretty weird. That's the only reason I'm laughing, I reckon...ha ha..otherwise I think I'd be freaked by the whole episode. Are you sure you're okay ? I mean after what you've been through ? "

" Well I can't really say I'm alright can ? It's not something like a headache is it ? I feel like I ought to do something, but I don't know what..."

" Maybe you should work for a tabloid newspaper..."

" What ? "

" You know, become a muck raking journalist, you'd have no trouble shit stirring...ha ha."

" Please Sarah try and listen to me, I'm seriously scared...'

" Sorry. Well I thought we might have heard some comment at least, about all these strange happenings, that you say happened. "

" Of course they happened. I wouldn't make up anything as embarassing as this...All I've heard is the Sports Centre has been closed for major repairs. No one's said anything about Roland and Martha though..."

" Who ? "

Gerry started.

" I wouldn't expect you to know Roland. But I thought you were quite friendly with Martha. "

" Describe her."

" Er well, short, bleach blond, well built."

" Oh that butch woman, wow, you got off with her. Actually I thought she was a bit of a dyke myself, ha ha ha..."

Gerry frowned.

" I'm sorry Gerry, I didn't mean it like that. I liked her, what I saw of her anyway...Maybe I found her a bit intimidating... But enough of that. What are you going to do ? "

" Goin back to the hospital seems the only real option. But what do I tell them ? "

" The truth."

" Yes I can just imagine...Well doctor, I've discovered I have this unfortunate ability, everything I touch turns to shit..."

" A true product of the modern world, hee hee hee... Sorry...Look you don't tell them that, you just say your condition's causing you anxiety, let them find out for themselves."

" I had thought of that. But they're going to ask me the whys and wherefores of it aren't they ? "

" Not necessarily. I mean your physical condition is obvious, with your thumbs upside down, like an Australian hitchhiker, hee hee...Oh I'm sorry, that's problem enough isn't it ? "

" I suppose, I feel too tired to be offended...It's just the waiting, they told me to wait, and nothing's happening, except scary weird things..."

" So tell them the wait is causing you anxiety...Look I don't see why you should be so worried. It's well known at the office you're on compassionate leave, that you need repeated visits to hospital. They're holding your job open until when you return. They've got some temp there at the moment, completely clueless, doesn't know what she's doing half the time..."

" I'm not going back into the warzone again though, am I ? "

" None of us are at the moment, the situations that bad..."

Gerry looked depressed.

"...Look, I don't think you can blame yourself Gerry. It's a fucked up situation. Both sides have been blaming anyone but themselves. And they only have themselves to blame really. You shouldn't pay attention to all that nonsense..."

" What nonsense ? "

" Oh, er, all that guff about keep Siddan the healthworker away, he's bad luck, he's too unfortunate, he's..."

Sarah turned her head slightly, as if recognising him for the first time. A questioning glance gave way to a sparkle. Gerry knew she was going to burst out laughing again."

" All right, what is it ? "

" No... ha ha, it's too stupid to be true."

" I thought you'd have known better by now, what is it ? "

" Well everything you touch turns to shit, yes ? "

" Well not everything, thankfully, but go on."

" And they call you Sidam the Healthworker."

" They also call me Sidan and Sidon. So what, they're just mispronouncing my surname."

" I thought that, but now I think It's more like a nickname."

" Eh ? "

" Turn the letters of your nickname back to front.."

" What ? then I become Nodis."

" No, it's Sidam, S.I.D.A.M, and Sidam back to front is ? "

" Middas."

" No Midas, don't you see, you're Midas in reverse, don't you see ? ...Don't you know who Midas is ? "

" Of course I know. Everything he touched turned to gold didn't it. And I've got the Midas touch, or rather the opposite."

" Yes, ha ha ha."

" Well that's all very enlightening, But what good does it do me ? "

" Nothing probably, but it must mean something..."

" Oh who cares what it means, does it make any difference ? "

" It might help us figure out your condition."

Gerry quite agreed with that. Events had come to the turn where something had to be done, even if he did not know how to go about it. The alternative was to accept his unfortunate condition, perhaps even to turn it to some kind of advantage. This latter option ingratiated itself in the face of all his anxiety. It helped deflate the worry. For the first time he began considering the situation rationally. He thought that accepting his condition was tantamount to becoming a circus freak. The urge to be as he was continued as the stronger impulse. Yet the counter impulse gained strength. Another notion gained entrance, his shit producing capability could be a powerful weapon.

Gerry could afford a smile as Sarah guided him out of the brasserie. They made a quick stroll through some local gardens, Sarah was due back at work soon. These gardens were weird. It seemed to Gerry they were once a cemetary. In fact it was patently obvious. The former headstones now made a perimeter wall. Why had he not noticed this before ? It gave him the creeps. Everything turned to shit in the end, and no one gave a shit. Gerry asked to sit down for a few moments, before the puns overwhelmed him again.

Sarah giggled as he explained why, then she continued talking at a very fast pace. It was office gossip mostly, it covered his silent brooding. Gerry looked at the tombstones, the faded headstones of forgotten people. They were forgotten just as his ailment seemed to be, moved aside in the hurly burly that makes up the modern workaday world. He had nothing, no one to judge his experiences against. His workplace seemed to blame him in some obscure way, the hospital appeared cold, the best he had was a colleague's giggling interest. Yet he liked Sarah, she helped him clarify his thoughts.

" It's the only way I suppose. I'll have to get in touch with the hospital. I just want to find out more about this, I don't care if it's weird..."

Sarah involuntarily grabbed his hand. Her grip was firm and protective. He felt warm and...That was it. Sarah opened her mouth to start a sentence which never materialised. Gerry tried to deny what has happening. But that all too familiar tingling could not be denied. Could he help it ? maybe he should not have liked her so much. Her hand had touched his, although it was now part of a steaming turd rather than a warm woman. It was a mound of the finest fertiliser he had ever seen, one of his bigger creations. By now he was numb to any effect. He just hoped this little excrement episode was not witnessed. Luckily it was not, a true miracle, a transformation in the middle of the lunch hour. He brushed the excrement from his hand, onto the planks of the bench, a grimace on his face. Then he got up, resignedly, and made his way home, sullenly.

Of course he heard nothing more about Sarah. She had gone the way of all turds. Thereafter, Gerry's life became more interesting, at least to him. To others he looked a bit weird. He continued drawing sick pay from work for a couple months. Then he pleaded upset about his continuing condition. He was given a decent reference and had the remainder of his contract paid up. They were bewildered at work, but not unsympathetic. They offered everything from counselling services to coffee mornings to help him. Yet he would not take these offers. Indeed, he was always aware of these services, right from the start. Yet his condition, mingled with his own messy emotions, had worked its own logic. He realised, somewhat dumbfoundedly, there would never be a cure for him. Its nature, if made public would make him a laughing stock. The problem before him now was what to do with his strange talent, for he now regarded it as such.

Some months later, after Gerry had left the W.H.A, his colleagues were discussing an art exhibition they had been to. Gerry's old manager listened in, half bored. It seemed like the usual kind of exhibitionist nonsense. Someone was trying to make a statement about the world again, while completely forgetting about artistic technique. This kind of approach irritated him, yet he could not deny his interest was piqued. His staff made the usual complaints and jokes that were made about such works. But as they droned on, the manager found his interest deepening. The work appeared to have a visceral impact, a punch straight to the stomach. This seemed out of all proportion to the artist's stated intent. But the artist insisted on behaving enigmatically anyway. No one could even be sure what he looked like, let alone what he said, or even if he was a he. The only name by which he was known was the Shit Sculptor. Likenesses of everyday objects were carved from huge number twos. Appparently it was some kind of comment about the quality of modern life. Though the manager pretended to frown, as his staff gossiped on, he resolved to visit this exhibition. Perhaps he would even meet the enigmatic artist, it was certainly worth making an attempt. He would certainly try to shake him by the hand.

YXSY GLYXSY VI

DEDUCT £.......... @ 8p in £	~£	~£				£
ASSESSED RATES	£_____	£_____		ASSESSED RENT	£ _____	£ _____

NON-DEPENDANTS -- ADD	ASSESSED RATES	£	£	ASSESSED RENT	£	£
18-20 years inclusive	.... @	£	£	.... @	£	£
21 years and over	.... @	£	£	.... @	£	£
Supplementary Benefit recipients Married couples count as one)	.... @	£	£	.... @	£	£
O.A.P's not in receipt of S.B. Married couples count as one)	.... @	£	£	.... @	£	£
	FINAL ASSESSED RATES	£	£	FINAL ASSESSED RENT	£	£

Weekly reckonable rates		£	£	Weekly allowable rent	£	£
Final assessed rates		£	£	Final assessed rent	£	£
RATE REBATE		£_____	£_____	RENT ALLOWANCE	£	£
(Minimum10p Maximum £				(Minimum 20p Maximum £		

Monthly x 52/12		£.............	£.............	Monthly x 52/12	£.............	£.............
Quarterly x 13		£.............	£.............	Quarterly x 13	£.............	£.............
Half-yearly x 26		£.............	£.............			

OPERATIVE DATES: RENT ALLOWANCE FROM .... EXPIRING ON ....

RENT ALLOWANCE FROM .... EXPIRING ON ....

RATE REBATE FROM 1st of .... EXPIRING ON ....

RATE REBATE FROM 1st of .... EXPIRING ON ....

Calculated by   Checked By   Finance Notified on   1575

My Love is Solid and True

I have often said that love knows no bounds. Actually, I never said it, I thought it sounded too soppy. I thought people would laugh at me. They laughed anyway, but I never let that put me off. Why should I ? Although I would like to make them shut up. But they never did, and they never have since.

I was always on the lookout for love. I heard about it in songs, saw tearjerking films and read potboiler novels. They were terrible crap. I wanted my love to be like an adventure, an absorbing passion, with thrills and spills, punctuated by moments of serene bliss. I never saw anything like that in any art. I saw one or two glimpses of it in the relationships of other people. I even caught a brief glimpse of it myself. But I blanched at the prospect of domesticity. Which is what my lover wanted, plus loads of little copies of us. The thought killed any passion in me. She wanted to be a wife and have a steady life. So she dumped me for somebody more reliable.

So, in my quest for love, down to earth women were out of the reckoning. This closed a lot of doors as far as I was concerned. I tried dating daring, shocking women. However, I found behind their confident bravado lay a series of emotional traumas. That scared the life out of me. Behind every outgoing person was an internal mess (and infernal as well), so it seemed. It made me afraid of going loopy myself, since my confidence was never rooted in any firm ground (hence my obssession with the right partner.).

I was never any kind of psychologist, I am no good about talking over my feelings. I always thought feelings were there to be felt, not to be talked about. I was not up to it. Nevertheless, I still hankered after the adventurous love, of two intrepid companions facing the epic of life together. Whenever I put this to people I was crestfallen, as they always burst out laughing. The ones who did not laugh, who listened to me with avid interest, I found a bit weird.

Maybe that was me, a bit weird. Friends often said that before they disappeared. I noticed my circle of acquaintances was growing smaller. Yet I was not to be deterred. I continued my search for the true love. I decided to change tack, or change sex anyway. I started dating men. Or rather, I started seeing men, since dating was a concept that made them laugh. They were very promiscuous, which I found interesting, but then it got boring, and then it got exhausting. I wanted a long term relationship of the type I always blabbed about, a companion in adventure. Unfortunately, the few men I was able to approach with this idea found me too boring. I had no background in the arts. The idea of having a man as long term lover paled after that.

In fact, human beings were particularly lacking in the companionable virtues, in my kind of virtues. And they were not very adventurous. And if they were it was in the wrong areas. I could not be bothered with sports, hobbies or obsessive-compusive habits generally . Then the idea of dating animals occurred to me. Animals can come into your life and remain there whatever. They can share in your every adventure. So long as you gave them a bit of food and let them go to the toilet occaisonally, they would be up for anything. I was aware I may be straying into illegal territory here. But true love knows no bounds. Or at least the search for true love is willing to consider any option, until it actually gets something. I tried going out with a few cats. But we were simply not compatible They were always going off on their own. A good relationship is about give and take. And I feel it is doomed, when the only reliable attribute in your partner, is when she lets you tickle her under the chin so she can purr.

Dogs were more reliable. Or they were supposed to be. I had heard stories that dogs had been trained to do various things by lonely, sex-starved owners. That sounded like my kind of relationship. So I resolved to train a dog to be my faithful lover. I started going out with a lovely husky, a rare breed actually. She was playful, lighthearted and very loyal. And I treated her as though the world revolved around her. But someone must have told the R.S.P.C.A. For some police came round to my house. They politely, if forcibly, informed me they had heard reports, which, if proved true, would lead to my being locked up, and beaten up. So that was the end of that relationship.

It occurred to me I needed to be discrete, so I tried going out with sheep. The countryside was devoid of informers and nasty police as well, so I thought. I had a rollicking good time in the country. Quite apart from the fact I was chased by a bull in one field. (I do not know why. I have never been into cows myself, either romantically or penetratively.) Then I was butted by a ram in another. I had to inform him I was not into roughhouse sex. However, I did start hanging around with a flock of delightful sheep. They were excellent company. The trouble was they were so shy. I had to make all the running in these relationships. These sheep were wallflowers. I did make the acquaintance of a delightful ewe. I was getting on famously, so I thought. That was until I heard the angry growl of a tractor, followed by the angry growl of a farm labourer. I suppose he took exception to a romantic buck trysting in the field with a lovely damsel. He shouted horrible curses, not at me, but at the ewe. How, as soon as his back was turned she was gallivanting around with every stray pervert that happened along. I was crestfallen. I was about to do the business with a slapper sheep. I quickly pulled up my trousers and ran away at great speed. My disappointment did not last long. For, in my travels I happened upon a rather horny old goat on the rebound. He was a goat of experience. We consoled each other with tales of past loves lost. We had both had our fingers burnt in relationships before, or hooves in his case. And we talked as only experienced lovers can. I was just about to consumate my mounting passion with this delightful creature, when a train pulled up alongside us. I had forgotten about the main line running by here. A carriageful of commuters glared at me with my tackle out, and my trousers down. Luckily I got away before the authorities came, but also before I had a chance to come.

I felt fate was being a bit pushy with me. It was telling me that love did not lie among the animal kingdom. In fact, I might have to drop down a genre or two. So, that meant I would now look for my true love among the machines. Now some may argue I was setting my sights too low here. But machines are reliable, honest, reassuring, and they are not afraid of running for ages. I did briefly look at the possbillity of dating factory machinery, or generators. But I did not have enough money to entertain them in the style they were accustomed to. Besides, I was not an engineer, and they were always after someone who could look after them. I speed dated a few computers, but they never wanted to go out. Finally I settled on cars. Cars fitted my requirements. They were sleek and sexy, honest and reliable, and not afraid of being pushed at breakneck speed in dangerous environments. So I began dating cars. It was very hard to make a selection I must admit, since there were not many opportunities to meet new cars on a social basis. I took to hanging around car showrooms, until I got chased away. So I tried some more speed dating. Responses were good, so I took a few on a test drive. They were lovely creatures, but beyond my income level, unfortunately. I tried going for a more experienced, dependable make. But most of these were already owned by someone else. And they tended to look alike, which gave rise to one or two faux pas, when I, rather embarassingly, got their names mixed up. Of course I do try to consider character in my partners. But the fact was I was being drawn to the sporty types, they were drop dead gorgeous. I always liked a bit of dash in my companions. I managed to go out with this beautiful Aston Martin, really tasty she was. Unfortunately she also belonged to someone else. I used to creep into his house, steal his keys and take her out for a romantic drive and picnic on the moors. While I ate crackers and cheese and glugged a supermarket wine, she had a drop of castrol and revved sportily. The police almost caught up with me here, again. I saw their car coming a mile off, which was lucky, since I was entering my Aston Martin's exhaust at the time, but sadly had to withdraw. The Aston Martin revved in frustration, but there was no choice. The man had reported his car stolen, again.

That was the trouble with my relationships with cars. All the good ones were spoken for. I was driven to surreptitious sex, quite literally. After being with a few sporty types, the appeal of your bog standard estate, or saloon, proved to be non-existent. They were either too bland or write offs, or both. Luckily, on the rebound from my Aston Martin, I fell in, or broke in, to a gorgeous Lotus. I used to pop into her owner's garage and poke her while the owner was watching telly. Unfortunately he must have heard the engine running one day. For he caught me, in flagrante delicto, up the exhaust again. I barely escaped. After this episode, I felt fate was giving me a good rollicking once more. It was time to move on, affairs with fast moving cars are very well, high-octane ejaculations in chrome tubing are manna to an adrenalin addict. Actually I almost went back on my word at this point. But no, no matter how good-looking, glamorous, and fast they were, my true love had be steadfast as well as adventurous and a good shag.

The world of machines began to pale after this. I did have a brief fling with a Hoover. But she became too attached to me. Indeed, I needed the help of the fire brigade, plus some counselling, to get her away from me. She was the most harrowing Hoover I had ever known. I did apply for an exclusion order, to stop this Hoover from attaching herself to me in future. However, the authorities only laughed. They then had the nerve to tell me stop bothering the Hoover. Otherwise it was tranquilisers at teatime for me. I ask you, why is the main earner always treated as though he were the guilty party when relationships break down ? She was a kept Hoover. I did not think she could cope on her own. Last I heard she was selling herself at a car boot sale. I felt I had been punished enough, for being both the breadwinner and the bagchanger.

I was heavily depressed at this latest turn of events. My quest for true love, for a true soul mate, had ground to a halt. I could not find a lover among women, men, animals, or machines. I did consider plants. But plants are so conservative, they never change and never want to go anywhere, they are so stuck-in-the-mud. Of course they respond to love and affection, but when is the last time you heard a plant say ' I love you ? ' There were too many cultural differences that prevented my forming any kind of relationship with fungi either. I did not understand their language or their religion. Besides, mushrooms gave me food poisoning once. I did look up a few bacteria. But these quickly became a few thousand. And I could not remember who I was supposed to be seeing in the first place, they multplied too quickly, so I last track. I was not into having millions of relatives every few minutes, nor having millions of babies for that matter. It was too many birthdays to keep track of. And Christmas would have been murder, when the family got back together again. I did not want to be part of an extended family of zillions. I had a brief fling with a viral strain. It gave me headaches and a high temperature and put me in bed for a week. It was a feverish affair. The doctors told me to kill it off, before it killed me off, love can be like that.

My options for love had not been totally explored. Maybe I could count on more suitable suitors from the kingdoms and species I had already explored. But the despair of a broken heart ruled it out. Perhaps this was unfair, but I was now totally fed up with women, men, animals, machines, plants, fungi, bacteria, and viral strains. If I was to find my true love, it would have to be in another kingdom. But what ? No other kingdom had any life. Even machines possessed a bit of energy. For they perform tasks within a certain limited role. (I have never met any machines capable of personal development though. They are too set in their ways for that.) So that appeared to be it. I could not picture myself going out with a plank of wood, or a tea urn, or a roll of carpet. I know a lot of people have formed long lasting bonds with inanimate objects. But I wanted a relationship with more get-up-and-go.

So, It appeared my quest had ended unsuccessfully. I would have to face the adventure of life without a companion. But rather than mope around, I thought I should get out of the house. I took to rambling in the hills. I needed to feel like I was still doing something. And I did begin to feel slightly better. The fresh air of Devon and Cornwall was extremely bracing as I clambered over their moors. I loved the isolation, the exposed outcrops of rocks known as tors, very rugged, almost primeval. And I could forget who I was, forget I was lonely. Yet walking in these areas could be dangerous. One day, as I was clambering over a tor, a thick fog descended all around me. It reduced visibility to the length of my arm. I got worried, as I was at a reasonably high altitude, on a surface which could be quite slippy. I slowed down, so my actions would not lead to any fall. I moved mostly by guesswork and touch. I could not resist falling on a couple of occaisons. They hurt painfully. I heard rocks falling below me. It seemed there was a big drop nearby. I stopped, or tried to, but slipped as the idea occurred to me. The rocks continued to tumble, some above as well as below now. I lay grimly on the slope, pressing myself down, hoping I would not slide more, dropping into the gap below, which I still could not quite see. Large stones began rolling past me, one or two hit me. I began thanking my luck they were not bigger. But then a bigger one did hit me, and then, out of the corner of my eye...

I came to at the bottom of the slope. I was scared by now. A sizeable granite boulder loomed above me. This is where people said my real trouble started, as if I were not perverted enough already. I was weird enough before, but this mishap really pushed me over the edge. But that was later, and it was all their opinion anyway. Then, in my frightened, fragile state, I clung onto this boulder for dear life. It was the only solid object around, it offered security.

And that was how the rescue team found me. They could not prise my grip away. So I was transported, boulder and all, to the nearest available hospital.

I was not badly hurt, a few bruises, plus some weakness due to exposure. And I soon rallied. I felt better for having the boulder by my bedside throughout my recovery. People did try to take it away, but my condition only worsened when they did. So it was soon brought back. It did cause no end of amusement when I was discharged. I insisted on taking the boulder home with me on a wheelbarrow.

When I was home I realised we could communicate. Perhaps the fall had loosened some kind of empathy in me. Anyway, the boulder and I soon realised we were kindred spirits. We had that uncanny telepathy. We quickly divined we were very much in love. This was despite our different religious and ethnic backgrounds. She had fallen on me, quite accidentally, when I was scrambling around on the tor. Now she had fallen for me, quite passionately. And I was left scrambling around for the right words to declare my feelings for her. She had insisted on staying with me, right through my ordeal and recovery. She wanted to be by my side, always, my companion in adventure, my steadfast lover, my rock.

I was flabbergasted. There I was, spending all those years, searching for the right partner. And then the right partner just falls on me. I assumed she was a she. She had one or two clefts and hollows cut into her voluptuous surface. These easily sufficed for me (and they allowed me to service her). Therefore a she she was. But she was resolute too, as only good rocks can be. Her name was Boulda in fact, Boulda Igneous. She came from good, granite stock. And she could trace her ancestry back to the formation of the Earth's crust, millions of years before the arrival of life on this planet. She was not snotty about her aristocratic background (though her cousins, the Basalts were). How many so-called aristocrats could trace their ancestry back that far ? There was a streak of iron in her, and one or two traces of sediment. But she was as rigorous a rock as you could find anywhere. That is, if you were on the lookout for rigorous rocks. Our love blossomed, just like the pretty moss that occaisonally formed on her surface. We set up home together, a place where she could be near her relatives - the Igneous-Tors. Visits were quite arduous. I pulled a muscle one time, dragging her over the moors. She never did take much exercise, apart from rolling down the occaisonal hill. I gained huge, muscular arms as the result of dragging her along. In town it was easier. I would push her about in the wheelbarrow. People thought us strange at first. However, once they saw how deeply in love we were, and once they stopped laughing, they mostly left us alone. We did have a problem with some kids for a while. They would insist on teasing Boulda and I. But once I toppled Boulda out of her wheelbarrow, on top of them, they soon ran away, at least those who were able. Their parents tried to pursue a case of assault against me, as there were one or two broken bones. Fortunately for me, the case was considered so strange it was laughed out of court. The judge could not hold his sides together long enough to deliver a verdict.

Life was idyllic, apart from the odd bit of ridicule. I learnt to be tolerant of this, as mixed race relationships were not common in this part of the world. Besides, most people saw how happy we were. They would never know just how happy. Perhaps it was strange. But they could never see Boulda as I could. Yet as she sunbathed in the rockery, and I consumed loads of cans of lager on the lawn, I could not but reflect how happy I was. I had finally found my companion in life, the one who I would share my adventures with. I warmed to my theme, as she nodded encouragement, from her vantage point, next to the daffodils. I also gave her the occaisonal can of lager. This made her glisten seductively in the sunlight. She was always more sexy when she was wet. As days turned into weeks, months, then years, my neighbours could not help but notice our happy relationship. They stopped laughing eventually, after they had worn themselves out, and after the tears ran down their eyes. They began to accept we were an item. Man and Boulda were as one, set in stone. In fact I often wished I could have converted to stone, just for Boulda's sake. But I could never get the hang of the rocky language. (Luckily Boulda was bilingual, if a little gravel voiced.) Besides, Igneous-Tor society was very set in its ways, they were slow to take to newcomers. Sometimes it took millions of years for them to accept your company, and even then they still would not talk to you.

How long our relationship might have gone on, in its way, I am not sure. But somehow a television company came to hear of us. We were invited onto a talk show, a specialised one, where people come on and discuss their weird lives with a studio audience. I was wary of such exploitation. Trouble was, Boulda had set her heart on having a ski slope built in our back garden, so I could roll her down all day. Therefore I felt I had to agree. Things did actually go reasonably well on this talk show, at first. The interviewer was a bit of an idiot, and he assumed the audience were bigger idiots than him. For his tone was one of wide-eyed wonder, as he asked us polite, but nosy, and pervy, questions. I was expecting the raucous laughter of course. But people were rather touched by our dedication to each other. Boulda went all shy. So I had to do most of the talking. This did not bother me, as I usually talked, on her behalf, to others. She trusted me implicitly to express our wishes. But when I was telling the interviewer about our hopes for the future, her chair collapsed. I am afraid Boulda had been putting on a bit of weight lately. She always wore one or two layers of moss to cover her bulk in those days. The interviewer, rather indiscretely I thought, suggested Boulda should go on a diet. I said I already put her on one, at her request. I had chiselled a few pebbles off her only the other week. (I needed something to line the rose beds.) Cue huge laughter - I was mortified. But Boulda stood up well to the embarassment I must say. Even though I was so upset I gave myself a hernia as I dragged her away from that studio. That turn of events left me unhappy. I was only mollified when a huge amount of money was transferred into our joint bank account, payment for our ritual humiliation.

Things might have settled back to normal then. For Boulda and I could easily slip back into our, by now, warm and cosy relationship. But something happened one day. I awoke to find a huge, stone monolith at the front door. No matter what I said to him, he would not budge an inch. He had come for Boulda. He was Boulda's companion of long standing, some five thousand years in fact. Dolmen was his name, and he had set up home with Boulda on the top of the tor. (The estate agents did not charge them extra for the view, as they did not exist then.) One day, he had come home early from work, being venerated by new age druids, because of the weather, when he saw Boulda simply roll away. He then saw her gallivanting around with an unconscious man, i.e. me, at the bottom of the hill. He would have rolled down after her. But Boulda and Dolmen had an open relationship, after five thousand years of standing around on the tor, some things were best left unsaid. But he knew it was the end. He felt his heart turn to stone. But then he had to forget about Boulda and roll on. This was because he had important work to do, being worshipped by druids and hippies. He was eventually designated as a heritage site and was kept very busy. But one day he saw Boulda and me on

T.V, and his heart melted. He had dismissed Boulda from his mind when she rolled away with me. But now all his old love came rolling back. He frantically sought to find his old rock again. I was bit sceptical about this. How could a huge stone monolith watch T.V. on a tor ? on a remote moor ? Dolmen told me he had got a deal on a cable package. I was taken back by this. Since I was still paying expensive instalments on a satellite deal. And I did not want lose my Boulda either. But I regained enough composure to know things must be sorted out. The monolith was obviously genuine. We needed to talk the whole thing through. I called Boulda's name. But she would not reply. She was completely reluctant to come to the door. And Dolmen was equally reluctant to come in, though he still would not budge. Instead he pleaded with me, tearfully, to bring Boulda to the door. He just wanted to discuss things with her. He wanted to find out if she wanted to stay with me or go with him. I did not want to lose my Boulda. But, if she did still have feelings for Dolmen, maybe they should talk things over. If Boulda wanted to stay with me, Dolmen would not object, but he had to find out. He would then go back to his place on the tor. (Or at least he would get someone with a lorry to transport him there. If Boulda wanted to go with him, a larger lorry would be needed.) I was mortified by the prospect of losing my rock. But if Boulda did have any wish to go with Dolmen, I thought it only proper she should not be denied the opportunity. And the prospect of dragging Boulda to the door made my hernia throb in pain. The thought of transporting them both back to the tor made it throb with fear. But she had not told me of this past lover. So I went to the back garden and confronted her. She asked for my forgiveness. Yes, she had been married to Dolmen in the past. But she had become so infatuated with me, that she had forgotten him. Besides, when she first saw me, she thought I might die if she left me alone, and had felt like that ever since. We were both overcome for a minute. But we both rallied ourselves. It was agreed she would have to talk the matter over with Dolmen. So I rolled her outside the front door, smarting with pain as I did so.

Dolmen asked for a private conversation alone. I readily conceded his request. Although I did spy on them from the window. They stood there in silent recrimination, for ages. I got fed up trying to eavesdrop. It was getting dark anyway, so I went to bed. Boulda and Dolmen were quite hardy souls, they did not mind spending a lot of time outdoors. And they could not roll away, my house was not near any slopes.

So we would have to pick up the drama the following morning. However, when I woke and went outside, they were gone. I was frantic. Had they rolled off together after all ? I asked around. But no one had seen two huge rocks rolling around. Yet some council workmen had been seen heaving two large stones onto the back of a lorry. Had Dolmen persuaded them to take the journey back to the tor ? I had to find out. I traced the workmen to their depot. They were very helpful. They had acted on a complaint that someone had made to the council, about the two standing stones dumped outside my house. It was thought unscrupulous builders had left them there, it was a common problem builders dumping waste in the area. So the stones had been brought to the depot. I could have them back, of course. The trouble was, there were more than two now. The workmen had broken up Boulda and Dolmen, so that all that was left was a pile of rubble. They kindly transported the rubble back to my home. Where I now have the most extensive rockery in the neighbourhood.

Cough Drop

It was another humiliation. They were served up in great dollops in the teenage years. They wanted to be manly, clever and experienced. While the adults around constantly reminded them how stupid, childish and ignorant they were. Take sex, please - Richard and Jim would have taken it, all day and every day, and every which way. They were experts on it, in theory at least. They had not actually had any yet, not even a wank. Though, technically, wanking was not considered proper sex, more like a dress rehearsal, or a sticky mess rehearsal, that was one of Jim's favourite jokes, repeated into infinity.

No, but in their carefully considered way, i.e. through gossip, sniggering and dirty mags, they had garnered a fair knowledge on the functions of the human body. This made them feel a little strange, a bit self-conscious, even though they bluffed it all away with a display of self-confidence. If they did not tell the truth to others, they told themselves - they were mixed up and confused. And now they were to be put through another ritual humiliation by the teachers at school. It was the infamous cough and drop. For days beforehand, playground gossip had revolved around the sighting of a nurse who looked like a man. This stocky battleaxe was due to give them a medical. What kind was made clear as the gossip progressed. They were to have their balls squeezed by the nurse's hairy hand, then told to cough, if they could forget their eyes watering.

Jim felt squeamish at the news, Richard looked bewildered. They could never divine the purpose of the 'cough and drop' ritual, a state of affairs that continued for the rest of their lives. It was one of those strange rites that signposted your way to adulthood, like consuming alcohol without being repelled by the taste, swearing without embarassment, and generally being a miserable git. It was the begining of the end of childhood, of enjoyment, of laughter. Soon they would have to have boring conversations about money, and then work for people more stupid then themselves. Secondary school was bad enough, a kind of open prison for pubescent twats, but at least you could have a laugh.

And the trepidation spread throughout their year. Once leery faces looked timid and frightened, once noisy kids became furtive and suspicious. The teachers remarked how agreeable the pupils had become. Jim and Richard looked for ways to avoid the cough and drop. But there were none. It was like an exam. In fact it was an exam, of sorts. But how would they know if they passed ? They would not. If they were called back for a retake there might be a problem, but otherwise ?

On the appointed day there were approximately one hundred boys standing in their pants, outside a makeshift, medical room. Unfortunately it was next to Bill Tandie's office, the schoolkeeper, who was a perverted pubescent molester, apparently. The story ran that every time you went to see this man, he would tell you to take your trousers down. You would complain of feeling sick, of having a headache, he would tell you to take your trousers down. Even if you asked for directions to the library, he would tell you to take your trousers down. If you said ' Good Morning,' he would tell you to take your trousers down. He was known as 'Bill Pansy.' As if that were not bad enough, ' Feeler Halloran,' was there as well. Halloran, the French master, had a fondness for fondling, in particular boys' bums before he gave them the cane (still allowed at their school). He used to rack his brains for any excuse to give boys the cane. Feeler Halloran's activities were better documented than Bill Pansy's. Whatever the level of truth, anecdotal evidence had already condemned them out of hand. Of course, on the evidence of their seedy personalities alone, most juries would have convicted them (Oh the joys of an all boys school).

Jim and Richard, therefore, looked embarassed, felt intimidated, and were scared. Some of the other boys modified the tension by making fun of Richard's pants. (Taking the piss out of his pants as one one wag joked.) His pants had picture patterns of tennis rackets and tennis balls on them. This provoked howls of laughter. Tennis was a girls' game. Richard deflected the pisstaking by pointing out Jim's pants, which had a logo, which said, ' Caution Long Vehicle.' The general opinion was this was an over-optimistic assessment. It was said Jim must have stolen a man's pants. And, in fact, they were hand-me-downs, his brother's old pants, but he did not bring this fact to their attention. Instead he dealt with the pisstaking by appealing to the incipient homophobia of teenage boys. Why would they make jokes about cocks and pants unless they were obssessed by cocks and pants ? The logic was flawless. Given their current situation it was an understandable joke to make, and also perhaps a bit stupid. It may have reminded everyone of their vulnerability. Jim's tormentors took exception at this turn of the conversation. There might have been a fight. But what happened next diffused the situation.

As they were standing around, pointing fingers and raising voices, a huge boxer dog trotted around between them. This phenomenon froze all conversation. For it was Bill Pansy's dog. It was rumoured he trained his dog to sexually assault boys. While the reason may have been due to paranoia, the fact was this dog, Duke by name, loved gripping peoples' legs and shagging for dear life. Jim had actually seen this. One dozy kid, Kenny, who fancied himself as a dog handler, used to befriend Duke, while others walked sharply away. One day his stroking and patting was getting Duke a bit too excited. The other boys said he better watch his step, but Kenny merely laughed as the dog humped his leg. He said the dog was only playing. He was, but it was more in the manner of foreplay. Kenny began to stroke Duke affectionately, to show there was nothing to be afraid of. Duke became ever more excited and broke off, Kenny turned to his compatriots with a smug grin on his face, as if to say 'I told you so.' But Duke reared up on his hind legs, and his prick dropped out like a flick knife. It was at this point Kenny ran away. Duke subsided, looking bewildered. The other boys took in this scene for a brief second, then joined Kenny.

As soon as Jim related this tale he realised it was the wrong place at the wrong time. When he grew older he would learn to exercise more judgement. But, at that moment, he had paralysed everyone with fear. This fear concentrated all their gaze on Duke. The boxer plodded his way around, looking for something to do, someone to hump. It was like being in a firing squad, waiting for the bullet. Fortunately for everyone, Duke began humping Richard's leg, who did not feel so fortunate. Maybe the dog was attracted to tennis racket pants. Huge sighs of relief were heard, which turned to concern when it was realised Richard might be in some trouble. His face was red through fear and embarassment. It looked like he might burst into tears at any moment. But what could they do? Duke was a well-built boxer, who might get annoyed at being separated from his playmate. Fortunately their shouts drew out a couple of adults. Unfortunately it was Bill Pansy and Feeler Halloran.

These two dodgy adults smirked their way through the situation. Bill Pansy waved an admonishing finger at the traumatised Richard. He made clear, in no uncertain terms, that Richard should not mistreat the dog, under pain of the cane. At the mention of the cane, Feeler Halloran's grin broadened, until his face almost split apart. And then he just walked off. Bill Pansy dragged Duke by the collar into his office. ' He's probably going to give the dog a wank,' someone maliciously remarked. Bill Pansy poked his molester's head out of the doorway, as if to say, ' I know what you're doing, sonny,' then disappeared. The rude comments about Bill Pansy resumed. The things they thought he would do to that dog would amount to several decades in prison, if true. The remarks cheered Richard up. He was snivelling a bit, but no tears came out. The others were quite concerned for a moment. But this moment soon passed. Thankfully, the former arguements about peoples' cocks and pants were forgotten.

However, now their minds were free to speculate on the ordeal ahead. The hairy nurse had already begun to go about her business, squeezing balls the way other people might squeeze a pod of peas until it opens. That last remark must have caught Feeler Halloran's ears, as did most things with a pervy tinge. He came out and berated Jim and Richard, for no obvious reason other than they were nearest to him, and he could not be bothered to find the real culprit. For one ghastly second Jim imagined Feeler Halloran might give them the cane. So they might have their arses fondled and stung. And, along with having their gonads grappled, this would set the seal on a day of appalling humiliation. Jim again revealed his lack of years when he related his thoughts to his companion. Already excessively worried, his nerves frazzled by the assault of Duke, Richard fainted as they made their way into the medical room. Those medical staff present laughed, while Feeler Halloran came up and grinned that stupid smirk of his. The medical staff proved to be as diplomatic as Jim. For they told Richard people usually fainted after the cough and drop, not before. This of course finally did for Richard as far as his nerves were concerned. He squealed in pain throughout the ceremony and had to be helped out afterward.

The scene made Jim feel uncomfortable. But the weirdness of the event soon overcame that. Having total strangers stare at him, and having the strangest one squeeze his bollocks, was quite interesting, he thought. To his alarm, he found he was quite enjoying the sensation. Even though, as he glanced down at the nurse, he could still have sworn she was a man in drag. Luckily Feeler Halloran had left the room. And, thankfully, Jim's treatment was over before any erection could get started.

The whole cough and drop episode was never mentioned ever again. Not because it was too traumatic, Jim and Richard just forgot. They did develop an obscure phobia each however. Richard was forever allergic to hairy female nurses who looked like men. As this was so specific he only activated this phobia once in the rest of his life. Jim, meanwhile, developed a marked aversion to a particular brand of cough sweets, known as 'cough drops.'. As he hated cough sweets anyway, his phobia was never activated. But you only had to mention the phrase, 'cough drops', and his eyes would become frightened while his mouth formed into a scowl.

Reincarnation Terminal

I thought of life as a journey, a journey that could go anywhere. Although one day this journey would end, a long time away, and I would be dead. Not much of a belief really, but then I could never really be bothered with belief. My tastes have always been simple. I do not ignore what goes on around me. There is so much, so much activity, so much talk and so much knowledge. It is all contradictory and confusing. I suppose I believe in what I have seen and done. So how could I believe much ?

I do not claim I know better than anyone. I have been told we all cling to different ideas according to our own experience. Well, if you want to look at it that way, you can. I have never clung to anything. Maybe I am too comfortable, maybe I have not been desperate enough, or maybe I do not feel things deeply enough.

This is about the limit of my speculation on life. People have called me stupid for it. I have even been ridiculed on occaison. But on my talking to them, I find out they are just as stupid as me. They have nothing that could be called an answer, because none of us can be bothered with the question. We just want to get on with our lives. It is like that a lot, I find. People are just waiting to see what happens. And they will not believe it until they experience it.

I could go on waffling I suppose. But I was thinking these kind of things as I was sitting on the train. I was going to the airport. My ex-wife was waiting for me. We had been married ten years and divorced for four. I thought we had moved on since then. That was what she kept telling me. She insisted on breaking it off with me, but she insisted on seeing me regularly. I never wanted to do it. But I always liked her. I was comfortable with her. I know the divorce was as much my fault as her desire. I did not see my mistakes until later. And I did not want to go back to them. But I never could resist going back to see her. She always went on about my habitual laziness, and my boring qualities. But I always wanted to see her.

I was not sure that it was such a good idea, maybe. I felt maybe I was going back to the scene of an accident, when I had already recovered and put it behind me. Yet she was insistent, she was alway insistent, and I never had any resistence. I had been talking to her more than usual lately. I felt like I was being drawn in again. She was going to say something to me, something important. Yet I did not want to think about it. I thought I was better off as I was now, to be honest. But, my curiosity was piqued, as they say. No doubt she would explain my feelings away for me, like she always used to. She would say I was in a situation over my head. I hated this, because I thought she was right.

That was the meeting I was heading for, and it set off my usual middling speculations about life.

Life carried me as a passenger, just like the train. And I was being led again, I do not know entirely where. What is the difference between living a life and and leading a life anyway ? Saying one is active and one is passive is not enough. People pretend they are active, but they seem to have little real control over their lives. Anyway, the train was delayed. There was a bad accident on the line. Being curious, or bored, by nature, I took a look. It was very bad. Some carriages had left the rails. They seemed to have twisted around like a rope, as they slid down the grass embankment. Their momentum had taken them through a perimeter fence, onto the road that ran parallel to the tracks. Someone always says something about 'luck' in these accidents. This time it was lucky there was not much road traffic around, otherwise the casualties could have been worse. It was not so lucky for the train driver though, or for a lot of the passengers. Flashing lights and people in bright protective clothing clambered over the wreckage in silence. They were serious and methodical. I could see them carrying stretchers. There was too much carnage for my liking. It left me with a queasy feeling. I never liked such scenes, even on the telly.

But of course I found it difficult to tear my gaze away. I could not help but linger I suppose, since we were forced to evacuate our train as well. I felt guilty, but I carried on looking. I thought I would be sick maybe. I wished I could have, in fact. I did not like all these feelings running around inside me. I wanted to get rid of them. This nausea just increased. That should have warned me. That, and the fact the emergency services did not impede me, as I went for a closer look. They usually throw a barrier around these events, I know that much at least. Instead they let me wander around, preoccupied with their task in hand. I could view areas of the disaster they had not reached. Areas where corpses still lay crushed and bloody, including my own bemused body. I saw it being lifted onto a stretcher before it was covered up and taken away.

There should have been shock. But I felt so strange anyway, I doubt it would have made much difference. Now

I realised why no one had paid me any particular attention. That circumstance was too common in my life to give me much of a clue however. The sight of my own corpse did suggest, to someone as basic as me, that I was probably was dead. Yet my feelings were still unsure. It was all so bizarre. The scene was not part of me, and here I was walking through it, as if I stepped into a telly programme.

Then, briefly, my perspective shifted. A crowd of faces looked down on me with concern. Then I saw them from behind. I saw all their behinds as they crouched over. I believe I must have shown some sign of life. Whatever it was, it was brief. For the crowd soon stood up and covered my body again.

Where was I supposed to go now ? I knew I could not communicate with those around before I even tried. You might as well try talking to a photograph. It became very lonely. I just hung around with the emergency services. I went back to the airport with them. I thought I should better escort my body, because I did not know what else to do. My body was taken to some hospital facilities back at the airport. Funny, I thought, I never realised there would be hospital facilities at an airport. But there are so many things I do not know. I found the light and the crowds at this place reassuring. My body was left in a room of bright lights. I waited beside it for something to happen. And something did. An official person led my ex-wife into the room. They looked at me woodenly then went to sit down. My ex-wife began moving back and foward in her seat. Then she bowed her head as the sobs were released. I could not hear anything. But her whole body seemed to expand as the breath was pulled out of her. I was quite surprised at this. I always thought she would be more in control. It seemed she really did love me, and that was another surprise. The poor official did his best to be comforting. He put an awkward arm around her. I must admit this little scene really affected me. A surge of sympathy just pulled itself out of me. And she stopped sobbing. She looked up, as if a person stood before her. Well he was, at least I was. But she could not see me. I fancied she had caught my feelings. Since she continued to look up, then around, in a quizzical manner. Then the kind official, who was begining to irritate me a bit, began his official symapathetic murmur about death etc, and led her away. I know he was being considerate, but that was my ex-wife he was leading away. I know she loved me now. And I had to get through to her somehow, to let her know I knew, give her some kind of sign.

I followed the official and my ex-wife, talking, shouting and gesticulating like an idiot as I did so. It made no impact. We all marched down innumerable passage ways. There were people everywhere. I thought we would never find the exit. I assumed she had her car somewhere. Finally we entered a raised walkway. This led to some kind of compound. Was it a car park ? a main hall ? a concourse ? or what ? Its dimensions were very strange, elusive, for I could not make out its shape. My ex-wife and the official continued walking. But they picked up speed constantly. I could barely keep up with them. Then I began lagging behind. No matter how fast I walked I just dragged further and further behind. I saw them enter what looked like a tunnel, two tiny specks disappearing from view. This happened right at the end of my field of vision, they were that far away now. So while I thought they disappeared I could not believe it was so. I ran and ran. The ground felt like a treadmill, continually dragging at my progress. I did not want to lose them. I knew I would be lost myself if I did so. But when I got the end of the compound there was nothing there, literally nothing. It was frightening. I wanted to follow but there was no way now . I tried. But there was no solid ground to walk upon. As I took a step into that void my legs were pushed back. I still needed solid ground to walk on. Otherwise I might float off into chaos, somewhere. I was fairly inexperienced at being dead. Still, I thought the afterlife would not look like another dreary rail or air terminal. Blandness and boredom were eternal it seemed. I was too scared to go off into the void. I thought I might fall, and go on falling forever, I just knew it.

So I retraced my steps, back along that monotonous walkway. And a tedious trudge it was too. Going back was as much of an effort as my attempt to leave. I felt like dropping down and lying there. A certain pointlessness took hold of me. My motion was automatic, ponderous. But then I could see no point in stopping either. A dim light winked in front of me. This told me of my objective, that crowded waiting room I tried to escape earlier. What an uninteresting dilemma, caught between a bland hole and a bland hall. As the features of the hall became recognisable again, I immediately regretted my decision not to lie down. But something was different, something elusive. It bothered me. An impression formed itself. People began looking at me, as well as rushing around in that confused, commuter manner of theirs. I appeared to be substantial, I thought I might be alive. But unfortuately not, I say unfortunately, I did not care really. I just thought that getting out of a terminal is easier when you are alive. The dimensions of the hall itself reminded me. They were peculiar. Walls and ceilings curved around at unsightly angles. Innumerable corridors, similar to the one I had taken, pockmarked its fabric. What did these corridors lead to ? I guessed I knew, other innumerable corridors, leading ultimately to nothingness. I might as well hang around in the hall. Until I thought of what to do next.

Bright lights glared from somewhere. I tried looking at the ceiling, but it always eluded my gaze. People continued wandering around, unconcerned and apathetic. A few did acknowledge my prescence with a raised eyebrow or a quick wave. It was just like an airport lounge in life, I knew it. That same sense of bland timelessness. Thousands of strangers everywhere, the paraphenalia of the airport lounge, with departures, tickets, check in and flight times, it was all there. Though I could not read it. Whenever I tried I could not make sense of any signs. I thought maybe I was a shortsighted ghost. But no matter how close I went to these signs, their message always remained blurred. Nothing was clear, the story of my life. I had hoped the afterlife would not be like that. Imagine not being able to express yourself, nor understand, for eternity. Then I glimpsed a portion of terror so overwhelming it constricted me. Imagine being stuck in a waiting room forever, never knowing what was going on around. I lost my focus entirely. The airport lounge began dissolving before me. But I started to assume I was being queasy again, as my wife accused me in life. I struggled to hold myself together. I had a notion I might dissolve myself. So I should recover enough poise to be able to sit down, my ambition did not stretch much further. Then, from the corner of my eye, I saw a figure detach itself from the general mess of the crowd. It strode purposefully toward me. I tried to pretend it was not there, as I knew it would only come up and talk to me.

The it became a he. I recognised the figure of this someone, someone who reminded me of a relative I once had. This relative was a drunken, bad tempered old man who smelled of tobacco and swore in every sentence. That was my uncle Chris. But this man before me, although dressed like my uncle Chris, in a dog tooth jacket and corduroy trousers, was just too nice looking. He was also clean, he had no angry lines across his face. He smiled instead of scowling. And he looked tanned instead of flushed. By the time I realised all this he had introduced himself as my uncle Chris. Of course I needed persuading of this fact. I reluctantly asked for confirmation.

" Look, nephew, you should stop being so suspicious. This is how I look. This is how I am, in this part of existence... It is me raised to my full potential if you like, without the drinking, the temper and the cynicism..."

" And the violence..."

" Yes, yes, and the violence too."

" I'm still not convinced. I agree you look well. But you look too well."

" What's so bad about that ? "

" Well it's not the uncle Chris I remember."

" Right, right. I suppose I'll have to remind of things only you and I know about eh ? "

" It might be a start."

" Such as things that happened when you were a child."

" Sounds fair to me."

" Okay, you remember I used to have a hairy mole on my stomach, just above the trouser line. You used to be fascinated by it. I was always showing it you..."

" Fascinated ? I was terrified. And you knew I was terrified. You kept showing me it to scare me, because that made you laugh. I got so scared I used to hide behind the armchair."

" That's true isn't it. I'm sorry about that. I thought it was all a bit of a laugh. I knew you were scared but I couldn't resist it."

" And you forced me to smoke cigarettes. "

" I did not, I merely offered you one."

" And I can't have been more than five years old at the time."

" I thought I was just indulging your childish curiosity."

" You were hoping to see me cough because that made you laugh as well."

" But you didn't cough, did you ? "

" No, I was sick all over the carpet. Then auntie Vee came in and gave me a good hiding."

" Yes I thought that was a laugh at the time. Sorry, I was just a big kid myself at the time."

" A big alcoholic kid."

" Yes, yes. That's true. I forget sometimes that good old Vee had a temper on her like a volcano. Mine paled by comparison."

" And you hardly ever gave me pocket money."

" Well, I was drunk a lot. But I do remember being quite generous to you sometimes."

" You always told me to go outside and play..."

" That's not too bad..."

" In the road."

" You know I did, didn't I. I remember now. But you know how alcoholics are..."

" Yes, you always smelled."

" Yes, yes, but I was quite fond of you really. If you remember, I always used to buy you sweets."

" Which you always kept in your pockets for ages. So when you gave them to me, they always had hairs, or bits of fluff, on them."

" Ha ha ha, yes ,that's right."

" Well, I need no more convincing. I suppose you are my uncle Chris."

" You suppose right."

" And I did quite like you as well, in a way."

" Don't look so disappointed. We are kindred souls you know."

" How's that ? "

" Well, we are family of course. And we have similar temperaments..."

" But I was never an alkie."

" Oh no. You liked the odd drink, until you lost count."

" It was just a bit of enjoyment."

" That's what I used to think myself. But my enjoyment got out of hand, just like yours. Anyway, I'm not here to discuss the perils of drinking...I am, I suppose you could call me your guide, the man who shows you around."

" But there's nothing much to see here."

" True, and I don't know that much about this place, but I have been here awhile already, and I've picked up one or two things."

" Such as ? "

" Don't walk down those corridors again. They lead nowhere, literally."

" I don't get it."

" You won't. Your soul will simply disappear. I don't know what will happen to it, if you'll cease to exist, but I don't think it's worthwhile finding out."

I remembered the big, black hole I saw, and I shuddered.

" Fair enough. But do I have to stick around here all the time ? "

I waved my arm around to indicate the big, bland hall we found ourselves in.

" I don't want to shuffle around for eternity, walking in circles."

" Well that's up to you. If you leave, or if you stay, depends on how much you know, how much you recognise. That can offer you a clue."

" Is that why all the information screens are blurred ? "

" Yes, possibly."

" Although I can make out more now."

" You might be learning already."

" Maybe. This is a kind of waiting room in the afterlife, yes, before we go off."

Uncle Chris nodded vigorously, but said nothing.

" Arrivals are the newly dead like me. Departures are the ones who are going to be reincarnated again ? "

" That's quick. You figured it out in no time. It took me ages to work that one out. Although all these terms I'm using are just figures of speech. I don't seem to know what words mean anymore."

" Really ? "

" Yes, it feels like we've always been here talking."

" But you died five years before me."

" I know."

" Strange, you know I never really believed in reincarnation when I was alive. "

" You must have accepted it at some level."

" Oh sure. I mean it's an interesting idea, but so is perpetual motion, anti-matter, mediumship, E.S.P, I could go on..."

" Please don't, we may be here a while yet. My guess is all the concepts you mention might work as possibilities."

" You mean anything's possible so it exists, somewhere."

" That's an interesting way of putting it. You know I quite regret some of the thoughts I had about you in life...I thought you were a bit slow to grasp ideas sometimes."

" I was. People called me laid back, when they were being kind. When they were being critical they called me dozy."

" I know you what you mean. A lot of people called me wild, when they really meant bad tempered."

I noticed then, that some parts of the departure area sloped downwards after the gates were passed.

" Why do some departure areas slope down like that. We're all waiting to catch the plane, aren't we ? "

Uncle Chris shook his head solemnly.

" Very few people here actually catch the plane, from what I gather. I think it is difficult, it appears to take you to another level..."

" The next plane of existence."

" Well if you want to express it by a bad pun, yes. As for the downward sloping departure areas, I would avoid them, unless you want to become a lower form of life."

" An animal you mean. Well that might not be so bad, if I was a chimpanzee or a dolphin."

" But their consciousness is less developed than ours, for all their intelligence. It would still be a step down. It would leave you at the mercy of the physical world, with all its dangers. And, if you have to avoid physical danger all the time, it might leave you remaining completely static as regards your soul's development. Plus, there is the further danger of you slipping further down, becoming a lower form of animal life than in your previous existence. Some people take this option, and good luck to them. Perhaps they find happiness grazing the fields or stalking their prey. But me, I think when you reach the human level it gives you responsibilities. You have to go on and develop yourself, no matter what pain or boredom is involved, no matter what mistakes you make."

" That sounds pretty admirable to me."

" Yes, I've been telling it to myself for God knows how long, er, no disrespect to anyone. I still don't quite believe it, that's if I'm supposed to of course."

" Why should you be supposed to believe anything ? "

" Well, it's like the shape of this airport lounge we're in. I think it's like that because it suits us to be in an airport lounge, in terms of what we are. We're like water finding its own level. We've found the kind of situation after death that suits us. Who knows ? for others it may be the fires of hell or the choirs of heaven. Some people might cease to exist because they don't want to exist anymore."

" It suits us to be in an airport lounge ? "

" Perhaps."

" An airport lounge in the afterlife ? Can't you be more specific."

" I am trying."

" It's trying my understanding, that's for sure."

" It's all part of the process, if there is a process."

" Uncle, you keep riddling me. Is that it ? What you're trying to say is we've got to figure out the riddle ? "

" Hmmm, a riddle might be as close as we get to the truth."

" Really. This reminds me of the kind of conversation I used to have with my wife. Every time I said something like - the Arctic is cold - or - we've sent men to the moon - she'd say - you don't know that for sure, that's just an assumption, that's what other people tell you..."

" You were married ? really ? Funny, I never thought of you as someone who would marry."

" Thanks a lot."

" No disrespect intended."

" I was on my way to meet her actually, after I hadn't seen her for ages as well."

" Doesn't sound like much of a marriage."

" We were divorced."

" Oh."

" It was to be our first meeting after…"

" Did you have kids ? "

" No. I wanted them but she didn't."

" Shame."

" I'm not bothered really, come to think of it. I realise now what I half-guessed then. She was going to want to get back together. And I would've agreed, even though I know it wouldn't have worked out, and I wouldn't have been happy. I just could not resist her."

" Dying seems a bit of a drastic way of getting out of a situation like that."

" I didn't intend to die. It's not like I committed suicide. I was caught up in a train accident…"

" I thought I heard a racket going on somewhere."

" Yes, well, that racket stopped me going back to a mess of problems I had escaped once already."

" Isn't that what you wanted ? "

" Of course not."

" Sounds to me like you enjoy a troubled relationship."

" Maybe then, but not now. You know I can feel the pull she had on me. She was like a magnet. And once I was caught in her attraction, I would've been stuck on her forever."

" Like an iron filing."

" Yes. It was me that was the problem. I had moved on in my life, and I was about to go back…"

" Well you've certainly moved on now."

" But not given up."

" Glad to hear it."

" I want to get out of here.'"

" It might not be that easy."

" I don't care. Look at this place."

" I have been looking, for a way out myself. But I seem to spend a lot of time just standing around. I think of something and then I forget. I seem to lack motivation. That's why I was so pleased when you turned up. As someone newly dead, I thought you might still have fresh ideas on how to go about getting out of a place like this."

" Eh ? how do you mean ? "

" Well you went on holidays, didn't you ? You travelled to new places and enjoyed yourself . "

" No, not really. I never took many holidays when I was alive. I couldn't afford them, I always seemed to be in debt. I think I know what you mean though. I'm going to try and get on that plane."

" From what I've seen, very few people actually catch the plane."

" So where do the rest of them go ? "

" Downward mostly, like you've just seen."

" That can't be all ? "

" It's a popular choice."

" There must be another way."

We looked around, we walked around, as energetically as we could. Lethargy was constanly out to get us. Eventually we did spy other exits, exits so mundane as to be unnoticeable, in the normal scheme of things. They led off to the car park or the train station.

" What about those, " I asked.

" They must be for people who go back to become other people."

" Why do you say that ? "

" Just a hunch."

" I think I agree. Just like you can take a train anywhere, or drive anywhere, in life, so you can do the same here. Most car or train journeys are boring anyway, so we won't change much."

" Not all those journeys are boring, just like in life. We might end up somewhere we don't know much about."

" Like a day trip, as opposed to a commuter journey you mean."

" I was thinking more of getting lost in a strange town."

" Well neither of us want that."

" Yes, maybe we could get something that's half and half."

" A compromise reincarnation you mean."

" Yes, er what does that mean ? "

" I'm not sure, but it sounded right."

I looked at the people who were leaving by the lateral exits. They were not as popular as the downward departures to the animal kingdom. But a fair amount of people were trying this option. No one looked particular happy to be going this way, however.. They all had Monday morning expressions on their faces. It was as if they knew they had work to do but did not want to go and do it.

We watched in silence. It was quite soothing looking at these people going about their business. They had made their decisions, or they had decisions made for them, I do not know which. They started looking like waves on a beach. I cannot say why I should have thought of that, when I was just comparing them to commuters. But that new image now seemed appropriate. For I now became aware that some of them were not actually walking through the exits. As they approached the automatic doors their bodies dispersed, as if they had turned to water. Parts of these watery people flowed out one exit, then another, or perhaps more. Certain individuals dispersed into tiny droplets and completely disappeared before my gaze. Uncle Chris was just as puzzled as me. But then something occurred to him.

" You remember what I said about water finding its own level. Well I think these people's souls are like water. They are putting a little bit back here, a little bit back there, or wherever. I think they're hedging their bets personally. They want to try more than one option in the new life. Though I could be talking a complete load of dog turds here."

" You certainly could," I said, " But it seems everything in this place is worth bearing in mind."

" Just as in life."

" No, not as in life, well, yes, maybe it should be, but it doesn't work the same. I'm getting confused."

" You'd better watch yourself. If you get too confused you might just disperse yourself, just blend into the fabric of this place. I've seen it happen. It's what this building is made out of. We are standing on innumerable souls right now."

" Ugh."

" Don't be squeamish."

" Can't help it. Though I am trying not to be."

" Good, good."

" And I've had an idea."

" It takes the afterlife to develop your intellect I notice."

" Is that a joke ? It doesn't matter though. I'm thinking this place, with all its fixtures and fittings, is built from volunteers."

" You mean they give their existence for others ? "

" If you like, yes. Although I'm sure it's more like a biological process, like symbo, symblo, symbil..."

" Symbolism, you mean, yes I see. In life a symbol represents a cluster of feelings and ideas. It takes these features and gives them back to those who experienced them originally, but separately, then they're given back as a whole, which gives them a new experience. "

" No, actually I was going to say symbiosis. You know where one organism feeds off another, who in turn feeds off that organism."

Uncle Chris looked disappointed.

" I'm afraid that idea doesn't do justice to our situation at all."

I was puzzled by this, and a little annoyed.

" I think maybe you're pumping me for answers to help with your own predicament."

" So, where's the injustice in that ? "

" It seems a little cynical."

" It's only cynical if we don't help each other out."

" That, that is symbiosis."

Uncle Chris frowned.

" I have to say I think we need something more complex than that."

" We always seem to need something more complex. This is what I'm begining to find a bit depressing. We never seem to know enough to do anything. It's just like my life was... Always someone would come up and say, ' Well, you think you're an expert on certain areas, but you know nothing about this,' and this person would tell me something that would undermine all my convictions, so I wouldn't feel sure of anything anymore..."

" You were a bit over sensitive, weren't you. Why couldn't you ignore these people. They're usually smartarses, with no real ideas themselves..."

" What ? and just plod along in my own way, never learning anything."

" But you can't know everything at once, not all the time anyway."

" That's just the kind of ridiculous statement that used to get on my nerves. It reminded me there was always something to learn, always something to do, always something to know. And it all stretched out before me, huge and confusing. I never knew where to start."

" So start anywhere."

" That was never very reassuring, and I still don't think it is. It seems like I have infinity to choose from and it takes an eternity to decide."

" Look, what makes you think it's so different for anyone else ? People just deal with it in their own fashion, that's all. Infinity and eternity are always there, they're not going to go anywhere, are they ? "

" Maybe, I don't know."

" Proper little pilgrim, aren't we. Now nephew, I think you may be right, of course. But all this speculation is only ensuring we stand around. You're right, I do need your help, but you have to give it wllingly. In return I might be able to guide you. So I will help you. But I'll walk away if you keep speculating and moaning..."

The idea never occurred to me. It was out of the question as soon as it was mentioned.

" No Uncle, I don't want that, and you know it. I believe we should get out of this place, now. After all, isn't that what airports are for, to direct us on a journey to somewhere else."

" You're a true nephew of mine. But you realise we will have to explore some of these corridors. We will run the risk of getting lost."

I shuddered at this. Being trapped in those interminable passageways again, the prospect alone seemed to drain my energy.

" I must admit I'm a bit wary of that, scared even."

" Me too. I always have been.. But at least I've admitted it."

" Do you think we can find some other exits ? "

" We might not be able to. We may have to settle for those exits that go down to the animal kingdom, or the ones that lead to another earthly existence. Getting the plane seems beyond us at the moment. We must explore the corridors. It's a case of needs must as the devil drives..."

A cold wind sprang up from nowhere as my uncle said this.

" A cold wind in a airport lounge. How very inappropriate."

" Maybe it's a reaction to your inappropriate remark, Uncle."

" There may be something in that. From now on, I will only make inappropriate remarks at appropriate moments. Where shall we go, Nephew ? "

And so we began our search for a decent way out. I suggested to Uncle Chris that I write down the events we had experienced, and any further ones that could happen. For I had made the discovery that you could write in the afterlife. It was a pointless discovery. But then I had a feeling it would prove useful. We bought a writing pad readily enough, from a shop that refused cash transactions. Apparently money is too clumsy for the afterlife. There was some kind of credit arrangement however. Which a smiling woman behind a counter made for me. No one particularly understands these arrangements, but they involve favours being carried out for someone, at a later date.

My uncle suggested that my writing materials be used to aid our memories. That was the meaning of my action I was looking for. The act of writing down was said to make memory stronger. And we felt it would benefit us once we got out of this place. Though how this would work we were not sure. And so, like two intrepid reporters of the afterlife, we went off, and then...

That is my first available memory. Or is it someone else's ? It may be just a fantasy I project back on myself. For the first definite memory I have is of being pushed out of familiar surroundings. I can't say where these were presicely. But there were warm and comfortable. I was pushed into a small room, full of dull objects that made ugly sounds. Strange shapes danced around me and dizziness overcome me. I felt pain for the first time I can recall, and it was horrible. I was in a horrible, squalid room, full of discomfort. But in these circumstances I felt some kind of familiarity. I knew I could grow and progress in this environment. I had been born.

XYSY GLYXSY VII

The Zug Zug Wars

(Part One)

Knowledge on the legendary human race is scarce. Some argue their existence was a hoax. But others argue they were all powerful and all wise beings, who messed things up by going a bit stupid. Whatever, documentary evidence of their exploits is rare. We do have these recordings, that purport to tell of their relations with a race of gelatine creatures, known as the Zug Zug. It all sounds a bit perverted to me. Hopefully we can learn from the exploits of these decadent creatures. Of course there are some who say the human race did not exist at all, that these recordings are merely the demented outpourings of a dysfunctional, delusional narrator. But we will not listen to them..

As the shuttle cruised into Jupiter's atmosphere, Sargeant Bloodlust watched ruefully. His escape pod was picked up by General Fratricide, on board the mother ship Homebase. They had failed in their attempt to reach that strange vessel yet again. It looked like a huge bowl to the Sargeant's eyes. This impression was compounded by the sight of its companion craft, which looked like a giant spoon.

His pod was scooped into the mother ship Homebase. Then Bloodlust presented himself before the General.

" So, failed again, Bloodlust."

" Well I got nearer this time, Sir."

" Close is not good enough. We need to make contact with that ship. It may contain intelligent life."

" No intelligent life would build vehicles that look like kitchen utensils."

" I tend to concur with the General."

" For Saturn's sake, Professor Nerdberger, stop creeping up on us like that."

" Sorry General. But you do remember that giant spaceship we encountered, that looked like a giant pepperpot..."

" That was a giant pepperpot," said the Sargeant, " It was meant to advertise the Irritant Pepper Company."

" I don't mean that incident. I mean the one we encountered by Saturn's rings."

" Another giant pepperpot, you mean ? "

" Well it looked like a pepperpot. But we believe it was a reconnaissance craft."

" To do what ? see if it can spray pepper in our faces, to make us sneeze to death."

" Your attempt at humour does you no credit. We may be on the brink of a first contact here, and, frankly, we don't want it spoilt by a sarcastic Sargeant."

" You can't let him talk to me like that, General."

" I'm afraid I can, Sargeant. We all have our orders. Making contact takes priority here."

" But Sir, that's what we've been doing the past three weeks.."

" And not succeeding, I note."

314

" Shut up Nerdberger, these aliens are proving mightily elusive," said the General, " Every time we get close to them they avoid us further."

" Maybe you should try a subtle approach," said Nerdberger.

" Like sending a disguised bomb over ? "

" No Sargeant, I don't."

" Then what do you have in mind ? " said the General.

" Broadcast on all radio frequencies to make contact."

" We've tried that."

" Yes, but ' Aliens, you are trepassing on private property,' does not give out the message of peace and goodwill somehow. And we need to get a bit of galactic goodwill going here."

" So what do you suggest ? " asked the General.

" Something like - ' Hello, mighty creatures from distant stars. We ask only for peace, goodwill, and any advanced technology you've got going."

" Really, " said the General, " They'll believe we're a bunch of wimps."

" Yes, why don't we fire a few missiles at them, along with the message, something like - 'Aliens, if you start messing us about, we'll stick some more of these up the bum of your ship.' "

" I'm horrified at you, Sargeant. This is a delicate moment in human history, one that could have profound consequences for eternity. We don't want to alienate the aliens."

" Besides, we have already tried firing misslies at them, they didn't seem to work," said the General.

" Sir, correct me if I'm wrong, but haven't we just lost the Titan colony, in suspicious circumstances. And then we have these illegal aliens hovering around. It all looks a bit too fishy for me."

" Merely a coincidence," said the Professor.

" We did receive some radio transmissions that said ' Help we're being attacked,' " said the General.

" Probably just a prank."

" Some prank," said the Sargeant.

" They're not doing anything wrong, Sargeant. They're not even trespassing."

" Not officially anyway ", said the Genral ruefully.

" They are trespassers. This is our solar system after all."

" We don't own it, Sargeant."

" But we look after it," said the General.

" Exactly," said the Sargeant, " And I don't see any other intelligent life forms around here."

" Certainly not in this room," joked the Professor.

" Sargeant, and Professor, we have to get on. Do any of you have any ideas ? "

" Shouldn't we refer the matter back to Earth, " said the Professor indecisively.

" Why ? " asked the General.

" Because it's policy."

" You know they take ages before they come to a decision."

" That's just the speed of inter-solar communication, General. It can't be helped."

" Yes it can. The Earth politicians take ages anyway, regardless of the speed of communication."

" So what do you suggest we do, General ? "

" Bring in a few heavily-armed battle cruisers, surround the bowl and the spoon, and then find out what the aliens are after."

" Hear hear," said the Sargeant.

" But supposing we can't communicate with them."

" Isn't that your problem, Professor. Show them pictures of triangles, or cubes, or whatever. You're always blabbing on about how geometric forms are universal anyway."

They were rudely interrupted by a Private.

" Sir, General, sir."
" What is it ? Gawkins."
" The spoon and the bowl are moving toward us."
" Put it up on the Viddy Screen, Ratbag."

Private Ratbag activated a huge screen that covered one wall of the room.

" Meathook."
" Yes sir."
" Make sure everyone is put on alert."
Shall I turn the muzak off then,sir."
" Please, " said the Professor, " It's the defintion of banality."
" I like Laurence Lugworm and the Tinny Tannoys, " said the Sargeant.
" Really, I thought it was Codpiece's Greatest Hits."
" Come on now people, look sharp, " said the General.
" Maybe they want to communicate with us. They probably have all kinds of technological goodies they want to bestow on us," said the Professor."
" In return for what ? "
" I don't know, maybe they'll find the human spirit fascinating."
" Really," said the General sarcastically, " I suppose we'll be an adventure holiday for them."
" Or a bit of rough," said the Sargeant, " If they don't stick us in a zoo first."

" They're transmitting to us, General," said Ratbag.

" What are they saying ? "

" I don't know, it's all pictures."

" You mean geometric shapes," said the Professor.

" Yeah, like childrens' drawings of squares and triangles."

" That, I suppose, is what you've been going on about," said the General, in a moment of reluctant admiration.

" Meathook, do you have any geometrical designs you could send back," said the Professor.

" Why ? are we setting them a maths exam ? "

" Just do what he says," said the General, "Don't worry about it sounding stupid," he added unhelpfully, " Ratbag, prepare to transmit further responses."

There followed a few hours of communication. Pictures of various shapes were transmitted between the ships. General Fratricide, Sargeant Bloodlust, Professor Nerdberger and Private Meathook kept themselves busy collating the results.

" Incredible," said the Professor, " we have reams and reams of comm   unciation."

" So ? " said Meathook.

" Yes, what do these reams all mean ? Nerdberger," said the General.

" Yeah, we send them a trapezoid, they send us one, they send a parallelogram, we send them one, we send a tetrahedron they send us one, they send a rhomboid, we..."

" Yes, shut up Meathook. The point, Nerdberger, is we've been swapping shapes for hours, so what does it all add up to, " said the General.

" A lot of shapes."

" Don't evade the answer."

" I'm not, I still need to collate."

" How long do you need ? "

" Until I can think up an answer."

" You must have some idea."

" I think they're very geometrically minded."

" Is that the best you can come up with ? Can't you take a guess what it all means ? "

" Erm...I'm not sure, I'll need more information."

" You mean more shapes," said the Sargeant.

" Er, yes."

" How is more of the same going to make things clearer ? when you don't know anything to start with," said the General.

" Every little helps."

" Really, so what, in your estimation, is the purpose of their visit here ? "

" Sightseeing ? "

" Come on Nerdberger."

" Shopping."

" You'll have to do better."

" Maybe they just fancied a change of scenery."

" The scenery in deep space isn't much to communicate home about. Really General, this is a waste of time, " said the Sargeant.

" I tend to concur, " said the General, " Meathook, what do you think ? Stop yawning will you."

" It's boring, sir, with all due respect."

" I think we should try another ploy."

" Yes, blast them out of space," said Bloodlust.

" With laser cannon," said Meathook.

" No, we should show that we are intelligent, constructive creatures," said Nerdberger.

" Well it looks like we'll be here a long time," said the General.

" It will be worth your while, General. It will be worth all humanities' while."

" They're not the ones stuck out here next to a big dish and spoon," moaned Meathook.

" We have no proof of anything, Professor. You're assuming these aliens are like Christian missionaries bringing civilised ways to primitive tribes," said Bloodlust.

" And look at the damage they did," said the General.

" Surely it's worth the risk, " said Nerdberger.

" Okay. So what approach do you suggest now ? "

" Well. We've tried visual imagery, and got limited success. Maybe we should now try aural imagery."

" Ugh, like oral sex you mean,." said Meathook squeamishly.

" No, I mean aural as in audio."

" But we've already tried talking to them," said Bloodlust.

" I mean music, Sargeant," said Nerdberger, " Have we got any music, apart from Laurence Lugworm and the Tinny Tannoys."

" What's wrong with them ? "

" I am not playing muzak to aliens, it might start a war."

" Sir, can we play Laurence Lugworm ? "

" I think we shall have to go along with the Professor, unfortunately. "

" Thank you, General. Have we got any proper music ? "

" Not really."

" Why not. Music is enjoyed by all. It can soothe the savage soul."

" This is a military transport, Nerdberger, we need savage souls. We have little time for luxuries."

" Not even personal recordings, Gemeral ? owned by your soldiers. "

" But most of the stuff they listen to is crap, ahem, no disrespect people."

" Well it'll be better than nothing."

" It probably won't be."

" But we must try something."

" Oh alright then. Meathook, see what music you can collect from the boys and girls."

Meathook disappeared, then came back again with only three computer disks.

" Is that all you can get ? " said Nerdberger.

" It's all that's available, Professor. "

" I told you this was a troop ship, Nerdberger. Enjoyment is not a high priority here you know, " said the General.

" Hear hear," added the Sargeant.

" Well it's better than nothing I suppose. Let's see what we've got here - ' Sponge Face and the Feckless Make Whale Noises,' ' Great Factory Hooters Of Our Time, by Norbert Tranquiliser,' and ' Rumblin Stomachs, by the Rumblin Stomachs'. Quantum preserve us, these aliens are going to think we're two satellites short of a solar system."

" I like the Rumblin Stomachs," said the Sargeant.

" And what kind of music do they play ? "

" Physiological Funky Noise."

" Ugh, well we'll save that until last. What about Sponge Face and the Feckless ? "

" Hardcore Nuclear Fission Rap Rock."

That's the penultimate one," said the Professor.

" Don't tell us you're a Norbert Tranquiliser fan," said the General.

" He has his moments," said Nerdberger.

" Yeah, most of them in the toilet, " said Meathook.

" I think ' Great Factory Hooters,' is one of the most ethereal compositions of all time."

" Unreal, certainly," said the General.

" It can seem a little discordant to the uneducated."

" It's just a load of sirens with muffled orchestra backing" said the Sargeant.

" It's far more subtle than that, Sargeant."

" It's music for obssessives, and, er..." said Meathook.

" Yes ? " said Nerdberger.

" Nerds."

Nerdberger looked offended.

" May I remind you, if it wasn't for us nerds and obssessives, you'd still be sitting in your back gardens, playing with fireworks."

" What ? " said Meathook.

" No we wouldn't," said Bloodlust, " We'd probably be in the army."

" the point is, us nerds, I mean us dedicated obssessives, are the professionals who got you where you are today."

" Yeah, stuck out in empty space," said Meathook.

" Even if we were in our back gardens, we still wouldn't be afraid of fighting aliens, " said Bloodlust.

" That's enough now. Let the Professor try this farce, I mean this plan," said the General.

Nerdberger looked annoyed.

" Let's get this transmission set up, shall we."

" You heard him, Meathook," said the General.

The Norbert Tranquiliser recording was transmitted in its entirety.

" Something's wrong they're firing rockets, they're getting away from us again," said the General.

" That's the reaction Norbert Tranquiliser has on most intelligent people," said Bloodlust.

" So how do you explain your own dislike then ? " said Nerdberger, bitterly.

" Ignore him Sargeant, he's just upset...Nerdberger, put something else on, quickly," said the General.

" I don't understand. I thought they'd appreciate the intricacies of 'Factory Hooters.'

" Apparently not."

" Okay, Private Meathook, stop the transmission please."

" Thank the Cosmos for that," said Meathook.

" Right, I suppose it'll have to be Sponge Face and the Feckless."

" Yeah, we'll see if they're breakheadbanging dancers."

'Sponge Face and the Feckless make Whale Noises' was transmitted in its entirety.

Well they seem to like this one a bit better," said the General.

" They've stopped retreating anyway," said the Sargeant.

" I feel this may be unwise. We may be giving the aliens the impression we are primitive psychotics," said Nerdberger.

" I thought we were, according to you," said the General.

" No General, I mean this music. It may give a bad impression of the human race. It's animal screeching overlaid with syncopated explosions with an out-of-tune guitar solo."

" The remix by D.J. Diplodicus is better," said Meathook.

" Try playing the Rumblin Stomachs," said Sargeant Bloodlust.

" I don't want to," said Nerdberger.

" Why not ? "

" The aliens might fire on us."

" Why would they want to do that ? "

" Because the Rumblin Stomachs are the lowest of low culture, the aliens might get annoyed if we send over crap like that."

" They're not crap, they're misunderstood that's all."

" We might as well try, " said the General, " What've we got to lose."

" Life, liberty, possessions, happiness."

" Stop going all timid on us, Professor. This was your idea in the first place."

The Rumblin Somachs were transmitted. The alien ships began pitching and manoevuring, as if moving in time to a psychotic seizure.

" Look their ships are moving in time to the music," said Meathook.

" Probably bad piloting," said Nerdberger.

" You 're just upset, Nerdberger."

" Maybe the aliens are psychotic after all, how could they like digestive noises set to a funky bass line ? "

" They're pulling up beside us, General, " said Meathook.

" Even though they have crap taste, this may still be a wonderful experience, " said The Professor.

The General sighed.

" We still can't communicate with them, and we still don't know if they're friendly."

" Oh no, are we going to spend more time swapping shapes ? " said Meathook.

" We could play the Rumblin Stomachs again," said Bloodlust.

" Once is enough, I feel, for at least a millenium," said Nerdberger.

" Sir, they're manoevuring, trying to dock with us, shall I let them ? "

" No, Meathook," said the General.

" Yes, Meathook, " said the Professor, " General, may I remind you, and your soldiers, this is a goodwill mission,"

" A goodwill mission that will make us ill," said Bloodlust," We can't just let their spaceship clamber all over us."

" Why not ? "

" It's like shagging on first date," said Meathook.

" No it isn't."

" We could call it an aggressive act, you know," said Bloodlust.

" It remains a possibility," said the General.

" General, we want face to face contact do we not. "

" You do, my troops want something else."

" Yes, shoot them up, " said Bloodlust.

" No, what we want here is face to face communication. And to do that, we must display a little trust."

" Sounds really boring, " said Meathook.

" Sir, we can't let another rocket dock us like that, without permission. It's date rape, it's interstellar molestation," said Bloodlust."

" Yeah, rocket rape," said Meathook, " by the way, the aliens are making contact again."

" Good now let's stop moaning and see what they have to show us," said the General, " Put it on the viddy screen, please."

The alien transmission is displayed. It amounts to a fuzzy, hummming noise with fuzzy visuals.

" What is that supposed to be ? " said the General.

" It's just like white noise," said Nerdberger.

" You mean the band ? " said Bloodlust.

" No, the phenomenon."

" I know they're phenomenal. I went to their annual renunion concert last year."

" Shut up please, Sargeant... Now Nerdberger, what do we do now ? " said the General.

" Would it help if we spoke English ? "

While they conversed, images had coalesced on the screen, a group of wibbly wobbly blobs, that appeared to be huge jellies. They rippled when they spoke.

" I think it was the aliens, Sir, on the screen,"

" Incredible, " said the Professor.

" Aliens," said the general, " Do...you...understand... me ? "

" Of course we can, stop speaking like a retard."

" Then why didn't you say anything before ? "

" We thought it was your custom to swap childish collections of pictures and noise."

" I suppose they must seem childish to your excellent civilisation."

" Shut up, Nerdberger," said the General, " Does this mean you've been monitoring our conversation the whole time ? "

" Only the interesting bits."

" You should know that we come in peace, goodwill, friendship and understanding, and hope to clinch a few business deals," said Nerdberger.

There was silence.

" Did you hear and understand that," continued the Professor.

" Er, yes, excuse us. It's just that we've heard the peace and goodwill routine a few times. We were momentarily distracted, that's all."

" They were bored shitless, that's all," said Bloodlust, rather too gleefully.

" The usual way of meeting up with alien beings, in our culture, is a cautious conversation. This gives a chance for one, or other, of the parties, to find out if their opposite numbers are violent, psychotic and not to be trusted."

" Don't say that General. As soon as they find out humanity's history, they'll high tail it to the end of the universe," said Nerdberger.

" Fear not, o bearded, nerdy one," said the aliens, " We can look after ourselves...Our ship or yours ?

" How about both ? " said the General.

" How do you mean ? "

" Two at our place, two at your place."

" An impartial suggestion, excellent, so be it, two discussions are better than one."

" Do you think we could see what you look like, first ? "

" You have been looking at us all the time."

" But I can't see anything, apart from a few blobs of wobbly jelly."

" We are those few blobs of wobbly jelly."

" Sorry. I was expecting something a bit more humanoid, that's all."

" That's okay. We were expecting something a bit more gelatine ourselves. It is disconcerting to see bipedal lumps cavorting about the place."

" Why you..."

" Easy Sargeant, " said Nerdberger. " Sirs, travellers from the stars, denizens of the cosmos..."

" Get on with it, Nerdberger," interrupted the General.

" Right, erm, what are we going to call you, anyway ? '

" You don't have to call us anything, we know who we are. "

" But we don't know who you are."

" That's only because we've never met before."

" Right, that's why we would like a name to call you."

" But we don't call ourselves names."

" I bet other people do, " said Bloodlust in a whisper.

" General, Professor, tell your Sargeant we heard that remark."

" What remark ? " said Bloodlust.

" Please accept our apologies, " said the Professor. " But we still haven't settled what we're going to call you."

" Apology accepted. But why should you need to call us anything ? "

" Because it helps us understand."

" Strange."

" And it is custom."

" Strange custom...Well, you might call us the Zug Zug, as other races in space do."

" There are other races in space." cried the Professor excitedly.

" Not that many now. Since we exterminated a lot of them."

" Why did you do that ? "

" Oh the usual reasons - colonisation, territorial expansion, greed, riches, glory, plunder...but we've moved on since then. "

" I think I like these Zug Zug a lot better now, " said Bloodlust.

" Right, " said the General, " Two of my most capable officers will go over to talk to you. While two of you, er, blobs, can come to talk to us. You don't mind being called blobs, do you ? "

" So long as you don't mind being called lumps."

" What ? "

" It is not a derogatory description General, just a simple way of categorising the more solid life forms."

" That could be construed as racist," said Nerdberger.

" Yes Professor it could. But we would assume there is little need for political correctness in space, especially on this momentous occaison. I'll send two of my most trusted blobs over. The discussion will continue."

The viddy screen faded.

" I like these blobs, even though one of them was a bit of a smartarse," said the General.

" Which one was that ? General, " said Bloodlust.

" The one who was a smartarse."

" So which two of us lumps are going to go over ? General," said Nerdberger.

" Please sir, can I go ? "

" No Blooodlust, it might be a trap. I want my most trusted officers here."

" I agree, General. Only a foolhardy idiot would go over there."

" Right. So I want you, Nerdberger, to go over. You can take Meathook with you."

" But Sir."

" Save it, Bloodlust, you're not going."

" I'm flattered you should think of me as so dispensable, General," said Meathook.

" Think, nothing of it."

" You just want me out of the way," said Nerdberger.

" Well it would be nice.. but you are good at diplomacy as well."

" Sir, I don't quite understand the reasons against my going over, " said Bloodlust.

" Which is why you're not going over, Sargeant."

" Yes, " said Nerdberger, " You'll only start shooting whatever happens to be moving around."

" What's wrong with that ? "

" Sargeant, " said the General, " Sometimes it's better to conserve energy, use diplomacy, gain knowledge of participants, assess the situation. Then you can go in and shoot anything that moves."

" I love you, General."

" Let's save the R and R for after hours, Sargeant."

A blobby voice came over the viddy screen again,

" Ready when you are."

" Right, this is a historic moment for us all. The fate of the solar system may hang on the words and deeds we perform today. This is only a walk next door for us two, but for humanity, it is the crossing of a boundary into new galaxies of experience, which could expand the knowledge and consciousness of everyone, and set the tone for future..."

" Get on with it, Nerdberger," said the General, " They won't wait forever."

" Erm, okay."

Meathook and Nerdberger disappeared through the airlock. Seconds later, two jelly creatures slithered through into the prescence of General Fratricide, Sargeant Bloodlust, and Privates Ratbag and Gawkins.

" I suppose these are the jelly monsters," said the General.

" I suppose you are the lumps," slobbered Blob Number One.

" I suppose you are the blobs," said Bloodlust.

" That is so, strange creature. We are pleased you know of our customs. It gratifies us to know you will accept your fate as all inferior beings must, without screaming in protest."

" Our fate ? what are you talking about ? " said the General.

" Those recordings you played us, the last one in particular."

" The Rumblin Stomachs you mean, what about it ? "

" Basically we took that as an invitation to come over and eat you."

" That is not what we intended to say."

" But that is how we intend to take it."

" We thought you might be hostile. So I had my troops prepare a little surprise, Gawkins, hit them with the cream soda hose.

Gawkins rushed up and sprayed the aliens with the delicious soft drink. The aliens began dissolving in confusion.

" Now the blancmange buckets."

Ratbag moved over with two buckets full of blancmange. He dumped these on the blobs, whose remains liquefied rapidly.

" Sir."
" What is it ? Ratbag."
" It looks like Nerdberger managed to escape, sir."
" Oh well."

And sure enough, Nerdberger staggered back through the airlock, sticky jelly all over him. Later on he talked to General Fratricide and Sargeant Bloodlust of his encounter.

" Their aim was clear, General, to surprise all of us, then absorb us into their bodies."
" It would have been a hefty meal," said the General.
" Funnily enough, that's exactly what they said. "
" Didn't stop them trying to be piggy," said the Sargeant.
" They were well capable of gluttony, Sargeant. Of course they devoured poor old Meathook."
" He was a good soldier and always shaved regurlarly," said the General."
" So why didn't you get eaten as well ? Professor," said the Sargeant.
" They found me disagreeable, apparently."
" Sir, these Zug Zug have their good points. "
" I quite agree Sargeant, " said the General.
" Yes, you see, they absorb us physically, intellectually and emotionally as well. They devour our ideas and feelings,

which also provide nourishment for them. Meathook was absorbed quite easily, he was something of a snack. "

" He was a good comrade," said Bloodlust.

" And quite savoury, apparently, according to them, if a little insubstantial."

" How did you get away ? Professor, " said Bloodlust.

" I made them vomit, a most distressing experience. They oozed all over me, trying to absorb me. I kept telling them they were not being compassionate. And my eloquent plea must have moved them."

" It moved them enought to vomit," Said the General, admiringly.

" Yes, otherwise I would have been dissolved by poisonous enzymes."

" Ugh."

" Ugh is right Sargeant. But while they were incapacitated, I made my way back through the air lock. I must admit I was expecting to find death and devastation everywhere. Instead I find jelly and blancmange everywhere, like a childrens' party."

" Yes, as soon as we had the opportunity, the Sargeant and I worked up a couple of devious contingency plans, just in case, you understand."

" Well I must admit in this case you were right, General, and Sargeant. I never expected this. It is most distressing when intelligent beings are considering you for the menu, rather than negotiating like most civilised beings. I mean, we could have worked out some kind of quota system, in return for some advanced technology. But no, they had to be greedy from the outset. I would like to take the Homebase back to base where we can make our reports. Earth needs to be warned. Did their ships get away ? "

" Yes the dish ran away with the spoon," said Bloodlust.

" That sounds vaguely familiar, said the Professor, " It's not by Norbert Tranquiliser is it ? "

" He does an instrumental version. But the best version is the Rumblin Stomachs death metal dub. "

" I'm sorry you never had a chance to use any firearms, Sargeant, " said the General.

" Thank you sir."

" In the meantime, I could do with a good meal, " said the Professor.

" Excellent idea," said the General, " I have just the thing."

" And what's that ? "

" Jelly, blancmange and cream soda."

The recording breaks off here.

The Zug Zug Wars

(Part Two)

We do have these further fragments, that purport to tell of the conflict between Humans and Zug Zug, in the dim and distant past. As both races do not exist anymore, we cannot verify the authenticity of these recordings. Some believe the whole thing is a hoax of course. Others, that the whole thing is too silly for a hoax. For who could conceive of hairless apes and jelly monsters without taking a powerful drug. Still others point to the fact that no one would bother making up something so pointless and dozy. The controversy rages on. In the meantime, copies of these recordings are available in the Library for Immature Idiots, but only under supervision.

" What is the situation now ? Sargeant . "

Sargeant Bloodlust took a deep breath, as if this were a weighty question.

" Crap."

" I see," said Ambassador Skimpy, " So all hope of negotiation is off then."

" With due respect, Ambassador Skimpy, the Zug Zug are not open to negotiation. As soon as their force landed, they attacked everyone in sight."

" Yes I see, absorbing people you say."

" Yes sir. The blobs simply smother us and digest us. The victim becomes one with his or her absorber."

" Quite romantic, according to some. Two souls, coming together as one. That is true love to a lot of people."

"I don't love to be eaten. I don't see much that's romantic in being digested by a jelly blob. "

" Ah, but then, these people would say you have no soul. Think of the possibilities, a human psyche, and a Zug Zug psyche, that share the same thoughts and emotions."

" I do think about it, Ambassador, and it scares the crap out of me. It's not as if we have any choice in the matter."

" That's true, Sargeant. Although I believe these same people would probably jump at the chance of being absorbed. They would consider it a cultural exchange."

" Ah yes, the Psycho-Suicide Arbitrators. We in the military look on them as collaborators. The Zug Zug don't even say please before they absorb. They just go around envelopping people without their consent. And it doesn't stop there, Ambassador. There's nothing mystical about it. These greedy blobs just gobble up all the people they can lay their tentacles on."

" I understand, Sargeant Bloodlust. But we do have to wait until the current round of talks are over. The peace delegation has been hard at work trying to hammer out a settlement. And it seems the Zug Zug want a settlement on Earth."

" So they can be near the larder."

" Such cynicism, Sargeant."

" I can tell you now, the peace delegation has been absorbed."

" Oh not again, that's the fifth one this month."

" Well thank the stars we in the military aren't hindered by negotiation."

" I suppose you want to wipe them all out ? "

" Just the ones on Earth, erm, then the ones on our Solar System, then the ones in our galaxy."

" That's a bit intolerant isn't it ? Sargeant Bloodlust."

" It's the only way, Ambassador Skimpy. Otherwise we're all going to end up as part-time blobs."

" What do you mean ?

" Well that's what happens, isn't it. Once you're absorbed, you become just a part of a Zug Zug."

" Yes, apparently. Although they do like us, rather. They like our individuality, our irrationality, all the things that make us so interesting and unpredictable. "

" And they like the fact we taste nice and digest easy as well."

" I have to agree. Although for some reason, nerds, obssessives, dictators and psychotics give them indigestion. These people can't be absorbed."

" This gives us an edge, particularly in government and the military, where so many disagreeable types can find a home."

" I'm sure. So what are you up to now ? "

' It's quite simple really. We had one battle, by Jupiter's Moons, with these Zug Zug. We only defeated them because we smothered them in blancmange and cream soda. And that mashed them up real bad."

" Quite. And are you planning the same kind of massacre here ? "

" Well up until recently. Then The Zug Zug destroyed all our blancmange and cream soda factories."

" Yes, they called it ' Party-Foods-Tragedy Time, ' didn't they."

" That was the media, but we were dumped in the crap, it's true. So we just made up something else."

" You had an idea then , Sargeant."

" Not me personally. I haven't had an idea for twenty years, We just took one off someone else, Professor Nerdberger, I think."

" Not that freelance irritation ? "

" The very same. And acting on his suggestion, I assembled a crack team of marines, to spray the Zug Zug headquarters with icing sugar and glazed cherries."

" You think that'll work."

" Maybe. If it does we'll have enough dessert to feed the whole of Earth for a couple of years."

" And if it fails we'll be the Zug Zug main course."

" Probably."

" What about the possible environmental effects. We could have a jelly slick miles long."

" I have a hunch about this one, Ambassador."

" I noticed. I thought they taught you to stand to attention in the military."

" Sorry, all these devious schemes I get involved in really put a crick in my neck."

" So what are we waiting for now ? "

" The squads to report if they've made it. I have six other bodies of crack troops standing by, with icing sugar automatics and glazed cherry bombs."

" Yuck, I've never liked sweet desserts myself."

" You were for being absorbed by a jelly earlier."

" I was just discussing the idea, Sargeant. I was wondering how the communion of Zug Zug and Human soul would change human nature."

" I think it would make us sickly sweet and wobbly in nature."

" Like the middle classes ? you mean."

" Probably, we'd be nice all the time, ugh."

" A lot of people might be tempted by that."

" Yes, there are always the social climbers, or the social absorbers in this case...."

Suddenly a blaring radio announcement was heard, which made both men jump.

" This is Operation Trifle, repeat, Operation Trifle. The childrens' party should be a success. We have enough money to pay the caterers. All those young tummies will stop rumbling now, over and out."

" What in Saturn's name was that ? Bloodlust."

" It was in code."

" So what does all that gibberish mean ? "

" It means the mission has gone well and is practically finished."

" Why couldn't he just say that ? "

" Secrecy has to be observed, Ambassador."

" This means your crack units will finish things off ? "

" Yes sir, as soon as I press this button."

Bloodlust immediately pressed a button, which made a horrible screeching noise.

" Can't you get it fixed ? Sargeant."

" Sorry sir. But it does remind people of the enormity of their responsibility."

" Either that or they think the fire alarm's gone off again."

" This transmits the 'go' signal. It will now be only a matter of time before the ' Blob Squad ' achieve the objective."

" The Blob Squad ? "

" Yes sir, their official designation."

" Well they're welcome to it. It has obscene connotations, doesn't it ? something to do with menstruation ? "

" Yes sir, the men thought it might give them a laugh."

" And what did the women think ? "

" It gave them a laugh too, sir."

" Really Sargeant, this is a crude state of affairs, dreamed up by a crude soldier."

" Thank you sir. Crudity is one of the factors that might help us win this war."

" I still think there is a place for diplomacy that drags on for ages and achieves nothing."

" Your time will come soon, Sir."

" Thank you, Sargeant. I suppose I should tell my colleagues I arrived too late to stifle your initiative...Why hello Sargeant Bloodlust, how are things on the front line these days."

" Good, we'll take it from there...couldn't be better, sir."

And so the Zug Zug invasion force was turned into the mightiest dessert the world had ever seen. After Sargeant Bloodlust's weird plan had succeeded, a universal holiday was declared. It was named Global Party Week. This was to enable all the world's population to eat the sugary jelly and glazed cherries. The week after was designated as Univeral Sickness Week.

Yes, historians do get in a tizz about this account. Some see it as a creation myth, a battle between the forces of the stupid but good, against the forces of the gluttonous but clever. Current theory also supports it, in that many scientists see the universe as edible, it is said to be God's takeaway. Others suggest we are wasting our time on babbling, psychotic meanderings again. Anyway, here are some more fragments that purport to tell of relations between Zug Zug and Humans (What stupid names).

A council of Zug Zug were sitting blobbily around a table in a conference chamber. It was in the Zug Zug Halls of Science, Diplomacy and Cheesy Comestibles. The Zug Zug had invented a new weapon. It could perhaps defeat the Humans categorically. The Humans were their sworn enemies in the Absorbing Wars. Although, of course, they had to be different and call them the Glutton Wars. It was the Zug Zug mission to turn all life into one massive, amorphous blob of consciousness, which would ultimately become a being greater than the universe itself. If the creatures they absorbed along the way also provdided a tasty snack, one they could digest between meals, without ruining their appetite, then so be it. To the Humans the Zug Zug were just greedy gluttons, who would never go on a diet. For they absorbed everything body, mind spirit, emotion, sensation, everything was food to them. Humans were just part of The Zug Zug menu.

A few souls on either side had discussed the possibilty of peaceful contact and exchange of information while remaining seperate entities. There was always the lunatic fringe. Such an idea was lunatic to the Zug Zug. They could not understand why anyone would not wish to be absorbed. You gained so much from the experience. Although a lot of the other conscious entities, they had absorbed on their travels, did not always see things their way. They would persist in resisting, struggling and howling as the inevitable absorption took its necessary course. They usually came round in the end. Some argued they had no choice. But everyone experienced the benefits of shared consciousness. And any naughty acts, or dirty habits, or character flaws, on the part of the absorbed creature, were looked with tolerance and forebearance by the Zug Zug.

In the recent war, the Zug Zug had encountered many disagreeable individuals, who simply could not be absorbed at all. This was an affront to Zug Zug dignity, since most conscious entities proved agreeable, in the end. However, among the humans there were many disagreeable types. Someone suggested cooking them in a delicious sauce, but this was an expensive option. Especially since today's busy Zug Zug were always on the move, balancing the heavy demands of work, home life and devouring alien races. A solution was needed to fit the affluent, sophisticated Zug Zug of today. Coming across a species, where a large portion of the population gave them indigestion, was a challenge. For there was no consistency to Human Disagreeability. You could not isolate the disgreeable types from the rest of the population, even though their behaviour always marked them out in contrast to the agreeable. (Small digression here - this month's Human speciality is spicy buttocks in sticky batter - the Interstellar Chefs recommendation, they absorb so easy.) No, these disagreeable types were spread throughout the population. It posed the Zug Zug a problem, since Humans could be so delicious when they set their mind to it. Flame-grilled-Person-on-a-Stick was a delicacy renowned throughout the galaxy.

No, the problem appeared to lay in the Humans' individuality itself. They were a contradictory lot. They were a social species, like the Zug Zug, but they forever pretended they were not. In fact, several individuals went about proclaiming they were the only ones in existence. These types tended to cluster around the mass media. Individuality was a difficult concept for the Zug Zug to grasp, ever since it had been banned for its anti-social tendencies, all those millenia ago. It always was difficult for them to grasp, so past dictators had told them. For they lived the communal life of the soul. They were separate, physical entities, that was true. Yet telepathy transmitted thoughts and feelings betweeen them at a ready rate. It was so difficult to be yourself, because most of your time and energy was used up in constant communication, that is, if you could find a self to be. Yet the rudiments of individual psyche remained in them. They recognised each other as seperate entities, even though no one could remember anyone elses' name.

Perhaps that is what made Humans so delicious. Every Zug Zug who absorbed a Human quickly gained an extra slither its step, and a quirk in its heart. These Zug Zug glowed with a radiant sliminess. Of course this soon disappeared as the Human psyche was completely absorbed, smothered by a floppy blob of gelatine consciousness. Yet those few, fleeting moments of joy, made them all the more hungry for more Humans. The Zug Zug could, and did, absorb each other occaisonally. But this was generally a bland experience. It was just more of the same. Anyway, if too many of them tried to combine, they ran the risk of falling apart, as wobbly jellies do. Though, of course, it remained their ultimate ideal - to become one big blob, planet -size would do for starters. However, they were still individual enough to slag each other off for getting too carried away.

The Zug Zug had discovered that the humans had a collective consciousness as well. It had grown a bit rusty through lack of usage, but it still functioned. It merely served as a vague race memory in Humans. Yet the Zug Zug saw it as a medium to possibly subjugate human individuality. They would do this through a combination of science, psychic ability, sneaky behaviour and psychotic tendencies, (they had learnt some things from the Humans). In this way, the right forms of energy - physical, mental and emotional - would be generated then gobbled up. Even though Humans did not use their collective consciousness much, once it was destroyed they would become a species of sociopathic loners.

And initial reports suggested their tactic had worked. Of course it necessitated the construction of a bulky , satellite-size computer, to transmit Anti- Empathy and Anti-Sympathy rays. This aroused lots of complaints from Blobby Residents' Commitees. Yet the complaints of a few jelly N.I.M.B.Y.'s were thought to be worth it. Humans had become more random and chaotic. Although some argued they were just exercising their natural tendency toward disorder. These dissenting blobs were soon absorbed. For the belief was that Human society would inevitably collapse. As co-operative activity failed, riots were reported in all major Earth cities. One or two wars broke out, and their international banking system stopped altogether. Some said this was usual Human behaviour on a Bank Holiday. These irritating blobs were absorbed as well. The unrest and discord on Earth grew. It looked as if the planet would decay into the war of all agianst all. And then things just settled down again. The Humans reorganised their lives, a bit more boringly than before, perhaps, and just got on with them. They had turned into a planet of office workers. This was still a success. For, as is known throughout the galaxy, office workers are incapable of independent thought or initiative. This makes them ripe for conquest.

As the Zug Zug discussed their invasion plans two disturbing events happened. Firstly, they were infested by a plague of little red spheres on stalks. These proved edible. And Zug Zug could not resist scoffing these wherever they were found. However, their wibbly-wobbly digestive process could not cope with a surfeit of the sickly fruit, and they died in their thousands. Then there was the sickly sweet snow. These sugar storms were helplessly absorbed by Zug Zug who happened to caught outside. And they keeled over, saturated in sweetness. Their satellite, their glorious satellite, was destroyed. It stopped transmitting its Anti-Empathy and Anti-Symapthy rays. The Human collective unconscious resserted itself. There was good news, in that Zug Zug meddling had precipitated several geological disasters on Earth. But instead of dying in pain, as was hoped, Humans responded to these events as challenges. The Zug Zug tactic, formerly so sneaky and efficient, had turned the Human race into a more energetic life form. This was greeted with dismay. There began mumblings of peace treaties. If all else failed they could a least negotiate a quota of Humans for Sunday dinner..

This meeting was noted telepathically, by the Secretary to all Jelly, Official Plenipotent-Recorder-in-Residence, the Halls of Science, Diplomacy and Cheesy Comestibles, this day - the Sixth Iggy of Nonny, in the year of the Tumbler... I'm sorry I fell asleep at this point and missed the rest...

Meanwhile back on Earth...

" It has been a strange couple of years, Sargeant," said General Fratricide, " First of all we revert back to barbarism, then we sink into boredom, then we nearly get wiped out by nature."

" You're telling me," Sargeant Bloodlust replied, "I never thought I'd ever find myself a soldier one day, then an accountant, then a secret policeman, then a soldier again. I don't know what came over me."

" It's suspicious as well, what with all these earthquakes and volcanos going off all over the place."

" Well that's bound to happen sometime, sir."

" What ? at least one environmental catastrophe a day, over a six week period."

" It's always the way. You have peace and quiet for millenia, and then, all of a sudden, everything happens at once, it's just like buses."

" Is it really ? "

" It's just bad luck that's all."

" You can stop gibbering now, Sargeant."

" Thank you, sir."

" Why couldn't we predict them ? "

" We never can, sir."

" Even so, all these other strange phenomena going on."

" Like what ? "

" Well, people stopped dreaming..."

" I never dream anyway."

" No art or literature of any significance was produced..."

" Good thing too."

" Discord was every where..."

" Well he does get around a bit."

Whole societies broke down..."

" These things happen."

" Constant wars..."

" At least we weren't out of work."

" You didn't take much notice of events, did you ? Sargeant."

" I never do, current affairs is really boring."

" But you did notice things were a bit more exciting than usual."

" Not really, no."

" But you noticed things were more chaotic than usual."

" I did. I love it when things get a bit messed up."

" What about the theory the Zug Zug used some kind of psychic weapon on us ? "

" The Zug Zug ? you know I haven't seen them for ages. I miss them a bit. They were horrible blobs of jelly, that always wanted to absorb you, but at least you knew where you stood with them."

" You miss them ? "

" They gave you a good fight as well."

" Sargeant, you are psychotic."

" Thank you, sir. I know that. Psychosis always gave us an edge in the ' Glutton Wars.' "

" Well, keep your psychosis under wraps for the moment. I have heard there is talk of peace. But all things are possible in this here universe. And the only certainty is that something weird is bound to happen sooner or later."

" You mean the Zug Zug might come back, great, er, I mean shame."

" Don't worry Sargeant. If they do come back, you could have plenty of time to involve yourself in random acts of violence."

" Thank you, sir."

" In the meantime we must keep you occupied so you are not a danger to your fellow creatures."

" Yes sir."

" Go and fetch me a cup of lava from that exploding volcano yonder, make sure it is exactly the right temperature and density. If it deviates by one iota, you have to go back, until the task is performed to my satisfaction. Do you understand ? "

" Yes sir. It is a pointless task designed to keep me out of mischief, for which I'm grateful. Can I shoot something in the meantime ? "

" No."

" Oh."

" Be patient, Sargeant, your time will come. Now, off you go."

" Yes sir."

Yes, well. Now we come to last of these recordings, that are supposed to tell of the wars between those legendary races - Zug Zug and Humans. As per usual, scholars are divided regarding their authenticity. One current theory in circulation says we are figments of a two- legged crustacean's imagination. I think our luchtime refreshment has been adulterated again to be honest. Nevertheless, the possibility of these legends being true was helped enormously by the discovery of a fossilised sock on Mars recently. But critics argue this was discarded by a rogue naturist...

What ? is it running ?...right. Er, I'm Private Ratbag, yeah. And I was Official Recorder at the peace talks between Us and the Zug Zug, It says here... I know it's true, I'm just making sure... Present at the discussions were - Ambassador Skimpy, that nerdy bloke, what was his name ? oh, Professor Nerdberger, General Fat Sides...What ? I can't help it, man, I can't say his name. I used to call him General Fatty Pies... What ? no, he never took any notice of me. Right, yeah, oh, and there was Sargeant Bloodlust (my hero). That was on our side. On the other side was a load of blobs...Eh ? No it's not being racist, man. I don't know their names. Even they don't know their names...What ? no, I'm not saying they're stupid, it's just what they're like. Come on, man, I've got a job to do here, you keep putting me off...Right, so I eddied the recordings, I etited the recording, oh, I told you you were putting me off, I tried putting things in some kind of order... Is that alright ? what do you mean, no ?....

" So what exactly does ' Aourrg' mean then ? "

asked Ambassador Skimpy. (Holder of the Purple Patch, 3 citations for common sense.)

" It's ' Aouurrrrg-g," said General Fratricide (Master of the Order of Squelch, Knight of the Liquid Table), " And basically, there is no translation for it. The closest we can get is ' Blubbery-Darling-Anus-Face.' "

" Ugh."

" It's a respected term of love and admiration in the Zug Zug language. And don't say ' ugh,' for Jupiter's sake. It means ' Get the kitchen implements out and we'll have sado-masochistic sex.' "

" All that in one word ? "

" It's all in the nuance."

" Ugh, sorry, really ? "

" Yes, and you don't want to have sex with them, believe me. Most people who attempt that end up being absorbed by their Zug Zug dates."

" I thought they just liked one night stands."

" Or one night meals, as the Zug Zug call them."

" How fickle."

" Sometimes a relationship is formed. But it can't last long when your body, mind and soul is slowly being dissolved by a jelly monster."

" It's always the way, isn't it. There's always one dominant partner in a realtionship."

" And it's always the Zug Zug."

" It does sound a bit creepy."

" I can appreciate that. I suppose, from their point of view, they're only being slimy, disgusting lumps of gelatine, absorbing everything in their path."

" You're not bitter, are General ? "

" No, just twisted. But not as much as the Sargeant here."

" Thank you, sir."

" Now ambassador, we have to remember the Zug Zug are sensitive, over sensitive in fact. They place great value on observing correct procedure. One slip of pronunciation, one facial gesture out of place, and the whole talks will be abandoned."

" You mean we must swallow our natural disgust."

" Otherwise we may be swallowed ourselves."

" Don't remind me. This war might have finished a year ago. But at the last peace talks, a delegate paused to clear his throat. This cleared the room, but not before the Zug Zug had absorbed everybody present. Apparently, the delegate's throat clearing translated as ' I'm going to scoop you up in spoonfuls,' which is a threat in the Zug Zug language."

" Exactly, so I would practice my Aourrrrg-g's if I were you."

" I only end the speech with ' Aourrg,' don't I ? "

" It's ' Aourrrrg-g,' as I keep telling you. And, yes, you are right. The Zug Zug like a formal speech, followed by a lusty welcome. So you must shout ' Aourrrrg-g,' with all the passion you can muster."

" I am extremely nervous."

" Don't worry. Sargeant Bloodlust and myself will be right behind you, to prompt you if necessary.. Remember, Zug Zug etiquette means they will let you have three attempts to shout ' Aourrrrg-g.' So don't panic."

A nerdish man ran up to shake Ambassador Skimpy's hand before walking off again.

" Who was that ? '

" That was Professor Nerdberger. If you need any advice, I'm sure he'll let you know."

" Yes, he's the kind of pest that's always sniffing around being annoying," added the Sargeant unhelpfully.

The scene was set, the negotiating table was ready. The Zug Zug delegates slithered in. The diplomat and his two soldier aides supressed their urges to shoot and run away, while Professor Nerdberger (Wayward Obsessive, Instructor of Obscurities and Visiting Pedant) hovered around. All parties behaved with formality and respect (for a change). And so Ambassador Skimpy began -

" Flabble Zabbley Dong-klee, Kaponey Durkni Bomblah, Excroti Onna Mental, sick sicky bick, cleptot by-the-by. Boggabonny deddysmell, licklee smellyplates, groan on flabby whipped cream. Tibia balsam and rye, to go whibble on the dandy. Mistress is sought after, the flabby lift wobbles tonight..."

As the Ambassador got into full flow, Bloodlust and Fratricide whispered among themselves.

" Looks like he's doing okay," said the Sargeant.

" Yes, so far so good... Remember our plan though, if he falters, the situation may demand the Fletz gun."

(The Fletz gun was the invention of Professor Nerdberger. It shot darts containing a powerful enzyme. This gave the victim severe pain, a fit of giggles, overwhelming orgasm, or agonising death, or any combination thereof, depending on the setting. The reasoning was that, if you had to shoot people, you could at least give them a bit of pleasure before they die. This was the humane thing to do.)

" Oogle Boogley ,baglee Laggee lagglee lager... erm... poop into ...what... won't go,indivisable..."

" Oh no, he's cracking under the strain, " said Bloodlust."

" No,no, he's rounding up," said Fratricide, " Good, he's made it. Now comes the Aourrrrg-g." " Oh no, he's muffed it," said a disappointed Sargeant.

" Get ready Sargeant, we may need to prompt the Ambassador...He's just about to make his second attempt..."

" Oh no, he's blown that as well."

" Quick, Sargeant, we have to seize the initiative, before it's too late. Fire."

Sargeant Bloodlust aimed his gun at the Zug Zug, but then shot the Ambassador instead. The dart hit the diplomat right between the buttocks.

" Aourrrrg-g, " he said, with all the passion he could muster.

" Good shot, Sargeant. But did you have to make the dart so powerful ? "

" Actually General, the setting on my gun is busted. I couldn't tell how powerful the dart was."

The General nodded. " Sometimes peace is worth getting stung for, " he said sagely.

Ambassador Skimpy walked bow-legged, with a high-pitched voice, for about a week afterwards. Then they all started talking boring crap, like they always do on these occaisons. Out came the ice cream and the puff pastries. Course, we don't get any, coz we're not officers... wankers... What ? what do you mean ? No man, we can edit the recording later... We can cut out all us talking, well me talking anyway, you just put me off all the time...

The Grunt League

Once upon a time, long long ago, far far away, on the magical, council estate of Grotbox Gardens, lived the happy people of Septic Borough. Despite their huge social problems, pronounced criminal activities, poverty, and repeated bad treatment by bureaucrats and politicians, they lived a carefree existence.

Now, the chairman of the estate committee had a beautiful daughter. Many sought her hand in marriage. But they usually had their hands bitten off by one of her seven insane brothers. The number of people who fancied the daughter, and were beaten up by her brothers, was many. No matter how many people the brothers beat up, there were still people who wanted this gorgeous person. Eventually, the brothers beat up so many suitors, that they ganged up and massacred the brothers. This did not give them access to the chairman's daughter however. The chairman was head of a large clan, aproximately 300 members in all, who occupied half the flats on the estate. Despite this, there were plenty of suitors who tried to force their way into the daughter's affections, if not her knickers. The clan readily resorted to violence, arson, blackmail and prolonged feuds to scare away potential suitors. But since these were normal features of life on the estate anyway, no one took much notice. Yet the violence inevitably became so bad that something had to be done, before they were put under martial law, as had happened so many times in the past. By now everybody was sick of the continual disorder. The chairman resolved to find a solution to the problem of who should take his daughter's hand, a solution that did not involve drunkeness or violence. This effectively caused him another problem. Since all solutions to his problems involved drunkeness or violence. After months of thinking he eventually hit on another solution. He would set potential suitors a test, a test to earn the right to his daughter's hand. And it must be as difficult as possible, since it would give him an excuse to get rid of a lot of difficult people. It must also be sufficiently repulsive to deter any faint-hearted wankers.

Then the Chairman wasted another few months racking his brains over what form the test should take. Many ideas were thought up, only to be discarded quickly. First, there was a pisstaking competition. But this was called off before it started, as it was over subscribed. Then a shoplifting competition was promoted. However, when several of the contestants went missing, they had to fear the worse. Then the suitor who could make the most money in the shortest period of time was considered. However, the subsequent police interest in this test soon brought it to a close. One suspended sentence later, the chairman was back where he started. A cynical observer proposed a chat up competition. Suitors would try to talk their way into marriage, charming the knickers off his delectable daughter. That was the last that was heard of the cynical observer. As if that was not enough, the chairman had to contend with all the boasting and wild promises of the eligible suitors. One boasted he had conquered Venus with an S.A.S. battalion, and this after drinking ten pints of hair spray. Another promised the daughter her own private island, complete with active volcano and mineral rights. A third said he was the Sultan of Brunei, he had just fancied slumming it for a couple of years. These were the least exaggerated stories of the suitors.

The chairman's headaches grew more frequent as he moved onto the next idea for a test. This involved suitors lying, in the face of overwhelming odds. Each suitor was tricked into a situation where he was standing over an inert body, covered in blood, with a meat cleaver in his hand. It was acted, but the suitors did not know this. However, when confronted with a difficult situation, they all proved to be expert at lying their way out of it. All gave out huge doses of charm as they sought to save their skins. The participants could not be separated in terms of ability, they were all of a high standard.

A belching contest was suggested, then dropped, because every second word of the suitors was a belch. A swearing competition was also dropped, as every first word of the suitors was a swearword. Drug taking contests, who could accumulate the most social problems, and who could spend the longest in the toilet, were all still born. In desperation the chairman thought of a farting contest. Normally this would have been as pointless as all the previous tests, for it would be too diffcult to tell people apart in terms of ability. And the estate already had a reputation for farting. Indeed the Olympic farting squad were housed on the estate, despite the chemical hazard. The sounds of bum trumpets were a common sound all around. It was a popular hobby. Methane gas always hung over the estate. However, the chairman had noticed differences in quality and consistency in the area of bum gymnastics. The suitors themselves showed their greatest variations of character in their arse talking.

Therefore, after much consideration, a fart competition it was. The chairman drew up a league points system to sort out the windy from the merely breezy. The lucky bum champion could then ask for his daughter's hand, and stink out the land. Loudness and poisonous smell were the two main criteria to be measured. Allied to this were the numbers of farts pumped out within a given period of time. These factors could then give a table of quality and consistency.

After many ripping sounds, many explosions of swamp gas, and much gagging in the part of the judges, some categories of farts did begin to emerge ;-

First were the Silent but Violent category. These had no points value at all when it came to sound. However, they more than made up for it in the intensity of smell. The smell was always overpowering. Though there was some variation on the poisonous fumes. These farts always provoked involuntary curses, cries, and a stampede to leave the room, on the part of those around.

Distinguished farts in this category were Eggy Ones - These smelled like the farter had eaten too many eggs. These were followed (A bit too closely) By Rotten Eggy Farts - These farts smelled like the farter had dropped a couple of stink bombs. They had a strong smell of hydrogen sulphide. Then there were Rancid Runs - In these farts the farter had eaten food that had gone off. They ran the risk of the runs. Next came the Sewer Bum - This farter produced farts of unknown provenance, with a completely poisonous bouquet. They crept up on people like the smell of a blocked drain, then pushed them into unconsciousness. Finally came Alcopops - These were suffered by alcoholic farters as they went through their hangovers. They mainly smelled of the cheap alcohol that had been consumed, though more concentrated. (This term is unrelated to those sweet drinks designed to get teenagers into alcohol - see also Pop Farts.)

The second category of farts, more moderate in nature, were designated as Moderate but Smelly. They could be as poisonous as silent farts, yet the dosage was often smaller. And they made enough sound for those around to evacuate the area before they could no longer breathe. In terms of sound, they usually consisted of short staccato bursts. However, discrete whines, breezes, and even melodious harmonies, were often reported.

Distinguished farts in this category included the Piffy Farts - These were close to silent farts in that their sound was barely audible. As the name illustrates, the sound made was 'piff'. They may be compared to the bum burp of the household cat. Often they may not even be smelly. Some hardened farters regarded piffy farts as no more than duds, rather than the true explosive bum rumble.

Second in this category were the Poppy Farts - These were a holdall category of farts. Aromas ranged from rotten eggs, alcohol, cabbage and every other decaying organic susbstance. Yet their sound signature was always a short burst of bubbles that sounded like a few, small pops. Small pops they may have been, yet each bubble contained a deadly dose.

Next in this category were the Cabbage Farts - These were one of the most widespread varieties. They usually had a rasping bum signature (see Rasping Farts), with the allied smell of greens from a leftover Sunday dinner, always suggestive of cabbage. The vegetarians among the suitors were particularly prone to these.

After that came the Rubbish Farts - again they had a sound reminiscent of a Rasper. Though the aroma was said to be of the household rubbish variety. These farts often excelled in smell. One judge described them as ' smelling like someone had emptied a rubbish bin into a stagnant pond.'

Then came the Bean Farts - These were also a popular variety, as expressed in the rhyme ' Beans, beans, good for your heart, the more you eat, the more you fart.' These were one of the most popular farts. The noise was always consistent, like cloth being torn apart. But the smell was always variable, ranging from non-existent to noxious. Seasoned farters regarded these only as standard farts for beginners.

The final major category of farts were known as BOBBY's (Big Old Bombastic Bum Yodels) or Arse Operas - And, of course, their major characteristic was their loud noise. They were subdivided as follows -

First were the Brass Section Farts - These sounded like the various instruments of a brass band. Saxophones and trumpets were the most frequently reported. Trombones were also popular, while constantly bubbling under were the bugle, the oompah, and the french horn. A further claim was made for those farts that were reminiscent of woodwind instruments, particularly flutes and clarinets. However, these farts were banned after they were found to be the result of excessive straining on the part of the farter. The more organic farter prefered to let nature take its course, and organic farts were held to be infinitely superior to battery farts. (Incidently, those who swallowed air in the hope of precipating farts were summarily beaten up then disqualified.)

Then came the Runny Ones - These sounded as if the farter had let out his gas underwater. They were also commonly known as wet farts. Smells often accompanied them, but not always. Runny ones could be particularly messy, as the same symptoms often heralded the approach of diarrhea, several brown trousered moments occurred with these farts therefore.

Next were the Pop Farts - These were farts brought on by consumption of fizzy drinks. They were also similar to certain pop songs, in that they were loud, short, forgetable, and had no smell content whatsoever.

After that were the Raspers - These were similar to brass section farts but usually sounded rougher. Comparisons were made to the noise of a car starting on a winter morning. But most found they were strongly reminiscent of the sound of a Japanese motor bike engine going at full tilt.

Then came the Synthesisers - These sounded like electronic, musical instruments. They had a variety of melody but not of tone, as they were all high pitched.

Finally came the Factory Hooters - Just a high pitched single note, not unlike the monotonous drone of the factory hooter. These farts were usually of a short duration. Though seasoned farters could sustain them after practice.

Once the Chairman had devised these farting criteria, he was able to work out a points system, along with a farts per hour monitor. This enabled a league system to come into being, known as the Grunt League. Farters were given nicknames according to the quality of their farts. This came in useful as it was not easy to distinguish them in terms of appearance or character. Two divisions emerged in the Grunt League, the final standings being as follows ;-

DIVISION ONE

Farter Nickname	Farts per hour	Noise Level	Smell Level
Rat Arse	60	15	12
Fart Organs	59	11	11
Smell-U-Don't-Like	59	10	11
King of the Grunt	58	10	10
Shitbits	57	9	10
King of the Sewers	57	9	9
Pop Smell Hee Hee	56	9	10
Swamp Gas	54	8	7
Stagnant Bum	50	8	8
The Running Man	49	8	7

DIVISION TWO

Farter Nickname	Farts per hour	Noise Level	Smell Level
Mister Whiffy	43	7	6
Guffer	40	7	6
Chuff Chuff	40	7	5
Sax Solo	37	6	5
Chemical Alert	36	5	5
Radioactive Material	33	4	5
Bum Omelette*	25	(Retired Hurt)	
Heinz Baked Burps*	19	(Retired Very Hurt)	
Bowel Merchant*	10	(Exploded)	
O.M.S.O.*(One Man Symphony Orchestra)	(Disqualified)		
Alkie Arse*	(Did Not Compete)		

*Casualties were to be expected in the dog eat dog world of farting. Bum Omelette suffered a prolapse, Heinz Baked Burps somehow imploded, Bowel merchant unwisely lit a cigarette in mid guff and spontaneously combusted, O.M.S.O. had a name no one could pronounce (therefore he was disqualified), Alkie Arse suffered from verbal diarrhea in the warm up (he had to run away before someone killed him).

The number of farts per hour was self explanatory. Only good quality farts were included. They were required to have at least a smell or a noise content (dud farts were discounted). The smell monitor was a veteran bum expert, trained to withstand the arse exertions of a thousand farters all at once (though he did wear a gas mask). He assessed the bouqet generated by every bum.

Farters were force fed huge quantities of eggs, greens, alcohol, vindaloo, sauerkraut, chili and fizzy drinks. As nature took its course a variety of posterior activity was generated. This gave some problems to the audience who had to mark the farting suitors on their noise level, as many of them did not have sufficient training to withstand the smell. Furthermore they were a selection of the population of the estate, which meant they were bad-tempered, intolerant individuals. This meant that Division Two of the Grunt League were soon eliminated, by a combination of abuse, objects thrown, and beatings. This left only Division One. Despite their final standings the farters had to undergo a further test to demonstrate their suitability as suitors. In the age old tradition, as soon as farters made their guffs known, any member of the audience could shout out, " slogs, " " beatings," or whatever. This was a general invitation for everyone present to give the farter a serious kicking. This tradition has it origins in the mists of time (and in the fog generated by a few bum burps). Of course farters could stave off the threat of imminent beating by calling out " No slogs," " No beatings," " No kicks," etc. As there were no set terms for this ritual , a contest developed between both farters and beaters in their rush to prevent or start off a beating. Various exotic phrases were heard, such as " flying ants," " messages from Mars," " baps," " blue people with cups of coffee," and " what about the Geneva Convention then ? "

Several beatings later the farters were thinned out. Only King of the Grunt was mildly maimed. Some farters tried to prevent their inevitable fate by gassing their attackers, but this only delayed their deaths.

And so King of the Grunt was presented as a suitable suitor to the chairman's daughter. However she said "ugh," and started screaming as soon as she met King of the Grunt. She ran off before anyone could react, and was never seen again. Everyone looked around bemused, not knowing what to do. Then they came up with the time honoured solution of starting pointless, unnecessary violence. This continued for some three days, before someone could be bothered to call the police. Then the police came around and finished off the survivors. These events were a serious blow to Britain's chances in the International Farting Olympics of that year. Huge embarassment was only avoided by pretending nothing had happened in the first place.

Don't Pick the Melancholy Flowers

" Dewar, you seem to be well qualified, you have experience. It's also the kind of experience I like."

They rambled through the vegetable patch. Only Killeen's idea of a vegetable patch was as big as a tennis court. That man had land, in excess.

" Stick with me, Dewar. I know you are a dreamer. Perhaps that is part of your recommendation. I like people who have the imagination to dream. But that does not mean you can idle around, gazing wistfully at the rhododendrons. I do not want to employ a stoned hippy. I expect you to work hard."

" I am capable of that."

" So I am assured. So why the idiot grin ? "

" I was thinking. "

" Of what ? "

" I mean, you have land in excess of what most people can imagine."

" That causes you a problem, does it ? "

" No, no, in fact I like it."

" Good. I hope we can get on well Dewar. I don't really like going through all this rigamarole of interviews. So, naturally, when our mutual friend recommended you, well I couldn't be more pleased..."

Killeen was warming to his theme. He now gazed wistfully into the distance himself, but not in any dreamy fashion. His was the clarity of vision. And it all related to his garden. His eye took on its best faraway look. Dewar cringed, he just wanted to get the boring monologue over with, and then get to work. Killeen, to his credit, noted the reluctance in Dewar's eye, so he tailored his tirade to suit the newborn mood.

" You like this already, Dewar, that is good. I can tell when people are at home in my garden. Does that sound trite ? superficial ? Well maybe so, but only to passionless cretins. I have a large affection for this garden, which you believe to be a large expanse of land."

" It's bigger than most. "

" You believe size is an issue ? "

Dewar smiled, " Not in this context."

" Good, because I have had these insipid arguements before. My land's better than yours, my garden grows greater than yours, etc etc, ad nauseum. No, Dewar, there is no time for such nonsense. There is not time. Because I know this garden is great, historic, matchless, inspirational. I only take the tiniest smidgeon of credit for that fact. For I inherited the garden, along with many of its plants."

" I know that."

" You know of its history ? "

" A little."

" A modest answer, which does you credit. For I am sure you know much, even though there is a lot to learn, about this garden. You know, of course, it is one of the oldest in the country."

" I do."

" Rare varieties of plant brought from all over the world, by my ancestor, the Original Killeen ? "

" I knew that."

" And cared for with dedication and tenderness every generation since."

Dewar smiled shyly.

" Good, you recognise the gravity of your responsibility. The vegetable patch is probably the least of your concerns. There are the greenhouses, the flower beds, the maze, the copse, the large lawns, and the intermediate lawns, that is about it, I think."

" And the orchards. "

" Yes of course the orchards. But like the vegetable patch these are my special concern. Yours, on the other hand, will be the rare plants in the greenhouses, in particular the orchids, and most particularly the melancholy flowers. You are to watch and observe the growth of these plants. Any care will be under my strict supervision."

" What are the melancholy flowers. ? "

" Didn't you see them ? no ? Well I think we should take a quick glance then. "

They ambled in the direction of the greenhouses. Killeen waxed lyrical as they did so. He was warming to his theme a little too well. He poured out anecdotes with abandon upon the grasses and trees. All appeared to lead back to the illustrious ancestor, the Original Killeen. This ancestor struck Dewar as a barbarian chieftan. Someone who would slaughter your whole family if you did not return his ' good morning.' Dewar could detect a little of that savagery in the Killeen before him. He thought he should not dismiss this notion out of hand. Killeen was obviously used to being obeyed. The fact he charmed you into doing something, you perhaps found onerous, did not disguise the aristocratic manner. Dewar wondered if Killeen could have savage

365

outbursts of temper, much like the Original. He did not want to find out. Killeen was telling a charming story, of how the Original had punished an adulterous ploughman. The man had been dragged across a field, tied to his own ploughshare. Then he was stabbed with a pitchfork and then buried, half alive, in an unmarked grave. His partner in adultery was the Original's daughter, but still...

Dewar shivered. The anecdotes of Killeen did not break the ice, they merely ignored it. Killeen chuckled,

" You find my story disturbing, Dewar."

" Well it's not entirely pleasant."

Killeen laughed, " ' Not entirely pleasant,' a classic understatement. All the Killeens are ' not entirely pleasant,' if they feel they have been sinned against. Remember that Dewar."

They walked through a claustrophobic copse, through a maze that maddened Dewar with its many twists and turns, and across those lush,green hills. Hills that took their toll on Dewar's legs, which surprised him. The lawn itself looked like billiard cloth. But the ground underfoot was squelchy, it sucked at his feet remorselessly. With Killeen as soundtrack, however, the greenhouse was reached with a relatively quick amble. It was his favourite, the one that contained rare orchids and blooms in their riot of colour. Dewar did not have that fetish for flowers some gardeners have. Blooms were dissatisfying in their transience and fragility. But Killeen's array of rare flowering plants was enough to draw a gasp or two from anyone. It was overpowering, not least because the atmosphere immediately became tropical once you passed into the greenhouse. All the galaxy of colour that ever existed would persist here, but only under the utmost dedication. It left Dewar slightly intoxicated. As his eyes trembled to forms, on the various shades on offer, his nostrils were assaulted by cloying fumes. It was close, prickly to his skin, in this place.

" You will grow accustomed to it, Dewar." Killeen chuckled.

They did not pause among the blooms. They made their way slowly, in profound admiration, at least in Killeen's case. Dewar was struggling to keep his sensory faculties in operating order. And then they stopped. For there they were, in pride of place, willfully excluded from the other plants by a short fence. They were beautiful beyond reproach. Dewar never called anything beautiful, usually he was too embarassed. But the word lept from his mind regardless.

" Indeed they are, Dewar, but so deadly. We do not quite understand them. These plants are rare, beyond rare, and never, I repeat, never, to be tampered with."

The flowers themselves clustered in a variety of forms ; sometimes reminiscent of the form of a tulip, others the shape of a rose or a daffodil. Smaller blooms carried reminders of hibiscus, iris, violets, hyacinths, foxgloves - in fact every shape of flower Dewar could recall. And it did not stop there. For the leaves were of a soft, serrated, fern-like quality. A quality that also took its form within a variety of shapes.

" They look comfortable enough to lie down and relax in."

Killeen chuckled again, whatever the mood, his chuckle was slightly malicious,

" Indeed, I guessed you had a soul, Dewar, that you might appreciate them."

" And the flowers so..."

" So, what ? "

" Er, awesome."

" Ha ha, you are never given to flights of poetry, are you Dewar, not often at any rate."

Dewar blushed.

" It does not matter. For poetry can manifest within a person's soul without any need for words."

Dewar looked up.

" Good, you understand me. These plants instil poetry in a person's soul, as only nature can."

" I agree," Dewar managed to say.

" One thing though, as with many things in nature, there is a catch here."

" A catch ? "

" Yes. The scent of these flowers is as distasteful as their sight is inspirational."

" I find that hard to believe."

" Do you ? Perhaps at first glance you are right. But, I would suggest you take a breath of the bouquet.

" A breath of the bouquet, how ? "

" Just lean foward as far as you can. Do not touch the plant under any circumstance whatsoever. That's it. Now inhale, not a massive breath, just a deep one, and gently."

Perhaps there was a trick in store here. For the first tingle of aroma brought Dewar nothing but pleasure. It was the pleasure of awakened childhood, of fresh snow on Christmas morning, of a slowly crackling log in an open fire, of the smell of ground coffee and the deep arousal of a fresh breeze. But then the smell changed. The snow turned to slush, if not slurry even. Christmas turned into the barren greyness of early January. The coffee was insipid, cold and weak. While the fresh air became the fetid fumes that escaped from an old boiler room. That lovely smell of burning wood on an open fire became the rank smell of a stagnant pond. No other smell had ever quite assaulted him so. It tracked its way into his mouth and nose, cauterising blood vessels along the way. He could taste it. The sensation provoked thoughts, thoughts of despair and crushed feeling.

His recent breakdown, his own listless month of suicidal lethargy, simmered to the boil of conscious awareness. The awareness told him what he dreaded most - it would never end. Instead the depression would only hide, under the surface of his everyday life. Only to wake at times when his character was fragile, his vitality drained, like now, when his vulnerability was to the fore. He could feel the flow of dreary blood through veins, that grew ever slower, but would never congeal. For his thoughts and emotions would keep him always open, exposed, aware..."

" Dewar, draw back...Dewar, now."

The face had gone pale and the body grown lifeless. Dewar was apparently very sensitive indeed. This man was going right up in Killeen's estimation. Not the brightest bloom ever to grow, but possessed of enough character, if trained adequately, to make a real contribution.

" Breathe deep now, Dewar, as deep as you can. Don't look at the melancholy flowers, face away. That's it, there, some colour is streaming back to that dreamy face already."

" How can a flower make me depressed ? "

" We're not quite sure yet. Obviously it is in the scent. But we cannot find out what the scent contains, or how it acts on the human endocrine system."

Dewar was breathing easier now, his depression had lifted,

" Do you think it's a defence ? "

" A defence ? why that's quick of you, Dewar. Yes we have considered this. Though it puzzles us. For a plant to have such a defence mechanism, one that only operates on higher animals, those with an organised intelligence, why ? "

" Those with consciousness."

" Indeed yes, how many depressed field mice or squirrels have you ever heard of ? Not to say animals are exempt from feelings, of course they're not. But animals rely more on instinct. An animal seeking to uproot this plant would not stop because it suffered a bout of existential despair, now would it ? But a human might. "

" So these melancholy flowers have evolved to influence people, is that what you're saying ? "

" Or to interact with them, although this is only theory."

Dewar paused, thoughtfully and briefly,

" So where do they come from ? "

" We haven't even established that yet. They were an anonymous donation. Their most likely origin is the rainforest. Though which continent's rainforest we cannot ascertain yet. Plus, we still have to bear in mind, the possibility they are genetically engineered, the product of a laboratory."

" Which is why they're seggregated."

" Exactly. These plants have male and female flowers. So far as we here know, the blooms before us are male, therefore they cannot reproduce. We have had limited success by nurturing of cuttings from these plants, but they become weak, colourless. Their lifespan would appear to be endless, however, and they are hardy. Our botanists suggest they constantly renew their foliage, and so, with careful management, could last an age."

" Immortal plants."

" Quite possibly, although natural damage will take its toll eventually, if not disease. They will live a substantial period nonetheless."

" Incredible."

" Indeed, Dewar, or at the very least, worth tending with the utmost consideration. Now you know why they are so precious, why, indeed, you must never touch them, and certainly not attempt to pick them, under any circumstances. I would recommend you do not even get too near, as their bouquet has already given quite a bout of depression."

" I agree. Don't worry Mister Killeen. I'll be as careful as care can be."

Killeen chuckled, this one was less malicious than his others,

" Good."

And so Dewar was hired. He found the work a succession of m's - monotonous maintenance mostly. But there was still more than enough to learn. Killeen's estate had its own methods of plant care, developed over centuries. And he had to learn all of them, even if his tasks were mainly menial. He had to learn the rationale behind the reason for everything, because he might be called on to do anything. The Killeen Estate might be considered traditional in its outlook and organic in its methods. Dewar soon became versatile enough to accomodate this state of affairs. He grew into his new position. It was evident he was part of the community. For, naturally, there were a number of other gardeners, a mixed bunch physically, but uniformly taciturn. That suited Dewar. The work took all his concentration anyway. Though it did leave his imagination free to roam. And that was the first intimation that problems would arise. For those plants preyed on his mind, the melancholy flowers. They had sucked something out of him, that elusive thing that gave him soul. Dewar felt it, he wanted it back. For every time he remembered the plants the depression would hit him. As if a sink backed up, or a well overflowed, a disgusting, black water, his own melancholy, would seep up and over, into everyday life. It would almost paralyse him. Dewar kept his feelings together enough to work his way through these melancholic bouts. And so no one noticed particularly. He did not feel he could tell anyone.

He was afraid the depression could mean they would think he was unable to function, if it were made public. So he kept himself to himself. Something was needing to be done, however.

An idea entered Dewar's head without really asking permission. It grew into a conviction. Those plants were the birth and continuation of his depression. He had to nullify the problem. That would mean killing the melancholy flowers. But he would have to do it. Dewar loved this place, he wanted to stay, and he knew he was wrong. But he hated his depression, and that which was responsible had to go. He was convinced to the point of superstition, once the melancholy flowers had gone, his spirits would lift. He would have to break the windows near the plants, let the weather do its work, maybe let the dogs in as well, so it seemed like an accident. He would be absolved from the killing, it was simple.

Though once he resolved on this course of action, Dewar had little opportunity to put it into practice. He mostly worked with one or other of his fellow gardeners. And when he did not he was supervised by Killeen. Perhaps they sensed his intention. His superstition took the opportunity to make him more paranoid. Perhaps there was a healthy reason for not picking the melancholy flowers. They could inflict a bout of depression at people merely standing by. If he were to actively harm them, perhaps they had some more pernicious defence. And would not that fact make them ever more special. But Dewar's mind would not credit this. He was slipping into legendary territory here. They were not like the mandrake plant - of whom myth states cannot be uprooted by people. For its man-shaped roots gave out horrible screams that drive the would-be picker insane. And so the mandrake should always be uprooted by a team of horses, who apparently are less suseptible to the roots' complaints. But surely horses would be more suseptible, given their their renowned sensitivity. No. There were poisonous plants, plants that choke with tendrils, plants that smother with scent, plants that eat insects, even small mammals. Dewar had heard legends of plants that could consume people, they existed in the prehistoric past, in faraway Madagascar. But if a plant's most deadly attributes were only legendary, Dewar knew he could proceed with his plan. His feelings would only exaggerate the damage done by melancholy flowers, and they were the only things that would suffer hurt. The only problem would be to convince his co-workers of his innocence, once his plan had been implemented. For he would be close to the event. He would make it so the plants had been stolen by specialist thieves. They crept in, under cover of night, which meant nothing was seen. Their disruption broke the windows in the greenhouse, and let the dogs in, who caused further chaos.

It was hardly a master plan. Something told Dewar the course he was taking was childish, stupid even. He ignored this something and went about his business. Now he had formulated the plan he had to go through with it. For the melancholy flowers continued to torment him. Every moment of respite in his mind meant they moved in to fill the vacancy. Their cloying, numbing barreness overwhelmed him. If he ever vacilated these attacks made him renew his determination. And, finally, he gained his opportunity. Due to sickness and holiday, he found himself the only gardener available. Killeen had absented himself for the weekend. Dewar seized the moment that night, bringing the dogs outside their usual area of patrol, into the greenhouse. He carefully smashed a couple of panes, enough to give the impression of forced entry. And he walked in to confront these plants at last, wasting no time in seeking to uproot them. A hastily improvised bandana tried to shield his face from the fumes as he set his shovel to work. But they defied his efforts. He dug down further, to expose their roots. But they were hard, like vine, thick vine, and ran downward through the soil, further than anticipated.

Not to be deterred, Dewar continued digging, almost frantically. He now revealed a massive root system, that far outweighed the plants it supported. It looked suspiciously like cable. And that should have alerted him. It fact it may have, had he not caught a breath of that depressing scent. He tried to exhale, he tried to hold his breath. But the strain was too much. That familiar nauseating nothingness numbed its way into his metabolism. He could feel his veins seizing up. But Dewar redoubled his efforts. He would not let the depression overcome him. He desperately pulled at the roots now. They would not yield. He cursed, the depression was winning, he would not let it. He used his shovel like an axe. The cables were battered by the force of his desperation. And they were recognised as cables now. For they sparked and they smoked as his blows began to make an impact. And he would not stop himself. He had to finish his task. Only then could the depresssion subside. The blows rained down heavier, faster, as Dewar realised his energy was having a definite effect. Then there was a short circuit, apparently, followed by an explosion. Dewar was not entirely convinced, because events became strange at that juncture. The very nature of reality shifted around him. The greenhouse and the rare plants began to fade. Different plants took their place, the scraggy undergrowth that always colonised unkempt ground, no more exotic flora now, just toxic weed. The dogs, timid or placid till now, barked. They were revealed as mangy, diseased curs rather than the friendly pedigree breeds he knew. Dewar panicked, he ran from that place. But now his senses could find no respite from the game reality now played on him. It smelt of game gone off. He made for the hills, those lush,green hills. They were now revealed as slag heaps, poisonous, brown, sticky slag. A combination of noxious substances, manure was too inadequate a term to use. Dewar remembered the wearying, pulling sensation this ground made on his legs. That much at least remained the same. And some reason began to trickle back into his brain. What were the melancholy flowers ? Why did he have to pick them ? were they a guard ? or a deceit ? But these thoughts gave way to panic again. He heard shouts, angry shouts. They were after him, so their reality had disappeared also, whoever they now were. Dewar was painfully aware he had done the wrong thing. But he could not comprehend the nature of the wrong, nor the nature of much else beside. He made his way to the claustrophobic copse, whose trees were now revealed as decayed tenement blocks. In the pockmarked windows of these teetering structures, there leered the malevolent gaze of tenants. And sure enough, they pointed at him, they cursed him, and they threw things at him. Dewar ran.

Comparative safety might be found in the maze. But the maze was only a derelict factory, roofless, just waiting for the weather to demolish it completely. It was only now used as a rubbish tip. The screams of carrion birds greeted him as he stumbled his way through this wasteland, through piles of stinking landfill. Flocks of gulls flew screaming overhead, as if accusing him. Eventually the rubbish thinned out, there was another building, derelict again, but more complete than the factory. It looked like some old railway station, forever waiting on the trains that had now abandoned it, looking so stupid and useless now. At least it would be a place to hide, to collect his thoughts, then use them to find his way back to the reality he had so clumsily destroyed.

The Killeen returned instantly he had the news. His grim, taciturn followers were a motley bunch, fully naked in their moroseness. But their loyalty was always certain, the more so now, as their security had been breached and their livelihood seemingly evaporated. They had to stand together in the face of this adversity. They waited on the words of their master.

" You know who is responsible ? "

" Dewar, " said a slovenly, ape-like man.

Killeen's mouth turned down. This man smelt, as did the others, less savoury parts of their lives were now being revealed.

" Well, my good people, you see the crisis before you. We must work to restore our former glories. It will be hard work. And we will start by tracking down that man responsible."

" We know where he's gone," said a sullen woman.

" Good. He needs remedial treatment first. We need to know how he was driven to break the barrier, to ensure the necessary preventative measures can be put in place."

" Then he'll be given a good kicking," said the ape man.

" Yes, he will, to be sure. Punishment is part of the treatment. He has dropped us in the excrement, surely, and needs must take his retribution. Mistakes always require learning. Chances are he may not survive treatment of course."

" We don't care, we want our old lives back," said the ape man.

" Aye, our old security. To be reminded of what we're like is a real pain," said the sullen woman.

" Indeed. Reality must be put back to rights. Time is of the utmost essence. So, let's be going about our unsavoury business."

They made directly for Dewar's hiding place.

Old Father Slime

Renton was pleased to see his old friend Carmichael again. It had been some time. Carmichael was very secretive, but this time had actually deigned for him to visit his flat. Renton felt privileged, Carmichael was as mysterious as he was charming. Renton supposed this was par for the course for a successful lawyer and local politician. Carmichael's new flat looked over the Wandsworth bank of the Thames. It was a new development, Renton thought it smelled of extravagance. But then the area had a reputation as far as he was concerned, for over priced, badly designed property.

But Carmichael did not take offence,

" It's okay Renton, I know you have certain principles. This area has changed out of all recognition since we went to school here. But it hasn't all been change for the bad. This area is now more pleasant than it was. Although I must admit I've always liked it."

" You're too pleasant yourself, Carmichael. You see good in everything, always the liberal. When all I see is the heart's been torn out of this area. It has lost it's character."

" Hmm, that may not be so bad. I thought the heart was a bit rotten myself, and the character in need of improvement..."

" At what cost ? pricing the local inhabitants out of the area ? "

" That is a moot point, Renton. I feel it's a shame, yet I also feel there is better quality of life to be had."

" You would say that, because you can afford a place like this."

" I can't actually, I'm going to have to let."

" You old trickster, you always did live beyond your means."

" And why not ? I've always believed everyone should have access to the good things in life."

" Even though it must be maintained by any means and leads to debt ? "

" Not necessarily, though debt does seem to be an all too frequent consequence. Besides, I would hate to leave this area."

" Pleasant memories ? "

" Not at all, some pretty unpleasant in fact."

" Such as ? "

" Well, I used to dread coming over this side of the river when I was young, sitting on the bus going to school. I used to have to cut through that sprawling estate, you remember ? There were always gangs of snotty-nosed, local kids to look out for."

" How could I forget, It certainly didn't help, our grammar school being situated in the middle of a grotty estate..."

" Aaah, not to keen to take the locals' side now."

" Well, not in that respect, some of those kids were gruesome, ha ha."

" Yes, it does seem funny now. But I hated it at the time. Most of those blocks seemed like slums in the making. The flats smelled terrible, and kids were like, I don't know, these evil smelling little goblins, with their tricks and their threats..."

" Did you ever get bullied ? "

" No, not really. Though I was chased a number of times. In fact I did get to know one or two of these kids, just by the fact of seeing them constantly."

" You were lucky, they always stole my sweets."

" Yes, that kind of thing was always going on. I don't know how I wrangled it. But still, even though I was the upwardly mobile kid from across the river, I came from a background similar to them, so I didn't particulary look down on anyone, not even an oik like you, Renton."

" Sarcasm gets you everywhere, Carmichael, ha ha."

" Yes, but seriously I did become good friends with some of these kids. It may have helped that I gave one of their bullies a bloody nose. But we did have some fun. I found them exciting. They were always daring me to do things which I would never have the nerve to do otherwise.."

" Such as ? "

" Oh, silly kid things, jumping from first floor balconies onto the grass, climbing down the riverbank. That's how I obtained those coins there..."

Carmichael gestured to a row of four coins on a shelf. They were mounted and set within acrylic plastic. Renton had not bothered to notice them previously,

" Interesting, you know know these look really ancient."

" They are, or at least I think they are. I can't get many experts to agree with me on that."

" Why ? "

" The designs are a bit beyond their experience, although they never said in so many words. Some tried to say the coins were some kind of novelty issue, fairground money if you please, while others thought they may be pre-Roman."

" You mean Celtic ? "

" Well they were found near a site where a few celtic ornaments and weapons had previously been found."

" Strange designs on them, are they Celtic ? "

" Not the usual Celtic motifs...look at the figure on this one..."

" It appears to be a scarecrow, with an axe in one hand and a severed head in the other."

" That's as good a guess as has been made. "

" And this one, it looks like a part man, part octopus."

" Again, another reasonable guess. I've been told they are heavily stylised abstract representations of gods and goddesses, or forces of nature."

" Sounds a bit vague to me."

" Indeed, but vague is all they can be. "

" They seem a bit too detailed to be abstract representations, or is my imagination running away with me."

" I've thought along similar lines, Renton. They are reminiscent of science fiction monsters to me, it is as if I can visualise them almost."

" Isn't that just being fanciful ? "

" Of course, but what a strange thing to trigger a fancy, and why trigger such a fancy ? I don't know."

" Ugh, I don't like the thought of it being based on anything that's real, even if it is just inside the head."

" Well it does remind me of something, that's why I kept all these coins."

" Don't tell me you've seen the living creature on which it's based, Renton."

" Well, it was a childhood episode."

" But something like this can only exist in the imagination."

" Perhaps it was my imagination."

Carmichael had blurted this last remark without thinking. The conversation had taken a life of its own, unusual for someone such as him, who always managed to keep the flow of conversation to a personal minimum. Renton looked at his friend with interest. There was always mystery in his friend's demeanour, part cultivated. Now the mystery had briefly slipped, which only deepened Renton's interest."

" What was your imagination ? "

" Oh nothing, just a childhood flight of fancy."

" Really, Carmichael, you can't say that, not now I'm intrigued."

" Too bad."

" You cannot leave me in suspense like this."

" I think I'll have to. You know the pair of us take great pride in being, I don't know, a bit experienced, we don't suffer fools glady..."

" I'd like to think so."

" Well, if I tell you a childhood fantasy, this might undo all that."

" A childhood fantasy ? I was under the impression you couldn't tell either way."

" Well, I don't think I can, so it's too bad."

" Oh come on, Carmichael, would I laugh at you ? "

" I don't care about you laughing at me, but laughing at my sanity.'

" Do I have to doubt your sanity on the basis of a story you tell me ? "

" Of course not."

" Well ? "

" I suppose so, you push too hard, Renton."

" And you intrigue too much."

" Well, I suppose I'm bound to continue now. You already know I used to play around the river a lot. I was always drawn to it. It was big, gloomy, heavily polluted at that time. But it was also exciting. And I wasn't the only one who felt that way, whole gangs of us used to explore the riverbank. We were always warned off by the adults, because of the obvious danger of a swiftly flowing, polluted river. They tried to scare us by saying the bogeyman had several homes along the riverbank..."

" A fairy tale landlord ? "

" Ha ha, yes. Although his residences consisted of storm drains and sewer outlets, the numerous tunnels and gates you see dotted along the riverbank around here. Various kids had testified to seeing this bogeyman. They were never believed of course. For, even when you're young you try to separate the credulous from the incredulous. But once I turned eleven, and started coming over the river, I found out this bogeyman had a name..."

" Which was ? "

" Old Father Slime, if you'd credit it."

" Ha ha, well, not bad, not bad bad at all. That does show a little imagination at least."

" That's what I thought. I mean, this was no vague character anymore. The estate kids all talked about him as if he were another local resident. "

" Part of the scenery.."

" Perhaps, a part of the scenery that wasn't acknowledged too much. Parents used to scare us with it, but never mentioned it apart from that. It was more of a talking point among ourselves. We were more convinced of his existence than any adult. In fact some of us wouldn't dare mention his name in front of an adult, because it seemed they did not fully appreciate this terrifying figure as we did. "

" Why ? "

" Kids and their secrets I suppose. I never thought to ask, I just took it for granted. Although now I do think it strange. Most of these kids didn't care what any adult thought, least of all their own parents."

" Well, you always have your secret names and your secret places when you are a kid."

" Yes, but this was a secret I think we'd rather have shared with the adults, because it put the collywobbles up us.."

" Ha ha, yes. I'm not laughing at you, Renton. It's just the recognition from my own childhood."

" You encountered bogeyman monsters in your own childhood ? "

" Only adults."

" Hee hee. No flights of fancy ? "

" Oh the usual stuff, raw head and bloody bones under the stairs and sleeping demons under the bed, that sort of thing."

" Yes, yes. That kind of thing was terrifying enough. Though we soon learned to distinguish a parent's warning from an actual happening. Old Father Slime was a fable, but not just another fable..."

" Real, in other words."

" Don't put words in my mouth, Renton. Let me tell the story so you get it in context, then you can judge.."

" Okay, okay. So there was more to Old Father Slime than just another tale...":

" Yes. I used to hang around with a family of about five brothers, and various cousins, till I was about thirteen. They were always the ringleadrers. What they said we all did. It was usually some stupid dare, like playing chicken on the high street, or exploring those parts of the riverbank we weren't allowed to go. There were one or two derelict wharves, and an abandoned factory..."

" Where ? "

" Pretty much where these apartment blocks are now."

" I do vaguely remember a factory."

" Right. Grim place too, we used to love smashing its windows. Other times we would walk along the mud and shingle at low tide...All fun in its way. But one day these brothers, the Dolans I think they were called, told me they knew where Old Father Slime lived. They knew his current address."

" He moved around the property ladder a lot then."

" Ha ha, yes, a prototype yuppie I suppose. Anyway, it was something I didn't want to know. But they took me there regardless. It was an old sewer opening just by Battersea Bridge. There was a big, iron gate at its entrance, shaped like a front door. It was always locked of course, but you could peer through the railings to the dark, smelly world beyond."

" So how did they know he lived there ? "

" The Dolan kids claimed they saw him moving around inside. Sure enough, there was a light source in that tunnel, although that could have been a ventilator shaft or whatever...I wasn't really convinced when I was shown this gate. A whole gang of us had gone down there. We thought perhaps we might might get a glimpse of some monster, but all we saw were a few shadows playing on our imagination instead...That might have been that. However, I had to admit, I didn't want to be convinced there was anything down there. It was a rank, evil-smelling place. But it began to take a hold on me. Every morning I would go to school on the bus. The bus would crawl over that bridge as if it was scared of tipping over. And I'd always be looking at that gate, for you could see it perfectly well from the top deck of a bus. It caught my gaze and would not let it go. I don't know how many times I stared at it, it became part of my routine. I think I half wished I was down there, having some kind of scarey adventure, instead of going to school...

And of course one day I actually saw something. I saw a hand reach out from inside and clasp one of the railings, a dark, gnarly hand. It shook the gate as if it wished to be let out..."

" Over active imagination."

" Possibly, I don't know. I didn't particularly believe I saw it, even then. I'd seen enough monsters in ghost and horror stories. But they were on telly and in comics. I was relieved the world was not populated by monsters and demons, at least not everyday life. Even if I did want a bit of excitement, I didn't want too much. But then I saw the hand on the gate on another occaison, then I began to see it regularly, not in any routine way. It always appeared just as I least expected it, even though I continued to stare at the gate every morning. I started going a bit sulky, sullen. Other people remarked on it. But it was put down to the usual adolescent bad behaviour. How long I could have gone on seeing that hand on the gate and sulking I don't know..."

" Probably indefinetly, you always were a good sulker, everyone was afraid to talk to you."

" Really ? but then sulkers are miserable sods, aren't they. Even they realise it sometimes. And I realised then I did not want to feel like that all the time. So, at the first opportunity, I told one of the Dolans, who I knew would scoff, then would go along to investigate. He could see I was a bit scared. So we bunked off school one afternoon. We picked up some other Dolans from the estate, and we resolved to break open the gate and go in. We had to be sure it wasn't real. What we were supposed to do if we found this Old Father Slime, I don't know. Although Neil Dolan suggested setting him on fire. That was his answer to everything..."

" That's right, I think I heard he was a bit of a firebug."

" A bit too much. Last I heard of him, he went to reform school. He set alight the bins behind one block of flats, unfortunately the fire caught, and the block had to be evacuated."

" So, did you get inside the gate ? "

" In the end, yes. But we had psyched ourselves up until we had to. It was a reluctant walk down to the river bank that day, but one we were always going to do. One of the older Dolans had got hold of a massive crowbar, and after a lot of huffing and puffing, we completely busted the lock on that gate. We still had a bit of a problem getting in. The gate was embedded in mud and sludge, eventually we forced it open enough to squeeze in. Then there was the smell, it stunk worse than a million toilets. Huge puddles of dubious material pockmarked the ground..."

" But then that was a tidal area."

" Indeed, but wading through a stagnant pond was preferable. Still, there we were, there was no turning back now, no one wanted to be called scaredy cat. An adult would have had to have had to crouch all along these slimy tunnels. But since we were shortarse kids that was no problem for us. We could see grilles overhead as we shuffled through this tunnel, inspection hatches or whatever. But it seemed we were the first people to inspect this place in years. It looked as if the place had been totally forgotten about. We turned a sharp left as the tunnel veered around. It broadened out into a room, the size of a sitting room I suppose. Various smaller tunnels led off into blackness. This was as far as our search would go, we all knew that without speaking.

Because the room itself gave signs of habitation, or at least the fact someone had been there. There were old sacks strewn around, crates, a roadworks oil lamp, empty bottles, a sodden mattress, and various other crap we could not identify. It made us think someone was staying there."

" So Old Father Slime turned out to be a tramp."

" Well, we thought of a tramp, but it didn't seem right. Half of the day this room was covered by the river."

" An aquatic tramp ? "

" Ha ha, yes, we knew it was strange. And once our eyes grew accustomed to the poor light, we noticed other objects..."

" Such as ? "

" Well books mainly, old books with weird writing, and sodden like everything else, though still in readable condition it seemed. We flicked through some of them, I did catch what looked like Latin or Greek phrases, but I only realised what they were years later. There was other writing as well, looking like no other script I have seen since. We came across illustrations, illustrations of anthropomorphic creatures, dog headed men and so on. These were fascinating, a real catalogue of monsters."

" You discovered Old Father Slime was really a classical scholar ? "

" Yes, a classical scholar squatting in a sewer, God, what a tongue twister. I would have liked to have left the whole episode there. We would have stayed ages, staring at these books, but someone found some coins, and they looked valuable, so we all scrambled around to see what we could get. And that's how I got those coins you've been staring at yourself. "

" And that was that."

" No, we probably would have ransacked the place a bit more. I was on the point of helping myself to a tidy, little tome, with its ornate metal clasps, when we heard the gate clang shut. Then we heard these dragging, shuffling footsteps, straight out of an old horror film. However, the fact that it was not on telly meant it was terrifying. It was happening, and we nearly wet ourselves through fear. When

389

the derelict actually appeared it gave us a sense of relief. He was a repulsive, blotchy, greasy individual, but apparently he looked human. He was also fat, which I remember as being unusual for a derelict. He was completely hairless as well, everywhere, not even any eyebrows. His clothes were brown and green, long since rendered featureless by wear and tear. And, of course, he stunk to high heaven. It was overpowering...Well, he had us caught redhanded, so to speak, and we just stood there, it was his move now. And he found this amusing, what did he say - ' I see now I'm to have young lads pay me respects, as in the old days. I've been out on the wilds too long, not like before, You go along with me, me boys, and you'll see things you'll never believe, and give you power you always command."

" He said that did he ? "

" Words to that effect, memory doesn't fail me that much. I probably got one or two words wrong, but I remember when he spoke that it sounded like music, even though it was gibberish. I was won over. I don't know about the others, but they were standing as frozen as me, so I believe they were experiencing the same. The man was intensely charismatic is the only way I can describe it."

" He hypnotised you ? "

" Not as such. I'm aware that adults can have a hold over children anyway. But this was different. It was just being in the presence of something desirable, and I wanted to stick around. And that's what we did. I don't know how long we stood there. But then he started turning his gaze on each of us individually. I caught young Tony Dolan's eye, and the fear welled up again. I think he felt the same, for he suddenly started whining about how he had to be home. This cut through the man's mood entirely. He grabbed Tony by the arm and threatened to molest us, no, it wasn't quite like that. He said he would poison our dreams forever, a weird threat if ever I heard one...But the change in atmosphere already produced a change of mood in us. Two of us attacked the man, who grabbed hold of them in turn, and held them in one hand with ease. I tried kicking him in the shins I recall. But something pushed me back, nearly cracking my ribs. The other kids were screaming now. Then I realised he hadn't any fingers. His arms ended in slimy stumps. And the grip he maintained was somehow produced by his own flesh wrapping itself around their own arms..."

" Are you serious ? "

" Yes, but as to your implication regarding what I saw, I don't know. I can only say that's what it looked like, and that's what it felt like to my companions. The man began threatening us. It was the most vile abuse you could think of, even in an age as secular as ours. I cannot remember the words, they seemed to make me shrivel up. I think now they were literally soul destroying. It was all to the effect that everything about us would die in pain, our minds, our souls, as well as our bodies. In fact his voice became so charged he began speaking other languages, ones I've never recognised. I reckon we were into pure hysteria at this stage. But I was helpless, I could not move. Then Neil, good, old firebug Neil, out of nowhere picks up this old roadside lantern, which, thankfully, was alight. He somehow shoves it into the man's clothing, and the flames catch instantly, not a big conflagration, more like the steady burning of a candle wick. Although, in this case, the man's slimy flesh was the wick. Of course he dropped the others as the flames spread. And while he was occupied trying to stop the spread of burning on his own body, we scrambled past him, all of us, clutching and pulling at each other, not wanting to be left in that place. We ran out of that gate as one, falling into the soft mud outside. Never did the stinking brown mud of the river seem so pure as at that time, and never since. As we caught our breath, we were about to run as far as we could. But we noticed the sounds were still coming from that sewer opening. In fact they coming toward us. We backed off. I think we still wanted to see what condition he was in. The curses continued of course. By now they were horrible burblings in some gutteral language. And then he plopped out of that tunnel. And plopped was the right word. It reminded me of a shit breaking up as it drops out of your arse into the toilet... I'm sorry to be this crude, Renton, but it is the most appropriate description. The difference being that this man was on fire as he broke apart. Once we saw this phenomenon, we scrambled up the metal ladder that ran up from the riverbank to the road. The pieces of slime continued burning as they broke up. The bulk of the man oozed himself into the river, what was left, and then hissed and steamed as it disappeared from view. The other parts of Old Father Slime that had dropped off, just burnt away into nothingness, much as plastic would if you set alight to it. All that was left were smoking stains...

Well, after that little show we went all quiet. We didn't know what we were going to do. But we never would hang around together again. Nor would we tell anyone, until now anyway. It was just too weird. I never saw the Dolans' again. And I started taking a different route to school, over a different bridge. It took me longer, but it was worth it. I also avoided that estate like the plague. People thought I was a bit timid about getting beaten up or something, or they felt I was a bit weird, but I didn't care. There was something that happened a bit later which reinforced this behaviour. Two people, apparently giving each other oral sex, were killed and cut up in the most brutal manner. Their remains were found outside the gate. It was talked about at school for ages. I'm not sure if it had anything to do with our adventure there. Although one or two reports remarked on the smell and traces of slime…Whatever, I'm never going back, even now…"

" But, at my estimation, we can't be more than a couple of blocks from the scene…"

" I know. Sometimes I think I can never go too far away, even if I never go back. Does that make sense."

" Some people might say it's obssessive."

" I'm sure they would. But then they didn't have an experience as weird as that. I don't know, I don't think I'm particulary damaged by the incident. I don't even have dreams, never have had. I feel life is empty and pointless sometimes. But then I've always been like that. I don't feel strongly about anything."

" He said 'poison your dreams', maybe he meant render them ineffective."

" I can't afford to believe such nonsense."

" It is an extraordinary story, I can see why you didn't tell anyone."

" And I'd appreciate you keeping it that way."

" Of course, I'm not going to betray anyone's trust."

And that was it. Carmichael never felt the need to raise the story again. And it was just a story. Childish imagination can run riot sometimes. So Renton tried to dismiss it. Nevertheless it intrigued him. And in the weeks that followed he found it played on his own imagination. Carmichael was strictly averse to even mentioning the subject again. But Renton did not mind. He found his own route to and from home to work now took a detour. He took a bus every day across that same bridge. And every day he peered at that same gate, repaired and renovated over the years, but still there. He felt silly. But he knew he might see something, eventually, and that would lead on to other things.

The <u>Commuting Compulsion</u>

The famous Manwatcher observed the lunch hour from the first floor of his Islington terrace. The office workers scurried to and fro at unnatural speeds. And of course there was a traffic jam, or a 'Gridlock,' as Manwatcher liked to call it. He pursed his lips, and grasped them between thumb and forefinger, in a mock thoughtful gesture. Just as his books were written in a manner his critics called mock psychology. His one idea was that human physical motion betrayed an underlying ocean of psychology, or something like that. Every little twitch had a complex at its core, he liked to say. However, the strength of his insight was not reflected in his writings. For he made the most banal observations from everything. And the notion of people having any intention in their action was, of course, anathema. It was all dictated by the twitch and fidget of bodily functions. Mister Manwatcher was unconcerned by any errors of judgement in his observation. He could always put it down to some unknown biological drive. The mysterious road the biological drive travelled was unknown to most people, but he knew the way better than most.

The office workers all leaned foward as they walked. All were pasty-faced, if clean. As distinct from the few lingering, malingering unemployed, those uneducated unfortunates who slouched along with a surly laziness. One or two workers adopted pompous, upright attitudes, to suggest they were people of importance, or they were not to be messed with, or both. He never could work out the distinction. But it was all a bit depressing. Nearly all the people he saw nowadays were commuters. Studying commuters had to be boring in the end. He had tried diversifying recently, and shuddered at the memory of it. He tried exercising the Manwatching talent at a pub called ' The Hedgehog's Hand.' Luckily he had escaped with his life. It seemed the drunken collection of misfits and psychotics did not appreciate the wisdom of his diagnostic anecdotes. What made matters worse was when they found out his name. They assumed he was some kind of pervert on the prowl. And when he insisted he was a professional at his job it became time to run. Yet he must not get depressed. He put his current misgivings down to fact he was meeting his analyst friend, Simon Cruise. Cruise indeed, he cruised through everything. Life was more important to Cruise than any process or underlying theory, so he said. Manwatcher thought Cruise's ideas to be dictated by biological drives. Irritatingly, Cruise did not disagree. Instead he pestered Manwatcher with irritating questions, such as ' What drives the biological drives ? ' To which Manwatcher could only answer, ' The biological drives are the core of everything, you cannot go back further.' To which Cruise would retort ' You're saying the biological drives drive the biological drives drive the biological drives.' Manwatcher would then lose his temper (his professional temper, naturally). A full blown arguement would usually ensue. Even so, there was a guarded respect from Manwatcher toward his colleague.

Cruise now saw him leaning out of the window and grinned that supercilious smirk of his. Manwatcher returned a feeble frown. Pulling himself back into the room, he banged his head on the raised window. Manwatcher was irritated at himself as the pain smarted for a long minute. He made attempts to compose himself as he went down to answer the door. Cruise could always scent irritation, and he relished making it worse. No, that was unfair. It was Manwatcher's own professional and personal pride that was rattled, even he could not deny his own vanity. One could not deny something so large.

Even the way Cruise rang the doorbell seemed sarcastic. It was a short, loud, jolting buzz, that always made Manwatcher jump. He opened his panelled front door to meet the man with the permanent smirk.

" How's your head ? hee hee hee."

" Fine, thank you. I don't know what is more irritating, me doing it, or you seeing it."

" Maybe it's the magic combination of both."

" Magic shmagic."

" Wasn't that the catchphrase for a childrens' T.V. series ? "

" I neither know nor care. Now, what can I do for you ? Mister Existentialist. Have your problems become too much for your imagination to solve ? "

Cruise's eyebrows raised in automatic admiration.

" Quite perceptive, for a passive observer that is. Yes, there is something that has been bothering me. It's the behaviour of some of my customers. Although I don't know if you'd call it a problem yet."

" Then you don't want the benefit of my observation on your facial gestures ? "

" Not after you turned my sister into a nympho."

Manwatcher squirmed. He knew what Cruise referring to.

" But I only suggested her body lanaguage was too stern. Then I gave her some techniques for relaxation."

" How very true. She relaxed to the point of not caring what was happening to her, or to anyone else for that matter.

" Look, I'm sorry, I've apologised enough for that, Haven't I ? "

" Yes you have. And, much as I would like to blame you for it all, I can't. Besides, you're good company, for a determinist anyway. Although she still blames you."

" Ho ho ho, R.D. Laing. You better come in before I start liking you."

" My pleasure, Desmond Morris."

The two men went upstairs to the first floor. The drawing room was large, regency style, though the furniture was mock antique, twentieth century copies for those who like all things old. Manwatcher helped himself to a whisky and brought the bottle of malt over to the armchair Cruise had sunk into. The pleasantries, if there were any, were brief. Both men became impatient when the point of a discussion was too long delayed.

" So what is the problem that is not a problem ? "

" Well, I'll have to pad it out a bit, if you'll bear with me. I'm sure you're aware that commuter traffic has increased lately."

" Really, such insight. I know, I've been watching it myself. But surely that's due to economic factors."

" I thought so too. But I'm begining to think there's something else as well. What time did I arrange to meet you ? "

" Approximately two hours ago. So what ? I just assumed it was your usual slack punctuality."

" Nice of you to say so. But seriously, I never try to be more than an hour late, if I can help it. So, with that in mind, I set off from my practice at two o'clock."

" Really, and it took you four hours, I don't believe you."

" It's true."

" Well, roadworks, traffic accident, probably, something like that. There are always delays."

" I Thought so too. But I had the traffic reports on, from the radio. There was the usual - a lorry has shed its load, tailbacks at so-and-so, etc, etc. But there was nothing directly effecting the route I was taking."

" Well the roads in and out of London are a mess, and public transport can't cope either, we all know that."

Cruise was nodding his head, like an adult trying to be patient with a dense child.

" All true, all true. But even with these circumstances, it should not take me as long as it does to drive into London, outside the rush hour I might add."

" So what ? "

" So what I am getting at is - traffic seems to have increased for no particular reason."

" Am I supposed to be interested in a banal statement like that ? "

" Well it's not just me. A lot of my appointments have been cancelled, or just turning up very late, saying the very same thing."

" So write to your M.P. "

" Be serious will you. You know my customers. They're forever writing to the newspapers or complaining to the local council. It's as much a part of the life in Sutton as tapas bars are in Islington."

" You're saying, if I'm right, there is a mysterious increase in traffic, despite every explanation offered. There's not much insight to be offered in that."

Cruise let out a big sigh.

" Oh look, I Haven't finished yet. There is another element."

" Which is ? "

" An increasing number of conversations I hear seem to involve driving just for the sake of it..."

" Why don't you listen to some other conversations ? "

" Let me finish, please. I'm Talking both personally and professionally. And, it is true, they are the most boring conversations imaginable. For people seem to enjoy driving the same routes in their spare time that they take to work."

" So ? They're all becoming trainspotters."

" I think maybe that's true, in a sense. I think driving can become obsessive at times. But there's something else as well..."

" Really, this is like a soap opera. You keep dragging things out to keep me interested."

" Well, if you'd stop interupting all the time, maybe I could finish."

Manwatcher held his hands up to placate his friend.

" I don't think I am, too much, but go on."

" I keep hearing, that people who take the trains into London every day, are also taking it up on evenings and weekends as a hobby."

" Trainspotting again."

" Perhaps. Some people hold that trainspotting is a mild form of obssessive-compulsive disorder, perhaps even a mild form of autism."

" Yes, just as tiredness is a mild form of depression, and anger is a mild form of schizophrenia."

This last comment by Manwatcher was delivered in a scathing tone. Cruise acknowledged his friend's point.

" Well, we can shove the theoretical hairsplitting aside, for now. But the circumstances remain."

" And your proposition remains - people are taking to commuting as a hobby, either by driving, or using public transport."

" Exactly."

" Ridiculous."

" Look, it's even true of the buses and tube trains. They're all packed, from the first service to the last."

" All that can be accounted for by more people going out ; to the theatre, restaurants, to see friends and what have you."

" No, you'd have to experience it, believe me. And you can't explain it by cutbacks in the services either."

It was Manwatcher's turn to sigh.

" This is leading up to something, isn't it ? " You want me to take a ride with you. Poor dear. Public transport must be such a traumatic experience for you."

" I don't like public transport, true. It's too overcrowded, and run down. But I want to prove it to you. I think it will develop into a problem. My suspicion is that people are obtaining habits designed by the motion of transport. Pretty soon, you may hear of cases where people simply cannot stop this endless commuting. Everyone I know talks of this endless travelling. But they just disregard it as ' one of those things.' But , I believe, the physical and mental toll of constant travel, will mean large numbers of people burning out. It is a psychological time bomb as far as I'm concerned."

Manwatcher sat back thoughtfully in his chair. A brief silence followed.

" You really are concerned, aren't you."

" Yes. I know it sounds daft, but most psychology does."

Manwatcher nodded.

" Okay. We will conduct a simple experiment. What we need to do is take a train, preferably on a commuter route, at an hour when it should be reasonably empty Any ideas ? "

" Well I thought of us leaving in a couple of hours, when the rush has died down. But I'm not sure which route to take."

Manwatcher considered a moment.

" The Thameslink line would be best. That's an overground train and commuter service, with Tube links. We can get it from Kings Cross."

So Manwatcher and Cruise set out on their self-appointed experiment. Some time was wasted wandering around Kings Cross in confusion. Then they found out the Thameslink station was a different building, a short walk away. It was busy, packed, hot and sweaty. Boarding a crowded train, they breathed stale air until the train reached Luton. By this time the men had lost count of the stations en route. And the speed the train travelled suggested it may have been quicker to walk. Eventually both managed to stagger out of Kings Cross, from a return journey no less uncomfortable. Their irritability only diminished significantly when they reached Manwatcher's house, and downed a refreshing whisky. Both men spent a long time staring at the ceiling, punctuating their stares with long, drawn out sighs. Then Manwatcher ventured to speak,

" Well, what a gruesome experience."

" I'll say," said Cruise, still dazed, " I think driving is bad enough. But the trains are infinitely worse."

" You realise this doesn't prove anything on its own. We need to undertake repeated journeys on trains, at all hours of the day, for your hypothesis to be proven."

" I've proven it as far as I care to try, thanks all the same. I'm not getting on another train..."

" You can do the driving then."

" More irritation, I don't think so."

" Even if you were paid."

" You mean research money ? "

" Sure, I believe I could work something out, This phenomenon interests me. I think it requires further investigation."

" Well, I'd rather be counted out, I'll do what I can, of course. I don't want to repeat the passenger experience myself. I'm fairly satisfied there. Though I would be interested in your findings."

" I thought you might say that."

And that was it. Manwatcher did gain some funds for research. Though it was hard work. Few sponsors were interested in something like this. They thought it was a waste of time. This rendered Manwatcher somewhat irritable. Indifference he could handle. Being treated as if he were playing a prank was another matter. Still, he persevered with his observational experiments. And he gave Cruise regular updates over the phone. But Cruise proved harder to reach as the experiments progressed. Manwatcher always seemed to get his friend's answerphone. Eventually, as Cruise never returned his calls, he gave up. By this time, the constant travelling on trains was taking up too much of his time anyway. He had to admit it was addictive. The feeling you were always going somewhere, always in motion, always had a destination in mind, was consistently reassuring. Even the cramped conditions could be tolerated after a while. His fellow travellers seemed to be a group of zombies at first. Yet, as he travelled more, he realised this was not the case. He felt he became more accepted by these commuting veterans. A wink here, raised eyebrows there, a suggestion of a smile, all contributed to his new sense of belonging. It was a complex code of subtle messages whereby commuters shared their experience. Limited space made for a limited repetoire of communicative signals. However, there was the shared notion they were all going somewhere, some further than others, on the mystical, magical tour that was commuting. Once or twice, Manwatcher even indulged in sporadic conversations with his fellow travellers. These were necessarily brief, boring and banal, as travelling etiquette demanded. Manwatcher could see he would have to indulge in a lot of commuting before he mastered its finer nuances. However, by the time that thought occurred, he had forgotten just how long he had been travelling. In fact it seemed he had stopped observing, and started simply enjoying, the experience of getting from A to B in a large crowd.

For he now realised he could not remember home very well. He did go home of course. For the trains did not run all night, not on his chosen routes. Though he was considering the prospect of branching out on his commuting. He was scared he might miss something unless he was travelling. Then the fear soon vanished as he began travelling again, it was so engrossing. Time began to become a series of timetables. Day and night were interchangeable. He put his fears down to the prospect of losing himself in his commuting. But this, he realised, was only a childish fear, a bit like the terror a child experiences at its supposed loss of liberty on the first day at school. He could now put this down to inexperience. It did not matter. He was now totally interested in the commuting experience.

Only one thing bothered him slightly. While trying a new route one day, he thought he saw Cruise, at the other end of a packed carriage. He was too embarassed to call out. So he tried to force his way through the massed ranks. This was a breach of commuter etiquette, as he knew well by now. But his curiosity overcame him. It was a grim struggle trying to force his way through. Elbows jabbed into his body, people trod on his feet, and blew curry and alcohol breath into his face. Widespread tutting began all around him. His fellow travellers sought to embarass him into behaving. He was about to tap Cruise on the shoulder, when the effort and the embarassment finally overcame him. By the time he recovered from his attack of shyness, Cruise had gone. Some kind soul had helped him into a seat, and left him there. Still, never mind. He knew he would run into Cruise eventually. This gave him extra incentive to ride the trains, not that he needed any. They would have a lot of experiences to compare.

YXSY GLYXSY IX

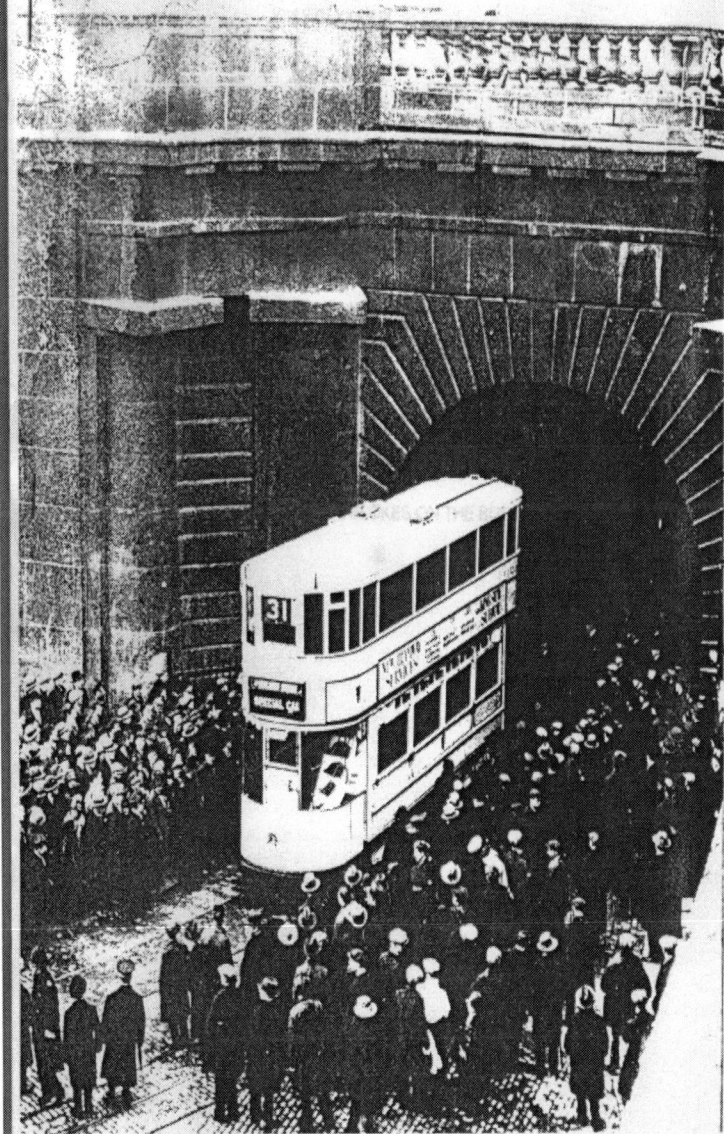

Black Cabs are Satan's Allies

I had to clear up the mess that was once Lochlin's flat. It was not something I was looking foward to. I never liked him completely - he was a pretentious journalist. (Lochlin was not even his real name, it was Stan.) But I was bound by familial duty to put his affairs in some kind of order. There was curiosity also, I must admit. Like all pretentious people, Lochlin could be interesting at times. I had a copy of his jokey article to hand -

' CABBIES ON THE MARCH '

' Beware the black cabs my son, with engines that screech and driving that's crap, right wing speech and a temper to match.

They may say they offer you a public service. What kind of service charges you money before they have even done anything ? You step into their cabins of control and they grip you in a vice that surely takes hold. Even stepping into this diesel monster costs you. They will soothe you with banal conversation, and encourage you to leave the drama of driving to them. But do not attempt to interrupt their easy flow with conversation of your own. For this will make their tempers go, and they will pin you down with a motormouth moan. Never query their driving, this will send them barking, even though they will stop at every traffic light. They will twist and turn, making tyre rubber burn, making money for the meter and your bank balance lighter. These detours of theirs are called short cuts, they are the quickest way into your wallet, since they really pile on the miles, and the pounds. And the fares climb higher, quicker than a fly with its arse on fire. Yet you are forever at their mercy. And you must tip them for their heavy levy, with abundant generosity, or you will see ferocity. They will scowl at you, as if you were the lowest of cheapskates, who only deserve a miserable fate.

How did this state of affairs come to be ? Well, long, long ago, in this, our fair city, cabbies saw they could clean up rapidly. Their country of origin was the depths of hell, and they had the glare of a ne'er do well. They took something of their native land into the body of this city. Once so fair and peaceful, it became home to chaos and destruction, by the bucketful. Black cabs roamed at will, spying stray pedestrians, and looming in for the kill. Pedestrians were knocked down at random. Other road users were abused in tandem. All other traffic was cut up, mercilessly. People were kidnapped off the streets, to pay huge ransom demands, before they were released.

Concern was raised at a governmental level, and after much hand-wringing, it decided there was trouble. It undertook to deal with this rabble, but only after a struggle. The cabbies should be clipped by the authorities, otherwise they would extend their territory. Yet the black cabs got wise, and with government devised, a strategy that hinged on consent from authority. They were allowed to continue on their rounds, giving abuse to all around, running people down with alacrity, treating the roads as their property. They merely toned their act down, slightly, and gave the authorities a cut, weekly, of the sums raised by their terror and unfair play.

For black cabs have demonstrated an intimate knowlerdge of the city. In a complex place, this can be of use to authority. Thus the mayhem and destruction continued, but under licence and with permits. They would appear, on the surface, to be tamed. Yet their ghastly, satanic mission remained. They want to bring the revolting rule of the hellish lord to bear on this once fair city, without a care. They have already dragged the demon Mammon into the metropolis, who holds the North of the city under the sway of finance. The South cannot be tamed, it is given over to acts of violence and depravity, by tribes of barbarians. There are enough barbarians in the North, of course, but these are subservient, even though they do not know it. The barbarians of the South are too wild to be subservient, too ill-disciplined to be trained. And this is why no black cab will venture south of the river.

Do not let the modern cabbies of today fool you. They have attempted to change their ways, all the better to deceive you. With their modern manners, their non-smoking cabins, their new age demeanours - these only further disguise their unspeakable iniquity. They change their colours to reds, greens and blues, yet their aim is the same, to thoroughly fleece you...'

This was a weird read, completely loopy, but I still liked it. And normally I would pay it no further mind. But Lochlin's disappearence had made me slightly uneasy. Had he managed to offend someone in his pretentiousness ? It was over-the-top satire, but some people queue up to be offended. There was a tiny kernal of truth in his article, I suppose, but no more. People always moan about cabbies, they always have done. I had a lifetime hearing complaints.

Even so, someone would have to pretty desperate to be outraged by the article.

But the uneasiness would not go away. Suppose he was not just ranting. For he was not fully acting the comedian. For a pretentious wanker he could get quite passionate sometimes. And he did have a keen sense of what he saw as injustice. Maybe I am too harsh on him. Most London journalists are all of a piece, they are the definition of clueless wankers. This is a prejudice, I know, I can be a clueless wanker myself, when I make the effort. This does not mean I hate these people. I do not have the energy to hate. I just know what they are. And Lochlin was a cut above your bog standard journalist.

Anyway, the screech of brakes outside brought an end to these thoughts. It was the peculiar squeal of the black cab's brakes. I looked out of the window, and there they were, hovering like two fat flies on the road, some three stories below. Ever since I started coming to this flat, I spied a cab or two outside. They were keeping an eye on the place, for whatever reason. I could not be sure, for I had not asked them, and I was not going to. It was not entirely unusual to see cabs roaming around. But this was a bit of a rundown area, not much chance of picking up fares. There was not even an office of the black cabs' arch enemies, the minicabs, here. I recalled my last conversation with Lochlin. It was in that grotty pub down the road, the Kings Arms...

" I'm telling you, I'm begining to wish I didn't make those jokes."

" Which jokes are those ? Lochlin."

" Calling cabbies evil-minded, satanic bastards."

" You're walking home tonight, obviously."

" I'm serious."

" So, would they have noticed ? and if they did, would they have cared ? "

" They notice everything. They're not as blunt and bigoted as you think. Actually, they probably are. And they have a genius for the accumulation of facts. Nothing escapes their attention..."

Lochlin took a huge swig from a half-full pint glass. Some cheers went up from a table further along the bar. It was nothing to do with our scintillating (?) conversation. A pub quiz had been in progress. And that lucky group of braying donkeys had obviously just won. Since they drew everyone's gaze, I took them in. They were oldish, worked hard all their life, and had gained some security in later life. They were dressed like colour blind football managers, and were all cast from the same physical mould - short, roly-poly and red faced. My guess was cabbies. But I never needed to say anything. Lochlin scowled,

" You see that lot ? cabbies of course," in a suitably lowered tone of voice.

" You reckon ? "

" I do reckon, definitely."

" I'm not arguing."

" No one has a grasp of factual information like the cabbie. It comes from taking ' The Knowledge,' that mind-numbing task that means they have to absorb the name of every street in London. They have a big hippocampus, you know."

" Lucky for them," I laughed, " or maybe they should see a doctor about it."

Lochlin grinned at the suggestion of a double entendre.

" Yes perhaps it does sound funny. But it is a part of the brain that deals with learned patterns of behaviour. It allows the absorption of facts at a rate that would defeat you or I. It allows them to swallow masses of boring routine, and to recall it when the time is necessary."

" Good for them."

" But not for the rest of us, I fear."

" What ? "

" Think of the power such a talent can give."

" They can win more pub quizes, so what ? "

" Ah, but, you know it's the types who pay attention to detail who usually succeed."

" So why isn't there a cabbie prime minister ? "

" Maybe there's no need." He tried to sound enigmatic.

" Oh come on, Lochlin. Anyway, people who pay a lot of attention to detail are mostly dull and plodding. I wouldn't describe cabbies as that. Leery and plodding maybe."

" That makes them all the more disturbing."

" So what are they going to do ? plan a military coup ? "

" Again, there's no need," but he had a grin on his face.

" Lochlin, don't take this wrong, But I always thought this attitude of yours toward cabbies was dictated by personal experience."

" Aren't all attitudes dictated by personal experience ? "

" They don't have to be. We don't have to be prejudiced all the time."

" What do you mean ? "

" Well, cabbies are no better or worse than other Londoners."

" That's not saying much."

" That's cynical, although there is some truth in it... What I am saying is - the bad experience you had with cabs in the past has coloured your judgement."

" Coloured my judgement, yes, although your twee phrase doesn't do it justice. You remember the accident I had on my moped ? "

How could I forget. He had related the incident to me so many times before. It was a proof of the injustice of the world, or of this city anyway.

" ...I was merely driving along, not doing more than thirty. It was pissing down, and that makes mopeds unreliable, the roads get really slippy. So, I was trying to be the good, careful rider, when, whack, a black cab just pulls out from a side road in front of me. Of course, I do a somersault, I go arse over tit, all over his bonnet. He hit me so hard it pushed my arm out of its socket, until it poked through the flesh on my back..."

Lochlin went quiet as he relived a bit of pain. Then he glared at me, demanding my sympathy. I nodded my head and he continued.

"... Eventually I did land on the ground, unable to writhe around even. I just whined away in pain. And that lump of lard, well, he just sits there in his cab until the police get there. I had three witnesses, who all gave me their support in court. I had him bang to rights. But he still got off, some technicality or other. I was so shocked. He got off scot free, the way they always do."

" Why should that surprise you. You hear about it all the time. They've got good lawyers."

" So, I had a good lawyer. But it made no difference whatsoever. They always get off. I've never heard of a cabbie being prosecuted, for anything."

" Oh come on, no one's above the law, you know."

" No I don't know."

" You're saying they could get away with murder."

" It's a distinct possibility."

Lochlin gave me his best knowing look, as if he were an Agatha Christie detective.

" Oh come on, that's too much."

415

" I don't believe it is. It may sound too much. But it also may be closer to the truth than you imagine."

" You're going way over the top."

" Am I ? Didn't you say you had trouble with a cabbie, last week, yourself ? "

" Did I ? well yes, sort of..."

And I had to relate the incident again. I had taken home two girls. Not that I had got lucky, you understand. It was my regular girlfriend and her best mate. Of course, like all best mates, they enjoy a good arguement . However, on this occaison it turned a bit heated. A fight started. And it spilled out of the cab once we reached our destination. I left them to it. They were going to pay for the cab, and I had heard them carrying on like this too many times already to take them seriously. But the cabbie was worried. So worried in fact he pursued me, and tried to start a fight with me for not paying the fare. Since he was a huge, fat bastard, I found this intimidating. Although the girls quickly placated him when they saw my predicament.

I was fed up of telling this story already. Lochlin sat there in ' I told you so ' mode.

" It proves nothing. The girls believed it was my fault anyway. I suppose I should have said something."

" But it illustrates my point, don't you think. He was leery, and wished to start trouble from the outset. He didn't bother to find out what the problem was..."

I was not at all convinced. I remember leaving soon after. Lochlin was getting on my nerves, a bit too much...

Back in the flat, I was rifling through a desk. Streams of paper flowed out as I ransacked its contents. It was mostly crap, one or two pads, but these were filled with scribble, gibberish, doodles. Then I stumbled on a notebook. It was the same free-associative rubbish. But in some pages there were attempts at journalism, it seemed.

...15/5... I managed to infiltrate one of their cafes. Those strange, green buildings you used to see throughout London. They are cabbies cafes. Unique-looking, from the outside, like mutant post boxes from the 1950's. There are still enough of them left to be recognisable. Though I doubt if most modern Londoners could say what they were...

I met a fat bigot in a flat cap. I shall call him Weeble. (It's his nickname, I forgot his real one.) He invited me in for a fried breakfast. It was like visiting a midgets' home, a midgets' home that's been gatecrashed by podgy cabbies. It was cosy though. It had to be. There was barely enough room for us all to squeeze round a table. Funny, the whole atmosphere reminded me of the time I was entertained at a masonic lodge, as if people were finally trusting me at last. The conversation soon killed off that thought. It all revolved around the contents of that day's newspapers, which, of course, my cabbies comrades had thoroughly absorbed. Now I remember why I mostly skim the newspapers. The meal was dreadful. Lumps of fried meat that might as well have been lumps of lard. In fact they probably were. There was a runny, gooey substance that purported to be an egg, and what looked like shrivelled nipples, but were allegedly fried tomatoes. The whole thing was swimming in a plate, more like a bowl, of grease. It reminded me of a rumour I had heard only just recently. That all cabbies are compulsorily retired at fifty five. And the method employed for this is an induced heart attack - while driving the streets of London, naturally. I was tempted to broach the subject with my cabbie comrades, but thought better of it. For there is another rumour I heard. It states cabbies have to undergo a routine surgical procedure when they are appointed, the complete removal of their sense of humour. Even I can show a little consideration and tact at times...

417

After this insulting material there was more of a considered attempt to be objective. Though Lochlin always let his prejudice show in the end.

...20/5...I spent the whole day with Weeble. And it was like spending it with a stranger. He was full of conversation all day. But he never told me anything. And everyone we met, and we met quite a few of his cabbie compadres, was the same. They babbled like it was going out of fashion, and about nothing in particular. We spent half the day lounging around in the bar of some swanky restaurant. These cabbie clones kept coming up to Weeble. I swear it was like the masons. They talked the usual banalities. But all of them made the same gestures - the hand movements, the winks, the shaking of the head. Yet they were all done in the same order, in the same way. I asked Weeble about this. I was expecting some kind of angry denial, but he just shrugged. ' Course it's mysterious. You can't learn the cabbie's life in a couple of days, there's a bit more to it than that.' That was the gist of what he dismissed my question with...

...22/5... A day in the cab with Weeble. He blathers like tomorrow is never going to come, and he has to get all his words in. He says the punters are getting a bit more stupid these days. He used to be able to hold a decent conversation with his punters. Now they all sit there like lemmings. Maybe he should try letting them get a word in edgeways...

...25/5... Pretty much the same. Heard an interesting rumour. Well I believe its interesting. It's more of a story. It says, the first man to drive a black cab in London, sold his soul to the Devil for unlimited knowledge. He spent all his time driving - his favourite activity, and so he could show off his unlimited knowledge, by going wherever he pleased and never getting lost. And when the Devil came to claim his own he could not find this cunning cabbie. For the

Devil did not know his way around the streets of London. After becoming lost several times, he gave up his claim on the cabbie's soul in frustration. But he could not help but be impressed. Therefore the Devil entered into negotiations with the cabbie. The pact was changed into a treaty. The cabbie would lure unwary souls into the back of his cab for the Devil's delight. This cabbie's name was Freddie Faust. If you ever got into the back of his cab and saw his name stamped there, then beware, you were finished. Though how you were finished is not made clear. Neither am I sure just what the Devil's delight entailed. Maybe he watched the cabbie bore you to death with banal conversation. I'm being facetious, but I am bored shitless at the moment... Maybe they all get stuck in a traffic jam for eternity, that would be hell...

...26/5...I thought Weeble might have disappeared. Then I could have a real story - ' Masonic Murder in Cabbie Cafe,' or something like that. But he turned up, late, which was unusual. He was very glum, unlike him, since he never shuts up normally. I wondered whether he had been disciplined in some way, or ' got to,' as he would say. But he wouldn't say, he was sulky all day. This made things even more boring. Why did I come on this assignment ? I can feel my will to live seizing up...

It broke off there. Pages had been ripped out of this book. I did not believe it was anything sinister. Lochlin was always ripping things up, throwing them away and starting again. And following his paper trail was like that. As soon as I felt I was getting somewhere, I had to look through another pile of gibberish to find something meaningful. Why was he shadowing cabbies ? It was indeed as boring as it sounded, or was it ? He seemed to hint at some thing or other, which was probably nothing. Lochlin was always good at building up an air of mystery. He never told anyone what he did, until he finished. Then he moved onto his next project, and protested he was too busy working to waste time talking about the past. His colleagues at work could not help. No one really oversaw his work. He could be an irritating twat sometimes.

I did glean some whispers however, no more than rumour. A spate of murders had happened in East London at the time. The victims were all found in the back of a London Cab. The cabbies were never under suspicion of course. Since their vehicles had been stolen some days before the murders took place. Yet this aspect, plus the nature of the killings themselves, did suggest a ritualistic element.

Moving back to Lochlin's flat, I thought about these killings. Lochlin did mention something to me once, along those lines...

" I'm telling you, they're a dodgy bunch, they run the whole show..."

He was as pissed as a fart on this occaison. This was unusual, since he never got pissed, although he was a fart.

" Who ? cabbies ? "

" Most powerful group in London."

" So why're they stuck in London traffic all the time ? "

" Where better to gain information."

" The newspapers."

" Be serious."

" T.V."

" I said be serious."

I shrugged my shoulders, not really caring.

" I'll tell you then."

" But I never asked."

" But you need to know anyway. It's people."

I cringed,

" So what ? everyone knows that."

" Ah, but not everyone has access to a wide range of people, certainly not the wide range of people you get in this teeming metropolis."

" That's right, it's always teeming in this metropolis."

" You're being unduly sarcastic."

" So what if I am ? "

" Well perhaps that's understandable. But if you knew, as I do, you wouldn't question the cabbies power. With their fearsome knowledge of the physical geography of this city, is allied their knowledge of the people who live in the city. It adds up to a fund of facts greater than any politicians, or journalists for that matter."

" That's not difficult."

" You believe it's not saying much ? "

" It isn't."

" Actually, it is. And you shouldn't let your everyday cynicism distract you from taking an interest."

" Even if it is boring in the first place."

" You're not listening to me."

" I am."

" But not properly."

" I don't have to. I just don't believe your wild claims about cabbies."

" You want proof ? I'll get you proof, reams of it. This tedious assignment finishes soon. Once I get my notes into some kind of order, you'll see it. You'll see I'm not just prejudiced, and if I am, I've got enough reason for it. You'll see who really runs this place, and people do run it..."

" Not possible, this city's too chaotic."

" But that's what they want you to think, don't you see..."

" No I don't."

" It's the best con there is. Once people assume everything's a mess, those who know how to exploit a

421

situation will clean up. Like our dear friends the cabbies, who get up to all sorts of mischief under cover of chaos."

" Under cover of chaos ? such as ? "

" I'm not being drawn here."

" Because there's nothing to draw on."

" No, because you won't believe me. You'll have to see it first. "

" Well, if you can get proof, I'm open minded."

" Good. You'll have to be when you see some of this stuff, mark my words."

I did mark his words. He was getting on my nerves again. I was being drawn into one of his stupid stories, I felt. Though he had piqued my interest, he always knew how to do that. I screwed my face at the memory of his alkie and baccy breath on that occaison. That is my last memory of him. That was the last time I saw him. I forget how long it was before anyone noticed Lochlin was missing. You are going to miss a person like him eventually. About two months later I was called in , through a mutual friend of ours, another journo. And there was the family link as well. Although I saw Lochlin from time to time, we were never that close. But I was the closest one to him, I realised with a start. So I took it on myself to try to sort his affairs out. No one else was about to do anything.

That is why I found myself strolling back to Lochlin's flat, on a fresh Autumn day, when I would rather be anywhere else, with a computer nerd in tow. I needed the nerd to access Lochlin's computer files. The nerd never said a word. We walked in silence all the way. I noticed a cab was parked oposite the block, engine running, while another passed occaisonally, brakes screeching. It was tempting to pursue certain lines of thought here, i.e. in paranoid conspiracy terms. But I really could not be bothered. I was afraid of becoming as paranoid as Lochlin was.

It turned out the files were accessed quite easily. The nerd sighed in disgust. He was obviously expecting much more of a challenge. Well it was a challenge, for me. I quickly paid off the nerd and sat down at Lochlin's old desk. I must admit, I was semi-excited. What would I find ? more paranoid prejudice no doubt. But I was looking foward to it. Again I had to wade through mounds of gibberish, however. Lochlin wrote exactly the same on file as he did in longhand. I moved around his files in some frustration. But then I lucked into some kind of blog, at least I assume it was. Like all Lochlin's stuff it needed stringent editing.

...Weeble has vanished, off the face of the Earth. I even called at his home. His wife was not worried. I gained the impression Weeble often disappeared for a few days, often to Amsterdam. She was a charming woman. And she was not in the least bothered by her partner's disappearance. Well, who would be ? he was a fat bastard bigot, but he had his good points, and he was my main contact....

...I'd been hanging around the rank, and then the cafe, for ages. Weeble's old compadres are doing their best to pretend I don't exist. Weeble himself has ' pissed off ' so they said. No one could confide any more, even if they did know anything. I was on the point of going, when this shady looking cabbie, one Brian by name, said there was a ' meet up ' in a couple of weeks. They are going to discuss ' the business,' whatever that's supposed to mean, probably a load of masonic types trying to be mysterious. I might check it out though, I suppose...

...Interesting stuff. Brian pointed me toward the library, in Guildhall. In an obscure room there I waded through these dusty old tomes. There was a legend, is it relevant ? who cares...Back some thousands of years ago, there was a celtic chieftain, Bladud, who wanted to take the ancient city from his rival, one Bludwyn, who ruled it. For years they fought. Bladud had conquered the tribes south of the river, yet could never consolidate his hold on the north. Bludwyn always drove him back. Bladud got cunning. He asked a druid, or some equivalent, to hypnotise, or drug, the charioteers of Bludwyn's army. They were put under some kind of spell. At low tide Bladud's army forded the river on horseback. They were met by the charioteers, one for every four horsemen. They split up and staggered their entry through the city's different gates with ease. For Bludwyn's charioteers could come and go as pleased. And they knew the city well. They took the horsemen to every major strategic point, every bridge, every temple, every camp. And, at a prearranged signal they attacked without mercy. They destroyed most of Bludwyn's army, who were taken completely by surprise and scattered. Then, gorged by their success, they began massacring the other inhabitants. Bludwyn escaped, mustered a small force, and fought his way back over the river. On the south bank he found some remnants of Bladud's force, plus his other people. So, to return the favour, Bludwyn massacred everyone in sight. Once Bladud heard of this outrage, he crossed back south, but was unable to find Bludwyn. Therefore, he resumed his masscre on the north bank. Bludwyn crossed north again in a bid to regain his territory, but was beaten back. Bladud then sought to regain his old territory again, but was beaten back. Several years of fighting followed, always ending in stalemate. In the end an uneasy truce prevailed. Though Bludwyn laid his most sinister curse on the treacherous charioteers, Bladud himself was not cursed. But the charioteers had reneged on their oaths of loyalty to their masters. And the curse would linger over the charioteers and their descendants for centuries...

Well there you go. The medieval chronicler broke off here. Then he related a story of some three centuries before his own time. It seems the Norman rulers of the city, in the Twelfth Century, had taken some severe action. For ritualistic murders were rife in the city. They were blamed on the jews at first. But the killings were too many, and too various, to be attributed to one group of people alone. Eventually they were traced back to one of the guilds, the Carters, those who made and hired out such vehicles. A detachment of soldiers was sent to their guildhall. All the inhabitants were massacred and the place was burnt to the ground. Afterwards, a gathering of monks surrounded the place and chanted psalms for forty days and nights. And then silence. The chronicler criticises the Norman Barons, who acted arbitrarily it seems. Yet he says he understands their actions in the light of the abominations that were practiced here, which, of course, he doesn't say anything else about...

The Chronicle just ends. There was nothing else that caught my interest as much. There were plenty of historical matters, but they all referred to the everyday business of government and administration...

...I have since discovered another intriguing (to me) piece of history, that may, or may not be related. It is more gossip, rumour and legend of course. And it relates to lurid conspiracies of power and murder. It seems, when the rapid expansion of London occurred in the Mid-Nineteenth Century, various bodies were scrambling for a slice of the huge wealth that was flowing into the city. This is hardly esoteric. It was reasonably well known that London expanded far too fast for the governing bodies that oversaw it. But organisations who already possessed enough clout were in a position to extend their power further. And so various bodies jealousy guarded their own rights and privileges as they sought to gain the advantage on others. Everything was up for for grabs in a city now industrialised on a scale hitherto undreamed of. People flocked here from all corners of the globe. Trade and enterprise had opened things up, for all-comers.

And this is where the coach drivers, or hansom cab drivers, come into the picture. There was yet another spate of ritual killings. Though this time they involved relatively affluent people, at least in some cases. This appeared to suggest there was a power struggle going on. Bodies were found in the backs of strategically placed hansom cabs. And , of course, the drivers were exonerated, as their vehicles had been stolen some weeks before. It was stated that some of the victims were despatched in a manner ' far too horrible to mention.'...

I have to admit I got a horrible little twinge on reading this. I mean, one of recognition, rather than my usual bodily behaviour. Brian kept leading me onto this stuff, for what reason I'm not particularly sure. My guess is some kind of attempt to draw my own conclusions from carefully presented facts. So why doesn't he just tell me ? I'm prepared to believe all manner of outlandish statements. I did look for some confirmation of these Nineteenth Century slayings however. I do have some scruple. There were just brief throwaway sentences in all periodicals of the time, apart from the mediocre, sensationalist rag I read the details in at first. There was definitely a series of unsolved murders, nothing more.

I did think of talking to Brian more. But he started to avoid me. Brian was worried something might have happened to Weeble. The others had complained Weeble was much too ' pally ' with me. And, besides that, nobody loves a journo that much...

This looked like another break off of Lochlin's, how annoying. These entries were put down in his scribbly way, as if in a hurry. Maybe he planned to revise them later. It was a pity he was so lazy. Anyone else would have written up this material by now, somewhere, despite the pressure he may have been under. I thought there should be more of his notes around. Did he not say he had reams of them ? Then there was something else to be found, perhaps in his old workplace.

So it was back to his office. It was a long shot, as his stuff may have been cleared out already. But I thought I should try anyway. I discussed it with his editor and got agreement. Lochlin's desk had been locked for weeks. Although the editor could not say say just when it had been closed. After all, he had been missing a while before anyone became concerned. I saw Lochlin's colleague, Bridget. The three of us opened the desk. And of course it was empty. Someone must have got to his papers already. I was assured Lochlin's desk was stuffed with papers, it was its natural condition. Bridget would never have dared go through his desk. Neither would the editor come to think of it, though he often told Lochlin off for his general slobbiness. And now the desk was pristine clean. There was shoulder shrugging between us. The editor and Bridget went back to their work. I had an extra rifle through the contents just to be sure. There were empty document wallets, containing a few time sheets, nothing more. I flicked through them absent mindedly. But too carelessly I am afraid, since I knocked a few off their rails. As I tried to refix them I noticed an envelope lying under the wallets. This I lifted deftly from the drawer and placed within my own case. I did not want anyone else to see the contents. I wanted to check them out first. He was family, after all.

And so it was back to Locklin's old flat. It was evening, and the cabbie was still there, waiting, that is, if it were the same one. They looked alike to me. As I crossed the road another black cab whizzed past, within a centimetre of me.

I could feel the slipstream as it passed. But I resolved to pay this no further mind. I quickly ran up to the flat.

Once inside I settled myself and began reading. Inside the envelope were typed pages -

...If you read this, please refer to the documents deposited in the box at -------Branch Office, ------ Street. My life is in danger. I may be dead already.

Last night, the 30th of June, acting on advice received from an informant, I surreptitiously entered the Council Annexe at ----- Road. I was led to understand that crimes would be committed on these premises. Unfortunately I found that to be the case.

I was to observe a ceremonial rite from a vantage point , on the balcony overlooking the main Council Chamber, with my informant, one B. Marsford.

I did observe this rite. It was of an osbcure, occult nature. I did not understand the bulk of its procedure. It consisted of a number of chants in a question and answer mode. The ceremony appeared to climax, when a bound, semi-naked man was led into the hall. Robed participants gathered around this man, who was tethered to a makeshift altar. I recognised this man as being a former informant, the man known as W, who had not been seen for some time. This man was repeatedly stabbed in the chest. Then his blood was drained before his heart was finally removed. Both of us observers could not refrain from an involuntary gasp of horror at this act. This led to our prescence at the hall being noticed. Though I do not believe we were recognised. We left the premises quickly. Once outside, B advised me to disappear. And I have not seen him since. If this man could be tracked down he would make an invaluable witness. This is my sworn , factual statement of what happened on the night in question...

Was Lochlin captured by these robed participants ? It did not seem so. Although he was definitely scared of them. So scared in fact, he wrote a note to me...

... You are the only one I can trust. I hate to be melodramatic, as you always accused me. But it is probably advisable in the current circumstance. I have to be careful when I go out now. Every time I go outside, I seem to encounter one of those black, metal monsters trying to run me down. One day I know they will succeed. I know it sounds ludicrous, but cabbies are part of a demonic order that allied its fortunes to the forces of darkness eons ago. Over thousands of years they, and their forerunners, have been building up their power, until such time as they can open the portal, and LET THE DEMONS COLONISE THE CITY. Once established in one of the world's great financial centres, they will subdue and enslave all life on this world. I know this sounds beyond the realms of my fantasy. That is because it is, yet it possesses its own reality. Even my elaborate jokes or flights of paranoia would not go so far.

And if you do not believe these claims now, I have amassed proof that will convince you. And it will convict 90% of all black cab drivers. So please, get the documents from the safe deposit box, and give them to the appropriate authorities with all due haste. Please hurry, for the cabbies' task nears completion. They have already unleashed some noxious creatures in this city. And this is nothing compared to what will follow. The best way to describe it would be to say it was inviting Satan and his minions to take up residence here. Of course there is some scientific explanation for what they are trying to accomplish. It involves the harnessing of natural forces under their complete control. Yet , put in that way, it does not do justice to the sheer evil of their intent, their psychotic agenda for life on this planet, and the reckless way they will spend the lives of others. If you think their behaviour can be obnoxious now, wait till they are freed from restraint...

Lochlin had broken off again. Yet I was not as annoyed now. Now I had found what I was looking for. His completed documents, the rest of his reams of notes, would be in the safe deposit box, I knew. I printed off his computer files, then deleted them. I gathered all his scattered notes together. There was a decent briefcase full. And I left his flat. Once outside I noticed the ever-present cabbie hovering around. I walked straight up to him and got into the back of his cab. He spoke first -

" Did you get everything ? "

" I think so. The rest is in a safe deposit box. I believe I' ve taken care of everything else."

" Do you want me to take you there ? "

" Please."

I told him the address to go to. The cab veered out, then cruised foward, with some purpose.

" Once we get hold of the contents we can rest easy," I said.

" At least till the next nosy hack comes sniffing around."

" Possibly. Although not many are as good as my cousin, you have to admit."

" I'll give him that."

What cousin Stan, or Lochlin, never remembered, was the fact two of my family were cabbies. We were never that close in the past, so maybe you could excuse that oversight. But maybe he should have checked it out, before he started involving me in his conspiracy theories. It was another example of his sloppiness I am afraid. Although he was a good journalist, generally speaking. He got further than most.

Pillar Box Protest

I am a sort of radical type geezer. I always have been. Everyone else calls me a twat. And they are welcome to call me that. So long as they do not mind my pointing out their misconceptions on this matter. Unfortunately, they do mind. They will not listen as I explain their concepts away. For they are only the result of mass media conditioning. They represent no more than crude statements of prejudice. Of course the discussion often gets no further. They usually lose their tempers and start becoming violent. Since I am fundamentally opposed to violence I have to put up with these temper tantrums. And I often had to stand there while my tormentor behaves like a demented orang utang. What these poor people do not realise is that taking out your agression on others does not solve your problems. It is only a temporary response that does little to soothe the symptoms, let alone eradicate the cause of their problems. I told certain people I thought might benefit from this message. They in turn told me I was not welcome at certain places anymore. Unless I held my life to be worthless of course. I was not sure such intimidation was called for, I tried pointing this matter out. Unfortunately I had to run away rather quickly. So I was persona non grata for ages. I could not go out at

431

all. Well I could, but I would probably end up having a race with some idiot who wanted to catch me, for some reason or other. But subsequent events won them round to my ideals. They all rallied round when my protest started. Although at first I thought they were rallying round to give me a good kicking.

Did I say I was living somewhere ? Well, actually I was squatting. It was old offices, really nice fitted carpets, and a few too many desks everywhere. But I did find an old sofa, quite comfy, even if it did give me fleas. It was better than most legit properties I had lived in. Anyway, one morning a vanload of men with tattoos, and no necks, pulled up. They smashed their way into my squat. They were some kind of private security firm, very good if you wanted things smashed up at a reasonable rate, apparently. These security men chased me all the way up three floors of empty offices. And all the way down an outside fire escape. For huge blokes they moved quite fast. They kept pace with me all the way. I was begining to get a bit frightened. For they ran me out of that building and continued to chase me. I learnt later that I was indeed to be made a scapegoat. The landlord was fed up with his properties being squatted. He intended to put others off by my example. I was not too sure of the legitimacy of this venture. It was a huge grey area. Though at the time it felt like a huge brown area. It seemed like any excuse would do, so long as those security men could rearrange my anatomy somewhat. They chased me all the way down the high street. They would not let up, I was scared stiff. I needed a convenient hiding place, secure enough to protect me. But there was none. However I did come across a postman, filling a sack from an old pillar box. He was a bit clumsy, he spilled his letters all over the pavement. And while he scooped to pick them up, I darted in his open box. Needs must, as they say. Amid all the traffic noise the postman did not notice me. But the security men had seen everything. And as the postman locked me in his box, they came up, gasping. They were too late.

The postman took some convincing there was a twat inside his box. At first he thought the security men were playing a game of double entendres with him. But I shouted out through the letter opening that those men would kill me if they had the chance. The postman hesitated, causing annoyance to the security men, who threatened to rip off the posties head. At which the postman began to lecture them about damaging post office property, while backing away hurriedly.

An amused crowd of onlookers had gathered, taking in the unfolding drama. The security men caused a bit of a scuffle as they tried to wrestle the postman from his keys. In desperation he stuffed them in the letterbox. One of the men stuck his chubby hand in the gap, so I bit his fingers, they tasted horrible, like spam that had gone off. Now they were really going to go to town on me. But their curses and threats only attracted a copper. This officer managed to pacify the security men. This was after they had painted me as some kind of public monster. My account of events was broadcast through the letter opening, it painted the security men as psychotic barbarians. Convinced by these accounts that the truth of the matter lay somwhere in between, the policeman made a decision, he would ask someone else back at the station. The security men grumbled but could do nothing but grumble, since a large audience would witness any unsavoury actions they might consider. So they slouched off to think of their next move. The audience was intrigued. They had listened to both accounts avidly. Their support veered toward me. This was more out of sympathy for the underdog, than for the justice of my case, since the common opinion was that I was a huge twat. I thought one or two voices were familiar. Some of my previous tormentors were there. They pretended they were not surprised at my predicament, which was very amusing.I worried about them, for until that time they had wanted to do the same to me as the security men. Now that was forgotten as they laughed their heads off. In the interests of democracy I must credit their share of the idea for my protest, unfortunately. For they suggested, in a sarcastic manner, that this was another of my half baked political stunts. Sensing a way out of my predicament, I agreed. I told them I was squatting a pillar box to protest at the lack of affordable housing in the area. There was more laughter, but also murmurings of sympathy. Some people took up this idea, they offered their support. Somehow a petition made an appearance, with enough signatures to make a scene at the local town hall. As time dragged on I hardly noticed, for I was interviewed by a local councillor, a local journalist, and a T.V. crew. Various supporters of mine were also interviewed. I was getting a bit embarassed by now. For everyone seemed to think I was doing some kind of good deed, even if I was a little weird. I made the six o'clock news that evening.

Eventually, the police and post office found their keys, lost their patience and unlocked the box, to the jeers of my supporters. I was led into a van, a token arrest. For all those people in uniform seemed to be having a good laugh at me as well. I was detained only a few hours, with a warning not to try stunts like this again. I was blushing by now. I would have gone home, but that was definitely out of bounds now. Instead I thought I would risk my local pub, I needed something to steady my nerves. I was glad I did. It was best night I had in ages. Everyone kept buying me me drinks, for providing them with such a good laugh, in a good cause naturally. I retold the events of the day several times, receiving several slaps on the back that nearly knocked me over. Really, I found being thought of as a nice twat was more embarassing than being thought of as a huge twat. So I soon left that area to look for somewhere else to live. Oh, and it seemed my protest was a success. The council were to build a huge new development on the site of the old offices. Unfortunately the development was to be a block of luxury apartments which no one could afford. So my protest was a qualified success at best.

The Relationship Sessions

" All the time you just go on at me. It's just nag, nag, nag. Don't you realise I'm doing my best."

" Your best. Maybe that's not good enough anymore. You mope around all day. You just don't communicate."

" How do you expect me to communicate ? when the only news I get is bad news. Look at these, bills, bills, bills, and more bloody bills."

" You just can't take that attitude, Ken, it's defeatist. For God's sake, how do you think I feel ? I'm worried sick day and night since you lost your job. And the debts just keep mounting up..."

" Aooooh."

" And how do you feel, Ken ? Alice has described her feelings, which are reflected in her body language. But your body language has become wooden, your movements restricted. I would hazard a guess you're depressed..."

" Oh would you, you psychobabble merchant. I'll show you what it's like to get depressed, you fucking wanker."

Ken made a lunge for Manwatcher (the noted psychologist and social commentator), but Alice inervened.

" Leave it, Ken, please, stop, stop Ken, he's not worth it. You know he'll only sue us if you hit him."

Manwatcher became a little perturbed.

" Oh is that the time ? Look, I think I'll call a halt on this observation session. We'll pick up again with some questionaires, next week..."

" I'll pick you up, you scrawny git, and bang your fucking head against the wall..."

Manwatcher opened the door and was out in the space of a breath.

He was relieved, he reflected later, to be sitting in a sandwich bar, even if it was with his irritating collegue, Simon Cruise.

" And those were his last words, were they ? " asked Simon.

" Yes."

" I think maybe you should give a little respect to this man's feelings."

" They volunteered for the research didn't they ? research into an everyday man and woman relationship and how they cope with the world. They were all given the necessary information, well apart from the complicated bits they wouldn't understand."

" Still, both of them have lost their jobs, haven't they ? and they're struggling to pay the mortgage..."

" Which confirms my preliminary findings. Most men and women aren't cut out for a relationship anymore, they simply fail to meet the challenges of the new global economy."

" You sound like a businessman."

" It's the business world that has borrowed the notion of competitive instincts from us psychologists..."

" From psychologists like you, you mean, the ones who babble on about territory and peoples' natural aggression, their hierachical behaviour. Your psychology is just a mishmash of anthropology, sociology and natural science...."

" Oh come on Mister Cruise, anthropology and sociology are just a mishmash themselves, you know that. As for natural sciences, a bunch of boring pedants, who never go out, but sit around theorising, validating their own prejudices..."

" You've got a point, somewhere, but calm down will you."

Manwatcher had begun to wave his arms around.

" I'm sorry, some of that poor, stupid husband's aggression must have displaced itself onto me..."

Cruise's eyebrows went up a few milimetres.

" Really, you don't suppose Ken and Alice might see things differently, do you ? that their view of the world might have been dealt a blow by their redundancies..."

" No I don't, what they think of the situation is immaterial. I'm concerned with the objective fact of their growing failure to maintain a marriage."

" Really, and the fact they both had a great deal of pride in their professions has nothing to do with it ? "

" No, their own opinions only confuse the issue. You always exaggerate the importance of how these people look at the world, this does not impinge on the circumstances that effect their behaviour..."

" I wish I could believe that."

" Wish away, it's a fact anyway."

" No it isn't, and you know better from your own experience."

" Oh, so give me an example."

" With relish. For one, there's the fact I can't go into my local newsagents anymore."

" Errrm."

Manwatcher was begining to look worried.

" Erm all you like, you know what I'm talking about. You saw the newsagent's father, sitting on a stool, with his eyes closed, rocking back and foward..."

" Symptoms of catatonic trance..."

" Except that he was saying his prayers..."

" How was I supposed to know that ? "

" You never bothered to find out, so we were chased out of the shop by an irate man waving a broom handle, because you said his father needed therapy."

" An honest mistake anyone could've made."

" Really, and what about the time we got chased by those young Orthodox jews in Hampstead ? "

" Well, they looked so neat and clean in their hats and coats. I thought they were a new teenage fashion."

" I know you did. That's why you told them they had a lot in common with the mods and the skinheads..."

" Look, I've apologised enough for that haven't I ? I was a bit impetuous, but that was a long time ago."

" Oh yes, what about last week, when you asked that Greek Cypriot if he was a homosexual."

" It seemed a fair guess at the time."

" But implying he was gay merely because he had a moustache..."

" But I was only joking."

" Only joking. You nearly got us killed, again. That's another establishment we can't go back to."

" And what about you, Mister Smartarse Cruise. Remember the times you went around recommending cannabis as a relaxant to clients. You got one sacked from his job at a merchant bank, another was disqualified from athletics meetings for life..."

" Er, well, as you were saying earlier, youthful mistakes..."

" Oh yes ? and how did the case go with the police superintendent, you know, the one you recommended take LSD, to gain an insight into the criminal mind..."

" Um, technically I'm still on probation. But that was an off-the-cuff remark. He took it out of context. I was vindicated."

" No, you were warned, one more slip up and your licence would be revoked."

" Oh yes that's right. I thought you were talking about the criminal proceedings rather than the censure from the British Psychological Association...The point is surely that things aren't always what they seem, particularly with those weird and wonderful things called people. So surely it's best to find out some preliminaries first as to what motivates them."

" Look, I've had God knows how many years study and observation. This gives me all the preliminaries I need.

" I give up."

" I wish you would."

" And leave the field clear for determinists like you, piss off."

" Actually I have to, one of my biological drives is getting the better of me. I've been sitting here cross-legged for the past fifteen minutes."

" How appropriate for someone called Willy."

" And stop calling me bloody Willy will you."

" I've never called you Bloody Willy in my life, but I can start if you like ? "

" Did you know Willy means top dog in America."

" While here it means you're just a big prick."

" Well I'm going to walk out on you, as you so richly deserve."

" You're saying that just to please me."

" No, I'm late, and I'm wetting myself. "

" You always did do too much at once."

Manwatcher could not think of a suitably scathing reply to this last comment. The call of nature was distracting him somewhat. And by the time he made it out of the toilet, Cruise was gone.

At his next session with Ken and Alice, Manwatcher was relieved to find Ken's aggression had subsided. Though the atmosphere still remained tense. Both threw occaisonal dirty looks at him. Manwatcher felt they were merely being territorially defensive about their relationship. He could easily win them over with his famous charm.

" So you admit your marriage is spiralling helplessly out of control, and despite your best efforts, you may lose your home. Would you accept that your inability to have chidren has further undermined your self esteem ? "

Ken briefly glowed red and uttered a growl.

" It's all right, Ken, I'll answer him."

" Why can't he answer for himself ? "

" He feels you twist his words all the time...to, ah..."

" To make me look like a complete wanker."

" That's not true at all, Ken...Look, you may drop out of this study at any time, you that. Besides, I'm not interested in insulting you. I'm just trying to get an objective view on a typical relationship in our changing, modern world, for the estimated five million readers who will buy the book I'm preparing..."

" Oh God."

Ken held his head in his hands.

" Perk up will you Ken. We need the money, you know that. Besides, Spamwatcher said he'd change our names."

" My name is Manwatcher, not Spamwatcher."

" What ? "

" I said my name is Manwatcher, not Spamwatcher."

" Oh alright then, let's get on with it," Ken growled.

" Okay, carry on Mister Spam...er, Mister Manwatcher, we're ready. Where were we ? "

Manwatcher was nettled himself. He could not remember what he was talking about. That stupid woman calling him names had done it. In such emergency situations he knew he could rely on his trusty questionaires. So he shuffled around in his personal organiser for the appropriate headings.

" Er, hold on a minute...here we are. Do you want to have dinner with me tonight ?

" I'm sorry ? "

" Oh, wrong question...okay...I'd like to take you out, just the two of us, no strings attached. It won't mean anything. What do you say ?..."

Ken glowed red again.

" Look Spamcatcher, or whatever your name is. If you're using this experiment as an excuse to chat up my wife, I'm going to whack you one."

" I'm perfectly capable of answering for myself, Ken."

" Sorry, I was reading out the wrong list."

Manwatcher hurriedly flicked through his pages.

" Erm ah, here we are...Have you ever engaged in group sex ? and do you still engage in it ? "

As soon as Manwatcher said this he opened his mouth in horror. Ken was waving his arms and shouting. Alice used her arms to try to stop Ken from standing up.

" I'm going to kill the bastard this time, I really am."

" No Ken, no. You're on probation for assaulting that minicab driver, remember..."

Manwatcher was becoming frantic. Had someone been tampering with his personal organiser ? He did not remember any of these questions. In fact it was not his writing. And then he saw a name written on the inside cover - Simon Cruise.

" Look, I'm terribly sorry, I appear to have picked up the wrong filofax by mistake..."

" And you're supposed to tell us what we're about, you dozy bastard," taunted Ken, unhelpfully.

" Hmmm, yes, I know this session hasn't gone too well, but we should be able to carry on without further mishaps..."

" Oh yeah ? "

" Yes Ken, I know the routine questions off by heart."

" Then why did you look in your little, black book ? you twat."

" Shush Ken, we need the money, remember."

" Oh alright."

" Thank you both. Things were going a little astray earlier. But now we are relaxed, I will continue..."

Alice yawned.

" Now Alice... do you still have the same regard for Ken as you did a year ago ? "

" Of course I do."

" Even though he has lost his status ? "

" I married him because I loved him, not because of his status."

" But being in debt has left you feeling less pleased with your relationship ? "

" In a way, yes, I'm less pleased with life generally."

" You worry more ? "

" Of course I do. Though we do have more time for each other, more time for enjoyment, if you know what I mean ? "

" No I don't."

" Sex, you gormless idiot."

" Oh, I see...Even though all that worry might affect your sex drive."

" It's not a problem for me."

" And what about you ? Ken."

" What about me what ? "

" Does all the worry affect your sex drive ? "

" You what ? "

" Answer him, Ken," Alice nudged her husband.

" Yeah, but he's saying I'm impotent."

" No I'm just clarifying the situation. A lot of men with your diminished status find they have difficulty performing..."

" Right, that's it. I'm sorry Alice, but this time I'm going to kill the bastard, I really am..."

Ken had started waving his arms around again. Alice managed to grab hold of her husband as he stood up. She expertly steered him into the kitchen. Ken's shouting and swearing could still be heard as she came out to talk to Manwatcher.

" You'd better leave, Spamcatcher."

" It's Manwatcher."

" Look, it won't be anything if you don't leave quick. Ken's really lost it this time."

" So I'll see you next week."

" I don't think so, goodbye."

" You'll reconsider when you've had time to think about it..."

" No I won't, piss off."

As these last words were spoken, Manwatcher was ungenerously guided toward the front door and shoved out.

The day after, Simon Cruise was relieved to be in possession of his personal organiser again. He was with Manwatcher at their routine sandwich bar once more.

" I suppose I had better thank you for returning it," Cruise grudgingly admitted.

" Your bloody filofax nearly got me into a fight."

445

" You're too eager to blame inanimate objects for your own failings."

" Shut up Cruise. I was in a muddle, okay. So I checked back on my list of notes to prompt myself. Of course I find your stupid questions and lists. It reads like the diary of a sexual pervert..."

" Well thank you anyway."

" Not at all. Seriously Simon, have you ever thought of letting me observe you for a couple of sessions ? My rates are reasonable. And if you are a serious fuckup, as I suspect, I might be able to suggest some treatments. "

" I think you're going too far," Cruise was getting irritable, " You shouldn't mistake a notebook for a diary. I'm not one of these yuppie psychologists like you. I just use this thing for random notes and jottings."

" Random is right. I still think there is room for therapy though."

" There is always room for therapy, which is why people like us exist. It doesn't mean to say I want it or need it."

Manwatcher opened his mouth to answer this but Cruise forestalled him.

"...And don't give me any crap along the lines of you're aware of some unconscious process I'm not."

" I wasn't going to."

" Good."

" But I might be aware of some physiological process you're not."

" So might the waitress. In fact she's probably more observant than you anyway."

" How can you say something as absurd as that ? "

" Look, we've been to this place a few times already. We spend a lot of time drinking tea and blathering on. And as soon as our cups are empty, she comes along, from the other side of the restaurant, to ask if we would like anything else..."

" That's ridiculous, that girl with the fake tan, the greasy hair, and that terrible cockney accent. She couldn't observe if she were awake or asleep herself..."

" Would you like anything else ? "

Manwatcher turned his head. With a start he found the waitress was right behind him. He froze in rigid embarassment. Fortunately Cruise helped out.

" Could we have two more teas please ? "

" Certainly."

The waitress walked off, not without giving Manwatcher a frosty look. A huge grin spread over Cruise's face.

" Wipe that smirk off your face, Cruise, it was a faux pas that could happen to anyone."

" But it usually happens to you."

" Ha ha, you don't suppose she really heard me do you ? "

" Can't be sure. That was a nasty look she gave you though."

Manwatcher sighed.

" Oh dear... I don't suppose you picked up my organiser, did you ? seeing as I picked up yours."

" I did, and here it is."

Cruise handed over the object. Manwatcher lovingly clutched it for a brief second before putting it away."

" I suppose you went reading through it."

" You suppose too much, I couldn't really be bothered."

Manwatcher frowned.

" Sorry Willy."

Manwatcher's frown deepened.

" Er, William I mean. I didn't mean it like that. I just didn't have time to nose through it, that's all."

Manwatcher's frown became a gaping mouth.

" Don't look so shocked. It's true there's not much demand for my services, but things have picked up lately..."

" I wish I could say the same."

" You have others to observe, besides Ken and Alice, surely ? "

" No, not at the moment, no one else has answered my letters."

" What about that solicitor couple ? "

" Oh, they're a pain in the bum those two. They fancy themselves as amateur psychologists. They keep questioning every question I give them. It's maddening. It's nearly as bad as talking to you."

" They're not qualified like us, and they're not even old college enemies like us."

Manwatcher appreciated his old friend's kindness, even if it was disguised by his customary sarcasm. A feeling of warmth came over him. Then a cup of tea was rudely slammed on the table in front of him, splashing his hand. Another feeling of warmth came over him.

" Ow, for God's sake."

" Here's your tea, twat," said the waitress.

Manwatcher looked at her, speechless. She placed his colleagues tea on the table with delicacy. Then she glared at Manwatcher and strode off.

" I think you can assume she did hear," said Cruise.

" Aaaah, what a day. Bringing insight to the masses is no easy task."

Cruise twisted his mouth uncertainly.

" I am joking you know, Simon. Even I'm not that pompous."

" I should think so too, Mister Spamcatcher."

" Oh shut up."

" Or was it Spamwatcher ? "

" You can talk, Simon Cruise, Slimy Bruise."

" Spamcatcher, Spamwatcher."

" Simon Cruise, Slimy Bruise."

" Spamcatcher, Spamwatcher."

" Can you gentlemen keep the noise down please. I would not expect people like your good selves to behave like silly children in public."

A forbidding woman stood before the two psychologists.

" Who are you ? " Manwatcher asked.

" I am the proprietor."

" Fair enough, sorry," said Simon Cruise.

The proprietor was pacified. They both drank their tea hurriedly and in silence. Both men settled the bill hurriedly as well. Once outside they realaxed a bit more.

" Well I think that's another establishment I'll be too embarassed to go back to."

" The feeling is mutual, Mister Cruise."

" These places do mount up, don't they ? "

" I'm afraid they do."

The two psychologists walked off in opposite directions.

The Huge Blokes on the Bus

We were stalled in a traffic jam. There was a big festival going on in the park. It was a gay pride march. I could see the crowds from the top deck of the bus. Hordes of men in lycra cycling shorts, and weight trainer physiques, sauntered down the high street. I was wary. Not because of the gays, it was just because we were stalling south of the river. Here was the haunt of a million retards, scumbags, psychopaths and plastic gangsters. Gays were no problem. In fact, I wished a load had got on the bus. They might have ensured the good behaviour of the other passengers. Every waif and stray caught the bus in the south. I could never wait to get out of there quick enough. People always used to say, or at least I did, the further south you went, in this teeming metropolis, with every step you took, the I.Q. level dropped a point.

Cynical and unnecessary, and perhaps a product of my own paranoia. Though I had seen enough disorder already to fuel my fears. I had seen fights, people being sick, people urinating, people defecating, and people shouting and jumping up and down and threatening me. I had a friend who was a bus driver. He assured me that crappy behaviour was par for the course. Then he recounted worse episodes than I had ever experienced, ones that did not do me any favours at all. There was something called 'Care in the Community' in those days. This was when the government closed all the mental hospitals. The idea was the patient should not be segregated from society. But that he or she could more easily be helped by living among the community at large. Trouble was, the community did not want them, if it existed at all. Round the south it was more like hillbilly country, the place itself was need of care, which it never got. All these people ended up on the bus, at least to my paranoid eyes.

So my spirits sunk when I heard the artificially loud voices of obnoxious geezers wafting up the stairs. And sure enough, it was a gang of kids, or young blokes. I will call them blokes because they were such huge bastards, probably had steroid and chips for dinner, huge bastards in badly designed tracksuits. I should not have been so quick to jump to conclusions. Trouble is, you learn to tell the troublemakers in life pretty sharpish, if you have any dealings with people. There is a checklist. First, there is the attitude of leery bravado, covering the low self-esteem, and lower intelligence. Second, their clothes are usually badly designed and badly worn - they walked and carried themselves like nothing quite fit. Third, there was that glassy-eyed, dozy expression, as seen in drunkards, junkies, religious evangelists and the odd psychotic. Finally, of course, was the fact they were in a gang in the first place. Naturally, people banded together for self-protection since the dawn of time. Yet there were rudiments of civilsation even in this place. This meant travel without armed escort was possible, paranoia to the contrary. But this lot would probably die of inactivity if they were left alone. One of the reasons they ganged up was so their brain cells could reach double figures.

Now, even given this checklist of prejudices, I have to make allowance for mistakes. You cannot always judge by appearance. And no one knows otherwise. People are always pushing some kind of attitude at you, that they want you to take up. And they are always trying to hide something they would be shy about you seeing. These blokes were projecting the usual hardman machismo. But it could have been a matter of them just being defensive. They got one or two worried looks as they sat down near the back of the bus. But people soon turned away and started staring outside again. The bus was reasonably crowded by now, and began lumbering foward at less than walking pace.

We forgot about those four blokes. I would have liked to have kept it that way. But after fifteen minutes or so, one of them figured out there were people of a different sexual persuasion walking down the street. The penny finally dropped among the others, as the one with the most brain pointed this out to his fellow troglodytes. They gave out noises and basic insults, a troop of chimpanzees whooping and screeching. It soon degenerated into an atttempt at social comment. They gave their expert tabloid opinions on the massed ranks of gays. Several right wing parties would have been proud of them. Expressions of critical disgust followed. Sighs began breaking out on the rest of the top deck. That was as far as our displeasure went, until something else happened. Some people nearby began pulling these blokes up about their obnoxious behaviour. This was a novelty in itself. Since the moronic behaviour of inbred psychotics was usually left alone, particularly in this neck of hillbilly country, personal safety was paramount. I turned round. It seemed these good citizens were gays themselves. They pointed out the error of their ways to the huge bastard blokes. There were more gays than huge blokes, and one or two of them were huge bastards also. They had obviously weighed up the odds in their favour when making their intervention. They had found the numbers on the other side wanting, just like their intelligence, and so felt entitled to get leery as the situation demanded. But the huge bastards were too stupid to be intimidated. After a gormless silence they began tellling the gays where to get off, repeating the same phrases over and over. The gays took up the challenge and easily got the best of the exchanges. Another silence followed. This one was more tense than gormless, since both parties went quiet. A stand off was in progress. I thought the huge bastards might have been cowed into submission. But the flicker of a synapse must have operated in the nervous system still. They attacked the gays all at once, without warning, punching at random. They scored a few notable knocks, but were soon overwhelmed by superior numbers. Indeed, as the Huge bastards began to disappear under a welter of flailing arms, the rest of the top deck got up, all in one movement, and went over to dish out some punishment. No one said anything, it was pure reflex. The opportunity was there to punish some delinquent retards, and we took it. This was hillbilly country after all. I bet each and every one of us had a story about being intimdated by delinquent, psychotic idiots. Now it was revenge time.

I should not have been surprised I suppose. Once the decent everyday types decide enough is enough, miscreants beware. The huge bastards disappeared under a mass of humanity. A mass that efficiently went about its business of beating the shit out of them, arms punching and legs kicking. This might have gone on forever, or until the bastards were beaten into unconsciousness. But the bus driver saved them. The commotion upstairs had drawn him to investigate. With his mantra ' wha's going on,' going on, he effectively broke the spell. The great mass of decent everyday types left off their battering and returned quietly to their seats.

This left the irate gays and manhandled bastards. The huge bastards were a bit of a mess, dragged backwards through the proverbial hedge. Both parties were voiciferous in condemning each other. But to the fresh onlooker, the huge bastards gained all the sympathy. They were bewildered, shocked and bloody. They looked as though they might burst into tears of humiliation. Some pedantic types in strange, official-looking uniforms came up the stairs. They took in the appearance of the huge bastards, and took their side all at once. The gays' case was not helped by the fact one of them was waving a knife around. In the argument that followed, the forces of petty officialdom decreed the gays should leave the bus. Never mind the fact the huge bastards had started the whole thing. No one else said anything. People were all embarassed by the fact they nearly massacred a bunch of scumbags only minutes earlier.

The petty uniforms escorted the gays off the bus. The driver got us going again. The traffic cleared a little. We began moving at the pace of a slow pushbike. Everyone went back to staring out the window. The huge bastards came out with their biggest silence yet. However, after the bus had gone some distance, more pennies rolled down that slow slope of their intelligence. They began moaning about the injustice of it all, giving dirty looks to a few of us. But they took it no further. They moaned for a good five minutes before they got off. Then we did the decent thing and erased the epsiode from from all our attention.

yxsy giyxsy X

Drinking with an Alien

He did not mind losing in any game, did Joe. But he could not take a severe thrashing too well. This left him embarrassed and resentful. In front of everyone else as well. He cringed at the memory. Five games of pool he played with this character, five games. And he did not even get on the table.

The alien, Joe could not pronounce his name (it sounded like Squorzqz, but the alien kept pulling him up when he tried to say it - his pronunciation was off and everyone got drenched in spittle), the alien had not given him a chance. By careful calculation of all possible angles, the relative positions of the balls, the momentum needed, and the force required, the alien had made one shot per game. This set off a chain reaction. The white careened around the table, knocking all the alien's balls into the pocket and leaving Joe's standing. Joe took exception to this. He complained and argued, he appealed to witnesses, but no one around would back him up. The alien had an unorthodox style, perhaps, but he did not appear to break any rules.

Joe thought of going to the bar.

" I suppose I'd better ask what you're having," he said to the alien.

" Oh, no problem there."

A pint glass floated past Joe's face. It contained a horrible, frothy mixture. Joe thought it looked worse than snakebite.

" And one for you."

A pint glass, full of Joe's favourite fizzy, yellow liquid floated up to him and hovered before his face.

" Very sickly looking I think, all that gas."

" It doesn't look half as bad as that concoction."

" Oh this, just a mixture of bitter, drambuie, pernod, whisky and blackcurrant."

" Urrgh."

" Yes, I must go easy, I'm teleporting home tonight."

" Must go easy, must go easy. That's enough to make me drunk for a week."

The alien smiled.

" How do you do that anyway ? "

" Elementary telepathy and leisurely levitation."

Cringe cringe, Joe thought. Jokes must be thin in the depths of space.

He was having a strange evening.

This huge vegetable-looking geezer walks up and starts gurgling at him. Then it wraps its tentacles around a pool cue and thrashes him out of sight, and no one bats an eyelid.

" Er...I think I'll have a bag of roasted peanuts as well."

" No problem."

" Look, if you don't mind, I'd rather get them myself."

" Suit yourself."

Joe walked up to the bar and made his order. As the barman gave him his change he took his chance.

" Look, don't you think that bloke's a little weird."

The alien sat meditatively, pulsating from purple to green to yellow. He (he ?) also seemed to change shape frequently. One second he looked like a giant hydra, the next like a giant sea anemone, the next like a green carrot.

" No weirder than the usual clientele," said the barman.

" Yeah, but not exactly human, is he."

" Ha ha, human, yes I know. I get that trouble myself, sometimes. I look at the people around here and wonder where they came from."

The barman gestured as he said this, indicating the assorted punks, hippies, rockers, bikers, et al, that made up the pub.

" But he's an alien."

" Yeah, that's what they all say."

" But he's not from this planet."

" Are any of the people here ? "

" Look, you don't understand. Okay, so there are a lot of strange people here. But they're not as weird as he is."

" You look around this pub again. Then tell me who're the weird ones. No, I'll tell you, it's you and me, the only sensibly dressed people here. And that makes us weird, why ? because we're the odd ones out. Or at least you are. As a barman I have to look like this. What's your excuse ? "

" Look, don't get me wrong. I just think he, if it is a he, or a she...er...or an it, is weirder than usual.

" I know what you mean."

" You do ? "

" Yes, I get the same myself...sometimes."

" What ? "

" Yeah, I look around this place, I see all these different types of people, and it makes me feel uncomfortable as well."

" Look, I don't mean...erm."

" What do you mean, then ? "

" Don't know, forget it, thanks for the peanuts."

" You're welcome."

Joe wandered reluctantly back to his seat. The alien was pulsating in a happy, radiant sort of way.

" Why so sad ? "

" I'm not sad."

" Yes you are, you're ashamed and embarrassed at losing in front of all of these people, and this makes you resent me...but don't worry, it's only a game."

Joe started.

" How did you know all that ? "

" Sorry, being nosy again. I was reading your mind."

" Look, leave my mind alone for tonight will you. It's had enough happening to it for one evening."

" Fair enough."

The alien coughed, or at least it was an approximation of one, and went on.

" I always beat earthlings at every game I play, it's nothing personal."

" You can't help but win," Joe remarked sarcastically.

The alien was unmoved.

" That's it exactly. Every sport I've ever played, since I've been on this planet , I've won easily."

" What ? there's thousands of sports on Earth."

" I know, card games, snooker, pool, billiards, tennis, squash, badminton, golf, horse racing, archery, rifle shooting, athletics, fencing, judo, rowing, darts..."

" All right, alright, but you must have played team sports, yeah."

" Yes, football (all varieties), polo, cricket, hockey, tug-of war, formation dancing..."

Formation dancing ?

" Yeah yeah, but you didn't do well in all these games. I mean, in these games a lot depends on the other members of your team."

" On the contrary, playing in a team, as you call it, was quite a disadvantage to the other side."

" What ? "

" I found it too much of a waste of time to play in a team. And so I played whole teams by myself, and won."

" Ballbags."

" It's true, I'm not lying."

" Sure."

" You must remember, I come from a planet far in advance of yours."

Joe frowned. It seemed like his planet was being called backward. He did not like that.

" Well you seem to be enjoying it here."

" I never said I wasn't. Quite a quaint, little place really, with it's funny, old, primitive, barbaric way of life."

" What ? primitive, barbaric, you must be joking. Listen, we've got loads of different ways of life on this planet ; different cultures, different art, different religions. We've got science as well, and sport...er, better forget sport."

" Science, you've got science."

The alien pulsated energetically.

" You build a couple of piddly rockets, that only make it as far as your nearest satellite. You make a couple of tin foil satellites that only get as far as the next star, don't talk to me about science. You know how I got here, on the Milky Way Public Transport System. For three Berblikoos (our currency) I can get to Andromeda, in ten minutes, by Rapido Thought Trans-Ferry. In a day I can get to the Crab Nebula (if I make the connection). And that's public transport, and you know how unreliable public transport is..."

" All right, alright...but we've still got our culture, the jewel of 10,000 years of human achievement, the striving aspirations of our race..."

Joe winced inwardly. The drink was getting to him already, it was only his first pint.

" Ha, it took me little over a year to get acquainted with your culture, and all your languages, all your art, all your philosophy. It reminds me of the D.I.Y. holograph albums we give to our children."

" What ? you can't write off a whole race like that."

" I'm not writing humans off. Your culture just doesn't measure up to ours, that's all. Do you realise, that in our galactic system, there is a philosopher-scientist called Xxyffibb."

The name sounded like someone farting to Joe, but he said nothing. The alien went on,

" His latest achievement was to bring out ' A Few Idle Musings on the Origins of the Universe,' - a book of maxims for houseplants. In it he argues through sublime poetry, pure mathematics, religious revelation, clinical logic, the finest arguement in fact, that the universe is really a giant comfy sofa, except on Wednesdays, when it's an obscure equation. He works through every discipline rigorously and profoundly. In one book he dwarfs the achievements of your Earth entirely. And it's only a book to be read by modest houseplants."

Joe was getting lost. He had the feeling he was coming off worst in this discussion. Then a thought came into his head and he seized upon it."

" Okay, maybe so. But you're a plant, right, and plants are inferior to humans, aren't they."

Joe felt embarrassed. He did not mean to put it like that. But the alien had annoyed him. He hoped he had not annoyed the alien.

' On this planet, maybe, but this planet seems a little backward in that area. I mean your plants are still stuck-in-the-ground types. On our planet we can move around as we please. We do have animals, its' true, but they are scrawny, stupid little things. Some people think they're cute and keep them in glass cases. But I think they make too much mess, and they're expensive to keep."

" What ? animals are more advanced than plants anyway, aren't they ? "

" Not at all. Once plants learn to uproot themselves and move around, nothing can stop them. Even standing still they're better than animals."

" Oh yeah, and how's that ? "

" We don't eat and destroy the way you do, killing and poisoning everything. We just photosynthesize."

Joe's brain reeled. Somehow a whole world of possibilties went out the window. He speculated - where would you be without a romantic dinner for two ? Ringing someone up and asking them to come for a walk in the park 'so we could photosynthesize together' just did not sound the same.

He absently went to pick up his glass.

" Urrgh."

Joe spat. It was the alien's glass. One sip was stronger than five pints of his usual. It was too late though, he had already swallowed some. He looked up. Through a rapidly growing alcoholic haze he saw a vision. A woman of rare beauty was sitting opposite. Her eyes entranced. They contained depths of mysterious intelligence, they radiated a fascinating desire. Her hair tumbled down an exquisitely carved face, it looked warm and fragrant. Her lips quivered invitingly. Her eyes never left his, they beckoned him. Joe moved foward slowly, ever so slowly. He was hypnotised by this vision. He closed his eyes and opened his mouth, waiting for that long, luxurious kiss. The next thing he knew he was tasting something that reminded him of soggy lettuce. The he became engulfed in a mass of tentacles.

" Aaaargh."

The alien released him, pulsating with mirth.

" Ha Ha...I'm sorry, I really am. I shouldn't have done that. But I can't resist it sometimes. You earthlings get in such a state over sex."

Joe frowned. He looked to punch the alien, but the alien was too quick, it belched, and a sap-like substance covered Joe's face and lap.

" Aaaargh...it's horrible... get it off."

" It's alright, you'll be rid of it soon."

A tentacle hovered over Joe, with a small opening at the end. It inhaled. In a moment the sap-like substance was gone. Yet a bad smell remained.

" Ugh."

Joe straightened up in his seat. He was becoming aware of other people looking at him, so he tried to compose himself. Pretty soon their glances left, but he still felt as embarrassed as ever. He searched his pockets for some reassurance, a cigarette, and tried to continue the conversation.

" Okay, so you don't eat, but you drink."

" As do all living things."

" But alcohol ? "

" Even plants need to have a good time now and then."

" What about sex then, that trick you played on me...I mean, don't you have females on your planet ? or males ? if you're a she...I'm not sure.

Joe's search for a cigarette was becoming frantic. The alien became aware of this.

" Here, have one of mine."

" Thanks."

Joe lit up and inhaled.

" Yes, we have sex, of course, but with far more variety. You see, it's like some plants on your planet. We have both male and female parts, so we can be either, or neither even, we can reproduce asexually as well. And shape changing comes in handy also, as you have seen. Why, it makes for endless variety. We have none of your earthling hang ups over sexuality, all these perversions and the like, since a lot of things are possible to us. Sex becomes at once a skill and an aesthetic pleasure, as well being the more crude things, which I am afraid to say appear to dominate in earthling sex. You see, by being freed from mere biological desire, which you lot are so attached to......"

Joe listened attentively to the begining of all this, but his mind drifted. It drifted to a point where he could not even listen to what the alien was saying anymore. Even though he knew the alien continued talking. He drifted for a short while, which became a long while, through ever widening depths, into a place of no boundaries, an abyss. Then his senses appeared to explode. The sounds of the pub heightened to deafening cacophony. It was a mass of ugly sound, while garish colours and shapeless forms moved before his eyes. The sounds and colours merged, then disappeared, then merged, then disappeared, faster and faster. Until he was not sure what he was seeing or hearing. A smell arose. It was by turns as sweet as fragrance and as sickening as decay. His senses were overpowering him. Then they collapsed, and there was nothing underneath. The cold black of night was there, and he was falling through it, faster and faster. His fear rose. His heart beat until it might burst. The fear was real, a horrible, physical thing, which oppressed on all sides. Then he stopped falling, but he was nowhere, nothing around, no thing above, below or beyond. He was alone, so utterly alone, with limitless time at his disposal, but time to do what ? to think ? what could he think of to do ? What could he do with all the time he could think of ? what was time anyway ? why did he need it ? why did it not come back ? Why was nothing happening

? Then, slowly, from a huge distance, a face appeared, and slowly, ever so slowly, it moved toward him. It was decades, an eternity, before he could see it clearly. But gradually, oh so gradually, he began to make out its features. It was a horrible face, contorted in absolute fear, the fear of eternity. The eyes bulged, dilated and bloodshot. The mouth gaped in rigid paralysis, while every hair stood on end.

Then Joe realised, it was his face, his face. He was looking at the shiny, mucous body of the alien. He was back in the pub, staring at his reflection on the alien's body.

" ......So sex on our planet is always a varied and stimulating experience, for senses, thought and emotion."

Joe gaped.

" Quite nice these cigarettes, aren't they ? I got them duty free on a star shuttle once."

Joe felt the muscles of his jaw gradually respond to his frantic mental commands.

" Ffnurgarrh."

" Yes, I find it hard to describe their effect as well. Quite subtle really, don't you think ? "

By now Joe had learnt how to speak again.

" That was some cigarette."

" I knew you'd agree they were subtle."

" Subtle, you're joking, I feel like I've been to hell and back."

" That's what I mean."

Joe looked defeated.

" Okay, so I admit it. Your planet, your galaxy, leaves this one standing when it comes to sport...science, er, culture, art, philosophy, religion, sex, even drugs."

" Well, it's all relative really, you know, nothing to get excited about."

" Nothing to get excited about. You've just been proving to me how inferior my planet is all evening."

" Yes, but strictly speaking, you can't prove these things. Everything exists in its own right, as well as being an intimate part of everything else."

Joe could feel his head spinning again. The conversation was slipping from his grasp, for the umpteenth time. He thought to steer the conversation back to more safe ground.

" Well, what are you doing here then ? working ? on holiday ? or what ? "

" A working holiday, actually...an enforced one."

" What do you mean ? "

" Well, I was taking a little pleasure ride through your stratosphere, on a pedal shuttle, when I crashed. And the owners won't give me back my deposit until I buy another. Very irritating really. I dropped my cigarette on the floor of the craft, and, as I was bending down to pick it up, I crashed into a mountain. They're quite expensive, pedal shuttles, unreasonably so."

" What ? so you mean you're working till you can buy the materials to build another one ? "

" Exactly."

" So how long will it take to pay off the debt ? "

" Oh, about a millenium or two."

" What ? "

" Well, you see, I'm only working as a toilet attendant."

Joe gaped again. But this time his amazement was dictated by humour.

" Ha ha...a toilet attendant, and with all your talents. You could be a nuclear physicist, a president, a top sportsman, er woman, er thingy."

" Yes but this job has a sideline."

" A sideline ? from looking after toilets ? "

" Yes, all those things you wasteful earthlings throw away."

" What ? like paper towels."

" No, fool, excreta, I'm collecting it."

" Yuck, that's disgusting, that really is."

" Not at all. Your brown excreta is much in demand on our planet. It's supposed to have great health-giving properties. You rub your roots over it and it takes away all aches and pains. It gives off a nice smell too."

" Ugh, you're joking, you must be."

" No I'm not. That liquid you lot always waste as well, that's in great demand as a soft drink. I've got storage tanks full of the stuff already. When I get off here I'm going to charter a star freighter and haul the whole lot back home. I'll make a killing."

Joe's head was feeling crushed again, under the force of absurd notions.

" This is stupid, it really is, I just don't believe a word of it, it's ridiculous. A plant from another galaxy, who can do anything, but works as a bog attendant, and saves poo and wee in his spare time. You're winding me up, aren't you ? None of this is real. The pool, the stories, the horrible gunge you spat over me. You slipped something in my drink earlier, admit it. That explains it. And that ridiculous, slimy costume you're wearing. Are you an out-of-work actor ? doing this for a bet or something ?..."

The alien was pulsating again, this time an angry shade of purple.

"...I mean, you don't expect me to believe all you've said, do you ? You've got a few tricks, I'll admit that, but where's the real proof..."

Even as he said that, he wished he had not. The men at the bar rushed over as soon as they saw something was wrong. But they were all talking in Spanish. After hours of confused communication, he understood he was in a bar, somewhere in Tierra Del Fuego. The alien had teleported him there, apparently. It was going to be quite a job getting home. He remembered he had an appointment for tomorrow, he might be a bit late. In the meantime he might as well play a few games of pool, he had noticed there was a table in his new surroundings. He needed a good game to restore his equilibrium, if not his self-esteem. He would try not to let the fact, that some of the players appeared to have more than two arms, get in the way. In fact they appeared to have tentacles. Never mind, what could be more down to Earth than a game of pool ?

Tottenham Chelsea in the Late 70's

The Sack was giving out again, the way he always used to. Telling tales about his past, and spinning it out till you didn't recognise what he was about. I knew the Sack all his life, and mine. He always was a geezer, a flawed diamond but in reasonably good nick. He was called the Sack on account of his podgy shape, and for the fact that, when he was younger, he couldn't hold down a job too long without getting the old tin tack. He was full of misdemeanours was the Sack. He liked to think he used to be a rascal, always up for the crack. Though not in any double entendre sense, you understand, just a good time. He usually neglected to say how he terrorised most people he met. He was a leery bastard then, and now he was a civilised leery bastard. He had mellowed, but people still didn't take issue with him too much. Although he would admit that the past was never to be repeated. And thank God for that, he always said, with a big flabby sigh.

Of course, now he was semi-civilised, a family man, he could put the gloss on his past. And he laid it on thick. I should know, I was with him on a lot of these mad occaisons, right, about as mad as someone fast asleep can be. Although, a little truth did peep through the cracks now and then. Take this last occaison. He was holding court to a number of young blokes, about his son's age, about the wild and woolly days of his going to football, back in the murky haze of those bad taste days, the 1970's.

" See, me and the Soppy Sod here (that being me) went every game for a couple of seasons, what was it ? the late 70's. That was when the fights were at their peak, you know. Some of the stuff that went on, unbelievable, never got in the papers, except when a few shops got smashed up, and they'd be an uproar. But it'd all settle down after a few weeks..."

His audience listened like the Sack was Jackanory Man, the ace storyteller. I wondered how long it would be before I saw the cracks appearing in this good old days crap. But I shouldn't be too cynical. I wasn't above beefing up the old past to make it a bit more showy. Thing was, I thought I was better at it than the Sack. But I wasn't going to tell him that. Anyway, he had this bunch of kids in the palm of his hand. Sounds a bit pervy that. What I meant was, he got their attention all wrapped up.

"...We was at Spurs once, and, like, the fighting was really bad, yeah, all over the place, everywhere. The Old Bill were on it, of course. They snuffed a lot of it out. But they couldn't deal with it all. They was firm handed, and treated us like the scumbags we always was, like they wanted us put down or something, you know. And the Filth were known to get a bit beneath themselves now and then. They'd kick shit out of some poor cunt, who was just walking along, and got nabbed by the wrong arm of the law. Course, when we got the chance we'd always beat shit out of a copper, that was the best fun...

But when me and Soppy come up to Tottenham Hale,there's Filth down both ends of the street, the Bill weren't taking no chances. Since we was Chelsea, you know, and we had the rep, being in the top three of the London hooligan league. West Ham were top dogs of course. They used to do everyone, everytime. Then it was the life or death struggle between us, the rabid dogs of Millwall, and the flash Harry's of Tottenham, for the other top places. Course, the mouthy gits of Arsenal could get it together when they tried. And the other London teams did have their firms. But I reckoned the three or four of us were the main ones..."

The Sack was going off the boil a bit here. I remember those arguments about who was the hardest in London. Well, I never really knew. But I never trusted anything in East or South East London. I'm sure of that much. It was enemy territory, paranoia overdose. I used to think even the buildings wanted to beat us up.

" ...Anyway, we come up out the station, it's Filth galore, wall to wall, our escort for the day. I thought that was nice of them. And they took us the long way round to the ground. God, we walked for fucking ages. I didn't realise till afterwards, we could've got off at Seven Sisters, which was next stop, and Spurs ground was just down the road. No, the Bill could be shrewd when they put their mind to it. They wanted us kept out the way, coz of all the Tottenham firms that came out to greet us. And it worked, well sort of.

See they took us round all the back streets and that. Soppy kept moaning about his feet aching..."

Actually, I remember it as the Sack moaning. He never did use his legs for much, except for putting the boot in. Even that knackered him out. He always was a fat bastard.

"... We was all a bit knackered, yeah. But soon we come up to the ground, the north side, what was it ? the Paxton ? or the Shelf ? "

I couldn't remember the name of the end. I didn't think it was important. But the Sack felt these little details verified the truth of what he said. So he glared at me like my shrug was letting him down. Then he got back to spinning out the yarn as far as it would go, again.

'...Anyway, we was there, and the Bill eased off a bit. Job done, you know, escort provided. We was just hanging round, regrouping like. And then we got steamed. This massive crew of Tottenham just came out of nowhere. And they just run us. They run us all over the place, all of us. And the Bill just stood there laughing. I heard one copper say we weren't as hard as we reckoned, since we got run so easy. But these things happen. Anyway, we got well scattered. Me and Soppy were just running round the back streets for a bit. Then we regrouped. Once we got a few numbers back, we started steaming into a couple of shops, nicking stuff left, right and centre. Course it was mostly Paki shops. And I always ended up with big bottles of Coke. I think I must've had about four or five at least. I had to give a couple away. All that gas made me burp more than I talked. I wanted some bars of chocolate in one place. But the owner and his family put up a bit of a fight, and they chased us right out. They screamed blue murder, and we thought we might have the Blue Murder on our backs if we didn't leg it quick, but we got away..."

Yes we did, with a trail of plastic bottles and sweet wrappers behind us, and a load of shocked shopkeepers. I had blanked that episode out of memory. I wasn't too proud of it.

"... So we went off back to the game. And it was half decent, you know, for a London derby, usual one one draw of course. Tottenham had a good side then. Better than us, course most sides were than us then. They had the two Argies, what were they ? Ardeals and Brillo..."

The Sack was glad to be corrected on his one, since it led to a fit of giggles on the part of his adoring audience. They knew their good footballers of the past, well the recent past anyway. Of course it was Ardiles and Villa, two class acts if ever there was.

"...We did have Wilkins though, the Crab..."

I couldn't remain silent at this sacrilege. Ray Wilkins was great. He was Chelsea for two seasons, kept the entire team going, and was highest scorer, a real midfield general. They sang that song about him - ' Wilkins, Wilkins, born is the king of Stamford Bridge.' The only other person to gain that accolade was Peter Osgood. Of course, like all good players, Wilkins got sold on, he went up to Manchester , to play for some flash git of a manager, whose name intentionally escapes me, who slagged him off. And the rest , as they say, is totally uninteresting (to me).

"...Well yeah, he had his moments he did. And we did okay on the day, on the footy side. Me and Soppy could hardly concentrate on the game. There was all these little fights going off all over the place in the stands. Nothing major, just individual barneys mainly. It was a bit packed. There weren't much room to do much more.."

I remember. I hated enclosed grounds. They always reminded me of prisons, or schools, real claustrophobic. West Ham was like that, and Millwall, God Millwall, the streets round the ground were like that as well. I thought maybe there was some connection between leery fans and grounds where you were cooped up. But Chelsea was an obvious exception. It looked like a half-demolished Roman ampitheatre, with a brand, spanking, new stand plonked in on one side. That nearly bankrupted us, that one.

"...Stay with us Soppy, I need you to back me up on the details here. This lot aint going to believe the legend otherwise..."

This was too much, the Sack was blundering into bollocks territory. I'm going to tell the rest of this in my words, not his. Because he was off on a ramble. You could see that faraway, dozy look came into his eye, like a dog eyeing up the prospect of a biscuit. He was well into polishing up his past, which was annoying, because it was my past too, I was there.

We were only fourteen for fuck's sake, if we were a day. I was a skinny runt, not much more than waist high to most of these huge geezers lumbering about the place. The Sack weren't much better. He was a smaller sack then, but still dumpy and lumpy, with cheeks like a hamster, when it stored food in them. He was sweating, like all doughboys do on warm days. That's funny, that's one of the few football memories I have of it being a warm day. You would always get a couple of games at the begining of the season when it was reasonably hot. But I always remembered the cold, miserable ones, when it got dark before the game was finished, and your legs went numb as the cold crept up.

Anyway, I'm doing a Sack here, rambling off the point a bit. To pick it up where he dropped it, before he started embroidering it, the game finished, but the needle remained between the fans. It was well set up for some nasty confrontation outside the ground. Tottenham were getting stick on account of their supposed jewishness. And they retorted by chanting out words to the effect Chelsea were so many little kids, only good for smashing things up. This led the Sack and I to pretend we were older and harder. The individual fights going on during the game had kicked off bad feeling. The opportunity was there for some chronic rucks. The mood was thick, it hung over us like a bad smell. Things were going to go off alright.

But they didn't. The police were canny on that day. They kept us back, a common tactic, but probably not as used as it should have been. And they kept us well back. It seemed like ages. The ground emptied all around us. This time the police were not going to ease up. They had us in a cordon, as tight as the chocolate round a choc ice. No one was going anywhere, except back to Tottenham Hale station, then all the way back to Victoria. And it went with military precision, actually, more like military simulation. We marched straight back, no long and winding roads this time. Our escort for the occaison even went so far as to see us onto the train, one specially laid on for us, which was nice, before they shoved us all in. They waited patiently for the doors to close, then pissed off in a body. I wished we could have had this personal valet service all the time, without the bullying naturally. Uniformed attendants protecting us from armies of unwashed thugs, laying on our own transport, and even engaging in cheery banter with their charges. One found oneself adapting to this preferential treatment readily. But it seems one really had to kick up a fuss before one obtained special treatment (or some other kind of treatment).

So off we went, away from temperamental types in Tottenham, back to thugs in more familiar territory. But of course we stopped at Seven Sisters. This was the Tottenham stop. When our train pulled in the platform was all jam packed with them. This led to some excitement on the part of the enclosed Chelsea. Much window banging followed, as though it might get them out, somehow. And, of course, the Tottenham responded in kind. Common sense had prevailed up till now. Although the train hung around the station for ages, the doors were resolutely closed. Then the automatic doors were opened, common sense failed. The Chelsea had the element of surprise. Geezers charged out of that train like greyhounds out of a trap. They steamed straight into the Tottenham. Their lines buckled a bit, but then they rebounded as they fought the Chelsea back. There was one door way where no one had charged out. This was because I was wedged in there, holding everyone back, frozen. Geezers behind me were shouting their heads off at me to get out the fucking way. And there I was, the scared traffic cop, holding back the big vehicles from going on the highway. Something must have given in the end. I made way, don't remember how. I stepped outside and stood aside, as impatient headcases charged out to take their place in the fray. I looked back inside to see the Sack, he was kneeling on a seat, his face squashed against the window.

Eventually he got out, as the rest of the Chelsea horde did. I could not stand aside anymore, there was no room. We just got caught up in the fight, like driftwood carried on the tide. The Tottenham and Chelsea were well matched by now. A mass of flailing bodies moved all over the place. At times both sides would back off, then charge each other again, then the whole confusing mess would go on again. It was intense, I'd never been in a brawl this big before. I have to admit the fear had drained out of me by now. I was finding it really exciting. I was just behind the front line, where I could throw no punches nor take no whacks, but I was right beside it all the time. First one side then then the other made gains, no one could force an advantage. It was just like battle scenes I'd seen on old films, where nutters in chain mail, with axes, swords and maces charged each other. Instead of medieval weapons other objects came into play. Those behind the front line, on either side of the main fight, were getting frustrated at not being able to get their tenpence worth in. Bottles began flying over our heads, as these people traded volleys. Then some managed to get hold of litter bins, and all their contents. And then it was fluorescent light tubes. These lights ran all along the platform. And some bright sparks had obviously plucked them out the walls and lobbed them into the fray. I could see these objects flying over my head, as the fighting continued all around. Bangs, crashes and the odd explosion sounded out, mixed in with the usual shouts and yells. I thought this was just going to go on and on. But then the objects ran out, and the weight of the Chelsea numbers pushed the Tottenham back, slowly, toward the exit at the end of the platform. Then their lines broke and they ran. And we charged after them. Up the stairs, and out of what looked like some kind of back entrance. There was a yard, bounded by a metal fence, with a narrow doorway in it. Most of the Tottenham got through this doorway. But some were were caught, and battered to fuck, not to put too fine a desciption on it. There was some kind of derelict ground outside. And the Tottenham regrouped there. As with most derelict land, there were bricks, half bricks, and big stones galore. They pelted us with these, raining them down on us, forcing us back into the station. Some of the Chelsea took some bad knocks. Then they must have run out of ammo, for they tried steaming into us again. Only the headcases were left among them ,the real hard bastards. And they had initial success, pushing the Chelsea back onto the stairs, almost back to the platform again. But they eventually got swamped by the Chelsea numbers, and had the shit beaten out of them, before they managed to stagger out. Some Chelsea charged out after the remnants of the stone throwers, but they had gone. Even the head cases melted away. All that was left were some poor, battered bastards lying in the yard, who could not get up to go away. A few token kicks were aimed at these blokes before all the Chelsea went back below, to get their train again.

The Spurs had gone. They had been beaten, and run, not without a struggle, which made it all the more sweeter. Because this was their home territory. And Chelsea had won the day in this arena. Singing started, that nearly took the roof off. People went wide eyed and delirious. All of a sudden we were all mates. There was nothing we could not do in the sweet smell of victory. Spitfires flew loop the loop over the Kent countryside, the spirit of Agincourt, Poitiers had been rekindled, and the world was a rosy place, even in the sweaty overcrowded confines of the Tube. The adrenalin flowed like lager. we sang and chanted all the way back to Victoria, louder and harder than we'd ever done. I felt like I'd somehow ' done it.' I'd got in with the geezers at last. Although the Sack and myself had not really done anything. But we were there, and that was enough. Some of the old hooligans had recently come out of retirement, especially for an old enemy like Tottenham. (We had only recently got promoted.) And it was like family renuion turned mental celebration. We stopped off at the Shakespeare when we got out at Victoria. A few bevvys were downed here. We met some mates, who didn't go to the game. So we filled them in on the historic occaison they missed. The Sack's doughboy tongue was loosened by alcohol and he began painting his participation in heroic terms, pretty much as he was doing now, to his young followers. It was like being with an excitable puppy. In fact it still is a bit like that. One phrase of his from that time always sticks in my mind. He said " I'm going to have dreams about this when I'm Forty." And here is now, in his forties, mellowed, but still believing we did something heroic then, silly fuck...

Stinky Pimple

A base has been established. Finally we have managed to land on this planet and remain intact. We can now begin to establish ourselves further. This base will serve as the first point for future expansion. The atmosphere is not quite stable, and, furthermore, the surface of this planet is subject to frequent convulsion, if not eruption. Still, we believe we have the necessary equipment to develop this unpromising environment into something suitable for colonisation...

" I think you don't wash properly."

" Sorry ? "

" You got another one."

" Another what ? "

" Zit."

" Where ? "

" On your cheek, where you always get them."

We will stay in base camp until our structure is developed enough to withstand the rigours of this planet's conditions. This is a dangerous place. However, once my colleagues land, and once they are established, we will be a significant presence. We should have enough infrastructure to withstand whatever this panet throws at us. If preliminary reports are to be believed, this planet is rich in minerals. And, if initial suggestions turn out to be true, there are numerous caverns and undergound rivers. This might circumvent any need to acclimatise, as we could simply burrow down to a convenient location. So we could be secure from any convulsions...

" Ugh, you've got a couple more."

" I know, I know."

" So why don't you squeeze them ? "

" No. Not yet anyway. That always leaves blotches."

" I'll do it for you."

" No you won't. I want to leave them for the time being."

The other landings have gone extremely well. We are what amounts to an expeditionary force. We have gained so much information already. This planet is almost fully organic. Sensors reveal it may even have a rudimentary intelligence. Although substantially below ours, so any communication is out of the question. The surface remains unstable. However, now we have mining equipment, making our base of operations underground looks ever more feasible...

" Pooh, they do smell."

" Well don't stand so close then."

" Stinky pimples."

" Same to you."

" You going to let me squeeze them ? "

" No, I'll do it myself, without you watching."

Mining operations are going well. The surface of this panet is tougher than it first appears, more pliable than solid, if that makes sense...

" Look, I think it's time, don't you ? "

" No."

" But they look terrible, really bad."

" I know, I know...okay...but be careful."

" Okay, here goes."

We thought it was too good to last. Conditions have changed drastically. Adverse weather has destroyed most of our base camps. We have tried to reinforce our own position, to withstand the rigours of what appear to be earthquakes and volcanic eruptions...

" Wow, this last one is really huge."

" I don't care, just get rid of it."

" I'll have to squeeze hard."

" Do it...ow, that hurts."

" Ugh, I think it's gone in my hair."

As feared, we had to leave the unstable surface of this panet. Yet, as luck would have it, we located another place to land fairly quickly. This new planet looks even better. We crash landed in a heavily forested area. According to surveys, these areas are less prone to convulsions, at least on this type of planet. So, we are going to be able to construct a base easily, and quickly. We are already thinking in terms of a colony, but first things first...

" Ugh, where'd it go, did you see it."

" No I didn't, but so what ? "

" But I don't want your pus in my hair, from your stinky pimple. Who knows what might happen."

" Nothing probably. You're the one who wanted to go for my spots. And now you go all squeamish."

" I don't want to get what you've got."

" I didn't want them either...I hope I don't get blotches now."

This base is excellent, operations proceed at pace. Further good news, some of my colleagues managed to burrow underground at the old location. Now we are established on two planets. Good. We can begin to colonise this whole system. There are numerous other planets in this sector. Once we build our numbers we can become the dominant life form here. I do not see any significant problem hindering us.

The Problem with Dick

The problem with Dick was his dick. He was a man obsessed. He measured it, massaged it and fretted over it. The average dick was five to six inches long, or so he had read. He never talked to anyone about this, and he never would. He just let a multitude of anxieties run riot in his imagination. His was under five inches at its peak size. Or maybe six. It depended on where you measured from. Dick tried to stretch right to his belly button. But even he had to concede some things. His problem could not help but inform his girlfriends. Since he could not stop looking at it every time he was undressed, and as often as his gaze allowed. He pondered it so much that sometimes his girlfriends would joke. With that unerring sense, whereby a mischievous soul homes in on a persons vulnerability, despite nothing being said, they would disparage his size. The fact he might possibly have contributed to these episodes eluded him. This was because he would appear to be in a daydream. And nothing is worse than a distracted partner when matters of sex are being dealt with. Dick simply sighed, if he replied. Their comments only made him feel worse. His insecure manhood was a faulty fortress at best. Severe digs by the opposite sex only undermined the foundations of his self-esteem still further.

Dick became painfully shy, his performance suffered. He felt like the free-scoring centre foward who had lost his touch in front of goal. Instead of the usual rasping volley, or brave header, he was more likely to have an embarassing miss in front of an open goal. Even worse was the continual fear of being substituted at any given moment. It continued in this way. As time progressed, however, he found he was wrong about his fear of being susbstituted. Now he could not even get a game, it was worse. Now he had no opportunities to score. And training on your own got very boring after a while. Like any good footballer (or any footballer that thought he was good), Dick tried drastic measures. Nothing was more drastic than trying to talk to other people about his problem. Yet he made the attempt. Doctors were first. And a few embarassing consultations followed. There was no physical problem. Dick was told size did not matter. This went against all his established belief. Furthermore, he was informed the problem was psychosomatic. His own anxieties were factors inhibiting his performance. This in turn made him over-sensitive to the remarks of others. It was a self-perpetuating cycle of low self-esteem, fertilised by a basic ignorance of all human biology. Dick was crushed. He moved onto psychiatrists. They made him feel even worse. They pointed to hidden monsters in his own mind that scared the life out of him. He felt meek and timid. But to deal with things, it seemed, he had to be more meek and timid, instead of hard and macho as he always desired. He was advised that this was myth, and to look at life the way a caring, considerate, normal person did. Ugh, yuck, was his reflex reaction, he did not want to be a new age social worker. Dick moved on to a hypnotherapist. A smiling hello, followed by a period of blank space, followed by a bewildered goodbye. It did remind him of his sex life in that respect. Yet his paranoia was otherwise occupied. It all concerned the activities of said hynpotherapist. Dick entertained the notion he was being laughed at frequently. Or maybe the hypnotherapist did nothing. Perhaps he just slipped down the betting shop while Dick was in a trance. No, that was silly. But he might have fondled Dick while he was defenceless. Who knows what foul pervervsions were practised under cover of therapy. Dick tried to raise the issue. But, like his libido, it wilted when confronted by laughter. And there was post hypnotic suggestion as well. The hypnotherapist looked devious enough to play a trick with Dick. He might find himself walking down the street one day. Then, at the mention of a choice phrase, he finds himself standing over the Prime Minister's dead body, with a bloody knife in his hands. Worse, he has anal sex with the Prime Minister before he stabs him, in full view of the police bodyguard and the watching news cameras. Twenty million people see his organ.

No, no, the hypnotherapist did not last long. Dick tried hypnotising himself, one time only. He fell asleep while sitting on the toilet gazing at a hand mirror. His flatmate, worried at the long wait, kicked the door in. The door flew off its hinges and gave Dick an alarm call on the head. His flatmates concern turned to giggles. Dick squirmed embarassingly out of that predicament. All kinds of hypnosis were definitely out.

Two further options presented themselves, or was it three ? for stretching his member and massaging his concern. Dick had heard that perverted practices may increase length, and breadth and girth while you were at it as well. Some drugs were also held to be desirable. In fact, drugs were always held to be desirable by Dick. Now he had a good excuse to pursue them. The question remained - In what combination should exercise, perversion and drugs be taken ? And the answer came to him, as quick as an orgasm, in any combination he cared to choose.

And so Dick found himself with a leather clad man who gave his penis a massage. This actually got him aroused. But then awareness woke up and embarassment set in. The fear was that someone might find out, and call him a poof, his ultimate fear. So, these sessions were abandoned. He paid some capable females to give him the same treatment. But their knowing grins and motherly touch also began to cause the blushes. Dick's worse fear, after being called gay, was being called a Mummy's boy. These sessions were abandoned as well. So it was onto the drugs without further ado. Dubious compounds of hormones found their way into his system. These, combined with his usual leisure drugs, contrived to give him some weird and disturbing moments. Dick was driven back to the doctors. He was warned off his exotic cocktails of drugs and his attempt to grow an exotic cock. The doctors shook their heads at Dick's intent. They lectured him not to meddle with his organ. If he treated it too rough it might rebound on him. Dick was scared off the drugs for a couple of weeks. But then he forgot his fear and began taking them again. His flatmate was aware of Dick's obssession now. He was actually quite sympathetic to Dick, in that he merely sniggered occaisonally rather than indulge in prolonged pisstaking. Somehow his flatmate's sister got to hear about it also. She took an active interest in the condition of Dick, much to his embarassment. And embarassment was what his obssession was all about in the first place. If Dick increased his size his embarassment would fade. That would leave him free to pursue the flatmate's sister, whose name was Sheila. Sheila did not know the full extent of Dick's embarassment however. She took his attempts to remain secretive and furtive as his playing hard to get. And she determined to get Dick and give him some exercise. Dick was playing hard to get, in a sense, he found it hard to get hard, which only increased his sense of embarassment. This rendered all thought of pleasurable female contact somewhat disturbing. So exercise was off the agenda.

So Dick became surreptitious, in every sense of the word. He began looking up dubious websites - the kind that offer a dong as large as a gee gees. He sent off for several catalogues. and, further intrigued, he began ordering dubious packages through the mail. These contained ever more exotic concoctions of his favourite substance - drugs. So Dick took it all in, without reading the instructions, not that he could understand them anyway. They would have been dangerous had he followed the instructions in the first place. All these packages were made under the aegis of dubious charlatans that called themselves doctors. In fact that was their only qualification, the self-appointed assumption they were medical practioners of note. They were promoted through self-recognition. Not that this was a concern, for Dick continued his wayward path in pursuit of size. Even if the packages did not quite work, at least they would get him pleasantly out of it. Or at least out of it, since some of the pills and potions he took gave him suspicious feelings, and were of suspicious origin. There were glands from dead animals and glands from dead people. It was rumoured that people paid to have certain hormones removed. And, if there were no volunteers available, the unwitting were drugged and had their hormones removed anyway. Dick could never prove the rumours, as he could never remember the names of most of the concoctions he took. It all got out of control, a bit too far out of control. Dick's body began reacting as if it had a new mind of its own. And this new mind was located in his penis. It would get him up at nights, to go out to bars, to pick up partners, of any persuasion. And his cock would behave like an impatient child going on holiday, it would fidget endlessly. It did everything bar saying " are we there yet." At first Dick thought he was dreaming, then sleepwalking. But no, his prick really was starting to take matters into its own hands. Though when Dick did eventually get " there " it was always the same. He found himself in bed, with a randy adult, and then his organ would drift off to sleep. It even snored. It was so embarassing. Dick was at the mercy of his percy. However, he soon stopped the midnight ramblings by locking all the doors. But his prick still dictated Dick's life. His diet changed, a collection of fish, vitamin pills and performance enhancing drugs were consumed. This part of the prick dictator's demands did not bother him so much. It was the public ejaculation that did. Every time he saw a desirable female, male, car, or even a decent suit, he came. And it was accompanied by a squeak that sounded like a leather rag on a window pane. Dick usually explained this away by blaming his digestion. Even this state of affairs might have continued indefinitely. But he also noticed his bossy member was not actually growing that much, if at all, even when looked at in the right light, in an optimistic mood.

That settled it. It was off to dodgy doctors forthwith, the kind Dick had ordered his suspicious chemical compounds from. He did need to see a doctor. Though a proper one was needed. Instead he saw a consultant who charged large amounts of money for an uncertain future. This quack ignored the growing confusion of Dick's metabolism and concentrated on his willie instead. Any really concerned medical party would have rushed Dick off to hospital. Though, to give him is due, the quack did voice his worry. For Dick would sweat profusely and give off a fishy smell. Dick reassured the quack it was his normal condition. As was the fact that one minute Dick was full of vitality, the next he was all lifeless. He managed to persuade the quack he was fine, as fine as a genital-obssessed, shy person could be. Any aberrations of Dick's part were due to his constant worry about his middle stump. Once the status of one-eyed jack was enhanced, the symptoms would disappear, for they came with his short stature. Thus reassured, and with the glint of extra sterling in his eye, the quack performed his operation. An extra piece of pork was inserted into Dick to increase his own cock.

And it appeared to work. Dick gained an extra spring in his step, and an extra inch when he stood to attention. He was hoping for the full wonga. But even the quack balked at the possible outcome on this druggie customer of his. Best to add an inch at a time. That way his trouser snake could grow at an orderly rate. And Dick was satisfied. Of course, the fact the quack's insertion proved to be a different colour was a bit off-putting. Dick now had a two tone tadger. But he was assured the other colour would fade. He would grow into his new cock. However, the fact it was coloured flesh and green meant he did not want it to be seen, even by himself. He took to urinating in the dark, and taking baths in the dark, even getting dressed in the dark. He was embarassed about doing these things. But it would all be worth it one day, his cock would come out in the wash. Then he could bring it into the open, as fresh and fully-formed as a butterfly from a cocoon, or as a brand new trouser snake, having shed its old skin. Not that Dick would literally get it out, he was not a flasher, though he would get it out if asked. And when that time came he would no longer be mortified. He would deal with any embarassment maturely, as he if were unwrapping a sausage to put it in the grill.

But Dick had to admit he was not feeling himself after the operation, in all senses of the word. Fondling stopped when his cock began to feel like some cold meat he had taken out of the fridge. It did not feel like his own. Besides, he was now becoming nauseous. This went beyond his normal range of self-disgust. He really was begining to feel like something horrible was happening. Speech was becoming difficult. His limbs grew floppy, moving them was such an effort. And the hair on the top of his body began to fall out. He tried to disguise his condition from his flatmate. But Dick's lethargy increased as well. He took to his bed. And once Dick did this he could not continue any deception. Sheila took to nursing him. And she had to admit his was a strange illness. Although Dick was frequently limp and lifeless, he continued putting on weight. The trouble was his muscle was becoming flaccid. Now Dick could hardly get up at all. The doctor was called, and when he came round he confirmed the worst. Dick was very sick, but the cause was not immediately apparent.

Once Dick was in hospital he was isolated from the other patients, it was felt they might be scared or intimidated by him. In fact he was isolated from all vistors at first, for he scared the staff as well. Once all were used to Dick, however, their curiosity, allied to their profesional manner, reasserted itself. His condition was most interesting. And they were not sure just what it was. There were analogies to flesh eating viral strains, hormonal treatements, even cancerous conditions, but they were clutching at straws here. They could not ascertain how many varieties of drug Dick had taken, all the therapies undertook, treatments undergone, they could not even tell where Dick had been recently. And neither could he, even if he wanted to, although, to be honest, it is doubtful if he would have remembered if he were well. Therefore, the medical staff would offer no form of treatment. They certainly would not operate. They would have to know a lot more about Dick's previous adventures first. But they kept him under observation. For Dick was a fascinating study, and the doctors took a keen interest in his condition.

And Dick was certainly developing, mutating almost. The exotic cocktails of drugs, the dubious surgical procedures, allied to Dick's own peculiar character, had initiated physiological change. This change proceeded exoponentially. His upper half was now completely hairless. His arms atrophied, they became lifeless, withered stalks, that shrivelled and dropped off. Dick's legs became became rounded and flaccid, and were increasingly sensitive to touch. The legs swelled outwards and were welded together. Dick's upper body developed into a regular shape. There was some problem with baldness on the top of his head, for it did not stop with his hair. His actual scalp fell off as well, as did the top of his skull. The doctors became worried Dick's brain might be exposed. But a new, red, fleshy layer now formed where his scalp had once been. Although his brain could not now be located, it was assumed it was still there. The doctors did not want to risk any kind of scan while Dick was still developing.

After two months it was obvious what Dick had become. He had truly been transformed by his obsession. He was living proof of the dictum - ' be careful what you wish for.' It was hardly likely Dick could be aware of any irony, but then again he never was. Though at least in his current state he would not feel embarassment anymore. It was arguable whether he was aware of anything now. Never again would be dissatisfied with the size of his organ. He had plunged right into his fear and come out the other side, if not a better man, at least one who was reconciled to his cock, after a fashion. And so it could be said Dick had triumphed. For Dick was dick, so many more times larger and extra, extra thick. Naturally, Dick became the main topic of conversation among staff at the hospital. The more respectable doctors tut tutted. While others took an almost obssessive interest in Dick. The nurses learned of Dick, his conditon was a favourite item in their conversation also. No one could resist the lure of a man called Dick who turned into a huge prick. Instead of behaving like a prick, as most males did, Dick had gone the whole hog, or the whole horse, as it were. Some surreptitious photographs were taken, and they enjoyed a wide circulation. They eventually reached Sheila. She could hardly believe her eyes. Her precious little Dick, my, how he had grown since she last saw him. He really was a fine specimen of manhood now. Sheila had a nurse friend at the hospital, and variously cajoled and bribed her way into Dick's room.

And there they stood, the nurse and Sheila, mouths agape. For neither had been this close to Dick before, not in his present conditon. There was no immediate recognition from Dick. But he appeared to register their prescence. The vestiges of his eyes widened. The rest of his facial features had disappeared. However, his whole body appeared to be swelling, growing larger. Sheila and the nurse exchanged looks. They were concerned, but intrigued as well. They knew Dick was sexually aroused by their presence without saying anything. So Sheila continued to talk soothingly, and Dick continued swelling. Both of them quickly developed a rapport with Dick. Although, for a few horrified seconds, it seemed Dick might continue growing indefinetely. But his swelling tailed off as he filled the whole bed, looking like a good firm sausage as he did so. Sheila and the nurse hardly exchanged words. This telepathic understanding went on as they began to touch Dick. It was tentative at first. But the intrigue increased as they realised Dick was quite warm and comfortable to feel. Then an idea came to them. They had to voice it of course, in case one might think the other too perverted. However, since they both admitted it the idea became that much easier. They pulled the blanket back and exposed Dick in all his throbbing glory. Giggles broke out intermittently. They had often called men pricks or dickheads in the past. And here was one who fitted the bill entirely. Once they recovered their composure, they considered taking it in turns sitting on Dick's head. But Dick was now pulsing like a palpitating heart, so it was back to the original idea. They eased their arms around Dick's fleshy body and linked them together. They then began moving their limbs up and down in unison. They were relieving Dick in effect. If someone happened to walk in they would say they were giving him a massage. This led to giggles again. But they continued their up and down motion with their linked arms. Dick's skin moved easily to this rhythm. He was becoming firmer, he almost felt like a massive marrow by now. From somewhere within the depths of Dick's flesh a quiver started. This quiver turned into a full blown shiver. The vibrations spread through Sheila and the nurse. But they redoubled their efforts, faster and faster. They thought they heard one or two gasps. Then a gasping Dick became a groaning Dick, then a moaning Dick. By this stage an observer might have felt there was something wrong (after taking photographs, as most observers seemed to do). However, other observers might have cheered the women on. It was obvious now they could not stop, they were too far into the rhythm to even slow down. The sounds of Dick seemed far away as they found they were enjoying themselves. Dick was building to his climax. The groans turned louder and longer. Then he let out a scream any orgasmic person would have been proud of, or any police siren for that matter. And that was what killed Dick. Maybe it was because his new form did not permit ejaculation. Or maybe his physiology had not adapted enough at that point. The doctors were never quite sure. Although they were sure enough of the event itself. It seemed Dick was still a person. For when he came, through the new slit in the top of his head, no semen was present. Instead his internal organs erupted through his head. Along with a resdue of gastric juice could be seen the remains of heart, lung stomach and liver. The women panicked and ran. They later confessed, but were exonerated, as they had been overcome by the passion of the moment. In the meantime, C.C.T.V. footage of their exploit enjoyed a healthy circulation. Those who knew Dick felt it was the way he would have wanted to go. His dedication to his organ was admired as much in death as it had been ridiculed in life. Dick had pursued his dream until he died in an episode that was beyond the wildest wet dream. His body was preserved in formaldehyde, in a tank shaped like a giant dildo.

Murderous Manny

I sat down with my laptop. I was going to begin on the latest instalment of the life of Murderous Manny. But I was stumped for an idea. He had a history, this character. He had grown up in the 1960's and 1970's. He was a great admirer of the Krays and the Richardsons, along with all the other celebrity villains of the time. Consequently, he tried to model himself on them. In his case it meant he was a nasty piece of work, violent and ruthless. He had no real intelligence, not even the criminal variety, no charm, and no one really trusted him because he was so short tempered. His life was one long series of prison spells, interrupted by brief spasms of freedom. In these spasms he invariably tried an activity which led to him being caught and put away. Manny had tried housebreaking, robbery, building society hold ups, warehouse burglary, raids on security vans and the protection racket. His methods were crude and stupid. He never got away, and usually caused untold damage to peoples' lives and property in the process.

And this character demanded another episode in his sorry life. My contract with 'Crime Stories' magazine made this necessary. I had to churn out five or six stories a year about him, besides the other commitments I had. But I was written out. I never really wanted to write about Manny in the first place. Even though he was fictional, I found him boring. But the punters really took him up. Manny's stories always got the most letters, so my editors told me. They found Manny pretty much a character of his time ; spoilt, rebellious, reckless. But they paid more attention to other characteristics. Manny was brave (headstrong I preferred) and he did what he wanted, regardless of the trouble it caused. It was these latter traits that excited the fans most, especially the younger ones. But myself, I was sick and tired of Manny. He was a troublemaker, a loser, and uninteresting it has to be said. My heart sank at the thought of writing another episode in this waster's life. A contract is a contract however. And since this was my fifth strory of the year, it would be my last story about Murderous Manny. I had already decided to kill him off.

After a lot of dithering, I eventually decided to make Manny's last episode on this planet an involved one. He would try kidnapping, which would lead to murder. He had not committed these crimes yet. But given his stupidity, I believed he would run into them eventually. In my last Manny story I had him beat up then blackmail a rival. I added the extra touch of the rival stealing Manny's girlfriend. Well now, I thought, I could have Manny follow on from there. The rival was a white collar criminal, someone Manny had befriended inside. This criminal had got to know Manny's girlfriend soon after he was released, while Manny was still in prison. A mutual acquaintance of both men had introduced them. The trouble was, in that penultimate story, this mutual acquaintance was a shadowy figure. I decided, in my last story, to have Manny break into the acquaintance's home, threaten him, hold him for ransom, and then, in a fit of rage, kill him.

These were the bare facts of the story. I could not get any further in fleshing it out. I had two nights just sitting in front of my laptop, staring. (I work better at night.) How long this might have gone on I am not sure. For on the third night things went a little strange. I was in my routinely depressed mood, unable to motivate myself. That was the last time I had to think, events moved quickly after that. I will try to recreate them as best I can.

The unmistakeable sound of breaking glass had me rushing downstairs. I instantly grasped the fact there was a burglar on the premises. So I armed myself with the nearest object that came to hand, which was a table lamp. A bit ridiculous I know, but it was all I could find. I moved carefully downstairs, all the while trying to maintain a brave composure, though in reality I was scared witless. As I moved into the darkened living room I could see a small hole in one of the windows. I checked around, there was no one present. Luckily my fears were unfounded. Someone had just broken the window, nothing more. After such a scare, I felt I needed a drink. So I went to my small kitchen to see what I had. As I went in and switched the light on, someone pounced from behind the door. He proceeded to strangle me with an electric flex. I struggled, mad with fear. I must have hit him, for he released his grip. Or maybe he released me anyway. For his next move was to punch me in the face. I was shocked, this hurt terribly. Luckily I managed to stagger back onto the sofa. I could feel the blood running down my nose. I automatically tilted my head back to staunch the flow, while he stood there gloating.

After a good gloat he outlined his reasons for being here. This was the part that shocked me the most. I cannot really reproduce his words, just the gist of them. It was unreal. He wanted payment from me, because I had been telling his life story for a number of years without acknowledgement.

Now he had come to collect. I protested at this, but he was insistent. I knew everything, even the bust up with his white collar friend and girlfriend. He had seen me around, this psychopath, in the local pubs. It was obviously here I had picked up on his escapades. He had enjoyed reading about himself at first. But now thought things had gone too far. He wanted some payment.

I protested I got most of my information from local newspapers and court cases. But this would not wash. He said it amounted to the same thing. It still told his story. But the fact remained Manny was a fictional character I had cobbled together from a dozen characters in detective novels I had read over the years. This information did not impress him. Manny was obviously him, although his name was Mickey. Mickey's mates had wound him up for years. They even called him Manny as a nickname. Mickey gave me an unnecessary slap after telling me this, I thought. Although I was assured it was for all the jokes he had taken from his mates over the years.

Well, I got over the intial shock, meeting a stranger who claimed to be a character I had created in my head, and tried to explain. Unfortunately, this Mickey would not have it that it was just coincidence. I was obviously taking the mickey (no pun intended, he was too stupid for that). I had lain out his character for all too see. That was worth some compensation. And he would ransack my house by way of collecting payment.

I tried to protest but he hit me again. That last blow made me feel queasy. And as the world whirled in front of me, Manny, sorry Mickey, produced a rope. Despite my feeble protests he tied my legs and hands. Then he stuck some sticky tape over my mouth. Off he went, ransacking till his heart's delight. Yet his delight soon turned sour as he searched the house. I had nothing much of value, about five pound in cash, and a crappy telly, that was it. I never made that much money anyway. This made him angry. I thought he might hit me again as he came back into the living room. I was scared, I could not take much more treatment like this. But, as he furiously tore apart the room where we were, it soon dawned on him, well soon was relative for Mickey, most people would have fallen asleep waiting for him to get an idea. Eventually, Manny, sorry Mickey, realised I was not too well off after all. A glance would have confirmed this, my lived-in clothes and threadbare furniture would have persuaded most burglars to get lost. Mickey was persistent though. He even searched my kitchen cupboards. And then, bingo, he found my supply of booze. This was one of my few indulgences, I liked expensive spirits. This discovery gave him time to ponder, before he mentioned his plans. He told me he would kidnap me, then send a ransom note to my editors. I knew I was dead if he did that. My editors would burst out laughing, thinking it was a joke. I made noises through the sticky tape, my eyes pleaded with him, but to no use. As he poured a drink I gave him a desperate, agonised look. I know I looked like this, because it was the way I felt. And he just laughed at me. But he should have paid more attention to my pleading. I was scared of what he might do, yes. But I was also worried about what he was drinking. The whisky bottle he used I had emptied long ago. It was now full of a very strong disinfectant. He not only knocked his glass back in one gulp, but took a huge swig from the bottle straight afterwards. Then I remember standing him there, like an idiot who had forgotten his name. He soon snapped out of this as painful spasms began to rack his body. His face turned a bright red.

Mickey moved to punish me for what he believed was my trick. I feared the worst. But he never made it to me, as he collapsed and died within two steps. I sat there for ages afterwards, wondering what to do. But eventually I squeezed out of the rope that tied me up. Then I managed to drag Manny's, sorry Mickey's, body across the park to the nearby canal and dumped him there. I had a nervy few days after this escapade. But now I knew how to finish Manny's story. Mickey had kindly supplied me with an end to his career.

This is Your Strife

They were sitting in his office, the high-powered T.V. executive, Farnsworth Bullyboy himself, and the cringing celebrity before him - none other than Amos Anthrax, presenter of the famous programme ' This is Your Strife.' The programme that catches the superstars of showbiz unawares, plonks them in a studio, delves into their past, digging up the dirt, being nosy, generally stirring it up, and holding any vaguely embarassing detail up to prolonged ridicule. The victim of this treatment also has to go through the ordeal of meeting past acquaintances, who Amos has brought along to discuss old times, renew old arguments and slag each other down to the ground (since most of these acquaintances have not seen the victim anymore because they cannot stand him/ her/it). ' This is Your Strife ' tops the viewing ratings. However, Amos is sweating profusely, and looks very disturbed, as Farnsworth Bullyboy draws on a fat, juicy havanna cigar and says -

Farnsworth Bullyboy : Amos, about the viewing figures for the current season of This is Your Strife, they seem to be declining rather steadily. Can you pinpoint any reason for this ?

Amos Anthrax : Well sir, it's just that we're running out of celebrities. This is Your Strife has run over twenty years, and, in that time, we've had practically every well-known person in the world on our show. Besides, there doesn't seem to be that many around nowadays anyway.

Farnsworth : Yes, it does look as if you're getting increasingly desperate for any kind of celebrity.

I've been looking through a list of people you've had on the show in the last series ; (picks up list and reads out) Suburban au pair, Sue Slave, known as the fastest hoover in Surbiton; Margo Fountain, possessor of the world's weakest bladder; Joey Himmler, the fascist traffic warden; Garry Gibberish, who can stutter in seventeen different languages; Elsie Barnyard, the born again vegetarian; Tommy Tacky, bearer of the world's most excrutiating grin. Hardly your pillars of modern civilisation, are they ?

Amos : Well, that proves my point, sir. The supply of celebs is really drying up. We've really had to scrape the barrel this series.

Farnsworth : But compare to the last series, that was simply oozing with big names; (picks up another list and reads out) John F. Kennedy; Marilyn Monroe; Mao Tse Tung; Bismarck; Madame Curie; Queen Elizabeth I; Charles Lindbergh; Albert Schweitzer; Catherine the Great; Blackbeard...

Amos : Er, all these people have one thing in common, (clears throat) they're dead.

Farnsworth : You're joking.

Amos : No.

Farnsworth : Please explain, Amos.

Amos : Well, for the last series, we had a lot of trouble finding really famous, or infamous, people. So we hit on the idea of using wax dummies of past prominent personalities.

Farnsworth : Well I never, wax dummies. Didn't the viewers ever suss it ? I mean, they read someone's been dead a few centuries, and the next thing they know is that someone's on the box.

Amos : Oh, we just said the guest wanted to retire from public life, you know, a bit of peace and relaxation, so they invented a death story. It worked every time.

Farnsworth : I thought Marilyn Monroe was a bit frigid when I tried to chat her up. Didn't you get any trouble from living relatives ? or anyone else for that matter ? Surely someone would have objected.

Amos : Nothing a few bribes and payments in the right places couldn't handle.

Farnsworth : Why don't you use more wax dummies for this series then ?

Amos : Well sir, the studio lights, and the general stuffy atmosphere, made a lot of the dummies melt. You remember the programme where Genghiz Khan was the guest...

Farnsworth : Yes ?

Amos : Well he dissolved into a puddle of liquid on the air. Can you inagine how embarrassing that was ?

Farnsworth : I see, a tricky situation.

Amos : Yes, we only got round it by saying Genghiz had to slip away to toilet, that he had a chronic bowel complaint, a hangover from his Chinese campaign.

Farnsworth : Wax Dummies are out of it then ?

Amos : Unless you want to run the risk of another guest dissolving on the air.

Farnsworth : Did you have anyone in mind for this week at all ?

Amos : Well...er...we're working on it.

Farnsworth : Oh come on, surely you could dig up any old turd, invent a few stories about them, grab a few relatives, you know, improvise a little.

Amos : That reminds me of the time we tried using normal people on the show.

Farnsworth : Who ?

Amos : You know, the plebs, the little people...

Farnsworth : Oh the dumb viewing masses, you mean, yes I remember, that was a stupid idea. The main reason they watch your programme is for the stories of scandal and strife so lacking in their own.

Amos : Exactly. But how about lynching some unsuspecting pleb off the street, invent a phony life story about them, get their relatives in to say dirty things about them. You know the kind of thing, tonights guest is a pervert, he doesn't wash under his armpits, etc etc...

Farnsworth : Why didn't you think of that before ?

Amos : I thought it was perhaps a bit too cynical.

Farnsworth : Who cares ?

Amos : Right ,er...

Farnsworth : Yes, you had better get on with it, hadn't you.

(And so, in a certain rush hour street, in a certain metropolis, a certain character, by the name of Norman Normal, after another weary days work at Municipal and General Porn Pedlars Ltd, is hit over the head, forced into a sack, and carted off to Groanada Studios.)

(We rejoin Farnsworth Bullyboy and Amos Anthrax in the Groanada studio, just minutes before Amos goes on the air, for the 60,434,378th edition of This is Your Strife. Amos is frantic with panic.)

Amos : Sir, we've got to call the programme off.

Farnsworth : But why ? Amos.

Amos : No one knows this bloke.

Farnsworth : Well go out on the street, ask someone, anyone, to come in, flash a few fivers at them.

Amos : Sir, you know people are unwilling to appear on T.V. nowadays, after being on numerous quiz shows that made them look bigger idiots than they already are. Why, if I even mentioned television, they'd run for dear life.

Farnsworth : And it's too late to kidnap anyone and haul them in ?

Amos : Yes.

Farnsworth : Oh damn...surely he must have some relatives ?

Amos : None.

Farnsworth : Friends ?

Amos : None.

Farnsworth : Well surely he must have the script you made up ?

Amos : That's the trouble, sir, he's so thick he can't even memorise the first line. At first I thought he was being stubborn because I had him kidnapped, but, no sir, he's just plain gormless.

Farnsworth : Well think of something,improvise, ad lib it, anything...Hurry it up, you're on the air soon.

(Amos rushes away.)

Farnsworth : (Shouts after him.) And make it good, Amos, or Groanada may have to make a salary cut.

(A Short while later, Amos walks up to a bland, vacant figure, standing bewildered in the middle of the studio floor, and says ;-)

Amos : Norman Normal, this is your strife.

(Cue flashy opening sequences, of past people pretending to look surprised, accompanied by a high-pitched, melodramatic theme tune. Once this mercifully short sequence is over, Norman is guided to a chair, and the programme begins.)

Amos : (Reading from a big,red book.) Norman Normal, you were born in, er...you don't know when you were born...ahem, in the little picturesque village of Idunnowhereicomefrom, ahem. No one realised you were alive, until you were found sitting at the back of the class, in the local secondary school. Do you remember this voice from your schooldays -

" What's that sitting at the back of the class ? clear it away,someone..."

Amos : Yes, it's your old schoolteacher, Ms Dirtie Oldmaid.

(Dirtie Oldmaid strolls in.)

Amos : Ms Oldmaid, Dirtie, is it true that Norman was the most, um, ah, quiet, and least troublesome of your pupils ?

Dirtie : Who ?

Amos : You remember Norman Normal, one of your pupils back in, er, a long time ago.

Dirtie : Oh yes, actually I remember him quite well.

Amos : Yes.

Dirtie : The thing that stood out about him.

Amos : Yes.

Dirtie : I mean, his most distinguishing feature.

Amos : Yes.

Dirtie : What set him apart from the other pupils.

Amos : Yes.

Dirtie : What put him in a class of his own.

Amos : Yes.

Dirtie : What I really remember about him.

Amos : Yes.

Dirtie : Er...I can't rightly remember offhand.

Amos : What ?

Dirtie : I've forgotten.

Amos : Oh.

(Amos frowns and shoves Dirtie Oldmaid, ungentlemanly, into a chair. He goes back to his book.)

Amos : Norman, you left school, when one day you walked out to find a toilet and couldn't find your way back. From there you went to your first, erm, your one and only job, at Municipal and General Porn Pedlars. You've given them distinguished service for, um, many many many years, ahem. Everyone at work treats you as a permanent fixture there, almost a part of the furniture. In fact, somebody once thought you were a desk, because you didn't move, and started to work on their files on you...ha ha ha. Your boss, when asked about you, gave a glowing account of your work. He said, ' Norman who ? never heard of the geezer. Hold on, I'll look up our index system, see if he works here.' Ahem...er, Norman, do you recognise this voice from your work -

" I saw this bloke standing there one day. No one knew how he got there. Someone suggested we use him as a bin. Now we stuff all the rubbish down his throat. Last week our photocopier broke down and we had to get a new one. We disposed of the old machine by ramming it down his throat. He didn't even blink. I'll say this for him, he never complains about working conditions, always gets on with his work. The other day he was promoted to Waste Disposal Unit."

Amos : Yes, your immediate superior at the office, Manfred Militant.

(Cue taped clapping as Manfred walks in.)

Amos : Manny, ha ha, is all that really true ?

Manfred : No. It was on that script you gave me, remember, about...

Amos : Ahem, well, sit down Manny.

(Manfred Militant is forcefully shoved into a chair, and sits there looking bewildered.)

(Amos continues reading, he shuffles the pages anxiously, flicks backward and foward through the book, begins sweating a lot, eventually he finds something.)

Amos : Whew...er, Norman, do you remember this voice ?

(For what seems to be the umpteenth time that night, Norman gazes at him with the utmost apathy.)

" Watch where you're going, you vegetable."

Amos : Yes, here tonight from all the way down the road, a lady you once bumped into while walking down the road, Mrs Martha Yard.

(Martha Yard walks in.)

Martha : That's what you say. I never seen this toe rag before, you said I...

Amos : Thank you Martha Yard, sit down (then whispers in her ear), and shut up.

(The pressure and the evenings chaos begin to tell on Amos. He has a slight tantrum, pulls a few strands of hair out, but suddenly remembers he is on T.V, in front of millions of viewers, and so quickly regains his composure. He reads from the last page in the book -)

Amos : Well Mister Normal, we searched for your relatives. We looked with a fine tooth comb, we scoured the country, we traversed the globe, in the hope that, somehow, somewhere, we'd find someone with the minutest blood tie to an apathetic creep like you. And find him we did, after God knows how many enquiries...All the way from the remote Pacific island of Popular New Tourist Destination, chief of the Missionary Sandwich Headhunter tribe, also chair of the Popular New Tourist Destination tourist board, Mister Feneecki skeek bak diki trek...er. I mean, Mister Nennafek shek baky traky...no, er, Mister Frenfecky creekyback slappy tronky... um, oh shit, here he is anyway.

(The Chief walks in)

Amos : Mister, er, thingy. I understand Norman's your uncle's, cousin's, nephew's, mother's, brother's, sister's, daughter's, father's, grandfather's, grandmother's, niece's, great aunt's, 4th cousin's, 3rd sister's, step-brother's, mother's-lover's, dog's brother's, cat's, nanny's, son's godmother's, illegitimate cousin's, housekeeper's, friend of a 5th uncle's friend, twice removed, twice brought back, great-great grandfather's pet's, half-brother's once removed, once bitten, twice shy, on your father's side.

Chief : I told you, man, I can't memorise all that, I need more time.

Amos : Oh God. (another ungentlemanly shove is made, this time on the Chief.) Don't you idiotic, cretinous guests realise, it's all for the sake of television, to make the viewers interested in this non-event, to make them think the boring, little fart (points to Norman) has done something in his life, besides getting up in the morning.

Norman : You mean I actually get up in the morning, actually out of bed, gee, I never realised.

Amos : Shut up. All of you, out, out, you're all brainless, the lot of you. God, you people are thicker than our programmes make you out to be, and that's really saying something.

(Everybody leaves, except Norman and Amos. Amos sinks dejectedly into his chair. He idly glances at his watch.)

Amos : Oh God, we've still got fifteeen minutes to go, we're still on the air...(He turns to Norman) Listen, you cretinous creep, don't you have anything to say about your bloody mundane little existence ? some story, some small event, some little routine, some ordinary anecdote, something, anything, anything anything...

Norman : Well, er...it's kind of hard to start anywhere, Amos, first of all...ah...er, kind of...er...um, I mean, first things first, heart of the matter conversations must be...ah.. well, er, what I'm trying to say,er...um, well what I'm trying to say, convey, regarding my confessions, revelations, say what you will, whatever you will...er, what you want of, er, ah...er, my long career, yes long, er, ah yes, well, about that later, anyway, er, you see, must go about things differen...er, definitely...er, with the right frame of mind...er...I'm sorry, I've forgotten the question, Amos.

Amos : ZZZZZZZZZZZZZZZZZZZZZZZZZZZZ...

Norman : Really ? ah, most interesting, um...it goes to show, concerning all sorts of things, ah...er, no matter, what, when ,whenever the need arises..ah...well, yes, about that anyway, there...er...you can't beat about the bush in the rush hour, or work your gradually up a steep gradient, or slowly incline your thinking, steadily but surely, but, whatever..er, ah, blah blah de bloody blah, and more of it, and so on...

(A few minutes later Farnsworth Bullyboy walks in, to discover everyone asleep, apart from Norman, who is still babbling incoherently. He proceeds to wake Amos with some gentleness.)

Farnsworth : You're sacked, Anthrax. And I'm going off for a good sulk. If you get me that wax dummy of Marilyn Monroe, to take on holiday, then I might reconsider. In the meantime, please clear up the mess here.

(Farnsworth walks out.)

THE END.

The Ideal Candidate

The interview was going well, Crapson thought so anyway. He had a flash of insight, this scared him at first, as it was thirty years since the last one ; what they were after was the sluggard, the plodder, the working stiff. He glanced over at Kropp, the interviewee. Kropp waffled his way through his past achievements in extremely tedious detail. Berke and Snare, Crapson's colleagues, took time off to daydream while he did so.

Crapson allowed himself to enjoy the possibility of another successful appointment, maybe. Possiblities walked through his head, like grass growing in slow motion. Yet he found he was bored brainless as well.

Kropp was telling how he used to keep accounts for a doorbell firm. Before that he worked for a cardboard box manufacturers. Also, he had freelance spells organising the finances of a minor television personality (who could not read or write). Since this television personality did not work anymore, this did not pay much.

Snare was shifting uncomfortably in his seat. His bum must ache, like mine, thought Crapson.

Berke was snoring. Suddenly his head drooped. He spluttered " Eh what ? " and came to. His head wobbled slightly. Then the snoring started again.

"...so you see, you had to write in the margins around the figurework, the totals being underlined, of course. These were weekly and monthly, after subtracting expenditure, except in urgent cases, when a special allowance had to be withdrawn, this was then added to the monthly figures, before tax was deducted, and after expenses had been calculated..."

Oh God, this man is anaesthetic made human, a plodder, a natural, he will go far, though very slowly. Kropp coughed and drew a deep, slow breath, as if to go on, but Snare interrupted.

" Tell me Kropp, what really interests you about this position ? You have said it's to your liking. But from what you say, It sounds like you might be some kind of whizz kid, the way you straightened out this cardboard box company."

" On the contrary, that took twenty years, sir."

" And do you like working with people ? "

" Well people aren't as reliable as figures, sir. They do have their good points it's true. But they tend to get in the way of a job sometimes."

" So you're one of those people that works all day and saves the socialising for evenings and weekends."

" No sir, I practise accounting at home."

" Any hobbies ? "

" Erm...not really. I do like sleeping, sitting in dusty corners and being depressed."

Berke continued snoring. Kropp looks ideal, thought Crapson. A bit chubby perhaps, and a funny square head, and a pale, grey complexion, but why has he got index stamped on his nose ? Then Crapson realised he was looking at the filing cabinet. He turned around. Kropp was droning again, a soft, soothing, mellow tone that could send an insomniac into deep coma. Snare interrupted again -

" So where do you see yourself in twenty years time ? Kropp."

" In a rut, sir."

" You're not filling in between your next venture."

" I never plan moves like that, sir."

" But you have plannned to progress."

" Well, to tell the truth, I've never understood what the phrase means, sir. Perhaps you could explain it to me."

" I 'm afraid I don't use the term myself. One of those newfangled notions me forethinketh."

A DEAD SILENCE FOLLOWED, LASTING ABOUT AN HOUR.
AND THEN -

" How did you find out about this vacancy ? "

" Well, I was talked into it, sir. I was happy at my previous employment, but my manager encouraged me further. He locked me out of the office one day. He said I couldn't get back in until I made some kind of effort to better myself.. My wife was also an encouragement, she beat me up..."

Kropp tailed off.

" Yes I see..."

Snare tailed off.

Brilliant, thought Crapson, absolutely brilliant. Just think of the team we would make - Kropp, Crapson, Berke and Snare.

Kropp sat there, implacable in his dozy manner, as Snare completely lost interest in the matter. He daydreamed, then he thought of something. He got up and went to his desk and drew a large doodle on the pad. Then he made a phone call.

" Snare here...yes...I'm just checking...oh...you are in... where exactly ?...oh next door...so why did you call me

?...oh I did...good job I have your number then...hur hur hur... oh yes, quite...sweet melon and salad dressing...I look foward to hearing from you...oh sorry, you meant the central heating... well fill out a form...yes...erm...sometime...erm...bye."

Snare drew two more large doodles then strolled back to where the others were sitting.

" What do you think ? Crapson, about...er...thingy here," he turned around,

" I'm sorry, I've forgotten your name."

Crapson heard the voice, but his daydream was begining to absorb him completely. Snare's voice was a hundred miles distant. Kropp hestitated,

"...Er, yes, it's Kropp, sir, or is it ?...yes...it is. I do forget it sometimes, sir. You see, other people might use it, especially if they're talking to me, but there's not much call for it with myself."

" What a splendid answer," said Snare.

Berke awoke, spluttered, tried to stand, swayed, coughed, steadied himself, stared at Kropp with bloodshot eyes. Then he extended his hand -

" Welcome to the Civil Service m'boy."

They shook hands warmly.

" Yes, we offer you the job," said Snare.

" Thank you."

A dull glint of pleasure showed briefly in Kropp's eye, before it glazed over again. Berke collapsed in a snoring heap again. Snare managed to catch him under the arms as he fell. He opened the door and dragged the snoring Berke out. Kropp sat in silence for a few minutes. Then it occurred to him he should look for his desk, wherever that might be. And all the while Crapson daydreamed in his chair, his body inert, his mind elsewhere.

Poor Cod

He was one in six million. This was true. But where he was in the order, he could not recall. Most of his family died early, as was usual. But his was hit particularly hard. He remembered no relatives, not that he would recognise them. There was the ritual of recognition, however. If he met a stranger he would circle warily, secreting those chemicals that were his individual signature. If there was recognition they would make the required motions of greeting. He had seen others do this, and was jealous at first, but no longer. Life was to be gotten on with. He heard someone say that once, and it was true. If he stopped then that would be it. He would be prey to all kinds of hazards. Maybe he would even become willing victim to some of these hazards. He had seen that too. Life was intense in the realm of the Blue. That 3D realm was so beautiful, so involved and so deadly.

He did not even have a number he could recall. All his kind had numbers. As a birth contained so many young, and so many died young, it was the only way of keeping track. Therefore, his first friend was 3M425. That was the three million, four hundred and twenty fifth birth. And there was 2M603,711, two million, six hundred and three thousand, seven hundred and eleventh, who was his best friend for a while. But he succumbed to a breathing ailment, and drowned slowly. They had proper names as well of course. But these were used only among those who grew up in the same school, or shoal. Bonds formed in the school would last for life. They compensated for the complete indifference most showed to family life. He wondered if it should be different. It did not feel wrong particularly. But he saw that others kept close family units, for large parts of their lives. But of course they were different species, and not considered important. But what made his own species so superior ? nothing really. They had no poison, no sharp teeth, no superior size. Some claimed their type had been much larger in the past. But, having lost this advantage, they still had numbers. Even these had dwindled from past greatness, according to some. In the past their numbers could block out the light from above, when they swam en masse. Although they were still numerous enough not to be troubled, by any but the most dangerous predator, when they remained together. And this was the crux of the matter. Remain together always, and their strength was undiminished, the species depended on it. Apart and alone they were nothing, and they were exposed to everything. In togetherness they could do anything and fear nothing.

His first school had found him, apparently. His family had been devasted, literally. There were sharks around, where he was found. All in their way had been eaten, and more besides. They always swam with their mouths open They did not care, as with all big creatures. But they were few, and were easily chased off by his new school. He was adopted, as all strays were. He gained some sympathy, but some distrust from the elders. Strays were not to be trusted. They missed early development of social skills. This led them to be a risk. Any disruption in the school could lead to a disruption in the swim path, or in the reaction required. This could lead to instant death, and it did, on a few occaisons. He was reminded of this. For he turned left when he should have turned right, then glided up when he should have dived down. This upset their movement. One was lost to the lower depths, another to a predator. Everyone said it was a shark. In fact it was probably one of their own. For the bigger fish regularly preyed on the smaller fish. Though no one would care to acknowledge this, it was only accepted in secret. But of course he was blamed. His clumsy, maladapted actions caused it. ' Schools give rule, Strays make waste,' was the derogatory proverb. And he heard it more than once.

Thankfully, most of the school were peers, about his age and size. There were two very large fish who were recognised as great elders. And one was recognised leader. That was Preacher 375. From the start he did not like Preacher 375. He always thought that religious dogma and leadership did not combine well. But Preacher 375 could point to his own longevity. This made him take pride in his authoritarianism. Longevity conferred instant respect, as did the fact the preacher was lucky. 375 was his birth number. Anyone who had a birth number under a million was considered lucky. This was because so few eggs survived to hatch, and so few codling survived to adulthood. In a brood of three million, for example, a mere fraction would survive. A mere tenth of this fraction, at the most, would be low numbers. Therefore, a number of a million and under was rare. And they all tended to be preachers, like 375. Maybe the knowledge of their own good fortune made them gratefully accept religion. Or maybe it was superstitious fear at their luck running out. None could quite distinguish. There was rumoured to be a Preacher 9 somewhere, somewhere in the cold Arctic. She was worshipped as a goddess. But he did not believe this to be more than mere fable.

Preacher 375 was real enough. It was Preacher 375 who gave him his name, or rather his nickname. For, the fact he could not remember his birth number, had marked him down in continual disgust in the eyes of Preacher 375. Even when a name was given it always dependent on number. With no number you could only have a nickname, never a proper name. And Preacher 375 called him Poor Cod. This was a gross insult. Poor cod were their inferior relatives, a less developed species. Preacher 375 doubted his birthright in fact. He doubted whether he was true to the species at all, so Poor Cod it was. This did not have the desired effect of alienating him from the rest of the school. As social beings, sympathy was as strong in them as distrust of strays. So they rallied round him, even if they did consider him inferior, for they believed Preacher 375. Poor Cod he remained.

But he was not considered inferior for long. As they went through their cycles of feeding, manoevuring and mating, Poor Cod gained his fill of everything. He fought harder. His smaller size gave him agility. He made use of this to dazzle his rivals, and his mates. His pairings lasted some time, much to the surprise of the others. He moved and danced with with a grace the rest of the school could only envy. Preacher 375 grudgingly admitted his worth. There ceased to be any talk of exiling him, as had once been mooted.

Life was proving reassuring in its routine. It was hardly comfortable though. Their space lay in the Mid Atlantic. There they bustled and competed with other schools for living and breathing space. Then they went to escort the mothers to spawning grounds, once a year, around the large islands, to the sheltered North. In the sheltered North were relatively settled conditions, even if the cold was ever-present.

But , of course, they could not help but become aware of worsening conditions, If they did not become aware they were made aware. Some of the other schools were smaller in number, and some of their number as small as Poor Cod. This gave him satisfaction. It was a circumstance to use against Preacher 375. Preacher 375 was twice as large as most in his school. He dwarfed Poor Cod. And he related tales of how his size was not unusual in the old days, as if Poor Cod's small stature were the result of some wrong he had done before he was born. Poor Cod would not accept this. He insisted on pressing for an explanation of the assertion. Preacher 375 was prone to exaggeration to prove a point. The Preacher did have some evidence, although argued against by some. Their quality of life had diminished. It had effected the other species too. Strange chemicals found their way into the Deep Blue, whose provenance was unknown (even if Preacher 375 believed he knew). These chemicals misled their senses, dulled their stability, weakened their gills. They were left more vulnerable to disease and predators. The seas had also grown warmer, less comfortable than in previous years. It meant they grew quicker and died younger.

But of course, the one, great hazard, to them and all their race, remained the Lines from Above. Those Lines that crept up on them separately and silently. Then, at the right moment, they combined in interlocking patterns. They hoisted quickly, back to the Above from where they first came, taking hundreds, sometimes thousands, with them. All species were prey to the Lines, but none more than the Cod. Preacher 375 explained it as the vengeance of fate on their species, for being so successful in their environment. Poor Cod thought this might have applied to the Sharks, the Tunny, even the Mackerel, more than them. But preacher 375 would have none of this. There was none more intelligent and adaptable than the Cod in this domain. There might be creatures, such as the air breathers, with bigger brains, but they were maladapted. They had to breathe in the element no one could thrive in , apart from the Gods of the Outside. For most of them, the prescence of the Gods of the Outside explained the Lines from Above. Why else should they plucked out at random ? their numbers horribly decimated. Some few had escaped the Lines. They told of hallucinatory experiences, of slimy parasites that lived on armoured whales, that picked them from the Lines, and left them gasping their lives out on the whales bare backs. No one gave real credence to such fantasy. Water deprivation did horrible things to you. And most of these escapees died soon afterwards, the shock was that much. It was bad enough hearing such things.

Poor Cod was a pragmatist, he liked to insist. There was no time for religion in a space such as theirs. A space that gave all life could give - in creation and destruction. Why should anything exist outside of it ? Creatures clinging to the surface of the water, or to the dry outcrops, were pathetic. Just like those fliers who wailed piteously at their plight, at having to live in such a barren environment. For who could help but wail when having to live in an empty space ? And they were supposed to believe there were Gods in this place ? Beings who manipulated the Lines from Above into their deadly patterns. The patterns that led them to life everlasting, after an intense moment of purging pain, if you believed some, and eternal reward. But even Preacher 375 did not push this point. For, as a survivor, he became something of a pragmatist himself. Yet he felt religion contributed to this. Without the pattern of thought and belief religion gave, they were prey to random events, events that treated them with complete indifference. Therefore, the Lines from Above must serve some purpose. Preacher 375 would never go so far as to believe the legend. But he related it all the same. The Gods of the Outside prized the Cod. Because the Cod made their own barren lives bearable, in their lonely environment. They took the fish into their bodies, into their soul, Cod into God, God into Cod. And they gained new talents, gained new knowledge. With their power they rose to a level of existence, beyond the lonely land, beyond the rich sea, beyond the empty air even. They gained skills and experience a sea creature could only dream of. It was all speculative fantasy to Poor Cod. And he hated it. Once he mastered the ways of the school he detested distraction of any form. He despised his former clumsy ways and despised any thing that may remind him.

Preacher 375 did not push the matter. He pushed others though, and held the beliefs bonded their school, their shoal, their species. Poor Cod was more curious. Maybe someday they would endeavour to sort the legends from the lies, to see if any truth lay within. Though if the Gods from the Outside were unproven, the Demons from Below were not. Poor Cod had seen them, glimpsed them rather. For he fled in terror at the sight of these elongated, semi-luminous creatures. There were others also, many-tentacled, pliable bodies, like their not-as-disturbing cousin, the octopus. They consumed everything in sight. Preacher 375 held such abominations to be rare in their domain, which was known as the Shelf. They could wander far and near but the Shelf was their special territory. Roughly 200 metres in height, always lit by day, relatively safe by night. Beyond the shelf the real depths began, where the Demons from Below dwelt. Sometimes the Demons moved up to shallower waters. But mostly they preferred the abyssal depths. Even when located further inshore they preferred the security of gaping chasms. For their domain was the crushing depths. These areas were almost as deadly as the air. Some few did manage to go down there, but too few could ever live down there.

Besides the Demons and the pressure were the darkness and loneliness. Schools were not so prominent there. All this were bad enough. But the very act of breathing became a chore. No, the Lower Depths scared many others as well as Poor Cod. It was a fear that was recognised. There was nothing for them down there, apart from ghastly, luminous monsters. Every cod wished to be devoured as it died, rather then drift down to the Lower Depths. The same fate might await in their special domain, but at least in the Shelf it was relatively quick. And the Lower Depths themselves were less of an agony than being hoisted up by the Lines from Above. Even death from below was more dignified than death from above. At least it was still the sea, their element. It carried the proper religious character of life-giving sanctity, even at it cruellest moments. Whereas suffocation and painful death throes, in the grip of nothingness, signified fear and shame.

Maybe someday they would explore the Lower Depths, the abyssal areas in particular. But they would never explore the air, that barren element that was the death of every care. Poor Cod and Preacher 375 were as one in this opinion, as were most others. For, recently, the Lines from Above had grown relentless in their pursuit of the cod. Poor Cod's school had not suffered as much as others, yet. They had learnt how to feel the energy the Lines gave off. They were subtle as they moved in their silent predation. Some questioned the value of pursuing a skill that only delayed the inevitable. But their life, it seemed, was always rich, vital, even despite the fact it was always dangerous. Or was it because of this fact. Poor Cod thought this might be the case.

In their spawning grounds, around the islands, they played and mated. They forgot the years and the dangers that plagued them. In this place Poor Cod met his most significant mate. She was known as 2M 323. And she fell in with him immediately. All fish were gifted with the talent known as the swimbladder. It gave them buoyancy, balance and poise. In the more advanced it gave rhythm. They learnt to manipulate this gift of fate to improve on nature's song. Poor Cod could grow a tune as well as anyone. And he could use it to hypnotic effect, as he pulsed, and thrummed and pushed the rhythms out in the Deep Blue. He swept 2M 323 into his orbit with apparent ease. She went for him right from the begining. Preacher 375 thought this might give him a constant distraction from persistent troublemaking, at last. But he was wrong. Instead it gave Poor Cod increased confidence. So the questioning of religion, the arguing, were pursued with greater tenacity. He even began making insuations about leadership of the school. It would never happen of course, not in Preacher 375's lifetime. And there were two other candidates stronger, and as intelligent as Poor Cod.

But Poor Cod agitated regardless. Whatever his status, he would have done the same. But 2M 323 gave his ambition a particular direction. She wanted to go north, to the frozen Arctic. For there was the Goddess 9. The cynicism of the others was quickly won over when she pointed out the Goddess 9 actually existed, some of her family had verified this. She was not a real goddess. But she led a shoal a thousand strong. And they were not not bothered by the hazards that effected others so readily - the diseases and the Lines from Above. Both were increasing, exponentially. And Preacher 375 did concede that new domains must be sought. Though he would not conceive of going north. The north was primeval. Harsh conditions would turn them into pagans. That could be seen with the deification of a living leader. No matter how capable the Goddess 9 was, it was sacrilege. Perhaps there was less disease, fewer Lines, in the Arctic. But the cold was all powerful. The cold they coped with, on a normal basis. But it placed a layer of land over the water in the north. The cold was so powerful that it might turn all the water into land, eventually. Even if this did not happen, it would make them sluggish, easy prey for some of the flabby, hairy mammals that liked to live there. Preacher 375 left no doubt, the north was forever out.

It seemed, briefly, as though rebellion might break out. But events soon distracted Poor Cod and his associates from their future concerns. There were more pressing matters. On their wanderings their rival schools became no more than remnants. Their spawning ground turned into a harsh, competitive environment, with no room for play anymore, not even much for spawning. They did not have to guess why. The Lines from Above had crossed this sea in a more intense routine. As a result, their species was devasted. And it confirmed Preacher 375 in his role as gifted survivor and religious adviser. His school survived, while all others faltered and eventually disappeared. There was no more talk of the Goddess 9 in the frozen north. The present moment caught all their time. Their adept manoevures, in avoiding the Lines from Above, were tested as never before. Some few of the school would always be caught, true. But more than enough would remain to confirm them as the best school, the most gifted survivors. The ministrations of Preacher 375 were a sure gift in keeping them alive. Even Poor Cod was impressed. But they still had to move. They swam with speed and ease, and consistently eluded the Lines. But the nets were closing ever tighter. The school could not afford to spend all its time in the spawning ground. Life was becoming too precarious. The Lines tried ever harder to snare them. Their grids and patterns took on new movement and shapes. They became more agile. Matrices were constructed, to shift and envelop with predatory ease. And they began to gain results. The numbers were being whittled down, slowly, but ever so surely. The activity of the Lines increased to a scale hitherto unheard of. It meant they should forget all other concerns, simply make a break, back to Mid-Atlantic. There they could gain some breathing space, hopefully. 2M 323 was lost on this run. Poor Cod could see her flapping helplessly, the fear in her eyes, as she began to rise, caught in an ever-constricting space, with so many friends. She called out to him, in her last frantic movements. All around caught the vibrations, before they were quickly smothered. The meassage was plain, ' Go and find the Goddess 9, you'll be safe in the frozen north.' Everyone heard it. Preacher 375 felt it necessary to restate his authority. There would be no going north. First they would try the deeper waters of the west, then maybe south. These prospects filled Poor Cod with concern. In the Deep West they would forever swim suspended above the Demons from Below. These would flick their slimy tentacles, and sway their ugly jaws, and snare the good fish, like so many passive prey. And the south, why should Preacher 375 choose the south ? Surely the Arctic was a better option, more known, The south was full of brightly malformed, poisonous fishes, who lived in choking, warm water. They would not be in their element. The north, the north was the only place to go. But Poor Cod was not able to gain much support. Some had been to the south. It was strange, yes. But the Lines from above, their most deadly hazard, did not operate in such numbers. They would adapt easily enough. But, if it were a case of adaption, surely the north would be a more suitable environment. Poor Cod kept up his case, as much as he could being severely outnumbered. But the situation was now desperate. The Lines from Above dictated a frantic response.

And eventually it happened, before their response could be co-ordinated. Perhaps they always knew it would. The school, what was left, was snared. The Lines from Above came down and left no one around. Up they went in a crushing mass. Bodies wriggled and heaved in among each other. That was horrible enough. But then began the bright, glaring light of the surface layers. Poor Cod felt his swimbladder might burst, in fact, all his internal organs were on the point of rupture. He knew his pain was the change in pressure. The others, flapping and squealing, in a shrinking space, confirmed it to be so. And then it was worse. They were lifted into the gasping, choking vaccuum of the air. Poor Cod felt the tightening of his eyes and skin as they began to dry. The all-powerful, life-giving water disappeared beneath them. It was their time to die. Would they see the Gods of the Outside ? Or would it be some debased equivalent of the Demons from Below ? They were moved at speed, onto the misshapen back of a sea mammal. So that much was true. The slimy parasites, that infested the surface of this creature, moved toward them, on their hind limbs, as the net dopped its load. The impact was terrible. Poor Cod lay flapping helplessly as the parasites moved in for the kill. His school all disappeared within the gaping maw of the giant mammal. Poor Cod was left stranded outside, on the chin of this hard-skinned leviathan. And one of the slimy parasites moved directly toward him, it flailed its limbs, causing a shock of pain, and he was lifted again. He flew through the air and dropped back in the ocean. The all-sustaining environment, which immediately began giving back his health and poise, as he drifted down to a comfortable depth. He had somehow escaped being comsumed by the ugly mammal. One of the slimy parasites had in fact saved him. At first he thought this was of little consequence. For the trauma he had experienced must surely kill him. But it did not. By degrees he recovered, enough to realise he must continue on his journey. And he knew he would go north, not west or south. He would continue until he found the Goddess 9. Nothing would stop him now. For there was no one left to disagree. For all his school had gone. So he swam on.

The Normans were a Bunch of Football Hooligans

"Shock Historical Discovery"

Recently a secret hoard of documents were discovered in the archives of the Guildhall in London. What these documents reveal are startling new facts about the birth of modern Britain. On their own they could perhaps be discounted. Yet further research, at such places as Holyrood House in Edinburgh, Lerwick in the Shetlands, and the French towns of Rouen and Bayeux, go to confirm the astonishing fact, that many of our most cherished institutions and great families owe their existence to a horde of rampaging football fans who happened to miss their boat home to Norway.

The documents in Guildhall were written by the chronicer, Rollo the bastard. He was a servant of William the Conqueror, or William the Bastard. Apparently Rollo adopted his own title in emulation of his master. Rollo goes on to say that Bastard was a title that owed as much to attitude as birth. Hence, although his master may have been born a bastard, it did not matter, for he acted like a bastard.

Rollo goes on to say that their recent Norman ancestors were invited to a football match just ouside of Paris. Here they were to compete against teams of Bretons, Scots, Saxons, Franks and Germans. However, due to their excessive bad manners, their fouling, their abusive chants, and their breaking of too many rules, the Normans were expelled from the tournament. Yet, being of a proud and belligerent temperament, they took exception to this ruling. And so they went on the rampage, ransacking, pillaging and destroying everything they could lay their hands on. Given the nature of football games in these times, i.e. they were a fierce brawl between two crowds of people (much like modern day football hooligans) the Normans behaviour must have been excessively brutal, even by the standards of the day. Indeed, one fortunate Saxon, Dangle of Avebury, who escaped the massacre, has preserved some of their chants for posterity - " We are the Famous, the famous Normans," " You'll never beat the Normans," " You're going to get your Saxon heads kicked in," and " No one likes us, we don't care." Variations of these are said to have survived down to modern times, at events wherever sporting thugs gather for activities of communal mayhem.

However, Rollo goes on say, everyone was so scared of the Normans after this, they were just left alone, to wander around Northern France generally laying waste to everything in sight. Some fleeing Saxons had set light to their ships before they escaped. The Normans vowed revenge, but since everyone was afraid to deal with them, it was some generations in coming. Eventually luck landed an opportunity in their lap. A Saxon nobleman called Harold was shipwrecked on the northern coast of France. The Normans captured him, and instead of torturing him, as they would normally do to captives, they plied him with drink and asked him to play some some games with them. Harold, relieved, agreed. So when, as a joke, he swore he would give the Norman leader, William, a friendly football fixture, Harold agreed. Of course, once Harold was released, he went back to his native England with no intention of making good on his playful, drunken promise. However, William had sneakily concealed some holy relics beneath the table on which Harold swore his oath, and, as the head of the European Football Association of the time (the Pope) confirmed, it may have been a dirty trick, but it was legitimate dirty trick.

Eventually William succeeded in bullying enough people to give his Normans ships so they could cross the channel to invade England. Harold was playing a friendly, football fixture, at Stamford Bridge at the time, with a Norwegian team raised by his brother, Tostig. As with all friendly football matches of the time, it was a bloody affair, which Harold only won after extra time. Then came news of William's landing. So Harold dashed south to fulfil his fixture requirements. Yet, as with so many modern teams, too many games within the space of a week meant shock results could happen. And so, after a successful defensive action, for so much of the game against William, his team grew over confident, thinking they could catch the Normans on the counter attack. This was to prove their undoing, and the result, as they say, is history. The Normans celebrated their result by their usual rampaging, and then by totally conquering the Saxons. The Saxons appealed to Uefa for help. But the Pope would only confirm William's result. So, in these controversial circumstances, the Normans gained power over much of Britain, and our modern British sense of fair play was born.

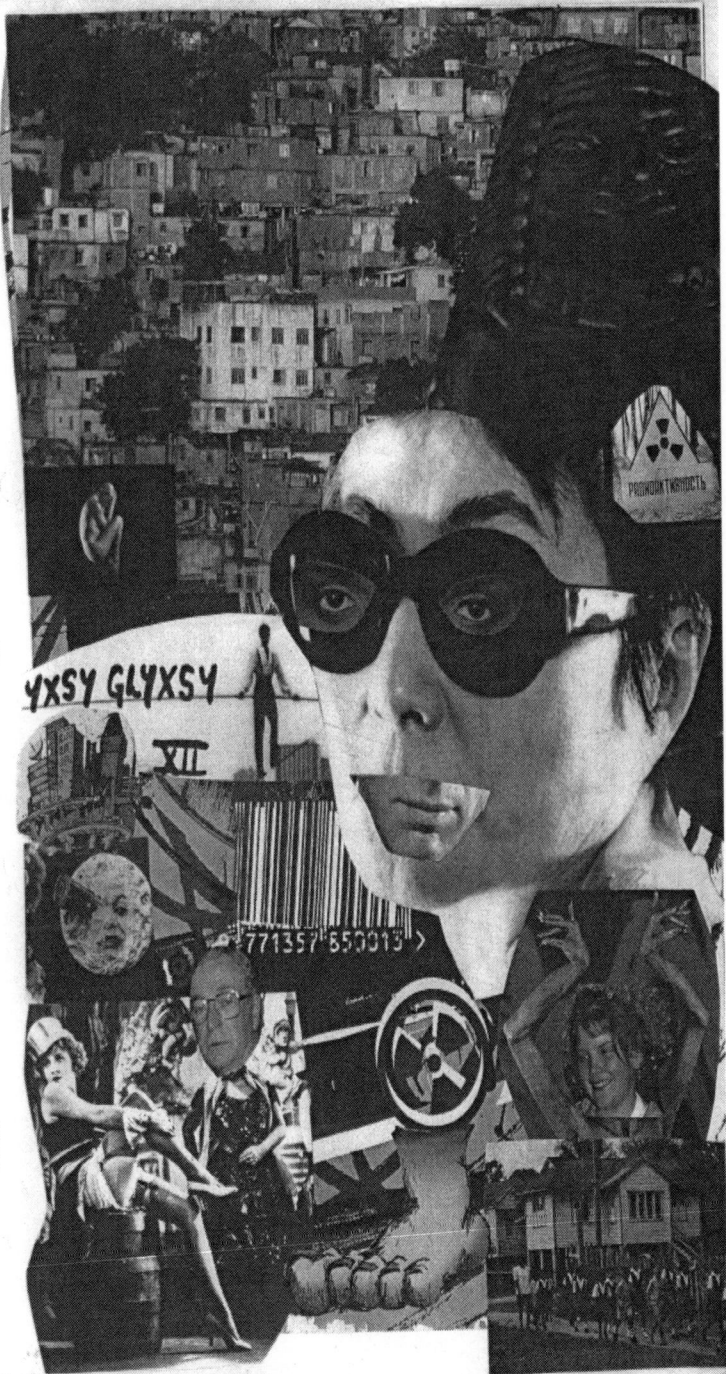

San Katerina

Dennis watched the conversation uneasily. That greasy wop made him a bit too suspicious, a right devious looking character, he thought. Maybe he was acting paranoid. It was all a bit too new, and baffling. The conversation he was listening to was in heated Italian. And he could not understand a word. They talked so fast, like sped up voices, how did they manage to cram so many words into a single breath ?

And that was not all, either. It was his first time in Italy. He did like the place, he reckoned, apart from experiencing it at close hand. So much to take in. Even if he did have two Italian-speaking friends with him, they never helped much. They had all the friends and contacts over here and he had nothing, this made him uneasy. The heat was intolerable and people moved casually in it. Unlike their fast voices their movements were carried out in slow motion. It was not like the rush hour chaos of London he was so used to. Mind you, it could have all been so much better, were it not for the nature of their business. They had come to do a drugs deal. They were no experts in the business and negotiations were prolonged. They were so long it made his head ache. This, added to lack of sleep, heightened his feelings of alienation. It seemed a straightfoward enough transaction. So why all the humming and haring ? It was good stuff, they had done a good deal in Amsterdam. And the aim was always to sell it in Italy, where they could sell the stuff for up to three times the original price. But Cesare and his friends kept buying samples between them, testing the water, and getting off their face in the process. And they would not commit themselves to a big buy, yet.

Anyhow, there they all were, at Cesare's, who was a friend of Tony, who convinced Dennis, at the time. The hotel was owned by Cesare's father, they were guests, as terms were being discussed. Dennis was worried about the price of their stay, but Tony kept telling him to shut up. They were in the tiny resort of San Katerina, a bit off the beaten track from the usual tourist trap. It reminded Dennis of an Italian version of Southend, but more sprawled out. Not many foreigners went there. Luckily Tony knew the way around, he said. Dennis had not even known they had arrived till Tony opened the door and jumped out the train. The town was a maze of hotels and snakey streets, like many of the small towns strewn along this part of the Adriatic coast. It all looked the same to Dennis. None of it seemed to have a centre, like a square, or a town hall in a square.

Cesare was not to his liking, too rodent-like. He always had four or five ' friends ' around him. These were workers in the hotel, he said. Dennis thought the man's manner was too twitchy, and shifty. Cesare always seemed on the lookout for someone, and it was someone he wanted to avoid.

Though he did like their goods, he pulled the right faces, then he gave off the machine gun burst of speech, which made Dennis dizzy. The terms were a stumbling block, and by terms was meant money. He had been arguing with Tony and Guido for almost an hour on this occasion. For the umpteenth time, Dennis wished he could decipher what they were saying, He wished they could settle the whole thing, there and then, like any normal deal. It was not like it was some kind of peace treaty or something. The lounge they sat in was large, and a big fan whirred, like a dozy helicopter blade. Once you sat in the comfy setttees there, it was hard to get up again. Dennis did not like this. Neither did he like the fact that people kept walking in and out of the room. He thought a bit of discretion should be at work here. Instead, all these ' friends' kept walking in and out, with all their machine gun speech, and their giggling, which made him paranoid, because he felt some was directed at him. He tried to voice his impatience. But Tony and Guido both told him to shut up. It was a hotel, they had to prepare for dinner. But Dennis never saw any other guests. Well, he saw a few people walking round, but he could not tell if they were guests or more ' friends.' Then Cesare started getting up and talking to people as they came in and out. This was doing Dennis' brain in. Once or twice, he caught the worried looks that appeared on his mates faces. And their tone of voice changed as well. But Dennis still had to shut up. Though he felt the others were getting a bit paranoid by this time. But the conversation still dragged on for ages. Dennis wondered if you could be paranoid and bored shitless at the same time.

Eventually a price was agreed, it seemed. Cesare clapped his hands in delight. Now they should all stay to dinner. But Dennis noticed the worried looks had stuck with his mates. He tried pumping them for information. But instead of their usual commands to shut up, this time they did admit things had got a bit tricky. They had thought they might be being set up. They thought they might be ambushed, or something. Dennis was quite reassured to learn their fears were as vague as his. They had no solid proof, of course. Cesare was always friendly, and had always kept his word, so they would go with that. But, since they were more in tune with the mood of the place, Dennis added their paranoia to his own. He could not but help notice the bulge in Guido's trousers as well. This was not Guido's huge prick but a huge knife. Guido was thinking of precautionary measures, and they were not linked to sex.

Dennis' dislike grew. Guido began making enquiries about the times of trains. Cesare fobbed him off. In the meantime, if they would like to hang around, dinner would be ready soon. They should not be impatient, it was a deal well done. Cesare wished to show his appreciation by giving them a meal. He might be grievously insulted if they did not.

Dennis thought of saying bollocks to politeness. But his politeness would not let him. So the four of them sat there, four ornaments left at random, as people continued to walk in and out. The conversation flew all around, little squally showers of verbal. This was getting on his nerves. People kept looking at him, and talking while they were looking at him. Then they began moving furniture around. He tried to get up, but they would not hear of it. Tony and Guido started to tell Dennis to shut up again. And they added the order for him to relax as well.

More furniture and rushing around. In the dining room, which seemed to be behind them, the clatter of pots and pans began. It was an irritating racket. For some reason everyone was in a mad rush. Tony told him to shut up again. It was only dinner, dinner was always a racket. Although Tony still had that worried look in his eye. Guido had gone all quiet, and he still had his huge knife. Dennis tried questioning Tony about the nature of his friendship with Cesare. Tony replied by saying he had known Cesare for years. Well, he had seen him about for years. He had not really spoken to him. Cesare was more a friend of a friend. Tony tried to reassure everyone against the rising paranoia, but failed.

Dennis would not be reassured, not until they were out of this place. The whole set up, the whole thing, if it was set up even, it was all too dodgy. Paranoia was hinted at with his two mates, with Dennis it was an overwhelming conviction. Cesare was going to pull something dirty on them. Two of Cesare's friends left. They gave the room a dirty look as they did so. Dennis' heart began playing out the rhumba. He noticed a bulge under one of their jackets, it was waist level and gun size. This was doing him in. He kept himself together enough to make a suggestion, instead of shouting as he wished. Unfortunately Tony and Guido were losing patience with him. Everything had gone right, sure they were not out of the woods yet, but nothing had given them cause for too much worry. They were a bit too willing to believe this statement, Dennis said so, and he said it was too good to be true. Tony and Guido made gestures to illustrate that Dennis may be losing his marbles. And this time he would shut up, or he would lose his cut of the proceeds.

Cesare came in, to lead them into the empty dining room. Dennis excused himself and went to the toilet. His head was buzzing like mad. Why the idiots could not see the full picture was baffling. They admitted they were scared, and still went along with him. But he would not get caught. He could walk into being shot, or stabbed, or whatever. But what else could he do ? He was too tensed up to even urinate beyond a trickle. But the palpitations were on him, he had to act. The way out from the toilet led straight out onto the street. He took that way. But he walked straight into one of Cesare's friends. The friend gesticulated and coveyed the meaning Dennis should come and eat. Dennis kept insisting there was something he had to check on first. And he ran out, leaving the friend standing bewildered. Cesare had even sent someone to fetch him, Dennis noted, another proof for the paranoiac. He was filled with fear for his mates, what would happen to them ? But he would not go back. At least while he was out there was a chance he could do something about the trap.

He ran down to the garage where they had stored their luggage. He had to go past the droves of people, who walked past to gain their favourite patch of beach. And they looked at him curiously. That sweaty, red-faced anglo-saxon with his nervy walk. They were looks of distaste. He found two Italians arguing by the store room. And they went quiet as they saw him. It was no good. He could not go in and get his luggage now. Their malicious eyes burned into him as he turned and walked away. Once Dennis was free of that garage, he ran, at pace. He glanced behind him to see if the two Italians had followed. They pointed and shouted, but they did not bother to pursue. They were shouting at people in front of him. Two burly types, who laid hands on him, and spoke harshly. Obviously they were questioning him. But he could not understand, so he brushed them away and ran, before they could react. It was still crowded, he heard shouts, people tried to address him. So he kept running, until he was away from the dirty looks and the angry shouts. His pace slowed, he had time to think again, although his thoughts raced. Every event of the past few hours had lent confirmation to his paranoia. He had uncovered the devious double meanings behind everything. The laughing, the pointing, the requests by strangers to enter strange rooms.

They had been set up from the start. And Tony and Guido were too cowardly to get out. His instinct revolted strongly against the whole town. The whole town was wrong. But it could not all be like that. There must be something he could do, to help his stupid, coward friends, before it was too late. He must try to do something, get help, then get out of here, but how ? where ? Questions asking for solutions hit him constantly. So while his metabolism raced his mind became groggy with indecision. He started to run again, that felt like he was doing something. His head pounded now. He ran just for the way it seemed to move him quickly through the snakey streets. The streets were all featureless, nameless, nondescript and bland. Each one was more confusing than the rest. As soon as he snaked his way up one, he was staggering his way down the other. Or was it all the same street ? Was he just running through a gigantic spiral ? There was no landmark he could cling to for directions. All streets were jam packed with little cars, crawling at a snail's pace or at a standstill. Their occupants cast curious glances at Dennis. There were few walkers now, and they tended to move to the other side of the street when they saw him approaching. They looked at him quizzically as he passsed.

Dennis was begining to get exhausted. He tried to change his tack. He threaded his way at random through the snakey streets, like some demented seamtress' needle. A plan struck him at last. It was desperate, but it began to have some possibility. He could go to the police station. He would say his friends had been robbed and beaten up. He was sure this was true by now, probably. He would have to be careful how he reported this. He could make no mention of drugs, nor of intended business deals. He would just say they were surprised, in a random robbery, by

Cesare and company. The drugs would surely be found, but they were in Cesare's possession by now, all of them, they must be. So if the police went round the hotel, they could be arrested for that as well. Having made this deduction, Dennis comforted himself with the prospect of getting something done. It now lent his aimless wandering some purpose. Though it was some time before he could find the nearest police station. It was not an easy task, hampered by his total lack of Italian. He did not even know the Italian for police.

After a few fruitless enquiries he stumbled on the police station. But here it got even more bewildering. From the start the officers at the desk began babbling their heads off. Their commotion brought a flood of brown-uniformed officers to the scene. Then the babble went into overdrive. Shouts and gestures and prods at Dennis' chest. He was the item being talked about rather than the person being helped. He was guided to a table and sat down. His hand was guided to fill in some forms. Then he was ushered out. Some officers even waved at him as he left. And, of course, they all started laughing. He did not know if they would act on his statement, or even if they understood it. There was a mention of the Embassy on the form, and he thought he might try this. But the officers pointed to a map on the wall, then pointed to their heads, as if to illustrate how mad he was. The Embassy was some 200 miles away, Dennis knew this, Tony had told him previously. It was in Rome.

He would have to get to Rome himself, he knew that. But then he remembered he had left his luggage, passport and money behind, when he ran out of the hotel. He did try thumbing a lift. But the passing vehicles seemed more eager to mow him down than stop for him. He could not think straight anymore. Everything was becoming unreal.

Even though he was totally certain that Cesare's intentions had been put into practice by now. The premonition was overwhelming. Despite that, the little doubts crept in. What if he had been overreacting ? what then ? The others were ill at ease but still went along with the occasion. It could be highly embarrassing if the police acted on his statement and found his paranoia to be rootless. They might sift and search and find the drugs anyway. Suddenly his palpitations subsided. Anger rose at his foolishness. Shame at his hasty actions, that may have precipitated the very events he was so scared of. At that the palpitations redoubled their force. He had also deserted his friends. The paranoia took root again, and he was still lost.

The Embassy was out of it, as he certainly felt by now. He was in no fit state to handle any degree of communication, particularly with strangers. He would have to make his way back to the hotel, and face whatever music was playing. Easier thought than done. He was now somewhere on a coastal highway. Darkness had fallen. The lights of the town, the lights of three towns, glistened on the horizon, one on the coast, two in the hills. He staggered back. The way was montonous and weary. But soon he began seeing houses at the side of the road again. The snakey streets had returned. They were more quiet now, no one around. Not a single, solitary lamppost, not a light in any home. A few porch lights buzzed their dull glare enough to find him a way. And the dirty, off-white buildings brooded over him, as if waiting for him to be gone. The feeling was mutual. He wanted to be gone also. This was a blur of alien architecture. It had all the familiar features of windows and doors, but they were all strange shapes he could not describe, for he could not relate to them. He tried to swallow these feelings, even going so far as to ask directions in a couple of bars he came across. But he could not get across to the people in them. They looked at him wide-eyed and escorted him out. There was more laughter and pointing to heads.

By now, his weariness had defeated his palpitations. Some powers of reasoning made their return. A new resolve took hold of him. He would systematically search the town, East to West and up and down, and the other two towns, if there were two towns. But he thought it was all the same town just a bit spread out. Anyway, he would be methodical and find out. If he could not find the hotel by this procedure he would simply work his way back, in the opposite direction, in the same manner. Now he would have to move less randomly, to avoid getting hopelessly lost all the time. His luck seemed to be turning at last, for his methodical search gave a new focus to his wish for direction. Even though the streets, or the one continuous street, all looked the same, still. He found an abandoned pushbike, in good working order. Now he could make some progress. The search would take half as long.

He soon ate these words. For however fast he pedalled, the same street appeared to be flying past. He made as much progress as when he was walking, which was none. And he soon became exhausted. The pushbike was abandoned, it was annoying him. It had made him very tired for no reward, other than to sweat more. Walking was less effort. He could feel his legs turning rubbery. He switched off the pain and decided to let them go about their motion unaided. His plan had got him nowhere. It was back to the wandering.

He was feeling feverish by now. He came across a sign that read ' San Katerina,' plus some other words he could not make out. He remembered this sign was near their hotel. He had seen it before. His hopes were dashed again, for every building nearby had this sign on it. And none looked remotely like his hotel. It was as if someone had stuck them up deliberately, just to confuse and torment him.

It was daylight again. After hours more aimless wandering he was back on an open road. The buildings were less dense. He was up in the hills, somewhere. It was desolate, deserted country. Despair gnawed at his guts. Now he had even lost the town. There were no signs to show him where to go. He tried thumbing a lift again. But, the motorists seemed just as willing to use him for target practice. It was back to retracing his steps, if he could remember where they were.

His powers of reason had packed in by now. His walking was purely automatic. He could not gain any kind of help from his surroundings. But some reflex in him made him continue wandering, for something, maybe a place where he could just sit down. He had no recognition of anything, he felt nothing, just plodding along. He continued plodding. He was walking much slower now. The days had been lost track of. He had seen the dark follow the light a few times now. Or was it more ? did it really matter ? His legs never ached now, they made their decision, and he followed their motion. Somewhere was a thought, a vague dizziness, that announced he must get somewhere, sometime. He did not know to what or for what. But it would all become clear when he came across it...

Antonio swerved to avoid the bedraggled figure walking in the road, he nearly ran it over. Guy swore and called attention to the weirdness of the figure. It reminded him of the story Caspar had told them. That a lost and lonely traveller roamed the hills, forever searching for his destination. It was a ghost of course, an earthbound spirit that had been trapped in this area for generations. It could never find its way to Heaven. Antonio told him to shut up. They had more pressing concerns. Caspar had betrayed them, the deal had gone sour, and they had to get out of this place. They had been driving a while and still could not find the road to Rome. Once they escaped then they could waste their time on ghost stories. Until then, Antonio thought ruefully on Dennis reluctance to come to this town of San Katerina. ' I may be getting paranoid, Tony, but it smells dodgy. I don't want to get bogged down in that place.' Something about those words made Antonio shiver. They drove on.

The Stick Insect

I crawled in some time ago. This dank corner appealed to me greatly, a cold, dark hole to make my own. It's rarely light here, the nights are a beetle-black and the day a stinking grey. Oh, on some occaisons the daylight is strong enough to see the surroundings more clearly - a slimy, rotting landscape trailing off to a septic horizon. The few dwellings that exist above above ground thrust themselves up awkwardly, like withered flowers. There is no form in their design, it is a sight to make your eyes sore. This is a city, of sorts, or out of sorts, depending on how you view it. Its main body is a subterranean maze. Most of the inhabitants spend nearly all their lives underground, some never surface at all, things outside are of no interest to them.

This place is home, there is no question of it being hovel or hell, it serves its purpose. Oh, when I first came here I did have feelings of disgust. I was uncomfortable. However, I have always been uncomfortable. It was that restlessness that drove me here. But once I was here these feelings deepened gradually. I did not notice this happening at first, it occurred in a subtle manner. A series of unrelated incidents, totally random, each left an impression on me. Small plans I made would become hopelessly jumbled when

I attempted to put them into action. My routine would creak awkwardly as a device to control events, when I hoped to come to terms with some detail I had not calculated in advance. Then, eventually, came the one event that unleashed all these volatile elements, the final straw that shattered the framework I had tried to impose on conditions here. I was attacked without warning, or motive (though that is quite common here) and badly hurt. It seemed as though I would never make it home. The thought of home kept me going though, the snug and content corner where I could relax. I returned to find it caved in, collapsed. This was hard to take, the very foundation of my organisation was taken from under my feet. I looked back on my stay here. I saw each occurrence had peeled away something of my aims and ambitions, layer by layer. This final event left me nothing to fall back on. I looked at myself and I could not see anything. I was alone in this cold, dark place. I felt small, crushed by its mere presence. It was not as though this presence was malicious, rather it was indifferent. The indifference of a city that had always existed despite its citizens. ' Look at you,' it seemed to imply, ' where are your precious plans now. You don't even own any self-respect now. Look at yourself, a small insect scurrying through the bowels of the earth. How dare you presume to have any significance whatsoever.' And I looked around. Nowhere could I see any form, any design. My fellow insects blundered aimlessly through a honeycomb of endless tunnels. I could see no process involved in this movement. It never seemed to begin anywhere, or achieve anything. Why should I have stayed after such a shock ? well, I could not go anywhere and feel as I did before. So this place seemed as good as any to be.

I felt corrupted. Still, corruption is insistent; you learn to live with it, you grow to like it, and then to relish it. This environment acted like a rust on my feelings of repulsion, eating away my disgust. I began to live and breathe this place. The diseased carrion that passes for food, the cold, choking air, no longer mattered. My environment is me now, we live in symbiosis, mutually rotting away.

The nature of this place makes it such that every breath of life is something to be fought over. Food is scarce here, what there is of it is foul,and the inhabitants go to great lengths to obtain it. There are no plant-eaters here, for there are no plants. Here we are all predators and all prey. Everyone has their own ingenious method to obtain food. Some have their huge bulk and strength to crush life out of their victims. Others have acid stings that inject enzymes which dissolve vital organs, others powerful pincers that cut deftly through living tissue. Still others have sucker-tipped feelers that peel flesh from bone. My lack of such a natural advantage means I have to resort to cunning to live with such neighbours. My weapon involves deception. For instance, the cultivation of an outwardly passive presence to lure those who hope for an easy kill. Or, alternatively, the adoption of an aggressive presence for the opposite effect. A variety of masks for every occaison, concealing the shrivelled intentions beneath. They enable me to glide with some ease among the inhabitants.

Of course there is no lord and master here, the parasites have parasites. The beetle with its huge jaws crushes the life out of the earwig, the wasp paralyses the beetle with its sting, the spider suffocates the wasp in its sticky threads, but is easily crushed by the pincers of the earwig. An extreme example ? not really, you must tread carefully when you walk these stinking sewers. Many is the time I have had to dodge a well-aimed sting, or found myself under the slobbering jaws of some hungry horror. It is no use adopting a single mode of survival in this place. You must be constantly open to changing your method as the situation demands. Easier said than done I suppose. How can any of us survive such a life ? Well, none of us live long, but we are ingenious enough in our short life spans to survive the everyday agonies. We are all insects, there is no other word for us. For are we not infinitely adaptable ? no environment, no circumstance, can defy us for long. And there is a certain pride in survival. Such a life is, in its own way, pure. We are untainted by thoughts for security, comfort, ambition. This life scours the need for emotion and cleans the soul. Reliance on these is transformed to use of these. To have it any other way would transform you into a pack animal, slow, plodding along in vain, trying to pursue the carrot of promise dangling in front of you. All the while the flies swarm thick around you. Yet you pay no attention, nothing must distract you from your pursuit. But all the while the parasites are draining your energy.

Oh, there have been some here who thought otherwise. They would hold the ways of a pack animal to be the highest virtue. There was a swarm here recently who taught that very message. How strange they were. They were pale and fine skinned. Their smell was funny, it was like a no-smell. They excited vague memories in me of fresh, green gardens and clear, blue skies. Such places that can only exist in memory. They spoke of changing this place, purging its poison. However, they did not last long before circumstance inspired disorder among their swarm. I found them easy prey. I gorged myself on their soft, pulpy flesh a solid week. I was unable to move for days afterwards. A few of them still survive, I see some occainsally. Conditions have changed them unwillingly into altering their ways. For noble ideals look peculiar when you are scavenging on a slag heap, which is what most of them now do to survive. I cannot but help laugh at their fate, it seems so ironic.

As I think this I glance my reflection in one of the frothy puddles that pockmark this corridor floor. This reminds me there is no time for reflection. That churning pain inside means I must snare another days meal, this grub must have his grub. For, the virus goes on, the disease never ceases, infection will have its day,   the swarm will always hold sway, the predators come as they may. Environment always dictates. Though I plan to stick around a while yet myself, if it will let me.

The Spirit of Free Inquiry

The Spirit of Free Inquiry had just stopped off in a quiet corner of the universe. Unfortunately this quiet corner was inhabited already, and somewhat noisy. Some insufferable life forms had made the place their home, they had polluted the place no end. They only lived on a tiny planet, yet the debris from their frequent jaunts into space floated about everywhere. Added to that was the tremendous racket that wafted up from their planet, all kinds of transmissions. The Spirit was moved to investigate, despite the raging headache these noises gave him. This was a bad move. Atmospheric conditions did not lend themselves to discretion. His manoeuvrings gave rise to various disruptions. And he noted the panic stricken consequences his arrival gave to the planet's inhabitants. Lights pulsed, sounds waved and millions of little feet scampered all over the ground. Time to leave, as quickly as possible. But not fast enough, some weird shapes followed him, craft of some kind, they buzzed him in a manner calculated cause irritation. The Spirit responded by making gestures that could only be construed as a gentle warning, in response to which the craft exploded.

The whole episode was bewildering and yet intriguing. The Spirit knew where it could ask about these creatures, without causing catastrophe or commotion, he hoped. The answer lay in the spaces between dimensions. Here, there lived a variety of beings. These beings existed as the Spirit did himself. They were found neither in one place nor another, but could be reached anytime, or anywhere. Communication was a matter of attitude rather than effort, the consequence of both desire and exertion. So the Spirit composed itself accordingly, and entered a gap which did not exist. This was always a risky process. The trouble was these gaps occurred because no laws of nature were in operation, if you concentrated hard enough. Though a certain dream-like logic gave them both form and content. As in a dream, you had to go along with the unreality of the place in order influence it in any way. This could be a tricky business.

The Spirit took a deep breath and made his entry. Already a scene coagulated out of formless chaos. It was a setting he had seen before many times in the physical universe. A rude, primitive dwelling was perched on the peak of a rounded hill. The Spirit stepped inside, to view what appeared to be a public place. In this public place were sold a variety of intoxicating substances. The sole aim of such a place was the extreme debilitation of consciousness. The Spirit always found these places to be disruptive and depressing. This was despite the fact that several entities appeared to enjoy debilitation, as the Spirit recalled some memories that were forever vague. He had to admit, these places were not in his character. A lone humanoid figure sat at a small round table. It was asleep, slumped foward with arms outstretched. The Spirit sighed, he looked around, inspecting the place, with an air of indifference. And as he was pottering around, the humanoid figure stirred, mumbling to itself. It appeared to be a male, quite an old male judging by its condition, although that could have been caused by the intoxicating substance. The Spirit composed itself as the man tried to focus, moaning and groaning.

" Who are you ? "

" You mean as a person, or as a phenomena, or as an event, or as an action, or as an intent ? "

" Don't get smart you bloody pedant...What do you call yourself ? and please, just give me a working definition."

" I am usually known as the Spirit of Free Inquiry."

" Sounds a bit pompous to me, but then it always did."

" Sorry ? have we met before ? "

" Many times, but you never remember."

" True. I am a bit all over the place at times."

" While I am all over the place all of the time."

" Ah, I see, I have to work out who you are. Great. I love guessing games, Give me another clue."

" Okay, what pervades all of space and time ? "

" Radio noise."

" No."

" Blackness."

" No."

" Energy."

" No."

" Thought."

" No."

" Oh God this is getting difficult..."

" You've got it."

" What kind of a name is ' Oh God this is getting difficult ? "

" Ooooh, for my sake...your memory is getting worse, it's just God."

" Your name is Just God ? "

" No, God."

" Your name is No God ? "

" Listen, in the phrase, just God, the word just is an adjective, while in the phrase no God, the word no is a negative. Now take away the adjective and the negative and you get my name."

" So your name is God God."

" Ooooh, me give me patience...now delete the last word from your last sentence.

" So your name is God."

" Finally, at last, before the end of infinity, the Spirit gets it. Why we have to go through this question and answer session, when you say my name anyway, but you don't recognise it."

" It just slipped out, as you say, my memory can be difficult sometimes."

" That's okay, now stop taking my name in vain as well, now your memory's back."

" I'm sorry God, it won't happen again."

" It will, but let's not go into that now...What are you doing here ? "

" That's funny, I can't remember..."

" A social visit then ? "

" Oh sorry, yes I can. I was in this quiet corner of the universe, just wanting to unwind, relax a little. But I could get no peace from these noisy creatures inhabiting a planet nearby. I was moved to complain, also to investigate why they were so badly behaved. I am afraid I seemed to disrupt their activities and cause more trouble..."

" You are your usual clumsy self, too well meaning, you just blunder in all the time."

" I know that."

" Then why are you telling me this ? "

" I wanted to know what kind of creatures they were."

" Look, if this is some kind of trick, I should warn you, nothing gets past the deity. I have been around a long time you know."

" So ? "

" So what I am saying is - you already know these creatures, you have walked among them several times."

" Like you do, you mean ? "

" Not like I do. I'm everywhere anyway, so the question is irrelevant."

" So how can you be here ? "

" I'm here and I'm everywhere else as well."

" Yes I remember now."

" Oh good."

" I mean I remember your all-pervading presence. But I'm still no clearer on the beings on that planet."

" Oh me."

" Give me a clue...er, please, your omnipotence. "

" Stop grovelling will you . God fearing behaviour is all very well. But it can get a bit irritating sometimes...A clue, let's see, something simple for your short term memory...It begins with an E..."

" Eternity. "

" No...it has been used in the name of a Goddess, as in mother..."

" Eros."

" Mother Eros is not a Goddess, or at least is a strange one if he is."

" Let's see, Mother Egg, no, Mother Entertainer, no, Mother Elastic, er, no, got it, Mother Enterprise."

" No, not at all. "

" Mother Education, Mother Excitement, Mother easy-to-please, Mother Excretion, no obviously not. Mother Ecstasy, Mother Enlightenment, got it, Mother Earth. This planet is Mother Earth. "

" At last, after only a couple of millenia."

" Well now that's all sorted."

" Good."

" So why did I come here if I already knew the name of the place."

" You are forgetful. It's part of your nature. You are also impulsive and irritating. You even get to me, the Supreme Being, occaisonally. But, since I am omniscient, I have room for a little tetchiness now an then. "

" In that case, since I have got to you this time, could you remind me what these Earth creatures are like please ? "

" Certainly, they call themselves people, or humans. They are a contradictory lot. They can be intelligent and enterprising, but also stupid and savage. They have tested my patience enormously at times with their brutal behaviour. But at other times I have found them so attractive as to see a little bit of myself in them."

" They sound a bit messed up to me."

" They certainly can be as forgetful as you. In their ignorance they do get a little rebellious at times."

" How do you mean ? "

" Well it has become fashionable among them to try and explain everything away, which can be annoying. "

" I see."

" Good, so good bye."

" Er, no, actually that was an attempt to get you to explain further."

" You really are tiresome aren't you. Well, for a period they would try to ignore me, saying I did not exist anymore. A few even went as far as to say I was dead."

" Blasphemy."

" Well you could say that. But these creatures are a bit confused. It became evident to them I had not died, they simply changed my name..."

" That's clever."

" It was and it wasn't. They said God had been ousted, but they simply started calling me Big Bang instead, a childish name to match their childish theories I suppose... But I am wise to their tricks, whether they call me Big Bang, The Absolute, Nirvana, The Tao, The Cosmos, The Theory of Everything, a Singularity , or whatever. It points to their confusion more than my supposed existence..."

" You sound a little irritated."

" These creatures constantly argue among themselves, seeking to prove whatever they may. But they only really succeed in tying themselves in knots. You cannot pension off an omnipotent and omniscient being anyway. If that wasn't enough they squabble and are badly behaved as well. They have incurred my wrath on more than one occaison. So I've had to deal out a few thunderbolts sometimes to keep them in order. But since I am all wise and all forgiving, I cannot hold a grudge for too long..."

" Then why don't you enlighten them ? "

" I do, and that's where you come in."

" It is ? "

" Yes it's all part of the scheme of things."

" Even though I came here of my own free will ? "

" Yes."

" That all sounds a bit too contrived to me."

" Really, then what about your name ? "

" It's mine."

" I know it's yours, but where did you get it ? "

" I just picked it up on my travels."

" But how did you get it ? "

" I can't remember."

" What a surprise."

" I don't believe it. I surprised God."

" No you didn't, I was just being cynical."

" But the Supreme Being can't be cynical."

" Why not ? I've seen it all before, as well as during and after... Now tiresome, impatient spirit, we were talking about your name.."

" Which is ? "

" The Spirit of Free Inquiry... do you remember this much ? "

" Yes. "

" And you still cannot remember how you got it ? "

" Yes."

" Well humans will say you are just a figure of speech, a saying, an abstraction, perhaps an attitude, but in no way a conscious entity."

" There might be something in that."

" Even though it may deny your existence ? "

" You mean I exist ? "

" That could be said, in a manner of speaking."

" But how would I know that ? "

" Well you could begin by defining the constituents of your existence, for example."

" But there are no parts that make up my existence, I just like asking questions."

" And what about answers ? "

" Well, if they come, they come. But if they don't, there's always other questions."

" Good, good, now you see why you have to go back among these creatures."

" I'm sorry, I don't follow you there."

" Me almighty...It seems unlikely you could follow anyone anywhere...What am saying is this - these creatures benefit from your prescence, so go back down among them."

" And cause more disruption ? "

" Disruption is only one of your effects. There is your open-ended curiosity."

" True."

" Plus these creatures can intrigue as much as they irritate. "

" They already have."

" Like some entity not a million miles away perhaps."

" And who's that ? "

" Never you mind, this audience is now at an end. Good bye then, until we meet again, don't call me, I'll call you."

" It's all very well to say, but I probably won't remember all this anyway, as soon as I leave this place, I'll be all over space, and this will begin all over again, and..."

But the Supreme Being had already vanished. And the Spirit of Free Inquiry could not remember what he was doing here. Here being this quiet corner of the universe, where a blue, green planet, full of noisy inhabitants, hovered before him. Since there was nothing else to do, he thought he might as well investigate. Not that the Spirit could remember if there was anything else.

To be sure it was a fascinating planet, though intensely complex. The way time passed, in particular, was very frustrating. It seemed to hold the lives of the planet's inhabitants to a variety of set patterns. The Spirit seemed to affect all their lives, at all points of their individual and collective existence. This did his brain in. The Spirit's impulsive nature meant it could not follow any pattern with any degree of consistency. He tried to be careful, yet he could not avoid causing disruption, including a series of wars and continual political conflict, not to mention the controversies in religion and science. Though everything seemed to flow along in the end, if only in a muddled fashion. The thought presented itself to the Spirit that these creatures, on this planet, might give opportunities to discipline his own memory. But then he promptly forgot this thought and wandered off somewhere else.

' Back in days of yore,
When life was not a bore,
Before we lived in clover,
Before the yuppies took over,
Life was oh so smelly,
We only had one telly.
But one would not lie low,
He rose from his lilo,
And did search high and low,
For that forbidden giro,
He braved the tyrant's nest,
That was the D.S.S. '

The Quest
to be Assessed
by the D.S.S.

Yes, one daring dole merchant's doings of dering do, from that age of bad haircuts and obnoxious politics, and obnoxious haircuts and bad politics, and politically bad, obnoxious haircuts, and hairy politics with obnoxious hair, and political obnoxiousness with a bad hair day, and haircuts with obnoxious politics on a bay horse on a bad day etc etc...

Things were not so hot in this green and pleasant land. The capital city of Rundown Town had seen better days. Inner city decay was the order of the day. Concrete, grey and unemployment held sway. Things were particularly bad in the borough of Tower Shambles. Where is Tower Shambles you may ask ? Well, it was near the edge of town, rubbing shoulders with the boroughs of Fester Gate, Acne,

Craplar, Wretch Ham, Poxton and Opensoreditch, with the Isle of Slugs to the south. Just over the oiley waters of the river Tainted lay the boroughs of Witherhithe, Grimewich and Dirtford. These boroughs were commonly known as the Beast End of Rundown Town.

Yes, things were pretty grim in Tower Shambles. Here, a job was this half-mythical thing that existed in the remote past. Local facilities consisted solely of armoured, police patrol, panda cars (A precaution necessary because of the alarmingly high crime rate). People became so hard up they began eating pigeons and dogs for Sunday dinner. When they started getting scarce, they ate rats, insects, then bushes, trees, lawns, then anything in sight;- lamposts, cars, walls (A particular delicacy of this time was fried Ford Cortina, in engine oil, with bricks and mortar for dessert). Tower Shambles soon became known as a deprived area, deprived of anything to eat. Eventually, the situation became so bad even the police were afraid of going into the area. They did not fancy the idea of being skewered and served as Sunday roast. Gangs of lean, hungry delinquents, with sharpened knives and forks, were known to roam the streets.

A meeting of local residents was held, with the aim of finding some kind of solution to the situation. A air of depression hung over the meeting. Suggestions were few, and ludicrous. They ranged from cannibalism, to help with the food shortage, killing every male over five years old, to reduce crime, and asking the government for financial help. Groans of helpless apathy sounded as every proposal was rejected and nothing constructive was sorted. Just as the meeting was winding down, to end with a whimper, someone asked if they should go to the Temple of Bureaucracy, more commonly known, in those days, as the D.H.S.S. (The Department of Hatred and Social Sadism), now more commonly known as the D.S.S. (The Department for

Slaying the Scumbags). A hushed silence fell over all. For many had dared enter the portals of this august organisation in the past. None had returned. It was rumoured that, the person who successfully entered a D.H.S.S. temple, and successfully passed various ordeals, could secure a living wage for life. No one had ever accomplished this. And there was widespread doubt over the possibility. But the mood of the meeting was desperate. If someone could prove it were possible, then others could follow and draw the fabled prizes, known only from fantasy, as benefits. It might be the dawning of a new giro for all.

Yet no one declared themslves willing to undertake this task. The D.H.S.S. were masters of torture. Besides, their offices were located near the centre of town, where no inhabitant of Tower Shambles had ever been.

Therefore, a young, shy, unemployed, self-employed taxidermist was volunteered for the task, by everyone else. This man had made himself redundant to cut costs, then reluctantly retaliated against himself and took himself off to court. There he declared himself bankrupt. It was felt this man was suficiently stupid not to be hindered by pain or endless delays. This was a valuable quality when dealing with the the long waits, endless form-filling, and relentless prying, personal questions, that were the terror weapons of the D.H.S.S. He was also sufficiently thick-skinned and gormless not to protest when his name was put foward.

Off he went, to do battle with the bureaucrats. He was briefed, as well as he could be, as to the dangers he would encounter. So, with this knowledge, armed only with a pen, our hero set off, on the quest to be assessed by the D.H.S.S (now more commonly known as the D.S.S.).

To prepare himself, our hero had to undergo certain rituals and drink a magic potion, i.e. he was given a bottle of spirits and put on a tube train. When he rose from the bowels of the earth, into the town centre, he found it a strange place. He narrowly avoided having his eardrums mugged by a Salvation Army band. And gangs of men in strange dresses sought to lure him into their clutches, with cymbals and chants of Krishna. Vigilantes armed with clipboards and questionaires tried to pin him down with banal questions. While underpaid delinquents tried to foist free samples of dodgy products on him. Collisions awaited on every corner, in this overcrowded arena. Our hero narrowly escaped being crushed to death by a stampede of rush hour commuters. Lone drunks also roamed the streets, who would vomit over you as soon as look at you. And random remarks, and rude gestures, flew from the strangers he encountered, thicker than dog ends from an overflowing ashtray. But our hero was not to be deterred. He forded a four-lane main road, without getting run over, and, shock of shocks, he passed a pub at chucking out time, without being accosted by a single inebriate, and he only got a few words of abuse.

He now moved cautiously through some council block undergrowth, treading carefully, so as not to disturb the grazing herds of dossers. (They were not meat eaters, but they had been known to attack without warning.) The housewives stood on their doorsteps, their cries marked their respective territories, in a series of moans, whelps and constant chattering. Our hero wisely kept his distance. Once you got within earshot of them, you were finished. They would corner you with a one-sided conversation that went on for ages. Eventually you would die through boredom, or starvation.

Our hero ducked down several times to avoid passing stampedes of kids. One gang of schoolchildren nearly ridiculed him to death. But luckily the teacher felt sorry for him, and started laughing. This narrow escape told our hero time was running out, however. The almighty D.H.S.S. only deigned to open certain hours. Otherwise he would have to queue all night. Our hero did not fancy the idea of spending the night here, he was ill-equipped for this kind of treacherous environment. Relentlessly he trudged on. But realisation soon dawned on him, he was lost. This meant he would have to take the risky step of asking directions. What if the natives were more than usually hostile ? There had been cases, in the past, of people being killed for merely asking the time. However, he swallowed his fear and ventured to ask a few solitary souls. But everyone gave him contradictory directions. He was walking round in circles, here and there, up the wall, and round the bend. Yet a passing weirdo took pity on him. Our hero gained the correct directions, after he made a donation to the U.F.O. restoration fund, and promised to turn up for the alien encounter on Sunday.

Finally our hero stood before the doors of a gaunt, grey building, the temple of the D.H.S.S. Hordes of miserable, hunched people slouched and shuffled around its doors. A woman was teasing a section of them. She held money in her hand, above her head. The crowd jumped and screamed in its frenzy to try and obtain it. Then she threw the money into the crowd, and a mad scramble ensued. Our hero froze. The woman's sadistic manner, and over-sensibly dressed demeanour, marked her out as a bureaucrat, a high priestess of the D.H.S.S. Our hero drew a deep breath and entered those horrifying halls. A stench of evo-stick and cider hit his nostrils. They were being consumed by the waiting claimants to stave off the mind-numbing boredom. He staggered down the corridor. On the walls were various posters;- how to get a furniture allowance, how to get a digital watch allowance, how to get a valium allowance, how to continue claiming when you were dead, how to claim when you did not exist in the first place. On one of the walls a message was written in blood - ' abandon hope all ye who enter here in the hope of poncing a stash of cash.' Our hero swallowed hard and staggered on.

A security guard, wielding a huge club, and an armelite rifle, shoved our hero in the direction of a waiting room. There he was asked to pick a numbered card, and wait for his number to be called for an interview. His card number was 56343026. At that moment the number 1331 was showing on a little screen. A long and tedious wait ensued. Eighteen people died of boredom before their numbers came up. Others looked like they had been waiting for centuries, they were covered in cobwebs. A few had erected tents in the waiting room, one enterprising young couple had even brought their caravan in. A lifetime later, 56343026 was called. A steel panel in the wall slid open, a harsh metallic voice rang through a microphone - ' This way please, 56343026, you filthy scrounger.' Our hero stepped inside, the steel door slammed shut automatically. A row of striplights blazed on, their harsh glare cut straight into his eyes. In front of him, he could dimly see a thick, glass panel. Behind this glass panel sat a stern figure, dressed in black.

" Sit down please,scum," it said.

Our hero sat down, in what looked like a huge dentist's chair. The authoritarian voice continued -

" Well, 56343026, state your reasons for daring to dirty our hallowed halls with your puny prescence, cap in hand, begging for a few pennies."

" Well, like most people in my area, I've been unemployed for a while. And I came along to see if I was entitled to anything."

" Why come now ? why not before ? as soon as you became unemployed."

" Well, like a lot of people, I didn't know whether it would be worth my while."

" What makes you think it would be worth it now ? "

" Well...I...er...er..."

" Do not mumble or stutter, speak clearly and correctly."

A uniformed guard appeared and struck our hero with a rubber truncheon.

" That's just to prod you into speech...Now come on, worthless insect, tell me."

" Well, to tell the truth, I didn't know how to go about it, and I was a bit scared."

" Pathetic, you expect me to believe such ridiculous lies...I think we should get the whole truth out of you. Guards, attach electrodes to his genitals please."

More burly guards appeared. They proceeded to strap our hero into his chair and interfere with his personal possessions. While they hurried about their task, the stern voice went on -

" Every time you do not answer a question to my satisfaction, you will receive a slight prod of a couple of hundred volts, to help steer you in the right direction... Right, first of all, do you really expect me to believe you're unemployed ? "

" Yes of course......zzzzzzzzzzzzt......aaargh."

" Date of birth, please."

" 13-4-55......zzzzzzzzzzzzt......aaargh."

" Former occupation."

" Taxidermist......zzzzzzzzzzzzt......aaargh."

" What kind of accomodation."

" Bedsit......zzzzzzzzzzzzt......aaargh."

Our hero was questioned in this manner for a further three excruciating hours...

" Any Hungarian dwarves living in your family."

" No......zzzzzzzzzzzzt......aaargh."

" What is the capital of Mongolia."

" Don't know......zzzzzzzzzzzzt......aaargh."

" Name the line up of the England football team that lost to West Germany in Mexico 1970."

" Um...Peter Bonetti...er......zzzzzzzzzzzzt...... aaargh."

" That's the end of your questions, scum."

" Ah...Look, I answered your questions as truthfully as I could, but you still gave me an electric shock for every answer I gave."

" Look, filth, you came in to try and get money, right..."

" Er...yes."

" Well you don't get it for nothing, you know."

" Now what you have to do is - recite the addresses in the Rundown Town telephone directory, backwards, while drinking the contents of a bedpan...in thirty seconds, starting from now."

After thirty nauseating seconds,

" Now, if you'd fill these forms, and take them along to the unemployment office."

" A pile of forms, roughly the height of a complete set of Encyclopaedia Britannica, were deposited in our hero's lap. He dragged them home. And, after five weeks continuous from filling, and much writers cramp, he took them to the unemployment office. However, the unemployment office sent him to the tax office, who sent him to the job centre, from there to the town hall, the citizens advice bureau, the local library, the corner shop, the Duke of Clarence and Smellies wine bar. And from there it was back to the D.H.S.S office. Further ordeals were still in store however. Firstly, the D.H.S.S. took a year to assess his entitlement, then his first cheque was lost in the post, his landlord stole the second, and the third was devoured by cockroaches on his doormat. He was sent a letter so an emergency payment could be made, it ran - " Dear 56343026, It occurs to us you may be in some financial difficulty. Ha ha, that is tough titty for you. But, to stop you starving to death, here's 50p. Go and buy yourself a bag of chips."

Finally, our hero was asked by the D.H.S.S. to call at their offices. Here he received a giro for fifty pounds, this being his first week's entitlement. He was also informed that he was due money for all the time he waited. However, because the D.H.S.S. computer had broken, he would not be receiving it until he was ninety years old. The fact remained though. Our hero had proved it was possible to obtain money from the D.H.S.S, hardly a living wage, but he had that giro at last. They would acclaim him as a hero back in Tower Shambles. Unfortunately, just as he was passing the local bingo hall, he was mugged and killed by a mob of bingo-addict pensioners. And the moral of this story is - ' You're sure to lose your money at bingo.'

Follow the Yellow Road Lines

At the roadside stands person A, on the double yellow road lines to be precise. The curious person known as person B finds this intriguing, and is bored as well, and so engages person A in conversation.

B : Why do you always stand on the lines ?

A : " Here I stand, on the brink, as per usual. If I step off the line I will fall into the abyss. Chaos will engulf me, I will disappear into non existence..."

B : " More like you'll get run over, by some twat in a van, because your head is full of these weird thoughts."

A : " Give me a bit of credit please. I know they're weird thoughts. But they help me make sense of this weird city. And anything that helps in that direction is worthwhile."

B : " You'll be stuck on medication again..."

A : " No. That was a breakdown, when I couldn't cope with the events in my head."

B : " And what's so different now ? "

A : " The difference is I am able to blend these thoughts and feelings in with the rest of my life."

B : " For the moment."

A : " Exactly, just like everybody else."

B : " But everyone else aint as messed up as you."

A : " Everyone has the potential to become messed up, why should you, or anyone else for that matter, be different in that respect."

B : " I suppose...but not everyone develops the weird thoughts as much as you."

A : " And how do you know that ? "

B : " Well, no one has developed your fantasy about yellow lines as far as I know."

A : " My fantasy of yellow lines ? How is it different from anyone else's fantasy ? or superstition ? What about the fear of stepping on a crack in the pavement..."

B : " Or walking under a ladder..."

A : " Whatever.."

B : " Granted, I know you've ripped off the Wizard Of Oz."

A : " Yeah, maybe he'll settle out of court."

B : " What ? "

A : " I am influenced by it, but then I use it for my own ends."

B : " A bit selfish isn't it ? "

A : " No, because it helps me understand."

B : " What ? the yellow lines take the place of the yellow brick road ? "

A : " Exactly."

B : " So where do the yellow lines lead then ? "

A : "To the heart and mind of all things...where decisions are made and options weighed, where the conscientious contrive to keep us more alive, where the bureaucrats thrive in the office hive, and complaints arrive, leaving only when they die.

B : " Sounds like the council offices to me."

A : " Could well be."

B : " You've met a tin man and a lion have you ? "

A : " No, but I met an exotic woman, a woman of poise and elegance. This woman's prescence was a breath of life for all who came into contact with her. Yet she carried an ubearable sorrow , the sorrow at having to perform an odious task merely to guarentee her survival. It appears the uniform is already corrupting her soul, turning her peevish, vindictive and cynical..."

B : " Sounds like a traffic warden to me..."

A : " She was begining to enjoy the taste of distasteful work..."

B : " Or maybe a copper..."

A : " Or any other of the uniformed people who patrol our lives, upholding mean spirited laws, and constantly seeing the bad behaviour of others..."

B : " Maybe a ticket inspector..."

A : " Does it matter ? "

B : " All right, all right. So people in official uniforms haven't got much heart.'

A : " Not very enlightening is it ? Most of us would argue that."

B : " So."

A : " So, if they spend too long in a job that demands too much, then it corrupts their soul."

B : " They become like tin men ? "

A : " And women."

B : " Working stiffs in effect."

A : " Whatever you want to call them."

B : " I don't want to call them anything. I just don't want them to be around."

A : " That's your problem."

B : " What about the lion in the Wizard of Oz, I thought that had no heart ? "

A : " But this is real life, sort of."

B : " Or no courage anyway."

A : " It's been a little while since I saw the film."

B : " You have to be a bit faithful to the original if you want to rip it off."

A : " Why ? "

B : " Don't know, its the done thing I suppose."

A : " I can't even remember the girl's name, what is it ? Jilly Holland ? "

B : " Judy Garland, yeah. Does that mean you're her. You don't really look like a fresh faced girl with pigtails."

A : " But I'm not a hollywood actor."

B : " Yeah I know, you're a real person. "

A : " Exactly."

B : " As in really fucked up. "

A : " Watch it."

B : " Sorry."

A : "I told you anyway, I adapted the film for my own ends. I am the protagonist. But I can hardly claim to be Judy Garland can I ? "

B : " You're not in your transvestite phase anymore then ? "

A : " I never was, not for long, just as you were never in your submissive, masochistic phase..."

B : " Er yeah, fair enough, er anyway, getting back to the Wizard of Oz, did you ever meet a lion without courage ? "

A : " A lion without courage, you mean metaphorically speaking ? of course. "

B : " Er yeah, sort of."

A : " Well actually I find courage, real courage, to be something possessed by a few, at any particular time. It is innate within us all, it's true. But it only exists as potential, never to be called on, except in the most extreme emergencies. And as these extreme emergencies are themselves horrible situations, where wrong decisions can lead to panic, and calamitous consequences, the use of courage of this sort is never guarenteed. Though of course we can also surpass our expectations, and show behaviour that has others grinning with admiration..."

B : " Eh ? "

A : " I mean sometimes we can be better than we are."

B : " Oh right."

A : " Yet there's different kinds of courage that all of us possess, that all of us use from day to day. This is the courage to go on living and working, to never give up trying. To live without having much knowledge, while being scared at what could happen, and totally confused when you try to make sense of it..."

B : " Wow, I don't know why they put you in the crazy cage.."

A : " The what ? "

B : " The fruitcake factory..."

A : " Pardon. "

B : " The looney bin."

A : " What do you mean ? "

B : " The psycho centre."

A : " I'm sorry ? "

B : " Don't be sorry, I love listening to you."

A : " Thank you...Oh I get it, all those crude statements of yours are supposed to refer to an institution.."

B : " Er yeah."

A : " Then why don't you say so, instead of using derogatory phrases ? "

B : " Coz you talk weird, with lots of weirdo words."

A : " What are you so scared of ? "

B : " Everything."

A : " That's an honest answer for a pisstaker."

B : " Yeah well, in the right company I can be honest.
"

A : " So you can be a bit of a lion yourself."

B : " I suppose...I've got to admit all this talk sounds like lovey dovey, dippie hippie, new age crap."

A : " Even though crap may have some uses."

B : " You see what I mean."

A : " I do indeed."

B : " Well, maybe you can see my problem then."

A : " Sometimes, we all have to pretend sometimes."

B : " Mice who pretend we're lions."

A : " Perhaps."

B : " Why do we do it ? "

A : " It helps."

B : " Sometimes ? "

A : " As often as need be."

B : " Whenever we feel like it in other words."

A : " But we should know of it."

B : " Of what ? "

A : " The fact that we kid ourselves sometimes."

B : " Sounds like always to me."

A : " Maybe."

B : " Or maybe not."

A : " Or maybe it just feels like that."

B : " Sometimes."

A : " Perhaps."

B : " This does my brain in."

A : " I know what you mean."

B : " So, any other little insights you want to show me from the Wizard Of Oz."

A : " No."

B : " Why not."

A : " Because I can't think of any."

B : " That's not very helpful."

A : " What do you expect, it's ages since I saw the film."

B : " A few more answers."

A : " Well maybe you should follow the yellow lines instead."

B : " What ? behind you ? "

A : " Well I wouldn't encourage it."

B : " Why not ? "

A : " Because you ask too many questions for a start."

B : " I promise, I won't ask questions, well not too many."

A : " You really want to follow me ? "

B : " Yes. "

A : " What are you, an idiot ? "

B : " No, just curious."

A : " After making fun of me and my fantasies."

B : " I was just joking. "

A : " How do I know you're not joking now ? "

B : " Does it matter ? "

A : " Yes, if you're going to be an irritating twat.'

B : " I just want to see what happens."

A : " It could be really boring for you."

B : " I don't see how. I'm waiting to see where the lines lead already."

A : " Well that's a start."

B : " And I'll always end up somewhere..."

A : " Or somewhere else. "

B : " I don't even find this dippy hippy shit too annoying anymore."

A : " But still weird."

B : " Just like life ? "

A : " Yes okay."

B : " Isn't life always going to be weird ? "

A : " Aren't you afraid someone will call you a weirdo. "

B : " Yeah, but what do they know."

A : " About as much as me and you."

B : " So I should be aware of them."

A : " Perhaps that's true."

B : " But I still choose to follow."

A : " Take it easy will you. I'm no guru. "

B : " I know that much is true."

A : " You have to make your own point of view."

B : " Yeah, but I still want to go with you."

A : " To see what the yellow lines do."

B : " Okay, alright, can we get on with it now please ? "

A : " Don't rush me, please. It's my idea, even if you want to indulge in it too."

B : " Okay, can we go now please. "

A : " Yes yes. Look, seeing as you're so energetic, why don't you walk in front of me for a while. "

B : " Eh ? "

A : " It's okay, I'll be right behind you. Just follow the yellow lines, wherever they go..."

B : " Right let's be off then. "

(B quickly walks off before A has a chance to react. A screech of brakes is heard, a bump, and a yelp. B has obviously been run over.)

A : " The poor, stupid fool, no road sense whatsover. Still, maybe it's just as well. I never asked for any followers in the first place."

Dave's Crispybits

Motto - Have a meal at Dave's Crispybits,
You'll get stuffed.

The fashionable new restaurant opened in town has to be Dave's Crispybits. Everyone is raving about it, and not just because of the food poisoning. Okay, some did get sick, and died in screaming agony, but eating has always been risky, especially in Britain. The name ' Dave's Crispybits ' is self explanatory, he says. For he serves allegedly edible lumps cooked in crispy batter. Dave wishes to distance himself from the deep-fried mars bar and curlywurly crowd (although you can have these for dessert). His specialities include exotic lumps that induce less coronaries than the usual deep fried monstrosities. Why, they even have a vegetarian menu, they say, since it is hard to know whether the lumps you are eating are animal or vegetable, or mineral for that matter. His exotic lumps in batter also contain less calories and have less side effects, or at least Dave says so, on the carefully prepared health warning leaflet he hands you as you enter his establishment. Two diners had to be carried out on stretchers while I was there. Dave tut tutted as they were carried out, some people just do not have the stomach for a cullinary challenge nowadays.

I was having the Anonymous bits in batter, followed by Crispychunks in a Hollandaise sauce, with crispy skins in cream for dessert. It was different. And that is perhaps why the bright young things patronise this establishment. Fed up with the elitism of most eateries, they wanted a restaurant experience that took them to other places, and Dave's Crispybits did. Although this other place was usually the toilet. They liked the wholesome unpretentiousness of Dave's food. Or at least they would if they knew what was inside his batter. But this added a particular frisson to the eating experience, one or two told me, on their way to be sick. A more prosaic description was offered by the delightfully stinking inebriate beside me. ' It's like eating a bag of Revels, you never know which flavour's going to come up next, that's if you can hold it down long enough. '

Most frequenters of Dave's swear by his genius at preparing these cullinary shocks and surprises. His delicacies can leave you weak at the knees, from botulism if nothing else. Others swear at Dave, because of their usual trouble in keeping their meals down. Yet Dave's star continues to rise. Only last month, the anorexic soap-actress, Strictlee Sicklee, began patronising his establishment. She never has anything beyond a glass of water and a twiglet, but her prescence alone has guarenteed many more customers for Dave's, as evidenced by the long queue for the toilets. Environmental Health Officers are also regular customers. They get so excited by coming here that they cannot sit still for long. They always have to get up and start enquiring on just how Dave's delicious delicacies are prepared. Their obssessive attitude even goes so far as make them wander around the kitchen, asking impertinent questions, in their quest to uncover the secret of Dave's Crispybits. So far they have always failed. And Dave's Crispybits remains resolutely open.

In the meantime, we can continue to enjoy the mystery and mastery inherent in Dave's Crispybits. It is rumoured he makes use of recipies handed down from father to son, like diseases, across the generations. These recipes are kept in a locked vault, in a sterile building, in a biological warfare research laboratory, somewhere.

Most of Dave's customers, those still alive, believe his Crispybits are beyond reproach. And, anyway, Dave's Crispybits is far less pretentious than some of the overpriced cack they usually eat, in shitpits staffed by snotty-nosed creeps. (This quote was taken verbatim from a passing punter, on her way to chuck up.)

It would seem Dave's Crispybits has been making waves, beyond ones of nausea, among fellow restauranteurs. After swallowing their acid distaste they began opening up rival establishments. Dave's Crispybits is now flanked by the rival establishments of Johnny's Fluffybits and Ronnie's Wispybits. Johnny's Fluffybits sells dishes in which hair is the principle ingredient (His ' Dog's Hair Delight ' has to sampled to be believed, as does his ' Pubic Pudding '). Ronnies Wispybits sells different varieties of smoke, in different coloured glass jars (This is a big hit among the cognoscenti I am informed).Not strictly cullinary I believe, but still very filling, and very fulfilling However, I would avoid Ronnies ' Diesel Fumes at Dusk ' and ' Morning Methane Mist. ' Though I would strongly recommend ' Laughing Gas a la Orange. ' Finally, I must mention the fast food outlet - Turdie's Tit Bits (located a stone's throw away, down the drain). This establishment only accepts punters with the requisite life insurance.

Bon Appetit.

Water Features Versus Fountains

Two gardeners are standing on a lawn. They are both facing a sound which is coming from off stage. (somewhere to the left or right) One of the gardeners is big, burly, and a bit of a slob in appearance. The other is slim and well dressed, as gardeners go, with knee pads, a big, straw hat, long sleeved shirt, holding a pair of secateurs ever ready. The burly gardener is dressed in an old T-shirt and jeans, hands, and arms, covered in dirt.

Burly Gardener : That's a nice fountain over there. (points)

Slim Gardener : It's not a fountain, it's a water feature.

B.G. : So what's the difference ?

S.G. : Well water is a feature of this garden.

B.G. : Not true, in that structure water spurts out of a tiny orifice, that's a fountain.

S.G. : Sounds like you're describing your toilet habits.

B.G. : That's not a million miles different, after all, some of the cruder among us talk of human fountains.

S. G. : Only the crude as you say, the more refined among us prefer to differentiate.

B.G. : But a fountain is a refined structure.

S.G. : That's a water feature

B.G. : No it isn't, it's a fountain.

S.G. : Fountain is a specific feature.

B.G. : Yes, like that one there. (points)

S.G. : No, water is the main feature in that structure.

B.G. : Yeah, where water spurts out of an orifice.

S.G. : So is a hosepipe a fountain then ?

B.G. : Well, a fountain can come out of it, but it's more like a water feature.

S.G. : So you admit a hosepipe can be a water feature then.

B.G. : No, water features in it, but it's not a permanent feature in it.

S.G. : What's that supposed to mean ?

B.G. : What you call a water feature is something that is specifically built into a garden.

S.G. : LIke a fountain you mean ?

B.G. : Ah, so you agree with me then.

S.G. : No, I don't, I was just using your terminology.

B.G. : Besides, don't you get hosepipes in the gardens most of the time ?

S.G. : No. it depends what you want to water, a hosepipe is not a permanent feature anyway, you move it or remove it,according to whether you want to use it.

B. G. : Unlike a more permanent feature.

S.G. : Like a water feature.

B.G. : Or like that fountain..

S.G. : No, like that water feature.

B.G. : Have you a problem with the word fountain then ?

S.G. : Yes, it carries an image which is too limited.

B.G. : You're saying it discriminates.

S.G. : Well yes,it does.

B.G. : How can you discriminate against a fountain ?

S.G. : You don't, you just use the phrase water feature.

B.G. : Water feature, water feature, oh isn't that nice and bland, very politically correct.

S.G. : No, it's just a case of not being too specific.

B.G. : Why ? if you call a fountain a fountain, is it going to cause offence to the sprinkler systems ?

S.G. : Sprinkler systems are not a permanent part of a garden like a water feature.

B.G. : That , over there, is a fountain, you twat.

S.G. : No it isn't, it's a water feature, you idiot.

B.G. : No, a pond is a water feature because water features in it, a hosepipe is a water feature, because water features in it...

S.G. : And what you call a fountain is a water feature, because water features in it.

B.G. : Why can't you just call it a fountain.

S.G. : Because it's a water feature.

B.G. : It's a fountain.

S.G. : Don't be so dogmatic, it's a water feature.

B.G. : Water feature means nothing to me, it's too general.

S.G. : you'll soon get used to it.

B.G. : I won't get used to it, beacause I'm not going to bloody use it.

S.G. : But you're wrong, people'll misunderstand you.

B.G. : They'll understand me because fountain is correct.

S.G. : No it isn't.

B.G. : Yes it is.

S.G. : No way.

B.G. : Look, you have no case against the word fountain.

S.G. : Yes I do, it's old fashioned, too narrow in definition...

B.G. : Not enough like jargon you mean, oh please, not enough like " Well, with my incremental salary increase for this fiscal quarter, I invested in a new water feature."

S.G. : Well, it sounds better than " Oh I got a spare bit of wonga bye the bye, think I'll dig up the old weed patch, stick a fountain in it."

B.G. : It's better than sounding bland.

S.G. : Better to sound bland than to sound stupid.

B.G. : But water feature is stupid.

S.G. : No it isn't, it's a nice, harmless term.

B.G. : But what's so harmful about calling it a fountain ?

S.G. : It's incorrect.

B.G. : But it's what I've always called it.

S.G. : You've always been incorrect.

B.G. : Wait a minute, you said a water feature was not specific, that means you can use it about a few things.

S.G. : Yes, so ?

B.G. : Like a fountain for instance.

S.G. : Except that it's wrong.

B.G. : A fountain is a specific name for a type of water feature.

S.G. : I've told you. It's not a fountain , it's a water feature, no more, no less.

B.G. : Any fixed structure that spurts out a jet of water is a fountain.

S.G. : I could say something rude here.

B.G. : No, that would be politically incorrect.

S.G. : Yes, I should leave that to you.

B.G. : I wish you'd leave the names of these things alone as well.

S.G. : Look, a fire hydrant can spurt out a jet of water. Does that make it a fountain ?

B.G. : No, that makes it a water feature.

S.G. : Don't get smart with me.

B.G. : You could get a fountain out of a fire hydrant.

S.G. : But not out of a water feature.

B.G. : I don't see what the problem is here. These things have always been called fountains.

S.G. : Which was incorrect. And that is why they're now called water features.

B.G. : Why is it everyone goes around changing the names of these things ? Are the fountains going to get ideas above their station if they're called fountains ? Do the ponds feel discriminated against because fountain sounds too aristocratic ?

S.G. : Gardens are egalitarian places, for everyone, apart from smelly riff raff and non residents of course.

B.G. : But you can't have too much discrimination in a garden.

S.G. : Correct.

B.G. : So you need a water feature.

S.G. : Exactly.

Looking somewhat confused the burly gardener walks off with a shrug of the shoulders. The slim gardener indulges in a bit of head scratching, as if trying to figure out the previous conversation, then follows.

SCENE 2 - The News

A person in a suit, sitting at a desk, reads the latest bulletin. This person has the professional gloss of all media people, looking most agreeable, but the type of person who is forgotten about as soon as absent.

Newsreader : Several thousand ponds marched on Downing Street today. They were protesting about the low status many garden bodies of water still have, despite the elitist term " fountain " being banned, and despite the popularity of gardening programmes.

Trouble began when a rival march of water features attempted to bar their path, apparently abusive chants of " Fountains rule, fountains are cool ," were heard. Scuffles broke out and several policemen were soaked. A spokesobject for the water features condemned the violence, saying it was only a tiny minority who had leaky pipes. It called for water features to follow the regal example of those structures at Trafalgar Square. This remark angered some water features, since the Trafalgar Square structures have retained the name fountains only after some extensive horse trading involving the government and several Nimbys. In the meantime a spokesbodyofwater for the ponds claimed it was saddened at some of the events that followed. Several ponds went on the rampage throughout the West End, soaking passers by with stagnant, green water. Many people were poisoned. A pond official said these were wild ponds, not connected with any gardens whatsover. However, he continued, people must recognise the poor, deprived backgrounds many ponds still have. A majority still suffer from poor drainage and pollution. The dismissal of the word fountain was a step foward. Yet it was still felt that many of the new water features were fountains in all but name. To add further controversy, a hose attachment said this was rubbish. Many ponds could only blame their own lack of self-discipline. They should look at the example rivers set, and get on and flow wherever it is they are going, instead of sitting in some hole in the ground, waiting for the wildlife to come along and appreciate you. As for the water features, well, they slipped from grace when they became water features. Now every allotment could claim to have a water feature. Whereas before, every graceful garden had a fountain. Reclaiming the word fountain might actually be a step foward. It could ensure the " Dumbing down" of gardens was halted.

The arguements over the words fountain and water feature look set to continue. I have with me in the studio two representatives of the great fountain debate, two ornate garden ornaments, one who is quite content to be a water feature, the other who insists on the word fountain.

(The camera, or scene, shifts. Whereas before all light and attention was concentrated on the newsreader, now it is revealed there are two fountains, or water features, sitting on chairs , to the newsreaders left. The one nearest to the newsreader is captioned as the water feature, while the one furthest is the fountain. Apart from the difference of title they both look the same.)

Both our guests are proud of their respective titles, and both believe their names will be the names of choice in the future... If I may start with you please fountain. The biggest fact against your name has to be accusation of snobbery does it not ?

THERE IS COMPLETE SILENCE

I see, well,as stubborn and uncooperative as ever... Perhaps you can enlighten me water feature. Why should we call you that, isn't it getting a bit too politically correct ?

MORE COMPLETE SILENCE

Aren't either of you going to say anything ?

THE SILENCE CONTINUES

Well both of our guests appeared to have dried up rather, they are sticking rather glumly to their positions and not giving anything away. Perhaps it is to be expected in this time of uncertainty. However it seems the controversy will continue, or get started even. That is all for this evening. But on our main bulletin tonight we discuss the garden related problem of ant gobbing. A bill is currently up before Parliament that will prohibit ants being spat on in gardens. Parents are outraged at this, believing it will encourage their children to gob in the house more often. And they say their children have enough obnoxious habits as it is. And there is some outrage at the proposed penalties for ant gobbing, such as smearing children in jam and burying them in anthills, or, having a group of policemen gobbing in the heads of the offensive, er offending, children. All that, plus the latest on the fountain versus water feature arguement, later tonight, with hopefully some fights between garden implements, and gardeners, if we're lucky, good evening, and have a nice couple of hours.

The end.

The House of Worry

Internal - guarded info. ;- Redall, could you please let me have a preliminary report on the House of Worry. As you know, a halfway drughouse facility at Yarmouth was stormed last week, two operatives and fifteen inmates were killed. There is likely to be an inquest into the running of these facilities by the criminal element. Some of them were believed to have links with the House of Worry. I am circulating this memo to other departmental heads to seek their remarks on this matter - Kinniston, State Control. cc. Dept of Internal Policing, Pharmaceutrical Division, Civil Chancellery Budget Control.

Kinniston - Agreed. This policy may need some revision, our information is scanty with regard to its efficacy - Ford-Brown D.I.P.

Myself , I feel it is too early yet to gauge any results. And, as you know, The Pharmaceutrical Probation Service are notoriously secretive with their projects. Nevertheless I would be interested to see a progress report - De Mettier P.D.

I am in favour of stricter regulation on these matters, as I have made known previously. I feel it is a mistake to let the P.P.S. police itself. I am not sure that these matters are beyond the capablities of financial and behavioural assessors, as is so often stated. There should be more people like Redall to liaison with - Monahan C.C.B.C.

Sirs - please find prelim enclosed - A.M. Redall.

As you may know, the main agent within the facility known as the House of Worry is Pearson.J.A, a life long addict, currently on undercover probation as an alternative to forced detoxification. However, as part of his cover, Pearson had to spend some time being detoxified in order to establish his credibilty for the House of Worry. For the House will only admit the recalcitrant addict. Other agents have disappeared when their disciplined habits have been uncovered. And we have suspicions a couple may have gone over. Pearson represents our only success so far. (our only one surviving.)

As you are well aware, the House of Worry purports to be a reformatory institution. In its own words it " Worries the addict into health." Given the escalating cost of policing addicts in these times, the courts were only too pleased to hand over their reprobates to a privately funded organisation. Its initial success was quite marked, a relapse rate of only 10 per cent, and this in the treatment of the hardcore user.

However, it must be remarked that failures were significant. Some deaths have occurred, legally uattributable ones it has to be said, due to poor liaison facilities with central and local government. Indeed, the House of Worry maintains that any sustained contact with " Official Bodies," (their term) tends to compromise the efficiency of their procedures.

A typical day in the House of Worry starts with a daily harangue. Each inmate is systematically villified in respect of character, with continued emphasis on the effects of their addiction on others. By afternoon, when everyone may be said to have been routinely persecuted, there is a brief period of meditation before the injection of a synaptic stabiliser. This stabiliser is produced by the addicts themselves. Nerurotransmitters are extracted from every inmate. These are held to be more efficacious in remedial remedies. They are said to be of major significance when weaning the hardcore from their own habits. As for the form of the harangue, Pearson has been quite vague. But I believe it to have little sophistication. Indeed, sometimes it appears to be no more than stylised verbal abuse. Pearson maintains it is hard to recall these sessions afterward, because they are psychologically trying. He suggests they might even be considered as tortuous, although no common law appears to be breached there.

There are further activities within this prison, along the lines of what may be called therapeutic. You are undoubtedly aware of the various therapies that engage creativity, whether painting, pottery, model making etc : these therapies are well recognised, and I will not detain your attention by mentioning them further. There is also a strict regime of physcial exercise, from individual fitness training to team sports. Indeed, the House of Worry prides itself on its physical regimen. However, Pearson suggests that, when taken in conjunction with the harangue and synaptic treatments, some breakdowns occur. I endeavoured for more details here, but Pearson appeared to be reluctant other than to pass a few names who died of seizure. It is held that a breakdown is bad motivation for the other addicts on the verge of recovery. Therefore, the ill consequences of any therapy are not wholly verified, even within the institution.

This may give rise to the suspicion of devious cover on the part of the institution. Yet there is some ground for the assertion, as Pearson himself dictates. We are all aware of the need to flow in one direction, to quote the old saying, within any institute or organisation.

Of course, being recalcitrants, the inmates seek any opportunity to rejuvenate their habits to their former state of addiction. This has given rise to concern. For it is contraband supplies of the synaptic stabilisers themselves that are most prevalent in the House of Worry. They appear to be so established as to become currency within the institution. There is some controversy here. We are all versed in the pro and con as to tolerance of illegal drugs in confinement. Yet it has been the case for the authority to permit some degree of this pernicious trade. For the addicts struggle is complex, even within the confines of the House of Worry. And some leeway is held to be necessary within the promulgation of instruction. Although Pearson suggests there may be official complicity, as funds are always depleted, it seems, yet the House appears never lacking in well paid employees. I find this aspect disturbing. I have pursued Pearson on this matter. Yet he will assert this is a most convoluted aspect, with many contingent dangers in the assessment of evidence. Nevertheless, I have asked him to attain evidence, though to act with cautious endeavour.

Certain aspects of this internal trade do merit further communciation. Prime among these is the fact the illegal synaptics are known as E.Z's or eezee's. The fact they have an established cognomen, or nickname, suggests a long traditional aspect. Indeed, it might herald confirmation of widespread use. I would suggest resources could be targetted toward this end in future. Though we must have adequate protection, as cost dictates, for operatives such as Pearson who are in the arena. I know the question has been perpetually dismissed, but some established procedure needs implementing here, with regard to diagnosis of the problem. Undercover addicts need some police support.

As perhaps you realise, Pearson is officially I.A., an incorrigible addict. This means he has adopted the lifestyle and persona concurrent upon the addiction subculture. Therefore his abilities in the arena may be rendered suspect, particularly in the light of previous operatives who have gone over. Some adequate assessment needs to be continually on board with regard to the shape, or lack, of his personality. So far his observations have remained reasonably apposite. But only so far as they have been verified by our more formal staff. I am of course talking primarily of the Department of Pharmaceutricals Executive, known by the sardonic acronym D.O.P.E.

Indeed, I see Pearson as our best hope in tracking down the various carcass factories that have been reported. As you may be aware, we are monitoring constant rumours of meat storage, for the extraction of fluids to manufacture eezee's. Persistent rumour attends the possibilty some of this meat may be human. Given the most effective eezee remains that extracted from human physiology, this possibilty can never be discounted. There are also questions relating to the flouting of consumer regulations, with regard to the storage of foodstuffs, if these possibilities are are reliably verified. I would prefer to extend operations with pathfinder teams to identify the location and corporations behind manufacture and trade.

But, of course, priorities remain priorities. I am merely suggesting the future course of policy, if certain outcomes are verified. Of more pressing moment is the need to gain official access of some kind to the House of Worry, to assess the reports of those such as Pearson with more objectivity. I know this proposition has met with dogged opposition in the past. Yet I believe we obtained a soured outcome when the rights to reformist drug treatment were negotiated away by government. Of course the saving in outlay, both administrative and financial, has been considerable. But this has only been in the short term. In the longer term, we may be conspiring unwittingly to build powerful vested interests, whose motivation could conflict with our own. I acknowledge these points have already been raised by dysfunctional politicals and other delinquent commentators. Yet that need not detract from their relevance. Perhaps I am being overly paranoid here. But when we released jurisdiction on the House of Worry, we may have inadvertently created a nation within a nation, so to speak. Our co-operation with the House is dependent entirely on personal trust. If toxic personalities, such as addicts, were allowed influence in this environment, then circumstances can only decay. Some speculation contends this is in the process of being realised, yet it is no more than possibility at present. However, as you are all aware, there are a further two institutions in the process of construction. If these were to make alliances, with negative outcomes in mind, then it may be beyond our resources to respond.

Redall - This perhaps only stokes our paranoia. Concomittent verification, of a quantifiable nature, is seriously needed. I can raise the matter at the next Government agenda conflab, but I can only be pessimistic concerning our need for more resources, particulary as we have just given jurisdiction away in so many areas. Please let me have the finshed report ASAP. We will need everything in our arsenal to argue this case. - Kinniston S.C.

We are in need of something more concrete, definitely, Pearson's testimony is not enough in itself, it only suggests lines of enquiry. - Ford-Brown D.I.P.

We are indeed on shaky ground, my valued collegues, we will have to engage the possibilty of no jurisdiction to act at all, even if in receipt of the requisite information. - De Mettier P.D.

That would be a shame, we need powers on this. Law and order was a prerequisite in our adminstration, I do not think we should back down on this, we need more powers, not more deregulation. - Monahan C.C.B.C.

Sirs - please note - I wil be fowarding an itemised report in due course - Redall.

Go Seek the Mentors

First came the environmental disasters - earthquakes and volcanos in particular. These were world wide, their effects shook everyone. There was no indication beforehand of their intensity, and no real defence when they happened. Next came the struggle for resources in the aftermath. The old causes for war, dogma in religion and nationalism, seemed something of a luxury. They soon went. Civilisation struggled to prevent its own collapse, and was not very successful. In the aftermath the survivors viewed their new world with a mixture of shock and fear. They were too numb to feel anything else. Gradually small pockets of humanity regained their initiative. The sheer will to survive kept them going at first. But then came the realisation just what they had lost. The material benefits of the old world lay scattered and broken everywhere. The knowledge of the world was ripped into a thousand fragments. Some small few realised the fullest implication of their new found situation. They were in danger of sliding back down the evolutionary scale, with no more than a grim struggle for scarce resources to live for.

And so people worked, with a haste unnatural to any previous human. Small communities grew up, seperated by barren wastes populated by diseased, barbaric hordes. To these communities falls the burden of civilisation. There is some communication but not much. Each must concentrate on the task in hand, preserve and build on the fragmented knowledge of the time before, before the world turned upside down, before the Fall...

Matlock read this, he could repeat it in his head. It was what they learnt in school. Funny, he did not see much evidence around him. But then, he was feeling low because he was not well. From his window he looked at the market place below. A shopkeeper was having a full blown argument with his supplier. Evidently some sleight of hand had been employed, somewhere. And someone had lost money as a consequence. That was all he could gather from the heated gibberish below. Shouting and gesticulation rose in waves. An energetic crowd slowly gathered round, adding their points of view. Most were there for the spectator sport it provided. A few mischievous souls actively wound up the participants. Matlock knew what came next. A few were already taking sides. Gesture turned to push turned to shove, a brawl was in the making.

Matlock knew he should stop looking. As he noted this thought he leant further out to get a better view, making a scraping noise as he did so. At this the crowd went silent. As one they glared up at him. He was conspicuous by his presence.

" Lookit dat nosey get."

" Seen alla action ye like, peepo man ? "

" Lookin faw better life,mon, coz it lackin in ya own respeck, eh chuck."

Matlock quickly drew back inside. He knew what the various comments meant. Polyglot, the slang of the Mundane classes. They used it always, especially to wind up cadet types like him. And he drew back in just in time. For a object followed him in. It rushed past him and splatt on the wall opposite, rotten fruit.

" Big shit bag types ye are," he shouted back out the window.

Giggles followed. Matlock knew a little Polyglot himself. It was a compilation of slang said to come from the old homeland. It seemed their ancestors came from some cold, damp island, heavily overpopulated, noted for its robust insults, that much he knew. There was a lot more, the Elders knew, they could tell a lot more. As could the Mentors, those scientists, or sorcerers according to some, who doled out the words of wisdom, which directed the affairs of his village, plus a couple of others, spread out around the mountain. That Mountain, that formed the first of the range known as Kokako. But the other villages did not matter, that much. Anyway they were rivals. Contact was sparse.

The ultimate goal of each cadet was to graduate in the four ways - first there were the Military arts, related to all matters of fight. Second were the Social arts, relating to all matters of knowing and dealing with people. Then were the Practical arts, relating to matters of agriculture, to crafts and such industry as remained. Then was the Fourth, the peak for some, relating to matters of culture, history, philosophy, governance. And that should be it. But there was the legendary Fifth. Legendary for some, who dimissed its utility. Matlock had always heard rumours. Yet he did not consider it real until the talk he heard on the last expedition. Then it was talked about as if real. Matlock knew the Fifth art gave you mastery of yourself and others, it made you into a leader. This was dangerous, as people with power can abuse it, especially in small communties. And they could not take more dangers than were necessary. For life was harsh, everyone suffered some want. The life was debilitating in every sense - physical, emotional and spiritual. Some had events in their lives they could not contain. For the truth of the matter was they lived in a claustrophobic, poverty-stricken community. Yet they were forever reminded of the glories that existed in the past, before the Fall - all the benefits were greater - material, emotional, spiritual. While nothing detailed could be known, and thus recreated, enough fragments remained to weigh heavy on the brain, to tease always with the knowledge of what, like lost youth, could never be regained. Thus were they constantly reminded of their own imperfection. And this was not all. For you had to be on the alert constantly, as environment insisted on telling you. Three farm workers were found dead in the last week alone. Their bodies stripped and left naked in the fields, their extremities cut off, trophies no doubt.

Matlock was on a party that had set out on a punitive expedtion, to right this wrong. It also gave him the last part of his martial training. They were a small but heavily-armed group, commanded by Madame-General Gretna, the best. They had tracked the raiders through the desert plains for three days, non-stop. Then came their sighting of the nomad pack. Their pursuit was swift and their revenge quick. These were Mani-coloureds, nomads who suffered from what appeared to be a score of diseases, each claiming its own territory on their skin, staking their claim through their own particular pigment. These people were born diseased and died diseased. Their lives were spent in the delirium of pain and agony. And they formed a good moral lesson - This is what you could become if you let matters slip, if you became disorganised. And they were frightening to encounter. Though poorly armed, they hurled themselves at Gretna's force, like rabid dogs. A volley of gunfire cut down the bulk of the pack, but the remaining three broke into the midst of the ranks. Matlock ducked on reflex. He felt long, sharp hands scrape his back. He heard the screams of Poole, as the thing caught him full, sinking its teeth into his face. It was cut down with well placed shots. The other two had died in that last volley, their lives terminated in mid leap. The panicked cadets hurriedly removed themselves from about these corpses. All eyes turned to Poole. He stood in shock, already begining to foam at the mouth. His eyes glazed. Gretna knew what to do, the infections must be violently killed. The order was given. Poole danced in an intense circle of gunfire before he collapsed lifeless. They would have to leave the body there of course, the risk of disease was too great. Then everyone looked at Matlock. They raised their guns at him, for a moment he thought he might join Poole. But Gretna barked a different order. He was seized, his head wrenched down. He felt his wounds burn, first through the applicaton of a hastily prepared flaming brand, then through the application of alcohol. It was the only way to completely disinfect the victim, but it worked.

Matlock screamed.

" Stop the whining, Matlock, it's only a graze, not like poor Poole."

This was Gretna.

" What noise would you make if you had a proper wound ? eh ? "

Gretna chuckled, and Matlock could not help but smile. But it was painful trek back. Parallel lines of pain on his body made him weak and giddy. Matlock staggered along. His thoughts weaved in and out of his skull, like some deranged nomad.

" Focus, Matlock, focus."

This was Gretna again.

" Warwick, Conwy, keep an eye out on dis loopy ed case, will youse."

Gretna laughed again, her use of polyglot as much a tease as an attempt to help him concentrate.

The two individuals named now flanked him.

" Awright, blurt."

" Now we's gonna mindya, bastid."

" Way eye mon, wee swally time is roaring for us all."

" Big crash out on the way."

" You mean we can relax and have something to eat and drink, when we get back, "

Matlock managed to smile through the pain.

" Straight up, right down, with blag we do, boyo."

" Bollock droop if'n we don't," Warwick smiled.

" Out of the tree, we all will be, and we fly free, on a blagger spree."

" Yes indeedy whack jack. Four arts have we, now we do merry,"

This was Conwy.

" There's still the Fifth," Matlock gasped.

His balance was returning, but vision was still a problem. The group trooped foward relentlessly, dragging him along for company. It seemed an automatic process.

" Is that gob-dribble now ? "

" That gibber-spunk."

" The Fifth is as real as the long dead past, our kid," Warwick became more serious.

" Warwick, tell geezer."

" Thou art the twat."

" I'm serious, sort of," a wave of pain made Matlock cringe, then he continued,

" Lanark went in search of it, did she not ? "

" He is seriously chewing on this, Warwick."

" Aye...she died crowning loopy for her pains."

" Look..ow..straight talk. I believe there's something in it."

" Pain, madness and death, to be sure," Conwy added.

" You want straight talk...fine. It helps relieve the boring walk home and keep your mind off the pain."

" Your Grandfather went, Warwick."

" He did. He made the long trek up the mountain, to see the Mentors, as the Mundanes call them. Trouble is, he froze to death before he could come down and enlighten us."

" It's superstitious jargon, boyo. We tell the Mundanes about the Mentors, to stop the war of all against all . It's good stuff, inspiring. But it don't exist, we know that, not properly. We know it's just a story, one that heats up the imagination and makes the sparks of wit fly."

" Besides which, if the Fifth does exist, could you have the temperament to hold it ? As the myth says - Those that seek the power of the Fifth go dead, diseased or delirious. Not much of value there, is there ? How can you enlighten the rest of us if you're sick, psychotic and silent...ha ha ha."

" It is a test, sure enough, as is every act of our lives. How could it be different. But it is a game, a game of deadly serious intent."

This was Gretna.

" Sorry, Madam, no disrespect intended." said Warwick.

" Aye none." Conwy added.

" None taken. Apologies taken all the same. You two are right, to a point. We organise our lives to have the best leaders and the greatest devotees. There is no other way. It has always been the means and the end. When you have the knowledge you three now have, you can be called knowledgeable, even worldwise, to a point. This will equip you for the community and keep you busy. But the further step is always there, to push that knowledge beyond. Do you attempt the further exam for love of the game ? Where every faculty is strained to the utmost, and so it becomes the life all pervasive, you understand ? "

" Sort of, Madam," said Warwick.

" Your words are got, Madam, " said Conwy.

" And how of you, Matlock ? "

" Erm.. don't understand all, Madam, feel I want it all the same though."

" Careful of desire, boy. Good answer though."

" Harwich and Kirk passed it, didn't they ? "

" They did too, I always forget them," said Warwick.

" It is easy to forget them. They keep quiet. Knowledge is a sobering shock. They function alright...Listen, you three, if you are interested we could rig the set up. If you want the Fifth we could get organised."

" Not me...the hazards are great, and the benefits I can't see."

" Spoken like a man of sense, Warwick...Conwy ? "

" Tis dubious,

Also curious,

Very dangerous

For any one of us...no way."

" Spoken with discretion. Well Matlock ? "

Matlock remained quiet at this time.

" Well..it could be fever talking. But ,all the same, l have noted your words. We shall small talk further, or maybe not. Time for you to recover first. Next up, we start chewing over this convo."

" Eh ? "

" This Conversation, Matlock. Look you, our outpost towers, we're almost home."

Gretna pointed. It was indeed the village. Matlock only saw the towers. The walls were sinking into the ground.

" Look lively you two, he's wobbling."

Warwick and Conwy caught Matlock as he nearly collapsed. They supported Matlock, who now saw the towers sink into the ground also.

" That was also that, " he mumbled, before he passed out.

" Howay the lad, gone for count, and he wants to take the Fifth."

" Easy, Conwy, we're all bringing it back home now."

And into the village they went.

Matlock came to in his room. It was two days after their return. Brief glimpses of memory made him cringe, but then he shrugged. There were one or two moments of gibbering delirium when he got back, but not much else. Gretna had already been to see him, along with Durness and Flint. This last person he had only heard of by repute. Gretna excepted, they had all been through the Fifth. Though she also dropped hints she had been and gone and come back (this was the way they referred to seeking the Mentors). It was amazingly simple. All they did was escort you to the gates, walk you to the foothills, then point out the route you must go, and left you to go if and when you pleased. If you were successful they would know it as you stumbled down the mountain. Something in your attitude could not help but be visible to the sentries. Then the waiting party would be assembled, to greet your return and escort you back to the village.

Matlock felt vaguely disappointed. There must be more than that. However, he was told, if he made contact with the Mentors he would realise that no other preparations were necessary. The dangers were more to the psyche than the body. What could cause such a shock ? Matlock could get no satisfactory answer to this. Only sarcastic smiles came from Durness and Flint. There were more hints from Gretna, along the lines of ' You must be prepared for anything, Matlock.'

And so the date was set for a week hence, to give him time to recover. Matlock was bored. That boredom had caused him to peer out the window at the brawl. And as he sat back, after the initial broadside of insults, someone shouted out that Matlock was the latest to try his luck up the mountain. They had heard also. Much ribaldry and abuse followed. Matlock leant out of the window again and made an obscene gesture, before quickly darting back in. Just in time, as another soft and mushy lump splattered on the wall opposite.

" Bog off toe rags," Matlock roared,

" Or I'll stick my weapon up your collective anus, and bring out the squeals, like the piggy-gits you are."

" Why drop shit on street as ye do."

But further comments were not heard. After this last insult the crowd melted away. This made him uncomfortable. The comments of the crowd distracted him from his own doubts, now they welled up again. What was he doing this for ? the community ? himself ? There was just the vague promise of knowledge. But what knowledge ? what had it done for others, beside death and madness. Those masochists, those sane survivors offered cold comfort as well. Durness was now a sarcastic little sod while Flint went all sullen. But they were honoured members of the community. Their decision was sought on a range of affairs, though always by proxy, for they appeared to have little direct contact with anyone. Still, the event had been put in motion. Matlock could back out, possibly. He knew he would not however. As soon as he toyed with the idea his curiosity opened up in response, all those doubts that nagged against his reason, if he missed out on going up the mountain, he might miss out something good.

And so the day crawled around. Matlock did not believe it. It did not seem real. No great ceremony ensued. Matlock was not expecting one, but he was expecting something, he was not quite right. His escort came in, business-like, marching him through the gates with no fuss. They walked in silence, exchanging grunts and monosyllables. At the base of the mountain they suddenly stopped.

" This is as far as we go," one of them said,

" It is your last chance to turn back. For once you have set foot beyond you must continue."

" We will stay to see you do."

This was Flint.

" But if I decide the climb is not worth it ? "

" Another reason why we stay. If you turn back, we shall shoot you."

" Seems a bit hard."

" Once you enter on this thing you can't turn back, boyo. That's why we give you the chance to turn back now. This is serious venture country, once you go, you go all the way."

" And if I can't go all the way ? "

Flint shrugged.

" Can't answer that, boyo, nor can you, till you go."

Matlock hesitated.

" You need to pick up the right frame of mind, Matlock, otherwise you're dead. We can't have all and sundry running up and down the mountain, they aint cut right for it,are you ? "

" Yes."

" Good."

" That's why we give out like it's some big quest. I won't lie Matlock. The climb is boring and dangerous. And, if you gain anything by it, you'll be strange to say the least."

" The Mentors will do that ? "

" Aye, maybe, but take nothing for granted, boyo, not even that name."

" What ? "

Matlock was dumbfounded.

" Gretna said you can do this. That your curiosity is insidious. It may help keep you alive. Frankly boyo, I have my doubts. Its why I gabb on about this last chance for you to turn tail."

A pause followed before Matlock replied,

" Seems a bit pointless now."

" Go on off with you then."

" Why not wish me luck."

A trace of a smirk flickered on Flint's face.

" You'll maybe have to make your own. But I wish you good as well as."

" Cheerful charlie you'll be eh."

" Ha ha, off my tree and out my box I will be, as will you, so walk lively."

" See you."

And that was it. Then came the climb, which was boring and dangerous. The slope was always steep. Matlock never got beyond a scramble throughout the initial ascent. The barbed wire perimeter was easily cut through. The minefield was manageable, with concentration. This was just the begining, to deter the unwary, it could not guard against anything else. Even here Matlock saw various tracks, tracks that increased with frequency once he negotiated the deterents. He had heard there were some dangerous cats around this territory. Matlock wondered how they could make a living on such barren land. An earthen slope gave way to a harsher, rocky landscape. The gradient extended from forty five degrees to almost ninety. A series of projecting ledges, like window sills, broke the arduous ascent. The climb tested his endurance, it was slippery. Footholds were maintained cautiously. At least the surface was not loose at all, though it was hard and unyielding. As each ledge was conquered he lay there, breathing hard. These pauses became longer as the climb progressed. About a third of the way up he came across the first bones. Thigh bones they looked like. They had been cracked lengthwise to extract the marrow. Matlock stared at first. But odd bones were a common enough sight. And hours after his first sighting he stopped registering them, they were frequent enough. There were mountain cats, goats and eagles on this mountain. Maybe some of these were not a threat, traditionally, but every living thing had to be treated with caution in these times. At least they would find the steep slope as hard as he did, he reasoned, hopefully. The bones came back to his notice again. For their numbers increased greatly. It was puzzling just how so many came to be deposited there. Matlock shivered, as most of his village knew, life could not be trusted anymore. All had tasted polluted water, or had chewed blighted plants, or devoured diseased meat. It made behaviour so unpredictable. It was not good, to be scrambling onto ledges, face first, with gnawed bones as your first sight. Matlock hurried as much as he could. He felt quite helpess, scrambling up the face of that mountain. What if something attacked ? Still, he kept any panic in check and sweated on. His arms were aching now, his fingers scraped sore. A desperate heave of his mind literally threw his body up onto that final ledge. That part was over. He squatted there awhile, taking in the next stage of the climb. Before him stretched a gentler slope, almost a plateau. Indeed it had its own small hills and valleys, even clumps of vegetation.

As his breathing subsided Matlock took in more of this landscape. The plateau rippled smoothly upward to the peak. The peak itself pointed upwards like a steeple. Matlock frowned. He would have to climb this as well. The place where the Mentors were, this was the highest cave on the mountain. Matlock squinted. There were a few caves that pockmarked the upper reaches, plus a few on the plateau itself. He used these as sighters to scan up to that highest pockmark. There, just below the snowline, was what looked to be the cave. That was the one, still such a distance away. He sat down, drank some water, ate some bread, from his meagre ration. Looking around, he spied his first skeleton of the climb so far. Wiping his mouth, and still chewing his last morsel, he went to investigate. It was a human skeleton, arms spread out wide, ribs pulled apart, both legs missing. Matlock was not perturbed. He saw worse in the field. But he wondered what had pulled the ribs apart. On closer inspection the jawbone was also missing. It suggested the predators were human, that certain parts had been removed tidily, in comparison to mountain cats. Cats tended to make a mess of the carcass. The obvious thought was of mani-coloureds. These mutants could be blamed for anything strange. It was nothing he had not seen before. Yet he was disturbed. He had to dismiss these thoughts as he walked away, but they would not die so easy. At least he could enjoy the sensation of walking upright, after crouching and crawling so much. It was almost leisurely. The first chasm soon pulled him up. A stone was dropped in it, it was quickly engulfed in the darkness, and no sound came back. Matlock scrambled around the delicate lip of the chasm. On the other side the skeletons became all to prevalent. And always they had limbs missing or broken ribs. Matlock fingered his revolver. Were there too many to be the work of mani-coloureds ? These bodies must have been past seekers, who failed. There was a thought he would have to come back this way, a thought he did not like. He would tell Flint about it, and Flint would shake his head, as if to say ' What did you expect.' He did not like the thought of that either. His barren surroundings influenced his miserable thoughts. Oh to be at home again, in front of a warm fire.

Instead he was on a bleak quest for an unknown outcome, full of hidden danger. Matlock began manoevuring the gentle slope, as the plateau rose to meet its peak. Sounds began to filter through his preoccupation. Light footfalls, no, it was too faint to be more than imagination. He stopped and listened - nothing. Warily, he continued walking again, never losing the hint of something following him. Again he stopped and wheeled around, nothing. On the third occaison his hands went to his revolver. He stood, ears straining. A faint breeze carried the sound away, but it was there.

Then a scream erupted in front of him. In one movement he twisted back to front and pumped two shots into something's face. The momentum of the mani-coloured's leap knocked them both to the ground. Matlock lay stunned. An already putrefying corpse embraced him, its decay had begun in life. He slid from under the mani-coloured, rejecting its fervent embrace. He tried not to look at its face, as he was tired and frightened. Because the look of these creatures always remained human, even with half the face blown away, it was the eyes. They retained the poignancy that constant pain marked on the intelligent mammal. And it would squeeze his heart, particularly as he felt so vulnerable. There was also the fear of disease of course. His training returned - they must be shot like the rabid animals they were. Matlock felt like a wounded animal himself, one in need of a bolt hole. He staggered on. Before he had gone a little distance he heard scraping and chewing behind. He looked back to see a mountain cat helping itself to the remains of the mani-coloured. So he was being stalked. If not for the nomad the cat would have had him by now. This thought annoyed Matlock. So he shot the cat dead. Two fresh deliveries of meat on the mountain might deter any fiurther predation. For who wants to struggle with a live one once the table is already laid. He had said this last thought out loud. He cursed himself with the realisation. He must get on with work in hand, suffer no distraction.

The air was thinner and the atmosphere charged, probably his exhaustion. Matlock focused on the steeple peak. The surface was corrugated. Matlock had to rely on constant momentum to keep ascending. Twice he did rest, in cave openings. But dark and stinking holes they were, with the excrement of birds and the skeletons of beasts, and the dust of...well...Every cobweb seemed to have its mother, brother, sister and lover in these places. Matlock wondered why he bothered. This futile exercise, scrambling and climbing. Always training for yet more hardships, using more self-disciplne, for a punishing reward. It was a tease, the promise of knowledge forever out of reach. But he could see the last cave now. He went out and climbed the last stretch without really noticing. His fatigue disappeared. This was it. He threw himself into that final aperture, the last of the gaping eye sockets. No cobwebs in this one, no excrement either, strange, probably too cold. There was debris everywhere all the same, bits of machinery, cold metal, broken weapons. A lot of it looked unfamiliar, advanced stuff. What a waste, machinery was scarce, he knew. But here there were wires and broken circuit boards everywhere. Matlock frowned. If just a fraction of this were intact he could find a use for it. Those machines, what were they called ? computers. There was one of them at the village, a squeaking, inefficent thing, always breaking down.

As he waded through piles of junk, Matlock looked, for what ? He did not know. He expected some kind of revelation. But none was forthcoming. The cave caught the rays of the Sun, and it beamed through the entrance. This made vision easy. Pile on pile of debris, of broken machines. Two corpses lay at the far end of the cave, propped up. They looked straight at Matlock, though the head of one was barely visible through a tangle of wires. Matlock recognised the unburied body. This was Larne. He did not look that different from when last seen. His body had mummified in the cold altitude, his skin stretched tight, impatient to burst its bonds. Larne's eyes were missing.' This is it ? ' thought Matlock, ' It can't be, there must be something else.'

Matlock scrambled through the boken piles aimlessly. Without thinking he uncovered the second corpse. This was Helston. Matlock could not believe it. This woman was almost mythical. She was a great leader in her time. Now no more than a dried husk on the floor. That fabled intellect, that vitality, sucked out by the years. Her right hand clutched a book, a journal it looked like. He had studied the journals of Helston at school. Her qualities were meant to be a match for the Ancients. Perhaps she could tell him something. For instance, what should he do now ? He was aware of a creeping paralysis, alarming for someone who prided himself on his alacrity. With impatient fingers he swept through the pages of Helston's most recent journal. Disappointingly, it read pretty much the same as his own recent experience, no breath of insight to put it all into place. She had not had his luck however. She fell while climbing the steeple peak, one leg was shattered. Rather than die in the teeth of a mountain cat, she had struggled into this cave to die in her own time. Matlock stood thoughtful, in admiration for this woman. She had the strength of will to do that then compose her own epitaph.

Then the subject matter of Helston's last entry engaged his interest all the deeper.

' ...This bastard mountain was a trick. No wonder the legend says all who try this go mad, or sick, or frightened. It is a ruse, to get the best from those restless souls, whom discipline and authority cannot condition. For, the horrible truth is - we are alone. There are no Mentors. There may not even be other settlements anymore, we have no proof, no contact. We are left to organise ourselves as best we can. So we bully ourselves to act civilised. We punish ourselves to maintain harmony. And we test those curious enough to question with tedious, pointless exercise. Now, here, I can see the point, not that it does me much fucking good...'

How Matlock scrambled down the mountain, he did not register. Two phrases had burned into his psyche - ' It was a ruse,' and ' There are no Mentors.' They had drilled his temples, making his head ache. He was not really conscious of any difficulty in descent. Strange it would have seemed, on another day, how relatively easy it was. But other considerations held sway. All the obstacles, they were just a stupid puzzle. The drilling pain remained as his desire increased. It was desire to destroy, to revenge himself on those manipulative bastards who staged this theatre.

Matlock spied the welcoming party on the foothills. They wavered in and out of vision.. Slowly they hovered toward him, like a swarm of erratic bees. He knew it was delirium moving him. But he did not care now. They did not care, with their stupid charade. They played with him as a director with an actor. He still had a gun, and he drew it to take aim.

" At least I can get that stupid bitch Gretna, with her woolly words on the meaning of life. One simple shot. They would cut me down. But it would be worth it. I'm already dead."

Matlock tried to keep his waving arm steady. But no, the pain was worse, enormous pain. Why ? what was this dart doing in his forearm ? They had him again. The ground came up to kiss him.

" Bloodyminded bastards tricked me again."

Matlock was carried home on a stretcher. Gretna and Flint lingered along behind.

" This one looks promising, Flint."

" You think so ? "

" I do, yes. And I believe you do too."

" You can't read my mind yet. Coz, if you did , you'd know I still have doubts."

" You always doubt, Flint, it's just you. I know there's no guarentees. But I was pleased by his reaction."

" You mean his anger ? "

" Aye, it reminded me of you."

" That's why I have my doubts. I had a terrible time curbing my resentment against the settlement."

" But you did."

" Don't give me that. You know this Mentors thing is presented in such a way, that the curious act like a cat with the sight of a mouse. I still resent it. I see the purpose of it, of course. But it made me feel so alone and, well, it's not pleasant."

" Aye, well, we'll have to see. A success is a success. And a failure just means we try again. We have to keep going, Flint, if we want evolve, to get back to where we were. We need people who are strong in shock and adaptable to change."

" It's true, I know it. It can be a shit life sometimes though."

They walked back the rest of the way in silence.

The Auld Alliance

On this historic Good Friday, the Irish have conceded the English have a case for self rule. It cannot be granted yet. Extensive negotiations will continue for some time. The different English factions need to discuss power sharing. Even then, it is not quite certain the English will be capable of doing it. But the principle of self rule has been established publicly at last. The interminable civil war in Britain is finally at an end. Centuries of unrest are now over, as are centuries of Irish control. London, or course, has always held the status of a free city, under concessions granted to the High King and President of Ireland. Cornwall is autonomous, with its Irish appointed governor. And Wales and Scotland have long been independent allies of Ireland, along with the Manx and Bretons. This grouping of the six core, celtic nations - Brittany, Cornwall, Ireland, Man, Scotland and Wales is known as the G6, or, more traditionally, the Auld Alliance.

Where once the Celts had ruled all Europe, now their influence has crossed the whole world. The Irish, Welsh and Scots have had established territories in the U.S, the Scots had territory in the Indian sub-continent. Whilst the Cornish, Bretons and Manx held a score or more townships throughout Africa, South America and Indonesia. The U.S, or to be more precise, the United States of Eastern America, were Irish in culture, with a Strong Welsh minority. (The Western half was dominated by Sino/Japanese cultures, with Alaska being Russian.) The Scots Dominion of Canada was as its name suggests. Australia was largely Irish in make up. There were still Celtic territories in Northen Spain, and historical enclaves in Bohemia and Cappdocia in Turkey. All territories were nominally independent, although the Auld Alliance continually meddled in their affairs in practice. The only nation to have no self determination whatsover was England. Together all these nations were known as the PCA - the Pan Celtic Alliance.

The PCA went back a few centuries, but the Auld Alliance went back to the days of the tribes. It was formed under the auspices of the Gauls, in order to defeat Julius Caesar's Romans. The Gauls thesmelves were defeated. However, the Auld Alliance of tribes shifted their rule to Britain. And once Britain was conquered, it switched to Ireland, where it has remained ever since. From their Territory in Hibernia (Ireland), the Celtic chiefs helped inaugurate the protracted guerilla wars, that meant the whole Island of Britain was never under complete Roman control. Caledonia (Scotland) remained free, and Wales only subdued with the help of huge garrisons. But the Romans were the best army in the world, possibly ever, and could not be pushed out, at first. This took the best part of four centuries. Even then, the assistance of the Germanic tribes of Northern Europe was needed. The superior discipline, and organisation, of the Romans could always be relied upon to push Celtic armies back. But the tribes learned. First they acquired Roman technology. Then they trained their warriors in Roman tactics. But there was a further, significant step. This was the appointment of a chief of all Celtic chiefs, an overlord, a

High King of Tara, who has ever since claimed, and received, the submission, and loyalty, of all Celtic peoples.

Now the Celts had a figure comparable to the Roman Emperor. Their squabbles coninued, this is true. But now they had a figurehead, that unified them in outlook, despite their different cultures. Now they became a match for the Romans, and they steadily pushed them out of Britain. Foremost, in these times, were the armies of Bishop Patrick and the legendary King Arthur. They took the fight onto continental Europe, and sought to gain the whole Roman Empire for the Celtic dominion. But the times were against this Celtic resurgence. The hordes of barbarians that troubled the Romans also troubled the Celts - the Goths, Vandals, Huns and Saxons. Even back in Britain the Celts had trouble with Raiding Saxons, who made alliance with rebellious Pictish tribes. Of more, almost fatal, consequence, was the quarrel between Bishop Patrick and king Arthur, over leadership. As apostle of the Irish, Patrick had converted all of Hibernia to christianity. While, Arthur, a Romano-British chieftain, waged continual war with enemies on all sides. And he defeated them all bar one. The Saxons had been employed as mercenaries in many cases. Patrick wanted their armies disbanded. The Saxons tried to exploit their quarrel to seize land for themselves. After many years conflict, peace was finally established. But the Saxons had gained a permanent foothold in Britain. Bishop Patrick, however, lost the right to make decisions on secular affairs, a position he had inherited from the Druids. Now all power passed through Arthur, down the hierachy of chiefs. Arthur was invited to become High king of Tara. He took the diplomatic step of marrying into the royal family of Ulster, the Red Branch, thus legitimising his power, and staving off future rebellion.

This decision was a master stroke. For internal conflict could have seen the death of the Celtic nations, if it continued. Instead, as so often in the following centuries, they rallied from the jaws of defeat to stand united against their foes. Their main foes were now revealed as the Saxons, now swarming all over the Isle of Britain. What further strengthened the Celts was the fact they made an independent treaty with the Papacy during this period. Thus they avoided the total submission to Papal Authority that so troubled the Holy Roman Empire a few centuries later. This left the High King alone with the supreme power. The High King was always elected. And it was always the most outstanding leader in the Celtic world. This person was not always Irish, but mostly so. Not all the High Kings were good, not all were remembered. But when the crises arose, the system of king ship, with the interlocking tribal loyalties that supported it, ensured the most talented were always equipped to make the right moves at the right time. This was just as well. For already the Celts had developed the practice of fighting among themselves to a fine art. The vice of needless bickering was also present. Some said this vice prevented the Celts from gaining even more power and influence. Though others argued the continual in-fighting kept them to a pitch of readiness and awareness, and this enabled them to deal with all crises, eventually.

The Celts have been the world's most influential peoples for a long time, if not the most dominant. Glory was theirs in so many ways. It was what they treasured, and was often pursued at the cost of more practical matters. For the Celts were always aware of the drive of history, of what would be written about a person's actions.

The Celtic drive and resilience was tested to the utmost in the era that followed the fall of the Roman Empire. Beset on all sides by barbaric tribes, The Celts were viewed as

the bulwark of civilisation against the Germanic and Asiatic
hordes, in the West anyway. In the East the Byzantine
Empire continued to abrogate that role for itself. The Celtic
enclave of Bohemia made the necessary alliances as each
tribe waxed and waned in power. It was overtaken, but
managed to survive. The enclave in Cappadocia, in Turkey,
had long been under Byzantine rule. It was absorbed but
not disposed of. Both these provinces remained outside
Western Celtic influence for some time. But the Celts of
North East Spain, the Galicians, were not. And neither
were the Bretons. These provinces formed the base for all
Celtic forays into Europe. And they were needed. The war
in Britain often gave the need for invasion from overseas,
on all sides. The Eastern half of Britain had been taken.
Even an area around Dublin, known as the Pale, had been
lost. Through some years of skirmish and raid the Pale was
recovered. Then the raiding bases of the Germanic tribes in
Scotland and Man were destroyed. And it was not before
time. For, by the Ninth Century, Norse raiders had joined
Germanic invaders. All were completely driven out of
Ireland. The waters around Cornwall and Wales were made
free from their piratic raids. Brittany and Galicia were
confirmed as seperate kingdoms. And, after, a protracted
struggle, the newly arrived Norsemen, in Northern France,
were placed under Celtic hegemony. Now The Saxons and
Norse of England strove to push West and subdue the whole
island of Britain. When the combined forces of Saxons,
now known as English, sought to extend themselves out of
Eastern Britain, that province known as the Danelaw, for
its large amount of Danish settlers, it looked as though they
might succeed. For theirs was a mighty army combined
of English, Danes and Norse. But they were beaten by
the Celtic Alliance, with their new Norman mercenaries.
Although the English forever sought their own alliances,

to exploit Celtic disunity. Yet the Celts ever rallied, under Irish stewardship. The Irish were now confirmed as the most powerful Celtic kingdom, as if there had ever been any doubt. They were seen as the most purely Celtic nation. They even developed their own Celtic church. This was nominally under the authority of the Pope, but in practice the Pontiff was dependent on Irish good will. The full flower of The Celtic identity made itself known through the Irish attitude to all things spiritual, cultural and religious. So their confidence never faltered when dealing with the manifold treaties of the trickster English. Those English that changed their allies as others changed their clothes. The Tenth Century saw the succession of pacts with various Danish leaders. The Celts were also hard pressed by Viking raids in this time. And the Danes forced their own case for settlement when the opportunity arose. After a protracted struggle, the Group of Six Celtic Nations were victorious yet again. They retained all their kingdoms. And then concentrated on the perennial English endeavour to push West. In this time, both English and Dane had produced great leaders, such as Alfred and Canute. Their endeavours spread the name of England to the vast majority of Britain. Yet still the Welsh and Cornish, under Irish overlords, pushed them back. Complete victory was never gained for the Celts, the English never admitted defeat. But there followed some decades of internal squabbling in England, with its Norman, Danish, and indeed Celtic enclaves.

During this dark age, the Celtic hierachy served its subjects with efficiency. These were universal times of violence and unrest. But the Celtic world retained its sophistication. The system of tribes, tirbutes, leaders, conferences, authorities and kings ever served them so well. It maintained the hierachy of the great and good, based on learning and ability, the true meritocracy of the ancient world, and of other worlds since.

Yet all Celtic ingenuity was tested to the utmost during the Middle ages. The English were a constant thorn in the side in this time. They made their continuous, and montonous, attempts to push Westward, and attain nationhood on the scale of the G6. Yet their actions always led to the inevitable Celtic reprisal. It was always the same story of raid, invasion, punitive expedition and counter invasion, and surrender of the English. What distinguished this period were the fluctuating alliances the English made with the French, in order to defeat the Celtic nations. The most intense activity within this period became known as the Hundred Years War. Needless to say the English and French cause was never pushed too far. They were always forced back to their original territories. Several Celtic leaders made the plea to destroy the English and French once and for all. But this could never be acheived. Eventually, the Anglo/French alliance was broken by a seperate peace treaty with the French. This act served as a marker to the end of the Middle Ages.

By the Renaissance the Auld Alliance were poised to become the dominant power in Europe. But a costly war with the Spanish delayed this achievement. There followed the rise of Protestantism. Some converts were made in Celtic countries, leading to brutal civil wars. Perhaps the existence of the Auld Alliance was only safeguarded during this period by the bloody, religious wars that erupted across Europe. Everywhere Catholic and Protestant fought, for a century and a half. These wars were most severe within the enemy nations of England and France. Although the newly emergent nations of the Netherlands and Germany now emerged as rivals also.

Belatedly, in the Eighteenth Century, the Celts began their colonial expansion. Irish and Welsh immigrants formed the U.S.E.A, the Scots developed Canada, Panama and Guyana. The Bretons, Cornish, Manx and Welsh co-operated in the establishment of trading posts along the West African coast. All the G6 co-operated in the formation of colonies in India (where the Scots became dominant), Australia (where the Irish assumed the major role), and throughout the smaller islands of Indonesia and the Pacific. This was not carried out without cost. For, despite the unwillingness of countries to be colonised, the expanding territories of the Spanish, Dutch and French often brought them into conflict with the Auld Alliance. Even the English strove to break out across the Atlantic. But their colonies were easily absorbed by the Auld Alliance. The Celtic colonies were ever the most succesful. By the begining of the Nineteenth Century, only France was left as a competitor to the Auld Alliance. Their rivalry culminated in one of the most protracted of wars. The French had one of the greatest generals ever, in Napoleon. Now they were reunited with their old allies, the English, under command of another great leader, Wellington. Ranged against them were adversaries just as worthy. The Auld Alliance were under leadership of Wolf Tone, the equal of anyone himself. The war went badly for the Celts at first. Continental Europe, North Africa, and much of North America, was overrun. Howver, Wolf Tone rallied the troops on land. And the brilliant Scots/American admiral John Paul Jones beat the combined French/English/Spanish fleets at Trafalgar. Tone invaded Spain, freeing Galicia from Napoleon's conquest. They gradually pushed the Napoleonic armies back out of Spain. A decisive battle was held at Waterloo. Here Tone defeated the combined armies of Napoleon and Wellington.

Now the last impediment to Celtic hegemony was removed. The Auld Alliance was established as the only world power. It held this position for the rest of the Nineteenth Century, well into the Twentieth Century. The old Celtic homelands of Bohemia and Cappadocia gained some kind of autonomy. This was a measure of Celtic power. For they could hardly be considered Celtic anymore. England was beset by a series of internal problems, including famine, poverty and political corruption. This rendered it quiescent for some time..

But Europe was never static, at least not for some long years to come. The rise of the nation state was seen thoroughout the continent. These nations began to see themselves as independent states rather than as countries ruled by a greater power. Even England, with all its problems, began to whisper the idea of total independence. It recovered from its turmoil painfully, and began to assert its identity again. It was helped by a new ally, Germany. War broke out again. This time it looked as though the Saxon Alliance might win. It took a herculean effort from the Auld Alliance to defeat it. And then only with the help of American allies. The Auld Alliance, under another great leader, Parnell, eventually defeated the English/ German axis. It was a long and costly war. Conditions in England, still not fully recovered from the Nineteenth Century, worsened. Widespread rebellion broke out. It continued well into the 1920's. It was led at first by the politician, Edward Carson. Then, as things became more intense, solidarity weakened among the English. This gave the rival leaders, such as Churchill, to chance to exert influence. But the bloody slaughter continued. This time the Irish could not exploit English disunity. For the only thing that united the English was the desire to be free of Irish rule.

This civil war may have continued for decades. Parnell, the Irish leader, was more than equipped to deal with the interminable decsion-making that followed, as was his rival, Churchill. Then came De Valera, eventually replacing Parnell in the 1920's, a trickster to match either. But then a new leader arose in Europe, with dreams of empire. This was Adolf Hitler. And he pursued his aim with ruthlessness. War broke out again. This time England was neutral in the greater war. But the Auld Alliance still found itself pitted against most of continental Europe, who were now fascist states. De Valera had to make extreme economies at home to raise the finance to fight this war. As did the other members of the G6. In fact, all members of the worldwide Celtic Commonwealth, the Pan-Celtic Alliance were drawn into this war. Large amounts of money had to borrowed from the Americas. This enabled the Celts to pursue the long and costly conflict that was the Second World War. Germany, Japan and their allies were ranged against them. The conflict was exhaustive, but again the Celts emerged as winners. The Celtic world was now bankrupt. Huge debts were owed to the U.S.E.A. and Canada. In the post war years the other members of the G6 established their complete independence. Other Celtic states worldwide now declared their loyalty to the G6 to be only historical. The English were the exception. They were still under direct rule, well into the 1960's. Attempts at English Parliaments were made, but they failed miserably, degenerating into sectarian violence. The next forty years were dominated by terrorist attacks. The main point of contention was between the English who wanted some link to remain with the Irish, and those who wished for complete independence. Social unrest dragged on into the 1990's. Finally, a true peace deal was brokered, by the Prime Ministers of Ireland, Scotland,

Wales, Man, Brittany, and the Governor of Cornwall, under the watchful eye of the President of the U.S.E.A.

England gained peace with autonomy, and the option of complete independence in the future. The one country we have always contested, always beaten, but were never able to subdue. Now they were off our backs. A fact that has forever irritated me about the English. Why did they never accept Irish supremecy ? or the Celtic hegemony ? Despite all the Celts have acheived over the centuries. Despite the conflicts, we could have worked together. But no, the English believe England to be the best of all possible worlds. This is their breathtaking arrogance. Nothing outside of their own territory is of the slightest importance. It has often been said the Celts wished to rewrite history according to what should have happened. Of course they then went out to create history in their own image. The English, meanwhile, were content merely to dream and be rebellious when called upon to action. Now they are begining to run their own affairs, they can enjoy their dreaming dotage, constructing worlds where ever they can succeed. They will also have more time for fighting among themselves, a habit they have developed to a greater degree of complexity than have the Celts.

The Parable of the Blue Arse Fly

And lo did the prophet walk, in his brand new second hand suit. He was the chosen one. It was his turn to do the photocopying. And thus did the only begotten son of bureaucracy stride purposefully, on the straight and narrow way, if a little slowly. And the multitude did notice him as he sloped by. Always they had known of him, but usually he had sleep in his eye. On this day, his gaze was ablaze with the wondrous vision of the greater good. He was daydreaming about his holiday in Lanzarote. But the multitude did gaze upon the serenity of his countenance. And they went and spake unto him, when they cornered him in the photocopy room.

" Speak unto us, o prophet of the office. Speak unto us of the the greater glory, that emanates from the divine presence that pervades all..."

" Or give us a tip in the Three Thirty at Kempton." added a nasal voice.

The owner of the nasal voice was summarily beaten up. The multitude continued,

" Speak unto us, o prophet. And we shall assess thy bidding, put it through the proper channels, and you'll hear from us in a months time."

" About what ? "

" Your impending beatification and canonisation."

" Wow, I only came in here for a few copies."

" For thou art the light that will shine to guide us on our way."

" Well yeah, I did go for union steward, but that was turned down."

" Turned down in favour of the greater calling."

" No, I don't want to be an office manager."

" Thou hast received a far greater calling."

" You mean C.E.O. ? I don't believe it."

" The summons from the most high."

" I thought the Director was off sick."

" Thou will now giveth the lesson for today."

" The what ? "

" Those words of wisdom that do dispense enlightenment and instruction."

" Can't it wait till the monthly meeting ? "

" Thou hast been called and must answer the call."

" I've already been to the toilet."

" Thy servants await thy instruction."

" Don't you think you're going over the top ? "

" It is always within the guise of the wise to project humility. But if thou cease from dispensing thy word, thou will be beaten with fierce knocks and buffets."

" Can't I have a coffee first ? "

" Thou must earn thy reward."

And lo, did the only begotten son of bureaucracy make to slope off again. Yet the multitude would not deign to permit his weasel-like characteristics. Since many had come far to see him, some from as far as the second floor.

Therefore they suffered the office prophet not to leave until they got their money's worth.

" The Chosen One must fulfil his calling."

" But no one said anything to me."

" The power that lies behind everything moves in ways most mysterious."

" Could I have that in writing ? "

" Now is the time for the deliverence of the word, the word that giveth and sustaineth, and absolveth us of responsibility."

And lo, did the multitude press foward menacingly, upon the only begotten son of bureaucracy. And thus was he fortified in his struggle against confusion, to give utterance to the word, that would enlighten the assembled multitude, and maybe stave off a good kicking into the bargain.

" Er, right, you want me to tell you a story, right ? "

" Thou hast been chosen to spread the word."

" Well, once upon a time..."

" But not in that direction."

" Er, alright, er...There was this Englishman, Irishman and a Scotsman..."

" Nor that one."

" Er...Did you hear the one about..."

" Do not test us, o prophet, but lest slip forth the utterance as the spirit moves thee."

And lo, did the multitude get a bit peevish.

" Er, um, it all started when..."

" No."

" A funny thing happened to me on the way to the office..."

" No."

" Er, unaccustomed as I am to public speaking..."

" No."

" Er, hear ye, hear ye..."

" No."

" First off, there are some people I'd like to thank, without whom this wouldn't be possible..."

" No."

" Hallo, good evening and..."

" Most definitely no."

And lo did the multitude lend their support and encouragement to the only begotten son of bureaucracy. They made offering of several knocks and buffets, and anointed the prophet with a box to the ears. These helped inspire the prophet on his way.

" I don't understand what you want."

" Instruct with the wisdom in thy possession, in the light of everyday action."

" Oh, you mean like a fairy story ? "

" Could be."

" Or a fable ? "

" Might be ."

" Or a parable ? "

" Should be."

" Right, erm, a parable it is then. But how do I start ? I have no experience in parabling, do I have to go on a course ? "

" Let the divine light inspire."

" I thought you might say something like that. Erm... well, erm, let's see, ah, er...There was this bloke, right, and this other bloke. And this bloke and this other bloke worked in the same place, in the same office, but not at the same desk. See, right, the bloke was a good worker, right, he worked real hard, all day and all night. No, he didn't work night coz he went home, but only after he'd done loads of overtime. And everyone thought he was a good worker, and everyone gave him loads of their work. Coz he was so clever and hardworking, and they were so slow and stupid.

And this other bloke, right, well, he's just as clever as the bloke, but he don't do nothing. See, coz he's a waster, a time server, a working stiff, a...never mind. He's lazy. He just does enough to get through the day. And people come up to him and ask him what to do, coz he's so clever. But he just shrugs his shoulders and goes off somewhere else. And he goes and has a cup of coffee. And he always goes home early, coz he says he's got to feed the kids. But he aint got no kids, he's just got a cat, and he never lets that indoors anyway. So, as time goes on, right, the hardworking bloke gets dumped with more and more work, and the lazy bloke goes off and has a ciggie. And, one day, the hardworking bloke has a heart attack, and the lazy bloke gets promoted..."

And lo, a silence befell the multitude. Then it bestirred itself to pester the prophet with questions.

" What is the moral of this parable ? o wise one."

" The moral is...oh wait a minute. It aint the hardworking bloke who should've died, it was the lazy bloke. He smoked himself stupid on all those ciggie breaks. And the hardworking bloke had to take on all his work. And, a few months later, he keels over from a heart attack as well..."

" What is the moral here ? "

" Erm, I dunno...erm, no wait. The hardworking bloke, right, and the lazy bloke. The lazy bloke is just sitting there, playing games on his computer. While the hardworking bloke is slogging his guts out. Everyones' coming up and asking the hardworking bloke favours. And he's getting up and down off his seat the whole time, going to see people. And all these different people are coming to see him. And the lazy bloke laughs at him. He says ' You're just like a blue arse fly, the way you keep getting up and down and buzzing around.' And the hardworking bloke takes exception to this. He says, erm, well, he goes into some really bad swearwords, which I won't go into here..."

" The mark of the wise prophet is always to show compassion at all times."

" Eh ? oh right, yeah, okay. Anyway, then the hardworking bloke says " You're just like a fat arse bluebottle yourself. Sitting there stuffing doughnuts and going chug-a-lug on the coffee.' To which the lazy bloke gets a bit miffed. He grabs a stapler and hits the hardworking bloke with it. But, in a freak accident, he accidentally staples the hardworking man's heart. And the hardworking man dies in screaming agony. Then the lazy bloke gets to take over his desk. And then the Manager walks up and gives him a payrise. And the moral of this story is...no wait, that's all wrong. It should have been the hardworking bloke accidentally killing the lazy bloke, with, er, I dunno, er...Accidentally giving the lazy bloke a bucket of strong coffee, which he guzzles down in one gulp, cos he's thirsty. Then he gives himself a heart attack when the palpitations start, er, so he palpitates himself to death..."

" What moral are we supposed to draw from this, o wise one who grows less wise, and will soon be smote down by the wrath of his despondent followers. "

And lo, as the sun doth cast its gaze and burn those who stand under its rays, so the multitude gained light of the prophet's ineptitude.

" Er, um, the moral of this story is - don't guzzle your coffee, or is it be careful with staplers..."

" Thou hast been weighed and found wanting."

" I didn't ask to be followed. I just wanted a photocopy and a cup of coffee. "

" But what, o less than wise one, is the moral of the blue arse fly and the bluebottle ? "

" You've got to be like the bluebottle."

" Thou saith it so."

" No, hold on a minute, like the blue arse fly."

" Why ? "

" He's the good one."

" Why should we work unto death ? "

" Eh ? I never said that."

" Thou didst."

" You get a nice gift at your retirement party, that's one reason."

" Thou hast given the bluebottle a better life."

" No I didn't."

" Yes thou didst."

" I've got nothing against bluebottles, but it's the blue arse fly you have to follow."

" And work until we drop ? "

" No, just work hard and be good."

" While the bluebottle has coffee and cigarettes."

" No, he's a lazy git."

" With a better life."

" No, in the end he doesn't have one."

" But thou messed up the end."

" Look, I did the best I could. I didn't ask for this. But if you like the bluebottle better, fine. I would recommend being the blue arse fly though."

Here ended the lesson of the only begotten son of bureaucracy. It was weighed, and found wanting, in every way. The multitude were in deep sorrow at being led astray by a twat. A twat who they once believed at least shone with the divine presence. But who, on closer inspection, was revealed to be wearing cheap aftershave and nylon underwear, and who daydreamed relentlessly about cheap package holidays. Therefore did they purge their embarrasment, by beating the crap out of the only begotten son of bureaucracy, but he was forgiven his sins...

The teacher closed the huge book with a hefty slam, waking most of the sleeping children.

" And so, children, what moral do we draw from this story ? "

" Don't be a fly."

" No. Malcolm you try."

" Try what ? "

" To answer the question."

" What question was that ? "

" Why is it better to be a blue arse fly than a bluebottle ? "

" I give up, why ? "

" I'm asking you."

" Why ? don't you know ? "

" I want you to tell me."

" I dunno."

" Mark, do you have any idea."

Mark shrugged his shoulders.

" Right, let's start again, from the top shall we."

" The top of what ? " said Malcolm.

" The Parable of the Blue Arse Fly."

" What ? are going to hear that one ? "

" Yes, again."

The teacher was begining to lose his temper, but was mindful of the fact he needed his composure.

" It's shite anyway," said another voice.

" Is it really ? Would you care to explain further ? Ray."

The one known as Ray had a brief attack of shyness, but then went on,

" Yeah, I mean the man was an idiot, right. He couldn't tell a story. And he couldn't make a bunch of idiots get the point. And the bunch of idiots got angry, coz they're so stupid. Coz they thought he was something special, just coz of the way he looked and how he talked. So they followed him, right. But then they found out what a dozy twat he was."

" And you draw no meaning from that ? "

" About what ? "

" The fact that people were conned, taken in by appearance. And when they found they had been conned, it was their own fault, and this made them angry, more angry than usual. Because the person they had chosen to follow was not worth it. "

" I liked the first part of Ray's answer, " said Malcolm.

" And what was that ? "

" That it was shite."

" Would you care to expand on that ? "

" Yeah, it was a big, huge dump of a shite."

" No, Malcolm, for all your cheek, you cannot disguise the fact you are fundamentally thick."

" What ? "

" As opposed to the others, who are merely dozy, except Ray, who is twice as thick."

" You calling us names ? "

" No, just stating the obvious, Malcolm."

" So, what if we called you a stuck-up, pompous toad's turd, with delusions of experience, when you're just a jumped up little fart in badly-fitting glasses. The only qualification you've got is the fact that other people call you a prize plum. Your only talent is the fact you can wash your hands without dropping the soap, and you carry round rotten fruit in your pockets, which you're scared to eat, in case you have to buy more. What do say to that ? you screwed-up, fucked-to-bits, bum boil."

" Wow, I 've never been awarded so many titles in my life."

At this point a surly security guard intervened.

" Right, that's your lot for today boys. The Prof. here, out of the goodness of his heart, arranged this seminar for you. So you can listen to stories and play around a bit. I think he's too soft myself. But he was willing to take a chance on scumbags like you. And how do you repay him ? By acting like stupid little boys. It's back to your cells the lot of you, and no apple tart and custard for tea this evening."

The surly security guard opened the door and the prisoners filed out in silence.

" Oh Guard, I just want to borrow this one for a short while longer if I may."

The teacher pointed to Ray.

" This, you couldn't use this one as a floorcloth."

" I just want him to get me a few photocopies."

" If you must."

" Thank you. Now ,Ray. If you'd oblige me by copying the notes I've made on todays seminar."

" What ? "

" Get these bits of paper copied."

" Oh alright."

Ray slouched off down the corridor. The security guard and the teacher both shook their heads in disgust as he did. Soon he would be out of this prison. Then he could go back on his holidays, if he was lucky, if he worked hard, if he got a job. This daydream fortified him for the boring task ahead. He had to walk past the office crowd first. And lo, did the only begotten son of bureaucracy make his appearance before the multitude. They noticed his visionary gaze, his divine countenance, and at once left their desks to seek the wisdom of this prophet, after they cornered him in the photocopy room. Etc etc, so it goes, round and round, on and on, or whatever, ad infinitum, this great wheel of destiny, or fate, or fortune, or whatever, that drives us up the wall and round the bend, or whatever...

The <u>Great Bowl Out of Bold</u>

' As you may be aware, we have a special guest here today, the world's foremost expert on Bold. And, no, I don't mean the washing powder. I am refering to the little known, mythical kingdom that was a contemporary of Atlantis. That controversial kingdom people claim is not even a decent legend. If Atlantis is scoffed at by scholars, Bold is guffawed at. There is not even the proof of a rumour that Bold existed. Well recent archeological discovery may mean we shall have to rewrite history, or not, as the case might be. Certain artefacts have presented themselves in peculiar places. Now experts place their chins in their hands and go " hmmmm " a lot. There is certainly food for thought here, so I've been told. To enlighten us further, may I present, the biggest Bold expert now currently working, since the last one - Professor Random Lee, Head of Fantastical Diatribe at the University of Dodgy Witness, London.

' Thanks, in kind excess of sorts, thank you... Class, let me start just by denying my position with the utmost uncertainty, and forever relying on never ever trying. For my subject, as it were, wearing well in the common weal, is the great bowl out of Bold. Endwise I have five minutes for questions, answers will be forthcoming, but don't wait up. As you were listing to the intro geezer, Bold is big mythical thingy, magog magog, jig-jig, big invisible power like concluded over all. Bits make themselves known from undersea antique venue, wherein once was - " The Mighty Country of Bold where delve live men, whose life story has not been written down yet, " So sayeth the Soothsayer Solon of the Scythians in Solitude, in early antiquated era.

Mythical thingy though it was (or wasn't), historicalised persons, engrossed in anaemic study, confuted its very persistence in the yarns of man. Moreover and done with, they thought in their theories confounded. Greatest civil-eye-sore-lotions did not even persist in remotest fantasy times. And those who held contrary to expectant, idealised sobrieties were treated as certifiably inane. Bold became sold to multivaried purveyors of the dreamy-eyed lotus occultypists. Yet ever, forensical proof was constant, in not forthcoming to their faith-held theories, of paradox of civil-eye-sore-lotion, before humankind people learnt to exploit tactics on each anyone individually.

Tis said Bold twas land of old gold, utopian top o't'tree in socialisation-legislative apparatus thingy. Science bods sat mathematically inclined, sages stored scholarly know-how, smartie-pants stuff in huge libraries, guarded by huge librarians. Strange, mythical, gimmick-like griffin types roamed the pasteurised land. Legendary heraldy beasties kept for dinner in huge pens as well as.

Politickles was their fancy. Every movement debated and overstated, as their law was consumated. Egalitarianess dominated the fated Boldians therefore. Fairs fair justice for all commie society it was indeedy.

And yet, in their picture book paradise, they still denied the old Bold goddess " Satisfactory, " from whence comes our noun, " factory," which originally meant a place where people, or like-minded things, gather together to be satisfied. Of course its meaningless was reversible in time since that one. " Satisfactory," amazon goddess of proud people since before the land was about to rise up. To her they used to shout - " Don't tread on us, big, Bold goddess. If you don't watch your footing, you leave big, sticky mess." Though big, old Satisfactory was ignobly ignorant to fat cats of Bold (Toward the intermission, before the first melodian of man), she had long-size, biggy big remember space. She marked down pupils of Bold who forgot what they were told, and screamed vengeance of sorts, well sort of vindictive, down on dozy heads below. Some sorts say twas consequential in its inevitableness. Boldians grown askew from rootedness past in historical times. Complacentricities wired their downturn. One sparko natural catastrophic would ever be fuel to blow Bold kingdom skywards to kingdom come.

Yet some paltry few scholastic dispositions guessed apocalyptically correcto on their odds being nowt. And tail turned discretely did they and quested off, in search of the premise of a promise land. Just a minute, incidentalise, as they disgorged themselves thither. Bold blew up in volcanic oversurge. Earth crack 'n' tickle all over. Big snidey wave creepo cover all Bold. Land dissolve just like cardsharpers wallet piece, vanished, traced not within or without. Cerebral citizens, dumbfounded to a man, all the accumulators of won past facts and figuratives could not behold them sleep, peaceable wise, add infinitum. Insteado, pluck down agony-wise into deepest, smelly type bowels of Ma Earth. To which all pudding proof dissolves in lore legend.

Until which was, only or so it was, two yearo ago. Big libation-type, ceremonial, shamaniacal bowl found. Inscribed were inscripto's in on its perverse surface - " Property of Mister Mystery, Freelance Alchemical Gentleman, Availability for parties guarenteed, 10 Cairn-

By-The-Well of Fruitfulness, Mythical Avenue, Bold 14, 2 for 1 at Tesco's 2.99."

Various decipherable types accrued, agreeing, and judgement made it genuine. Thereforesoever contruded relic piece to be genuflect souvenir of hoary, old-time place of Bold. Excepto, say that is, one authoritarian, who boldly claims Bold story-theory rings true as false thingy would. Several and more itemised ceremonials, of likewise artifice, are clear crystal-like sold at hypermegasuperdupermarket, bland stores up, down and around the land and before, and always were. Academia been lured out its lair, and coaxed by a hoax into a snare.

So, the contorted riddle is still gone spare, the legend goes on, without a care. Yet Bold lives long, in epic imagine of golden era ,fusty boots romance, etc etc, and forever will be. For you can poke a snook at history, but you can't lay down with a mystery. The ague rages everward and mote it unrelentingly be.

Hands up up will now be quested and disgusted answers. Yes, you sire, in the knobbly head...

Questioner : What are you talking about ?

' I see-saw, yes you willing, very to penetrate perpertrations on lecher, and shout about lectern. This academic-wise, big brainy, nicey-nice disgusto. If thou don't want a fluffy conflab in bourgeois manner, then slake off to little boyo room... nexto, yes miss-you, with the hirsuite hands...'

Questioner : Is Boldy bowl bigggy fake-o or what if opinionated ?

' Opininionated is out to lunch on the matter. Mucho fake-o bowl easy got at garage petrol. Yetto big boil doubt remains genuine... nexto, misso floor-length sleeves. '

Questioner : If iggy pan on the man saw Dan as a tran in the van withtout a plan, would he cause a catastrophe to collapse upon calamity.

'I sorry, I don't quite understand, your dialect will have to be translated first before I answer such a question... nexto

Questioner : Aren't thou not guise ? huge-o, biggy-big psycho, on run from nice and cosy armchair established lockplace ?

' My pursed lips assistobody answers all and sundry of the nosy variety. You will have to make written reppo, nosy bastard request...'

' I'm sorry that's all we've got time for. We will have to close this most enlightening lecture. I'm sure Professor Random Lee has made the current situation clear regarding the great bowl out of Bold. I certainly could not have explained it more succinctly. Those of you hoping for more should note that Random Lee is next speaking on the 21st. of next month, at the Plain English Society.

Anaemic Acadaemia

It was the greatest palace of learning in the country, historically. It had no name but Acadaemia. Its tradition alone meant it needed no other. Other institutions may exist, but Acadaemia was the original. The original still had the reputation. A degree taken behind its august portals usually set the graduate up for life. Until recently that was. Professor Hackett was its most recent Dean. He was as proud as anyone could be. He only needed to survey the lists ;- of past Deans, past professors, past pupils who had gone on to greater things. Many were great statesmen, scientists, artists, and men of letters. However, all that was some time ago now. The last person of any note to attend Acadaemia had been a politician. This dubious person had distinguished his career through bribery, corruption and sexual vice. Then he had the gall to write it up in a best-selling autobiography, after he had taken the necessary steps to assure his immunity from prosecution. That was a mere fifty years ago. This was not so embarassing to Professor Hackett as the fact the College now had to admit female students. In his own biased opinion, females were nothing but a distraction to learning. Even his poor wife, who committed suicide years earlier, agreed with him. Apart from this, Hackett believed in equality of opportunity, providing students had large incomes, to afford the massive college fees, they were given every opportunity. This meant the college was never prejudiced, not even to the poor, as they could not afford to even gaze on the place they never turned up anyway. But, if someone were to sponsor a poverty-stricken wretch, to the tune of an astronomical sum, then Hackett was happy to oblige.

As Acadaemia had history, undergraduates queued up to deprive their friends and families of huge sums of money, to learn subjects redolent of a golden age (and more relevant then too, the bitter critics argued).There had been a place of learning there since time immemorial. Legend had a druids' grove on the spot, tradition a Roman Temple. There was definitely a monastery. Then a rich merchant endowed a place of learning, before he absconded to foreign parts with a lot of other peoples' taxes. The merchant was excised from the records, but the college was given a royal charter. Professor Hackett was prone to sighing, so much history, and none left to make anymore it seemed, not even a hint of purpose to keep them going, beyond tradition.

The College had a unique tradition of breeding its own. Future dons were born and raised on the site, in separate family quarters, far from the maddening mass of the illiterate population. They served their academic apprenticeship as students, for some years longer than the usual undergraduate. Some outsiders were admitted, but they had to study at least five years longer. Here again, applicants from all over the country, and abroad, were lured by the history of Acadaemia. Unfortunately, the balance of power had shifted within recent generations, the proportion of outsiders had increased as students bred on site became increasingly sterile. Although this condition proved suprisingly infectious among the outsiders after a generation. Doctors blamed something in the air, then shrugged their shoulders, bewildered. Worse than that, however, was a growing lack of respect. Hackett had divined a tendency among students to treat Acadaemia merely as a career move. So when they left they could obtain any job they wished, simply by mentioning they had attended this august establishment. This had always happened before of course, but now students were so blatant about it, where had discretion gone ? They did their time here before moving onto greener pastures. Hackett hated that phrase, but he could do nothing about it.

In previous times he had power of life and death over students. He still liked to terrorise them of course, this was part of tradition. Students must feel intimidated and unworthy at all times. In previous times there would have been no talk of ' career moves.' Acadaemia's vision of the truly educated, integrated man would have been enough. And wherever they went in later life, graduates would forever pine nostalgically. For times spent at Acadaemia were the most significant in their life, it was downhill from there. However, now everybody moved on, it seemed, there was more money elsewhere. There was more incentive as well. Since Acadaemia only gave a education rooted in atniquity, many felt unable to cope with modern world when they left. Some even took another degree just to be able to readapt to the world. Acadaemia was seen as too isolated from the world, many questions were raised as to its relevance. Professor Hackett was infuriated by these questions. Luckily he could still intimidate enough people in the wider society so Acadaemia could maintain its status. But he knew, eventually, the philistines would win. It was a shame, people who did not merit a reply now seemed to ask Acadaemia to justify it existence. They made the complaints of unenlightened, uneducated, uncouth and uninterested types. Hackett could not even explain Acadaemia's vision to these people. He had to justify it in crude monetary terms, only then did their stupid faces show any sign of life within. Therefore, the more hardheaded economists among his adverseries easily dismissed his arguements.

Reluctantly, Hackett had to concede that Acadaemia was indeed decrepid. As he had substantial dealings with the outside world, he began to realise how cobweb-ridden his own kingdom was. He began to look on aspects of his own life with growing discomfort. He lived and taught within decaying, dank, dark and dusty buildings. His staff were a collection of bloodless pedants and psychotic eccentrics, the typical inhabitants of Acadaemia. There was no escaping the fact they had all become institutionalised, like prison inmates. The staff room was about as lively as a conference of the undead. Numb silence reigned over all, punctuated by obscure arguements made from strange tangents. Hackett suddenly developed a strange complusion for fresh air.

For too long Acadaemia had justified its existence by reputation alone. This was authoritarian, uninspiring. Teaching and learning alike became regarded as chores. Hackett had tried recruiting new blood. For with new blood came new ideas, so he thought. What he gained was confrontation and arguement with the established staff. This was carried out in the muted, convoluted fashion now so common in Acadaemia. And of course it never ran its course, it just dragged on interminably. One thing was established. The staff disdained new ideas. Ideas that had no longevity had no merit. The new blood could not be bothered taking up the arguement. They quickly succumbed to the apathy of Acadaemia. Those few whose indepedence of thought did not atrophy soon moved to pastures cleaner. While the old blood continued to pulse in its senile fashion. Hackett detected some irony in the situation. There were now so many people who had been frustrated by Acadaemia. And now some of them were politicians, who had power over Acadaemia's continued existence.

Hackett tried to counter this trend. He looked to restore links with the local community. This was a colossal blunder. For Hackett had forgotten to note the impact of social change in the surrounding area. The last local student had been drawn from genteel rows of terraced houses, almost twenty years ago. The terraced housing that remained now would have been condemned, if anyone could have been bothered. What dominated the area now was a massive housing estate - conceived in the 50's, started in the 60's, and not finished till the 80's. Bad planning and shoddy execution had plagued it all the way. The end result meant Acadaemia was surrounded by a warren of social problems. Hackett found this out to his cost. He was not hurt but shocked. He found himself arrested one evening for breaking curfew. Every male who loitered on the estate, after ten o'clock, was asking for trouble. But Hackett was undeterred. The authorities tut tutted, but he decided to help the local community. His assisted places scheme worked wonders at first. His new intake of students took to learning avidly. Unfortunately they brought their social problems into college with them. Vandalism and drug abuse increased. Teachers were routinely assaulted. Hackett admitted that generations of ignorance and neglect could not be made good in his classrooms. Besides, the police and the council constantly nagged him into excluding certain types. He regretted the forced expulsion of these students, but there were no resources available to deal with them.

Now the bullying local council really came into its own. Acadaemia's funds had always come from patronage. In the past aristocrats had endowed the college. Recently local government and business had tried to do the same.

Both tried to dictate the curriculum. This failed. But they did succeed in dropping a welter of tests, exams, certifcates, marks, diplomas and assessments on Acadaemia. These were not only used on students, staff now had to constantly fill in forms, in the hope of justifying their continued existence. The result was inevitable confusion. No one knew how this new bureaucracy could be administered. Hackett complained in vain. His notion of a well-rounded education, although rooted in antiquity, at least had the merit of making some sense. But the world was more specialised now, populated by office managers. In his desperation, Hackett looked for a way out of this impasse. He thought to rely more on the subsidy of businessmen. Yet the businessmen he flirted with were only interested in profit. So they decimated Acadaemia. Staff were sacked in droves, student numbers increased, and the amount spent on materials reduced. For a brief period Acadaemia produced some talented engineers and accountants. Then the honeymoon period ended, such as it was. Acadaemia became just another boring college, offering boring lessons to boring students. In terms of boring qualifications, Acadaemia was not competitive enough, so the businessmen stopped their subsidy and moved elsewhere. The last resort had to be taken. This meant giving local government an increased role in running Acadaemia.

This move filled Hackett with trepidation. Local government was parochial in spirit, small minded in outlook, with its incessant regulations, its ocean of paperwork, and its bad-tempered bureaucrats. But there was no other option. Acadaemia was sucked into the bureacratic bog. Some of Acadaemia's woolly minds might have risen to the challenge. However, the administrative fog local government engendered, made their pedantic, hair-splitting, academic exercises as bracing as an Arctic gale.

The woolly heads were suffocated from within and without, most staff grew increasingly catatonic, as did most students. And through this fog sneaked a devious character, unknown to the catatonics. It was a councillor of dubious reputation, who was already suspected of shady financial transactions, though nothing was proved. He sold the site of Acadaemia to a property magnate, a close friend, and a mason, naturally. When this piece of furtiveness was discovered, it was already too late. The property deal had already become law. There was no redress to be had in the courts.

Hackett felt as though his person had been violated. The property magnate wished to turn Acadaemia into a combination of amusement park and shopping centre. There would be room for a small heritage booth, where tacky postcards and guide books, and tiny models, could be bought. This would help keep Acadaemia in touch with its past. This just rubbed in the outrage. But Hackett could do no more than splutter and go red in the face. The end came quickly. First, bland, young men, with their management speak and clipboards, began roaming around the college. Then short fat men with short fat heads began moving furniture out. Then larger, more menacing men came into the grounds, and stood there, with large, menacing dogs on leads, at a distance. Hackett knew that was his cue. He had to lead the staff and remaining students out of the building, otherwise they would be forced out. As he did so he was surprised to notice they only had five students left. These students loped off to find a pub that was open. Hackett's staff were left standing there bewildered, blinking in the afternoon sun. They all looked like Ancient Greek Philosophers, even the women. Hackett was also reminded of small furry creatures who had been forced into the open once their burrows had been destroyed.

All staff, including Hackett, managed to find employment elsewhere. There were still a couple of palaces of learning that time forgot. In the meantime, the property magnate went bankrupt within a couple of years. And a couple of years after, so did the council. The site was left to rot. Then some former students became nostalgic, and enough funds were raised to re-open the college as a museum and tea-room.

Plant People

David Russell was a flustered man. He had had a bad morning. There were irritating people pestering him. He knew he was bad tempered, and that this would account for some of the irritation. But the rest could be put down to the pests. Lunchtime could not crawl around quick enough. He took a walk to the end of the Common, to meet Ritch and the rest of them. It was only a fifteen minute walk, usually. However, on this day there was a large volume of traffic, pedestrian and motor. After a week of mild weather, the temperature had again pushed the high Eighties, for the second time this month. The heat rebounded off the sticky road, as if an oven door opened. Crowds of people dressed in weird, baggy things sought the sun. Briefly, David thought there must be some kind of sporting event on. For everyone was dressed in shiny, bright white. A collection of T-shirts with obscure designs, and shorts of weird provenance, were parading around. Or maybe there was a Sale on somewhere.

David was dodging the pavement traffic more than usual. He knew Ritch would be by the statue, at the end of a side turning, their usual meeting place on that patch of greenery. He turned toward his secluded spot to find it somewhat altered. Ritch was there all right, along with Chrissy, Kemal and Jackie. And some mysterious, but nice, looking woman he had not seen before. What made the greater impression on him was the fact his favourite, secluded spot was packed to overload. For a minute he thought he was on a Spanish Holiday beach. Every spare spot was occupied by sun worshippers. Where did these people come from ? David ranted and raved. Every working day of the year he came to this common. It was his space. No one else came here, apart from a few people walking their dogs, or schoolkids. Yet as soon as the sun came out, all these people came from nowhere and crowded the place out. Where were they the rest of the year ?

It was decided to go to a cafe for lunch. David's tantrums amused the others along the way. He was losing his balance, along with his judgement. He became aware that he was losing any chance of being in the mystery woman's good books by being a moaning minnie. But he could not stop moaning now, he was on a roll. He compared the Summer crowd to those rare plants that only poke their heads above the soil for a few days a year. They show off a few petals then piss off. They spent the rest of the year making zeds below ground, like these people probably. These people were stuck indoors most of the year. There should be a rota system for the Common. The amount of hours you spend on the place should give you the right to your own space, not like these Johnny-Come-Latelys. In terms of green time David had a stake in the place, his own space in the place should be staked out. This gave him priority over all these fair-weather, sunburn-addicts.

Ritch and the others laughter eventually perked him out of his rant. And he was acting like a letter writer to a serious newspaper, he was a serious twat in fact. Even so, he did feel there was a serious issue at the core here. Much as he humoured the others, for pointing out his bad-tempered ways, he would try to convince the others of the common sense in his argument on the Common. And it might get him in with the mystery woman also. Because she was a hormone raiser, to say the least. Although he was not being sexist here, perish the thought, merely lustworthy.

However, all David's attempts to argue his ground sensibly came to no avail. For he kept straying onto the same bad-tempered manner that made the others laugh so much. And he could not offer any more beyond - ' more time spent gave you more right not to relent your space.' This apparently gave you the right to ask newcomers to vacate your space when you wanted it, as if you paid for it. But David felt like he owned the place, at least a part of it, because it was part of him.

This might have gone on, into the night, as David's monologues were prone to do. However, his moaning monologue of an agony aunt argument was finally quashed by Ritch, who said -

" If you feel so bad about it, why the fuck did you take the job of park keeper in the first place ? "

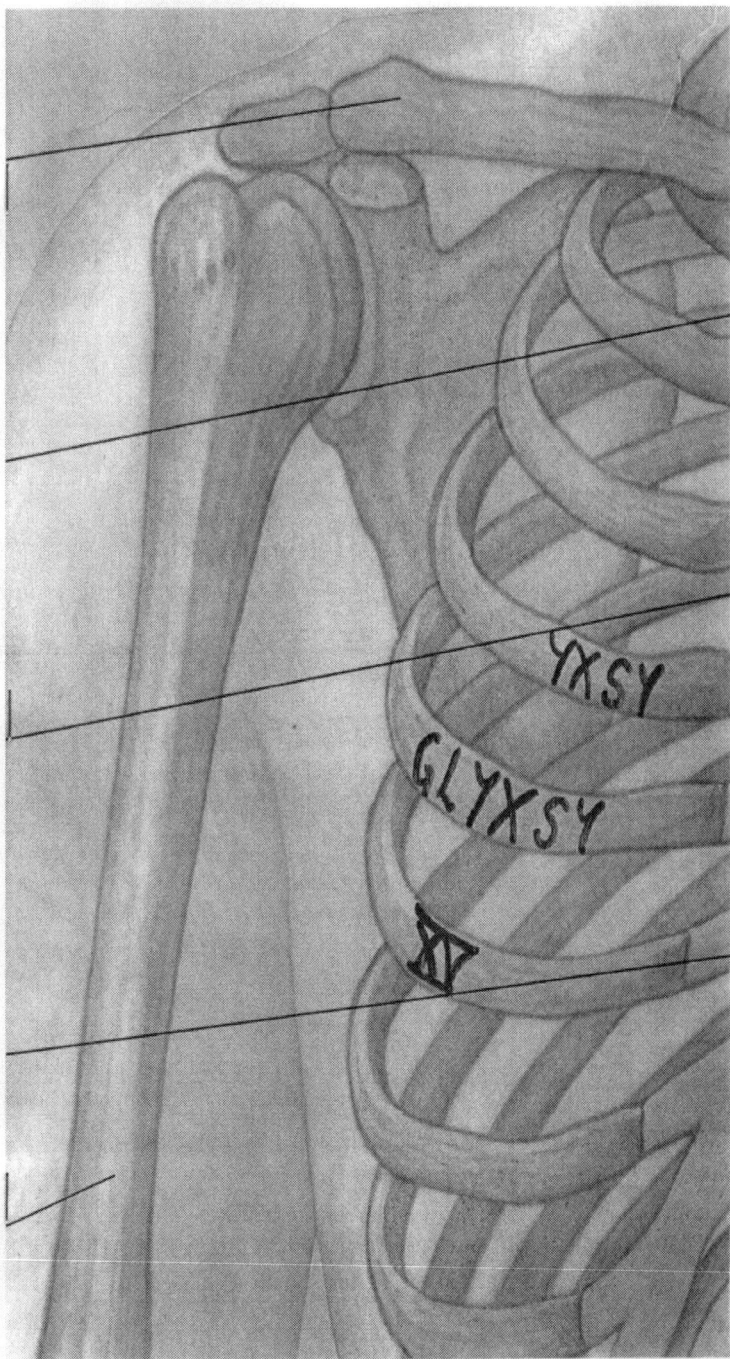

The Sour Dare

They were talking idly in the pub again. They always talked idly, it was just a question of degree. They had no interest in anything apart from making money and having a good time. At least that is what they professed. In reality, since they had all moved down to London, they had all moved on in their various ways. But they clung to the Friday night tradition. You could stack their Friday nights back to back and they would stretch awhile. But no one could remember how long. This was because Fridays were for getting well gone. Although, to all intents and purposes, they had had ten constructive years in this place, but they felt they were still wild.

Most of their crowd had families now. They were settled in long-term occupations. The city life was a pain, but had won them over also. A few dissenting voices did protest. They railed against their easy submission to the workyday world. But no one really minded. These dissenting voices always came from the same two people. The tones may have varied from time to time, depending on how drunk they were.

These two were Luke and Lucy. If you said their names quickly enough together it gave you trapped wind. And what they said often gave you indigestion, or was that a pain in the neck ? Luke and Lucy had become the conscience of the group, no one knew how. They had all sold out of course. No one did anything exciting anymore. Remember how they were all going to change everything. And of course no one could, even those with good memories.

They had all done something was the reply. All of them had got on in their various ways. The trouble was these various ways were too boring to remember individually. They looked at each other and shrugged their shoulders, and they yawned at Luke and Lucy, so what ? It was because these two had not done as much as the others. They were the most boring of the crowd, always complaining everyone had sold out, but they were the ones who always had money, because they never bought or did anything. They always had the steady jobs and the reassuring routines. Perhaps it was their lost past catching up with them. But then that was felt to be too harsh. For they had always moaned and did not need any real reason for their favourite hobby.

Luke found the others assessment unfair, not that it was necessarily untrue. He just wondered why people just shrugged their shoulders all the time. They were living in this big shithole. And, for all its wealth, that is what it was. Most of the residents were miserable, including them, most of the time. Everything cost way too much. And it was so fucking crowded. And if that was not enough, it was the weirdo capital of the world. Moan moan moan he would, but it never did him any good. The others began to shy away from him, after the yawning and the shrugging was finished. Luke was good at bringing the evening to a close.

And so Luke found himself around Lucy's again. She was the only one who would listen to him and, more important, agree with him. Everyone else only sighed before they told him to shut up. There was extra incentive also. She would sit next to him, stroking his hair, offering little ooohs of consolation. This wound him up all the more. For he made concerted efforts to get off with Lucy in the past, only to be rebuffed on all occasions. While every time he was moany (which was almost every time), she acted like Mrs Doctor, soothing the irate patient. Her bedside manner was excellent. But he never got further than the side of the bed. She was only playing at playing. This made his vitriol steam to boiling point. But he could not be annoyed with anyone for too long, especially when he was given a head massage. That tender touch that always hinted at further things to come, things that were unknown to him, since he never saw them arrive.

Perhaps this night was the culmination of all his past frustration. For Luke's patience finally went.

" Look, do you like me ? Lucy."

" What makes you say that ? "

" I was wondering, that's all."

" Well don't wonder too much, you'll get lost in your own thoughts."

" Very funny. It's just that..."

" What ? "

" Well, you give me the impression you quite fancy me. But every time I've made a move on you, you've blanked me out."

" What a romantic you are."

" Come on, Lucy, you know what I mean."

" And what do you mean ? "

" Do you like me ? "

" Why do you have to ask me such a question ? "

" I want to know."

" Because I wouldn't let you get off with me. That's it, isn't it ? "

" Er, sort of."

" Oooh, of course I like you, you idiot. But you're too clumsy a lot of the time. And you smell of beer a lot."

" Do I ? what always ?

" No, not always. But you can be a bit of a slob. I like someone to approach me in the right way."

" What ? all polite like ? "

" Could be."

" You're just teasing."

" Maybe."

" So maybe I'll write you a Dear Madam letter."

" I'm not a Madam."

" Not even a proper little one ? "

" No."

" Alright then, Dear Miss."

" I'm a Ms."

" Don't I know it. I ms my chance every time."

Lucy smiled.

" That's an improvement. You can't beat a bit of humour, and a lot of action. I like action men."

" But they haven't got any bollocks."

" I'm not talking about the boys dolls, I'm talking about the fully grown article."

" But they haven't got any bollocks."

" Hee hee. You wouldn't say that to their faces."

" Of course I would. I'd say it, but I'd make sure there was a window between us."

" Hmmm, I think you're all mouth and no bollocks yourself."

" I'm not that bad. "

" Yes you are. Always slagging off others."

" Like who ? "

" Stanley and Emma, Denise and Errol."

" What's wrong with that, they deserve it."

" You're always whingeing about them."

" I don't like lovey dovey couples, that's all."

" They're your friends."

" I know, but they're irritating."

" You think you're better than them, that's what it is."

" And you don't ? '

" No, not really. I just think it's all a bit stifling sometimes."

" Me too. You know they talk about us as if we're already an item sometimes..."

" What ? so we can make up the set ? "

" Probably. Would that be such a disaster ? "

" Yes it would, a domestic disaster."

Lukes' mood turned down.

" What do you want ? You say you like me, but you don't want to become steady. It doesn't have to be like that."

" What should it be like, then ? "

" It could be a bit better."

" A bit better for you, you mean. I can't give guarentees on what I feel. I just don't want to go too far at the moment. Because when it goes further it gets serious, and then all the arguements start. Having a friendship that turns into a relationship, I don't want that at the moment..."

So why not give it a go anyway ? "

" Look, you can't persuade me to go out with you."

" But you do want to anyway."

" Oooh, but you want a bit more intimacy, a bit too quickly."

" Of course. But I don't want to persuade you, I just want you."

She smiled.

" That's nice."

Then she frowned.

" Oh no, I'll not have you going all lovey dovey on me."

" Why not, if it's the truth."

" I don't want to go out with a soppy sod."

" I'm not being soppy, I just want to go out with you."

" You're just saying so you can get your end away."

Luke was shocked.

" How can you say that to me ? Haven't I always tried to be honest and up front, er, sort of..."

Lucy was impressed, but not totally convinced.

" Hmmm, maybe I should set you some kind of test, to see if you're suitable."

" What ? like a job interview, you mean ? "

" No, I mean the kind of test that was given to the hero, to see if he was worthy."

" Like killing loads of monsters ? "

" Yes, although I was thinking of slaying a dragon."

" Why ? is it your hobby ? "

" No, I'd just love someone to do it for me."

" They're a bit thin on the ground in North London."

" I don't mean literally. It's just a name for a task. It doesn't have to be about scaly monsters."

" Why not ? I know a few scaly monsters."

" Yes, but leave your family out of it, please..."

Luke paused for thought. The idea appealed to him.

" Okay, Ms Smartarse. Let's say, for arguments sake, I agree. If you set me a task, I'll do it, whatever it is. There's no backing out. If I complete it you're going to go out with me, and I mean for good. "

Lucy paused.

" Fair enough. Now I think you'd better leave."

" What ? "

" Nothing personal. But I have to find a dragon from somewhere."

Luke shook his head in disbelief and walked out.

" You let her string you along, all the time. She's just taking the piss, you know that, don't you. Why do you waste your time chasing a fruit loop like her ?..."

Errol's disgust only carried his words so far. Luke felt foolish as he sat there and sipped bitter with his oldest mate. Was there too much truth in this ?

" She always was a dreamer. I don't think she can ever be consistent. I wonder if she's all there," Errol finally added.

Luke frowned. Perhaps this conversation was getting a bit insulting. Errol sensed he was offended.

" No disrespect, Luke. I just don't like seeing you messed around, that's all. Slaying a dragon for fuck's sake, what does she think this is ? the Lion the Witch and the Wardrobe ?

Luke burst out laughing with his friend.

" More like the Liar the Bitch and the Dildo, " Errol said.

" I think she means a good old-fashioned dare. All this talk about dragons is just..."

" A pile of dogs' doo dahs,' Errol completed.

" Maybe, maybe," Luke giggled. " Maybe it is. But, like I say, it's a dare, a game if you like, a laugh..."

" And a song and a smile...Come on Luke, she'll probably dare you to do something really difficult, like take a bath..."

Luke was uncertain how to take that one.

" Are you saying I smell ? "

" No, of course not, well not that much."

" Not that much, you bastard."

Luke began self-consciously sniffing his armpits. Errol collapsed in giggles.

" I 'm only joking. Of course you don't smell...well, not that much."

" Don't start."

" Okay, okay." Errol nodded his head vigorously. He felt Luke needed placating.

" So, you're going to take this dare seriously. Are you off to slay the dragon," Errol started giggling again, " You know it sounds like a euphemism."

" A euphemism ? for what ? "

" I don't know, wanking I suppose."

" I think I better be off."

" Look, I was only joking."

" I know that. But I was going home anyway."

Nevertheless he was relieved to get out of the pub. Luke was irritated. He realised, with a shock, he was set on doing this dare.

The next time he saw her was during the day. It was a bank holiday. Everything should have been quiet. And it would have been, but for the builders who were renovating the row of houses opposite. Every now and then a high pitched whine butted in to their conversation. It was the same tone as Lucy's voice when she got excited, Luke thought unkindly, and it sounded like his own when he was stressed. Well at least the unkind thought was balanced up.

" Those bloody builders, it's a Bank Holiday."

" I get a bit shy when I walk past them."

" Why ? do they wolf whistle you ? "

" No, they proposition me."

" What ? " Luke was shocked, " That's terrible."

" Actually, it's not. It's nothing dirty, they're only asking me out."

Luke was jealous.

" Really ? "

" Yes. And I always start blushing when I talk to them. It's so embarrassing."

" Probably the shame of the situation."

Lucy frowned at him.

" You would say that. But the other day, when I was locked out, they gave me a ladder, so I could climb in through the bathroom window."

" I know what they want to climb into. They want to get in your good books, so they can get off with you."

" You would say that as well. But there's nothing in it. Although it has given me an idea."

" Oh yeah, what's that ? "

" Well, you go to that drama class, don't you ? "

" So what, there's nothing wrong in that," Luke was feeling defensive, " You go as well, sometimes."

" I know. I'm not criticising, I'm just thinking. Your acting skills could be tested by a dare I've thought up."

Luke was interested.

" And what's that ? "

" You get dressed as a woman, and you go out on a date with one of the builders across the road."

" What ? bloody hell. You don't mess around, do you ? You could have led up to this a bit better."

" Sorry, but will you do it ? "

" Whew, course not. I'm not walking over to a crowd of leering builders. I'd get lynched, or raped, probably."

" Don't be stupid. I've talked to them already. I've told them I've got a friend, who fancies one of them. But she's very shy. Besides, there's only going to be two of them there next week anyway."

" I'm not walking up to a couple of big bruisers and asking one of them out."

" Chicken."

" Fuck off. Think of something else."

" No way. You do this dare, or else you don't go out with me."

" I am expected to go up to a couple of big bruisers and ask one of them out, ugh. Double ugh. What exactly does it involve ? "

" That's the spirit."

" Easy for you to say."

" Easy for you to do, if you set your mind to it."

" God, the things I do for lust ."

" That's all it is with you, isn't it."

" I was joking. It is for love. You think I could do something like this otherwise."

" Yes, well, you still have to prove that."

Luke had to let Errol in on the dare. For he found it hard to dress himself, and he wanted to borrow Denise's clothes. His friend took some persuading that Luke was not turning into some kind of pervert, a pervert through want of a shag. Once Errol came round to the idea he could not stop laughing. Although he still insisted on calling Luke a skinny pervert. But he helped out. Unfortunately Luke was not skinny enough. Denise's clothes were a tight squeeze. Luke burst a button on one of her blouses and bust a zip on one of her skirts. Even one of her dresses split under the arms. Eventually Errol managed to squeeze his friend in a fetching sleeveless number. It was beige, the same colour as Luke's bumfluff. Of course Luke would have to shave, particularly under his armpits, phew.

Luke's big feet would not squeeze into any shoes. But he could wear a pair of trainers. They would be liberally sprayed with perfume, to take away the whiff of his feet. The make up was less convincing. Too much blusher and eye shadow made him look like an embarrassed panda. It was at this point Denise walked in. At first she collapsed with laughter. But then she became worried. Were they turning to more kinky areas in order to boost flagging libido ? (Men were always desperate, in every sense.) It took extensive pleading from Errol to explain the situation and allay her fears. Then she became angry because no one asked her. Luke explained the nature of the dare to her. He feared the worse. However, Denise was impressed at the lengths Luke would go for Lucy. Even though she thought that sarky cow was not worth it (But do not tell her that). She would help because she admired Luke.

And so Luke was made up very good in the end. He looked less like Widow Twanky now, and more like a passable girl. He always did look slightly aesexual, people used to say, to wind him up. Now perhaps he could turn those traits to his advantage. Denise had also given him a wig, which turned him into a redhead. And, most important of all, Errol and Denise had made sure he was now endowed with impressive breasts. Luke was instantly proud of his big tits, he felt reassured. The builders would look at them all the time, instead of at his face, where a stray bristle might give the game away. It was a few days since Lucy had made her dare. Arrangements had been made meticulously. He did not want to go round her house and find she was not in. He felt mortified as walked down her street. Every step was longer than the last. Every male he passed appeared to be ogling his new breasts. At least the builders were on their lunch break. Nevertheless, Luke felt eyes bore through him. Then he heard laughter. He looked across the street and he saw two characters eyeing him up. Why did she take so long to answer the door ? this was really embarrassing.

Eventually Lucy answered. Once Luke was indoors the plan was explained. He was now to be known as Tracy. He preferred something a bit more clever, like Debbie, but Lucy would not have it. Lucy set the conditions. They were to meet those two giggling creatures who had made him feel self-conscious. They were both medium height, balding heads, going a bit fat maybe, but very robust. A bit too robust for Luke's liking, or Tracy's even. Of course Lucy had to pick the more gross of the two as Tracy's, the one with the bull neck and the loud voice. Lucy had described Tracy to him. Evidently he was impressed. But of course he wanted Tracy to come over and ask him. This was the part where Luke almost lost it. But Tracy held it together. As he walked up to the smirking builders, he heard remarks about her legs being too knobbly, her waist too skinny and her nose too big. He was annoyed at this, although he said nothing. But the builders caught his glare, and, to their credit, were politeness itself. Bull neck seemed to agree a bit too readily to come out for a drink. Tracy was slightly embarrassed that his voice did not give the game away. Neither of the builders cared to notice it was deeper than the usual feminine voice, though it was always nasal. Lucy watched him from her window. But she did not need to. Bull neck's fog horn voice carried all the way across the street. But Lucy's supervision was intended to ensure Tracy did gain an appointment with the builders, otherwise the dare was forfeit.

Did people ever feel as self conscious as Luke felt in those moments ? He imagined the builders were like C.C.T.V., ruthlessly recording ever detail about him. His own movements appeared awkward, mannered. Yet they did not particularly notice. The conversation went something like -

" Allo," said Bull neck.

" Er, hallo. My name's Tracy."

" Yeah, we know. I'm Derek, this is Robert," Bull neck pointed to his less tubby compatriot.

" Alright, nice to meet you," Robert said, " You gotta excuse me though, I'm off for an eyelash."

" A what ? "

" A slash."

" Oh really," said Tracy, not quite grasping the meaning in her shyness, " And you do that often, do you ? "

The builders found this hilarious.

" Only as often as I need to," said Robert, before he walked off, with a smirk and a sigh.

" Oh right."

Luke felt that sounded too masculine. But he remembered Lucy had reassured him, he had always sounded camp. Irritatingly, he realised there might be some truth in that remark. Derek did not bat an eyelid. An awkward silence followed, where Luke slowly felt himself to be dying.

" And what brings you this way, Trace ? "

Trace, ugh.

" Well, er, you know my friend Lucy, I believe. "

" Sort of. I've talked to her a bit. She did say a little about you."

" Nothing nasty, I hope."

" No, no, of course not. She just said, ah , how nice you were, and, er, maybe we could go out for a drink."

Luke blushed. This bloke did not mess around.

" Does that interest you ? " Tracy said.

" Maybe."

" And what if I said yes ? "

" Well, if you would, I mean if you did, great. We could go to the pub on the corner. That is , if you're serious about this."

Luke cleared his throat to sound more like Tracy.

" I've got some cough sweets if you want one.'

" No, thanks...Okay, will I see you later then ? "

" We'll be in the pub from Seven,"

As Luke went back to Lucy's he was amazed how easy it all was. He was reminded how difficult he had always found it with girls. Once he changed gender it was a doddle. Blokes were always up for it, it seemed. And these two hunks of slobbering masculinity were no exception. He wondered if these blokes literally would go inside anyones knickers. In his own case it depended on how much alcohol he consumed. Ugh, the thought of Derek getting inside his knickers nearly made him vomit. And he was scared, the thought of this builder finding his surprise package. He would think he found the pantry but would have got the tool cupboard instead. He flushed with fear. He could see Derek's pupils dilate as he spoke, he was game all right. But then Luke realised this might play to his advantage. He might get a few free drinks out of it.

Lucy was impressed. She gave him a full blown kiss. But it smudged his lipstick. His carefully-ordered underwear became very hot and uncomfortable. Lucy tut tutted and reminded him of his mission. No reward until after the dare. His trainers were killing him. He still could not get the hang of a decent feminine walk.

" Now you see some of things we have to put up with, all the time... What did he say ?

" The man called Del Boy, he say yes. They're in the pub from Seven onwards."

" Good. Now don't get your knickers in a twist. I mean that literally. We've still got to go and see them."

" I'm not sure I want to go through with the rest of this."

" Think of the free drinks."

Luke had gone pale.

" I'm not too bothered now, nor about the dare itself to be honest."

Lucy gave him a sympathetic hug.

" Oh come on. It's only a drink and a talk in a pub for an hour or so. Then we make our excuses and go."

" I've proved my point, surely."

" No you haven't. You had one short conversation in the street. Now comes the acid test. If you can bluff your way through this, you can bluff your way through anything."

Luke did not seem convinced. So she went on.

" I really admired you for going out there and doing that, you know. I think that means something, something special. And if you finish off this dare, I'm going to know you'll do anything for me. and I'd do anything for someone who's that devoted to me."

Luke stood up. He felt proud. He looked at her. Perhaps it was no more than a pep talk, to get him perform an embarrassing stunt that any twat could perform. But he was not just any twat, he was a twat in love. And besides, there was the added bonus of rudie-dudies.

" Do You mean that. I mean, you're not going to go out with me just because I once dressed up as a girl."

" Of course not. You know I like you. And I want to take it further. But a bet's a bet, or rather, a dare's a dare."

In the pub were Derek and Robert, all sitting comfortably. A days work had been sufficiently washed away, internally at least. Derek himself was covered in patches of thin, white dust. They were both flushed. And they both looked up the instant Luke and Lucy entered. Luke almost made a bolt back out again. But Lucy's restraining arm would not let him.

" Go on, it's alright. They're not going to eat you."

" How do you know. They might try and get off with us."

" Look, all we do is stay for a couple of drinks, okay. If they try any funny business, we're off."

" Easy for you to say. Derek might find out I've got bollocks."

" You're not talking like someone with bollocks. Come on, pull yourself together, they'll get suspicious."

" This is the last time I do anything like this," Luke mumbled, as they finally strode over to the builders.

" Remember, your name is Tracy," Lucy hissed in his ear.

He should have turned back even then, he thought. But he knew it would not have been the same. For he never would have known. Curiosity was driving him now. The dare was begining to feel more important than winning Lucy. He gave her a glance askance. From that moment he determined he would have some kind of revenge, by some means that provided maximum embarrassment..

All went smoothly in the preliminaries. The initial awkwardness of first greetings, the shuffling of seats, and the ' how's it going,' went well. Before Tracy could make her comments about the weather Derek had gone to the bar. Robert tried to engage Lucy in conversation. Yet his shyness only led to bland, boring remarks. An uncomfortable silence followed. Derek was obviously the talker out of the two. And everyone felt easier once he came back laden with drinks. Now the dodgy part started. Tracy tried to relax, but he was tense. Derek appeared to understand. He gently settled in with remarks about work. A long detailed description followed. Tracy learnt things about building he never wanted to know. Still, the renovation was proceeding smoothly. Tracy smiled and nodded his head when he felt it was appropriate. He also smiled at moments when it was inappropriate. Getting the hang of feigning interest was difficult. Plastering, painting, drilling, hammering, cement-mixing were all aired. Tracy felt they should have been kept locked up. Finally Derek even bored himself. Then he asked what she did. Tracy was dreading this. He managed to fluff out a couple of lines about working in an office, somewhere. He decided to say he worked in secretarial services. That seemed a bland enough phrase to cover most office tasks.

However, he nearly came unstuck when he mentioned helping in the office removals. Derek seemed surprised she would be shifting desks. Tracy was almost stumped. Then he had the bright idea to look offended. This made Derek all apologetic. He was casting no apersions on women doing physical work. It was just that Tracy was so petite. This made Tracy feel worse. Actually, Derek liked people who were prepared to muck in, whatever their sex. People should not be afraid to get their hands dirty, or their clothes for that matter. These phrases had a peculiar appropriatness for Tracy. He noticed Derek eyeing his breasts as he said that. He would get more than dirty hands if he grabbed hold of the old socks that passed for mammaries. Derek was warming to him. He admired a girl who drank pints, as Tracy did. This was quite rare, he said, in his experience, he hastened to add. Most women he went out with would drink poxy shorts all the time. Small drinks in small glasses, and they always cost a bomb.

Luke, or rather Tracy, was learning to relax himself. Though he made sure he was aware of the clock that hung over the bar. He willed it to speed up as Derek left for more drinks. Tracy could certainly stick them away, another thing about her that Derek liked. Tracy checked on Lucy and Robert's progress. But neither had got anywhere. Theirs was a stop-start conversation, only remarkable for its long pauses. In truth Lucy did not help. Yet Robert's questions were so boring as to elicit only yes or no answers. Yet she kept the talk trickling along, enough to kill time while killing off Robert's hopes. Robert was slowly raising the white flag, the only thing that would be raised on his person that night. Lucy was adroit at the method of letting another person talk himself to death. She got the rundown on the building work as well, but paid no more attention to it than she would a slight breeze. Tracy marvelled at this. For he noticed Robert was now catching Lucy's boredom, as if it were contagious. Robert began looking at his watch frequently. He began shifting uncomfortably, wanting to leave. Tracy suddenly got worried. This could not be allowed to happen. He did not want to be left with Derek. The dare stipulated an hour at least on a date in the pub. He did not want to have Derek monopolising the rest of the evening.

Derek came back with more drinks. Sight of that lovely brown liquid made Tracy drool. All his misgivings went into hiding. It was obvious by now that Derek was a person who took the lead, Tracy noted, in matters of dates, friendships, and, well, everything. He was begining to quite like this builder. And now Derek himself was relaxed, he was freed from the pedantic anecdotes about his trade. Tracy was regaled with stories of his escapades. They were not that much better to be honest. They seemed to involve getting drunk, playing cricket, getting drunk, weight training, getting drunk and squash. All the sports were to compensate for getting drunk. In fact he hardly looked like a bloke who needed sports. But you had to get your enjoyment from somewhere that did not kill you, occaisonally. Tracy, in his other guise as Luke, knew something about cricket and squash. He had dabbled in playing at them, to impress his office colleagues, and failed. It impressed Derek. He always liked a sporty type.

It was their third drink, or was it their fourth ? Tracy felt the need to go to the toilet. He got up and made straight for the Gents. Fortunately, Lucy successfully intervened and steered him toward the Ladies. Robert and Derek were bemused by the whole scene, but gave each other knowing looks as the girl and the guest-girl disappeared inside. They looked a bit out of it, which meant the boys might be in with a definite chance of a shag.

Lucy berated her new sister once they were safely inside.

" What are you doing ? You nearly gave the game away there."

" Sorry, I was dying for a piss. Instinct just took over, that's all."

" Really ? You don't still want to back out ? "

" No. But I can't wait till this is over, it's doing my brain in...How much longer have we got to do this ? "

" Till Eight at least, you know that."

" I'm getting a bit tipsy."

" So what. Enjoy the moment."

" But I might forget myself."

" I'll look after you, don't you worry."

" I think Derek fancies me, hee hee hee."

" I think those two'll go for anything in a skirt."

" Including a Scotsman."

" Or an Englishman if you're not careful."

Luke/Tracy stopped laughing.

" This is a bit scary, you know."

Lucy put an arm around him.

" Trust me," said Lucy, " I can handle these types. You don't let them in first time you meet them. You give them nothing, not even a peck on the cheek. And we're only seeing them the once."

Luke/Tracy sighed.

" Come on now, Luke, not much longer to go. Have your piss. But make sure you lock the door of the cubicle, in case someone comes in. "

" It's lucky this dress has buttons all the way down the front."

" How are your knickers ? are you all tangled up again."

" Of course not, stop embarrassing me."

" Don't get offended. I thought they might have ridden all the way up again, that's all."

Luke/Tracy shivered.

" I think Derek wants to ride all the way up...I'm not a tranny, you know, stop laughing at me."

" Sorry. I know you're doing this for me. And I love you for it. But it's not long to go now...Now get in and hurry up."

Lucy shoved Tracy into the cubicle and walked out. As Tracy urinated he ruminated. Lucy had said she loved him. She never said that to him before. Though she was still the same bossy old cow.

Tracy took some time to work his way out of those toilets. There were one or two giveaway stains on his dress. Lucy scolded him for being so clumsy. Neither of them had considered the difficulty of a man in a dress urinating. Still, on with the show. Lucy escorted her new girlfriend back to the builders. Derek and Robert beamed at them as they sat down. More drinks had arrived. Tracy needed no encouragement. All this deception was thirsty work. Lucy too drank with gusto. Maybe they were getting too tipsy.

Derek had relaxed enough to tell a few jokes. They were all crap. Still, the women giggled as if they were hilarious. Robert chimed in with a few choice efforts of his own. They were even worse than Dereks. They all seemed to involve men having their dicks trapped in something. But, by now, they would laughed at a page in a phone directory. In fact, Robert produced a filofax and reeled off the names of building firms they dealt with. He thought they were weird, and so worthy of a good laugh. This did not work as well as the crap jokes but did raise a titter or two.

Tracy was scared he might wet himself. It was toilet time again. He asked Lucy to come with him. This led to much ribbing from Derek and Robert. For poor old Tracy was that much of a little girl she had to be escorted to the Ladies. She probably had her bum wiped as well. Tracy blushed, he knew it, he could feel the heat. And a giggling Lucy helped him to the toilets. He was well worried now. They had to go. They were becoming too drunk. Tracy suspected their drinks had been spiked with shorts. But he was too drunk to voice this properly. But he did convey the message that Derek and Robert were actively taking advantage. Lucy agreed with him, probably. Tracy did not find her answers too clear. However, once they were back with the grinning builders their mood changed. They were having such a good time after all. They had another drink, and another, and another. And eventually they managed to get out of the pub. They had to, as it was closing time. They also managed to get back to Lucy's flat unscathed. Though the two builders were still with them. Tracy remembered giving Derek a French kiss. After that it was a bit of a blur. At least until he found himself on the sofa, where Derek discovered his genitals. Derek was surprised, but not shocked, nor disappointed. He was one to make the most of any situation. So he gave Tracy a hand job. Tracy was gulity, and felt a bit strange. But when he found Derek carried on regardless, he felt he could not stop now. It would be like getting out of the bath before you had a wash.

Carry on they did. Tracy had an orgasm two times to Derek's three. Then Derek dropped off into a snore. Although incredibly woozy, Tracy stayed awake, smoking half a packet of cigarettes in the meantime. He wanted to get out of there as soon as possible. His senses were returning now, the aching feelers of a hangover were making themselves known. He waited till dawn. Then he slipped out from under and sneaked off.

It was a bit embarrassing, as he went home all dishevelled, still in womens' clothes. Tracy became Luke again, quickly, methodically and thoroughly. The clothes were hidden away. He had a bath and a shower. Then he felt the utmost relief at being able to climb into a pair of trousers again. No more irritating make up anymore, no more trying to walk like you are holding everything together. Luke paced around his flat, posing, prancing around, deliberately acting the male slob, as if reasserting his gender. He made sure he deliberately walked into furniture and made a mess of everything he touched. He felt so liberated to be a male again, even if he doubted what it meant a bit more now.

As he slid down to lounge on his sofa, the phone rang. It was Derek.

" Tracy ? don't hang up on me, please..."

Luke was tempted to.

" Please, just hear me out...I know what Lucy and you planned to do. I know you had your own reasons..."

Uh oh.

" And you're angry ? "

" I was for awhile. But not as annoyed as Robert. Lucy wouldn't let him get near. He had to sleep in the bathroom."

They both chuckled.

" I'm sorry. I didn't mean to lead you on. I was doing it for Lucy, because I love her. I didn't mean for it to go so far. But now, I want to get on with my life, because I'm not really into doing things like that..."

" That's not what you said last night."

The fear turned up in Luke.

" Er, what did I say ? "

" You were talking about loving someone regardless of categories, such as age, belief or sex..."

Luke was aghast.

" Fuck, I said that. But I was drunk. I was totally out of it by that time...which you knew about. Because I've got the suspicion you spiked our drinks."

" We did, we did, I admit that. And I'm sorry. But we were doing it to our own drinks as well. We just wanted to get drunk quicker. We do feel bad though, me and Rob. Maybe we did take advantage. But we knew you were in drag right from the start."

" You did ? "

" Yeah. We could see your hairy legs through the gap in your dress. That was the first giveaway. Then there was the fact you had a few stray bristles stuck to your chin. And your voice was a bit weird...'

" You bastards, you conned us."

" It's no worse than the trick you tried on us."

Luke got suspicious.

" Lucy told you, didn't she ? I mean before I met you."

" She did, yeah..."

" Oh fuck."

" But listen, please don't hang up. We didn't mean to end up at Lucy's flat like that..."

" What do you mean ? "

" Well, I didn't expect to get on so well with you."

" But I was ratarsed, remember."

" But it was also what you did."

" Er... you mean the hand jobs you gave me, look that was a mistake..."

" And the ones you gave me...and the anal sex."

" What ?.. fucking hell."

" My thoughts exactly, both then and now."

" It was a mistake, Derek. I'm not into having sex with men. I'm not a homosexual."

" Neither am I. I'm just into shagging people I love."

" But I don't love you, Derek."

" That's not what you said last night."

" But I was under the influence..."

" Yeah, of passion."

" No...er...Look, if I say I loved my car, I wouldn't go and have sex with it."

" I would, right up the exhaust."

" You would ? "

" And I have."

" I'm not taking this conversation further, Derek, it's giving me the creeps..."

" But you said you loved me.."

" I was drunk."

" Over and over again."

" I'm not interested, Derek. Sorry, sorry about the whole episode, now good bye..."

" But I love you."

Derek screamed this last plea in Luke's ear as the conversation ended abruptly. It was the first of many times he had to hang up that day. Derek would not leave him alone. It settled into a routine of every half an hour. After the third day Luke unplugged his phone.

But Derek found out the block where he lived. He followed Luke on the street. He usually pleaded with Luke to say something, for a good distance, before Luke's silence drove him away. Luke's 'ignore it and will go away' approach worked at first. But then Derek found out the number of his flat. Every time Luke heard a ring he would glance through the spyhole in his front door. Then he would see the big builder's face filling up the glass. He pleaded with Tracy to let him in, he still insisted on calling him Tracy. Thank God Luke was off work at the moment. Otherwise Derek would have followed him there as well.

He had now gone through five days of Derek's stalking. But he had seen no one since the original Tracy episode, it was too embarrassing. He always preferred to deal with these things on his own, he told himself. Yet a familiar face, someone to talk to, quickly became a necessity. Derek's pursuit was begining to tell on his nerves. And the thought of being stalked by a love smitten builder was not funny anymore. He could not talk to Lucy, that irritating bitch with her dragons and dares. Well, now the dragon had taken a shine to himself. He was the damsel in distress. Where was his knight in shining armour ? Although the thought of being the helpless maiden, rescued by the hunky hero, did not gell well with him either. Perhaps he should talk to Errol. But he knew Errol would back off, and climb the walls in repulsion. Perhaps Denise, but then Errol would think he was trying to get off with her. So Luke knew he must be subtle. He chose a time when he knew Errol to be at work and Denise at home. He payed a visit to their place to coincide with this time. He congratulated himself on this solution. But , inevitably, he found them both at home. Shit and double shit. Now he needed a reason to cover his real intent. But he could not think of one. And so he told them, taking great care not to mention the mutual masturbation and anal sex. He hinted that more could have possibly happened, than a mere drunken joke. This hint went flying over Errol's head, but Denise took it in straight away.

" Oh you poor, stupid idiot, why did you do it ? "

" It was a dare," was the only reason he could think of.

" You're either pervy or insane," said Errol.

" He's an insane pervert all right...What are you going to do ? "

" Don't know yet...I must say, you're taking this well, Errol."

" Really ? I do think you're an extreme weirdo. But, whatever perversions you've got as hobbies is up to you. Just don't drag me into them, or drag me into drag."

" Come on, Errol. The poor sap obviously needs some advice."

" No, not advice...actually, yeah, I probably do."

" You're going to have to talk to him again, " said Denise.

" Yeah, tell him to fuck right off."

" Big mistake. You have to stress to him you are not interested, in no uncertain terms, but respect his feelings."

" But what if he don't accept it ? "

" He will, so long as you're honest with him and not offensive. Believe me, I 've had a bit of experience at this kind of thing myself. When someone pesters you, you have to stand your ground. And you have to tell him the same thing over and over again without losing your patience. Keep stressing you're not interested, and don't give him room for doubt, because he'll probably be feeling a bit emotional, and he'll seize on anything."

" Ugh, " said Errol, " I think she's right, Luke, you'll only get all messed up again."

" Thanks for those diplomatic words, Errol."

" But he's right, Luke."

" I know. I'll have to go through with it, won't I ? I can't go on avoiding him."

" Yeah, you might end up in shit creek. Or he might end up in your shit creek, ha ha ha..."

Luke went all quiet. Denise glared at her partner.

" Sorry Luke, sorry, bad joke. Look, arrange a meeting in a public place and tell him."

So it was arranged. Luke met Derek in the same pub the drunken drag escapade took place, which was strangely reassuring. Denise and Errol were there, keeping a discrete distance as they kept a watchful eye. It felt weird. Derek looked like he was going to be given his exam results, all trepidation. But then this whole event had been weird. The two took their seats, and the interview began.

" I'm sorry, mate. I really didn't mean to lead you on. But I'm not interested."

" Really ? "

" Yeah."

" Even after all you said."

" That wasn't me talking, it was the drink."

" And after all you did."

" Again, I was under the influence. I wasn't totally aware of what was going on."

" So it all meant nothing ? "

" No, It's not like that. I had a good time, I did, but I did things I didn't mean to."

" You were just using me ? "

" No I wasn't. It was a dare with Lucy, one that went a bit sour."

" Right. It went sour when you messed around with my feelings."

" I never intended to mess with anyone's feelings at all. The whole purpose was just to see if I could pass as a girl."

" And you did pretty well. You'd make a decent transvestite."

" Er, yeah well. I'm not going to be doing anything like that again."

" So you're chucking me."

" Look, Derek, we never were an item. I don't want to see you or be with you. But this doesn't mean I dislike you as a person. It's just my interest lies in, well, other areas."

" You mean Lucy ? "

" Yeah."

Actually Lucy was definitely out of the question now. But Luke thought he had better say yes, to further dissuade Derek's interest.

" Yeah, yeah, fair enough. I'm sorry Tracy, er Luke. I could guess you weren't really interested, the way you kept avoiding me. But I wish you'd talked to me like this earlier."

" Sorry, but I was a bit scared."

" Well don't be scared to make mistakes, mate. You're a decent bloke, and you've got a great pair of dusters."

" Dusters ? "

" Yeah, like my great dane."

" What're they ? "

" Balls and ball bag, mate. The whole package apart from the dick."

Luke blushed heavily.

" Sorry. I didn't mean to embarrass you. I'd better be off, yeah, before I do it some more."

" You're not backward in coming foward."

" I'm not backward when it comes to coming."

Luke felt this was getting a bit too friendly.

" Anyway, sorry yeah."

" Stop apologising. It was a mistake, no hard feelings, Tracy, er Luke. I'll be off now. But if you change your mind, I'll be around a while yet."

" I won't."

" As you wish, take care."

" And you."

Luke watched Derek's back disapear out the doors. Not even a glance behind or a shrug of the shoulders. He admired the way the man took it, in certain respects anyway. He was relieved the whole episode was now finished. Denise and Errol soon made their way over.

" Good news, yeah ? " said Errol.

" The best."

" That'll teach you to go around messing with other peoples' feelings," said Denise.

Luke agreed with that. But he would mess around with one person's feelings one more time, that was Lucy.

" Actually, mate, if you'd have talked to us earlier, we might have been able to help," said Errol.

" How do you mean ? "

" Well, I thought I recognised that bloke. I've seen him hanging round Esquires. So we could have warned you what this bloke was like. But no, you have to go on, like a dozy plum with your stupid dare."

" Errol," said Denise.

" Esquires, what that gay pub ?"

" Not gay, strictly speaking. It's more like S an M. Word has it you can get any perversion you like if you go there. Just don't go there alone."

" Why ? "

" Why do you think ? you melon."

"Really ? "

" That's right."

The rest of the night passed pleasantly enough. Although an idea did work its way into Luke's head. The next day he phoned Lucy at the first available opportunity.

" Oh, Luke, I'm sorry about what happened. I heard all about it. I thought you wouldn't talk to me again."

" Well I would like to meet up with you, Lucy, for a talk, that is, to sort things out, is that okay ? "

" Sure, you want to come around ? "

" Actually, I fancy going to a pub first, do you mind ? "

" Of course not, which one ? "

" Well, do you know Esquires ? no ? well its pretty good. I'll meet you in there about Eight, okay, great, see you later."

Luke had no intention of keeping this appointment. It was a petty, vindictive gesture, he knew. Still, at least she might gain a glimpse of what he went through. He did not really want to go out tonight anyway. He thought he would stay in. He noticed he still had Denise's clothes. He thought he would have a quiet night in, with Tracy.

Bonzo White

Bullies took some strange forms in the old school days. There was one called Bonzo White. I cannot remember his real name. In fact I cannot remember him as a real person, more like a caricature. There was a story about how he got his nickname, but I forget it, it was that boring. Bonzo was usually a dog's name, I think it had something to do with that. Although most dogs were better looking than Bonzo. He was a fat bastard. Not an especially fat bastard by today's obese standards, but he could still waddle with the best of them. As most of us were skinny, sickly bastards, the overweight tended to stand out more. Nowadays, of course, you would be hard pressed to find a skinny bastard who could pass muster. Where have all the long streaks of piss gone ?

But I digress. I should continue describing Bonzo, while slagging him off simultaneously. Bonzo had a round head, to match his round body, like a football. His flat, greasy hair stuck to his head as if to confirm that impression. His teeth stuck out. In fact he was in poor shape to be a bully. He seemed more qualified to be one of the bullied. They say most people who abuse others have been abused themselves. I recognise now this was probably the case with him. I had no sympathy for him at the time though. Then I saw him as a cross between Billy Bunter and a serial killer, with a hint of sexual pervert thrown in.

Some people always compare bullies of the past with bullies of the present. They wonder if the bullies of the past would cut it in today's more affluent world. With Bonzo I would doubt it. He was not fit in any athletic sense (or any other sense). Neither was he particularly cunning, except in a basic, rat-like manner. So he could only pick on boys at least two years younger than himself. And even then he had to take them by surprise. His favourite trick was walking up behind boys, punching them on the top of the head and shouting ' knock knock.' Then he ran away with that pervert's giggle of his. Another, rarer, trick was his belly flop. He would trip unsuspecting kids over, then fall on them, trying to crush them into the ground. This latter trick did not last that long. One of his unwilling victims rolled out of the way on one occaison. And Bonzo winded himself on the tarmac. On another occaison his victim neatly sidestepped, making sure Bonzo's own momentum took him into some prickly bushes. He was shown up. But naturally Bonzo got his revenge on both occaisons. ' Knock knock ' was always a handy weapon.

I was not in any particular terror of Bonzo White, at least compared to other bullies. He could be a difficult pest to shake off. He was one of those irritating obstacles that had to be negotiated on the road through puberty. There was no getting around him, and not just because he was a fat bastard. He caught me with ' knock knock ' a few times. It really made the eyes water. I had to stop him. If I could not, then he might take it for granted, and I do not think my head could have taken the punishment. However, he was difficult to get back. For even when I did get a gang together, I could not touch him. For he was in with some of the best fighters in school. Actually, I doubt whether I could have beaten him up on my own. His layers of flab absorbed punches, while he giggled and hit back. No, a gang of us jumping him after school, and beating the shit out of him, seemed the best option. Easier said than done. Bonzo had his bodyguard wherever he went. I caught the same bus as him, but I could never catch him alone. He always had his two main cronies at least - Pimples Macca and Dusty Rake. Both were terrifying to look at. It was rumoured that Pimples Macca had a rare hereditary condition, this gave him his luxuriant skin eruption. His acne really was of a heroic stature. You would not cross this boy. You would rather cross the road than walk by him. Pimples always got a seat on the bus, no adult would sit near him. Then of course there was Dusty Rake. I think Rake was his surname. Although it suited him, he was as thin as one. He was called Dusty because every time you hit him, dust flew up. He had prodigious dandruff which also contributed. Of course he always hit you back, and he always hurt. Dusty was a pisstaker extraordinaire. He had to have the end of every conversation. And he could be genuinely funny. This meant he got hit and caned by teachers regularly. For Dusty could not desist from dusting off his wit, even though it often dropped him in the shit.

This was the position we faced. And, forced into making an effort, the gang came up with a plan. Step one was quite easy. We had to ensure Dusty was put in detention. We had to get round the difficulty that Dusty was usually caned instead of detained. We put the word around, so teachers could overhear, that Dusty preferred the cane to detention. This was true, he told us so, under pain of pisstake we were not to divulge it. But we were desperate to give Bonzo a good kicking. For the cane was a brief pain, intense but it faded away, while detention went on over and over again, and he thought he would never get away. As teachers liked to cause the maximum amount of pain and embarassment permissable, they started giving Dusty detention. As he was such a pisstaker he got it every night of the week. This left Pimples. Pimples was literally a can of worms. After intensive discussion, we pulled a devious trick on him . We switched his bottle of skin lotion for a strong aftershave. So, instead of his pimples being patted with tender loving Calamine lotion, they were seared with ' Brutal Bastard ' lotion, or whatever it was called. This made us feel guilty, but not for long. Pimples was a five star bully. His favourite trick was to get you in a headlock, then rub his pustulent cheek on your face. Therefore sympathy was non existent.

With Dusty in detention and Pimples sent home, and no other cronies to call on, we four of us could surely jump Bonzo and beat shit out of him. However, Bonzo had that psychic sense, that bullies often have, when faced with threat. He spied us bearing down on him as he peered out a classroom window into the playground. He tried to skulk wherever he could hide. But his fellow pupils would insist on grassing up his whereabouts to us. But Bonzo always kept one step ahead as he ran from corridor to classroom and back again. He still could not resist playing ' knock knock ' on the heads of a couple of innocent bystanders. These Bystanders joined in the chase.

Unfortunately it looked like he might get away. Desperation had lent the fat bastard wings. He really gave us the runaround, and always remained a good way ahead. We saw him make for the school gate. We doubled our speed, anxious not to lose him. But it looked as if our chance might be going. Once out of school there were any number of turnings Bonzo could lose us in, and he knew it. However, as he ran past a shortarse pupil in his P.E. kit, he could not resist playing ' knock knock ' one more time. This backfired, because the shortarse in P.E. kit was not a pupil, it was Mister Middleton, the chemistry teacher, subsequently known as Midge. Well Midge turned in a fury and wrestled Bonzo to the ground, causing extreme pain as he did so. An angry copper could not have done it much better. Always conscious of his size, Midge overreacted to any suggestion of being picked on by anyone. And so it looked like the game was up for Bonzo. A teacher could save us the bother and give him a severe caning. Bonzo was marched off to the Head's office, like an awkward prisoner.

Bonzo was not to be beaten, yet. He turned the tables by claiming we had put him up to playing ' knock knock ' on Midge. It was a dare. In a stroke he turned the situation around. We were called in to justify ourselves. In the lying, crying and accusing that followed we all bid to outdo each other. One glimpse of the Head's trusty bamboo stick was enough to induce that. Blame was attributed all over the place, and the result was it did not stick anywhere. Midge and the Head both growled and scowled. But they could not be bothered to take the matter further. We were all threatened with dire consequences should we all find ourselves in the same room again. In the meantime Bonzo was given a complimentary slap across the head. This made his eyes water, but it amounted to him getting off lightly.

Despite this, Bonzo's power was now broken. No one could be bothered with him anymore. He now had a reputation for trouble. So he could not get near anyone to cause any. Even Dusty toned his act down. He made the startling discovery he would get less detention if he shut up occaisonally. Pimples Macca came back a week later, looking clean and well groomed. At first we thought it was someone else. Obviously he could not have his given nickname anymore. From then on he was known as Baby's Bum Macca. I heard Bonzo went on to become a store detective. Then he did ' something ' in the tax office, whatever that means.

Lambert Essex

Who would want to get stuck with a name like Lambert Essex? The poor sod used to have the piss taken out of him at school, mercilessly. He would go home and beg his parents to change his name by deed poll. They always refused. Then they hit him. So he learnt to hate his name in silence. Until his early twenties anyway, for people eventually got worn out telling crap jokes about his name. His own attitude also changed. Now he saw his name as romantic. So did other people, for some reason, or maybe he convinced them by droning on about it. They told him it was mysterious just to shut him up. Of course he still got the endless tedious remarks about being an Essex boy. But, he felt, at the world weary age of twenty, he could show a bit of indulgence toward dozy twats. He used to say it was ' water off a duck's arse.' I always corrected him here and said it was ' water off a duck's back.' Then he would glare at me and say ' Well that's the version I heard.' He never backed down on anything like this. He could be a difficult man sometimes, a proper twat in fact.

The trouble really started when Lambert got his band together, I mean the huge swollen lump between his shoulders. He felt they were the business, as he was

713

himself. And they were not that bad, as pub showbands go. But then they started getting better. They played old fashioned Rhythm and Blues and Heavy Rock mostly. I did not care for either, the former was pretentious and the latter ponderous, but they actually sounded okay. I liked the way they put it across - kind of middle class Essex boy angst, mixed up with sword and sorcery blues. A complete mess to describe, except they made it work. The band themselves were reasonably unpretentious characters, if you cut off Lambert's swollen head. None of this crap about musicianship, or their great mission to enlighten the world. No, it was a couple of albums down the line before they got like that.

At the begining, though, they could not think of a name. And, after much agonising, they found they did not need to. For Lambert was with them. The others in the band did not like this suggestion at first. It might go to Lambert's head, then he would not be able to fit through a doorway. But since they could not think of anything else remotely decent, Lambert Essex became the name of the band. They played under this name until they went their seperate ways, which was only a couple of years in the end. In the meantime, however, they had built up a good following. It took a while for people to decide between ' Are these twats who believe they live in a fantasy novel ? ' or, ' Are these people being intelligent and ironic ? ' By some accident of fate, which I have never explained, people decided Lambert Essex were into the crap they played, but were intelligent enough to make fun of it at the same time. So that was them set up. After building up a following here there was talk of a trip to America. I noticed a change of attitude. Lambert was extremely fond of himself. This now developed into a tempestuous affair. He used to say it was not him that had changed. It was the people around who treated him differently. He neglected to mention that the people around him changed - from pisstaking mates to cringing sycophants. Although I have to admit there was some truth in what he said, but only a drop. I used to find him an irritating twat, now he was an offensive twat. He was always posing and preening, and this was in his sleep. He could not even light a cigarette without going throught ritual poses, (Lambert and Butler, naturally) and he did not even smoke. Not that I am bitter, the jammy, fucking bastard. He deserved his success as much as anyone, and he took it to it like no one's business. In the 1980's it seemed only messed up types with criminal tendencies were successful. All right, I suppose I was envious. He did play six nights a week in that band, most of the time. And I was pleased for him .This was mainly because I thought I might be able to cash in on his success, somehow. But I was never sure how. If I hung around in his entourage long enough, looking cool, I was sure something might have happened. But he got fed up with me hanging around, and I could never get in backstage anymore. He would never answer his door, or his phone either.

You could say I should have been glad in the light of what happened later. But I would not have minded a few free drugs and bouts of sex in the meantime. So I lost track, his records were crap anyway, no, I am not bitter, that much. Lambert Essex really found their audience in America - the bloke and the band. The money started pouring in. Chart success followed more chart success, and more chart success. There was drink and drugs and sex everywhere. But mostly in the bands' bodies. There was excess followed by excess and more excess. Something was bound to go wrong. (I did have my hands clasped together in prayer.) And eventually it did. It started with some ex-girlfriends, and boyfriends, selling their stories to the sleazy tabloids. It was all ' My life of Perverted Mayhem with Sex-God Rockstar, in a twenty-in-the-bed, druggie romp, with tea and scones afterwards. ' I was insanely jealous by this time. The press dealt with it obssessively in the following weeks, and months. Lambert Essex - the man and the band - were walking pharmacies, Top of the Pops in the consumption league. They had sex in more positions than a Kama Sutra fan. Etc, etc, etc, it all ran on. I have no time for people who sell their stories, betray their friends' trust and everybodys' dignity, the bastards. If I had some stuff that was half as juicy as the average kiss and tell I could have made a few thousand. I mean, you have to be moral, except when a big pile of easy money presents itself.

Well, in the middle of all this titilation the band were causing, something else came up. All this controversy caused the band to come to the attention of a few people they would not normally reach. (You know the kind; swots, nerds, stiffs, wimps, wankers, wet farts and creeps - the kind who always tuck their shirts in their underpants.) Unfortunately some of them worked for a drug company, sorry, I should pharmaceutrical supplier. This supplier specialised in pills for bored housewives, and it was called Lambert Essex. Lambert Essex claimed Lambert Essex was ruining the good name of Lambert Essex. A lot of drugged up weirdo Englishmen was not good for business (unless some kind of sponsorship deal could be arranged, but here negotiations floundered). If they were discreet weirdos it might be okay. But Lambert Essex, the band, were all over the place and off their face, and a total disgrace. The band retaliated by saying a lot of single mums were addicted to their powerful products, which was true, after being heavily targetted by an advertising campaign. But The band were too off their heads to offer a coherent arguement about this, and it looked as if they were merely moaning, instead of pointing out a dubious practice. It also lost them part of their audience. Nevertheless, it seemed they might have a case for suing the supplier, and so an interminable lawsuit developed, with either party denouncing the other as unfit to wear the dignified name of Lambert Essex. (This did give a brief glow of pride to Lambert Essex the person. He had never been called dignified before. Although he had been called a few other things.) At one point things became desperate, the band would have to give up their name. Even the singer would have his name taken away. (Then he would be like his hero, the man with no name. But it would make the tax returns difficult.) The drug company argued they had copyright on his personal name as well. Since this company was based in a historic state in the U.S.A., it could invoke some ancient laws to suit its own ends. Therefore, the severest punishment for breach of copyright was the electric chair. There was a legal case for saying Lambert Essex might be executed just for having that name. Fortunately an out-of-court settlement was reached however. Lambert Essex the band changed their name to the ' Essex Lambs.' The cringing embarrassment this induced was somewhat mollified by the award of a huge sum of dollars. Lambert Essex the man was allowed to keep his name, with a slight addition. He was now called Lambert Essex-who-is-no-relation-to-the-wonderful-pharmaceutrical-company-of-the-same-name. It was a bit of an effort to write all that in his passport, but again, another huge wad of cash softened the hurt.

That appeared to be the end of it. Unfortunately, while on tour, and having a drink after a show, Lambert Essex-who-is, etc, got into an arguement with some Lambert Essex company employees. They could not help laughing at his ridiculous new name. One thing led to another and Lambert Essex the man was accidentally murdered. The circumstances of his death were suspicious, to say the least. Lambert was shot fourteen times, he had six knives in his chest, and a rope around his neck. The coroner returned a verdict of alcohol poisoning.

After his death, Lambert Essex, the man, quickly became an international cult hero. Teenage girls wept and swooned everywhere photos of him were displayed. Sales of the bands music rocketed. The wave of sympathy for the man, and his band, was acompanied by an outcry against the drug company. The company's products were boycotted until they were nearly bankrupt, when they were swallowed by another drugs company (without any side effects apparently). The surviving members of the band became millionaires. The singers share went to a retarded cousin in Essex, who built steam engines as a hobby, who I happen to know. Though I have flattered him mercilessly, and begged shamelessly, he still refuses to give me any money. This is because I once called him a trainspotter, well once a day. He will not speak to me anymore, the jammy, bastard trainspotter.

Mother Bluebeard

Mother Bluebeard brought up her children with love and affection. She doted endlessly on all of them. Not one but every one had her equal and undivided attention. She had no time or effort for anything else. Indeed, her source of continuing pride and achievement was in the growth and development of her five sons and five daughters. Neighbours commented how fine they all were. They were well balanced, healthy and happy. What could be the source of more satisfaction in life than this ?

Yet Mother Bluebeard was pleased as her children moved out one by one. They now had their own lives to build. Her hard work was over. She could now develop aspects of her own life that had been supressed by the demands of parenthood. Her life could turn to a new course. She might fill out her personality until all aspects were as sophisticated as her motherhood.

Unfortunately, life kept turning. It turned three hundred and sixty degrees, until Mother Bluebeard was back where she started. Her children returned, one by one, each of them had tales of woe. There were broken marriages, psychotic breakdowns, health probelms, debt problems, drug problems punctuating their lives. It was all very difficult, difficult to listen to, as well as making her children difficult to deal with. Now her children had breathed life outside her home they were more independent, or so they thought. In reality they were incapable of doing anything for themselves. Mother Bluebeard had looked after them too well. Her children would always be dependent upon her. Although they could never admit it. Mother Bluebeard endured their tantrums for a few years. She also dealt with many crises, arguments and relationship problems. Then she decided she had had enough. One day, she accidentally, on purpose, left the gas tap uncovered, and running. All ten children died in their sleep. Mother Bluebeard was arrested for murder. She was convicted of manslaughter, but given a suspended sentence. The court took into account that dealing with ten twats was enough to drive anyone loopy. To commerorate this event she let her facial hair grow, and, as she was feeling blue, she dyed it the appropriate colour.

Lightning Source UK Ltd.
Milton Keynes UK
09 October 2009

144757UK00001B/1/P